The Bean Trees
Animal Dreams
Pigs in Heaven

BY BARBARA KINGSOLVER

FICTION

THE BEAN TREES
PIGS IN HEAVEN
ANIMAL DREAMS
HOMELAND AND OTHER STORIES
THE POISONWOOD BIBLE
PRODIGAL SUMMER

NONFICTION

HIGH TIDE IN TUCSON: ESSAYS FROM NOW OR NEVER
HOLDING THE LINE: WOMEN IN THE GREAT ARIZONA MINE STRIKE OF 1983

POETRY

ANOTHER AMERICA

The Bean Trees
Animal Dreams
Pigs in Heaven

Barbara Kingsolver

Quality Paperback Book Club
New York

Printed in the United States of America

The Bean Trees

For Ismene,
and all the mothers who have lost her

ONE

The One to Get Away

I have been afraid of putting air in a tire ever since I saw a tractor tire blow up and throw Newt Hardbine's father over the top of the Standard Oil sign. I'm not lying. He got stuck up there. About nineteen people congregated during the time it took for Norman Strick to walk up to the Courthouse and blow the whistle for the volunteer fire department. They eventually did come with the ladder and haul him down, and he wasn't dead but lost his hearing and in many other ways was never the same afterward. They said he overfilled the tire.

Newt Hardbine was not my friend, he was just one of the big boys who had failed every grade at least once and so was practically going on twenty in the sixth grade, sitting in the back and flicking little wads of chewed paper into my hair. But the day I saw his daddy up there like some old overalls slung over a fence, I had this feeling about what Newt's whole life was going to amount to, and I felt sorry for him. Before that exact moment I don't believe I had given much thought to the future.

My mama said the Hardbines had kids just about as fast as they could fall down the well and drown. This must not have been entirely true, since they were abundant in Pittman County and many survived to adulthood. But that was the general idea.

Which is not to say that we, me and Mama, were any better than Hardbines or had a dime to our name. If you were to look at the two of us, myself and Newt side by side in the sixth grade, you could have pegged us for brother and sister. And for all I ever knew of my own daddy I can't say we weren't, except for Mama swearing up and down that he was nobody I knew and was long gone besides. But we were cut out of basically the same mud, I suppose, just two more dirty-kneed kids scrapping to beat hell and trying to land on our feet. You couldn't have said, anyway, which one would stay right where he was, and which would be the one to get away.

Missy was what everyone called me, not that it was my name, but because when I was three supposedly I stamped my foot and told my own mother not to call me Marietta but *Miss* Marietta, as I had to call all the people including children in the houses where she worked Miss this or Mister that, and so she did from that day forward. Miss Marietta and later on just Missy.

The thing you have to understand is, it was just like Mama to do that. When I was just the littlest kid I would go pond fishing of a Sunday and bring home the boniest mess of blue-gills and maybe a bass the size of your thumb, and the way Mama would carry on you would think I'd caught the famous big lunker in Shep's Lake that old men were always chewing their tobacco and thinking about. "That's my big girl bringing home the bacon," she would say, and cook those things and serve them up like Thanksgiving for the two of us.

I loved fishing those old mud-bottomed ponds. Partly because she would be proud of whatever I dragged out, but also I just loved sitting still. You could smell leaves rotting into the cool mud and watch the Jesus bugs walk on the water, their four little feet making dents in the surface but never falling through. And sometimes you'd see the big ones, the ones nobody was ever going to hook, slipping away under the water like dark-brown dreams.

By the time I was in high school and got my first job and all the rest, including the whole awful story about Newt Hardbine which I am about to tell you, he was of course not in school anymore. He was setting tobacco alongside his half-crippled daddy and by that time had gotten a girl in trouble, too, so he was married. It was Jolene Shanks and everybody was a little surprised at her, or anyway pretended to be, but not at him. Nobody expected any better of a Hardbine.

But I stayed in school. I was not the smartest or even particularly outstanding but I was there and staying out of trouble and I intended to finish. This is not to say that I was unfamiliar with the back seat of a Chevrolet. I knew the scenery of Greenup Road, which we called Steam-It-Up Road, and I knew what a pecker looked like, and none of these sights had so far inspired me to get hogtied to a future as a tobacco farmer's wife. Mama always said barefoot and pregnant was not my style. She knew.

It was in this frame of mind that I made it to my last year of high school without event. Believe me in those days the girls were dropping by the wayside like seeds off a poppyseed bun and you learned to look at every day as a prize. You'd made it that far. By senior year there were maybe two boys to every one of us, and we believed it was our special reward when we got this particular science teacher by the name of Mr. Hughes Walter.

Now *him.* He came high-railing in there like some blond Paul McCartney, sitting on the desk in his tight jeans and his clean shirt sleeves rolled up just so, with the cuffs turned in. He made our country boys look like the hand-me-down socks Mama brought home, all full of their darns and mends. Hughes Walter was no Kentucky boy. He was from out of state, from some city college up north, which was why, everyone presumed, his name was backwards.

Not that I was moony over him, at least no more than the standard of the day, which was plain to see from the walls of the girls' bathroom. You could have painted a barn with all the lipstick that went into "H. W. enraptured forever" and things of that kind. This is not what I mean. But he changed my life, there is no doubt.

He did this by getting me a job. I had never done anything more interesting for a living than to help Mama with the for-pay ironing on Sundays and look after the brats of the people she cleaned for. Or pick bugs off somebody's bean vines for a penny apiece. But this was a real job at the Pittman County Hospital, which was one of the most important and cleanest places for about a hundred miles. Mr. Walter had a wife, Lynda, whose existence was ignored by at least the female portion of the high school but who was nevertheless alive and well, and was in fact one of the head nurses. She asked Hughes Walter if there was some kid in his classes that could do odd jobs down there after school and on Saturdays, and after graduation maybe it could work out to be a full-time thing, and he put the question to us just like that.

Surely you'd think he would have picked one of the Candy Stripers, town girls with money for the pink-and-white uniforms and prissing around the bedpans on Saturdays like it was the holiest substance on God's green earth they'd been trusted to carry. Surely you would think he'd pick Earl Wickentot, who could dissect an earthworm without fear. That is what I told Mama on the back porch. Mama in her armhole apron in the caned porch chair and me on the stepstool, the two of us shelling out peas into a newspaper.

"Earl Wickentot my hind foot" is what Mama said. "Girl, I've seen you eat a worm whole when you were five. He's no better than you are, and none of them Candy Stripers either." Still, I believed that's who he would choose, and I told her so.

She went to the edge of the porch and shook a handful of pea hulls out of her apron onto the flowerbed. It was marigolds and Hot Tamale cosmos. Both Mama and I went in for bright colors. It was a family trait. At school it was a piece of cake to pick me out of a lineup of town girls in their beige or pink Bobbie Brooks matching sweater-and-skirt outfits. Medgar Biddle, who was once my boyfriend for three weeks including the homecoming dance, used to say that I dressed like an eye test. I suppose he meant the type they give you when you go into the army, to see if you're color blind, not the type that starts with the big E. He said it when we were breaking up, but I was actually kind of flattered. I had decided early on that if I couldn't dress elegant, I'd dress memorable.

Mama settled back into the cane chair and scooped up another apronful of peas. Mama was not one of these that wore tight jeans to their kids' softball games. She was older than that. She had already been through a lot of wild times before she had me, including one entire husband by the name of Foster Greer. He was named after Stephen Foster, the sweet-faced man in the seventh-grade history book who wrote "My Old Kentucky Home," but twenty-two years after naming him that, Foster Greer's mother supposedly died of a broken heart. He was famous for drinking Old Grand Dad with a gasoline funnel, and always told Mama never to pull anything cute like getting pregnant. Mama says trading Foster for me was the best deal this side of the Jackson Purchase.

She snapped about three peas to every one of mine. Her

right hand twisted over and back as she snapped a little curl of string off the end of each pod and rolled out the peas with her thumb.

"The way I see it," she said, "a person isn't nothing more than a scarecrow. You, me, Earl Wickentot, the President of the United States, and even God Almighty, as far as I can see. The only difference between one that stands up good and one that blows over is what kind of a stick they're stuck up there on."

I didn't say anything for a while, and then I told her I would ask Mr. Walter for the job.

There wasn't any sound but Henry Biddle using a hay mower on his front yard, down the road, and our peas popping open to deliver their goods out into the world.

She said, "Then what? What if he don't know you're good enough for it?"

I said, "I'll tell him. If he hasn't already given it to a Candy Striper."

Mama smiled and said, "Even if."

But he hadn't. After two days passed with nothing more said about it, I stayed after class and told him that if he didn't have his mind made up yet he'd just as well let me do it, because I would do a right smart job. I had stayed out of trouble this long, I said, and didn't intend to let my effort go to waste just because I was soon going to graduate. And he said all right, he would tell Lynda, and that I should go up there Monday afternoon and she would tell me what to do.

I had expected more of a fight, and when the conversation went straight down the road this way it took me a minute to think what to say next. He had to have about the cleanest fingernails in Pittman County.

I asked him how come he was giving the job to me. He said because I was the first one to ask. Just like that. When I think of all the time and effort girls in that school put into daydreaming about staying after school to make an offer to Hughes Walter, and I was the only one to do it. Though of course it was more a question of making the right kind of offer.

It turned out that I was to work mainly for Eddie Rickett, who was in charge of the lab—this was blood and pee and a few worse things though I was not about to complain—and the x-rays. Eddie was an old freckled thing, not really old but far enough along that everybody noticed he hadn't gotten married. And Eddie being the type that nobody made it their business to ask him why not.

He didn't treat me like teacher's pet or any kind of prize-pony thing, which was okay with me. With Eddie it was no horseradish, I was there to do business and I did it. Lab and x-ray were in two connected rooms with people always coming in and out through the swinging doors with their hands full and their shoes squeaking on the black linoleum. Before long I was just another one of them, filing papers in the right place and carrying human waste products without making a face.

I learned things. I learned to look in a microscope at red blood cells, platelets they are called though they aren't like plates but little catchers' mitts, and to count them in the little squares. It was the kind of thing I'm positive could make you go blind if you kept it up, but luckily there were not that many people in Pittman County who needed their platelets counted on any given day.

I hadn't been there even one whole week when hell busted loose. It was Saturday. These orderlies came in from the emergency room yelling for Eddie to get ready for a mess in x-ray. A couple of Hardbines, they said, just the way people always said that. Eddie asked how much of a hurry it was, and if he'd need help to hold them still, and they said half and half, one of them is hot and the other cold.

I didn't have time to think about what that meant before

Jolene Shanks, or Hardbine rather, was rolled in on a wheelchair and then came a stretcher right behind her, which they parked out in the hallway. Jolene looked like the part of the movie you don't want to watch. There was a wet tongue of blood from her right shoulder all the way down her bosom, and all the color was pulled out of her lips and face, her big face like a piece of something cut out of white dough. She was fighting and cursing, though, and clearly a far cry from dead. When I took one of her wrists to help her out of the wheelchair it twisted away under my fingers like a sleeve full of cables. She was still yelling at Newt: "Don't do it," and things like that. "Go ahead and kill your daddy for all I care, he's the one you want, not yourself and not me." Then she would go still for a minute, and then she'd start up again. I wondered what Newt's daddy had to do with it.

They said Doc Finchler was called and on his way, but that Nurse MacCullers had checked her over and it wasn't as bad as it looked. The bleeding was stopped, but they would need x-rays to see where the bullet was and if it had cracked anything on its way in. I looked at Eddie wanting to know would I have to get her out of her top and brassière into one of the gowns, and couldn't help thinking about bloodstains all over the creation, having been raised you might say in the cleaning-up business. But Eddie said no, that we didn't want to move her around that much. Doc would just have to see around the hooks and the snaps.

"Lucky for you he was a bad shot," Eddie was telling Jolene as he straightened her arm out on the table, which I thought to be rude under the circumstances but then that was Eddie. I held her by the elbows trying not to hurt her any more than she was already hurt, but poor thing she was hysterical and fighting me and wouldn't shut up. In my mind's eye I could see myself in my lead apron standing over Jolene, and this is exactly what I looked like: a butcher holding down a calf on its way to becoming a cut of meat.

Then Eddie said we were done, for me to keep her in the room next door until they could see if the pictures came out; they might have to do them over if she'd moved. Then he yelled for the other one, and two guys rolled in the long stretcher with the sheet over it and started hoisting it up on the table like something served up on a big dinner plate. I stood there like a damn fool until Eddie yelled at me to get on out and look after Jolene, he wasn't needing me to hold this one down because he wasn't going anyplace. Just another pretty picture for the coroner's office, Eddie said, but I couldn't stop staring. Maybe I'm slow. I didn't understand until just then that under that sheet, that was Newt.

In the room next door there was a stretcher intended for Jolene, but she would have none of it. She took one of the hard wooden seats that swung down from the wall, and sat there blubbering, saying, "Thank God the baby was at Mom's." Saying, "What am I going to do now?" She had on this pink top that was loose so it could have gone either way, if you were pregnant or if you weren't. As far as I know she wasn't just then. It had these little openings on the shoulders and bows on the sleeves, though of course it was shot to hell now.

Jolene was a pie-faced, heavy girl and I always thought she looked the type to have gone and found trouble just to show you didn't have to be a cheerleader to be fast. The trouble with that is it doesn't get you anywhere, no more than some kid on a bicycle going no hands and no feet up and down past his mother and hollering his head off for her to look. She's not going to look till he runs into something and busts his head wide open.

Jolene and I had never been buddies or anything, she was a year or two ahead of me in school when she dropped out, but I guess when you've just been shot and your husband's dead you look for a friend in whoever is there to hand you a Tylenol with codeine. She started telling me how it was all Newt's daddy's fault, he beat him up, beat her up, and even had hit the baby with a coal scuttle. I was trying to think how a half-dead old man could beat up on Newt, who was built like a side of beef. But then they all lived together in one house and it was small. And of course the old man couldn't hear, so it would have been that kind of life. There wouldn't be much talk.

I don't remember what I said, just "Uh-huh" mostly and "You're going to be okay." She kept saying she didn't know what was going to happen now with her and the baby and old man Hardbine, oh Lord, what had she got herself into.

It wasn't the kindest thing, maybe, but at one point I actually asked her, "Jolene, why Newt?" She was slumped down and rocking a little bit in the chair, holding her hurt shoulder and looking at her feet. She had these eyes that never seemed to open all the way.

What she said was "Why not, my daddy'd been calling me a slut practically since I was thirteen, so why the hell not? Newt was just who it happened to be. You know the way it is."

I told her I didn't know, because I didn't have a daddy. That I was lucky that way. She said yeah.

By the time it was over it seemed to me it ought to be dark outside, as if such a thing couldn't have happened in daylight. But it was high noon, a whole afternoon ahead and everybody acting like here we are working for our money. I went to the bathroom and threw up twice, then came back and looked in the microscope at the little catchers' mitts, counting the same ones over and over all afternoon. Nobody gave me any trouble about it. The woman that gave up that blood, anyway, got her money's worth.

I wanted Mama to be home when I got there, so I could bawl my head off and tell her I was quitting. But she wasn't, and by the time she came in with a bag of groceries and a bushel basket of ironing for the weekend I was over it for the most part. I told her the whole thing, even Jolene's pink bow-ribbon top and the blood and all, and of course Newt, and then I told her I'd probably seen the worst I was going to see so there was no reason to quit now.

She gave me the biggest hug and said, "Missy, I have never seen the likes of you." We didn't talk too much more about it but I felt better with her there, the two of us moving around each other in the kitchen making boiled greens and eggs for dinner while it finally went dark outside. Every once in a while she would look over at me and just shake her head.

There were two things about Mama. One is she always expected the best out of me. And the other is that then no matter what I did, whatever I came home with, she acted like it was the moon I had just hung up in the sky and plugged in all the stars. Like I was that good.

I kept that job. I stayed there over five and a half years and counted more platelets than you can think about. A person might think I didn't do much else with all that time other than keeping Mama entertained and off and on dating Sparky Pike—who most people considered to be a high-class catch because he had a steady job as a gas-meter man—until I got fed up with hearing who laid out in their backyards by their meters wearing what (or nothing-but-what) in the summer-time.

But I had a plan. In our high school days the general idea of fun had been to paint "Class of '75" on the water tower, or maybe tie some farmer's goat up there on Halloween, but now I had serious intentions. In my first few years at Pittman County Hospital I was able to help Mama out with the rent and the bills and still managed to save up a couple hundred dollars. With most of it I bought a car, a '55 Volkswagen bug with no windows to speak of, and no back seat and no starter. But it was easy to push start without help once you got the hang of it, the wrong foot on the clutch and the other leg out the door, especially if you parked on a hill, which in that part of Kentucky you could hardly do anything but. In this car I intended to drive out of Pittman County one day and never look back, except maybe for Mama.

The day I brought it home, she knew I was going to get away. She took one look and said, "Well, if you're going to have you an old car you're going to know how to drive an old car." What she meant was how to handle anything that might come along, I suppose, because she stood in the road with her arms crossed and watched while I took off all four tires and put them back on. "That's good, Missy," she said. "You'll drive away from here yet. I expect the last I'll see of you will be your hind end." She said, "What do you do if I let the air out of the front tire?" Which she did. I said, "Easy, I put on the spare," which believe it or not that damned old car actually had.

Then she let out the back one too and said, "Now what?" Mama had evidently run into trouble along these lines, at some point in her life with Foster and an Oldsmobile, and she wanted to be sure I was prepared.

I thought, and then I said, "I have a bicycle pump. I can get enough air in it to drive down to Norman Strick's and get it pumped up the rest of the way." And she just stood there with her arms crossed and I could see that she nor God nor nobody else was going to do it for me, so I closed my eyes and went at that tire for everything I was worth.

Mama hadn't been there that day. She couldn't know that all I was seeing behind those shut eyes was Newt Hardbine's daddy flying up into the air, in slow motion, like a fish flinging sideways out of the water. And Newt laid out like a hooked bass.

* * *

When I drove over the Pittman line I made two promises to myself. One I kept, the other I did not.

The first was that I would get myself a new name. I wasn't crazy about anything I had been called up to that point in life, and this seemed like the time to make a clean break. I didn't have any special name in mind, but just wanted a change. The more I thought about it, the more it seemed to me that a name is not something a person really has the right to pick out, but is something you're provided with more or less by chance. I decided to let the gas tank decide. Wherever it ran out, I'd look for a sign.

I came pretty close to being named after Homer, Illinois, but kept pushing it. I kept my fingers crossed through Sidney, Sadorus, Cerro Gordo, Decatur, and Blue Mound, and coasted into Taylorville on the fumes. And so I am Taylor Greer. I suppose you could say I had some part in choosing this name, but there was enough of destiny in it to satisfy me.

The second promise, the one that I broke, had to do with where I would end up. I had looked at some maps, but since I had never in my own memory been outside of Kentucky (I was evidently born across the river in Cincinnati, but that is beside the point), I had no way of knowing why or how any particular place might be preferable to any other. That is, apart from the pictures on the gas station brochures: Tennessee claimed to be the Volunteer State, and Missouri the Show-Me State, whatever that might mean, and nearly everyplace appeared to have plenty of ladies in fifties hairdos standing near waterfalls. These brochures I naturally did not trust as far as I could throw them out the window. Even Pittman, after all, had once been chosen an All-Kentucky City, on the basis of what I do not know. Its abundance of potato bugs and gossip, perhaps. I knew how people could toot their own horn without any earthly cause.

And so what I promised myself is that I would drive west

until my car stopped running, and there I would stay. But there were some things I hadn't considered. Mama taught me well about tires, and many other things besides, but I knew nothing of rocker arms. And I did not know about the Great Plain.

The sight of it filled me with despair. I turned south from Wichita, Kansas, thinking I might find a way around it, but I didn't. There was central Oklahoma. I had never imagined that any part of a round earth could be so flat. In Kentucky you could never see too far, since there were always mountains blocking the other side of your view, and it left you the chance to think something good might be just over the next hill. But out there on the plain it was all laid out right in front of you, and no matter how far you looked it didn't get any better. Oklahoma made me feel there was nothing left to hope for.

My car gave out somewhere in the middle of a great emptiness that according to the road signs was owned by the Cherokee tribe. Suddenly the steering wheel bore no relation to where the car was going. By the grace of some miracle I surely did not yet deserve, I managed to wobble off the highway all in one piece and find a service station.

The man who straightened out my rocker arm was named Bob Two Two. I am not saying he didn't ask a fair price—I should have been able to fix it myself—but he went home that night with his pocket full of something near half the money I had. I sat in the parking lot looking out over that godless stretch of nothing and came the closest I have ever come to cashing in and plowing under. But there was no sense in that. My car was fixed.

I had to laugh, really. All my life, Mama had talked about the Cherokee Nation as our ace in the hole. She'd had an old grandpa that was full-blooded Cherokee, one of the few that got left behind in Tennessee because he was too old or too ornery to get marched over to Oklahoma. Mama would say, "If we run out of luck we can always go live on the Cherokee Nation." She and I both had enough blood to qualify. According to Mama, if you're one-eighth or more they let you in. She called this our "head rights."

Of course, if she had ever been there she would have known it was not a place you'd ever go to live without some kind of lethal weapon aimed at your hind end. It was clear to me that the whole intention of bringing the Cherokees here was to get them to lie down and die without a fight. The Cherokees believed God was in trees. Mama told me this. When I was a kid I would climb as high as I could in a tree and not come down until dinner. "That's your Indian blood," she would say. "You're trying to see God."

From what I could see, there was not one tree in the entire state of Oklahoma.

The sun was headed fast for the flat horizon, and then there would be nothing but twelve hours of headlights in front of me. I was in a hurry to get out of there. My engine was still running from Bob Two Two's jumper cables, and I hated to let a good start go to waste, but I was tired and didn't want to begin a night of driving without a cup of coffee and something to eat. I drove across the big patch of dirt that lay between the garage and another small brick-shaped building that had a neon Budweiser light in the window.

When I drove around to the front, a swarm of little boys came down on my car like bees on a bear.

"Wash your windows, lady," they said. "Dollar for the whole car."

"I got no windows," I told them. I reached back and put my hand through the side window hole to show them. "See, just the windshield. Lucky me, because I got no dollar either."

The boys went around the car putting their hands through all the window holes again and again. I thought twice about leaving my stuff in the car while I went into the restaurant. I didn't have anything worth taking, but then it was all I had.

I asked them, "You boys live around here?"

They looked at each other. "Yeah," one of them said. "He does. He's my brother. Them two don't."

"You ever hear of a Polaroid memory?"

The big one nodded. The others just stared.

"Well, I got one," I said. "It's just like a camera. My memory just took a picture of what y'all look like, so don't take any stuff out of my car, okay? You take any stuff, you're in for it."

The kids backed off from the car rubbing their hands on their sides, like they were wiping off anything their hands might have already imagined grabbing onto.

After the cool night, the hot air inside the bar hit me like something you could swim through. Near the door there was a wire rack of postcards. Some had Indians in various hokey poses, but most were views-from-the-air of Oral Roberts University, which apparently was in the vicinity—although I'm pretty sure if it had been within two hundred miles I could have seen it from the parking lot.

I picked out one with two Indian women on it, an older and a younger, pretty one, standing side by side next to some corn-grinding thing. I had often wondered which one-eighth of me was Cherokee, and in this picture I could begin to see it. The long, straight hair and the slender wrist bones. The younger one was wearing my two favorite colors, turquoise and red. I would write on it to Mama, "Here's us."

I sat down at the counter and gave the man a dime for the postcard. I nodded when he pointed the pot of coffee at me, and he filled my cup. The jukebox was playing Kenny Rogers and the TV behind the counter was turned on, although the sound was off. It was some program about, or from, Oral Roberts University, which I recognized from the postcards. Frequently a man with clean fat hands and a crest of hair like a woodpecker would talk on and on without sound. I presumed this was Oral Roberts himself, though of course I can't say for certain that it was. From time to time a line of blue writing would run across the bottom of the screen. Sometimes it gave a telephone number, and sometimes it just said "Praise the Lord." I wrote my postcard to Mama. "Grandpa had the right idea," I told her. "No offense, but the Cherokee Nation is crap. Headed west. Love, M." It didn't seem right just yet to sign it Taylor.

The place was cleared out except for two men at the counter, a white guy and an Indian. They both wore cowboy hats. I thought to myself, I guess now Indians can be cowboys too, though probably not vice versa. The Indian man wore a brown hat and had a brown, fine-looking face that reminded me of an eagle, not that I had ever actually seen an eagle. He was somewhere between young and not so young. I tried to imagine having a great grandpa with a nose like that and such a smooth chin. The other one in the gray hat looked like he had a mean streak to him. You can tell the kind that's looking for trouble. They were drinking beers and watching Oral on the silent TV, and once in a great while they would say something to each other in a low voice. They might have been on their first couple of beers, or they might have been drinking since sunup—with some types you can't tell until it's too late. I tried to recall where I had been at sunup that day. It was in St. Louis, Missouri, where they have that giant McDonald's thing towering over the city, but that didn't seem possible. That seemed like about a blue moon ago.

"You got anything to eat that costs less than a dollar?" I asked the old guy behind the counter. He crossed his arms and looked at me for a minute, as if nobody had ever asked him this before.

"Ketchup," the gray-hat cowboy said. "Earl serves up a mean bottle of ketchup, don't you, Earl?" He slid the ketchup bottle down the counter so hard it rammed my cup and spilled out probably five cents' worth of coffee.

"You think being busted is a joke?" I asked him. I slid the bottle back and hit his beer mug dead center, although it did not spill. He looked at me and then looked back to the TV, like I wasn't the kind of thing to be bothered with. It made me want to spit nails.

"He don't mean nothing by it, miss," Earl told me. "He's got a bug up his butt. I can get you a burger for ninety-nine cents."

"Okay," I told Earl.

Maybe ten or fifteen minutes passed before the food came, and I kept myself awake trying to guess what the fat-hands man was saying on the TV screen. Earl's place could have done with a scrub. I could see through the open door into the kitchen, and the black grease on the back of the stove looked like it had been there since the Dawn of Man. The air in there was so hot and stale I felt like I had to breathe it twice to get any oxygen out of it. The coffee did nothing to wake me up. My food came just as I was about to step outside for some air.

I noticed another woman in the bar sitting at one of the tables near the back. She was a round woman, not too old, wrapped in a blanket. It was not an Indian blanket but a plain pink wool blanket with a satin band sewed on the edge, exactly like one Mama and I had at home. Her hair lay across her shoulders in a pair of skinny, lifeless plaits. She was not eating or drinking, but fairly often she would glance up at the two men, or maybe just one of them, I couldn't really tell. The way she looked at them made me feel like if I had better sense I'd be scared.

Earl's ninety-nine-cent burger brought me around a little, though I still felt like my head had been stuffed with that fluffy white business they use in life preservers. I imagined myself stepping outside and the wind just scattering me. I would float out over the flat, dark plain like the silvery fuzz from a milk-weed pod.

Putting it off, I read all the signs on the walls, one by one, which said things like THEY CAN'T FIRE ME, SLAVES HAVE TO BE SOLD and IN CASE OF FIRE YELL FIRE. The television kept on saying PRAISE THE LORD. 1-800-THE LORD. I tried to concentrate on keeping myself all in one place, even if it wasn't a spot I was crazy about. Then I went outside. The air was cool and I drank it too fast, getting a little dizzy. I sat with my hands on the steering wheel for a few minutes trying to think myself into the right mood for driving all night across Oklahoma.

I jumped when she pecked on the windshield. It was the round woman in the blanket.

"No thanks," I said. I thought she wanted to wash the windshield, but instead she went around to the other side and opened the door. "You need a lift someplace?" I asked her.

Her body, her face, and her eyes were all round. She was someone you could have drawn a picture of by tracing around dimes and quarters and jar tops. She opened up the blanket and took out something alive. It was a child. She wrapped her blanket around and around it until it became a round bundle with a head. Then she set this bundle down on the seat of my car.

"Take this baby," she said.

It wasn't a baby, exactly. It was probably old enough to walk, though not so big that it couldn't be easily carried. Somewhere between a baby and a person.

"Where do you want me to take it?"

She looked back at the bar, and then looked at me. "Just take it."

I waited a minute, thinking that soon my mind would clear and I would understand what she was saying. It didn't. The child had the exact same round eyes. All four of those eyes were hanging there in the darkness, hanging on me, waiting.

The Budweiser sign blinked on and off, on and off, throwing a faint light that made the whites of their eyes look orange.

"Is this your kid?"

She shook her head. "My dead sister's."

"Are you saying you want to give me this child?"

"Yes."

"If I wanted a baby I would have stayed in Kentucky," I informed her. "I could have had babies coming out my ears by now."

A man came out of the bar, gray hat or brown hat I couldn't tell because my car was parked some distance from the door. He got into a pickup truck but didn't start the ignition or turn on the lights.

"Is that your man in there, in the bar?" I asked her.

"Don't go back in there. I'm not saying why. Just don't."

"Look," I said, "even if you wanted to, you can't just give somebody a kid. You got to have the papers and stuff. Even a car has papers, to prove you didn't steal it."

"This baby's got no papers. There isn't nobody knows it's alive, or cares. Nobody that matters, like the police or nothing like that. This baby was born in a Plymouth."

"Well, it didn't happen this morning," I said. "Plymouth or no Plymouth, this child has been around long enough for somebody to notice." I had a foggy understanding that I wasn't arguing the right point. This was getting us nowhere.

She put her hands where the child's shoulders might be, under all that blanket, and pushed it gently back into the seat, trying to make it belong there. She looked at it for a long time. Then she closed the door and walked away.

As I watched her I was thinking that she wasn't really round. Without the child and the blanket she walked away from my car a very thin woman.

I held the steering wheel and dug my fingernails into my

palms, believing the pain might force my brain to wake up and think what to do. While I was thinking, the woman got in the pickup truck and it drove away without lights. I wondered if that was for a reason, or if it just didn't have headlights. "Praise the Lord," I said out loud. "At least my car has headlights."

I thought: I can take this Indian child back into that bar and give it to Earl or whichever of those two guys is left. Just set it on the counter with the salt and pepper and get the hell out of here. Or I can go someplace and sleep, and think of something to do in the morning.

While I was deciding, the lights in the bar flickered out. The Budweiser sign blinked off and stayed off. Another pickup truck swung around in the gravel parking lot and headed off toward the highway.

It took everything I had to push-start the car. Naturally I had not found a hill to park on in Oklahoma. "Shit!" I said. "Shit fire son of a bitch!" I pushed and pushed, jumped in and popped the clutch, jumped out and pushed some more. I could see the child's big eyes watching me in the dark.

"This isn't as dumb as you think," I said. "It's easier in Kentucky."

My car has no actual way of keeping track of miles, but I believe it must have been fifty or more before we came to a town. It was getting cold with no windows, and the poor little thing must have been freezing but didn't make a peep.

"Can you talk?" I said. I wondered if maybe it spoke something besides English. "What am I supposed to do with you tonight?" I said. "What do you eat?"

I believe that flat places are quieter than hilly ones. The sounds of the cars on the highway seemed to get sucked straight out over the empty fields where there was nothing, not even a silo, to stop them from barreling on forever into the night. I began to think that if I opened my mouth nothing would come out. I hummed to myself to keep some sound in my ears. At that time I would have paid my bottom dollar for a radio. I would even have listened to Oral Roberts. I talked to the poor, dumbstruck child to stay awake, although with every passing mile I felt less sleepy and more concerned that I was doing something extremely strange.

We passed a sign that said some-odd number of miles to the Pioneer Woman Museum. Great, I thought. Now we're getting somewhere.

"Are you a girl or a boy?" I asked the child. It had a cereal-bowl haircut, like pictures you see of Chinese kids. She or he said nothing. I supposed I would find out eventually.

After a while I began to wonder if perhaps it was dead. Maybe the woman had a dead child, murdered or some such thing, and had put it in my car, and I was riding down the road beside it, talking to it. I had read a story in Senior English about a woman who slept with her dead husband for forty years. It was basically the same idea as the guy and his mother in *Psycho*, except that Norman Bates in *Psycho* was a taxidermist and knew how to preserve his mother so she wouldn't totally rot out. Indians sometimes knew how to preserve the dead. I had read about Indian mummies out West. People found them in caves. I told myself to calm down. I remembered that the baby's eyes had been open when she put it down on the seat. But then again, so what if its eyes were open? Had it blinked? What was the penalty for carrying a dead Indian child across state lines?

After a while I smelled wet wool. "Merciful heavens," I said. "I guess you're still hanging in there."

My plan had been to sleep in the car, but naturally my plans had not taken into account a wet, cold kid. "We're really in trouble now, you know it?" I said. "The next phone booth we come to, I'm going to have to call 1-800-THE LORD."

The next phone booth we did come to, as a matter of fact, was outside the Mustang Motel. I drove by slowly and checked the place out, but the guy in the office didn't look too promising.

There were four or five motels pretty much in a row, their little glass-fronted offices shining out over the highway like TV screens. Some of the offices were empty. In the Broken Arrow Motor Lodge there was a gray-haired woman. Bingo.

I parked under the neon sign of a pink arrow breaking and unbreaking, over and over, and went into the office.

"Hi," I said to the lady. "Nice evening. Kind of chilly, though."

She was older than she had looked from outside. Her hands shook when she lifted them off the counter and her head shook all the time, just slightly, like she was trying to signal "No" to somebody behind my back, on the sly.

But she wasn't, it was just age. She smiled. "Winter's on its way," she said.

"Yes, ma'am, it is."

"You been on the road long?"

"Way too long," I said. "This place is real nice. It's a sight for sore eyes. Do you own this place?"

"My son owns it," she said, her head shaking. "I'm over here nights."

"So it's kind of a family thing?"

"Kind of like. My daughter-in-law and me, we do most of the cleaning up and all, and my son does the business end of it. He works in the meat-packing plant over at Ponca City. This here's kind of a sideline thing."

"You reckon it's going to fill up tonight?"

She laughed. "Law, honey, I don't think this place been filled up since President Truman." She slowly turned the pages of the big check-in book.

"President Truman stayed here?"

She looked up at me, her eyes swimming through her thick

glasses like enormous tadpoles. "Why no, honey, I don't think so. I'd remember a thing like that."

"You seem like a very kind person," I said, "so I'm not going to beat around the bush. I've got a big problem. I can't really afford to pay for a room, and I wouldn't even bother you except I've got a child out in that car that's wet and cold and looking to catch pneumonia if I don't get it to bed someplace warm."

She looked out toward the car and shook her head, but of course I couldn't tell what that meant. She said, "Well, honey, I don't know."

"I'll take anything you've got, and I'll clean up after myself, and tomorrow morning I'll change every bed in this place. Or anything else you want me to do. It's just for one night."

"Well," she said, "I don't know."

"Let me go get the baby," I said. "You won't mind if I just bring the poor kid in here to warm up while you decide."

The most amazing thing was the way that child held on. From the first moment I picked it up out of its nest of wet blanket, it attached itself to me by its little hands like roots sucking on dry dirt. I think it would have been easier to separate me from my hair.

It's probably a good thing. I was so tired, and of course I was not in the habit anyway of remembering every minute where I had put down a child, and I think if it had not been stuck to me I might have lost it while I was messing with the car and moving stuff into the little end room of the Broken Arrow. As it was, I just ended up carrying it back and forth a lot. It's like the specimens back at the hospital, I told myself. You just have to keep track. It looked like carrying blood and pee was to be my lot in life.

Once we were moved in I spread the blanket over a chair to dry and ran a few inches of warm water in the tub. "First order of business," I said, "is to get you a bath. We'll work out the rest tomorrow." I remembered the time I had found a puppy and wanted to keep it, but first Mama made me spend thirty-five cents a word to run an ad in the paper. "What if it was yours?" she had said. "Think how bad you'd want it back." The ad I wrote said: FOUND PUPPY, BROWN SPOTS, NEAR FLOYD'S MILL ROAD. I had resented how Floyd's Mill Road was three whole words, a dollar and five cents.

I thought to myself, I'd pay a hundred and five to get this one back to its rightful owner. But what kind of ad would you run to find out if anybody had lost an Indian child?

All of the baby's clothes were way too big, with sleeves rolled up and shirt tails wrapped around, and everything wet as mud boots and as hard to get off. There was a bruise twice the size of my thumb on its inner arm. I threw the soggy shirt in the sink to soak. The child's hands constantly caught my fingers and wouldn't let go. "You little booger," I said, shaking my finger and the little fist. "You're like a mud turtle. If a mud turtle bites you, it won't let go till it thunders." I hadn't any sooner gotten the hands pried loose from my fingers before they grabbed onto my shirt sleeves and my hair. When I pulled off the pants and the diapers there were more bruises.

Bruises and worse.

The Indian child was a girl. A girl, poor thing. That fact had already burdened her short life with a kind of misery I could not imagine. I thought I knew about every ugly thing that one person does to another, but I had never even thought about such things being done to a baby girl. She sat quietly in the bathtub watching me, and I just prayed she had enough backbone not to fall over and drown, because I had to let her go. I doubled up on the floor at the base of the toilet and tried not to throw up. The floor was linoleum in a pattern that looked like rubber bricks set in mortar. Nothing, not Newt Hardbine or anything else I had ever seen, had made me feel like this.

The kid was splashing like a toad frog. Her fingers were wiggling and slapping at the surface of the water, no doubt trying to grab hold of something. "Here," I said, and handed her a washcloth that had BROKEN ARROW written on the selvage in indelible magic marker. She hugged that wash cloth and smiled. I swear to God.

After I washed and dried her I put her to bed in a T-shirt that one of Mama's people had brought me one summer from Kentucky Lake. It was tight on me, and said DAMN I'M GOOD. I am skinny and flat-chested like a model, and always looked great in that T-shirt if I say so myself. It was turquoise with red letters, and came down past the baby's knees. "These are good colors," I said, trying to pull it over her sleepy, bobbing head. "Indian colors." Finally her hands were empty and relaxed. She was asleep.

I took out the stamps I had brought from home wrapped in waxed paper, and licked one and stuck it on my souvenir postcard from the Cherokee Nation. I added a line at the bottom:

"I found my head rights, Mama. They're coming with me."

TWO

New Year's Pig

Lou Ann Ruiz lived in Tucson, but thought of herself as just an ordinary Kentuckian a long way from home. She had acquired her foreign last name from her husband, Angel. As it turned out, this was the only part of him that would remain with her. He left on Halloween.

Three years before on Christmas Day Angel had had a bad accident in his pickup truck. It left him with an artificial leg below the knee, and something else that was harder to pin down. Lou Ann often would get the feeling he didn't really like her, or anyone else for that matter. He blamed people for things beyond their control. Lou Ann was now pregnant with her first, which was due in two months. She hoped more than anything that it wouldn't be born on Christmas Day.

She had been thinking about herself and Angel splitting up for even longer than she had been pregnant, but she didn't particularly do anything about it. That was Lou Ann's method. She expected that a divorce would just develop, like a pregnancy—that eventually they would reach some kind of agreement without having to discuss it. This isn't how it worked out.

When she began to turn away from him in bed at night, and to get up quietly in the mornings to cook his eggs, Angel seemed to accept this. Possibly he thought she was worried about the baby. Later, when the arguments resumed, they had a hopeless quality that Lou Ann had not experienced before. The arguments made her feel that her bones were made of something like the rubber in a Gumby doll, that her body could be bent into any shape and would stay that way. She would sit at the kitchen table tracing her fingers over the artificial knots in the wood-look Formica table top while Angel paced back and forth and accused her of thinking he wasn't good enough. He listed names of people, mostly friends of his she could barely remember having met, and asked her if she had slept with them, or if she had wanted to. Angel limped so slightly it was barely noticeable, but there was just the faintest jingling sound with every other step. It was probably something he could have gotten adjusted if he hadn't been too proud to take it into the prosthetic shop. No matter how loud his voice became, Lou Ann could still hear the jingle. She could never think of anything to say that would change the course of these arguments, and so they went on and on. Once, several years before, she had become so frustrated with Angel that she threw a package of baloney at him. They both laughed, and it ended the argument. Now she didn't have the strength to get up and open the refrigerator.

Finally he had said it was because of his leg, and no matter what she said he wouldn't hear it any other way. She more or less gave up talking, and when she lay on her back at night she felt it was the guilt weighing down on her aching spine, instead of the baby.

She could remember wheeling him down the white corridor at the hospital to bring him home, just two and a half weeks after the accident. She had felt filled-up and proud; everything she loved in the world was in that chair. Having nearly lost Angel made him all the more precious. One of the doctors said that his boot had probably saved his life, and she felt like kissing it, although in all the confusion no one knew exactly where it had ended up. The boot had caught on the door frame, causing him to be dragged several hundred yards along with the truck as it spun into an irrigation ditch along Highway 86 west of Tucson. The damage to the truck was surprisingly minor. There was a bottle of Jim Beam in the cab that wasn't even broken. He lost his leg because of being twisted and dragged, but the doctor said if he had been thrown from the vehicle at such a high speed he would have died instantly. It crossed Lou Ann's mind that he might have just been saying this because Angel was so upset about losing a leg, but she decided it would be best to take the doctor's word for it.

When he came home Lou Ann gave up her part-time job at the Three Bears Day School to be with him, insisting that they would get along fine on his disability pay until he was able to go back to work at the bottling plant. She spent weeks playing gin rummy with Angel on the bed and running out to Lee Sing's market to get whatever he wanted. She loved the way he asked for things specifically, like Mrs. Smith's pound cake or Beefaroni. She wouldn't have guessed Angel had even noticed that things came in different brand names, other than beer. It was their best time together.

Never at any time was Lou Ann repulsed by the amputation. After his stump had healed it did not bother her to touch it, which Angel himself would never do. It had a smooth, defenseless look to it that reminded her of a penis, something she had always thought seemed out of place on a man's body. When he got the prosthesis she was fascinated at first by the way it was put together, and then thought nothing of it at all. It was something that lay on the floor by his side of the bed at night while the cat, Snowboots, lay curled up by hers. It took Angel some time to get used to the new leg, but in the long run there was very little he couldn't do with it, except that he was no longer able to wear cowboy boots. For some reason the ankle hinges were not flexible enough to fit into a boot. Other than this, Lou Ann could never see why the accident needed to change his life at all. He hadn't been a cowboy for years, anyway.

On the Friday Angel left, he had long since gone back to work. He probably didn't think about it being Halloween, only that it was payday. Lou Ann didn't think of any of this, of course, since she had no idea that it was the particular day her husband had decided to leave her.

Lou Ann was in Dr. Pelinowsky's waiting room waiting for her seventh-month prenatal exam. She had a magazine on her lap, or what was left of her lap, but preferred to stare instead at an enormous wall calendar that showed all the months at once. She was anxious about her child's birthday. Christmas had been difficult for Angel and Lou Ann since the accident, naturally, and they had just about stopped celebrating it altogether. Having a baby on that day would just be a reminder. And besides she had read in *McCall's* that children with Christmas birthdays often feel cheated out of having their own special day. Lou Ann thought being born the day after, when everybody is fed up with celebrating, would just be that much worse. She decided to ask the doctor if there was some way to make sure the baby would come before Christmas, although she was pretty sure there wasn't.

Dr. Pelinowsky's nurses seemed to like him, and called him "Dr. P." Lou Ann thought this was a hoot because he was OB-GYN, a maternity doctor, which all starts when you bring in a jar of pee. She had to keep from laughing out loud whenever she heard the nurses call out over the intercom. "Doctor Pee, Doctor Pee."

A nurse with crispy-looking white hair and a lavender pants suit came out and called Lou Ann's name. She called her Mrs. Angel Ruiz. Angel would always correct Anglos when they pronounced his name wrong. "Ahn-*hel!*" he would say. "I'm not a damn baseball team!" But Lou Ann rarely corrected anybody on anything. Her mother, Mrs. Logan, still pronounced neither Angel's first name nor their last name correctly, saying it something like Ruins. She hadn't wanted Lou Ann to marry Angel in the first place, but for the wrong reasons. She disliked him because he was Mexican, which didn't make the slightest difference to Lou Ann. In Tucson, she tried to explain to her mother, there were so many Mexicans that people didn't think of them as a foreign race. They were doctors, bank clerks, TV personalities, and even owned hotels. "You can see them any day of the week eating in a Black Angus Steak House," she told her mother. Mrs. Logan, who lived in eastern Kentucky and had never seen a Mexican, thought Lou Ann was making this up.

When Dr. Pelinowsky examined her he warned again that she was gaining too much weight. Originally he had thought it might be twins, but now they knew for sure it was just Lou Ann and the baby. This time his warning about her weight was more severe. For Lou Ann, who had always been practically underweight according to the doctor's office charts, it was impossible to imagine she wouldn't be exactly the same after it was all over. But she had to admit the baby made her want to eat constantly. She told Dr. Pelinowsky that it's hard when you're in the kitchen cooking for someone all the time. He told her to put her husband on a diet too. He meant it as a joke.

On her way out the nurse gave her a pamphlet with a special diet written out in both English and Spanish. She thought about asking for a second copy to send to her mother. After four years Lou Ann still felt that she had to prove her point about Mexicans, and so she would send clippings from the newspaper when they were promoted to company vice presidents and such. Lou Ann realized, though, that this pamphlet didn't fall into that category. Her mother was no doubt already convinced that Mexicans had babies like anyone else. In fact, she had told Lou Ann that from what she heard they had too many, that they were trying to take over the world like the Catholics.

Lou Ann hadn't yet broken the news that, when the baby was born, the plan was to give it a Catholic baptism. This would be for the sake of Angel's mother, who frequently claimed to be dying from any one of various causes. The only English words she knew were the names of diseases. Lou Ann made the baptism decision purely for practical reasons: if one of the grandmothers was going to have a conniption, it might as well be the one who was eighteen hundred miles away rather than the one who lived right across town.

Lou Ann looked over the pamphlet while she waited for the bus. Like most of the other literature she had received, it had a picture on the front of a mother holding a baby. Sometimes the women in the pictures were white, sometimes Mexican, and sometimes black. They were shown holding their babies in various positions, but they were never shown as pregnant. Lou Ann wondered about this, since all the pamphlets were about prenatal care.

On the bus she decided it must have to do with the fact that the pamphlets were put together by men, who in her opinion liked the looks of a mother and baby better than a pregnant woman. She was fairly sure about this. On the bus, for instance, several men would stand up to offer her a seat, but they wouldn't quite look at her. The high school boys didn't make remarks under their breath or try to rub up against her when the bus made sudden stops and turns. To be able to relax this way on a crowded bus was a new experience for Lou Ann, and she thought that in some ways it would not be so bad to go through your life as a pregnant lady.

She watched the houses and telephone poles go sailing by. Some of the telephone poles had advertisements for Tania Maria, a woman leaning forward in a loose sweater and spike heels. She was a singer, and had enough hair for at least two people. Other telephone poles had black posters with letters that appeared to be cut out of a newspaper, like the ransom notes in mystery novels, but they were ads for bands with names like Audio Confusion and Useless Turmoil and the Meat Puppets. She thought of naming her baby Tania Maria. Angel would suggest naming it something like Meat Puppet. That would be his idea of a joke.

It was pure pleasure not to have men pushing into her and touching her on the bus. It allowed her mind to drift far away from her strange, enormous body. When she was nine her Grandfather Ormsby had given her a jackknife, and had told her that for safety's sake she should always keep a magic circle around her when she used it. She would sit in the backyard and draw a circle in the dirt that no one could come into while she whittled for hours and hours on thick brown bars of soap. The jackknife was long gone now, but once again there was something like a magic circle around her.

She got off at the Roosevelt Park stop, which was a half block from the park itself. Sprawled over the large corner lot was a place called Jesus Is Lord Used Tires. You couldn't make a mistake about the name—it was painted in big, cramped blue letters over the door, with periods inserted between the words: JESUS.IS.LORD.USED.TIRES. On the side of the pleated tin building there was a large picture of Jesus with outstretched hands and yellow streamers of light emanating from His head. There was also a whitewall tire, perhaps added to the mural as an afterthought and probably meant to have no direct connection with the Lord, but it hung in the air below His left hand very much like a large yoyo. Jesus appeared to be on the verge of performing an Around the World or some other fancy trick.

Top-heavy, chin-high stacks of Firestones and Michelins at the edge of the paved lot formed a wall between Jesus Is Lord and a combination nightclub and pornography shop next door called Fanny Heaven. There was no mistaking this place either. The front windows were whitewashed, and large signs painted over them declared GIRLS GIRLS GIRLS on one side of the door and TOTAL NUDITY on the other. On the front door of Fanny Heaven was a life-size likeness of a woman with long red hair and a leopard-skin bikini. Public art of various types was popular on this block.

Lou Ann walked past both of these establishments nearly every day. Something about the Jesus Is Lord place reminded her of Kentucky, and she always meant to ask (if she only had the nerve) if the people there came from her part of the country. Fanny Heaven she just tried to ignore. There was something innocent and primitive about the painting on the door, as though the leopard-bikini lady might have been painted by a schoolchild, except that she was positioned in such a way that the door handle, when a person pushed it, would sink into her crotch. This door always gave Lou Ann the shivers, though she tried not to give it a second thought.

She rounded the corner and stopped to do some grocery shopping at the Lee Sing Market, which faced the park directly across from where she and Angel lived. She bought most of the items recommended by the diet pamphlet, but some of them, like yogurt, were too expensive. She bought a package of macaroons because they were Angel's favorite.

The Chinese woman at the cash register was Lee Sing. Her

mother, who was said to be more than one hundred years old, lived with her in the back of the store. Lee Sing told Lou Ann she was going to have a girl. "She's high, up here," Lee Sing said, tapping her bony fist above her stomach. She said this to Lou Ann every time she came in.

"Either way is okay with me," Lou Ann said, although she was somewhat curious to see if Lee Sing would be right.

Lee Sing shook her head as she rang the cash register, and muttered something that sounded to Lou Ann like "New Year pig."

"Beg your pardon?" Lou Ann was a little afraid of Lee Sing, who often said peculiar things like this.

"Feeding a girl is like feeding the neighbor's New Year pig. All that work. In the end, it goes to some other family."

Lou Ann felt offended, but didn't really know how to answer. She was a long way from her own family in Kentucky, but she didn't see this as being entirely her fault. And it wasn't as if her brother had stuck any closer to home, either. He had gone north to work on the Alaska Pipeline and had married a Canadian dog trainer. They had four daughters with Eskimo names that Lou Ann couldn't keep straight—things that sounded like Chinook and Winnebago.

Outside it was beginning to get dark. Lou Ann crossed the park in a hurry, skirting around an old wooden trellis where several transients were congregating. As usual she tried to concentrate on not being afraid. Angel had told her that some people, like dogs, can smell fear.

When she got home she saw that Angel had already been home from work and had left again, for good. She was confused at first and thought they had been robbed, until she began to see a pattern to what was taken. She wandered around the house with her grocery bag looking at the half-empty house. After four years there was very little, other than clothes, that she thought of as belonging clearly to one or the other. In a strange way she was fascinated to see what he had claimed for his own. It revealed more to her about his personality, she thought, than she had learned during their whole marriage.

He left all of the sheets and blankets, the knickknacks, and all the kitchen things except for three matching beer mugs. He had taken some of the old magazines and paperback mysteries from the shelf. She didn't miss the books so much as she was hurt by the ugly empty spaces left behind, like missing teeth, the books on either side falling and crowding into the gaps.

Gone from the bedroom was a picture of Angel taken at a rodeo in 1978. In the picture he was sitting on top of a bull named S.O.B., which was supposed to be the meanest bull in the history of rodeo. In the entire year of 1978 only one rider had stayed on S.O.B. for eight seconds. Angel wasn't the one. At the time of this particular photo the animal was doped up on PCP, which the rodeys used to drug the bulls and horses when they moved them around. PCP was common as dirt in that line of work. Angel's rodeo name had been Dusty, which was short for Angel Dust.

He also had taken one clean towel, the only tube of toothpaste, and the TV.

Lou Ann had forgotten it was Halloween, and was completely bewildered when a mob of children came to the door. She was frightened by their dark, darting pupils peering through the little holes in their bright plastic masks. She knew they were neighborhood children she had seen a thousand times, but in their costumes she couldn't tell who they were. To calm herself down she talked to them and tried to guess whether each one was a boy or a girl. She guessed correctly on the princess, the green-faced witch, Frankenstein, and the Incredible Hulk (also green). The Extra Terrestrial she got wrong.

Now she remembered why she had needed to go to the Lee

Sing Market: she didn't have any candy to give out. She considered giving them pieces of fruit or macaroons, but this would be a waste of money. Their mothers would probably go through their bags and throw things like that away, fearing cyanide and razor blades. On television they said everything should be sealed in the original wrapper. The children seemed to feel sorry for her, but were growing impatient. They expected adults to be prepared.

"You better give us something or we'll have to soap your windows, Mrs. Ruiz," the Extra Terrestrial said half-heartedly. Lou Ann decided to go and shake out the Mickey Mouse bank, in which she had been saving pennies to buy a washing machine for the baby's diapers. Angel had laughed at her, saying the baby would have kids of its own before she could save that many pennies.

The children seemed satisfied with the pennies and went away. She left Mickey by the door so she would be better organized for the next round.

By eleven o'clock Lou Ann's feet were killing her. She could feel her heartbeat in her ankles. For three or four weeks Lou Ann's feet had been so swollen that she could only wear one particular pair of shoes, which had a strap across the ankle, and now she was going to have to go to bed with these shoes on. She couldn't bend over far enough to unbuckle the straps, and Angel was not there to do it for her. If she had thought of it she might have asked the last bunch of trick-or-treat kids to do it, but it was too late now.

As she was getting ready for bed she caught sight of herself in the mirror and thought she looked disgusting and pornographic in her nightgown and panty hose and shoes, like someone who would work at Fanny Heaven. Though of course they wouldn't have pregnant women there. Still, the thought upset her. She turned out the light but kept listening for sounds that might be more kids coming to the door, or might be Angel changing his mind, coming home. In her other ear, pressed against the pillow, she could hear the blood pumping all the way down to her feet. It sounded something like the ocean, which she had seen once with Angel in Mexico. The baby nudged and poked at her with what felt like fingers, but must be tiny elbows or feet. She thought about the baby playing in waves of her blood, on the smooth, dark beach of her insides. Her feet hurt and she couldn't find a comfortable place in the bed.

Finally, late in the night, she cried until her eye sockets felt empty. At the beach she had gotten seawater in her eyes and they felt like this. Angel had warned her to keep them shut, but she had wanted to see where she was going. You never knew what kind of thing could be down there under the water.

THREE

Jesus Is Lord Used Tires

We crossed the Arizona state line at sunup. The clouds were pink and fat and hilarious-looking, like the hippo ballerinas in a Disney movie. The road took us through a place called Texas Canyon that looked nothing like Texas, heaven be praised for that, but looked like nothing else I had ever seen either. It was a kind of forest, except that in place of trees there were all these puffy-looking rocks shaped like roundish animals and roundish people. Rocks stacked on top of one another like piles of copulating potato bugs. Wherever the sun hit them, they turned pink. The whole scene looked too goofy to be real. We whizzed by a roadside sign on which I could make out a dinosaur. I wondered if it told what kind of rocks they were, or if it was saying that they were actually petrified dinosaur turds. I was laughing my head off. "This is too much," I said to the Indian child. "This is the best thing I've seen in years." Whether my car conked out or not, I made up my mind to live in Arizona.

It was the second day of the new year. I had stayed on at the Broken Arrow through most of the holidays, earning some money changing beds. The older woman with the shakes, whose name was Mrs. Hoge, was determined that I should stay awhile. She said they could use the extra help during the Christmas season, especially since her daughter-in-law's ankles were giving her trouble. Which is no wonder. A human ankle is not designed to hold up two hundred and fifty pounds. If we were meant to weigh that much we would have big round ankles like an elephant or a hippopotamus.

They did get quite a few folks at Christmastime passing through on their way to someplace on one side or the other of Oklahoma, which was where I longed to be. But on the other hand, I was glad for the chance to make some bucks before I headed on down the pike. Mrs. Hoge's ulterior motive, I believe, was the child, which she looked after a great deal of the time. She made it plain that her fondest wish was to have a grandbaby. Whenever fat Irene would pick up the baby, which was not too often, Mrs. Hoge would declare, "Irene, you don't know how becoming that looks." As if someone ought to have a kid because it looked good on them.

By this time I had developed a name for the child, at least for the time being. I called her Turtle, on account of her grip. She still wasn't talking but she knew her name about as far as a cat ever does, which means that when you said it she would look up if she was in the right mood. Mrs. Hoge hinted in every imaginable way that she was retarded, but I maintained that she had her own ways of doing things and wasn't inclined to be pushed. She had already been pushed way too far in her lifetime, though of course I didn't tell this to old Mrs. Hoge or her daughter-in-law.

I was in hog heaven to be on the road again. In Arizona. My eyes had started to hurt in Oklahoma from all that flat land. I swear this is true. It felt like you were always having to look too far to see the horizon.

By the time we were in sight of Tucson it became clear what those goofy pink clouds had been full of: hail. Within five minutes the car was covered with ice inside and out, and there was no driving on that stuff. The traffic was moving about the speed of a government check. I left the interstate at an off ramp and pulled over next to what looked like the Flying Nun's hat made out of bumpy concrete, held up by orange poles. Possibly it had once been a gas station, although there were no pumps and the building at the back of the paved lot looked abandoned. All over the walls and boarded-up windows someone had painted what looked like sperms with little smiles in red spray paint, and sayings like "Fools Believe."

I rubbed my hands on my knees to keep them from freezing. There was thunder, though I did not see lightning. I thought of all the mud turtles in Arizona letting go. Did Arizona even have mud turtles? An old man my mama used to clean for would say if it thunders in January it will snow in July. Clearly he had never been to Arizona. Or perhaps he had.

We got out of the open car and stood under the concrete wings to stay dry. Turtle was looking interested in the scenery, which was a first. Up to then the only thing that appeared to interest her was my special way of starting the car.

"This is a foreign country," I told her. "Arizona. You know as much about it as I do. We're even steven."

The hail turned to rain and kept up for half an hour. A guy came out of the little boarded-up building and leaned against one of the orange poles near us. I wondered if he lived there, or what. (If he did live there, did he paint the sperms?) He had on camouflage army pants and a black baseball cap with cloth flaps hanging down in the back, such as Gregory Peck or whoever it was always wore in those old Foreign Legion movies. His T-shirt said VISITOR FROM ANOTHER PLANET. That's me, I thought. I should be wearing that shirt.

"You from out of town?" he asked after a while, eying my car.

"No," I said. "I go to Kentucky every year to get my license plate." I didn't like his looks.

He lit a cigarette. "What'd you pay for that bucket of bolts?"

"A buck two-eighty."

"Sassy one, aren't you?"

"You got that one right, buster," I said. I wished to God I wasn't going to have to make such a spectacle of myself later on, starting the car.

The sun came out even before the hail stopped. There was a rainbow over the mountains behind the city, and over that another rainbow with the colors upside down. Between the two rainbows the sky was brighter than everywhere else, like a white sheet lit from the back. In a few minutes it was hot. I had on a big red pullover sweater and was starting to sweat. Arizona didn't do anything halfway. If Arizona was a movie you wouldn't believe it. You'd say it was too corny for words.

I knew I had better stay put for a few more minutes to give the engine a chance to dry out. The guy was still hanging around, smoking and making me nervous.

"Watch out," he said. There was this hairy spider about the size of a small farm animal making its way across the pavement. Its legs jerked up and down like the rubber spiders on a string that you get from a gumball machine.

"I've seen worse," I said, although to tell you the truth I hadn't. It looked like something that might have crawled out of the Midnight Creature Feature.

"That's a tarantula," he said. "You got to watch out for them suckers. They can jump four feet. If they get you, you go crazy. It's a special kind of poison."

This I didn't believe. I never could figure out why men thought they could impress a woman by making the world out to be such a big dangerous deal. I mean, we've got to live in the exact same world every damn day of the week, don't we?

"What's it coming around here for?" I said. "Is it your pet, or your girlfriend?"

"Nah," he said, squashing out his cigarette, and I decided he was dumber than he was mean.

There were a lot more bugs crawling up on the cement slab. A whole swarm of black ants came out of a crack and milled around the cigarette butt trying, for reasons I could not imagine, to take it apart. Some truck had carried that tobacco all the way from Kentucky maybe, from some Hardbine's or Richey's or Biddle's farm, and now a bunch of ants were going to break it into little pieces to take back to their queen. You just never knew where something was going to end up.

"We had a lot of rain lately," the guy said. "When the ground gets full of water, the critters drown out of their holes. They got to come up and dry off." He reached out with his foot and squashed a large, shiny black bug with horns. Its wings split apart and white stuff oozed out between. It was the type that you wouldn't have guessed had wings, although I knew from experience that just about every bug has wings of one kind or another. Not including spiders.

He lit another cigarette and threw the match at the tarantula, missing it by a couple of inches. The spider raised its two front legs toward the flame like a scared lady in an old movie.

"I got things to do," I said. "So long." I put Turtle in the car, then went around to the other side and put it in neutral and started to push.

He laughed. "What is that, a car or a skateboard?"

"Look, buster, you can help give me a push, or you can stand and watch, but either way I'm out of here. This car got me here from Kentucky, and I reckon she's got a few thousand left in her."

"Not on them tires, she don't," he said. I looked back to see the rear tire flapping empty on the wheel. "Shit," I said, just as the engine caught and the car zoomed forward. In the rear-view mirror I could see broken glass glistening on the off ramp, dropping away behind me like a twinkly green lake.

I had no intention of asking the dumb guy for help. The tire looked like it was done-for anyway so I drove on it for a few blocks. There were a bank, some houses, and a park with palm trees and some sick-looking grass. Some men with rolled-up blankets tied around their waists were kicking at the dirt, probably looking for bugs to step on. Just beyond the park I could see a stack of tires. "Will you look at that," I said. "I'm one lucky duck. We should have gone to Las Vegas."

The stacked-up tires made a kind of wall on both sides of a big paved corner lot. Inside the walls a woman was using an air hose to chase bugs off the pavement, herding them along with little blasts of air. She was wearing blue jeans and cowboy boots and a red bandana on her head. A long gray braid hung down the middle of her back.

"How do," I said. I noticed that the name of the place was Jesus Is Lord Used Tires. I remembered wanting to call 1-800-THE LORD, just to see who you'd get. Maybe this was it.

"Hi, darlin," she said. "These bugs aggravate the dickens out of me after it rains, but I can't see my way clear to squashing them. A bug's just got one life to live, after all. Like us."

"I know what you mean," I said.

"Oh, bless your heart. Looks like you've got a couple of flats."

I did. I hadn't seen the rear on the right side.

"Drive it up onto the big jack," she ordered. "We'll get them off and have a look. We'll fix your little wagon right up."

I asked if Turtle could ride up on the jack, but she said it wasn't safe, so I took her out of the car and looked for a place to put her down. All those tires around made me nervous. Just out of instinct, more or less, I looked up to see if there was anything tall overhead to get thrown up onto. There was nothing but clear blue sky.

Off to one side there were some old wheel rims and flat tires. An empty tire couldn't possibly explode, I reasoned, so I sat Turtle down in one of those.

"What's your little girl's name?" the woman wanted to know, and when I told her she didn't bat an eye. Usually people would either get embarrassed or give me a lecture. She told me her name was Mattie.

"She's a cute little thing," Mattie said.

"How do you know she's a girl?" I wasn't lipping off, for once. Just curious. It's not as if I had her dressed in pink.

"Something about the face."

We rolled the tires over to a tub of water. Mattie rubbed Ivory soap on the treads and then dunked them in like big doughnuts. Little threads of bubbles streamed up like strings of glass beads. Lots of them. It looked like a whole jewelry store in there.

"I'm sorry to tell you, hon, these are bad. I can tell you right now these aren't going to hold a patch. They're shot through." She looked concerned. "See these places here along the rim? They're sliced." She ran her hand along the side of the tire under the water. She had a gold wedding band settled into the flesh of her finger, the way older women's rings do when they never take them off.

"I'm sorry," she said again, and I could tell she really was. "There's a Goodyear place down the road about six blocks. If you want to roll them down there for a second opinion."

"That's okay," I said. "I'll take your word for it." Turtle was slapping at the side of her flat whitewall with one hand. The other had caught hold of the doohickey where the air goes in. I tried to think what in the world we were going to do now. "How much for new ones?" I asked.

Mattie considered for a minute. "I could give you a pair of good retreads, five thousand miles guaranteed, put on and balanced for sixty-five."

"I'll have to think on that one," I said. She was so nice I didn't want to tell her flat out that I couldn't afford new tires.

"It's too early in the morning for bad news," Mattie said. "I was just brewing up a pot of coffee. You want a cup of coffee? Come sit."

"Okay," I said. I collected Turtle out of the tire and carried her to the back of the shop. It was a big old two-story place, and there at the back of the garage was an area with a sink and some shelves, some folding chairs painted blue, a metal table, and a Mr. Coffee. I scooted another flat over next to the chairs and set Turtle down in it. I was glad to be away from that wall of tires, all of them bulging to burst. Hanging around here would be like living in a house made of bombs. The sound of the air hose alone gave me the willies.

"These come in pretty handy," I said, trying to be cheerful. "I know what I can use those two flat tires for."

"I've got some peanut-butter crackers," Mattie said, leaning over Turtle. "Will she eat peanut butter?"

"She eats anything. Just don't let her get hold of anything you don't want to part with. Like your hair," I said. Mattie's braid was swinging into the danger zone.

She poured coffee into a mug that said "BILL with a capital B," and handed it to me. She poured a cup for herself in a white mug with cartoon rabbits all over it. They were piled all over each other like the rocks in Texas Canyon. After a minute I realized that the rabbits were having sex in about a trillion different positions. I couldn't figure this woman out. This was definitely not 1-800-THE LORD.

"You must have come a ways," she said. "I saw your plates were Kentucky. Or plate, rather. You don't have to have them both front and back in Kentucky?"

"No. Just the back."

"Here you've got to have one on the front too. I guess so the cops can get you coming and going." She handed Turtle a peanut-butter cracker, which she grabbed with both hands. It broke to smithereens, and she got such big sad eyes I thought she was going to cry.

"It's all right, honey," Mattie said. "You put that one in your mouth and I'll give you another one." Turtle did. I was amazed. She had never been this kind to Mrs. Hoge. Mattie was clearly accustomed to dealing with kids.

"Are you on the road?" she asked me.

"Have been up to now. From Kentucky, with a stopover in Oklahoma. We're out to see what we can see. Now I guess we'll see how we like Tucson."

"Oh, you will. I ought to know, I've lived my whole life here. And that's a rare breed, let me tell you. I don't think there's hardly a soul in Tucson anymore that was born here. Most of them come, you know, from out of state. My husband, Samuel, was from Tennessee. He came out as a young man for his asthma and he never could get used to the dry. I love it, though. I guess it's all in what you're used to."

"I guess," I said. I was dying to know about the name of the place, but couldn't think of a polite way to bring it up. "Is this tire place part of a national chain, or something like that?" I finally asked. That sounded polite, but dumb.

She laughed. "No, me and my husband started it up. His dad was a mechanic, so Sam was a grease monkey born and raised. He was the one that named the place. He was kind of fanatical, you might say. Bless his soul." She handed Turtle another cracker. The kid was eating like a house on fire. "He got some

Mexican kids to do the painting out front. I never did change it, it's something different. Lots of people stop in for curiosity. Does that baby want some juice? She needs something to wash that peanut butter down with."

"Don't put yourself out. I can get her some water out of the tap."

"I'll run get some apple juice. I won't be a minute." I had thought she meant she was actually going to a store, but she went through a door at the back of the shop. Apparently there was more to this building, including a refrigerator with apple juice in it. I wondered if Mattie lived on the premises, maybe upstairs.

While she was gone two men stopped by, almost at exactly the same time, although they were not together. One of them asked for Matilda. He wanted an alignment and to pick up a tire for his ORV. He said it as though everybody ought to know what an ORV was, and maybe have one or two at home. The other man had on a black shirt with a white priest's collar, and blue jeans, of all things. I wondered if maybe he was some kind of junior-varsity priest. I really had no idea. They didn't have Catholics in Pittman.

"She'll be back in about two seconds," I told them. "She just went to get something."

The ORV fellow waited, but the priest said he would come back later. He seemed a little jumpy. As he drove away I noticed there was a whole family packed into the back of his station wagon. They looked like Indians.

"Well, how in the world are you, Roger?" Mattie said when she came back. "Just make yourself at home, hon, this won't take a minute," she told me, and handed me an orange cup with a little drinking spout, which must have been designed especially for small children. I wondered if it was hard to fill it through that little spout. Once Turtle got her hands on this cup she wasn't going to want to give it up.

Roger drove his car onto a platform that was attached to a red machine with knobs and dials on it. Mattie started up the machine, which made the front tires of Roger's Toyota spin around, and after a minute she lay down on one shoulder and adjusted something under the front. She didn't get that dirty, either. I had never seen a woman with this kind of know-how. It made me feel proud, somehow. In Pittman if a woman had tried to have her own tire store she would have been run out of business. That, or the talk would have made your ears curl up like those dried apricot things. "If Jesus is indeed Lord," I said to myself, "He surely will not let this good, smart woman get blown sky-high by an overfilled tire. Or me either, while He's at it."

The two of them went out to the wall of tires and pulled down a couple of smallish fat ones. They hit the ground with a smack, causing both Turtle and me to jump. Roger picked one of them up and dribbled it like a basketball. He and Mattie were talking, and Roger was making various vibrating sounds with his lips. I supposed he was trying to describe something that was wrong with his ORV. Mattie listened in an interested way. She was really nice to Roger, even though he was bald and red-faced and kind of bossy. She didn't give him any lip.

When she came back Turtle had drunk all her juice and was banging the cup against the tire, demanding more in her speechless way. I was starting to get embarrassed.

"You want more juice, don't you?" Mattie said to Turtle in a grownup-to-baby voice. "It's a good thing I brought the whole bottle down in the first place."

"Please don't go out of your way," I said. "We've put you out enough already. I have to tell you the truth, I can't even afford to buy one tire right now, much less two. Not for a while, anyway, until I find work and a place for us to live." I picked up Turtle but she went on banging the cup against my shoulder.

"Why, honey, don't feel bad. I wasn't trying to make a sale. I just thought you two needed some cheering up." She pried the cup out of Turtle's hand and refilled it. The top snapped right off. I hadn't thought of that.

"You must have grandbabies around," I said.

"Mmm-hmmm. Something like that." She handed the cup back to Turtle and she sucked on it hard, making a noise like a pond frog. I wondered what, exactly, could be "something like" grandbabies.

"It's so dry out here kids will dehydrate real fast," Mattie told me. "They'll just dry right up on you. You have to watch out for that."

"Oh, right," I said. I wondered how many other things were lurking around waiting to take a child's life when you weren't paying attention. I was useless. I was crazy to think I was doing this child a favor by whisking her away from the Cherokee Nation. Now she would probably end up mummified in Arizona.

"What kind of work you looking for?" Mattie rinsed the coffee cups and set them upside down on a shelf. A calendar above the shelf showed a bare-chested man in a feather headdress and heavy gold arm bracelets carrying a woman who looked dead or passed out.

"Anything, really. I have experience in housecleaning, x-rays, urine tests, and red blood counts. And picking bugs off bean vines."

Mattie laughed. "That's a peculiar résumé."

"I guess I've had a peculiar life," I said. It was hot, Turtle was spilling or spitting juice down my shoulder blade, and I was getting more depressed by the minute. "I guess you don't have bean vines around here," I said. "That kind of limits my career options."

"Well, heck yes, girl, we've got bean vines!" Mattie said. "Even purple ones. Did you ever see purple beans?"

"Not that were alive," I said.

"Come on back here and let me show you something."

We went through the door at the back, which led through a little room jam-packed with stuff. There was a desk covered with papers, and all around against the walls there were waist-high stacks of old *National Geographics* and *Popular Mechanics* and something called *The Beacon,* which showed Jesus in long, swirling robes floating above a lighthouse. Behind the desk there was a staircase and another door that led out the back. I could hear someone thumping around overhead in stocking feet.

Outside was a bright, wild wonderland of flowers and vegetables and auto parts. Heads of cabbage and lettuce sprouted out of old tires. An entire rusted-out Thunderbird, minus the wheels, had nasturtiums blooming out the windows like Mama's hen-and-chicks pot on the front porch at home. A kind of teepee frame made of CB antennas was all overgrown with cherry-tomato vines.

"Can you believe tomatoes on the second of January?" Mattie asked. I told her no, that I couldn't. Frankly that was only the beginning of what I couldn't believe. Mattie's backyard looked like the place where old cars die and go to heaven.

"Usually we'll get a killing frost by Thanksgiving, but this year it's stayed warm. The beans and tomatoes just won't quit. Here, doll, bite down, don't swallow it whole." She handed me a little tomato.

"Okay," I said, before I realized she had popped one into Turtle's mouth, and was talking to her. "It hailed this morning," I reminded Mattie. "We just about froze to death for a few minutes there."

"Oh, did it? Whereabouts?"

"On the freeway. About five blocks from here."

"It didn't get here; we just had rain. Hail might have got the tomatoes. Sometimes it will. Here's the beans I was telling you about."

Sure enough, they were one hundred percent purple: stems, leaves, flowers and pods.

"Gosh," I said.

"The Chinese lady next door gave them to me." She waved toward a corrugated tin fence that I hadn't even noticed before. It was covered with vines, and the crazy-quilt garden kept right on going on the other side, except without the car parts. The purple beans appeared to go trooping on down the block, climbing over anything in their path.

"They're originally from seeds she brought over with her in nineteen-ought-seven," Mattie told me. "Can you picture that? Keeping the same beans going all these years?"

I said I could. I could picture these beans marching right over the Pacific Ocean, starting from somebody's garden in China and ending up right here.

Mattie's place seemed homey enough, but living in the hustle-bustle of downtown Tucson was like moving to a foreign country I'd never heard of. Or a foreign decade. When I'd crossed into Rocky Mountain Time, I had set my watch back two hours and got thrown into the future.

It's hard to explain how this felt. I went to high school in the seventies, but you have to understand that in Pittman County it may as well have been the fifties. Pittman was twenty years behind the nation in practically every way you can think of, except the rate of teenage pregnancies. For instance, we were the last place in the country to get the dial system. Up until 1973 you just picked up the receiver and said, Marge, get me my Uncle Roscoe, or whoever. The telephone office was on the third floor of the Courthouse, and the operators could see everything around Main Street square including the bank, the drugstore, and Dr. Finchler's office. She would tell you if his car was there or not.

In Tucson, it was clear that there was nobody overlooking us all. We would just have to find our own way.

Turtle and I took up residence in the Hotel Republic, which rented by the week and was within walking distance of Jesus Is Lord's. Mattie said it would be all right to leave my car there for the time being. This was kind of her, although I had visions of turnips growing out of it if I didn't get it in running order soon.

Life in the Republic was nothing like life at the Broken Arrow, where the only thing to remind you you weren't dead was the constant bickering between old Mrs. Hoge and Irene. Downtown Tucson was lively, with secretaries clicking down the sidewalks in high-heeled sandals, and banker and lawyer types puffy-necked in their ties, and in the evenings, prostitutes in get-ups you wouldn't believe. There was one who hung out near the Republic who wore a miniskirt that looked like Reynolds Wrap and almost every day a new type of stockings: fishnets in all different colors, and one pair with actual little bows running down the backs. Her name was Cheryl.

There was also a type of person who lived downtown full time, not in the Republic but in the bus station or on the sidewalk around the Red Cross plasma center. These people slept in their clothes. I know that living in the Republic only put me a few flights of stairs above such people, but at least I did sleep in pajamas.

And then there was this other group. These people did not seem to be broke, but they wore the kinds of clothes Mama's big-house ladies used to give away but you would rather go naked than wear to school. Poodle skirts and things of that kind. Standing in line at the lunch counters and coffeeshops they would rub the backs of each other's necks and say, "You're holding a lot of tension here." They mainly didn't live downtown but had studios and galleries in empty storefronts that had once been J. C. Penney's and so forth. Some of these still had the old signs on the faces of the brick buildings.

Which is to say that at first I had no idea what was going on in those storefronts. One of them that I passed by nearly every day had these two amazing things in the front window. It looked like cherry bombs blowing up in boxes of wet sand, and the whole thing just frozen mid-kaboom. Curiosity finally got the better of me and I walked right in. I knew this was no Woolworth's.

Inside there were more of these things, one of them taller than me and kind of bush-shaped, all made of frozen sand. A woman was writing something on a card under one of the sand things that was hanging on the back wall, kind of exploding out of a metal frame. The woman had on a pink sweater, white ankle socks, pink high heels, and these tight pants made out of the skin of a pink silk leopard. She came over with her clipboard and kind of eyed Turtle's hands, which were sticky I'll admit, but a good two feet clear of the sand bush.

"This is terrific," I said. "What's it supposed to be?"

"It's non-representational," she said, looking at me like I was some kind of bug she'd just found in her bathroom.

"Excuse me for living," I said. She was about my age, no more than twenty-five anyway, and had no reason I could see for being so snooty. I remembered this rhyme Mama taught me to say to kids who acted like they were better than me: "You must come from Hog-Norton, where pigs go to church and play the organ."

The thing was sitting on a square base covered with brown burlap, and a little white card attached said BISBEE DOG #6. I didn't see the connection, but I acted like I was totally satisfied with that. "Bisbee Dog #6," I said. "That's all I wanted to know."

Turtle and I went all around checking out the ones on the walls. Most of them were called something relief: ASCENDANT RELIEF, ENDOGENOUS RELIEF, MOTIVE RELIEF, GALVANIC RELIEF. After a while I realized that the little white cards had numbers on them too. Numbers like $400. "Comic Relief," I said to Turtle. "This one is Instant Relief," I said. "See, it's an Alka-Seltzer, frozen between the plop and the fizz."

On some days, like that one, I was starting to go a little bit crazy. This is how it is when all the money you have can fit in one pocket, and you have no job, and no prospects. The main thing people did for money around there was to give plasma, but I drew the line. "Blood is the body's largest organ," I could just hear Eddie Ricketts saying, and I wasn't inclined to start selling my organs while I was still alive. I did inquire there about work, but the head man in a white coat and puckery white loafers looked me over and said, "Are you a licensed phlebotomist in the state of Arizona?" in this tone of voice like who was I to think I could be on the end of the needle that doesn't hurt, and that was the end of that.

Down the block from the plasma center was a place called Burger Derby. The kids who worked there wore red caps, red-and-white-striped shirts, and what looked like red plastic shorts. One of them, whose name tag said, "Hi I'm Sandi," also wore tiny horse earrings, but that couldn't have been part of the uniform. They couldn't make you pierce your ears; that would have to be against some law.

Sandi usually worked the morning shift alone, and we got to know each other. My room in the Republic had a hot plate for warming cans of soup, but sometimes I ate out just for the company. The Burger Derby was safe. No one there was likely to ask you where you were holding your tension.

Sandi turned out to be horse-crazy. When she found out I was from Kentucky she treated me like I had personally won the Derby. "You are so lucky," she said. "My absolute *dream* is to have a horse of my own, and braid flowers in its mane and prance around in a ring and win ribbons and stuff." She had this idea that everyone in Kentucky owned at least one Thoroughbred, and it took me some time to convince her that I had never even been close enough to a horse to get kicked.

"In the part of Kentucky I come from people don't own Thoroughbreds," I told her. "They just wish they could live like one." The Thoroughbreds had their own swimming pools. My whole county didn't even have a swimming pool. I told her what a hoot we all thought it was when these rich guys paid six million for Secretariat after his running days were over, since he was supposedly the most valuable stud on the face of the earth, and then he turned out to be a reticent breeder, which is a fancy way of saying homosexual. He wouldn't go near a filly for all the sugar in Hawaii.

Sandi acted kind of shocked to hear this news about Secretariat's sex life.

"Didn't you know that? I'm sure that made the national news."

"No!" she said, scouring the steam table like a fiend. She kept looking around to see if anyone else was in the restaurant, but no one was, I'm sure. I always went there around ten-thirty, which is a weird time of day to eat a hot dog, but I was trying to get Turtle and me onto two meals a day.

"What's it like to work here?" I asked her. There had been a HELP WANTED sign in the window for going on two weeks.

"Oh, it's fan*tas*tic," she said.

I'll bet, I thought. Serving up Triple Crown Chili Dogs and You Bet Your Burgers and chasing off drunks and broke people who went around the tables eating nondairy creamer straight out of the packets would be fan*tas*tic. She looked about fourteen.

"You should apply for it, really. They couldn't turn you down, being from Kentucky."

"Sure," I said. What did she think, that I was genetically programmed to fry chicken? "What's it pay?"

"Three twenty-five an hour. *Plus* your meals."

"What am I even talking about? I've got this kid," I said. "I'd have to pay somebody more than that to take care of her."

"Oh no! You could just do what I do, take her to Kid Central Station."

"You've got a kid?"

"Yeah, a little boy. Twenty-one months."

I had thought Pittman was the only place on earth where people started having babies before they learned their multiplication tables. I asked her what Kid Central Station was.

"It's free. See, it's this place in the mall where they'll look after your kids while you shop, but how do they know? See what I mean? The only thing is you have to go and check in every two hours, to prove you're still shopping, so I just dash over there on my breaks. The number five bus just goes right straight there. Or I'll get some friend to go. The people that work there don't know the difference. I mean, they've got these jillion kids crawling all over the place, how are they going to know if somebody's really one of 'em's mother?"

Sandi was sliding the little white buckets of cauliflower and shredded carrots and garbanzo beans into the holes in the salad bar, getting ready for the lunch crowd. For some odd reason they had artificial grapes strewed out over the ice all around the buckets.

"I'll go check it out," I said, although I already had a good notion of what it would be like.

"If you're going right now, could you check in for my little boy? His name's Seattle. I'm sure he's the only one there named Seattle. Just make sure he's okay, will you?"

"Like Seattle, Washington?"

"No, like Seattle Slew, the racehorse. He's a little towhead, you can't miss him, he looks just like me only his hair's blonder. Oh, they have a requirement that they have to be able to walk. Can your daughter walk?"

"Sure she walks. When there's someplace she wants to go."

A celery stick fell out of the bucket onto the floor, and Sandi swiped it up and took a bite. "Well, I couldn't very well let a customer eat it," she said.

"Don't look at me," I said. "It's no skin off my teeth if you want to eat the whole bucket of celery, and the artificial grapes besides. For three twenty-five an hour I think you're entitled."

She munched kind of thoughtfully for a minute. Her eyelashes were stuck together with blue mascara and sprung out all around her eyes like flower petals. "You know, your little girl doesn't look a thing like you," she said. "I mean, no offense, she's cute as a button."

"She's not really mine," I said. "She's just somebody I got stuck with."

Sandi looked at both of us, her elbow cocked on her hip and the salad tongs frozen in midair. "Yeah, I know exactly what you mean."

FOUR

Jug Fork Water

Lou Ann's Grandmother Logan and Lou Ann's new baby were both asleep in the front room with the curtains drawn against the afternoon heat. For the last two weeks Granny Logan had stomped around the house snapping the curtains shut just as fast as Lou Ann could open them, until finally Lou Ann gave up the effort and they all moved around in the gloom of a dimly lit house. "You'd think somebody had died, instead of just being born," Lou Ann complained, but the old woman declared that the heat was unnatural for January and would cause the baby to grow up measly and unwholesome.

When she woke up, Granny Logan would deny she had been sleeping. She had said she only needed to rest her eyes for the trip back to Kentucky, three days on the Greyhound.

In the kitchen Ivy Logan and Lou Ann were packing a paper bag with baloney sandwiches and yellow apples and a Mason jar of cold tea. Ivy's heavy arms and apron-covered front moved around like she was the boss, even in her daughter's unfamiliar kitchen. Under her breath she hummed one line of a hymn, "All our sins and griefs to bear," over and over until Lou Ann thought she would scream. It was an old habit.

Lou Ann pushed her damp blond hair back from her face and told her mother she wished she would stay a few days more. Whenever Ivy looked at her Lou Ann could feel the tired half-moons under her own eyes.

"You haven't hardly had time to say boo to Angel. He'll have Tuesday off and we could take the truck and all go someplace. We could all fit in some way. Or otherwise I could stay here with Dwayne Ray, and you all go. It's a shame for you to come all this way from home and not see what you can see."

Surprisingly, Angel had agreed to move back in until after her mother and grandmother's visit. He might be hard to talk to and unreasonable in every other way but at least, Lou Ann realized, he knew the power of mothers and grandmothers. If Granny Logan had known they were getting a divorce she would have had an apoplectic. At the very least, she and Ivy would insist that Lou Ann come back home.

"Oh, honey, we seen plenty from the bus," Ivy said. "Them old big cactus and every kind of thing. Lordy, and them big buildings downtown, all glass it looked to me like. I expect we'll see a good sight more on the way home."

"I guess, but it seems like we haven't done a thing since you got here but set around and look at the baby."

"Well, that's what we come for, honey. Now we've done helped you have him, and get settled with him, and we're anxious to get on home. The heat puts Mother Logan in a mood."

"I know it." Lou Ann breathed in slowly through her nose. She was beginning to believe that the hot, dry air in her chest might be the poison her grandmother claimed it to be. "I wish I could have put you up better than we did," she said.

"You put us up just fine. You know her, it wouldn't make no difference if it was the Queen a Sheba a-putting us up, she'd be crosspatch. She just don't sleep good out of her own bed." Ivy untied the borrowed apron and smoothed down the front of her navy-blue dress. Lou Ann remembered the dress from about a hundred church potluck suppers. Just the sight of it made her feel stuffed with potato-chip casseroles and Coca-Cola cake.

"Mama," she said, and then started over because her voice was too low to hear. "Mama, when Daddy was alive . . . " She was not sure what she meant to ask. Did you talk to each other? Was he the person you saved things up to say to, or was it like now? A houseful of women for everything, for company. Ivy was not looking at her daughter but her hands were still, for once. "Did Granny Logan always live with you, from the beginning?"

Ivy peered into the brown bag and then rolled the top down tightly. "Not her with us. We lived with her."

"Is that how you wanted it?" Lou Ann felt embarrassed.

"I guess I always thought it would have been something to go off on our own, like you done. But there was so much work in them days, no time for fun, and besides I'd of been scared to death out someplace all by myself."

"It wouldn't be all by yourself. You would have been with Daddy."

"I s'pose," Ivy said. "But we didn't think about it that way." She turned back to the sink to wash her hands, then pulled the dish towel down from the wooden ring over the sink, refolded it, and hung it back up. "I want you to run on in there now and tell Mother Logan we've got to get ready to go."

Ivy and her mother-in-law were not speaking, on account of one thing or another. Lou Ann could never keep track. She wondered what the trip would be like for them, all those days and nights on the Greyhound. But they were sure to find some way of having a conversation. In the past, in times of necessity, she had seen her mother and grandmother address one another through perfect strangers.

"Granny Logan." Lou Ann put her hand gently on the old woman's shoulder, feeling the shoulder bones through the dark, slick cloth of her dress. At the same time she opened her eyes the baby started to cry. "You have a nice catnap, Granny?" she asked, hurrying to pick up the baby and bounce him on her hip. She always thought he sounded like he was choking.

"It was just my eyes, needed a rest. I weren't sleeping." She held tightly to the arms of the chair until she knew where she was. "I told you, the heat's done put that baby into a colic. He needs a mustard plaster to draw out the heat."

"Mama says tell you it's time to get your grip packed. She says you all are fixing to leave tonight."

"My grip's done packed."

"All right then. You want a bite of supper before you go?"

"Why don't you come on home with us, honey? You and the baby."

"Me and *Angel* and the baby, Granny. I've been married now for practically five years, remember?" She felt like such a sneak, letting on as though her marriage was just fine. It was like presenting her mother and grandmother with a pretty Christmas package to take back with them, with nothing but tissue paper inside. She had never lied to them before, that she could remember, but something in her would not let them be right about Angel.

"Angel's got good work at the bottling plant," she told Granny Logan. This, at least, was true. "We like it here."

"I don't see how a body could like no place where it don't rain. Law, I'm parched. Get me a glass of water."

"I'll get it for you in a minute," she said, switching the baby to her other hip, knowing that in a minute Granny Logan would have forgotten her request. "You get used to it. When we first moved out I had sore throats all the time. I was scared to death I'd caught throat cancer like that what's her name on TV. You know, that had to stop singing?" Lou Ann realized Granny Logan wouldn't know NBC from pinto beans. "But I turned out to be fine, of course. And it don't bother him one bit, does it?" She crooked a finger under the baby's chin and looked into the foggy blue eyes. "Dwayne Ray's a Tucson boy, aren't you?"

Lou Ann's baby had not been born on Christmas, or even the day after. He had come early on the morning of January 1, just missing First Baby of the Year at St. Joseph's Hospital by about forty-five minutes. Lou Ann later thought that if she had just pushed a little harder she might have gotten the year of free diapers from Bottom Dollar Diaper Service. That was the prize. It would have come in handy now that her washing-machine fund, which was meager enough to begin with, had been parceled out to all the neighborhood kids.

"I don't see how a body can grow no tobaccy if it don't rain," Granny Logan said.

"They don't grow tobacco here. No crops hardly at all, just factories and stuff, and tourists that come down here for the winter. It's real pretty out in the mountains. We could have showed you, if you hadn't had to go back so soon." The baby coughed again and she jiggled him up and down. "And it's not usually this hot in January, either. You heard it yourself, Granny, the man on the radio saying it was the hottest January temperatures on record."

"You talk different. I knowed you was going to put on airs."

"Granny, I do not."

"Don't talk back to me, child, you do. I can hear it. I expect you'll be persuadin' the baby that his people's just ignorant hill folks."

Ivy brought in the bags of food and her suitcase, which was

held together with a leather belt. Lou Ann recognized the belt as one she had been whipped with years ago, when her father was alive.

"Honey," Ivy said, "tell Mother Logan not to start in on you again. We've got to git."

"Tell Ivy to mind her business and I'll mind mine. Here, I brung you something for the baby." Granny Logan retrieved her black velvet purse, purpled with age and wear around the clasp, and rummaged through it with slow, swollen knuckles. Lou Ann tried not to watch.

After a minute the old woman produced a Coke bottle filled with cloudy water. The bent metal cap had been pushed back on and covered with cellophane, tied around and around with string.

Lou Ann shifted the baby onto her hip, pushed her hair behind her ear, and took the bottle with her free hand. "What is it?"

"That's Tug Fork water. For baptizing the baby."

The water inside the bottle looked milky and cool. A fine brown sediment stuck to the glass bottom when she tipped it sideways.

"I remember when you was baptized in Tug Fork, you was just a little old bit of a thing. And scared to death. When the reverend went to dunk you over, you hollered right out. Law, I remember that so good."

"That's good, Granny. You remember something I don't." Lou Ann wondered how Granny Logan was picturing a baptism in one bottle of water. Of course, the original plan had been to have Dwayne Ray sprinkled as a Catholic, but Granny would die if she knew that. And everything was up in the air now, anyway, with Angel gone.

"Doll baby, I reckon we're all set," Ivy said. "Oh, I hate to go. Let me hold my grandbaby again. You see he gets enough to eat now, Lou Ann. I always had plenty of milk for you and your brother, but you're not as stout as I was. You never was a stout girl. It's not my fault you wouldn't eat what I put down in front of you." She gave the baby a bounce on her pleated bosom. "Lordy mercy, he'll be all growed up before we see him again, I expect."

"I'm as fat as a hog since I had him, Mama, and you know it."

"Remember you have to use both sides. If you just nurse him on one side you'll go dry."

"Don't expect I'll see him again a-tall," Granny Logan grunted. "Not his old great-grandmaw."

"Mama, I wish you'd wait till Angel gets home and we could drive you down to the station. You're going to get all confused if you try to take the bus. You've got to change downtown." The way they had both managed to avoid Angel he might as well not have moved back in.

"It's a sin to be working on Sunday. He ought to be home with his family on the Lord's day," Granny Logan said, and sighed. "I guess I oughtn't expect better from a heathern Mexican."

"It's shift work," Lou Ann explained again. "He's just got to go in when they tell him to, and that's that. And he's not a heathen. He was born right here in America, same as the rest of us." Just because he wasn't baptized in some old dirty crick, Lou Ann added in a voice way too low for Granny Logan to hear.

"Who tells him to?" the old woman demanded. Lou Ann looked at her mother.

"We'll manage, with the bus and all," Ivy said.

"That don't make it right, do it? Just because some other heathern tells him to work on the Lord's day?"

Lou Ann found a scrap of paper and wrote down the name of the stop and the number of the bus they would have to take downtown. Ivy handed back the baby and took the paper. She looked at it carefully before she folded it twice, tucked it in her purse, and began helping Granny Logan on with her coat.

"Granny, you're not going to need that coat," Lou Ann said. "I swear it's eighty degrees out there."

"You'll swear yourself to tarnation if you don't watch out. Don't tell me I'm not going to need no coat, child. It's January." Her old hand pawed the air for a few seconds before Ivy silently caught it and corralled it in the heavy black sleeve.

"Lou Ann, honey, don't let him play with that ink pen," Ivy said over her shoulder. "He'll put his eyes out before he even gets a good start in life."

The baby was waving his fist vaguely in the direction of the blue pen in Lou Ann's breast pocket, although he couldn't have grabbed it or picked it up if his little life depended on it.

"All right, Mama," Lou Ann said quietly. She wrapped the baby in a thin blanket in spite of the heat because she knew one or the other of the two women would fuss if she didn't. "Let me help you with the stairs, Granny," she said, but Granny Logan brushed her hand away.

Heat waves rising from the pavement made the brown grass and the palm tree trunks appear to wiggle above the sidewalk, making Lou Ann think of cartoons she had seen of strange lands where palm trees did the hula. They reached the little bus stop with its concrete bench.

"Don't sit on it," she warned. "It'll be hot as a poker in this sun." Granny Logan and Ivy stepped back from the bench like startled children, and Lou Ann felt pleased that she was able to tell them something they didn't already know. The three women stood beside the bench, all looking in the direction from which the bus would come.

"Pew, don't they make a stink," Mother Logan said when the bus arrived. Ivy put her arms around both Lou Ann and the baby, then picked up the two bags and boarded the bus, lifting her feet high for the two big steps. At the top she turned and reached down for her mother-in-law, her sturdy, creased hand closing around the old knuckles. The bus driver leaned on his elbows over the steering wheel and stared ahead.

"I just wish you wasn't so far away," Ivy said as the doors hissed together.

"I know," she mouthed. "Wave bye to your great-grandmaw," Lou Ann told the baby, but they were on the wrong side to see.

She imagined herself running after the bus and banging on the door, the bus driver letting her climb up and settle herself and the baby onto the wide seat between her mother and grandmother. "Tell your mother to hand me that jar of tea," Granny Logan would say to her. "I'll be dry as a old stick fence before we get back to Kentucky."

One block down and across the street, old Bobby Bingo sold vegetables out of his dilapidated truck. Lou Ann had been tempted by his tomatoes, which looked better than the hard pink ones at the grocery; those didn't seem like tomatoes at all, but some sickly city fruit maybe grown inside a warehouse. She had finally collected the nerve to ask how much they cost and was surprised that they were less than grocery tomatoes. On her way home she made up her mind to buy some more.

"Hi, tomato lady," Bingo said. "I remember you."

She flushed. "Are they still forty-five a pound?"

"No, fifty-five. End of the season."

"That's okay," she said. "It's still a good price." She looked at every one in the box and picked out six, handing them to the old man one at a time with her free hand. With her other hand she adjusted the baby on her hip taking extra care, as she had been instructed, to support his wobbly head. "Your tomatoes are the first good ones I've had since back home." She felt her heart do something strange when she said "back home."

Bobby Bingo had skin like a baked potato. A complete vegetable man, Lou Ann thought, though she couldn't help liking him.

He squinted at her. "You're not from here? I didn't think so." He shook out a wad of odd-sized plastic bags, chose one with red letters on it, and bagged the tomatoes. "Seventy-five," he said, weighing them up and down in his hand before he put them on the scales. "And an apple for Johnny," he said, picking out a red apple and shaking it at the baby.

"His name's Dwayne Ray, and he thanks you very much I'm sure but he don't have any teeth yet." Lou Ann laughed. She was embarrassed, but it felt so good to laugh that she was afraid next she would cry.

"That's good," Bingo said. "Soon as they get teeth, they start to bite. You know my boy?"

Lou Ann shook her head.

"Sure you do. He's on TV every night, he sells cars. He's a real big guy in cars."

"Sorry," she said. "I don't have a TV. My husband took it to his new apartment." She couldn't believe, after deceiving her own mother and grandmother for two entire weeks, that she was admitting to a complete stranger on the street that her marriage had failed.

He shook his head. "Don't worry about it. Makes me sick every time he comes on. Don't even call himself by his own name—'Bill Bing' he says. 'Come on down to Bill Bing Cadillac,' he says. 'Bill Bing has just the thing.' I always wanted him to be a real big guy, you know. Well, look at him now. He don't even eat vegetables. If he was here right now he would tell you he don't know who I am. 'Get rid of that old truck,' he says to me. 'What you need to sell this garbage for? I could buy you a house in Beverly Hills right now,' he says to me. 'What?' I tell him. 'You crazy? Beverly Hills? Probably they don't even eat vegetables in Beverly Hills, just Alaska King Crab and bread sticks!' I tell him.

'You want to make me happy, you give me a new Cadillac and I can sell my vegetables out of the trunk.'" Bingo shook his head. "You want grapes? Good grapes this week."

"No, just the tomatoes." She handed him three quarters.

"Here, take the grapes. Johnny can eat the grapes. Seedless." He put them in the bag with the tomatoes. "Let me tell you something, tomato lady. Whatever you want the most, it's going to be the worst thing for you."

Back at the house she laid down the baby for his nap, then carefully washed the produce and put it in the refrigerator, all the while feeling her mother's eyes on her hands. "The worst thing for you," she kept repeating under her breath until she annoyed herself. She moved around the edges of the rooms as though her big mother and demanding grandmother were still there taking up most of the space; the house felt both empty and cramped at the same time, and Lou Ann felt a craving for something she couldn't put a finger on, maybe some kind of food she had eaten a long time ago. She opened the curtains in the front room to let in the light. The sky was hard and bright, not a blue sky full of water. Strangely enough, it still surprised her sometimes to open that window and not see Kentucky.

She noticed the Coke bottle sitting on the low wooden bureau along with two of Granny Logan's hairpins. The old-fashioned hairpins gave her a sad, spooky feeling. Once she had found a pair of her father's work gloves in the tobacco barn, still molded to the curved shape of his hands, long after he was dead.

The bottle had leaked a wet ring on the wood, which Lou Ann tried to wipe up with the hem of her jumper. She was concerned about it staining, since the furniture wasn't actually hers. The house had come furnished. She thought for a long time about what to do with the bottle and finally set it on the glass shelf of the medicine cabinet in the bathroom.

Later, while she was nursing the baby in the front room, she closed her eyes and tried to remember being baptized in Tug Fork. She could see the child in a white dress, her sunburned arms stiff at the elbows, and could hear her cry out as she went over backwards, but she could not feel that child's terror as the knees buckled and the green water closed over the face. The strong light from the window took on a watery look behind her closed eyelids and she could see it all perfectly. But couldn't feel it. She thought of her mother and automatically switched the baby to her other breast.

She was still nursing when Angel came home. She opened her eyes. The late-afternoon light on the mountains made them look pink and flat like a picture postcard.

She heard Angel in the kitchen. He moved around in there for quite a while before he said anything to Lou Ann, and it struck her that his presence was different from the feeling of women filling up the house. He could be there, or not, and it hardly made any difference. Like a bug or a mouse scratching in the cupboards at night—you could get up and chase after it, or just go back to sleep and let it be. This was good, she decided.

When he came into the front room she could hear the jingle of his leg.

"They gone?" he asked behind her.

"Yes."

"I'm packing my shaving stuff," he said. Angel had a moustache but shaved the rest of his face often, sometimes twice a day. "Did you see my belt buckle? The silver one with the sheepshank on it?" he asked her.

"The what on it?"

"Sheepshank. It's a rope tied in a knot."

"Oh. I wondered what that was on there."

"So did you see it?"

"No. Not lately, I mean."

"What about my Toros cap?"

"Is that the blue one?"

"Yeah."

"You left that in Manny Quiroz's car. Remember?"

"Damn it, Manny moved to San Diego."

"Well, I can't help it. That's what you did with it."

"Damn."

He was standing close enough behind her so she could smell the faint, sweet smell of beer on his breath. It was a familiar smell, but today it made Lou Ann wonder about bars and the bottling plant and the other places Angel went every day that she had never seen. She turned her head in time to watch him leave the room, his work shirt rolled up at the elbows and dirty from doing something all day, she did not know exactly what. For a brief instant, no longer than a heartbeat, it felt strange to be living in the same house with this person who was not even related to her.

But of course he's related. He's my husband. Was my husband.

"What the hell is this?" he called from the bathroom.

She leaned back in the rocking chair where she sat facing east out the big window. "It's water from Tug Fork, the crick at home that I was baptized in. Me and I guess practically everybody else in my family. Granny Logan brought it for baptizing Dwayne Ray. Wouldn't you know she'd bring something weird like that?"

She heard the chugging sound of the water as he poured it down the drain. The baby's sucking at her felt good, as if he might suck the ache right out of her breast.

FIVE

Harmonious Space

The Republic Hotel was near the exact spot where the railroad track, which at one time functioned as a kind of artery, punctured Tucson's old, creaky chest cavity and prepared to enter the complicated auricles and ventricles of the railroad station. In the old days I suppose it would have been bringing the city a fresh load of life, like a blood vessel carrying platelets to circulate through the lungs. Nowadays, if you could even call the railroad an artery of Tucson, you would have to say it was a hardened one.

At the point where it entered the old part of downtown, the train would slow down and let out a long, tired scream. Whether the whistle was for warning the cars at the crossings up ahead, or just letting the freeloaders know it was time to roll out of the boxcars, I can't say. But it always happened very near six-fifteen, and I came to think of it as my alarm clock.

Sometimes the sound of it would get tangled up into a dream. I would hear it whistling through my sleep for what seemed like days while I tried to lift a heavy teakettle off a stove or, once, chased a runaway horse that was carrying off Turtle while she hollered bloody murder (something I had yet to hear her do in real life). Finally the sound would push out through my eyes and there was the daylight. There were the maroon paisley curtains made from an Indian bedspread, there was the orange-brown stain on the porcelain sink where the faucet dripped, there was the army cot where Turtle was asleep, safe and sound in the Republic Hotel. Some mornings it was like that.

On other days I would wake up before the whistle ever sounded and just lie there waiting, feeling that my day couldn't begin without it. Lately it had been mostly this second way.

We were in trouble. I lasted six days at the Burger Derby before I got in a fight with the manager and threw my red so-called jockey cap in the trash compactor and walked out. I would have thrown the whole uniform in there, but I didn't feel like giving him a free show.

I won't say that working there didn't have its moments. When Sandi and I worked the morning shift together we'd have a ball. I would tell her all kinds of stories I'd heard about horse farms, such as the fact that the really high-strung horses had TVs in their stalls. It was supposed to lower their blood pressure.

"Their favorite show is old reruns of Mr. Ed," I would tell her with a poker face.

"No! You're kidding. Are you kidding me?"

"And they *hate* the commercials for Knox gelatin."

She was easy to tease, but I had to give her credit, considering that life had delivered Sandi a truckload of manure with no return address. The father of her baby had told everyone that Sandi was an admitted schizophrenic and had picked his name out of the high school yearbook when she found out she was pregnant. Soon afterward the boy's father got transferred from Tucson and the whole family moved to Oakland, California. Sandi's mother had made her move out, and she lived with her older sister Aimee, who was born again and made her pay rent. In Aimee's opinion it would have been condoning sin to let Sandi and her illegitimate son stay there for free.

But nothing really seemed to throw Sandi. She knew all about things like how to rub an ice cube on kids' gums when they were teething, and where to get secondhand baby clothes for practically nothing. We would take turns checking on Turtle and Seattle, and at the end of our shift we'd go over to the mall together to pick them up. "I don't know," she'd say real loud, hamming it up while we waited in line at Kid Central Station. "I can't decide if I want that La-Z-Boy recliner in the genuine leather or the green plaid with the stainproof finish." "Take your time deciding," I'd say. "Sleep on it and come back tomorrow."

Turtle would be sitting wherever I had set her down that morning, with each hand locked onto some ratty, punked-out stuffed dog or a torn book or another kid's jacket and her eyes fixed on some empty point in the air, just the way a cat will do. It's as though they live in a separate universe that takes up the same space as ours, but is full of fascinating things like mice or sparrows or special TV programs that we can't see.

Kid Central Station was not doing Turtle any good. I knew that.

After six days the Burger Derby manager Jerry Speller, this little twerp who believed that the responsibility of running a burger joint put you a heartbeat away from Emperor of the Universe, said I didn't have the right attitude, and I told him he was exactly right. I said I had to confess I didn't have the proper reverence for the Burger Derby institution, and to prove it I threw my hat into the Mighty Miser and turned it on. Sandi was so impressed she burned the french fries twice in a row.

The fight had been about the Burger Derby uniform. The shorts weren't actually plastic, it turned out, but cotton-polyester with some kind of shiny finish that had to be dry-cleaned. Three twenty-five an hour plus celery and you're supposed to pay for dry-cleaning your own shorts.

My one regret was that I didn't see much of Sandi anymore. Naturally I had to find a new place to eat breakfast. There were half a dozen coffeeshops in the area, and although I didn't really feel at home in any of them I discovered a new resource: newspapers. On the tables, along with their gritty coffee cups and orange rinds and croissant crumbs, people often left behind the same day's paper.

There was a lady named Jessie with wild white hair and floppy rainboots who would dash into the restaurants and scrounge the leftover fruit and melon rinds. "It's not to eat," she would explain to any- and everybody as she clumped along the sidewalk pushing an interesting-smelling shopping cart that had at some point in history belonged to Safeway. "It's for still-lifes." She told me she painted nothing but madonnas: Orange-peel madonna. Madonna and child with strawberries. Together we made a sort of mop-up team. I nabbed the newspapers, and she took the rest.

Looking through the want ads every day gave new meaning to my life. The For Rents, on the other hand, were a joke as far as I was concerned, but often there would be ads looking for roommates, a possibility I hadn't considered. I would circle anything that looked promising, although people seemed unbelievably picky about who they intended to live with:

"Mature, responsible artist or grad student wanted for cooperative household; responsibilities shared, sensitivity a must."

"Female vegetarian nonsmoker to share harmonious space with insightful Virgo and cat."

I began to suspect that sharing harmonious space with an

insightful Virgo might require even greater credentials than being a licensed phlebotomist in the state of Arizona.

The main consideration, though, was whether or not I could locate the address on my Sun-Tran maps of all the various bus routes. At the end of the week I made up my mind to check out a couple of possibilities. One ad said, among other things, "Must be open to new ideas." The other said, "New mom needs company. Own room, low rent, promise I won't bother you. Kids ok." The first sounded like an adventure, and the second sounded like I wouldn't have to pass a test. I put on a pair of stiff, clean jeans and braided my hair and gave Turtle a bath in the sink. She had acquired clothes of her own by now, but just for old time's sake I put her in my DAMN I'M GOOD T-shirt from Kentucky Lake. Just for luck.

Both places were near downtown. The first was a big old ramshackle house with about twelve kinds of wind chimes hanging on the front porch. One was made from the silver keys of some kind of musical instrument like a flute or clarinet, and even Turtle seemed interested in it. A woman came to the door before I even knocked.

She let me inside and called out, "The prospective's here." Three silver earrings—a half moon, a star, and a grinning sun—dangled from holes in her left ear so that she clinked when she walked like some human form of wind chime. She was barefoot and had on a skirt that reminded me of the curtains in my room at the Republic. There was no actual furniture in the room, only a colorful rug and piles of pillows here and there, so I waited to see what she would do. She nested herself into one of the piles, flouncing her skirt out over her knees. I noticed that she had thin silver rings on four of her toes.

Another woman came out of the kitchen door, through which I was relieved to see a table and chairs. A tall, thin guy with a hairless chest hunkered in another doorway for a minute, rubbing a head of orange hair that looked like a wet cat. He had on only those beachcomber-type pants held up by a fake rope. I really couldn't tell how old these people were. I kept expecting a parent to show up in another doorway and tell Beach Blanket Bingo to put on his shirt, but then, they could have been older than me. We all settled down on the pillows.

"I'm Fay," the toe-ring woman said, "spelled F-E-I, and this is La-Isha and that's Timothy. You'll have to excuse Timothy; he used caffeine yesterday and now his homeostasis is out of balance." I presumed they were talking about his car, although I was not aware of any automotive uses for caffeine.

"That's too bad," I said. "I wouldn't do anything with caffeine but drink it."

They all stared at me for a while.

"Oh. I'm Taylor. This is Turtle."

"Turtle. Is that a spirit name?" La-Isha asked.

"Sure," I said.

La-Isha was thick-bodied, with broad bare feet and round calves. Her dress was a sort of sarong, printed all over with black and orange elephants and giraffes, and she had a jungly-looking scarf wrapped around her head. And to think they used to stare at me for wearing red and turquoise together. Drop these three in Pittman County and people would run for cover.

F-E-I took charge of the investigation. "Would the child be living here too?"

"Right. We're a set."

"That's cool, I have no problem with small people," she said. "La-Isha, Timothy?"

"It's not really what I was thinking in terms of, but I can see it happening. I'm flex on children," La-Isha said, after giving it some thought. Timothy said he thought the baby was cute, asked if it was a boy or a girl.

"A girl," I said, but I was drowned out by Fei saying,

"Timothy, I *really* don't see that that's an issue here." She said to me, "Gender is not an issue in this house."

"Oh," I said. "Whatever."

"What does she eat?" La-Isha wanted to know.

"Mainly whatever she can get her hands on. She had half a hot dog with mustard for breakfast."

There was another one of those blank spells in the conversation. Turtle was grumpily yanking at a jingle bell on the corner of a pillow, and I was beginning to feel edgy myself. All those knees and chins at the same level. It reminded me of an extremely long movie I had once seen about an Arabian sheik. Maybe La-Isha is Arabian, I thought, though she looked very white, with blond hair on her arms and pink rims around her eyes. Possibly an albino Arabian. I realized she was giving a lecture of some kind.

"At least four different kinds of toxins," she was saying, more to the room in general than to me. Her pink-rimmed eyes were starting to look inflamed. "In a hot dog." Now she was definitely talking to me. "Were you aware of that?"

"I would have guessed seven or eight," I said.

"Nitrites," said Timothy. He was gripping his head between his palms, one on the chin and one on top, and bending it from side to side until you could hear a little pop. I began to understand about the unbalanced homeostasis.

"We eat mainly soybean products here," Fei said. "We're just starting a soy-milk collective. A house requirement is that each person spend at least seven hours a week straining curd."

"Straining curd," I said. I wanted to say, Flaming nurd. Raining turds. It isn't raining turds, you know, it's raining violets.

"Yes," Fei went on in this abnormally calm voice that made me want to throw a pillow at her. "I guess the child . . . "

"Turtle," I said.

"I guess Turtle would be exempt. But we would have to make adjustments for that in the kitchen quota. . . ."

I had trouble concentrating. La-Isha kept narrowing her eyes and trying to get Fei's attention. I remembered Mrs. Hoge with her shakes, always looking like she was secretly saying, "Don't do it" to somebody behind you.

"So tell us about you," Fei said eventually. I snapped out of my daydreams, feeling like a kid in school that's just been called on. "What kind of a space are you envisioning for yourself?" she wanted to know. Those were her actual words.

"Oh, Turtle and I are flex," I said. "Right now we're staying downtown at the Republic. I jockeyed fried food at the Burger Derby for a while, but I got fired."

La-Isha went kind of stiff on that one. I imagined all the little elephants on her shift getting stung through the heart with a tiny stun gun. Timothy was trying to get Turtle's attention by making faces, so far with no luck.

"Usually little kids are into faces," he informed me. "She seems kind of spaced out."

"She makes up her own mind about what she's into."

"She sure has a lot of hair," he said. "How old is she?"

"Eighteen months," I said. It was a wild guess.

"She looks very Indian."

"Native American," Fei corrected him. "She does. Is her father Native American?"

"Her great-great-grandpa was full-blooded Cherokee," I said. "On my side. Cherokee skips a generation, like red hair. Didn't you know that?"

The second house on my agenda turned out to be right across the park from Jesus Is Lord's. It belonged to Lou Ann Ruiz.

Within ten minutes Lou Ann and I were in the kitchen drinking diet Pepsi and splitting our gussets laughing about homeostasis and bean turds. We had already established that our hometowns in Kentucky were separated by only two counties, and that we had both been to the exact same Bob Seger concert at the Kentucky State Fair my senior year.

"So then what happened?" Lou Ann had tears in her eyes. I hadn't really meant to put them down, they seemed like basically good kids, but it just got funnier as it went along.

"Nothing happened. In their own way, they were so polite it was pathetic. I mean, it was plain as day they thought Turtle was a dimwit and I was from some part of Mars where they don't have indoor bathrooms, but they just kept on asking things like would I like some alfalfa tea?" I had finally told them no thanks, that we'd just run along and envision ourselves in some other space.

Lou Ann showed me the rest of the house except for her room, where the baby was asleep. Turtle and I would have our own room, plus the screened-in back porch if we wanted it. She said it was great to sleep out there in the summer. We had to whisper around the house so we wouldn't wake the baby.

"He was just born in January," Lou Ann said when we were back in the kitchen. "How old's yours?"

"To tell you the truth, I don't even know. She's adopted."

"Well, didn't they tell you all that stuff when you adopted her? Didn't she come with a birth certificate or something?"

"It wasn't an official adoption. Somebody just kind of gave her to me."

"You mean like she was left on your doorstep in a basket?"

"Exactly. Except it was in my car, and there wasn't any basket. Now that I think about it, there should have at least been a basket. Indians make good baskets. She's Indian."

"Wasn't there even a note? How do you know her name's Turtle?"

"I don't. I named her that. It's just temporary until I can figure out what her real name is. I figure I'll hit on it sooner or later."

Turtle was in a high chair of Lou Ann's that must have been way too big for a kid born in January. On the tray there were decals of Kermit the Frog and Miss Piggy, which Turtle was slapping with her hands. There was nothing there for her to grab. I picked her up out of the chair and hefted her onto my shoulder, where she could reach my braid. She didn't pull it, she just held on to it like a lifeline. This was one of our normal positions.

"I can't get over it," Lou Ann said, "that somebody would just dump her like an extra puppy."

"Yeah, I know. I think it was somebody that cared for her, though, if you can believe it. Turtle was having a real rough time. I don't know if she would have made it where she was." A fat gray cat with white feet was sleeping on the windowsill over the sink. Or so I thought, until all of a sudden it jumped down and streaked out of the kitchen. Lou Ann had her back to the door, but I could see the cat in the next room. It was walking around in circles on the living-room rug, kicking its feet behind it again and again, throwing invisible sand over invisible cat poop.

"You wouldn't believe what your cat is doing," I said.

"Oh yes, I would," Lou Ann said. "He's acting like he just went potty, right?"

"Right. But he didn't, as far as I can see."

"Oh, no, he never does. I think he has a split personality. The good cat wakes up and thinks the bad cat has just pooped on the rug. See, we got him as a kitty and I named him Snowboots but Angel thought that was a stupid name so he always called him Pachuco instead. Then a while back, before Dwayne Ray was born, he started acting that way. Angel's my ex-husband, by the way."

It took some effort here to keep straight who was cats and who was husbands.

Lou Ann went on. "So just the other day I read in a magazine that a major cause of split personality is if two parents treat a kid in real different ways, like one all the time tells the kid it's good and the other one says it's bad. It gives them this idea they have to be both ways at once."

"That's amazing," I said. "Your cat ought to be in *Ripley's Believe It or Not*. Or one of those magazine columns where people write in and tell what cute things their pets do, like parakeets that whistle Dixie or cats that will only sleep on a certain towel with pictures of goldfish on it."

"Oh, I wouldn't want anyone to know about Snowboots, it's too embarrassing. It's just about proof-positive that he's from a broken home, don't you think?"

"What does Pachuco mean?"

"It means like a bad Mexican boy. One that would go around spray-painting walls and join a gang."

Pachuco alias Snowboots was still going at it in the living room. "Seriously," I said, "you should send it in. They'd probably pay good money—it's unbelievable what kinds of things you can get paid for. Or at the very least they'd send you a free case of cat chow."

"I almost won a year of free diapers for Dwayne Ray. Dwayne Ray's my son."

"Oh. What does he do?"

Lou Ann laughed. "Oh, he's normal. The only one in the house, I guess. Do you want some more Pepsi?" She got up to refill our glasses. "So did you drive out here, or fly, or what?"

I told her that driving across the Indian reservation was how I'd ended up with Turtle. "Our paths would never have crossed if it weren't for a bent rocker arm."

"Well, if something had to go wrong, at least you can thank your stars you were in a car and not an airplane," she said, whacking an ice-cube tray on the counter. I felt Turtle flinch on my shoulder.

"I never thought of it that way," I said.

"I could never fly in an airplane. Oh Lord, never! Remember that one winter when a plane went right smack dab into that frozen river in Washington, D.C.? On TV I saw them pulling the bodies out frozen stiff with their knees and arms bent like those little plastic cowboys that are supposed to be riding horses, but then when you lose the horse they're useless. Oh, God, that was so pathetic. I can just hear the stewardess saying, 'Fasten your seat belts, folks,' calm as you please, like 'Don't worry, we just have to say this,' and then next thing you know you're a hunk of ice. Oh, shoot, there's Dwayne Ray just woke up from his nap. Let me go get him."

I did remember that airplane crash. On TV they showed the rescue helicopter dropping down a rope to save the only surviving stewardess from an icy river full of dead people. I remember just how she looked hanging on to that rope. Like Turtle.

In a minute Lou Ann came back with the baby. "Dwayne Ray, here's some nice people I want you to meet. Say hi."

He was teeny, with skin you could practically see through. It reminded me of the Visible Man we'd had in Hughes Walter's biology class. "He's adorable," I said.

"Do you think so, really? I mean, I love him to death of course, but I keep thinking his head's flat."

"They all are. They start out that way, and then after a while their foreheads kind of pop out."

"Really? I never knew that. They never told me that."

"Sure. I used to work in a hospital. I saw a lot of newborns coming and going, and every one of them's head was flat as a shovel."

She made a serious face and fussed with the baby for a while without saying anything.

"So what do you think?" I finally said. "Is it okay if we move in?"

"Sure!" Her wide eyes and the way she held her baby reminded me for a minute of Sandi. The lady downtown could paint either one of them: "Bewildered Madonna with Sunflower Eyes." "Of course you can move in," she said. "I'd love it. I wasn't sure if you'd want to."

"Why wouldn't I want to?"

"Well, my gosh, I mean, here you are, so skinny and smart and cute and everything, and me and Dwayne Ray, well, we're just lumping along here trying to get by. When I put that ad in the paper, I thought, Well, this is sure four dollars down the toilet; who in the world would want to move in here with us?"

"Stop it, would you? Quit making everybody out to be better than you are. I'm just a plain hillbilly from East Jesus Nowhere with this adopted child that everybody keeps on telling me is dumb as a box of rocks. I've got nothing on you, girl. I mean it."

Lou Ann hid her mouth with her hand.

"What?" I said.

"Nothing." I could see perfectly well that she was smiling.

"Come on, what is it?"

"It's been so long," she said. "You talk just like me."

SIX

Valentine's Day

The first killing frost of the winter came on Valentine's Day. Mattie's purple bean vines hung from the fence like long strips of beef jerky drying in the sun. It broke my heart to see that colorful jungle turned to black slime, especially on this of all days when people everywhere were sending each other flowers, but it didn't faze Mattie. "That's the cycle of life, Taylor," she said. "The old has to pass on before the new can come around." She said frost improved the flavor of the cabbage and Brussels sprouts. But I think she was gloating. The night before, she'd listened to the forecast and picked a mop bucket full of hard little marbles off the tomato vines, and this morning she had green-tomato pies baking upstairs. I know this sounds like something you'd no more want to eat than a mud-and-Junebug pie some kid would whip up, but it honestly smelled delicious.

I had taken a job at Jesus Is Lord Used Tires.

If there had been any earthly way around this, I would have found it. I loved Mattie, but you know about me and tires. Every time I went to see her and check on the car I felt like John Wayne in that war movie where he buckles down his helmet, takes a swig of bourbon, and charges across the minefield yelling something like "Live Free or Bust!"

But Mattie was the only friend I had that didn't cost a mint in long distance to talk to, until Lou Ann of course. So when she started telling me how she needed an extra hand around the place I just tried to change the subject politely. She had a lot of part-time help, she said, but when people came and went they didn't have time to get the knack of things like patching and alignments. I told her I had no aptitude whatsoever for those things, and was that a real scorpion on that guy's belt buckle that was just in here? Did she think we'd get another frost? How did they stitch all those fancy loops and stars on a cowboy boot, was there a special kind of heavy-duty sewing machine?

But there was no steering Mattie off her course. She was positive I'd be a natural at tires. She chatted with me and Turtle between customers, and then sent us on our way with a grocery bag full of cabbage and peas, saying, "Just think about it, hon. Put it in your swing-it-till-Monday basket."

When Mattie said she'd throw in two new tires and would show me how to fix my ignition, I knew I'd be a fool to say no. She paid twice as much as the Burger Derby, and of course there was no ridiculous outfit to be dry-cleaned. If I was going to get blown up, at least it would be in normal clothes.

In many ways it was a perfect arrangement. You couldn't ask for better than Mattie. She was patient and kind and let me bring Turtle in with me when I needed to. Lou Ann kept her some days, but if she had to go out shopping or to the doctor, one baby was two hands full. I felt a little badly about foisting her off on Lou Ann at all, but she insisted that Turtle was so little trouble she often forgot she was there. "She doesn't even hardly wet her diapers," Lou Ann said. It was true. Turtle's main goal in life, other than hanging on to things, seemed to be to pass unnoticed.

Mattie's place was always hopping. She was right about people always passing through, and not just customers, either. There was another whole set of people who spoke Spanish and lived with her upstairs for various lengths of time. I asked her about them once, and she asked me something like had I ever heard of a sanctuary.

I remembered my gas-station travel brochures. "Sure," I said. "It's a place they set aside for birds, where nobody's allowed to shoot them."

"That's right. They've got them for people too." This was all she was inclined to say on the subject.

Usually the people were brought and taken away by the blue-jeans priest in the station wagon I'd seen that first day. He also wore an interesting belt buckle, not with a scorpion but with an engraving of a small stick figure lost in a kind of puzzle. Mattie said it was an Indian symbol of life: the man in the maze. The priest was short, with a muscular build and white-blond, unruly hair, not really my type but handsome in a just-rolled-out-of-bed kind of way, though I suppose that saying such things about a priest must be some special category of sin. His name was Father William.

When Mattie introduced us I said, "Pleased to meet you," making an effort not to look at his belt buckle. What had popped into my head was "You are old, Father William." Now where did *that* come from? He was hardly old, and even if he were, this isn't something you'd say.

He and Mattie went to the back of the shop to discuss something over coffee and pie while I held down the fort. It came to me a little later while I was testing a stack of old whitewalls, dunking them in the water and marking a yellow chalk circle around each leak. I remembered three drawings of a little round man: first standing on his head, then balancing an eel straight up on his nose, then kicking a boy downstairs. "You Are Old, Father William" was a poem in a book I'd had as a child. It had crayon scribbles on some pages, so it must have been a donation from one of Mama's people whose children had grown up. Only a rich child would be allowed to scribble in a hardback book.

I decided that after work I would go down to one of Sandi's New To You toy stores and find a book for Turtle. New To You was just like Mama's people, only you had more choice about what you got.

After I had marked all the tires I rolled them across the lot and stacked them into leaky and good piles. I congratulated myself on my steady hand, but later in the day Mattie saw me jump when some hot-dog Chevy backfired out in the street. She was with a customer, but later she came over and said she'd been meaning to ask what I was always so jumpy about. I thought of that column in *Reader's Digest* where you write in and tell your most embarrassing moment. Those were all cute: "The Day My Retriever Puppy Retrieved the Neighbor's Lingerie Off the Clothes Line." In real life, your most embarrassing moment is the last thing in the world you would want printed in *Reader's Digest.*

"Nothing," I said.

We stood for a minute with our hands folded into our armpits. Mattie's gray bangs were more salt than they were pepper, cut high and straight across, and her skin always looked a little sunburned. The wrinkles around her eyes reminded me of her Tony Lama boots.

Mattie was like a rock in the road. You could stare at her till the cows came home, but it wouldn't budge the fact of her one inch.

"Just don't tell me you're running from the law," she said finally. "I've got enough of that on my hands."

"No." I wondered what exactly she meant by that. Out on the street a boy coasted by on a bicycle, his elbow clamped over a large framed picture of a sportscar. "I have a fear of exploding tires," I said.

"Well, of all things," she said.

"I know. I didn't ever tell you because it sounds chickenshit." I stopped to consider if you ought to say "chickenshit" in a place called Jesus Is Lord's, but then the damage was done. "Really it's not like it sounds. I don't think there's a thing you could name that I'm afraid of, other than that."

"Of all things," she said again. I imagined that she was looking at me the way you do when you first notice someone is deformed. In sixth grade we had a new teacher for three weeks before we realized his left hand was missing. He always kept his hanky over it. We'd just thought it was allergies.

"Come over here a minute," Mattie said. "I'll show you something." I followed her across the lot. She took a five-gallon jerry can, the type that Jeeps have strapped on their backs, and filled it a little better than halfway up with water.

"Whoa!" I said. While I wasn't paying attention she'd thrown the heavy can at me. I caught it, though it came near to bowling me over.

"Knocked the wind out of you, but it didn't kill you, right?"

"Right," I said.

"That's twenty-eight pounds of water. Twenty-eight pounds of air is about what you put in a tire. When it hits you, that's what it feels like."

"If you say so," I said. "But I saw a guy get blown up in the air once by a tire. All the way over the Standard Oil sign. It was a tractor tire."

"Well that's another whole can of beans," Mattie said. "If we get a tractor tire in here, I'll handle it."

I had never thought of tire explosions in relative terms,

though it stood to reason that some would be worse than others. By no means did this put my fears to rest, but still I felt better somehow. What the hell. Live free or bust.

"Okay," I said. "We'll handle it together, how's that?"

"That's a deal, hon."

"Can I put this down now?"

"Sure, put it down." She said it in a serious way, as if the can of water were some important damaged auto part we'd been discussing. I blessed Mattie's soul for never laughing at any point in this conversation. "Better yet," she said, "pour it out on those sweet peas."

There was a whole set of things I didn't understand about plants, such as why hadn't the sweet peas been killed by the frost? The same boy sped by again on his bike, or possibly a different boy. This time he had a bunch of roses in a white paper funnel tucked under his arm. While the water glugged out over the sweet peas I noticed Mattie looking at me with her arms crossed. Just watching. I missed Mama so much my chest hurt.

Turtle had managed to get through her whole life without a book, I suppose, and then had two of them bought for her in one day. I got her one called *Old MacDonald Had an Apartment House,* which showed pictures of Old MacDonald growing celery in windowboxes and broccoli in the bathtub and carrots under the living-room rug. Old MacDonald's downstairs neighbors could see the carrots popping down through the ceiling. I bought it because it reminded me of Mattie, and because it had stiff pages that I hoped might stand up to Turtle's blood-out-of-turnips grip.

While I was downtown I also looked for a late Valentine's card to send Mama. I still felt kind of awful about leaving her, and changing my name just seemed like the final act of betrayal, but Mama didn't see it that way. She said I was smarter than anything to think of Taylor, that it fit me like a pair of washed jeans. She told me she'd always had second thoughts about Marietta.

I found just the right card to send her. On the cover there were hearts, and it said, "Here's hoping you'll soon have something big and strong around the house to open those tight jar lids." Inside was a picture of a pipe wrench.

Lou Ann, meanwhile, had bought one of those name-your-baby books in the grocery checkout line. When I came home she had it propped open on the stove and was calling out names from the girl section while she made dinner. Both Turtle and Dwayne Ray were propped up at the table in chairs too big for them. Dwayne Ray's head was all flopped over, he was too little to hold it up by himself, and he was wiggling toward the floor like Snake Man escaping from his basket. Turtle just sat and stared at nothing. Or rather, at something on the table that was as real to her as Snowboots's invisible poop was to him.

Lou Ann was banging pot lids to wake the dead and boiling bottles. She had stopped nursing and put Dwayne Ray on formula, saying she was petrified she wouldn't have enough milk for him.

"Leandra, Leonie, Leonore, Leslie, Letitia," she called out, watching Turtle over her shoulder as though she expected her to spew out quarters like a slot machine when she hit the right combination of letters.

"Lord have mercy," I said. "Have you been doing this all the way from the Agathas and Amys?"

"Oh, hi, I didn't hear you come in." She acted a little guilty, like a kid caught using swear words. "I thought I'd do half today and the rest tomorrow. You know what? Lou Ann is on the exact middle page. I wonder if my mother had a book like this."

"The book our mothers had was the Bible, not some fifty-cent dealie they sell from the same rack as the *National*

Enquirer." I knew very well that none of my various names had come out of a Bible, nor Lou Ann's either, but I didn't care. I was just plain in a bad mood. I put Turtle over my shoulder. "What do you really expect her to do if you say the right name, Lou Ann? Jump up and scream and kiss you like the people on those game shows?"

"Don't be mad at me, Taylor, I'm just trying to help. She worries me. I'm not saying she's dumb, but it seems like she doesn't have too much personality."

"Sure she does," I said. "She grabs onto things. That's her personality."

"Well, no offense, but that's not personality. Babies do that automatically. I haven't worked in a hospital or anything, but at least I know that much. Personality has to be something you learn."

"And reading off a list of every name known to humankind is going to teach her to have personality?"

"Taylor, I'm not trying to tell you what to do, but all the magazines say that you have to play with children to develop their personality."

"So? I play with her. I bought her a book today."

"Okay, you play with her. I'm sorry." Lou Ann ladled soup out of the big pot on the stove and brought bowls over to the table. Her bowl held about two teaspoons of the red-colored broth. She was starving herself to lose the weight she'd gained with Dwayne Ray, which was mostly between her ears as far as I could see.

"This is Russian cabbage-and-beet soup," she announced. "It's called borscht. It's the beets that turn it pink. You're supposed to put sour cream on top but that just seemed like calories up the kazoo. I got it out of *Ladies' Home Journal.*"

I could imagine her licking her index finger and paging through some magazine article called "Toasty Winter Family

Pleasers," trying to find something to do with all that cabbage I kept bringing home from Mattie's. I fished out a pink potato and mushed it up in Turtle's bowl.

"It's good, Lou Ann. Nothing personal, I'm just in a crappy mood."

"Watch out, there's peas in there. A child's windpipe can be blocked by anything smaller than a golf ball."

For Lou Ann, life itself was a life-threatening enterprise. Nothing on earth was truly harmless. Along with her clip file of Hispanic bank presidents (which she had started to let slide, now that Angel was talking divorce), she saved newspaper stories of every imaginable type of freak disaster. Unsuspecting diners in a restaurant decapitated by a falling ceiling fan. Babies fallen head-first into the beer cooler and drowned in melted ice while the family played Frisbee. A housewife and mother of seven stepping out of a Wick 'N' Candle store, only to be shot through the heart by a misfired high-pressure nail gun at a construction site across the street. To Lou Ann's way of thinking, this proved not only that ice chests and construction sites were dangerous, but also Wick 'N' Candle stores and Frisbees.

I promised her that I wouldn't give Turtle anything smaller than a golf ball. I amused myself by thinking about the cabbage: would you have to take into account the size of one leaf compressed into golf-ball shape? Or could you just consider the size of the entire cabbage and call the whole thing safe?

Lou Ann was fanning a mouthful that was still too hot to swallow. "I can just hear what my Granny Logan would say if I tried to feed her Russian cabbage soup. She'd say we were all going to turn communist."

Later that night when the kids were in bed I realized exactly what was bugging me: the idea of Lou Ann reading magazines for child-raising tips and recipes and me coming home grouchy after a hard day's work. We were like some family on a TV commercial, with names like Myrtle and Fred. I could just hear us striking up a conversation about air fresheners.

Lou Ann came in wearing her bathrobe and a blue towel wrapped around her hair. She curled up on the sofa and started flipping through the book of names again.

"Oh, jeez, take this away from me before I start looking at the boy section. There's probably fifty thousand names better than Dwayne Ray, and I don't even want to know about them. It's too late now."

"Lou Ann, have a beer with me. I want to talk about something, and I don't want you to get offended." She took the beer and sat up like I'd given her an order, and I knew this wasn't going to work.

"Okay, shoot." The way she said it, you would think I was toting an M-16.

"Lou Ann, I moved in here because I knew we'd get along. It's nice of you to make dinner for us all, and to take care of Turtle sometimes, and I know you mean well. But we're acting like Blondie and Dagwood here. All we need is some ignorant little dog named Spot to fetch me my slippers. It's not like we're a *family,* for Christ's sake. You've got your own life to live, and I've got mine. You don't have to do all this stuff for me."

"But I want to."

"But I don't *want* you to."

It was like that.

By the time we had worked through our third beers, a bag of deep-fried tortilla chips, a pack of individually-wrapped pimiento-cheese slices and a can of sardines in mustard, Lou Ann was crying. I remember saying something like "I never even *had* an old man, why would I want to end up acting like one?"

It's the junk food, I kept thinking. On a diet like this the Bean Curd kids would be speaking in tongues.

All of a sudden Lou Ann went still, with both hands over her mouth. I thought she must be choking (after all her talk about golf balls), and right away thought of the Heimlich Maneuver poster on the wall at Mattie's store. That's how often she fed people there. I was trying to remember if you were or were not supposed to slap the person on the back. But then Lou Ann moved her hands from her mouth to her eyes, like two of the three No-Evil monkey brothers.

"Oh, God," she said. "I'm drunk."

"Lou Ann, you've had three beers."

"That's all it takes. I *never* drink. I'm scared to death of what might happen."

I was interested. This house was full of surprises. But this turned out to be nothing like the cat. Lou Ann said what she was afraid of was just that she might lose control and do something awful.

"Like what?"

"I don't know. How do I know? Just something. I feel like the only reason I have any friends at all is because I'm always careful not to say something totally dumb, and if I blow it just one time, then that's it."

"Lou Ann, honey, that's a weird theory of friendship."

"No, I mean it. For the longest time after Angel left I kept thinking back to this time last August when his friend Manny and his wife Ramona came over and we all went out to the desert to look at the shooting stars? There was supposed to be a whole bunch of them, a shower, they were saying on the news. But we kept waiting and waiting, and in the meantime we drank a bottle of José Cuervo plumb down to the worm. The next morning Angel kept saying, 'Man, can you believe that meteor shower? What, you don't even remember it?' I honestly couldn't remember a thing besides looking for the star sapphire from Ramona's ring that had plunked out somewhere. It turned out she'd lost it way before. She found it at home in their dog's dish, can you believe it?"

I was trying to fit Angel into some pigeonhole or other in the part of my brain that contained what I knew about men. I liked this new version of an Angel who would go out looking for shooting stars, but hated what I saw of him the next morning, taunting Lou Ann about something that had probably never even happened.

"Maybe he was pulling your leg," I said. "Maybe there never was any meteor shower. Did you ask Ramona?"

"No. I never thought of that. I just assumed."

"Well, why don't you call her up and ask?"

"She and Manny moved to San Diego," she wailed. You'd think they had moved for the sole purpose of keeping this information from Lou Ann.

"Well, I'm sorry."

She persisted. "But that's not even really the point. It wasn't just that I'd missed something important. I kept on thinking that if I could miss a whole meteor shower, well, I'd probably done something else ridiculous. For all I know I could've run naked through the desert singing 'Skip to My Lou.'"

I shuddered. All those spiny pears and prickly whatsits.

She stared mournfully into the empty bag of chips. "And now it's Valentine's Day," she said. "And everybody else in the whole wide world is home with their husband smooching on the couch and watching TV, but not Lou Ann, no sir. I ran off both my husband *and* the TV."

I couldn't even think where to begin on this one. I thought of another one of Mama's hog sayings: "Hogs go deaf at harvest time." It meant that people would only hear what they wanted to hear. Mama was raised on a hog farm.

Lou Ann looked abnormally flattened against the back of the sofa. I thought of her father, who she'd told me was killed when his tractor overturned. They'd found him pressed into a mud bank, and when they pulled him out he left a perfect print. "A Daddy print" she'd called it, and she'd wanted to fill the hole with plaster of Paris to keep him, the way she'd done with her hand print in school for Mother's Day.

"I always wondered if that night we got drunk had something to do with why I lost him," she said. I was confused for a second, still thinking of her father.

"I thought you were glad when Angel left."

"I guess I was. But still, you know, something went wrong. You're supposed to love the same person your whole life long till death do you part and all that. And if you don't, well, you've got to have screwed up somewhere."

"Lou Ann, you read too many magazines." I went into the kitchen and checked the refrigerator for about the fifteenth time that night. It was still the same: cabbages and peanut butter. I opened a cabinet and peered behind the cans of refried beans and tomato sauce. There was a bottle of black-strap molasses, a box of Quick Hominy Grits, and a can of pink salmon. I considered all of these things in various combinations, then settled for another bag of tortilla chips. This is what happens to people without TVs, I thought. They die of junk food.

When I came back to the living room she was still depressed about Angel. "I'll tell you my theory about staying with one man your whole life long," I said. "Do you know what a flapper ball is?"

She perked up. "A whatter ball?"

"Flapper ball. It's that do-jobbie in a toilet tank that goes up and down when you flush. It shuts the water off."

"Oh."

"So one time when I was working in this motel one of the toilets leaked and I had to replace the flapper ball. Here's what it said on the package; I kept it till I knew it by heart: 'Please Note. Parts are included for all installations, but no installation requires all of the parts.' That's kind of my philosophy about men. I don't think there's an installation out there that could use all of my parts."

Lou Ann covered her mouth to hide a laugh. I wondered who had ever told her laughing was a federal offense.

"I'm serious, now. I'm talking mental capacity and everything, not just parts like what they cut a chicken into." By this time she was laughing out loud.

"I tell you my most personal darkest secret and you laugh," I said, playing vexed.

"They can always use a breast or a thigh or a leg, but nobody wants the scroungy old neckbones!"

"Don't forget the wings," I said. "They always want to gobble up your wings right off the bat." I dumped the rest of the bag of chips out into the bowl on the ottoman between us. I was actually thinking about going for the jar of peanut butter.

"Here, let me show you this Valentine's card I got for Mama," I said, digging through my purse until I found it. But Lou Ann was already having such a fit of giggles I could just as well have shown her the electric bill and she would have thought it was the funniest thing in recorded history.

"Oh, me," she said, letting the card fall in her lap. Her voice trailed down from all those high-pitched laughs like a prom queen floating down the gymnasium stairs. "I could use me a good wrench around here. Or better yet, one of them . . . what do you call 'ems? That one that's shaped like a weenie?"

I had no idea what she meant. "A caulking gun? An angle drill? A battery-head cleaner?" Come to think of it, just about every tool was shaped like either a weenie or a pistol, depending on your point of view. "The Washington Monument?" I said. This set Lou Ann off again. If there really had been a law against laughing, both of us would have been on our way to Sing Sing by now.

"Oh, Lordy, they ought to put that on a Valentine's card," she said. "I can just see me sending something like that to *my* Mama. She'd have a cow right there on the kitchen floor. And Granny Logan jumping and twisting her hands saying, 'What is it? I don't get it.' She'd go running after the mailman and tell him, 'Young man, come back in here this minute. Ask Ivy what's supposed to be so funny.'

"Oh, Lordy, Lordy," Lou Ann said again, drying her eyes. She put a chip in her mouth with a flourish, licking each of her fingers afterward. She was draped out on the sofa in her green terry bathrobe and blue turban like Cleopatra cruising down the Nile, with Snowboots curled at her feet like some insane royal pet. In ancient Egypt, I'd read somewhere, schizophrenics were worshiped as gods.

"I'll tell you one thing," Lou Ann said. "When something was bugging Angel, he'd never of stayed up half the night with me talking and eating everything that wasn't nailed down. You're not still mad, are you?"

I held up two fingers. "Peace, sister," I said, knowing full well that only a complete hillbilly would say this in the 1980s. Love beads came to Pittman the same year as the dial tone.

"Peace and love, get high and fly with the dove," she said.

SEVEN

How They Eat in Heaven

"A red Indian thought he might eat tobacco in church!" Lou Ann had closed her eyes and put herself in a trance to dig this item out of her fourth-grade memory, the way witnesses at a holdup will get themselves hypnotized to recollect the color of the getaway car. "That's it! Arithmetic!" she cried, bouncing up and down. Then she said, "No offense to anyone present, about the Indian." No one seemed offended.

"Oh, sure, I remember those," Mattie said. "There was one for every subject. Geography was: George eats old gray rutabagas and picks his—something. What would it be?"

"Oh, gross," Lou Ann said. "Gag a maggot."

I couldn't think of a solitary thing George might pick that started with Y. "Maybe you haven't got it quite right," I told Mattie. "Maybe it's something else, like 'pulls his yarn.'"

"Plants his yard?" offered Lou Ann.

"Pets his yak," said the dark, handsome man, who was half of a young couple Mattie had brought along on the picnic. Their names I had not yet gotten straight: Es-something and Es-something. The man had been an English teacher in Guatemala City. This whole conversation had started with a rhyme he used to help students remember how to pronounce English vowels. Then we'd gotten onto spelling.

"What's a yak?" Lou Ann wanted to know.

"It's a type of very hairy cow," he explained. He seemed a little embarrassed. Lou Ann and I had already told him three or four times that he spoke better English than the two of us combined.

We were flattened and sprawled across the rocks like a troop of lizards stoned on the sun, feeling too good to move. Lou Ann's feet dangled into the water. She insisted that she looked like a Sherman tank in shorts but had ended up wearing them anyway, and a pink elastic tube top which, she'd informed us, Angel called her boob tube. I'd worn jeans and regretted it. February had turned mild again right after the frost, and March was staying mainly on the sweaty end of pleasant. Lou Ann and Mattie kept saying it had to be the warmest winter on record. The old-timers, somewhere down the line, would look back on this as the year we didn't have a winter, except for that freeze God sent on Valentine's Day so we'd have green-tomato pie. When the summer wildflowers started blooming before Easter, Mattie said the Lord was clearly telling us to head for the hills and have us a picnic. You never could tell about Mattie's version of the Lord. Mainly, He was just one damn thing after another.

We'd come to a place you would never expect to find in the desert: a little hideaway by a stream that had run all the way down from the mountains into a canyon, where it jumped off a boulder and broke into deep, clear pools. White rocks sloped up out of the water like giant, friendly hippo butts. A ring of cottonwood trees cooled their heels in the wet ground, and overhead leaned together, then apart, making whispery swishing noises. It made me think of Gossip, the game we played as kids where you whisper a message around a circle. You'd start out with "Randy walks to the hardware store" and end up with "Granny has rocks in her underwear drawer."

It had been Lou Ann's idea to come here. It was a place she and Angel used to go when she first came to Tucson with him. I didn't know if her choice was a good or bad sign, but she didn't seem unhappy to be here without him. She seemed more concerned that the rest of us would like it.

"So is this place okay? You're sure?" she asked us, until we begged her to take our word for it, that it was the most wonderful picnic spot on the face of the earth, and she relaxed.

"Me and Angel actually talked about getting married up here," she said, dipping her toes in and out. There were Jesus bugs here, but not the long-legged, graceful kind we had back home. These were shaped like my car and more or less careened around on top of the water. The whole gang of them together looked like graduation night in Volkswagen land.

"That would have been a heck of a wedding," Mattie said. "A hefty hike for the guests."

"Oh no. We were going to do the whole thing on horseback. Can't you just see it?"

I could see it in *People* magazine, maybe. What with my disgust for anything horsy, I always forgot that Angel had won Lou Ann's heart and stolen her away from Kentucky during his days as a rodeo man.

"Anyway," she went on, "we could never have gone through with it on account of Angel's mother. She said something like, 'Okay, children, go ahead. When I get thrown off a horse and bash my brains out on the rocks, just step over me and go on with the ceremony.'"

The English teacher spoke softly in Spanish to his wife, and she smiled. Most of our conversation seemed to be getting lost in the translation, like some international form of the Gossip game. But this story had come from Mrs. Ruiz's Spanish (Lou Ann claimed that the only English words her mother-in-law knew were names of diseases) into English, and went back again without any trouble. A certain kind of mother is the same in any language.

Esperanza and Estevan were their names. It led you to expect twins, not a young married couple, and really there was something twinnish about them. They were both small and dark, with the same high-set, watching eyes and strong-boned faces I'd admired in the bars and gas stations and postcards of the Cherokee Nation. Mattie had told me that more than half the people in Guatemala were Indians. I had no idea.

But where Estevan's smallness made him seem compact and springy, as though he might have steel bars inside where most people had flab and sawdust, Esperanza just seemed to have shrunk. Exactly like a wool sweater washed in hot. It seemed impossible that her hands could be so small, that all the red and blue diamonds and green birds that ran across the bosom of her small blouse had been embroidered with regular-sized needles. I had this notion that at one time in life she'd been larger, but that someone had split her in two like one of those hollow wooden dolls, finding this smaller version inside. She took up almost no space. While the rest of us talked and splashed and laughed she sat still, a colorful outgrowth of rock. She reminded me of Turtle.

There had been something of a scene between her and Turtle earlier that day. We'd driven up in two cars, Lou Ann and me and the kids leading the way on my brand-new retreads and the other three following in Mattie's pickup. When we got to the trail head we parked in the skimpy shade you find under mesquite trees—like gray lace petticoats—and pulled out the coolers and bedspreads and canteens. The last two things out of the car were Dwayne Ray and Turtle.

Esperanza was just stepping out of the cab, and when she saw the kids she fell back against the seat, just as if she'd been hit with twenty-eight pounds of air. For the next ten minutes she looked blanched, like a boiled vegetable. She couldn't take her eyes off Turtle.

As we hiked up the trail I fell in behind Estevan and made small talk. Lou Ann was in the lead, carrying Dwayne Ray in a pouch on her back and holding his molded-plastic car seat over her head like some space-age sunbonnet. Behind her, ahead of us, went Esperanza. From behind you could have mistaken her for a schoolgirl, with her two long braids swinging across her back and her prim walk, one small sandal in front of the other. The orange plastic canteen on her shoulder looked like some burden thrust upon her from another world.

Eventually I asked Estevan if his wife was okay. He said certainly, she was okay, but he knew what I was talking about. A little later he said that my daughter looked like a child they'd known in Guatemala.

"She could be, for all I know." I laughed. I explained to him that she wasn't really my daughter.

Later, while we sat on the rocks and ate baloney sandwiches, Esperanza kept watching Turtle.

Estevan and I eventually decided to brave the cold water. "Don't look," I announced, and stripped off my jeans.

"Taylor, no! You mustn't," Lou Ann said.

"For heaven's sake, Lou Ann, I've got on decent underwear."

"No, what I mean is, you're not supposed to go in for an hour after you eat. You'll drown, both of you. It's something about the food in your stomach makes you sink."

"I know I can depend on you, Lou Ann," I said. "If we sink, you'll pull us out." I held my nose and jumped in.

The water was so cold I couldn't imagine why it hadn't just stayed frozen up there on the snow-topped mountain. The two of us caught our breath and whooped and splashed the others until Lou Ann was threatening our lives. Mattie, more inclined to the direct approach, was throwing rocks the size of potatoes.

"If you think I'd go in there to drag either one of you out, you're off your rocker," Mattie said. Lou Ann said, "If you all want to go and catch pee-namonia, be my guest."

Estevan went from whooping to singing in Spanish, hamming it up in this amazing yodely voice. He dog-paddled over to Esperanza and rested his chin on the rock by her feet, still singing, his head moving up and down with the words. What kind of words, it was easy to guess: "My sweet nightingale, my rose, your eyes like the stars." He was unbelievably handsome, with this smile that could just crack your heart right down the middle.

But she was off on her own somewhere. From time to time she would gaze over to where the kids were asleep on the blue bedspread. And who could blame her, really? It was a sweet sight. With the cottonwood shade rippling over them they looked like a drawing from one of those old-fashioned children's books that show babies in underwater scenes, blowing glassy bubbles and holding on to fishes' tails. Dwayne Ray had on a huge white sailor hat and had nodded forward in his car seat, but Turtle's mouth was open to the sky. Her hair was damp and plastered down in dark cords on her temples, showing more of her forehead than usual. Even from a distance I could see her eyes dancing around under eyelids as thin as white grape skins. Turtle always had desperate, active dreams. In sleep, it seemed, she was free to do all the things that during her waking life she could only watch.

We went back at that time of evening when it's dusky but the headlights don't really help yet. Mattie said she was stone-blind this time of night, so Estevan drove. "Be careful now," she warned him as the three of them climbed into the cab. "The last thing we need is to get stopped." Lou Ann and the kids and I followed in my car.

Fortunately the parking lot had a good slant to it so getting started was a piece of cake. I hardly had time to curse, and we caught right up. Mattie needn't have worried; Estevan was a careful driver. As we puttered along Lou Ann had to keep reaching into the back seat, which wasn't really a seat but a kind of pit where one used to be, to get the kids settled down. They had both slept through the entire hike back, but now were wide awake.

"Oh, shoot, I've sunburned the top half of my boobs," she said, frowning down her chest. "Stretch marks and all."

Mattie's pickup stopped so fast I nearly rear-ended it. I slammed on the brakes and we all pitched forward. There was a thud in the back seat, and then a sound, halfway between a cough and a squeak.

"Jesus, that was Turtle," I said. "Lou Ann, that was her, wasn't it? She made that sound. Is her neck broken?"

"She's fine, Taylor. Everybody's fine. Look." She picked up Turtle and showed me that she was okay. "She did a somersault. I think that sound was a laugh."

It must have been true. She was hanging on to Lou Ann's boob tube for dear life, and smiling. We both stared at her. Then we stared at the tailgate of the truck in front of us, stopped dead in the road.

"What in the tarnation?" Lou Ann asked.

I said I didn't know. Then I said, "Look." In the road up ahead there was a quail, the type that has one big feather spronging out the front of its head like a forties-model ladies' hat. We could just make out that she was dithering back and forth in the road, and then we gradually could see that there were a couple dozen babies running around her every which way. They looked like fuzzy ball bearings rolling around in a box.

Our mouths opened and shut and we froze where we sat. I suppose we could have honked and waved and it wouldn't have raised any more pandemonium than this poor mother already had to deal with, but instead we held perfectly still. Even Turtle. After a long minute or two the quail got her family herded off the road into some scraggly bushes. The truck's brakelights flickered, like a wink, and Estevan drove on. Something about the whole scene was trying to make tears come up in my eyes. I decided I must be about to get my period.

"You know," Lou Ann said a while later, "if that had been Angel, he would've given himself two points for every one he could hit."

Knowing that Turtle's first uttered sound was a laugh brought me no end of relief. If I had dragged her halfway across the nation only to neglect and entirely botch her upbringing, would she have laughed? I thought surely not. Surely she would have bided her time while she saved up whole words, even sentences. Things like "What do you think you're doing?"

I suppose some of Lou Ann had rubbed off on me, for me to take this laugh as a sign. Lou Ann was the one who read her horoscope every day, and mine, and Dwayne Ray's, and fretted that we would never know Turtle's true sign (which seemed to me the least of her worries), and was sworn to a strange kind of logic that said a man could leave his wife for missing a meteor shower or buying the wrong brand of cookies. If the mail came late it meant someone, most likely Grandmother Logan, had died.

But neither of us could interpret the significance of Turtle's first word. It was "bean."

We were in Mattie's backyard helping her put in the summer garden, which she said was way overdue considering the weather. Mattie's motto seemed to be "Don't let the grass grow under your feet, but make sure there's something growing everywhere else."

"Looky here, Turtle," I said. "We're planting a garden just like Old MacDonald in your book." Mattie rolled her eyes. I think her main motive, in insisting that Turtle watch us do this, was to straighten the child out. She was concerned that Turtle would grow up thinking carrots grew under the rug.

"Here's squash seeds," I said. "Here's pepper seeds, and here's eggplants." Turtle looked thoughtfully at the little flat disks.

"That's just going to discombobble her," Mattie said. "Those seeds don't look anything like what you're saying they'll grow into. When kids are that little, they don't take much on faith."

"Oh," I said. It seemed to me that Turtle had to take practically everything on faith.

"Show her something that looks like what you eat."

I scooped a handful of big white beans out of one of Mattie's jars. "These are beans. Remember white bean soup with ketchup? Mmm, you like that."

"Bean," Turtle said. "Humbean."

I looked at Mattie.

"Well, don't just sit there, the child's talking to you," Mattie said.

I picked up Turtle and gave her a hug. "That's right, that's a bean. And you're just about the smartest kid alive," I told her. Mattie just smiled.

As I planted the beans, Turtle followed me down the row digging each one up after I planted it and putting it back in the jar. "Good girl," I said. I could see a whole new era arriving in Turtle's and my life.

Mattie suggested that I give her some of her own beans to play with, and I did, though Lou Ann's warning about windpipes and golf balls was following me wherever I went these days. "These are for you to keep," I explained to Turtle. "Don't eat them, these are playing-with beans. There's eating beans at home. And the rest of these in here are putting-in-the-ground beans." Honest to God, I believe she understood that. For the next half hour she sat quietly between two squash hills, playing with her own beans. Finally she buried them there on the spot, where they were forgotten by all until quite a while later when a ferocious thicket of beans came plowing up through the squashes.

On the way home Turtle pointed out to me every patch of bare dirt beside the sidewalk. "Humbean," she told me.

Lou Ann was going through a phase of cutting her own hair every other day. In a matter of weeks it had gone from shoulder length to what she referred to as "shingled," passing through several stages with figure-skaters' names in between.

"I don't know about shingled," I said, "but you've got to draw the line somewhere or you're going to end up like this guy that comes into Mattie's all the time with a Mohawk. He has 'Born to Die' tattooed onto the bald part of his scalp."

"I might as well just shave it off," said Lou Ann. I don't think she was really listening.

She was possessed of the type of blond, bone-straight hair that was, for a brief period in history, the envy of every teenaged female alive. I remember when the older girls spoke so endlessly of bleaching and ironing techniques you'd think their hair was something to be thrown in a white load of wash. Lou Ann would have been in high school by then, she was a few years older than me, but she probably missed this whole craze. She would have been too concerned with having the wrong kind of this or that. She'd told me that in high school she prayed every night for glamour-girl legs, which meant that you could put dimes between the knees, calves, and ankles and they would stay put; she claimed her calves would have taken a softball. I'm certain Lou Ann never even noticed that for one whole year her hair was utterly perfect.

"It looks like it plumb *died,*" she said, tugging on a straight lock over one eyebrow.

I was tempted to remind her that anything subjected so frequently to a pair of scissors wouldn't likely survive, but of course I didn't. I always tried to be positive with her, although I'd learned that even compliments were a kind of insult to Lou Ann, causing her to wrinkle her face and advise me to make an appointment with an eye doctor. She despised her looks, and had more ways of saying so than anyone I'd ever known.

"I ought to be shot for looking like this," she'd tell the mirror in the front hall before going out the door. "I look like I've been drug through hell backwards," she would say on just any ordinary day. "Like death warmed over. Like something the cat puked up."

I wanted the mirror to talk back, to say, "Shush, you do not," but naturally it just mouthed the same words back at her, leaving her so forlorn that I was often tempted to stick little notes on it. I thought of my T-shirt, Turtle's now, from Kentucky Lake. Lou Ann needed a DAMN I'M GOOD mirror.

On this particular night we had invited Esperanza and Estevan over for dinner. Mattie was going to be on TV, on the six-o'clock news, and Lou Ann had suggested inviting them over to watch it on a television set we didn't have. She was constantly forgetting about the things Angel had taken, generously offering to loan them out and so forth. We'd settled it, however, by also inviting some neighbors Lou Ann knew who had a portable TV. She said she'd been meaning to have them over anyway, that they were very nice. Their names were Edna Poppy and Virgie Mae Valentine Parsons, or so their mailbox said. I hadn't met them, but before I'd moved in she said they had kept Dwayne Ray many a time, including once when Lou Ann had to rush Snowboots to the vet for eating a mothball.

Eventually Lou Ann gave up on berating her hair and set up the ironing board in the kitchen. I was cooking. We had worked things out: I cooked on weekends, and also on any week night that Lou Ann had kept Turtle. It would be a kind of payment. And she would do the vacuuming, because she liked to, and I would wash dishes because I didn't mind them. "And on the seventh day we wash bean turds," I pronounced. Before, it had seemed picayune to get all bent out of shape organizing the household chores. Now I was beginning to see the point.

The rent and utilities we split fifty-fifty. Lou Ann had savings left from Angel's disability insurance settlement—for some reason he hadn't touched this money—and also he sent checks, but only once in a blue moon. I worried about what she would do when the well ran dry, but I'd decided I might just as well let her run her own life.

For the party I was making sweet-and-sour chicken, more or less on a dare, out of one of Lou Ann's magazines. The folks at Burger Derby should see me now, I thought. I had originally planned to make navy-bean soup, in celebration of Turtle's first word, but by the end of the week she had said so many new words I couldn't have fit them all in Hungarian goulash. She seemed to have a one-track vocabulary, like Lou Ann's hypochondriac mother-in-law, though fortunately Turtle's ran to vegetables instead of diseases. I could just imagine a conversation between these two: "Sciatica, hives, roseola, meningomalacia," Mrs. Ruiz would say in her accented English. "Corns, 'tato, bean," Turtle would reply.

"What's so funny?" Lou Ann wanted to know. "I hope I can even fit into this dress. I should have tried it on first, I haven't worn it since before Dwayne Ray." I had noticed that Lou Ann measured many things in life, besides her figure, in terms of Before and After Dwayne Ray.

"You'll fit into it," I said. "Have you weighed yourself lately?"

"No, I don't want to know what I weigh. If the scale even goes up that high."

"I refuse to believe you're overweight, that's all I'm saying. If you say one more word about being fat, I'm going to stick my fingers in my ears and sing 'Blue Bayou' until you're done."

She was quiet for a minute. The hiss of the steam iron and the smell of warm, damp cotton reminded me of Sunday afternoons with Mama.

"What's Mattie going to be on TV about? Do you know?" she asked.

"I'm not sure. It has something to do with the people that live with her."

"Oh, I'd be petrified to be on TV, I know I would," Lou Ann said. "I'm afraid I would just blurt out, 'Underpants!' or something. When I was a little girl I would get afraid in church, during the invocation or some other time when it got real quiet, and I'd all of a sudden be terrified that I was going to stand up and holler, 'God's pee-pee!'"

I laughed.

"Oh, I know it sounds ridiculous. I mean, I didn't even know if God had one. In the pictures He's always got on all those robes and things. But the fact that I even wondered about it seemed like just the ultimate sin. If I was bad enough to think it, how did I know I wasn't going to stand up and say it?"

"I know what you mean," I said. "There's this Catholic priest that comes to Mattie's all the time, Father William. He's real handsome, I think he's your type, maybe not. But sometimes I get to thinking, What if I were to strut over and say something like, 'Hey good looking, whatcha got cooking?'"

"Exactly! It's like, did you ever have this feeling when you're standing next to a cliff, say, or by an upstairs window, and you can just picture yourself jumping out? The worst time it happened to me was in high school. On our senior trip we went to the state capitol, which is at Frankfort. Of course, you know that, what am I saying? So, what happened was, you can go way up in the dome and there's only this railing and you look down and the people are like little miniature ants. And I saw myself just hoisting my leg and going over. I just froze up. I thought: if I can think it, I might do it. My boyfriend, which at that time was Eddie Tubbs, it was way before I met Angel, thought it was fear of heights and told everybody on the bus on the way home that I had ackero-phobia, but it was way more complicated than that. I mean, ackero-phobia doesn't have anything to do with being afraid you'll holler out something god-awful in church, does it?"

"No," I said. "I think what you mean is a totally different phobia. Fear that the things you imagine will turn real."

Lou Ann was staring at me, transfixed. "You know, I think you're the first person I've ever told this to that understood what I was talking about."

I shrugged. "I saw a *Star Trek* episode one time that was along those lines. All the women on this whole planet end up naked. I can't remember exactly, but I think Captain Kirk gets turned into a pipe wrench."

The six o'clock news was half over by the time we got the TV plugged in. There had been a mix-up with the women next door, who were waiting for us to come over and get the television. They didn't realize they had been invited for dinner.

Meanwhile, Estevan and Esperanza arrived. Estevan played the gentleman flirt, saying how nice I looked, and didn't he perhaps know my tomboy sister who worked with a used-tire firm? "Exquisite" was what he actually said, and "tom boy" as if it were two words. I batted my eyelashes and said yes indeed, that she was the sister who got all the brains of the family.

I suppose I did look comparatively elegant. Lou Ann had parted my hair on the side ("What you need is one of those big blowzy white flowers behind one ear," she said, and "God, would I kill for black hair like yours." "Kill what?" I asked. "A skunk?") and forced me into a dress she had purchased "before Dwayne Ray" in an uptown thrift shop. It was one of those tight black satin Chinese numbers you have to try on with a girlfriend—you hold your breath while she zips you in. I only agreed to wear it because I thought sharing our clothes might shut her up about being a Sherman tank. And because it fit.

But Esperanza was the one who truly looked exquisite. She wore a long, straight dress made of some amazing woven material that brought to mind the double rainbow Turtle and I saw on our first day in Tucson: twice as many colors as you ever knew existed.

"Is this from Guatemala?" I asked.

She nodded. She looked almost happy.

"Sometimes I get homesick for Pittman and it's as ugly as a mud stick fence," I said. "A person would have to just ache for a place where they make things as beautiful as this."

Poor Lou Ann was on the phone with Mrs. Parsons for the fourth time in ten minutes, and apparently still hadn't gotten it straight because Mrs. Parsons and Edna walked in the front door with the TV just as Lou Ann ran out the back to get it.

One of the women led the way and the other, who appeared to be the older of the two, carried the set by its handle, staggering a little with the weight like a woman with an overloaded purse. I rushed to take it from her and she seemed a little startled when the weight came up out of her hands. "Oh my, I thought it had sprouted wings," she said. She told me she was Edna Poppy.

I liked her looks. She had bobbed, snowy hair and sturdy,

wiry arms and was dressed entirely in red, all the way down to her perky patent-leather shoes.

"Pleased to meet you," I said. "I love your outfit. Red's my color."

"Mine too," she said.

Mrs. Parsons had on a churchy-looking dress and a small, flat white hat with a dusty velveteen bow. She didn't seem too friendly, but of course we were all dashing around trying to get set up. I didn't even know what channel we were looking for until Mattie's face loomed up strangely in black and white.

Signatory to the United Nations something-something on human rights, Mattie was saying, and that means we have a legal obligation to take in people whose lives are in danger.

A man with a microphone clipped to his tie asked her, What about legal means? And something about asylum. They were standing against a brick building with short palm trees in front. Mattie said that out of some-odd thousand Guatemalans and Salvadorans who had applied for this, only one-half of one percent of them had been granted it, and those were mainly relatives of dictators, not the people running for their lives.

Then the TV showed both Mattie and the interview man talking without sound, and another man's voice told us that the Immigration and Naturalization Service had returned two illegal aliens, a woman and her son, to their native El Salvador last week, and that Mattie "claimed" they had been taken into custody when they stepped off the plane in San Salvador and later were found dead in a ditch. I didn't like this man's tone. I had no idea how Mattie would know such things, but if she said it was so, it was.

But it was all garbled anyhow. Mrs. Parsons had been talking the whole time about not being able to sit in a certain type of chair or her back would go out, and then Lou Ann flew in the back door and called out, "Damn it, they're not home. Oh."

Mrs. Parsons made a little sniffing sound. "We're here, if you want to know."

"What program did you want to see?" Edna asked. "I hope we haven't spoiled it by coming late?"

"That was it, we just saw it," I said, though it seemed ridiculous. Thirty seconds and it was all over. "She's a friend of ours," I explained.

"All I could make out was some kind of trouble with illegal aliens and dope peddlers," said Mrs. Parsons. "Dear, I need a pillow for the small of my back or I won't be able to get out of bed tomorrow. Your cat has just made dirt in the other room."

I went for a cushion and Lou Ann rushed to put the cat out. Estevan and Esperanza, I realized, had been sitting together on the ottoman the whole time, more or less on the fringe of all the commotion. I said, "I'd like you to meet my friends . . . "

"Steven," Estevan said, "and this is my wife, Hope." This was a new one on me.

"Pleased to make your acquaintance," Edna said.

Mrs. Parsons said, "And is this naked creature one of theirs? She looks like a little wild Indian." She was talking about Turtle, who was not naked, although she didn't exactly have a shirt on.

"We have no children," Estevan said. Esperanza looked as though she had been slapped across the face.

"She's mine," I said. "And she *is* a little wild Indian, as a matter of fact. Why don't we start dinner?" I picked up Turtle and stalked off into the kitchen, leaving Lou Ann to fend for herself. Why she would call this old pruneface a nice lady was beyond my mental powers. I did the last-minute cooking, which the recipe said you were supposed to do "at the table in a sizzling wok before the admiring guests." A sizzling wok, my hind foot. Who did they think read those magazines?

A minute later Esperanza came into the kitchen and quietly helped set the table. I touched her arm. "I'm sorry," I said.

It wasn't until everyone came in and sat down to dinner that I really had a chance to look these women over. The fact that they couldn't possibly have had time to dress up for dinner made their outfits seem to tell everything. (Though of course Mrs. Parsons would have had time to powder her nose and reach for the little white hat.) Edna even had red bobby pins in her hair, two over each ear. I couldn't imagine where you would buy such items, a drugstore I suppose. I liked thinking about Edna finding them there on the rack, along with the purple barrettes and Oreo-cookie hair clips, and saying, "Why, look, Virgie Mae, red bobby pins! That's my color." Virgie Mae would be the type to sail past the douche aisle with her nose in the air and lecture the boy at the register for selling condoms.

Estevan produced a package, which turned out to be chopsticks. There were twenty or so of them wrapped together in crackly cellophane with black Chinese letters down one side. "A gift for the dishwasher," he said, handing each of us a pair of sticks. "You use them once, then throw them away." I couldn't think how he knew we were going to have Chinese food, but then I remembered running into him a day or two ago in the Lee Sing Market, where we'd discussed a product called "wood ears." The recipe called for them, but I had my principles.

"The dishwasher thanks you," I said. I noticed Lou Ann whisking a pair out of Dwayne Ray's reach, and could hear the words "put his eyes out" as plainly as if she'd said them aloud. Dwayne Ray started squalling, and Lou Ann excused herself to go put him to bed.

"What is it, eating sticks?" Edna ran her fingers along the thin shafts. "It sounds like a great adventure, but I'll just stick to what I know, if you don't mind. Thank you all the same." I noticed that Edna ate very slowly, with gradual, exact movements of her fork. Mrs. Parsons said she wasn't game for such foolishness either.

"I never said it was foolishness," Edna said.

The rest of us gave it a try, spearing pieces of chicken and looping green-pepper rings and chasing the rice around our plates. Even Esperanza tried. Estevan said we were being too aggressive.

"They are held this way." He demonstrated, holding them like pencils in one hand and clicking the ends together. I loved his way of saying, "It is" and "They are."

Turtle was watching me, imitating. "Don't look at me, I'm not the expert." I pointed at Estevan.

Lou Ann came back to the table. "Where'd you learn how to do that?" she asked Estevan.

"Ah," he said, "this is why I like chopsticks: I work in a Chinese restaurant. I am the dishwasher."

"I didn't know that. How long have you worked there?" I asked, realizing that I had no business thinking I knew everything about Estevan. His whole life, really, was a mystery to me.

"One month," he said. "I work with a very kind family who speak only Chinese. Only the five-year-old daughter speaks English. The father has her explain to me what I must do. Fortunately, she is very patient."

Mrs. Parsons muttered that she thought this was a disgrace. "Before you know it the whole world will be here jibbering and jabbering till we won't know it's America."

"Virgie, mind your manners," Edna said.

"Well, it's the truth. They ought to stay put in their own dirt, not come here taking up jobs."

"Virgie," Edna said.

I felt like I'd sat on a bee. If Mama hadn't brought me up to do better, I think I would have told that old snake to put down her fork and get her backside out the door. I wanted to scream at her: This man you are looking at is an English teacher. He did not come here so he could wash egg foo yung off plates and take orders from a five-year-old.

But Estevan didn't seem perturbed, and I realized he must hear this kind of thing every day of his life. I wondered how he could stay so calm. I would have murdered somebody by now, I thought, would have put a chopstick to one of the many deadly uses that only Lou Ann could imagine for it.

"Can I get anybody anything?" Lou Ann asked.

"We're fine," Edna said, obviously accustomed to being Virgie Mae's public-relations department. "You children have made a delightful meal."

Esperanza pointed at Turtle. It was the first time I ever saw her smile, and I was struck with what a lovely woman she was when you really connected. Then the smile left her again.

Turtle, wielding a chopstick in each hand, had managed to pick up a chunk of pineapple. Little by little she moved it upward toward her wide-open mouth, but the sticks were longer than her arms. The pineapple hung in the air over her head and then fell behind her onto the floor. We laughed and cheered her on, but Turtle was so startled she cried. I picked her up and held her on my lap.

"Tortolita, let me tell you a story," Estevan said. "This is a South American, wild *Indian* story about heaven and hell." Mrs. Parsons made a prudish face, and Estevan went on. "If you go to visit hell, you will see a room like this kitchen. There is a pot of delicious stew on the table, with the most delicate aroma you can imagine. All around, people sit, like us. Only they are dying of starvation. They are jibbering and jabbering," he looked extra hard at Mrs. Parsons, "but they cannot get a bite of this wonderful stew God has made for them. Now, why is that?"

"Because they're choking? For all eternity?" Lou Ann asked. Hell, for Lou Ann, would naturally be a place filled with sharp objects and small round foods.

"No," he said. "Good guess, but no. They are starving because they only have spoons with very long handles. As long as that." He pointed to the mop, which I had forgotten to put away. "With these ridiculous, terrible spoons, the people in hell can reach into the pot but they cannot put the food in their mouths. Oh, how hungry they are! Oh, how they swear and curse each other!" he said, looking again at Virgie. He was enjoying this.

"Now," he went on, "you can go and visit heaven. What? You see a room just like the first one, the same table, the same pot of stew, the same spoons as long as a sponge mop. But these people are all happy and fat."

"Real fat, or do you mean just well-fed?" Lou Ann asked.

"Just well-fed," he said. "Perfectly, magnificently well-fed, and very happy. Why do you think?"

He pinched up a chunk of pineapple in his chopsticks, neat as you please, and reached all the way across the table to offer it to Turtle. She took it like a newborn bird.

EIGHT

The Miracle of Dog Doo Park

Of all the ridiculous things, Mama was getting married. To Harland Elleston no less, of El-Jay's Paint and Body fame. She called on a Saturday morning while I'd run over to Mattie's, so Lou Ann took the message. I was practically the last to know.

When I called back Mama didn't sound normal. She was out of breath and kept running on about Harland. "Did I get you in out of the yard?" I asked her. "Are you planting cosmos?"

"Cosmos, no, it's not even the end of April yet, is it? I've got sugar peas in that little bed around to the side, but not cosmos."

"I forgot," I told her. "Everything's backwards here. Half the stuff you plant in the fall."

"Missy, I'm in a tither," she said. She called me Taylor in letters, but we weren't accustomed to phone calls. "With Harland and all. He treats me real good, but it's happened so fast I don't know what end of the hog to feed. I wish you were here to keep me straightened out."

"I do too," I said.

"You plant things in the fall? And they don't get bit?"

"No."

At least she did remember to ask about Turtle. "She's great," I said. "She's talking a blue streak."

"That's how you were. You took your time getting started, but once you did there was no stopping you," Mama said.

I wondered what that had to do with anything. Everybody behaved as if Turtle was my own flesh and blood daughter. It was a conspiracy.

Lou Ann wanted to know every little detail about the wedding, which was a whole lot more than I knew myself, or cared to.

"Everybody deserves their own piece of the pie, Taylor," Lou Ann insisted. "Who else has she got?"

"She's got me."

"She does not, you're here. Which might as well be Red Taiwan, for all the good it does her."

"I always thought I'd get Mama out here to live. She didn't even consult me, just ups and decides to marry this paint-and-body yahoo."

"I do believe you're jealous."

"That is so funny I forgot to laugh."

"When my brother got married I felt like he'd deserted us. He just sends this letter one day with a little tiny picture, all you could make out really was dogs, and tells us he's marrying somebody by the name of She-Wolf Who Hunts by the First Light." Lou Ann yawned and moved farther down the bench so her arms were more in the sun. She'd decided she was too pale and needed a tan.

"Granny Logan liked to died. She kept saying, did Eskimos count as human beings? She thought they were half animal or something. And really what are you supposed to think, with a name like that? But I got used to the idea. I like to think of him up there in Alaska with all these little daughters in big old furry coats. I've got in my mind that they live in an igloo, but that can't be right."

We were sitting out with the kids in Roosevelt Park, which the neighbor kids called such names as Dead Grass Park and Dog Doo Park. To be honest, it was pretty awful. There were only a couple of shade trees, which had whole dead parts, and one good-for-nothing palm tree so skinny and tall that it threw its shade onto the roof of the cooler-pad factory down the block. The grass was scraggly, struggling to come up between shiny bald patches of dirt. Mostly it put me in mind of an animal with the mange. Constellations of gum-wrapper foil twinkled around the trash barrels.

"Look at it this way, at least she's still kicking," Lou Ann said. "I feel like my mama's whole life stopped counting when Daddy died. You want to know something? They even got this double gravestone. Daddy's on the right hand side, and the other side's already engraved for Mama. 'Ivy Louise Logan, December 2, 1934—to blank.' Every time I see it it gives me the willies. Like it's just waiting there for her to finish up her business and die so they can fill in the blank."

"It does seem like one foot in the grave," I said.

"If Mama ever got married again I'd dance a jig at her wedding. I'd be thrilled sideways. Maybe it would get her off my back about moving back in with her and Granny." Dwayne Ray coughed in his sleep, and Lou Ann pushed his stroller back and forth two or three times. Turtle was pounding the dirt with a plastic shovel, a present from Mattie.

"Cabbage, cabbage, cabbage," she said.

Lou Ann said, "I know a guy that would just love her. Did you ever know that fellow downtown that sold vegetables out of his truck?" But Turtle and Bobby Bingo would never get to discuss their common interest. He had disappeared, probably to run off with somebody's mother.

"Your mother wouldn't be marrying Harland Elleston," I told Lou Ann, getting back to the subject at hand.

"Of course not! That big hunk is already spoken for."

"Lou Ann, you're just making a joke of this whole thing."

"Well, I can't help it, I wouldn't care if my mother married the garbage man."

"But Harland Elleston! He's not even . . . " I was going to say he's not even related to us, but of course that wasn't what I meant. "He's got warts on his elbows and those eyebrows that meet in the middle."

"I'll swan, Taylor, you talk about men like they're a hangnail. To hear you tell it, you'd think man was only put on this earth to keep urinals from going to waste."

"That's not true, I like Estevan." My heart sort of bumped when I said this. I knew exactly how it would look on an EKG machine: two little peaks and one big one.

"He's taken. Who else?"

"Just because I don't go chasing after every Tom's Harry Dick that comes down the pike."

"Who else? You never have one kind thing to say about any of your old boyfriends."

"Lou Ann, for goodness' sakes. In Pittman County there was nothing in pants that was worth the trouble, take my word for it. Except for this one science teacher, and the main thing he had going for him was clean fingernails." I'd never completely realized how limited the choices were in Pittman. Poor Mama. If only I could have gotten her to Tucson.

"Well, where in the heck do you think I grew up, Paris, France?"

"I notice you didn't stick with home-grown either. You had to ride off with a Wild West rodeo boy."

"Fat lot of good it did me, too."

"Well, you did get Dwayne Ray out of the deal." I remembered what Mama always said about me and the Jackson Purchase.

"But oh, Taylor, if you could have seen him. How handsome he was." She had her eyes closed and her face turned up toward the sun. "The first time I laid eyes on him he was draped on this fence like the Marlboro man, with his arms out to the sides and one boot up on the bottom rung. Just chewing on a match and hanging out till it was time to turn out the next bull. And do you know what else?" She sat up and opened her eyes.

"What?" I said.

"Right at that exact moment there was this guy in the ring setting some kind of a new world's record for staying on a bull, and everybody was screaming and throwing stuff and of course me and my girlfriend Rachel had never seen a rodeo before so we thought this was the wildest thing since Elvis joined the army. But Angel didn't even look up. He just squinted off at the distance toward the hay field behind the snack bar. Rachel said, 'Look at that tough guy over by that fence, what an asshole, not even paying attention.' And you know what I thought to myself? I thought, I bet I could get him to pay attention to me."

A child in a Michael Jackson tank shirt rumbled down the gravel path on a low-slung trike with big plastic wheels, making twice as much noise as his size would seem to allow for. "This is a O-R-V," he told us. Now I knew.

"I know you." He pointed at Lou Ann. "You're the one gives out money at Halloween."

Lou Ann rolled her eyes. "I'm never going to live that down. This year they'll be coming in from Phoenix and Flagstaff to beat down our door."

"Watch out when the bums come," he told us. "Go straight home." He tore off again, pedaling like someone possessed.

The gravel path cut through the middle of the park from a penis-type monument, up at the street near Mattie's, down to the other end where we liked to sit in a place Lou Ann called the arbor. It was the nicest thing about the park. The benches sat in a half-circle underneath an old wooden trellis that threw a shade like a cross-stitched tablecloth. The trellis had thick, muscly vines twisting up its support poles and fanning out overhead. Where they first came out of the ground, they reminded me of the arms of this guy who'd delivered Mattie's new refrigerator by himself. All winter Lou Ann had been telling me they were wisteria vines. They looked dead to me, like everything else in the park, but she always said, "Just you wait."

And she was right. Toward the end of March they had sprouted a fine, shivery coat of pale leaves and now they were getting ready to bloom. Here and there a purplish lip of petal stuck out like a pout from a fat green bud. Every so often a bee would hang humming in the air for a few seconds, checking on how the flowers were coming along. You just couldn't imagine where all this life was coming from. It reminded me of that Bible story where somebody or other struck a rock and the water poured out. Only this was better, flowers out of bare dirt. The Miracle of Dog Doo Park.

Lou Ann went on endlessly about Mama. "I can just see your mama. . . . What's her name, anyway?"

"Alice," I said. "Alice Jean Stamper Greer. The last thing she needs is an Elleston on top of all that."

". . . I can just see Alice and Harland running for the sugar shack. If she's anything like you, she goes after what she wants. I guess now she'll be getting all the paint and body jobs she needs."

"He's only half owner, with Ernest Jakes," I said. "It's not like the whole shop belongs to him."

"Alice and Harland sittin' in a tree," she sang, "K-I-S-S-I-N-G!"

I plugged my ears and sang, "I'm going back someday! Come what may! To Blue Bayou!" Turtle whacked the dirt and sang a recipe for succotash.

I spotted Mrs. Parsons and Edna Poppy coming down the gravel path with their arms linked. From a great distance you could have taken them for some wacked-out geriatric couple marching down the aisle in someone's sick idea of a garden wedding. We waved our arms at them, and Turtle looked up and waved at us.

"No, we're waving at them," I said, and pointed. She turned and folded and unfolded her hand in the right direction.

Now and again these days, not just in emergencies, we were leaving the kids with Edna and Virgie Mae on their front porch to be looked after. Edna was so sweet we just hoped she would cancel out Virgie's sour, like the honey and vinegar in my famous Chinese recipe. It was awfully convenient, anyway, and Turtle seemed to like them okay. She called them Poppy and Parsnip. She knew the names of more vegetables than many a greengrocer, I'd bet. Her favorite book was a Burpee's catalogue from Mattie's, which was now required reading every night before she would go to bed. The plot got old, in my opinion, but she was crazy about all the characters.

"Ma Poppy," Turtle said when they were a little closer. She called every woman Ma something. Lou Ann was Ma Wooahn, which Lou Ann said sounded like something you'd eat with chopsticks, and I was just Ma. We never told her these names, she just came to them on her own.

The two women were still moving toward us at an unbelievably slow pace. I thought of a game we used to play in school at the end of recess: See who can get there last. Edna had on a red knit top, red plaid Bermuda shorts, and red ladies' sneakers with rope soles. Virgie had on a tutti-frutti hat and a black dress printed all over with what looked like pills. I wondered if there was an actual place where you could buy dresses like that, or if after hanging in your closet for fifty years, regular ones would somehow just transform.

"Good afternoon, Lou Ann, Taylor, children," Mrs. Parsons said, nodding to each one of us. She was so formal it made you want to say something obscene. I thought of Lou Ann's compulsions in church.

"Howdy do," Lou Ann said, and waved at a bench. "Have a sit." But Mrs. Parsons said no thank you, that they were just out for their constitutional.

"I see you're wearing my favorite color today, Edna," I said. This was a joke. I'd never seen her in anything else. When she said red was her color, she meant it in a way most people don't.

"Oh, yes, always." She laughed. "Do you know, I started to dress in red when I was sixteen. I decided that if I was to be a Poppy, then a Poppy I would be."

Edna said the most surprising things. She didn't exactly look at you when she spoke, but instead stared above you as though there might be something wonderful hanging just over your head.

"Well, we've heard all about that before, haven't we?" said Mrs. Parsons, clamping Edna's elbow in a knucklebone vice-grip. "We'll be going along. If I stand still too long my knees are inclined to give out." They started to move away, but then Mrs. Parsons stopped, made a little nod, and turned around. "Lou Ann, someone was looking for you this morning. Your husband, or whatever he may be."

"You mean Angel?" She jumped so hard she bumped the stroller and woke up Dwayne Ray, who started howling.

"I wouldn't know," Virgie said, in such a way that she might as well have said, "How many husbands do you have?"

"When, this morning while I was at the laundromat?"

"I have no idea where *you* were, my dear, only that *he* was *here*."

"What did he say?"

"He said he would come back later."

Lou Ann bounced the baby until he stopped crying. "Shit," she said, quite a few minutes later when they'd moved out of earshot. "What do you think that means?"

"Maybe he wanted to deliver a check in person. Maybe he wants to go on a second honeymoon."

"Sure," she said, looking off at the far side of the park. She was still jiggling Dwayne Ray, possibly hadn't noticed he'd stopped crying.

"Why do you think she puts up with that coot?" I asked.

"What coot, old Vicious Virgie you mean? Oh, she's harmless." Lou Ann settled the baby back into his stroller. "She reminds me of Granny Logan. She's that type. One time Granny introduced me to some cousins by marriage of hers, I was wearing this brand-new midi-skirt I'd just made? And she says, 'This is my granddaughter Lou Ann. She isn't bowlegged, it's just her skirt makes her look that way.'"

"Oh, Lou Ann, you poor thing."

She frowned and brushed at some freckles on her shoulder, as though they might suddenly have decided to come loose. "I read a thing in the paper this morning about the sun giving you skin cancer," she said. "What does it look like in the early stages, do you know?"

"No. But I don't think you get it from sitting out one afternoon."

She pushed the stroller back and forth in an absent-minded way, digging a matched set of ruts into the dust. "Come to think of it, though, I guess that's a little different from the way Mrs. Parsons is. Somehow it's more excusable to be mean to your own relatives."

She rubbed her neck and turned her face to the sun again. Lou Ann's face was small and rounded in a pretty way, like an egg sunny side up. But in my mind's eye I could plainly see her dashing out the door on any given day, stopping to say to the mirror: "Ugly as homemade sin in the heat of summer." No doubt she could see Granny Logan in there too, staring over her shoulder.

After a while I said, "Lou Ann, I have to know something for Turtle's and my sake, so tell me the honest truth. If Angel wanted to come back, I mean move back in and have everything the way it was before, would you say yes?"

She looked at me, surprised. "Well, what else could I do? He's my husband, isn't he?"

There may have been a world of things I didn't understand, but I knew when rudeness passed between one human being and another. The things Mrs. Parsons had said about aliens were wrong and unkind, and I still felt bad even though weeks had passed. Eventually I apologized to Estevan. "She's got a mean streak in her," I told him. "If you're unlucky enough to get ahold of a dog like that, you give it away to somebody with a big farm. I don't know what you do about a neighbor."

Estevan shrugged. "I understand," he said.

"Really, I don't think she knew what she was saying, about how the woman and kid who got shot must have been drug dealers or whatever."

"Oh, I believe she did. This is how Americans think." He was looking at me in a thoughtful way. "You believe that if something terrible happens to someone, they must have deserved it."

I wanted to tell him this wasn't so, but I couldn't. "I guess you're right," I said. "I guess it makes us feel safe."

Estevan left Mattie's every day around four o'clock to go to work. Often he would come down a little early and we'd chat while he waited for his bus. "Attending my autobus" was the way he put it.

"Can I tell you something?" I said. "I think you talk so beautifully. Ever since I met you I've been reading the dictionary at night and trying to work words like constellation and scenario into the conversation."

He laughed. Everything about him, even his teeth, were so perfect they could have come from a book about the human body. "I have always thought you had a wonderful way with words," he said. "You don't need to go fishing for big words in the dictionary. You are poetic, mi'ija."

"What's miha?"

"Mi hija," he pronounced it slowly.

"My something?"

"My daughter. But it doesn't work the same in English. We say it to friends. You would call me mi'ijo."

"Well, thank you for the compliment," I said, "but that's the biggest bunch of hogwash, what you said. When did I ever say anything poetic?"

"Washing hogs is poetic," he said. His eyes actually twinkled.

His bus pulled up and he stepped quickly off the curb, catching the doorway and swinging himself in as it pulled away. That is just how he would catch a bus in Guatemala City, I thought. To go teach his classes. But he carried no books, no graded exams, and the sleeves of his pressed white shirt were neatly rolled up for a night of dishwashing.

I felt depressed that evening. Mattie, who seemed to know no end of interesting things, told me about the history of Roosevelt Park. I had just assumed it was named after one of the Presidents, but it was for Eleanor. Once when she had been traveling across the country in her own train she had stopped here and given a speech right from a platform on top of her box car. I suppose it would have been a special type of box car, decorated, and not full of cattle and bums and such. Mattie said the people sat out in folding chairs in the park and listened to her speak about those less fortunate than ourselves.

Mattie didn't hear Eleanor Roosevelt's speech, naturally, but she had lived here a very long time. Thirty years ago, she said, the homes around this park belonged to some of the most fortunate people in town. But now the houses all seemed a little senile, with arthritic hinges and window screens hanging at embarrassing angles. Most had been subdivided or otherwise transformed in ways that favored function over beauty. Many were duplexes. Lee Sing's was a home, grocery, and laundromat. Mattie's, of course, was a tire store and sanctuary.

Slowly I was coming to understand exactly what this meant. For one thing, people came and went quietly. And stayed quietly. Around to the side of Mattie's place, above the mural Lou Ann and I called Jesus Around the World, there was an upstairs window that looked out over the park. I saw faces there, sometimes Esperanza's and sometimes others, staring across the empty space.

Mattie would occasionally be gone for days at a time, leaving me in charge of the shop. "How can you just up and go? What if I get a tractor tire in here?" I would ask her, but she would just laugh and say, "No chance." She said that tire dealers were like veterinarians. There's country vets, that patch up horses and birth calves, and there's the city vets that clip the toenails off poodles. She said she was a city vet.

And off she would go. Mattie had numerous cars that ran, but for these trips she always took the four-wheel Blazer and her binoculars, and would come back with the fenders splattered with mud. "Going birdwatching" is what she always told me.

After she returned, a red-haired man named Terry sometimes came by on his bicycle and would spend an hour or more upstairs at Mattie's. He didn't look any older than I was, but

Mattie told me he was already a doctor. He carried his doctor bag in a special rig on the back of his bike.

"He's a good man," she said. "He looks after the ones that get here sick and hurt."

"What do you mean, that get here hurt?" I asked.

"Hurt," she said. "A lot of them get here with burns, for instance."

I was confused. "I don't get why they would have burns," I persisted.

She looked at me for so long that I felt edgy. "Cigarette burns," she said. "On their backs."

The sun was setting, and most of the west-facing windows on the block reflected a fierce orange light as if the houses were on fire inside, but I could see plainly into Mattie's upstairs. A woman stood at the window. Her hair was threaded with white and fell loose around her shoulders, and she was folding a pair of men's trousers. She moved the flats of her hands slowly down each crease, as if folding these trousers were the only task ahead of her in life, and everything depended on getting it right.

True to his word, Angel came back. He didn't come to move in, but to tell Lou Ann he was going away for good. I had taken Turtle for a doctor's appointment so I didn't witness the scene; all I can say is that the man had a genuine knack for dropping bombshells at home while someone was sitting in Dr. Pelinowsky's waiting room. But of course, I had no real connection to Angel's life. It was just a coincidence.

Turtle was healthy as corn, but as time went by I got to thinking she should have been taken to a doctor, in light of what had been done to her. (Lou Ann's main question was: Shouldn't you tell the police? Call 88-CRIME or something? But of course it was all in the past now.) I had thought of asking Terry, the red-haired doctor on the bicycle, but couldn't quite get up the gumption. Finally I called for an appointment with the famous Dr. P., on Lou Ann's recommendation, even though he wasn't exactly the right kind of doctor. His nurse agreed that he could see my child this once.

We found the doctor's office all right, but checking her in was another story. They gave me a form to fill out which contained every possible question about Turtle I couldn't answer. "Have you had measles?" I asked her. "Scabies? Date of most recent polio vaccination?" The one medical thing I did know about her past was not on the form, unless they had a word for it I didn't know.

Turtle was in my lap but had turned loose of me completely, since she needed both arms to turn through the pages of her magazine in search of vegetables. She wasn't having much luck. Every other woman in that waiting room was pregnant, and every magazine was full of nursing-bra ads.

I knew how to trample my way through most any situation, but you can't simply invent a person's medical history. I went up and tapped on the glass to get the nurse's attention. I saw that she was actually pregnant too, and I felt an old panic. In high school we used to make jokes about the water fountains outside of certain home rooms.

"Yes?" she said. Her name tag said Jill. She had white skin and broad pink stripes of rouge in front of her ears.

"I can't answer these questions," I said.

"Are you the parent or guardian?"

"I'm the one responsible for her."

"Then we need the medical history before we can fill out an encounter form."

"But I don't know that much about her past," I said.

"Then you are not the parent or guardian?"

This was getting to be a trip around the fish pond. "Look," I said. "I'm not her real mother, but I'm taking care of her now. She's not with her original family anymore."

"Oh, you're a foster home." Jill was calm again, shuffling through a new stack of papers. She blinked slowly in a knowing way that revealed pink and lavender rainbows of makeup on her eyelids. She handed me a new form with far fewer questions on it. "Did you bring in your DES medical and waiver forms?"

"No," I said.

"Well, remember to bring them next time."

By the time we got in to see Dr. Pelinowsky I felt as though I'd won this man in one of those magazine contests where you answer fifty different questions about American cheese. He was fiftyish and a little tired-looking. His shoulders slumped, leaving empty space inside the starched shoulders of his white coat. He wore black wing-tip shoes, I noticed, and nylon socks with tiny sea horses above the ankle bones.

Turtle became clingy again when I pulled off her T-shirt. She squeezed wads of my shirt tail in both fists while Dr. Pelinowsky thumped on her knees and shined his light into her eyes. "Anybody home?" he asked. The only time she perked up at all was when he looked in her ears and said, "Any potatoes in there?" Her mouth made a little O, but then she spaced out again.

"I didn't really think she'd turn out to be sick, or anything like that. She's basically in good shape," I said.

"I wouldn't expect to turn up anything clinically. She appears to be a healthy two-year-old." He looked at his clip board.

"The reason I brought her in is I'm concerned about some stuff that happened to her awhile ago. She wasn't taken care of very well." Dr. Pelinowsky looked at me, clicking his ballpoint pen.

"I'm a foster parent," I said, and then he raised his eyebrows and nodded. It was a miracle, this new word that satisfied everyone.

"You're saying that she was subjected to deprivation or abuse in the biological parents' home," he said. His main technique seemed to be telling you what you'd just said.

"Yes. I think she was abused, and that she was," I didn't know how to put this. "That she was molested. In a sexual way."

Dr. Pelinowsky took in this information without appearing to notice. He was scribbling something on the so-called encounter form. I waited until he finished, thinking that I was going to have to say it again, but he said, "I'll give her a complete exam, but again I wouldn't expect to turn up anything now. This child has been in your care for five months?"

"More or less," I said. "Yes."

While he examined her he explained about abrasions and contusions and the healing process. I thought of how I'd handled Jolene Shanks exactly this way, as calm as breakfast toast, while her dead husband lay ten feet away under a sheet. "After this amount of time we might see behavioral evidence," Dr. P. said, "but there is no residual physical damage." He finished scribbling on the form and decided it would be a good idea to do a skeletal survey, and that sometime soon we ought to get her immunizations up to date.

I was curious to see the x-ray room, which was down a hall in another part of the office. Everything was large and clean, and they had a machine that turned out the x-rays instantly like a Polaroid camera. I don't believe Dr. Pelinowsky really understood how lucky he was. I used to spend entire afternoons in a little darkroom developing those things, sopping the stiff plastic sheets through one and another basin of liquid, then hanging them up on a line with tiny green clothespins. I used to tell Mama it was nothing more than glorified laundry.

We had to wait awhile to see him again, while he saw another patient and then read Turtle's x-rays. I hung around asking the technician questions and showing Turtle where the x-rays came out, though machines weren't really her line. She had one of her old wrestling holds on my shoulder.

When we were called back to Dr. Pelinowsky's office again he looked just ever so slightly shaken up. "What is it?" I asked him. All I could think of was brain tumors, I suppose from hanging around Lou Ann, who had learned all she knew about medicine from *General Hospital.*

He laid some of the x-rays against the window. Dr. Pelinowsky's office window looked out onto a garden full of round stones and cactus. In the dark negatives I could see Turtle's thin white bones and her skull, and it gave me the same chill Lou Ann must have felt to see her living mother's name carved on a gravestone. I shivered inside my skin.

"These are healed fractures, some of them compound," he said, pointing with his silver pen. He moved carefully through the arm and leg bones and then to the hands, which he said were an excellent index of age. On the basis of height and weight he'd assumed she was around twenty-four months, he said, but the development of cartilage in the carpals and metacarpals indicated that she was closer to three.

"Three years?"

"Yes." He seemed almost undecided about telling me this. "Sometimes in an environment of physical or emotional deprivation a child will simply stop growing, although certain internal maturation does continue. It's a condition we call failure to thrive."

"But she's thriving now. I ought to know, I buy her clothes."

"Well, yes, of course. The condition is completely reversible."

"Of course," I said.

He put up more of the x-rays in the window, saying things like "spiral fibular fracture here" and "excellent healing" and "some contraindications for psychomotor development." I couldn't really listen. I looked through the bones to the garden on the other side. There was a cactus with bushy arms and a coat of yellow spines as thick as fur. A bird had built her nest in it. In and out she flew among the horrible spiny branches, never once hesitating. You just couldn't imagine how she'd made a home in there.

Mattie had given me the whole day off, so I had arranged to meet Lou Ann at the zoo after Turtle's appointment. We took the bus. Mattie and I hadn't gotten around to fixing the ignition on my car, so starting it up was a production I saved for special occasions.

On the way over I tried to erase the words "failure to thrive" from my mind. I prepared myself, instead, for the experience of being with Lou Ann and the kids in a brand-new set of hazards. There would be stories of elephants going berserk and trampling their keepers; of children's little hands snapped off and swallowed whole by who knows what seemingly innocent animal. When I walked up to the gate and saw her standing there with tears streaming down her face, I automatically checked Dwayne Ray in his stroller to see if any of his parts were missing.

People were having to detour around her to get through the turnstile, so I led her to one side. She sobbed and talked at the same time.

"He says he's going to join up with any rodeo that will take a one-legged clown, which I know isn't right because the clown's the hardest job, they jump around and distract them so they won't tromple on the cowboys' heads."

I was confused. Was there an elephant somewhere in this story? "Lou Ann, honey, you're not making sense. Do you want to go home?"

She shook her head.

"Then should we go on into the zoo?"

She nodded. I managed to get everybody through the turnstile and settled on a bench in the shade between the duck pond and the giant tortoises. The sound of water trickling over a little waterfall into the duck pond made it seem cool. I tried to get the kids distracted long enough for Lou Ann to tell me what was up.

"Look, Turtle, look at those old big turtles," I said. The words "childhood identity crisis" from one of Lou Ann's magazines sprang to mind, but Turtle seemed far more interested in the nibbled fruit halves strewn around their pen. "Apple," she said. She seemed recovered from her doctor's visit.

"He said something about the Colorado-Montana circuit, which I don't even know what that means, only that he's leaving town. And he said he might not be sending any checks for a while until he'd got on his feet. He actually said on his foot, can you believe that? The way Angel sees himself, it's like he's an artificial leg with a person attached."

A woman on a nearby bench stopped reading and tilted her head back a little, the way people do when they want to overhear your conversation. She had on white sneakers, white shorts, and a visor. It looked as if she must have been on her way to a country club to play tennis before some wrongful bus change landed her here.

"It's her husband that's the problem," I told the woman. "He's a former rodeo man."

"Taylor!" Lou Ann whispered, but the woman ignored us and took a drag from her cigarette, which she balanced beside her on the front edge of the bench. She shook out her newspaper and folded back the front page. It showed a large color picture of Liz Taylor with a black man in a silver vest and no shirt, and there was a huge block headline that said, WORLD'S YOUNGEST MOM-TO-BE: INFANT PREGNANT AT BIRTH. Apparently the headline wasn't related to the picture.

A kid with orange foam-rubber plugs in his ears whizzed by on a skateboard. Another one whizzed right behind him. They had a fancy way of tipping up their boards to go over the curbs.

"They shouldn't allow those in here. Somebody will get killed," Lou Ann said, blowing her nose. I noticed that one of the giant tortoises in the pen was pursuing another one around and around a clump of shrubby palm trees.

"So what about Angel?" I asked.

A woman in a flowery dress sat down on the bench with the country-club woman. She had very dark, tightly wrinkled skin and wore enormous green high-heeled pumps. The country-club woman's cigarette, on the bench between them, waved up a little boundary line of smoke.

"He said there would be papers to sign for the divorce," Lou Ann said.

"So what's the problem, exactly?" I didn't mean to be unkind. I really didn't know.

"Well, what am I going to do?"

"Well, to be honest, I don't think it much matters what you do. It probably doesn't make any difference what kind of a divorce you get, or even if you get one at all. The man is gone, honey. If he stops sending checks I don't imagine there's anything to be done, not if he's out riding the range in God's country. I guess you'll have to look for a job, sooner or later."

Lou Ann started sobbing again. "Who would want to hire me? I can't do anything."

"You don't necessarily have to know how to do something to get a job," I reasoned. "I'd never made a french fry in my life before I got hired at the Burger Derby." She blew her nose again.

"So how'd she get born pregnant?" the green-shoes woman asked the woman with the newspaper.

"It was twins, a boy and a girl," the woman told her. "They had sexual intercourse in the womb. Doctors say the chances against it are a million to one."

"Yeah," the green-shoes woman said in a tired way. She bent over and shuffled through a large paper shopping bag, which was printed with a bright paisley pattern and had sturdy-looking green handles. All three of us waited for her to say something more, or to produce some wonderful answer out of her bag, but she didn't.

Lou Ann said to me, in a quieter voice, "You know, the worst thing about it is that he wouldn't ask me to come with him."

"Well, how in the world could you go with him? What about Dwayne Ray?"

"It's not that I'd *want* to, but he could have asked. He did say if I wanted to come along he wouldn't stop me, but he wouldn't actually say he wanted me to."

"I don't follow you, exactly."

"You know, that was always just the trouble with Angel. I never really felt like he would put up a fight for me. I would have left him a long time ago, but I was scared to death he'd just say, 'Bye! Don't let the door hit your butt on the way out.'"

"Well, maybe it's not that he doesn't want you, Lou Ann. Maybe he's just got better sense than to ask you and a four-month-old baby to come along on the Montana-Colorado circuit, or whatever. I can just see it. Dwayne Ray growing up to be one of those tattooed midgets that do somersaults in the sideshow and sell the popcorn at intermission."

"It's not a circus, for God's sake, it's a rodeo." Lou Ann honked in her handkerchief and laughed in spite of herself.

At the edge of the pond there was a gumball machine full of peanuts, for feeding to the ducks, I presumed. But these ducks were so well fed that even where peanuts were scattered by the fistful at the water's edge they just paddled right on by with beady, bored eyes.

Turtle dug one out of the mud and brought it to me. "Bean," she said.

"This is a peanut," I told her.

"Beanut." She made trip after trip, collecting peanuts and

mounding them into a pile. Dwayne Ray, in his stroller, was sleeping soundly through his first zoo adventure.

I couldn't stop thinking about the x-rays, and how Turtle's body was carrying around secret scars that would always be there. I wanted to talk to Lou Ann about it, but this wasn't the time.

"So why are you taking his side?" Lou Ann wanted to know.

"I'm not taking his side. Whose side?"

"You are too. Or at least you're not taking mine. Whenever I complain about Angel you won't agree with me that he's a scum bucket. You just listen and don't say anything."

I picked up a green bottle cap and threw it in the duck pond. The ducks didn't even turn their heads. "Lou Ann," I said, "in high school I used to lose friends that way like crazy. You think he's a scum bucket now, but sooner or later you might want him back. And then you'd be too embarrassed to look me in the eye and admit you're still in love with this jerk whose anatomical parts we've been laughing about for the last two months."

"It's over between me and Angel. I know it is."

"Just the same. I don't want you to have to choose him or me."

She dug through her purse looking for a clean handkerchief. "I just can't get over him leaving like that."

"When, now or last October?" I was starting to get annoyed. "He moved out over six months ago, Lou Ann. Did you think he'd just stepped out for some fresh air? It's April now, for God's sake."

"Did you see that?" Lou Ann pointed at Turtle. Her head had bobbed up like an apple on a string, and her eyes fixed on me as if she had seen the Lord incarnate.

"What's up, Turtle?" I asked, but she just stared fearfully from her pile of peanuts.

"She did that one other time that I know of. When we were

talking about the phone bill you thought we'd got gypped on," Lou Ann said.

"So what are you saying, that she understands when we're mad? I already knew that."

"No, I'm saying that bill was for April. She looks up when you say April, especially if you sound mad."

Turtle did look up again.

"Don't you get it?" Lou Ann asked.

I didn't.

"That's her name! April's her name!" Now Lou Ann was kind of hopping in her seat. "April, April. Looky here, April. That's your name, isn't it? April!"

If it was her name, Turtle had had enough of it. She had gone back to patting the sides of her peanut mound.

"You have to do it scientifically," I said. "Say a bunch of other words and just casually throw that one in, and see if she looks up."

"Okay, you do it. I can't think of enough words."

"Rhubarb," I said. "Cucumber. Porky Pig. Budweiser. April." Turtle looked up right on cue.

"May June July August September!" Lou Ann shouted. "April!"

"Lord, Lou Ann, the child isn't deaf."

"It's April," she declared. "That's her legal name."

"Maybe it's something that just sounds like April. Maybe it's Mabel."

Lou Ann made a face.

"Okay, April, that's not bad. I think she's kind of used to Turtle though. I think we ought to keep calling her that now."

A fat duck with a shiny green head had finally decided Turtle's cache of peanuts was too much to ignore. He came up on shore and slowly advanced, stretching his neck forward.

"Ooooh, oooh!" Turtle shouted, shaking her hands so vigorously that he wheeled around and waddled back toward the water.

"Turtle's okay for a nickname," Lou Ann said, "but you have to think of the future. What about when she goes to school? Or like when she's eighty years old? Can you picture an eighty-year-old woman being called Turtle?"

"An eighty-year-old Indian woman, I could. You have to remember she's Indian."

"Still," Lou Ann said.

"April Turtle, then."

"No! That sounds like some weird kind of air freshener."

"So be it," I said, and it was.

We sat for a while listening to the zoo sounds. There were more trees here than most places in Tucson. I'd forgotten how trees full of bird sounds made you sense the world differently: that life didn't just stop at eye level. Between the croaks and whistles of the blackbirds there were distant cat roars, monkey noises, kid noises.

"I'll swan, the sound of that running water's making me have to go," Lou Ann said.

"There's bathrooms over by where we came in."

Lou Ann took a mirror out of her purse. "Death warmed over," she said, and went off to find a bathroom.

The giant tortoise, I noticed, had caught up to its partner and was proceeding to climb on top of it from behind. Its neck and head strained forward as it climbed, and to tell the truth, it looked exactly like a bald, toothless old man. The knobby shells scraping together made a hollow sound. By the time Lou Ann came back from the bathroom, the old fellow on top was letting out loud grunts that rang out all the way down to the military macaws.

"What on earth? I could hear that noise up by the bathrooms," Lou Ann declared. "Well, I'll be. I always did wonder how they'd do it in those shells. That'd be worse than those panty girdles we used to wear in high school to hold our stockings up. Remember those?"

A teenage couple holding hands bounced up to investigate, giggled, and moved quickly away. A woman with an infant on her hip turned the baby's head away and walked on. Lou Ann and I laughed till we cried. The country-club woman gave us a look, folded her paper, stabbed out her cigarette, and crunched off down the gravel path.

NINE

Ismene

Esperanza tried to kill herself. Estevan came to the back door and told me in a quiet voice that she had taken a bottle of baby aspirin.

I couldn't really understand why he had come. "Shouldn't you be with her?" I asked.

He said she was with Mattie. Mattie had found her almost immediately and rushed her to a clinic she knew of in South Tucson where you didn't have to show papers. I hadn't even thought of this—all the extra complications that must have filled their lives even in times of urgency. Mattie once told me about a migrant lemon picker in Phoenix who lost a thumb in a machine and bled to death because the nearest hospital turned him away.

"Is she going to be all right?"

How could he know? But he said yes, that she was. "They might or might not have to vacuum her stomach," he explained.

He seemed to know the whole story, including the ending, and I began to suspect it was something that had happened before.

It was after sunset and the moon was already up. A fig grew by the back door, an old, stubborn tree that was slow to leaf out. The moon threw shadows of fig branches that curled like empty hands across Estevan's face and his chest. Something inside this man was turning inside out.

He followed me into the kitchen where I had been cutting up carrots and cubes of cheese for Turtle's lunch tomorrow.

To keep my hands from shaking I pushed the knife carefully through stiff orange carrot flesh against the cutting board. "I don't really know what to say when something like this happens," I told him. "Anything I can think of to talk about seems ridiculous next to a person's life or death."

He nodded.

"Can I get you something? Did you eat?" I opened the refrigerator door, but he waved it shut. "At least a beer, then," I said. I opened two beers and set one on the table in front of him. From my earliest memory, times of crisis seemed to end up with women in the kitchen preparing food for men. "I can see right now that I'm going to do one of two things here," I told Estevan. "Either shove food at you, or run off at the mouth. When I get nervous I fall back on good solid female traditions."

"It's okay," he said. "I'm not hungry, so talk." I had never heard him say, "It's okay," before. Restaurant work was corrupting Estevan's perfect English.

I took his statement to mean that it was okay to talk about things that weren't especially important, so I did. "Lou Ann took the baby over to her mother-in-law's for some kind of a weekend-long reunion," I said, swallowing too much beer. "They still consider her part of the family, but of course she won't go over when Angel's there so they have to work it all out, but now of course it's easier since Angel's left town. It's totally nuts. See, they're

Catholic, they don't recognize divorce." I felt my face go red. "I guess you're Catholic too."

But he wasn't offended. "More or less," he said. "Catholic by birth."

"Did you have any idea she was going to do this?"

"No. I don't know."

"There's not a thing you could have done, anyway. Really." I swept the carrot pieces into a plastic bag and put it in the refrigerator. "I knew this kid in high school, Scotty Richey? Everybody said Scotty was a genius, mainly because he was real quiet and wore these thick glasses and understood trigonometry. He killed himself on his sixteenth birthday, just when everybody else was thinking, 'Well, now Scotty'll learn to drive and maybe get a car and go out on dates,' you know, and that his complexion was bound to clear up and so forth. Bang, they find him dead in a barn with all these electrical wires strung around his neck. In the paper they said it was an accident but nobody actually believed that. Scotty had done probably five hundred different projects with electricity for 4-H."

"Four-H?"

"It's a club for farm kids where you raise lambs or make an apron or wire a den lamp out of a bowling pin, things like that. I never was in it. You had to pay."

"I see."

"Do you want to sit in the living room?" I asked him. He followed me into the other room and I scooted Snowboots off the sofa. When Estevan sat down next to me my heart was bumping so hard I wondered if I was going to have a heart attack. Just what Estevan needed would be another woman falling apart on him.

"So nobody could understand about Scotty," I said. "But the way I see it is, he just didn't have anybody. In our school there were different groups you would run with, depending on your station in life. There were the town kids, whose daddies owned the hardware store or what have you—they were your cheerleaders and your football players. Then there were hoodlums, the motorcycle types that cut down trees on Halloween. And then there were the rest of us, the poor kids and the farm kids. Greasers, we were called, or Nutters. The main rule was that there was absolutely no mixing. Do you understand what I mean?"

"Yes," he said. "In India they have something called the caste system. Members of different castes cannot marry or even eat together. The lowest caste is called the Untouchables."

"But the Untouchables can touch each other?"

"Yes."

"Then that's it, exactly. The Nutters were the bottom of the pile, but we had each other. We all got invited to the prom and everything, from inside our own group. But poor Scotty with his electricity and his trigonometry, he just didn't belong to any group. It was like we were all the animals on Noah's ark that came in pairs, except of his kind there was only the one."

It struck me how foolishly I was chattering about something that was neither here nor there. Mama would call this "rattling your teeth." I drank about half my beer without saying another word.

Then I said, "I could kind of see it with Scotty, but Esperanza had somebody. Has somebody. How could she want to leave you? It's not fair." I realized I was furious with Esperanza. I wondered if he was too, but didn't dare ask. We sat there in the shadowy living room thinking our thoughts. You could hear us swallowing beer.

Then out of the clear blue sky he said, "In Guatemala City the police use electricity for interrogation. They have something called the 'telephone,' which is an actual telephone of the type they use in the field. It has its own generator, operated by a handle." He held up one hand and turned the other one in a circle in front of the palm.

"A crank? Like the old-fashioned telephones?"

"Operated with a crank," he said. "The telephones are made in the United States."

"What do you mean, they use them for interrogation? Do you mean they question you over the telephone?"

Estevan seemed annoyed with me. "They disconnect the receiver wire and tape the two ends to your body. To sensitive parts." He just stared at me until it hit me like a truck. I felt it in my stomach muscles, just the way I did when I realized that for nearly an hour I had been in the presence of Newt Hardbine's corpse. There is this horrible thing staring you in the face and you're blabbering about bowling-pin lamps and 4-H.

"I'll get us another beer," I said. I went to the kitchen and brought back the rest of the six pack, carrying it by the plastic rings like a purse. I popped two of them open and plumped back down on the sofa, no longer caring what I looked like. The schoolgirl nerves that had possessed me half an hour ago seemed ridiculous now; this was like having a crush on some guy only to find out he's been dating your mother or your math teacher. This man was way beyond me.

"I don't know exactly how to say this," I said. "I thought I'd had a pretty hard life. But I keep finding out that life can be hard in ways I never knew about."

"I can see that it would be easier not to know," he said.

"That's not fair, you don't see at all. You think you're the foreigner here, and I'm the American, and I just look the other way while the President or somebody sends down this and that, shiploads of telephones to torture people with. But nobody asked my permission, okay? Sometimes I feel like I'm a foreigner too. I come from a place that's so different from here you would think you'd stepped right off the map into some other country where they use dirt for decoration and the national pastime is having babies. People don't look the same, talk the same, nothing. Half the time I have no idea what's going on around me here."

A little shadow moved in the doorway and we both jumped. It was Turtle.

"You're a rascal," I said. "You hop back to bed this minute."

She took one hop backwards, and both Estevan and I tried not to smile. "This minute," I said, in the meanest voice I could muster. She hopped backwards through the door, clapping her hands one time with each hop. We could hear her hopping and clapping all the way back through the kitchen and into bed. Snowboots jumped onto the back of the sofa and sat behind my neck, waiting for something. He made me nervous.

"All I am saying is, don't be so sure until you have all the facts," Estevan said. "You cannot know what Esperanza has had to live through."

I was confused. He was picking up the middle of a conversation I didn't even know we'd started.

"No," I said. "I don't. Or you either."

He looked away from me and touched the corners of his eyes, and I knew he was crying in the secret way men feel they have to do. He said something I couldn't hear very well, and a name, "Ismene."

I shoved Snowboots gently away from the back of my neck. "What?" I asked.

"Do you remember the day we walked in the desert? And you asked why Esperanza was staring at Turtle, and I told you she looked very much like a child we knew in Guatemala." I nodded. "The child was Ismene."

I was afraid to understand this. I asked him if he meant that Ismene was their daughter, and Estevan said yes, that she was. She was taken in a raid on their neighborhood in which

Esperanza's brother and two friends were killed. They were members of Estevan's teachers' union. He told me in what condition they had found the bodies. He wasn't crying as he told me this, and I wasn't either. It's hard to explain, but a certain kind of horror is beyond tears. Tears would be like worrying about watermarks on the furniture when the house is burning down.

Ismene wasn't killed; she was taken.

Try as I would, I couldn't understand this. I was no longer so stupid as to ask why they didn't call the police, but still I couldn't see why they hadn't at least tried to get her back if they knew the police had taken her, and where. "Don't be upset with me," I said. "I know I'm ignorant, I'm sorry. Just explain it to me."

But he wasn't upset. He seemed to get steadier and more patient when he explained things, as if he were teaching a class. "Esperanza and I knew the names of twenty other union members," he said. "The teachers' union did not have open meetings. We worked in cells, and communicated by message. Most people knew only four other members by name. This is what I am saying: In Guatemala, you are careful. If you want to change something you can find yourself dead. This was not the—what do you call? The P.T.A."

"I understand."

"Three members had just been killed, including Esperanza's brother, but seventeen were still alive. She and I knew every one of those seventeen, by name. Can you understand that this made us more useful alive than dead? For us to go after Ismene is what they wanted."

"So they didn't kill her, they just held her? Like . . . I don't know what. A worm on a goddamn hook?"

"A goddamn hook." He was looking away from me again. "Sometimes, after a while, usually . . . these children are adopted. By military or government couples who cannot have children."

I felt numb, as if I had taken some drug. "And you picked the lives of those seventeen people over getting your daughter back?" I said. "Or at least a chance at getting her back?"

"What would you do, Taylor?"

"I don't know. I hate to say it, but I really don't know. I can't even begin to think about a world where people have to make choices like that."

"You live in that world," he said quietly, and I knew this, but I didn't want to. I started to cry then, just tears streaming out all over and no stopping them. Estevan put his arm around me and I sobbed against his shoulder. The dam had really broken.

I was embarrassed. "I'm going to get snot on your clean shirt," I said.

"I don't know what it is, snot."

"Good," I said.

There was no way on earth I could explain what I felt, that my whole life had been running along on dumb luck and I hadn't even noticed.

"For me, even bad luck brings good things," I told him finally. "I threw out a rocker arm on my car and I got Turtle. I drove over broken glass on an off ramp and found Mattie." I crossed my arms tightly over my stomach, trying to stop myself from gulping air. "Do you know, I spent the first half of my life avoiding motherhood and tires, and now I'm counting them as blessings?"

Turtle showed up in the doorway again. I don't know how long she had been there, but she was looking at me with eyes I hadn't seen on her since that night on the Oklahoma plain.

"Come here, pumpkin," I said. "I'm okay, just sprung a leak, don't you worry. Do you want a drink of water?" She shook her head. "Just want to cuddle a few minutes?" She nodded, and I took her on my lap. Snowboots jumped onto the sofa again. I could feel the weight of him moving slowly across the back and down the other arm, and from there he curled into Estevan's lap. In less than a minute Turtle was asleep in my arms.

When I was a child I had a set of paper dolls. They were called the Family of Dolls, and each one had a name written on the cardboard base under the feet. Their names were Mom, Dad, Sis, and Junior. I played with those dolls in a desperate, loving way until their paper arms and heads disintegrated. I loved them in spite of the fact that their tight-knit little circle was as far beyond my reach as the football players' and cheerleaders' circle would be in later years.

But that night I looked at the four of us there on the sofa and my heart hurt and I thought: in a different world we could have been the Family of Dolls.

Turtle wiggled. "No," she said, before she was even awake.

"Yes," I said. "Time for bed." I carried her in and tucked her under the sheet, prying her hand off my T-shirt and attaching it to her yellow stuffed bear, which had a pink velvet heart sewed onto its chest.

"Sleep tight, don't let the potato bugs bite."

"Tato bite," she said.

When I came back Snowboots had moved from Estevan's lap and curled into the little depression where I had been. I sat in the space between them with my feet tucked under me. I no longer felt self-conscious, though I could feel almost a pull, like a flow of warm water, at the point where our knees touched.

"It seems like, if you get to know them well enough, everybody has had something awful happen to them. All this time I've been moping around because of having the responsibility of Turtle forced on me, and now I feel guilty."

"That responsibility is terrible if you don't want it."

"Oh, big deal. The exact same thing happened to about sixty percent of the girls in my high school, if not the whole world."

"If you look at it that way," he said. He was falling asleep.

"I guess that's just the way the world has got to go around. If people really gave it full consideration, I mean, like if you could return a baby after thirty days' examination like one of those Time-Life books, then I figure the entire human species would go extinct in a month's time."

"Some people wouldn't send them back," he said. "I would have kept Ismene." His eyes were closed.

"Did you get up in the middle of the night to do the feeding and diapering?"

"No," he said, smiling a little.

"I can't believe I'm even asking you that. Does it hurt you a lot to talk about Ismene?"

"At first, but not so much now. What helps me the most is to know her life is going on somewhere, with someone. To know she is growing up."

"Sure," I said, but I knew there was another side to this, too. Where she was growing up, what they would raise her to be. I thought of Turtle being raised by Virgie Mae Parsons, learning to look down her nose and wear little hats, and then I got it mixed up with police uniforms. A little later I realized I had been asleep. We both rolled in and out of sleep in a friendly way. You can't be nervous if you're sleeping on the same sofa with somebody, I thought. Letting your mouth fall open any old way.

Snowboots jumped off the sofa. I heard his claws scratch the carpet as he covered up his sins.

"Why did they call you Nutters?" I remember Estevan asking at some point. I thought and thought about it, trying to fight my way out of some dream where Turtle and I were trying to get to the other side of a long, flat field. We had to follow the telephone wires to get to civilization.

"Nutters," I said finally. "Oh, because of walnuts. In the fall, the kids that lived in the country would pick walnuts to earn money for school clothes."

"Did you have to climb the trees?" Estevan amazed me. That he would be interested in details like that.

"No. Basically you waited till they fell, and then picked them up off the ground. The worst part was that to get the hulls off you'd have to put them in the road for cars to run over, and then you'd pick the nuts out of the mess. It stained your hands black, and then you were marked. That was the worst part, to go to school with black hands and black fingernails. That was proof positive you were a Nutter."

"But otherwise you would have no new clothes."

"Right. So you were damned if you didn't and damned if you did. I guess the ideal thing," I conjectured, half dreaming, "would have been to get clothes with good, deep pockets." I meant so that you could hide your hands, but I had a picture in my mind of skirts and trousers with pockets full of pounds and pounds of walnuts. Ten cents a pound is what we got for them. A hundred and fifty pounds equaled one pair of Levi's.

Later I woke up again, feeling the pressure of Snowboots's feet walking down my leg, then hearing them thump on the floor. Estevan and I were curled like spoons on the sofa, his knees against the backs of my knees and his left hand on my ribs, just under my breast. When I put my hand on top of his I could feel my heart beating under his fingers.

I thought of Esperanza, her braids on her shoulders. Esperanza staring at the ceiling. She would be lying on a cot somewhere, sweating the poison out of her system. Probably they had given her syrup of ipecac, which makes you keep throwing up until you can feel the sides of your stomach banging together. All of Esperanza's hurts flamed up in my mind, a huge pile of burning things that the world just kept throwing more onto. Somewhere in that pile was a child that looked just like Turtle. I lifted Estevan's hand from my ribcage and kissed his palm. It felt warm. Then I slid off the sofa and went to my own bed.

Moonlight was pouring in through the bedroom window like

a watery version of my mother's potato soup. Moon soup, I thought, hugging myself under the covers. Somewhere in the neighborhood a cat yowled like a baby, and somewhere else, closer by, a rooster crowed, even though it was nowhere near daybreak.

TEN

The Bean Trees

Even a spotted pig looks black at night. This is another thing Mama used to tell me quite often. It means that things always look different, and usually better, in the morning.

And they did. Mattie called first thing to say that Esperanza was going to be all right. They hadn't pumped her stomach after all because she hadn't taken enough to do much harm. I made Estevan a big breakfast, eggs scrambled with tomatoes and peppers and green chile sauce, and sent him home before I could start falling in love with him again over the breakfast dishes. Turtle woke up in one of those sweet, eye-rubbing moods that kids must know by instinct as a means of saving the human species from extinction. Lou Ann came home from the Ruiz family reunion singing "La Bamba."

It's surprising, considering Roosevelt Park, but we always heard birds in the morning. There must be transients in the bird world too, rumple-feathered outcasts that naturally seek out each other's company in inferior and dying trees. In any case, there were lots of them. There was a type of woodpecker that said, "Ha, ha, ha, to hell with you!" I swear it did. And another one, a little pigeony-looking bird, said, "Hip hip hurroo." Lou Ann insisted that it was saying "Who Cooks for Who?" She said she had read it in a magazine. I had a hard time imagining what kind of magazine would go into something like that, but I wasn't about to argue. It was the first time I could remember her hanging on to her own opinion about something—Lou Ann not normally being inclined in that direction. One time in a restaurant, she'd once told me, a waiter mistakenly brought her somebody else's dinner and she just ate it, rather than make trouble. It was beef shingles on toast.

Gradually Lou Ann and I were changing the house around, filling in the empty spaces left behind by Angel with ABC books and high chairs and diaper totes and all manner of toys, all larger than a golf ball. I had bought Turtle a real bed, junior size, from New To You. We turned the screen porch in the back into a playroom for the kids, not that Dwayne Ray did any serious playing yet, but he liked to sit out there strapped in his car seat watching Turtle plant her cars in flowerpots. The fire engine she called "domato," whereas the orange car was "carrot." Or sometimes she called it "Two-Two," which is what I had named my Volkswagen, after the man who profited from my rocker arm disaster.

I had considered putting Turtle's bed out there on the porch too, but Lou Ann said it wouldn't be safe, that someone might come along and slash the screen and kidnap her before you could say Jack Robinson. I never would have thought of that.

But it didn't matter. The house was old and roomy; there was plenty of space for Turtle's bed in my room. It was the type of house they called a "rambling bungalow" (the term reminded me somehow of Elvis Presley movies), with wainscoting and steam radiators and about fifty coats of paint on the door frames, so that you could use your thumbnail to scrape out a history of all the house's tenants as far back as the sixties, when people were fond of painting their woodwork apple green and royal blue. The ceilings were so high you just learned to live with the cobwebs.

It wasn't unreasonably hot yet, and the kids were bouncing around the house like superballs (this was mainly Turtle, with Dwayne Ray's participation being mainly vocal), so we took them out to sit under the arbor for a while. The wisteria vines were a week or two past full bloom, but the bees and the perfume still hung thick in the air overhead, giving it a sweet purplish hue. If you ignored the rest of the park, you could imagine this was a special little heaven for people who had lived their whole lives without fear of bees.

Lou Ann was full of gossip from her weekend with the Ruiz cousins. Apparently most of them spoke English, all the men were good-looking and loved to dance, and all the women had children Dwayne Ray's age. She had about decided that every single one of them was nicer than Angel, a conclusion to which they all heartily agreed, even Angel's mother. A large portion of the flock were preparing to move to San Diego.

"I can't believe it," she said, "first Manny and Ramona, you remember, the friends I told you about that saw the meteor shower? And now two of Angel's brothers and their wives and kids. You'd think they'd discovered gold out there. Angel used to always talk about moving to California too, but I'll tell you this right now, Mama would have had an apoplectic. She thinks in California they sell marijuana in the produce section of the grocery store."

"Maybe they do. Maybe that's why everybody wants to live there."

"Not me," Lou Ann said. "Not for a million, and I'll tell you why, too. In about another year they're due to have the biggest earthquake in history. I read about it someplace. They say all of San Diego might just end up in the ocean, like noodle soup."

"I guess the sharks will be happy," I said.

"Taylor, I swear! These are my relatives you're talking about."

"Angel's relatives," I said. "You're practically divorced."

"Not to hear them tell it," Lou Ann said.

Turtle was staring up at the wisteria flowers. "Beans," she said, pointing.

"Bees," I said. "Those things that go bzzzz are bees."

"They sting," Lou Ann pointed out.

But Turtle shook her head. "Bean trees," she said, as plainly as if she had been thinking about it all day. We looked where she was pointing. Some of the wisteria flowers had gone to seed, and all these wonderful long green pods hung down from the branches. They looked as much like beans as anything you'd ever care to eat.

"Will you look at that," I said. It was another miracle. The flower trees were turning into bean trees.

On the way home Lou Ann went to the corner to buy a newspaper. She was seriously job-hunting now, and had applied at a couple of nursery schools, though I could just hear how Lou Ann would ask for a job: "Really, ma'am, I could understand why you wouldn't want to hire a dumb old thing such as myself."

Turtle and I walked the other way, since we needed to stop in at the Lee Sing Market for eggs and milk. Lou Ann refused to set foot in there these days, saying that Lee Sing always gave her the evil eye. Lou Ann's theory was that she was mad at her for having had Dwayne Ray instead of a girl, going against some supposedly foolproof Chinese method of prediction. My theory was that Lou Ann suffered from the same disease as Snowboots: feeling guilty for things beyond your wildest imagination.

In any case, today Lee Sing was nowhere to be seen. She often went back to check on her famous century-old mother, the source of Mattie's purple beans, whom neither Lou Ann nor I had ever laid eyes on, though not for lack of curiosity. According to Mattie no one had sighted her for years, but you always had the feeling she was back there.

Lee Sing had left her usual sign by the cash register: BE BACK ONE MINUTE, PLEASE DO NO STEAL ANY THING. LEE SING. I spotted Edna Poppy in paper goods, the next aisle over from the dairy case. As best I could see, Edna was sniffing different brands of toilet tissue.

"Edna! Miss Poppy!" I called out. When I needed to call her by name I generally hedged my bets and used both first and last. Her head popped up and she seemed confused, looking all around.

"It's me, Taylor. Over here." I came around into the aisle where she had parked her cart. "Where's Mrs. Parsons today?" I stopped dead in my tracks. Edna had a white cane.

"Virgie is ill in bed with a croup, I'm sorry to say. She sent me out to get fresh lemons and a drop of whiskey. And of coursc a few other unmentionables." She smiled, dropping a package of orange toilet paper into the cart. "Can you tell me, dear, if these are lemons or limes I have?" She ran her hand over her goods and held up a lopsided plastic bag of yellow fruits.

Edna Poppy was blind. I stood for a minute staring, trying to reorganize things in my mind the way you would rearrange a roomful of furniture. Edna buying all her clothes in one color, ever since age sixteen. Virgie's grip on her elbow. I remembered the fantasy I'd constructed the day of our dinner party: Edna happily discovering red bobby pins in the drugstore. I'd had it completely wrong. It would have been Virgie Mae who found them, plucked them down off the rack of Oreo-cookie barrettes, and purchased them for her friend.

"Are you with me, dear?"

"I'm sorry," I said. "Lemons. They're kind of small, but they look just fine."

When I got home I asked Lou Ann if she knew. She insisted I was making the whole thing up. "Is this a joke?" she kept asking. "Because if it is, it's a sick one."

"It's not a joke. She had a white cane. She asked me if what she had was lemons or limes. Think about it, the way she kind of looks over your head when she talks. The way Virgie leads her around. How Virgie always says everybody's name when the two of them come into a room."

Lou Ann was horrified. "Oh my God," she said. "Oh my merciful heavens, I feel about this big. When I think about all the times I've just bounced over there and said, 'See ya this! See ya that! Thanks for keeping an eye on Dwayne Ray.'"

"I don't think she'd mind. Her eyes are her hands. And Virgie. She has her own special ways of keeping an eye on things," I told Lou Ann, and this seemed to make her feel better.

On Monday afternoon I asked if it would be okay if I went up to see Esperanza. I had never been upstairs at Mattie's and for some reason I felt it was off limits, but she said fine, to go on up. I went through the cramped study, which of course was still piled high with Mattie's dead husband's magazines (I knew by now that he had been dead many years, so it seemed unlikely that his mess would clear up any time soon) and on up the staircase into Mattie's living room.

It had the same crowded, higgledy-piggledy look as the office downstairs, though the stuff here had more to do with everyday living: junk mail, bills, pencils, magazines with color pictures of people like Tom Selleck and the President (not Jesus), a folded newspaper with a half-worked crossword puzzle, the occasional pliers or screwdriver. It was the type of flotsam and jetsam (a pair of words I had just learned from the dictionary) that washes up on your coffee table, lies around for a week or so, and then makes way for whatever comes in on the next tide.

Every surface was covered: tables, chairs, walls. Over the fireplace there was a big cross made up of hundreds of small, brightly glazed pieces of tile, each one shaped like something: a boy, a dog, a house, a palm tree, a bright blue fish. Together they all added up to a cross. I had never seen anything like it.

The wall across from the fireplace was covered with pictures of every imaginable size and shape. There were snapshots of people squinting into the sun, a few studio portraits of children, pictures of Mattie flanked by other people, all of them dark and shorter than herself. There were a number of children's drawings. I remembered Mattie telling me when we'd first met that she had "something like" grandchildren around, how that had struck me as such a peculiar thing to say.

I noticed that practically all the kids' drawings had guns in them somewhere, and huge bullets suspended in the air, hanging on the dotted lines that flowed like waterfalls out of the gun barrels. There were many men in turtle-shaped army helmets. One picture showed a helicopter streaming blood.

The living room had no windows, just doors opening off in four directions. An older woman came in with a cardboard box and looked at me with surprise, asking something in Spanish. I had never before seen anyone whose entire body looked sad. Her skin just seemed to hang from her, especially from her arms above the elbows, and her jaw.

"Esperanza," I said, and she nodded toward a door at the back.

That room seemed to belong in another house—it was empty. The walls were an antique-looking shade of light pink, completely bare except for a cross with two palm fronds stuck behind it, over one of the beds. The two beds were neatly made up with rough-looking blue blankets that surely no one would sleep under in this weather. Esperanza was not in either bed, but sitting up in a straight-backed chair by the window. She looked up when I knocked on the door casement.

"Hi, I came to see how you were doing."

She got up from the chair and offered it to me. She sat on the bed. I don't believe she had been doing anything at all, just sitting with her hands in her lap.

We looked at each other for a second, then looked at other things in the room, of which there were painfully few. I didn't know why I'd thought I'd have the nerve to do this.

"How are you feeling now? Are you feeling better? Your stomach's okay?" I put my hand on my stomach. Esperanza nodded, then looked at her hands.

I had lost my directions somewhere when I came into the house. I looked out the window expecting to see Roosevelt Park, but this was not that window. We were at the back of the house. From here you got a terrific bird's-eye view of Lee Sing's back garden. I wondered if you might catch a peek at Lee Sing's old mother from up here, if you stayed at your post long enough.

"I've been meaning to tell you," I said, "I think Esperanza's a beautiful name. Estevan told me it means to wait, and also to hope. That in Spanish the same word means both things. But I thought it was pretty even before I knew it meant anything. It reminded me of, I don't know, a waterfall or something."

She nodded.

"Taylor doesn't mean anything that interesting. A tailor hems up people's pants and stuff like that."

Her mouth stretched a little bit in the direction of a smile. But her eyes looked blank. Dark, black holes.

"You understand basically everything I'm saying, right?"

She nodded again.

"I think that's how Turtle is, too, but people always forget.

They think she doesn't take in any more than she puts out, but I know better, I can tell she understands stuff. It's something about the way she looks at you."

Esperanza kept staring at her empty hands. I wished I had something to put in them, something that would be wonderful for her to look at.

"I hope you don't mind me talking about Turtle."

Her eyes flew up at me like a pair of blackbirds scared out of safe hiding.

"Estevan told me about Ismene," I said. "I'm sorry. When I first found out you'd taken pills, I couldn't understand it, why you'd do such a thing to yourself. To Estevan. But when he told me that. God, how does a person live with something like that?"

She looked away. This conversation would have been hard enough even with two people talking. No matter what I said, it was sure to be the exact wrong thing to say to someone who recently swallowed a bottle of baby aspirin. But what would be right? Was there some book in the library where you could look up such things?

"I guess the main thing I came up here to tell you is, I don't know how you go on, but I really hope you'll keep doing it. That you won't give up *esperanza.* I thought of that last night. *Esperanza* is all you get, no second chances. What you have to do is try and think of reasons to stick it out."

She had tears in her eyes, but that seemed better somehow than nothing at all. "It's terrible to lose somebody," I said, "I mean, I don't know firsthand, but I can imagine it must be. But it's also true that some people never have anybody to lose, and I think that's got to be so much worse."

After a long time I said, "He's crazy about you."

I went over and took one of the hands in her lap and held it for a second. Her skin felt cold and emptied-out, like there was nobody home.

As I left to go back to work I saw the woman with the cardboard box, still in the living room. She was sorting through a handful of possessions she had laid out on the sofa—a black skirt, a small book bound in red vinyl, a framed photograph, a pair of baby's sneakers tied together by the laces—and carefully putting them back into the box.

On Wednesday, just as I was finishing up the last patch of the day and getting ready to head for home, I spotted Lou Ann stepping off the bus at the Roosevelt stop. I yelled for her to wait up, and she came over and talked to me while I used the water hose to wash the black dust off my hands. One thing I can tell you right now about tires: they're dirty business.

Lou Ann had just been for a job interview at a convenience store on the north side. She'd left Turtle and Dwayne Ray with Edna and Mrs. Parsons.

"So the first thing the guy says to me is 'We get a lot of armed robberies in here, sweetheart.' He kept on calling me sweetheart and talking to my boobs instead of my face, this big flabby guy with greasy hair and you just know he reads every one of those porno magazines they keep behind the counter. 'Lots of stickups, sweetheart, how do you hold up under pressure?' he says. Holdup, that was his idea of a big hilarious joke. Jeez, the whole thing gave me the creeps from the word go."

I could see that she had dressed up for this interview: a nice skirt, ironed blouse, stockings, pumps. In this heat. The humiliation of it made me furious. "Something better's bound to come along," I said. "You can hold out." I wiped my hands on a towel, hollered goodbye to Mattie, and we headed down the sidewalk.

"I hate that place," she said, nodding back over her shoulder at Fanny Heaven.

"Yeah," I said. "But on the bright side, Mattie says they don't do a whole lot of business. She thinks having a place called

Jesus Is Lord right next door kind of puts a hex on it."

Lou Ann shuddered. "That door's what gets me. The way they made that door handle. Like a woman is something you shove on and walk right through. I try to ignore it, but it still gets me."

"Don't ignore it, then," I said. "Talk back to it. Say, 'You can't do that number on me you shit-for-brains,' or something like that. Otherwise it kind of weasels its way into your head whether you like it or not. You know those hard-boiled eggs they keep around in jars of vinegar, in bars? It's like that. After a while they get to tasting awful, and it's not the egg's fault. What I'm saying is you can't just sit there, you got to get pissed off."

"You really think so?"

"I do."

"The thing about you, Taylor, is that you just don't let anybody put one over on you. Where'd you ever learn to be like that?" Lou Ann wanted to know.

"Nutter school."

ELEVEN

Dream Angels

In the third week of May, Lou Ann got a job as a packer in the Red Hot Mama's salsa factory. This meant that she stood elbow to elbow with about a hundred other people in a sweaty packing line dicing chiles and tomatillos and crushing garlic cloves into moving vats, with so much salsa slopping onto the floor that by the end of the day it sloshed around their ankles. The few who hoped to preserve their footwear wore those clear, old-fashioned rainboots that button on over your shoes. Most people gave up the effort. On days when they were packing extra hot, their ankles burned as if they were standing on red ant hills.

The ones that handled the chiles grew accustomed to tingling fingertips, and learned never to touch their eyes or private parts (or anyone else's), not even on their days off. No matter how they scrubbed their hands, the residue of Red Hot Mama had a way of sticking around, as pesty and persistent as a chaperone at a high school dance.

Truly this was a sweatshop. Half the time the air conditioner didn't work at all, and all the time the fumes made everyone's eyes water so furiously that contact lenses could not be worn on the premises. Lou Ann's vision was 20/20, so this wasn't a problem, nor was any of the rest of it for that matter. Lou Ann loved her job.

If Red Hot Mama's had given out enthusiastic-employee awards Lou Ann would have needed a trophy case. She brought home samples and tried out recipes, some of which would eventually be printed on the jar labels, and some of which would not, God willing. She gave us lectures on how the tiniest amount of cilantro could make or break the perfect salsa. Six months ago I'd never heard of salsa. Now I was eating it on anything from avocados to pot roast.

It came in three speeds: the jars with green lids were "mild," whereas pink meant "hot." The red-lidded jars were so-called "firecracker style." The latter was not a big hit with the kids. Turtle would cry and pant at just the slightest taste, fanning her tongue and eying Lou Ann like she was some spy that had tried to poison us. Dwayne Ray had better sense than to let the stuff enter his mouth.

"Enough already," I told Lou Ann. "How about we just put the jar on the table and use the honor system?" On my nights to cook I made the blandest things I could think of: broiled white fish and mashed potatoes and macaroni and cheese, to give our taste buds a chance to grow back.

But Lou Ann had bought the company propaganda, hook, line, and sinker. "It's good for you," she said. "Some doctors recommend a teaspoon a day to prevent ulcers. Plus it clears your sinuses."

I informed Lou Ann that, thank you very much, my sinuses had just about vacated the premises.

Telling it this way it sounds like a lot of fights, but actually I was liking Lou Ann a great deal these days. In the few weeks since she'd started working, she had begun to cut her hair far less often and finally stopped comparing her figure to various farm animals. Having a job of her own seemed to even out some of Lou Ann's wrinkled edges.

She mostly worked swing shift, which meant that she left at three in the afternoon, leaving the kids with Edna Poppy and Mrs. Parsons until I came home a couple of hours later. For the longest time Lou Ann was scared to say two words to Edna, for fear she might let slip some reference to eyes. Finally I cleared the air, just stating right out to Edna that for a great while we hadn't realized she was blind, because she got on so well. Edna had just assumed we knew all along. She took it as a compliment, that it wasn't the first thing we noticed about her.

Once she started swing shift Lou Ann's experimental family dinners, featuring Five-Alarm Casserole and so forth, were limited to her days off. Most of the time I fed the kids and put them to bed before Lou Ann came home at eleven. Then she and I would eat a late supper, or on nights when it was still too hot to look a plate of food in the eye, we'd sit at the kitchen table fanning ourselves in our underwear, reading the paper, and drinking iced coffee. Sleep was hopeless anyway. But mostly we'd talk. At first all she could ever talk about was cilantro and tomatillos and the people at Red Hot Mama's, but after a time things got back to normal. She would leaf through the paper and read me all the disasters.

"Listen at this: 'Liberty, Kansas. The parents and doctor of severely deformed Siamese twins joined at the frontal lobe of the brain have been accused of attempting to murder the infants by withholding medical care.' Lord, you can't really blame them, can you? I mean, what would you do? Is it better to be totally retarded and deformed and miserable, or just plain old dead?"

"I honestly couldn't say," I said. "Not having been either one." Although, when I thought about it, being dead seemed a lot like not being born yet, and I hadn't especially minded that. But I didn't give it a lot of thought. I was interested in the weather forecast. We hadn't had a drop of rain since that double-rainbow hailstorm back in January, and the whole world was looking parched. When you walked by a tree or a bush it just looked like it ached, somehow. I had to drag the water hose around to the back every day for Mattie's squash and beans. The noise of the cicadas was enough to drive you to homicide. Mattie said it was their love call, that they mated during the hottest, driest weeks of the year, but it was beyond belief that any creature—even another cicada—would be attracted by that sound. It was a high, screaming buzz, a sound that hurt your eyes and made your skin shrink, a sound in the same class with scratched-up phonograph records and squeaking chalk.

Lou Ann, who had lived here long enough to make the association, said the sound of the cicadas made her hot. For me it went way beyond that. I used the air hose to blast the accursed insects out of the low branches of the Palo Verde trees around Mattie's, sending them diving and screaming off through the air like bottle rockets. Every time I walked past the mural of Jesus Is Lord I begged Him for rain.

But every day the paper said: No precipitation expected.

"Remember that time at the zoo?" Lou Ann asked, still occupied with the Liberty, Kansas, horror. "About those Siamese twins born pregnant, or whatever it was?"

"I remember the giant turtles," I said.

Lou Ann laughed. "Now how's a turtle manage to be pregnant, I'd like to know. Do they get maternity shells? I almost feel like going back to see how she's doing."

"Do you know what Estevan told me?" I asked Lou Ann. "In Spanish, the way to say you have a baby is to say that you give it to the light. Isn't that nice?"

"You give the baby to the light?"

"Mmm-hmm." I was reading a piece about earthquakes under the ocean. They cause giant waves, but in a ship you can't feel it at all, it just rolls under you.

I twisted my hair into a knot to try and get it off my sweaty neck. I looked enviously at Lou Ann's blond head, cropped like a golf course.

"I was so sure Dwayne Ray was going to be a Siamese twin or something," she said. "Because I was so big. When he was born I had to ask the doctor about fifteen times if he was normal, before it sunk in. I just couldn't believe he was okay."

"And now you just can't believe he's going to get through a day without strangling or drowning in an ice chest," I said, but in a nice way. I put down the paper and gave Lou Ann my attention. "Why do you think you're such a worry wart, if you don't mind my asking?"

"Taylor, can I tell you something? Promise you won't tell anybody. Promise me you won't laugh."

"Cross my heart."

"I had this dream, one week after he was born. This angel came down, I guess from the sky—I didn't see that part. He was dressed kind of modern, in a suit, you know? With a brown tie? But he was an angel, I'm positive—he had wings. And he said: 'I was sent to you from the future of this planet.' Then he told me my son would not live to see the year two thousand."

"Lou Ann, please."

"But no, that's not even the scariest part. The next morning my horoscope said, 'Listen to the advice of a stranger.' Now don't you think that's got to mean something? That part's real, it's not a dream. I cut it out and saved it. And Dwayne Ray's said something about avoiding unnecessary travel, which I took to mean, you know, traveling through life. Not that you could avoid that. So what on earth was I supposed to do? It scared me to death."

"You were just looking for a disaster, that's all. You can't deny you hunt for them, Lou Ann, even in the paper. If you look hard enough you can always come up with what you want."

"Am I just completely screwed up, Taylor, or what? I've always been this way. My brother and I used to play this game when we were little, with a cigar box. That box was our best toy. It had this slinky lady in a long red dress on the inside of the lid, with her dress slit way up to here. It's a wonder Granny Logan didn't confiscate it. She was holding out a cigar I think, I s'pose she was a Keno girl or something, but we said she was a gypsy. We'd make believe that you could say to her, 'Myself at the age of fourteen.' Or whatever age, you know, and then we'd look in the box and pretend we could see what we looked like. My brother would go all the way up to ninety. He'd say, 'I see myself with a long beard. I live in a large white house with seventeen dogs' and on and on. He loved dogs, see, and Mama and Granny would only let him have just Buster. But me, I was such a chicken liver, I'd just go a couple of weeks into the future at the very most. I'd look at myself the day school was going to start in September, maybe, and say, 'I am wearing a new pink dress.' But I'd never, never go up even to twenty or twenty-five. I was scared."

"Of what?"

"That I'd be dead. That I'd look in the box and see myself dead."

"But it was just pretend. You could have seen yourself any way you wanted to."

"I know it. But that's what I thought I'd see. Isn't that the most ridiculous thing?"

"Maybe it was because of your father. Maybe you got kind of hung up on death, because of him dying."

"I'm just totally screwed up, that's all there is to it."

"No, Lou Ann. You have your good points too."

Usually Lou Ann spit out compliments you tried to feed her like some kind of nasty pill, but that night her blue eyes were practically pleading with me. "What good points?" she wanted to know.

"Oh gosh, tons of them," I faltered. It's not that it was a hard question, but I was caught off guard. I thought a minute.

"The flip side of worrying too much is just not caring, if you see what I mean," I explained. "Dwayne Ray will always know that, no matter what, you're never going to *neglect* him. You'll never just sit around and let him dehydrate, or grow up without a personality, or anything like that. And that would be ever so much worse. You read about it happening in the paper all the time." I meant it; she did. "Somebody forgetting a baby in a car and letting it roast, or some such thing. If anything, Lou Ann, you're just too good of a mother."

She shook her head. "I'm just a total screwed-up person," she said. "And now I'm doing the same thing to poor Dwayne Ray. But I can't help it, Taylor, I can't. If I could see the future, if somebody offered to show me a picture of Dwayne Ray in the year 2001, I swear I wouldn't look."

"Well, nobody's going to," I said gently, "so you don't have to worry about it. There's no such thing as dream angels. Only in the Bible, and that was totally another story."

In June a package came from Montana, all cheery and colorful with stamps and purple postage marks. It contained, among other things, a pair of child-sized cowboy boots—still years too big for Dwayne Ray—and a beautiful calfskin belt for Lou Ann. It was carved or stamped somehow with acorns, oak leaves, and her name. There was also a red-and-black Indian-beaded hair clip, which was of course no use to Lou Ann at this particular point in the life of her hair.

Angel had changed his mind about the divorce. He missed her. He wanted her to come up and live in Montana in something called a yurt. If that was not an acceptable option, then he would come back to Tucson to live with her.

"What in the heck is a yurt anyway?" Lou Ann asked. "It sounds like dirt."

"Beats me," I said. "Look it up."

She did. "A circular domed tent of skins stretched over a lattice framework," she read, pronouncing each word slowly without a Kentucky accent. She pronounced "a" like the letter "A." "Used by the Mongol nomads of Siberia."

As they say in the papers, I withheld comment.

"So what do you think, Taylor? Do you think it would have a floor, or plaster walls inside, anything like that? Think the bugs would get in?"

What popped into my head was: George eats old gray rutabagas and plasters his yurt.

"The part I can't get over is that he asked for me," she said. "He actually says here that he misses me." She mulled it over and over, twisting her gold wedding band around her finger. She had stopped wearing it about the time she started working at the salsa factory, but now had put it on again, almost guiltily, as though Angel might have packed a spy into the box along with the belt and the boots.

"But I've got responsibilities now," she argued, with herself certainly because I was giving no advice one way or the other. "At Red Hot Mama's."

This was surely true. In just three weeks' time she had been promoted to floor manager, setting some kind of company record, but she refused to see this as proof that she was a good worker. "They just didn't have anybody else to do it," she insisted. "Practically everybody there's fifteen years old, or worse. Sometimes they send over retardeds from that Helpless program, or whatever the heck it's called."

"It's called the Help-Yourself program, and you know it, so don't try to change the subject. The word is handicapped, not retardeds."

"Right, that's what I meant."

"What about that woman you told me about that breeds Pekingeses and drives a baby-blue Trans Am? What's-her-name, that gave you the I Heart My Cat bumper stickers? And what about the guy that's building a hot-air blimp in his backyard? Are they fifteen?"

"No." She was flipping the dictionary open and closed, staring out the window.

"And Sal Monelli, how old's he?"

Lou Ann rolled her eyes. Sal Monelli was an unfortunate fellow whose name had struck such terror in her heart she forbade him to touch any food item that wasn't sealed and crated. Lou Ann's life was ruled by the fear of salmonella, to the extent that she claimed the only safe way to eat potato salad was to stick your head in the refrigerator and eat it in there.

"He actually wants me to go," she kept repeating, and even though she said she wasn't going to make up her mind right away, I felt in my bones that sooner or later she'd go. If I knew Lou Ann, she would go.

It seemed like the world was coming apart at the gussets. Mattie was gone more than she was home these days, "birdwatching." Terry, the red-haired doctor, had moved to the Navajo reservation up north (to work, not because he had head rights). Father William looked like he had what people in Pittman call a case of the nerves.

The last time I'd really had a chance to talk with Mattie,

she'd said there was trouble in the air. Esperanza and Estevan were going to have to be moved to a safe house farther from the border. The two best possibilities were Oregon and Oklahoma.

Flat, hopeless Oklahoma. "What would happen if they stayed here?" I asked.

"Immigration is making noises. They could come in and arrest them, and they'd be deported before you even had time to sit down and think about it."

"Here?" I asked. "They would come into *your* house?"

Mattie said yes. She also said, as I knew very well, that in that case Estevan's and Esperanza's lives wouldn't be worth a plugged nickel.

"That just can't be right," I said, "that they would do that to a person, knowing they'd be killed. There's got to be some other way."

"The only legal way a person from Guatemala can stay here is if they can prove in court that their life was in danger when they left."

"But they were, Mattie, and you know it. You know what happened to them. To Esperanza's brother, and all." I didn't say, To their daughter. I wondered if Mattie knew, but of course she would have to.

"Their own say-so is no good; they have to have hard proof. Pictures and documents." She picked up a whitewall and I thought she was going to throw it across the lot, but she only hoisted it onto the top of a pile beside me. "When people run for their lives they frequently neglect to bring along their file cabinets of evidence," she said. Mattie wasn't often bitter but when she was, she was.

I didn't want to believe the world could be so unjust. But of course it was right there in front of my nose. If the truth was a snake it would have bitten me a long time ago. It would have had me for dinner.

TWELVE

Into the Terrible Night

At three o'clock in the afternoon all the cicadas stopped buzzing at once. They left such an emptiness in the air it hurt your ears. Around four o'clock we heard thunder. Mattie turned over the "Closed" sign in the window and said, "Come on. I want you to smell this."

She wanted Esperanza to come too, and surprisingly she agreed. I went upstairs to phone Edna and Mrs. Parsons, though I practically could have yelled to them across the park, to say I'd be home later than usual. Edna said that was fine, just fine, the kids were no trouble, and we prepared to leave. At the last minute it turned out that Estevan could come too; he had the night off. The restaurant was closed for some unexpected family celebration. We all piled into the cab of Mattie's truck with Esperanza on Estevan's lap and me straddling the stick shift. The three of us had no idea where we were headed, or why, but the air had sparks in it. I felt as though I had a blind date with destiny, and someone had heard a rumor that destiny looked like Christopher Reeve.

Mattie said that for the Indians who lived in this desert, who had lived here long before Tucson ever came along, today was New Year's Day.

"What, July the twelfth?" I asked, because that's what day it was, but Mattie said not necessarily. They celebrated it on whatever day the summer's first rain fell. That began the new year. Everything started over then, she said: they planted their crops, the kids ran naked through the puddles while their mothers washed their clothes and blankets and everything else they owned, and they all drank cactus-fruit wine until they fell over from happiness. Even the animals and plants came alive again when the drought finally broke.

"You'll see," Mattie said. "You'll feel the same way."

Mattie turned onto a gravel road. We bounced through several stream beds with dry, pebbled bottoms scorched white, and eventually pulled over on high ground about a mile or so out of town. We picked our way on foot through the brush to a spot near a grove of black-trunked mesquite trees on the very top of the hill.

The whole Tucson Valley lay in front of us, resting in its cradle of mountains. The sloped desert plain that lay between us and the city was like a palm stretched out for a fortuneteller to read, with its mounds and hillocks, its life lines and heart lines of dry stream beds.

A storm was coming up from the south, moving slowly. It looked something like a huge blue-gray shower curtain being drawn along by the hand of God. You could just barely see through it, enough to make out the silhouette of the mountains on the other side. From time to time nervous white ribbons of lightning jumped between the mountaintops and the clouds. A cool breeze came up behind us, sending shivers along the spines of the mesquite trees.

The birds were excited, flitting along the ground and perching on thin, wildly waving weed stalks.

What still amazed me about the desert was all the life it had in it. Hillbilly that I was, I had come to Arizona expecting an endless sea of sand dunes. I'd learned of deserts from old Westerns and Quickdraw McGraw cartoons. But this desert was nothing like that. There were bushes and trees and weeds here, exactly the same as anywhere else, except that the colors were different, and everything alive had thorns.

Mattie told us the names of things, but the foreign words rolled right back out of my ears. I only remembered a few. The saguaros were the great big spiny ones, as tall as normal trees but so skinny and personlike that you always had the feeling they were looking over your shoulder. Around their heads, at this time of year, they wore crowns of bright red fruits split open like mouths. And the ocotillos were the dead-looking thorny sticks that stuck up out of the ground in clusters, each one with a flaming orange spike of flower buds at its top. These looked to me like candles from hell.

Mattie said all the things that looked dead were just dormant. As soon as the rains came they would sprout leaves and grow. It happened so fast, she said, you could practically watch it.

As the storm moved closer it broke into hundreds of pieces so that the rain fell here and there from the high clouds in long, curving gray plumes. It looked like maybe fifty or sixty fires scattered over the city, except that the tall, smoky columns were flowing in reverse. And if you looked closely you could see that in some places the rain didn't make it all the way to the ground. Three-quarters of the way down from the sky it just vanished into the dry air.

Rays of sunlight streamed from between the clouds, like the

Holy Ghost on the cover of one of Mattie's dead husband's magazines. Lightning hit somewhere nearby and the thunder made Esperanza and me jump. It wasn't all that close, really, about two miles according to Mattie. She counted the seconds between the lightning strike and the thunder. Five seconds equaled one mile, she told us.

One of the plumes of rain was moving toward us. We could see big drops spattering on the ground, and when it came closer we could hear them, as loud as pebbles on a window. Coming fast. One minute we were dry, then we were being pelted with cold raindrops, then our wet shirts were clinging to our shoulders and the rain was already on the other side of us. All four of us were jumping and gasping because of the way the sudden cold took our breath away. Mattie was counting out loud between the lightning and thunderclaps: six, seven, boom! . . . four, five, six, boom! Estevan danced with Esperanza, then with me, holding his handkerchief under his arm and then twirling it high in the air—it was a flirtatious, marvelous dance with thunder for music. I remembered how he and I had once jumped almost naked into an icy stream together, how long ago that seemed, and how innocent, and now I was madly in love with him, among other people. I couldn't stop laughing. I had never felt so happy.

That was when we smelled the rain. It was so strong it seemed like more than just a smell. When we stretched out our hands we could practically feel it rising up from the ground. I don't know how a person could ever describe that scent. It certainly wasn't sour, but it wasn't sweet either, not like a flower. "Pungent" is the word Estevan used. I would have said "clean." To my mind it was like nothing so much as a wonderfully clean, scrubbed pine floor.

Mattie explained that it was caused by the greasewood bushes, which she said produced a certain chemical when it rained. I asked her if anybody had ever thought to bottle it, it was so wonderful. She said no, but that if you paid attention you could even smell it in town. That you could always tell if it was raining in any part of the city.

I wondered if the smell was really so great, or if it just seemed that way to us. Because of what it meant.

It was after sunset when we made our way back to the truck. The clouds had turned pink, then blood red, and then suddenly it was dark. Fortunately Mattie, who was troubled by night-blindness, had thought to bring a flashlight. The night was full of sounds—bird calls, a high, quivery owl hoot, and something that sounded like sheep's baahs, only a hundred times louder. These would ring out from the distance and then startle us by answering right from under our feet. Mattie said they were spadefoot toads. All that noise came from something no bigger than a quarter. I would never have believed it, except that I had seen cicadas.

"So how does a toad get into the middle of the desert?" I wanted to know. "Does it rain toad frogs in Arizona?"

"They're here all along, smarty. Burrowed in the ground. They wait out the dry months kind of deadlike, just like everything else, and when the rain comes they wake up and crawl out of the ground and start to holler."

I was amazed. There seemed to be no end to the things that could be hiding, waiting it out, right where you thought you could see it all.

"Jeez," I said, as one of them let out a squall next to my sneaker.

"Only two things are worth making so much noise about: death and sex," Estevan said. He had the devil in him tonight. I remembered a dream about him from a few nights before, one that I had not until that minute known I'd had. A very detailed dream. I felt a flush crawling up my neck and was glad for the dusk. We were following Mattie's voice to keep to the trail, concentrating on avoiding the embrace of spiny arms in the darkness.

"It's all one to a toad," Mattie said. "If it's not the one, it's the other. They don't have long to make hay in weather like this. We might not get another good rain for weeks. By morning there'll be eggs in every one of these puddles. In two days' time, even less, you can see tadpoles. Before the puddles dry up they've sprouted legs and hit the high road."

We were following behind Mattie in single file now, holding to one another's damp sleeves and arms in the darkness. All at once Esperanza's fingers closed hard around my wrist. The flashlight beam had found a snake, just at eye level, its muscular coils looped around a smooth tree trunk.

"Better step back easy, that's a rattler," Mattie said in a calm voice. With the flashlight she followed the coils to the end and pointed out the bulbs on the tail, as clear and fragile-looking as glass beads. The rattle was poised upright but did not shake.

"I didn't know they could get up in trees," I said.

"Sure, they'll climb. After birds' eggs."

A little noise came from my throat. I wasn't really afraid, but there is something about seeing a snake that makes your stomach tighten, no matter how you make up your mind to feel about it.

"Fair's fair," Mattie pointed out, as we skirted a wide path around the tree. "Everybody's got her own mouths to feed."

I knew right away that something had gone wrong. Lou Ann was standing on the front porch waiting and she looked terrible, not just because she was under a yellow light bulb. She had been crying, possibly screaming—her mouth looked stretched. She wasn't even supposed to be home yet.

I ran up the sidewalk, almost tripping twice on the steps. "What is it? Are you okay?"

"It's not me. Taylor, I'm so sorry to have to tell you this. I'm so sorry, Taylor. It's Turtle."

"Oh God, no." I went past her into the house.

Edna Poppy was sitting on the sofa with Turtle in her lap, all in one piece as far as I could see, but Turtle was changed. All these months we had spent together were gone for her. I knew it from her eyes: two cups of black coffee. I remembered exactly, exactly, how the whites of her eyes had been thin slivers of moon around the dark centers, how they had glowed orange, on and off, with the blinking neon sign from that Godforsaken bar.

I didn't go to her, because I couldn't. It is that simple. I didn't want any of this to be happening.

Mrs. Parsons was standing in the kitchen door with a broom. "A bird has got into the house," she explained, and disappeared into the kitchen again, and for a confused second I thought she meant that this was the terrible thing that had happened.

But Lou Ann was right behind me. "They were in the park, Edna and Turtle. It was so cool after the rain they thought they'd enjoy the air for a little bit, and Virgie was to come tell them if it looked like another storm was coming. But Virgie didn't come, and Edna never realized it was getting dark."

"So what happened." I was sick to my stomach.

"We don't know, exactly. I've called the police and they're coming over with a medical examiner or a social worker or, Christ, I don't know, somebody that can talk to Turtle."

"But what happened? How much do you *know* happened?"

Edna's eyes looked more glassy than usual. I noticed, now that I looked at her, that her clothes were a little messed up. Just traces, the red sweater pulled down on one shoulder, a hole in her stocking.

"I heard a peculiar sound," Edna said. She seemed almost in

another world, a hypnotized person speaking out of a trance. "It sounded just like a bag of flour hitting the dirt. Turtle had been talking, or singing I suppose would be more like it, and then she was quiet, just didn't make a peep, but I heard struggling sounds. I called out, and then I swung my cane. Oh, I swung it high, so I wouldn't hit the baby. I know how tall she is." She held her hand just where Turtle's head would be, if she had been standing on the floor in front of Edna.

"Did you hit anything?"

"Oh, yes, dear. Yes. I don't know what, but something that had some—I'd say some *give* to it. Do you understand what I mean? Oh, and I shouted too, some terrible things. The next thing I knew, I felt a great heavy weight on the hem of my skirt, and that was Turtle."

"It took us twenty minutes to get her to turn loose," Lou Ann said. Now she was holding on to Edna's sleeve instead of her hem.

"Oh my dear, I feel terrible. If I had only thought to come in a little sooner."

"It could have happened to anybody, Edna," Lou Ann said. "You couldn't have known what was going to happen, I might have done the exact same thing. You saved her, is what you did. Anybody else might have been scared to swing at him."

Anybody else, I thought, might have seen he had a gun, or a knife.

Someone knocked at the door and we all jumped. It was the police, of course, a small man who showed his detective badge and a woman who said she was a social worker, both of them dressed in ordinary clothes. Edna told what there was of her story again. The social worker was a prim-looking strawberry blonde who was carrying two rag dolls with yarn hair, a boy and a pigtail-girl. She asked if I was the mother. I nodded, a dumb animal, not really a mother, and she took me into the hallway.

"Don't you think a doctor should look at her?" I asked.

"Yes, of course. If we find evidence that she's been molested we'll need to talk with the child about it."

"She won't talk," I said. "Not now. Maybe not ever."

The social worker put her hand on my arm. "Children do recover from this kind of thing," she said. "Eventually they want to talk about what's happened to them."

"No, you don't understand. She may not talk again at all. Period."

"I think you'll find that your daughter can be a surprisingly resilient little person. But it's very important that we let her say what she needs to say. Sometimes we use these dolls. They're anatomically accurate," she said, and showed me. They were. "A child generally doesn't have the vocabulary to talk about these things, so we encourage her to play with these dolls and show us what has happened."

"Excuse me," I said, and went to the bathroom.

But Mrs. Parsons was in there with the broom. "A bird is in the house," she repeated. "A song sparrow. It came down the chimney."

I took the broom out of her hands and chased the bird off its perch above the medicine cabinet. It swooped through the doorway into the kitchen, where it knocked against the window above the sink with an alarming crack, and fell back on the counter.

"It's dead!" Virgie cried, but it wasn't. It stood up, hopped to a sheltered place between a mixing bowl and Lou Ann's recipe file, and stood blinking. In the living room they were asking about medical records. I heard Lou Ann spelling out Dr. Pelinowsky's name.

Virgie moved toward the bird slowly, crooning, with her hand stretched out in front of her. But it took off again full tilt before she could reach it. I batted it gently with the broom, heading it off from the living room full of policemen and anatomically accurate dolls, and it veered down the hallway toward the back porch. Snowboots, at least, didn't seem to be anywhere around.

"Open the screen door," I commanded Virgie. "It's locked, you have to flip that little latch. Now hold it open."

Slowly I moved in on the terrified bird, which was clinging sideways to the screen. You could see its little heart beating through the feathers. I had heard of birds having heart attacks from fright.

"Easy does it," I said. "Easy, we're not going to hurt you, we just want to set you free."

The sparrow darted off the screen, made a loop back toward the hallway, then flew through the open screen door into the terrible night.

The medical examiner said that there was no evidence Turtle had been molested. She was shaken up, and there were finger-shaped bruises on her right shoulder, and that was all.

"All!" I said, over and over. "She's just been scared practically back into the womb is all." Turtle hadn't spoken once in the days since the incident, and was back to her old ways. Now I knew a word for this condition: catatonic.

"She'll snap out of it," Lou Ann said.

"Why should she?" I wanted to know. "Would you? I've just spent about the last eight or nine months trying to convince her that nobody would hurt her again. Why should she believe me now?"

"You can't promise a kid that. All you can promise is that you'll take care of them the best you can, Lord willing and the creeks don't rise, and you just hope for the best. And things work out, Taylor, they do. We all muddle through some way."

This from Lou Ann, who viewed most of life's activities as

potential drownings, blindings, or asphyxiation; who believed in dream angels that predicted her son would die in the year 2000. Lou Ann who had once said to me: "There's so many germs in the world it's a wonder we're not all dead already."

I didn't want to talk to her about it. And she was furious with me, anyway, saying that I had practically abandoned Turtle since that night. "Why didn't you go to her and pick her up? Why did you just leave her there, with the police and all, chasing that dumb bird around for heaven's sake? Chasing that bird like it was public enemy number one?"

"She was already good and attached to Edna," I said.

"That's the biggest bunch of baloney and you know it. She would have turned loose of Edna for you. The poor kid was looking around the whole time, trying to see where you'd gone."

"I don't know what for. What makes anybody think I can do anything for her?"

I couldn't sleep nights. I went to work early and left late, even when Mattie kept telling me to go home. Lou Ann took off a week from Red Hot Mama's, putting her new promotion at risk, just to stay home with Turtle. The three of them—she, Edna, and Virgie—would sit together on the front porch with the kids, making sure we all understood it was nobody's fault.

And she stalked the neighborhood like a TV detective. "We're going to catch this jerk," she kept saying, and went knocking on every door that faced onto the park, insisting to skeptical housewives and elderly, hard-of-hearing ladies that they must have seen something or somebody suspicious. She called the police at least twice to try and get them to come take fingerprints off Edna's cane, on the off-chance that she'd whacked him on the hand.

"I know it was probably some pervert that hangs out at that sick place by Mattie's," Lou Ann told me, meaning Fanny Heaven of course. "Those disgusting little movies they have, some of them with kids. Did you know that? Little girls! A guy at work told me. It had to have been somebody that saw those movies, don't you think? Why else would it even pop into a person's head?"

I told her I didn't know.

"If you ask me," Lou Ann said more than once, "that's like showing a baby how to put beans in its ears. I'm asking you, where else would somebody get the idea to hurt a child?"

I couldn't say. I sat on my bed for hours looking up words. Pedophilia. Perpetrator. Deviant. Maleficent. I checked books out of the library but there weren't any answers in there either, just more words. At night I lay listening to noises outside, listening to Turtle breathe, thinking: she could have been killed. So easily she could be dead now.

After dinner one night Lou Ann came into my room while the kids were listening to their "Snow White" record in the living room. I'd skipped dinner; I wasn't eating much these days. When I was young and growing a lot, and Mama couldn't feed me enough, she used to say I had a hollow leg. Now I felt like I had a hollow everything. Nothing in the world could have filled that space.

Lou Ann knocked softly at the door and then walked in, balancing a bowl of chicken-noodle soup on a tray.

"You're going to dry up and blow away, hon," she said. "You've got to eat something."

I took one look and started crying. The idea that you could remedy such evil with chicken-noodle soup.

"It's the best I can do," Lou Ann offered. "I just don't think you're going to change anything with your own personal hunger strike."

I put down my book and accepted her hug. I couldn't remember when I had felt so hopeless.

"I don't know where to start, Lou Ann," I told her. "There's just so damn much ugliness. Everywhere you look, some big guy kicking some little person when they're down—look what they do to those people at Mattie's. To hell with them, people say, let them die, it was their fault in the first place for being poor or in trouble, or for not being white, or whatever, how dare they try to come to this country."

"I thought you were upset about Turtle," Lou Ann said.

"About Turtle, sure." I looked out the window. "But it just goes on and on, there's no end to it." I didn't know how to explain the empty despair I felt. "How can I just be upset about Turtle, about a grown man hurting a baby, when the whole way of the world is to pick on people that can't fight back?"

"You fight back, Taylor. Nobody picks on you and lives to tell the tale."

I ignored this. "Look at those guys out in the park with no place to go," I said. "And women, too. I've seen whole families out there. While we're in here trying to keep the dry-cleaner bags out of the kids' reach, those mothers are using dry-cleaner bags for their children's *clothes,* for God's sake. For raincoats. And feeding them out of the McDonald's dumpster. You'd think that life alone would be punishment enough for those people, but then the cops come around waking them up mornings, knocking them around with their sticks. You've seen it. And everybody else saying hooray, way to go, I got mine, power to the toughest. Clean up the neighborhood and devil take the riffraff."

Lou Ann just listened.

"What I'm saying is nobody feels sorry for anybody anymore, nobody even pretends they do. Not even the President. It's like it's become unpatriotic." I unfolded my wad of handkerchief and blew my nose.

"What's that supposed to teach people?" I demanded. "It's no wonder kids get the hurting end of the stick. And she's so little, so many years ahead of her. I'm just not up to the job, Lou Ann."

Lou Ann sat with her knees folded under her, braiding and unbraiding the end of a strand of my hair.

"Well, don't feel like the Lone Ranger," she said. "Nobody is."

THIRTEEN

Night-Blooming Cereus

Turtle turned out to be, as the social worker predicted, resilient. Within a few weeks she was talking again. She never did anything with the anatomical rag dolls except plant them under Cynthia's desk blotter, but she did talk some about the "bad man" and how Ma Poppy had "popped him one." I had no idea where Turtle had learned to talk like that, but then Edna and Virgie Mae did have TV. Cynthia was concerned about Turtle's tendency to bury the dollies, believing that it indicated a fixation with death, but I assured her that Turtle was only trying to grow dolly trees.

Cynthia was the strawberry blonde social worker. We went to see her on Mondays and Thursdays. Of the two of us, Turtle and me, I believe I was the tougher customer.

It was a miserable time. As wonderful as the summer's first rains had been, they soon wore out their welcome as it rained every day and soaked the air until it felt like a hot, stale dishcloth on your face. No matter how hard I tried to breathe, I felt like I couldn't get air. At night I'd lie on top of the damp sheets and think: breathe in, breathe out. It closed out every other thought, and it closed out the possibility of sleep, though sometimes I wondered what was the point of working so hard to stay alive, if that's what I was doing. I remembered my pep talk to Esperanza a few months before, and understood just how ridiculous it was. There is no point in treating a depressed person as though she were just feeling sad, saying, There now, hang on, you'll get over it. Sadness is more or less like a head cold—with patience, it passes. Depression is like cancer.

Cynthia had spent a lot of time talking with both of us about Turtle's earlier traumas, the things that had happened before I ever knew her. The story came out of me a little at a time.

But apparently it was no news to a social worker. Cynthia said that, as horrible as it was, this kind of thing happened often, not just on Indian reservations but in the most everyday-looking white frame houses and even places a whole lot fancier than that. She told me that maybe one out of every four little girls is sexually abused by a family member. Maybe more.

Surprisingly, hearing this wasn't really what upset me the most. Maybe by then I was already numb, or could only begin to think about the misfortunes of one little girl at a time. But also, I reasoned, this meant that Turtle was not all alone. At least she would have other people to talk to about it when she grew up.

But there was other bad news. During the third week of sessions with Cynthia she informed me that it had recently come to the attention of the Child Protection Services Division of the Department of Economic Security, in the course of the police investigation, that I had no legal claim to Turtle.

"No more legal claim than the city dump has on your garbage," I said. I think Cynthia found me a little shocking. "I told you how it was," I insisted. "Her aunt just told me to take her. If it hadn't been me, it would have been the next person to come down the road with an empty seat in the car. I guarantee you, Turtle's relatives don't want her."

"I understand that. But the problem is that you have no legitimate claim. A verbal agreement with a relative isn't good enough. You can't prove to the police that it happened that way. That you didn't kidnap her, for instance, or that the relatives weren't coerced."

"No, I can't prove anything. I don't understand what you're getting at. If I don't have a legal claim on Turtle, I don't see where anybody else does either."

Cynthia had these tawny gold eyes like some member of the cat family, as certain fair-haired people do. But unlike most people she could look you straight in the eye and stay there. I suppose that is part of a social worker's training.

"The state of Arizona has a claim," she said. "If a child has no legal guardian she becomes a ward of the state."

"You mean, like orphan homes, that kind of thing?"

"That kind of thing, yes. There's a chance that you could adopt her eventually, depending on how long you've been a resident of the state, but you would have to qualify through the state agency. It would depend on a number of factors, including your income and stability."

Income and stability. I stared at Cynthia's throat. In this hot weather, when everybody else was trying to wear as little as they could without getting arrested, Cynthia had on a pink-checked blouse with the collar pinned closed. I remembered hearing her say, at some point, that she was cool-blooded by nature.

"How soon would this have to happen?" I asked.

"It will take two or three weeks for the paperwork to get to a place where it's going to get noticed. After that, someone from Child Protection and Placement will be in touch with you."

The pin at her throat was an ivory and flesh-colored cameo that looked antique. As Turtle and I were leaving I asked if it was something that had come down through her family.

Cynthia fingered the cameo and laughed. "I found it in the one-dollar bin at the Salvation Army."

"Figures," I said.

Lou Ann had a fit. I had never seen her so mad. The veins on her forehead stood out and her face turned pink, all the way up to her scalp.

"Who in the hell do those people think they are? That they have the right to take her out of a perfectly good home and put her in some creepy orphanage where they probably make them sleep on burlap bags and feed them pig slop!"

"I don't think it's quite that bad," I said.

"I can't believe you," she said.

But I was ready to give in. "What else can I do? How can I fight the law?" I asked her. "What am I going to do, get a gun and hold Turtle hostage in here while the cops circle the house?"

"Taylor, don't. Just don't. You're acting like it's a lost cause, and that I'm telling you to do something stupid. All I'm saying is, there's got to be some way around them taking her, and you're not even trying to think of it."

"Why should I, Lou Ann? Why should I think Turtle's better off with me than in a state home? At least there they know how to take care of kids. They won't let anything happen to her."

"Well, that's sure a chickenshit thing to say."

"Maybe it is."

She stared at me. "I cannot believe you're just ready to roll over and play dead about this, Taylor. I thought I knew you. I thought we were best friends, but now I don't hardly know who in the heck you are."

I told her that I didn't know either, but that didn't satisfy Lou Ann in the slightest.

"Do you know," she told me, "in high school there was this girl, Bonita Jankenhorn, that I thought was the smartest and the gutsiest person that ever walked. In English when we had to work these special crossword puzzles about *Silas Marner* and I don't know what all, the rest of us would start to try out different words and then erase everything over and over again, but Bonita worked hers with an *ink pen.* She was that sure of herself, she'd just screw off the cap and start going. The first time it happened, the teacher started to tell her off and Bonita said, 'Miss Myers, if I turn in a poor assignment then you'll have every right to punish me, but not until then.' Can you even imagine? We all thought that girl was made out of gristle.

"But when I met you, that day you first came over here, I thought to myself, 'Bonita Jankenhorn, roll over. This one is worth half a dozen of you, packed up in a box and gift-wrapped.'"

"I guess you were wrong," I said.

"I was *not* wrong! You really were like that. Where in the world did it all go to?"

"Same place as your meteor shower," I said. I hadn't intended to hurt Lou Ann's feelings, but I did. She let me be for a while after that.

But only for a while. Then she started up again. Really, I don't think the argument stopped for weeks, it would just take a breather from time to time. Although it wasn't an argument, strictly speaking. I couldn't really disagree with Lou Ann—what Cynthia and the so-called Child Protectors wanted to do was wrong. But I didn't know what was right. I just kept saying how this world was a terrible place to try and bring up a child in. And Lou Ann kept saying, For God's sake, what other world have we got?

*   *   *

Mattie had her own kettle of fish to worry about. She hadn't been able to work out a way to get Esperanza and Estevan out of Tucson, much less all the way to a sanctuary church in some other state. Apparently several people had offered, but each time it didn't work out. Terry the doctor had made plans to drive them to San Francisco, where they would meet up with another group going to Seattle. But because of his new job on the Indian reservation the government liked to keep track of his comings and goings. Mattie always said she trusted her nose. "If I don't like the smell of something," she said, "then it's not worth the risk."

Even with this on her mind, she spent a lot of time talking with me about Turtle. She told me some things I didn't know. Obviously Mattie knew what there was to know about loopholes. She was pretty sure that there were ways a person could adopt a child without going through the state.

But I confessed to Mattie that even if I could find a way I wasn't sure it would be the best thing for Turtle.

"Remember when I first drove up here that day in January?" I asked her one morning. We were sitting in the back in the same two chairs, drinking coffee out of the same two mugs, though this time I had the copulating rabbits. "Tell me the honest truth. Did you think I seemed like any kind of a decent parent?"

"I thought you seemed like a bewildered parent. Which is perfectly ordinary. Usually the bewilderment wears off by the time the kid gets big enough to eat peanut butter and crackers, but knowing what I do now, I can see you were still in the stage most mothers are in when they first bring them home from the hospital."

I was embarrassed to think of how Mattie must have seen straight through my act. Driving up here like the original tough cookie in jeans and a red sweater, with my noncommittal answers and smart remarks, acting like two flat tires were all in a day's work and I just happened to have been born with this kid growing out of my hip, that's how cool I was. I hadn't felt all that tough on the inside. The difference was, now I felt twice that old, and too tired to put on the show.

"You knew, didn't you? I didn't know the first thing about how to take care of her. When you told me that about babies getting dehydrated it scared the living daylights out of me. I realized I had no business just assuming I could take the responsibility for a child's life."

"There's not a decent mother in the world that hasn't realized that."

"I'm serious, Mattie."

She smiled and sipped her coffee. "So am I."

"So how does a person make a decision that important? Whether or not they're going to do it?"

"Most people don't decide. They just don't have any choice. I've heard you say yourself that you think the reason most people have kids is because they get pregnant."

I stared at the coffee grounds that made a ring in the bottom of the white mug. Back in Pittman I'd heard of a fairly well-to-do woman who made her fortune reading tea leaves and chicken bones, which she kept in a bag and would scatter across her kitchen floor like jacks. On the basis of leaves and bones, she would advise people on what to do with their lives. No wonder she was rich. It seems like almost anything is better than having only yourself to blame when you screw things up.

"Taylor, honey, if you don't mind my saying so I think you're asking the wrong question."

"How do you mean?"

"You're asking yourself, Can I give this child the best possible upbringing and keep her out of harm's way her whole life long? The answer is no, you can't. But nobody else can either. Not a state home, that's for sure. For heaven's sake, the best they can do is turn their heads while the kids learn to pick locks and snort hootch, and then try to keep them out of jail. Nobody can protect a child from the world. That's why it's the wrong thing to ask, if you're really trying to make a decision."

"So what's the right thing to ask?"

"Do I want to try? Do I think it would be interesting, maybe even enjoyable in the long run, to share my life with this kid and give her my best effort and maybe, when all's said and done, end up with a good friend."

"I don't think the state of Arizona's looking at it that way."

"I guarantee you they're not."

It occurred to me to wonder whether Mattie had ever raised kids of her own, but I was afraid to ask. Lately whenever I'd scratched somebody's surface I'd turned up a ghost story. I made up my mind not to bring it up.

I called for an appointment to meet with Cynthia alone, without Turtle. In past appointments she had talked about legal claim and state homes and so forth in Turtle's presence. Granted Turtle had been occupied with the new selection of toys offered by the Department of Economic Security, but in my experience she usually got the drift of what was going on, whether or not she appeared to be paying attention. If either I or the state of Arizona was going to instill in this child a sense of security, discussing her future and ownership as though she were an item of commerce wasn't the way to do it. The more I thought about this, the madder I got. But that wasn't what I intended to discuss with Cynthia.

The appointment was on a Friday afternoon. I started to lose my nerve again when I saw her in her office, her eyes made up with pale green shadows and her hair pulled back in a gold barrette. I don't believe Cynthia was much older than I was, but you put somebody in high-heeled pumps and sit her behind a big desk and age is no longer an issue—she is more important than you are, period.

"Proof of abandonment is very, very difficult," she was explaining to me. "In this case, probably impossible. But you're right, there are legal alternatives. The cornerstone of an adoption of this type would have to be the written consent of the child's natural parents. And you would need to be named in the document."

"What if there are no natural parents? If they were to be dead, for instance."

"Then it would have to come from the nearest living relative, the person who would normally have custody, and a death certificate would have to be presented as well. But the most important thing, as I said, is that the document would name you, specifically, as the new guardian."

"What kind of document exactly?"

"The law varies. In some states the mother would have to acknowledge her consent before a judge or a representative of the Department of Economic Security. In others, a simple written statement, notarized and signed before witnesses, is sufficient."

"What about on an Indian reservation? Do you know that sometimes on Indian reservations they don't give birth or death certificates?"

Cynthia wasn't the type that liked to be told anything. "I'm aware of that," she said. "In certain cases, exceptions are made."

Cynthia's office was tiny, really, and her desk wasn't actually all that big. She didn't even have a window in there.

"Don't you miss knowing what the weather's like?" I asked her.

"I beg your pardon?"

"You don't have a window. I just wondered if you ever kind of lost touch with what was going on outside, being cooped up in here all day with the air conditioning and the fluorescent lighting." It was the first time in my life I'd ever said anything like "fluorescent lighting" out loud.

"As you recall, I came to your house on the evening that your, that April was assaulted." Cynthia always called Turtle by her more conventional name. "I do my share of field work," she said.

"Of course."

"Have I answered your questions, Taylor?"

"Mostly. Not completely. I'd like to know how a person would go about finding the information you mentioned. About the laws in different states. Like Oklahoma, for instance."

"I can look that up and get back to you. If you like, I can get you the name of someone in Oklahoma City who could help you formalize the papers."

This took me by surprise. "You'd be willing to help me out?"

"Certainly. I'm on your side here, Taylor." She leaned forward and folded her hands on her desk blotter, and I noticed her fingernails were in bad shape. It's possible that Cynthia was a nail-biter.

"Are you saying that you'd rather see Turtle stay with me than go into a state home?"

"There has never been any doubt in my mind about that."

I stood up, walked around the chair, and sat down again. "Excuse my French, but why in hell didn't you say so before now?"

She blinked her gold-coin eyes. "I thought that ought to be your decision."

At the end of my hour I was halfway out the door, but then stopped and came back, closing the door behind me. "Thank you," I said.

"You're welcome."

"Can I ask you a kind of personal question? It's about the cameo brooch."

She looked amused. "You can ask," she said.

"Do you have to shop at the Salvation Army? I mean, is it because of your pay, or do you just like rummaging through other people's family heirlooms?"

"I'm a trained therapist," Cynthia said, smiling. "I don't answer questions like that."

Out in the lobby I stopped to chat with one of the secretaries, who asked where my little girl was today. The secretary's name was Jewel. I had spoken with her several times before. She had a son with dyslexia, which she explained was a disease that caused people to see things backwards. "Like the American flag, for instance," she said. "The way he would see it would be that the stars are up in the right-hand corner, instead of the left. But then there's other things where it doesn't matter. Like you take the word WOW, for instance. That's his favorite word, he writes it all over everything. And the word MOM, too."

Before I had gotten around to leaving the building, another secretary came hustling over and handed me a note, which she said was from Cynthia. It said, "I appreciate your sensitivity in not wishing to discuss April's custody in her presence. I'm sorry if I have been careless."

There was also a name: Mr. Jonas Wilford Armistead—along with an Oklahoma City address—and underneath, the words "Good luck!"

All evening, after I'd fed the kids and put them to bed, I paced the house. I couldn't wait for Lou Ann to get home, but then when she did I wasn't sure I wanted to tell her anything yet. I hadn't completely made up my mind.

"For heaven's sake," Lou Ann said, "you're making me nervous. Either sit down or wash the dishes." I washed the dishes.

"Whatever's on your mind, I hope you get it settled," she said, and went to the living room to read. She had been reading a novel called *Daughter of the Cheyenne Winds,* which she claimed she had found in her locker at Red Hot Mama's, and had nothing whatever to do with Angel being on the Montana-Colorado Circuit.

I followed her into the living room. "You're not mad are you? Because I don't want to talk about it?"

"Nope."

"I'll tell you tomorrow. I just have to think some more."

She didn't look up. "Go think," she said. "Think, and wash the dishes."

I didn't sleep at all that night. I was getting used to it. I watched Turtle roll from her side to her stomach and back again. Her eyes rolled back and forth under her eyelids, and sometimes her mouth worked too. Whoever she was talking to in her dream, she told them a whole lot more than she'd ever told me. I would have paid good money to be in that dream.

In the morning I left her asleep and went to Mattie's to finish an alignment and front-and-rear rotation I'd left undone the previous afternoon. The guy was coming in sometime that day to pick it up. I didn't look at a clock but it must have been early when I went in because I was already finished and ready to go home before Mattie came downstairs. I hung around a while longer, making coffee and dusting the shelves and changing the calendar (it was still on May, and this was August). I stared for a long time at the picture of the Aztec man carrying the passed-out woman, thinking about whatever Latin American tragedy it stood for. Thinking, naturally, of Esperanza and Estevan. Though I knew that more often than not it was the other way around, the woman carried the man through the tragedy. The man and the grandma and all the kids.

Finally Mattie came down. We had a cup of coffee, and we talked.

Afterward I found Lou Ann and the kids in the park. Turtle was amusing herself by sweeping a patch of dirt with an old hairbrush, presumably Edna's since it was red, and Lou Ann had momentarily put aside *Daughter of the Cheyenne Winds* to engage in a contest of will with Dwayne Ray. Lou Ann was bound to win, of course.

"I said no! Give it to me right now. Where'd you get that from?" She grabbed his fist, which was headed on an automatic-pilot course for his mouth, and extracted a dirt-covered purple jelly bean. "Where in the heck do you think he got that? My God, Taylor, just imagine if he'd eaten it!"

Dwayne Ray's mouth remained in the shape of an O for several seconds, still expecting the intercepted jelly bean, and then he started to scream.

"I used to know this old farm woman that said you've got to eat a peck of dirt before you die," I said.

Lou Ann picked up Dwayne Ray and bounced him. "Well, maybe if you don't eat a peck of dirt before your first birthday then you won't die so quick, is what I say."

I sat down on the bench. "Listen, I've made up my mind about something. I'm going to drive Esperanza and Estevan to a safe house in Oklahoma. And while I'm there I'm going to see if I can find any of Turtle's relatives."

She stared at me. Dwayne Ray came down on her knee with a bump, and was stunned into being quiet.

"What for?"

"So they can sign her over to me."

"Well, what if they won't? What if they see how good she's turning out and decide they want her back?"

"I don't think they will."

"But what if they do?"

"Damn it, Lou Ann, you've been telling me till you were blue in the face to do something, take action, think positive, blah, blah, blah. I'm trying to think positive here."

"Sorry."

"What other choice have I got than to go? If I just sit here on my hands, then they take her."

"I know. You're right."

"If her relatives want her back, then I'll think of something. We'll cut that fence when we come to it."

"What if you can't find them? Sorry."

"I'll find them."

Lou Ann, uncharacteristically, had overlooked the number-one thing I ought to be worried about. Over the next few days Mattie asked me about fifty times if I was sure I knew what I was doing. She told me that if I got caught I could get five years in prison and a $2,000 fine for each illegal person I was assisting, which in this case would be two. To tell the truth, I couldn't even let these things enter my head.

But Mattie persisted. "This isn't just hypothetical. It's actually happened before that people got caught."

"I don't know why you're worried about me," I told her. "Esperanza and Estevan would get a whole lot worse than prison and a fine."

I did suggest to Mattie, though, that it might be a good idea to fix the ignition on Two-Two, my VW, now that we were setting out across the country again. She looked at me as though I had suggested shooting an elected official.

"You are *not* taking that old thing," she said. "You'll take the Lincoln. It's got a lot of room, and it's reliable."

I was offended. "What's wrong with my car?" I wanted to know.

"What's wrong with it, child, I could stand here telling you till the sun went down. And just about any one of those things could get you pulled over by a cop. If you think you care so much about Esperanza and Estevan, you'd better start using that head of yours for something besides thinking up smart remarks."

Mattie walked off. I'd seen her bordering on mad before, but never at me. Clearly she did not want me to go.

The night before I was to leave, Virgie Mae Parsons came knocking on the door. It was late but Lou Ann and I were still up, going round and round about what I ought to pack. She thought I should take my very best clothes in case I might have to impress someone with my financial security. She was sure that at the very least I ought to take a pair of stockings, which I would have to borrow from Lou Ann, not being in the habit of owning such things myself. I pointed out to her that it was the middle of summer and I didn't think I'd need to impress anyone that much. We didn't notice a timid little peck at the door until it grew considerably louder. Then Lou Ann was afraid to answer it.

I looked out the window. "It's Virgie Mae, for heaven's sake," I said, and let her in.

She stood looking befuddled for a second or two, then pulled herself together and said, "Edna said I ought to come over and get you. We have something the children might like to see, if you don't think it would do too much harm to wake them."

"What, a surprise?" Lou Ann asked. She was back in less than a minute with Dwayne Ray in one arm and Turtle by the other hand. Turtle trailed grumpily behind, whereas Dwayne Ray chose to remain asleep, his head bobbing like an old stuffed animal's. In the intervening minute I had not extracted any further information from Virgie.

We followed her out our front door and up the walk to their porch. I could make out Edna sitting in the glider, and in the corner of the porch we saw what looked like a bouquet of silvery-white balloons hanging in the air.

Flowers.

A night-blooming cereus, Virgie Mae explained. The flowers

open for only one night of the year, and then they are gone.

It was a huge, sprawling plant with branches that flopped over the porch railing and others that reached nearly as high as the eaves. I had certainly noticed it before, standing in the corner in its crumbling pot, flattened and spiny and frankly extremely homely, and it had crossed my mind to wonder why Virgie Mae didn't throw the thing out.

"I've never seen anything so heavenly," Lou Ann said.

Enormous blossoms covered the plant from knee level to high above our heads. Turtle advanced on it slowly, walking right up to one of the flowers, which was larger than her face. It hung in the dark air like a magic mirror just inches from her eyes. It occurred to me that she should be warned of the prickles, but if Lou Ann wasn't going to say anything I certainly wasn't. I knelt beside Turtle.

There was hardly any moon that night, but gradually our eyes were able to take in more and more detail. The flowers themselves were not spiny, but made of some nearly transparent material that looked as though it would shrivel and bruise if you touched it. The petals stood out in starry rays, and in the center of each flower there was a complicated construction of silvery threads shaped like a pair of cupped hands catching moonlight. A fairy boat, ready to be launched into the darkness.

"Is that?" Turtle wanted to know. She touched it, and it did not shrivel, but only swayed a little on the end of its long green branch.

"It's a flower, dear," Virgie said.

Lou Ann said, "She knows that much. She can tell you the name of practically every flower in the Burpee's catalogue, even things that only grow in Florida and Nova Scotia."

"Cereus," I said. Even its name sounded silvery and mysterious.

"See us," Turtle repeated.

Lou Ann nosed into a flower at eye level and reported that it had a smell. She held Dwayne Ray up to it, but he didn't seem especially awake. "I can just barely make it out," she said, "but it's so sweet. Tart, almost, like that lemon candy in a straw that I used to die for when I was a kid. It's just ever so faint."

"I can smell it from here." Edna spoke from the porch swing.

"Edna's the one who spots it," Virgie said. "If it was up to me I would never notice to save my life. Because they come out after dark, you see, and I forget to watch for the buds. One year Edna had a head cold and we missed it altogether."

Lou Ann's eyes were as wide and starry as the flower she stared into. She was as captivated as Turtle.

"It's a sign," she said.

"Of what?" I wanted to know.

"I don't know," she said quietly. "Something good."

"I can get the pruning shears and cut one off for you, if you like," Virgie Mae offered. "If you put it in the icebox it will last until tomorrow."

But Lou Ann shook her head. "No thanks. I want to remember them like this, in the dark."

"After you pluck them they lose their fragrance," Edna told us. "I don't know why, but it just goes right away."

If the night-blooming cereus was an omen of anything, it was of good weather for traveling. The morning was overcast and cool. Once again we rolled the children out of bed, and Lou Ann and Dwayne Ray came with us over to Mattie's. Turtle wanted to be carried, like Dwayne Ray, but we had the bags to deal with.

"We'll just walk this little way," I told her. "Then you can sleep in the car for a long time."

Estevan and Esperanza had one suitcase between them and

it was smaller than mine, which did not even include Turtle's stuff. I had packed for a week, ten days at the outside, and they were packed for the rest of their lives.

Several people had come to see them off, including the elderly woman I had once seen upstairs at Mattie's and a very young woman with a small child, who could have been her daughter or her sister, or no relation for that matter. There was lots of hugging and kissing and talking in Spanish. Mattie moved around quickly, introducing people and putting our things in the car and giving me hundreds of last-minute instructions.

"You might have to choke her good and hard to get her going in the mornings," Mattie told me, and in my groggy state it took me a while to understand whom or what I was supposed to be choking. "She's tuned for Arizona. I don't know how she'll do in Oklahoma."

"She'll do fine," I said. "Remember, I'm used to cantankerous cars."

"I know. You'll do fine," she said, but didn't seem convinced.

After we had gotten in and fastened our seat belts, on Mattie's orders, she leaned in the window and slipped something into my hand. It was money. Esperanza and Estevan were leaning out the windows on the other side, spelling out something—surely not an address—very slowly to the elderly woman, who was writing it down on the back of a window envelope.

"Where did this come from?" I asked Mattie quietly. "We can get by."

"Take it, you thick-headed youngun. Not for your sake, for theirs." She squeezed my hand over the money. "Poverty-stricken isn't the safest way to go."

"You didn't answer my question."

"It comes from people, Taylor, and let's just leave it. Some folks are the heroes and take the risks, and other folks do what they can from behind the scenes."

"Mattie, would you please shut up about heroes and prison and all."

"I didn't say prison."

"Just stop it, okay? Estevan and Esperanza are my friends. And, even if they weren't, I can't see why I shouldn't do this. If I saw somebody was going to get hit by a truck I'd push them out of the way. Wouldn't anybody? It's a sad day for us all if I'm being a hero here."

She looked at me the way Mama would have.

"Stop it," I said again. "You're going to make me cry." I started the engine and it turned over with an astonishing purr, like a lioness waking up from her nap. "This is the good life, cars that start by themselves," I said.

"When I hired you, it was for fixing tires. Just fixing tires, do you understand that?"

"I know."

"As long as you know."

"I do."

She reached in the window and gave me a hug, and I actually did start crying. She put kisses on her hand and reached across and put them on Esperanza's and Estevan's cheeks, and then Turtle's.

"Bless your all's hearts," she said. "Take good care."

"Be careful," Lou Ann said.

Mattie and Lou Ann and the others stood in the early-morning light holding kids and waving. It could have been the most ordinary family picture, except for the backdrop of whitewall tires. Esperanza and Turtle waved until they were out of sight. I kept blinking my eyelids like windshield wipers, trying to keep a clear view of the road.

On Mattie's advice we took one of the city roads out of town, and would join up with the freeway just south of the city limits.

Outside of town we passed a run-over blackbird in the road, flattened on the center line. As the cars and trucks rolled by, the gusts of wind caused one stiff wing to flap up and down in a pitiful little flagging-down gesture. My instinct was to step on the brakes, but of course there was no earthly reason to stop for a dead bird.

FOURTEEN

Guardian Saints

We werc stopped by Immigration about a hundred miles this side of the New Mexico border. Mattie had warned me of this possibility and we had all prepared for it as best we could. Esperanza and Estevan were dressed about as American as you could get without looking plain obnoxious: he had on jeans and an alligator shirt donated from some church on the east side where people gave away stuff that was entirely a cut above New To You. Esperanza was wearing purple culottes, a yellow T-shirt, and sunglasses with pink frames. She sat in the back seat with Turtle. Her long hair was loose, not braided, and as we sped down the highway it whipped around her shoulders and out the window, putting on a brave show of freedom that had nothing to do with Esperanza's life. Twice I asked if it was too much wind on her, and each time she shook her head no.

Every eastbound car on the highway was being stopped by

the Border Patrol. The traffic was bottled up, which gave us time to get good and nervous. This kind of check was routine; it had not been set up for the express purpose of catching us, but it still felt that way. To all of us, I believe. I was frantic. I rattled my teeth, as Mama would say.

"There's this great place up ahead called Texas Canyon," I told them, knowing full well that none of us might make it to Texas Canyon. Esperanza and Estevan might not make it to their next birthday. "Wait till you see it. It's got all these puffy-looking rocks," I chattered on. "Turtle and I loved it."

They nodded quietly.

When our turn came I threw back my head like a wealthy person, yanked that Lincoln into gear and pulled up to the corrugated tin booth. A young officer poked his head in the car. I could smell his aftershave.

"All U.S. citizens?" he asked.

"Yes," I said. I showed my driver's license. "This is my brother Steve, and my sister-in-law."

The officer nodded politely. "The kid yours or theirs?"

I looked at Estevan, which was a stupid thing to do.

"She's ours," Estevan said, without a trace of an accent.

The officer waved us through. "Have a nice day," he said.

After we had passed well beyond the checkpoint Estevan started apologizing. "I thought it would be the most believable thing. Since you hesitated."

"Yeah, I did."

"You looked at me. I thought it might seem suspicious if I said she was yours. He might wonder why you didn't say it."

"I know, I know, I know. You're right. It's no problem. The only thing that matters is we made it through." It did bother me though, just as it bothered me that Turtle was calling Esperanza "Ma." Which was a completely unreasonable thing to resent, I know, since Turtle called every woman Ma something. There's no way she could have managed "Esperanza."

We got out at the rest station in Texas Canyon. It turned out there weren't rest rooms there, just picnic tables, so I took Turtle behind a giant marshmallow-shaped boulder. Ever since I'd found out she was three years old, we'd gotten very serious about potty training.

When we came back Estevan and Esperanza were standing by the guard rail looking out over an endless valley of boulders. A large wooden sign, which showed dinosaurs and giant ferny trees and mountains exploding in the background, explained that this was the lava flow from a volcanic explosion long ago. Along with the initials and hearts scratched into the sign with pocket knives, someone had carved "Repent."

The setting did more or less put you in that frame of mind. There wasn't a bush or tree in sight, just rocks and rocks, sky and more sky. Estevan said this is what the world would have looked like if God had gone on strike after the second day.

It was a peculiar notion, but then you had to consider Estevan's background with the teachers' union. He would think in those terms.

They seemed uncomfortable out of the car so we stayed on the move after that, driving down an endless river of highway. After my VW, driving Mattie's wide white car felt like steering a boat, not that I had ever actually steered anything of the kind. Estevan and Esperanza didn't have proper drivers' licenses, of course—that was the very least of what they didn't have—so to be on the safe side I did all the driving. The first night we would try to go straight through, pulling over for naps when I needed to. Lou Ann had made us a Thermos of iced coffee. For the second night, I told them, I knew of a nice motor lodge in Oklahoma where we could most likely stay for free.

Estevan and I talked about everything you can think of. He asked me if the alligator was a national symbol of the United

States, because you saw them everywhere on people's shirts, just above the heart.

"Not that I know of," I told him. It occurred to me, though, that it might be kind of appropriate.

He told me that the national symbol of the Indian people in Guatemala was the quetzal, a beautiful green bird with a long, long tail. I told him I had seen military macaws at the zoo, and wondered if the quetzal was anything like those. He said no. If you tried to keep this bird in a cage, it died.

Shortly after sunset we left the interstate to take a two-lane road that cut through the mountains and would take about two hundred miles of New Mexico off our trip. I wished we could keep New Mexico in and cut out two hundred miles of Oklahoma instead, but of course Oklahoma was where we were going. I had to keep reminding myself of that. For some reason I had in the back of my mind that we were headed for Kentucky. I kept picturing Mama's face when we all pulled up in the driveway.

I squinted and flashed my lights at a car coming toward us with its brights on. They dimmed.

"Do you miss your home a lot?" I asked Estevan. "I know that's a stupid question. But does it make you tired, being so far away from what you know? That's how I feel sometimes, that I would just like to crawl in a hole somewhere and rest. Go dormant, like those toad frogs Mattie told us about. And for you it's just that much worse; you're not even speaking your own language."

He let out a long breath. "I don't even know anymore which home I miss. Which level of home. In Guatemala City I missed the mountains. My own language is not Spanish, did you know that?"

I told him no, that I didn't.

"We are Mayan people; we speak twenty-two different

Mayan languages. Esperanza and I speak to each other in Spanish because we come from different parts of the highlands."

"What's Mayan, exactly?"

"Mayans lived here in the so-called New World before the Europeans discovered it. We're very old people. In those days we had astronomical observatories, and performed brain surgery."

I thought of the color pictures in my grade-school history books: Columbus striding up the beach in his leotards and feathered hat, a gang of wild-haired red men in loin cloths scattering in front of him like rabbits. What a joke.

"Our true first names are Indian names," Estevan said. "You couldn't even pronounce them. We chose Spanish names when we moved to the city."

I was amazed. "So Esperanza is bilingual. You're, what do you call it? Trilingual."

I knew that Esperanza spoke some English too, but it was hard to say how much since she spoke it so rarely. One time I had admired a little gold medallion she always wore around her neck and she said, with an accent, but plainly enough: "That is St. Christopher, guardian saint of refugees." I would have been no more surprised if St. Christopher himself had spoken.

Christopher was a sweet-faced saint. He looked a lot like Stephen Foster, who I suppose you could say was the guardian saint of Kentucky. At least he wrote the state song.

"I chose a new name for myself too, when I left home," I said to Estevan. "We all have that in common."

"You did? What was it before?"

I made a face. "Marietta."

He laughed. "It's not so bad."

"It's a town in Georgia where Mama's and my father's car broke down once, I guess, when they were on their way to Florida. They never made it. They stayed in a motel and made me instead."

"What a romantic story."

"Not really. I was a mistake. Well, not really a mistake, according to Mama, but an accident. A mistake I guess is when you regret it later."

"And they didn't?"

"Mama didn't. That's all that counts, in my case."

"So Papa went on to Florida?"

"Or wherever."

"Esperanza also grew up without her father. The circumstances were different, of course."

In the back seat Esperanza was stroking Turtle's hair and singing to her quietly in a high, unearthly voice. I had heard enough Spanish to understand that the way her voice was dipping and gliding through the words was more foreign than that. I remembered Estevan's yodely songs the day of our first picnic. They had to have been Mayan songs, not Spanish. Songs older than Christopher Columbus, maybe even older than Christopher the saint. I wondered if, when they still had Ismene, they had sung to her in both their own languages. To think how languages could accumulate in a family, in a country like that. When I thought of Guatemala I imagined a storybook place: jungles full of long-tailed birds, women wearing rainbow-threaded dresses.

But of course there was more to the picture. Police everywhere, always. Whole villages of Indians forced to move again and again. As soon as they planted their crops, Estevan said, the police would come and set their houses and fields on fire and make them move again. The strategy was to wear them down so they'd be too tired or too hungry to fight back.

Turtle had fallen asleep with her head in Esperanza's lap.

"What's with everybody always trying to get rid of the Indians?" I said, not really asking for an answer. I thought again of the history-book pictures. Astronomers and brain surgeons.

They should have done brain surgery on Columbus while they had the chance.

After a while Estevan said, "What I really hate is not belonging in any place. To be unwanted everywhere."

I thought of my Cherokee great-grandfather, his people who believed God lived in trees, and that empty Oklahoma plain they were driven to like livestock. But then, even the Cherokee Nation was *someplace*.

"You know what really gets me?" I asked him. "How people call you 'illegals.' That just pisses me off, I don't know how you can stand it. A human being can be good or bad or right or wrong, maybe. But how can you say a person is illegal?"

"I don't know. You tell me."

"You just can't," I said. "That's all there is to it."

On the second day we got into flatlands. The Texas panhandle, and then western Oklahoma, stretched out all around us like a colossal pancake. There was no way of judging where you were against where you were going, and as a consequence you tended to start feeling you were stuck out there, rolling your wheels on some trick prairie treadmill.

Estevan, who had apparently spent some time on a ship, said it reminded him of the ocean. He knew a Spanish word for the kind of mental illness you get from seeing too much horizon. Esperanza seemed stunned at first, then a little scared. She asked Estevan, who translated for me, whether or not we were near Washington. I assured her we weren't, and asked what made her think so. She said she thought they might build the President's palace in a place like this, so that if anyone came after him his guards could spot them a long way off.

To keep ourselves from going crazy with boredom we tried to think of word games. I told about the secretary named Jewel with the son who sees things backwards, and we tried to think of words he would like. Esperanza thought of *ala,* which means wing. Estevan knew whole sentences, some in Spanish and some in English. The English ones were "A man, a plan, a canal: Panama!" (which he said was a typical gringo way of looking at that endeavor), and "Able was I ere I saw Elba," which was what Napoleon supposedly said when he was sent into exile. I hadn't known, before then, where or what Elba was. I'd had a vague idea that it was a kind of toast.

Turtle was the only one of us who didn't seem perturbed by the landscape. She told Esperanza a kind of ongoing story, which lasted for hundreds of miles and sounded like a vegetarian version of Aesop's Fables, and when she ran out of story she played with her baby doll. The doll was a hand-me-down from Mattie's. It came with a pair of red-checked pajamas, complete with regular-sized shirt buttons, that someone had apparently sewn by hand. Turtle adored the doll and had named it, with no help from anyone, Shirley Poppy.

We bypassed Oklahoma City and headed north on I-35, reversing the route I had taken through Oklahoma the first time. We reached the Broken Arrow Motor Lodge by late afternoon. At first I thought the place had changed hands. Which it had, in a way: Mrs. Hoge had died, and Irene was a different person, a slipcover of her former self. She had lost 106 pounds in 24 weeks by eating one Weight Watchers frozen dinner per day and nothing else but chamomile tea, unsweetened.

"I told Boyd if he wanted something different he could learn to cook it himself. Anybody that can butcher a side of beef can learn to cook," she explained. She had started the diet on her doctor's advice, when she decided she wanted to have a baby.

Irene seemed thrilled to see Turtle and me again and insisted on feeding the whole bunch of us. She made a pot roast with onions and potatoes even though she couldn't touch it herself.

She told us Mrs. Hoge had passed away in January, just a few weeks after I left.

"We knew it was coming, of course," she said to Esperanza and Estevan. "She had the disease where you shake all the time."

"That was a disease?" I asked. "I had no idea it was something you could die from. I thought it was just old age."

"No," Irene shook her head gravely. "Parkerson's."

"Who?" I asked.

"That's the disease," she said. "I notice she's talking now." She meant Turtle, who was busily naming every vegetable on Esperanza's plate. She named them individually so it went like this: "Tato, carrot, carrot, carrot, carrot, tato, onion," et cetera. Toward the end of the meal she also said "car," because underneath all the food the plates had pictures of old-timey cars on them.

After the others went to bed I stayed up with Irene, who was expecting her husband in from Ponca City after midnight. We sat on high stools behind the desk in the bright front office, looking out through the plate glass at the highway and the long, flat plain behind it. She told me she missed Mrs. Hoge something fierce.

"Oh, I know she wasn't *kind,*" Irene said, her thinned-down bosom heaving with a long, sad sigh. "It was always 'Here's my daughter-in-law Irene that can't make up a bed with hospital corners and is proud of it.' But really I think she meant well."

The next morning we had to make a decision. Either we would go straight to the sanctuary church, which was a little to the east of Oklahoma City, or we could all stay together for another day. They could come with me to the bar where I'd been presented with Turtle, to help me look for whatever I thought I was going to find in the way of Turtle's relatives. I admitted to them that I could use the moral support, but on the other hand I would understand if they didn't want to risk being on the road any more than they had to be. Without hesitation, they said they wanted to go with me.

Retracing my original route became a little more complicated. I had left the interstate when my steering column set itself free, that much I knew, and I'd stayed on a side road for several hours before joining back up with the main highway. I could remember hardly any exact details from that night, in the way of landmarks, and of course there were precious few there to begin with.

The clue that tipped me off was a sign to the Pioneer Woman Museum. I remembered that. We found a two-lane road that I was pretty sure was the right one.

As soon as we left the interstate, trading the fast out-of-state tourist cars for the companionship of station wagons and pickup trucks packed with families, we were on the Cherokee Nation. You could feel it. We began to understand that Oklahoma had been a good choice: Estevan and Esperanza could blend in here. Practically half the people we saw were Indians.

"Do Cherokees look like Mayans?" I asked Estevan.

"No," he said.

"Would a white person know that?"

"No."

After a little bit I asked him, "Would a Cherokee?"

"Maybe, maybe not." He was smiling his perfect smile.

I asked Turtle if anything looked familiar. When I looked in the rear-view mirror I caught sight of her on Esperanza's lap, playing with Esperanza's hair and trying on Esperanza's sunglasses. Later I saw them playing a clapping-hands game. The two of them looked perfectly content: "Madonna and Child with Pink Sunglasses." Nobody, not even a Mayan, could say they weren't. One time I thought—though I couldn't swear it—I heard her call Turtle Ismene. I was getting a cold feeling in the bottom of my stomach.

I tried to keep myself cheerful. "I always tell Turtle she's as good as the ones that came over on the *Mayflower,*" I told Estevan. "They landed at Plymouth Rock. She just landed in a Plymouth."

Estevan didn't laugh. In all fairness, I might not have told him before that she was born in a car, but also he was preoccupied, going over and over the life history he had invented for himself and his Cherokee bride. He was quite imaginative. He had a whole little side plot about how his parents had disapproved of the marriage, but had softened their hearts when they saw what a lovely woman Hope was.

"Steven and Hope," he said. "But we need a last name."

"How about Two Two?" I said. "That's a good solid Cherokee name. It's been in my family for months."

"Two Two," he repeated solemnly.

I missed my own car. I missed Lou Ann, who always laughed at my jokes.

I was positive I wouldn't recognize the place, if it was even still there, but as soon as I laid eyes on it I knew. A little brick building with a Budweiser sign, and across the parking lot a garage. The garage looked closed.

"That's it," I said. I slowed down. "What do I do?"

"Stop the car," Estevan suggested, but I kept going. My heart was pounding like a piston. A quarter of a mile down the road I stopped.

"I'm sorry, but I can't do this," I said.

We all sat quietly for a minute.

"What is the worst thing that can happen?" Estevan asked.

"I don't know. That I won't find anybody that knows Turtle. Or that I will, and they'll want her back." I thought for a minute. "The worst thing would be that we lose her, some way," I said finally.

"What if you don't go in?"

"We lose her."

Estevan gave me a hug. "For courage," he said. Then Esperanza gave me a hug. Then Turtle did. I turned the car around and drove back to the bar.

"First let me go in alone," I said.

It looked like a different place. I remembered all the signs—IN CASE OF FIRE YELL FIRE. They were gone. Blue gingham curtains hung in the windows and there were glasses of plastic roses and bachelor buttons on all the tables. I would have walked right out again, but I recognized the TV. Good picture, but no sound. And there was the same postcard rack too, although it seemed to have changed its focus, placing more emphasis on scenic lakes and less on Oral Roberts University.

A teenaged girl in jeans and an apron came through a door from the kitchen. She had a round Indian face behind large, blue-rimmed glasses.

"Get you some coffee?" she asked cheerfully.

"Okay," I said, and sat down at the counter.

"Now, what else can I do for you?"

"I'm not sure. I'm looking for somebody."

"Oh, who? Were you meeting them here for lunch?"

"No, it's not like that. It's kind of complicated. I was in here last December and met some people I have to find again. I think they might live around here. It's very important."

She leaned on her elbows on the counter. "What was their names?"

"I don't know. There was a woman, and two men in cowboy hats. I think one of them might have been her husband, or her boyfriend. I know, this isn't getting anywhere. Ed knew their names."

"Ed?"

"Isn't that who runs this place?"

"No. My parents own it. We bought it in March, I think. Or April."

"Well, would your parents know Ed? Would he be around here?"

She shrugged. "The place was just up for sale. I think whoever owned it before musta died. It was gross in here."

"You mean he died *in here?*"

She laughed. "No, I just mean all the dirt and stuff. I had to scrub the grease off the back of the stove. It was *black.* I was thinking about running away and going back home. We're not from here, we're from over on tribal land. But I like some kids here now."

"Do any of the same people come in here that always did? Like men, drinking after work and that kind of thing."

She shrugged.

"Right. How would you know."

I stared at my cup of coffee as though I might find the future in it, like the chickenbone lady back home. "I don't know what to do," I finally said.

She nodded out the window. "Maybe you should bring your friends in for lunch."

I did. We sat at one of the spick-and-span tables with plastic flowers and had grilled-cheese sandwiches. Turtle bounced in her seat and fed tiny pieces of grilled cheese to Shirley Poppy. Estevan and Esperanza were quiet. Of course. You couldn't speak Spanish in this part of the country—it would be noticed.

After lunch I went up to the register to pay. No other member of the family had materialized from the kitchen, so I asked the girl if there was anyone else around that might help me. "Do you know the guy that runs the garage next door? Bob Two Two?"

She shook her head. "He never came over here, because we serve beer. He was some religion, I forget what."

"Are you telling me he's dead now too? Give me a break."

"Nah, he just closed. I think Pop said he was getting a place closer to Okie City."

"It wasn't even a year ago that I was here."

She shrugged. "Nobody ever comes out here anyway. I never could see who would go to that garage in the first place."

I put the change in my pocket. "Well, thanks anyway," I told her. "Thanks for trying to help. I hope your family does all right by this place. You've fixed it up real nice."

She made a small gesture with her shoulders. "Thanks."

"What did you mean when you said you came from tribal land? Isn't this the Cherokee Nation?"

"*This!* No, this is nothing. This is kind of the edge of it I guess, they do have that sign up the road that says maintained by the Cherokee tribe. But the main part's over east, toward the mountains."

"Oklahoma has mountains?"

She looked at me as though I might be retarded. "Of course. The Ozark Mountains. Come here, look." She went over to the postcard rack and picked out some of the scenery cards. "See how pretty? That's Lake o' the Cherokees; we used to go there every summer. My brothers like to fish, but I hate the worms. And this is another place on the same lake, and this is Oologah Lake."

"That looks beautiful," I said. "That's the Cherokee Nation?"

"Part of it," she said. "It's real big. The Cherokee Nation isn't any one place exactly. It's people. We have our own government and all."

"I had no idea," I said. I bought the postcards. I would send one to Mama, although she was married now of course and didn't have any use for our old ace in the hole, the head rights. But even so I owed an apology to great grandpa, dead though he was.

As we were leaving I asked her about the TV. "That's the one thing that's still the same. What's with it anyway? Doesn't anybody ever turn the sound up?"

"The stupid thing is broke. You get the sound on one station and the picture on the other. See?" She flipped to the next channel, which showed blue static but played the sound perfectly. It was a commercial for diet Coke. "My gramma likes to leave it on 9, she's just about blind anyway, but the rest of us like it on 8."

"Do you ever get the Oral Roberts shows?"

She shrugged. "I guess. I like Magnum P.I."

Somehow I had been thinking that once we got back in the car and on the road again, everything would make sense and I would know what to do. I didn't. This time I didn't even know which way to head the car. If only Lou Ann were here, I thought. Lou Ann with her passion for playing Mrs. Neighborhood Detective. I knew she would say I was giving up too easily. But what was I supposed to do? Stake out the bar for a week or two and see if the woman ever showed up again? Would I recognize her if she did? Would she be willing to go to Oklahoma City with me to sign papers?

There had never been the remotest possibility of finding any relative of Turtle's. I had driven across the country on a snipe hunt. A snipe hunt is a joke on somebody, most likely some city cousin. You send him out in the woods with a paper bag and see how long it takes for him to figure out what a fool he is.

But it also occurred to me to wonder why I had come this far. Generally speaking, I am not a fool. I must have wanted something, and wanted it badly, to believe that hard in snipes.

"I can't give up," I said as I turned the car around. I smacked my palms on the steering wheel again and again. "I just can't. I want to go to Lake o' the Cherokees. Don't even ask me why."

They didn't ask.

"So do you want to come with me, or should we take you to your church now? Really, I can go either way."

They wanted to come with me. I can see, looking back on it, that we were getting attached.

"We'll have a picnic by the lake, and stay in a cabin, and maybe find a boat somewhere and go out on the water. We'll have a vacation," I told them. "When's the last time you two had a vacation?"

Estevan thought for a while. "Never."

"Me too," I said.

FIFTEEN

Lake o' the Cherokees

Esperanza and Estevan were transformed in an unexplainable way over the next two hours. They showed a new side, like the Holy Cards we used to win for attendance in summer Bible school: mainly there was a picture of Jesus on the cross, a blurred, shimmering picture with flecks of pink and blue scattered through it, but tip it just so and you could see a dove flying up out of His chest. That was the Holy Ghost.

We must have been getting closer to the heart of the Cherokee Nation, whatever or wherever it was, because as we drove east we saw fewer and fewer white people. Everybody and his mother-in-law was an Indian. All the children were Indian children, and the dogs looked like Indian dogs. At one point a police car came up behind us and we all got quiet and kept an eye out, as we had grown accustomed to doing, but when he passed us we just had to laugh. The cop was an Indian.

It must have been a very long time since Esperanza and Estevan had been in a place where they looked just like everybody else, including cops. The relief showed in their bodies. I believe they actually grew taller. And Turtle fit right in too; this was her original home. I was the odd woman out.

Although, of course, I supposedly had enough Cherokee in me that it counted. I knew I would never really claim my head rights, and probably couldn't even if I wanted to—they surely had a statute of limitations or some such thing. But it was a relief to know the Cherokee Nation wasn't a complete bust. I read a story once, I might have this confused but I think the way it went was that this lady had a diamond necklace put away in a safe-deposit box all her life, thinking that if she ever got desperate she could sell it, only to find out on her deathbed that it was rhinestones. That was more or less the way I felt on that first terrible trip through Oklahoma.

It was nice to find out, after all, that Mama's and my ace in the hole for all those years really did have a few diamonds in it: Lake Oologah, Lake o' the Cherokees.

"The Cherokee Nation has its own Congress and its own President," I reported to Esperanza and Estevan. "Did you know that?" I wasn't sure if I actually knew this or was just elaborating on what the girl in the restaurant had told me.

The scenery grew more interesting by the mile. At first it was still basically flat but it kind of rolled along, like a great green, rumpled bedsheet. Then there were definite hills. We passed through little towns with Indian names that reminded me in some ways of Kentucky. Here and there we saw trees.

Once, all of a sudden, Turtle shouted, "Mama!" She was pointing out the window.

My heart lost its beat for a second. To my knowledge she had never referred to anyone as Mama. We looked, but couldn't see anybody at all along the road. There was only a gas station and a cemetery.

Turtle and Esperanza were becoming inseparable. Turtle sat on her lap, played with her, and whined at the rest stops when Esperanza wanted to go to the bathroom by herself. I suppose I should have been grateful for the babysitting. I couldn't quite imagine how I would have kept Turtle entertained by myself, while I was driving. We'd managed a long trip before, of course, but that was in Turtle's catatonic period. At that stage of her life, I don't think she would have minded much if you'd put her in a box and shipped her to Arizona. Now everything was different.

Lake o' the Cherokees was a place where you could imagine God might live. There were enough trees.

I still would have to say it's stretching the issue to call the Ozarks mountains, but they served. I felt secure again, with my hopes for something better tucked just out of sight behind the next hill.

We found a cottage right off the bat. It was perfect: there were two bedrooms, a fireplace with a long-tailed bird (stuffed) on the mantel, and a bathroom with an old claw-foot tub (one leg poked down through the floor, but the remaining three looked steadfast). It was one of a meandering row of mossy, green-roofed cottages lined up along a stream bank in a place called Saw Paw Grove.

They didn't want to take it for the night, but I insisted. We had the money from Mattie, and besides, it wasn't that expensive. No more than we would have spent the night before if I hadn't had connections at the Broken Arrow. It took some doing, but I convinced Estevan and Esperanza that we weren't doing anything wrong. We deserved to have a good time, just for this one day.

I told them to think of it as a gift. "As an ambassador of my country I'm presenting you with an expenses-paid one-day vacation for four at Lake o' the Cherokees. If you don't accept, it will be an international incident."

They accepted. We sat on the cottage's little back porch, watching out for Turtle and the holes where the floorboards were rotted out, and stared at the white stream as it went shooting by. No water in Arizona was ever in that much of a hurry. The moss and the ferns looked so good I just drank up all that green. Even the rotten floor planks looked wonderful. In Arizona things didn't rot, not even apples. They just mummified. I realized that I had come to my own terms with the desert, but my soul was thirsty.

Growing all along the creek there were starry red-and-yellow flowers that bobbed on the ends of long, slender stems. Turtle informed us they were "combines," and we accepted her authority. Estevan climbed down the slick bank to pick them. I thought to myself, Where in the universe will I find another man who would risk his neck for a flower? He fell partway into the creek, soaking one leg up to the knee—mainly, I think, for our benefit. Even Esperanza laughed.

Something was going on inside of Esperanza. Something was thawing. Once I saw a TV program about how spring comes to Alaska. They made a big deal about the rivers starting to run again, showing huge chunks of ice rumbling and shivering and bashing against each other and breaking up. This is how it was with Esperanza. Behind her eyes, or deeper, in the arteries around her heart, something was starting to move. When she held Turtle on her lap she seemed honestly happy. Her eyes were clear and she spoke to Estevan and me directly, looking at our eyes.

Estevan survived his efforts and handed a flower to each of us. He kissed Esperanza and said something in Spanish that included "mi amor," and fixed the flower in her buttonhole so that it sprang out from her chest like one of those snake-in-the-can tricks. I could imagine them as a young couple, shy with each other, doing joky things like that. I braided the stem of my flower into my hair. Turtle waved hers up and down like a drum major's baton, shouting, "Combine, combine, combine!" None of us, apparently, was able to think of any appropriate way of following this command.

I was supposed to be calling them Steven and Hope now so they could begin getting used to it. I couldn't. I had changed my own name like a dirty shirt, but I couldn't help them change theirs.

"I love your names," I said. "They're about the only thing you came here with that you've still got left. I think you should only be Steven and Hope when you need to pull the wool over somebody's eyes, but keep your own names with your friends."

Neither of them said anything, but they didn't urge me again to call them by false names.

Later we found a place that rented boats by the half hour and Estevan and I took one out onto the lake. Esperanza didn't want to go. She didn't know how to swim, and I wasn't sure about Turtle, so the two of them stayed on the shore feeding ducks.

Estevan and I took turns rowing and waving at the shore until Turtle was a tiny bouncing dot. By then we were in the very middle of the lake, and we let ourselves drift. The sun bounced off the water, making bright spangles and upside-down shadows on our faces. I rolled my jeans up to my knees and dangled my bare feet over the side. There was a fishy-smelling assortment of things in the bottom of the boat, including a red-and-white line floater and a collection of pop-top rings from beer cans.

Estevan took off his shirt and lay back against the front of the boat, his hands clasped behind his head, exposing his smooth Mayan chest to the sun. And to me. How could he possibly have done this, if he had any idea how I felt? I knew that Estevan had walked a long, hard road beyond innocence, but still he sometimes did the most simple, innocent, heart-breaking things. As much as I have wanted anything, ever, I wanted to know how that chest would feel against my face. I looked toward the shore so he wouldn't see the water in my eyes.

I pulled the wilted flower out of my braid and twisted the stem in my fingers. "I'm going to miss you a lot," I said. "All of you. Both, I mean."

Estevan didn't say he was going to miss all of me. We knew this was a conversation we couldn't afford to get into. In more ways than one, since we were renting by the half-hour.

After a while he said, "Throw a penny and make a wish."

"That's wasteful," I said, kicking my toes in the water. "My mother always said a person that throws away money deserves to be poor. I'd rather be one of the undeserving poor."

"Undeservedly," he corrected me, smiling.

"One of the undeservedly poor." Even my English was going to fall apart without him.

"Then we can wish on these." He picked up one of the pop-top rings. "These are appropriate for American wishes."

I made two American wishes on pop tops in Lake o' the Cherokees. Only one of them had the remotest possibility of coming true.

At dusk we found picnic tables in a little pine forest near the water's edge. Both Mattie and Irene had packed us fruit and sandwiches for the road, most of which were still in the Igloo cooler in the trunk. We threw an old canvas poncho over the table and spread out the pickle jars and bananas and apples and goose-liver sandwiches and everything else. Other picnickers here and there were working on modest little balanced meals of things that all went together, keeping the four food groups in mind, but we weren't proud. Our party was in the mood for a banquet.

The sun was setting behind us but it lit up the clouds in the east, making one of those wraparound sunsets. Reflections of pink clouds floated across the surface of the lake. It looked like a corny painting. If I didn't let my mind run too far ahead, I felt completely happy.

Turtle still had a good deal of energy, and was less interested in eating than in bouncing and jumping and running in circles around the trees. Every so often she found a pine cone, which she would bring back and give to me or to Esperanza. I tried very hard not to keep count of whose pile of pine cones was bigger. Turtle looked like a whirling dervish in overalls and a green-striped T-shirt. We hadn't realized how cooped up she must have felt in the car, because she was so good. It's funny how people don't give that much thought to what kids want, as long as they're being quiet.

It's also interesting how it's hard to be depressed around a three-year-old, if you're paying attention. After a while, whatever you're mooning about begins to seem like some elaborate adult invention.

Estevan asked us which we liked better, sunrise or sunset. We were all speaking in English now, because Esperanza had to get into practice. I couldn't object to this—it was a matter of survival.

"Sun set, because sun rise comes too early," Esperanza said, and giggled. She was very self-conscious in English, and seemed to have a whole different personality.

I told them that I liked sunrise better. "Sunset always makes me feel a little sad."

"Why?"

I peeled a banana and considered this. "I think because of the way I was raised. There was always so damn much work to do. At sunrise it always seems like you've got a good crack at getting everything done, but at sunset you know that you didn't."

Esperanza directed our attention to Turtle, who was hard at work burying Shirley Poppy in the soft dirt at the base of a pine tree. I had to laugh.

I went over and squatted beside her at the foot of the tree. "I've got to explain something to you, sweet pea. Some things grow into bushes or trees when you plant them, but other things don't. Beans do, doll babies don't."

"Yes," Turtle said, patting the mound of dirt. "Mama."

It was the second time that day she had brought up a person named Mama. I registered this with something like an electric shock. It started in my hands and feet and moved in toward the gut.

I kneeled down and pulled Turtle into my lap. "Did you see your mama get buried like that?" I asked her.

"Yes."

It was one of the many times in Turtle's and my life together that I was to have no notion of what to do. I remembered Mattie saying how it was pointless to think you could protect a child from the world. If that had once been my intention, it should have been clear that with Turtle I'd never had a chance.

I held her in my arms and we rocked for a long time at the foot of the pine tree.

"I'm sorry," I said. "It's awful, awful sad when people die. You don't ever get to see them again. You understand that she's gone now, don't you?"

Turtle said, "Try?" She poked my cheek with her finger.

"Yeah, I'm crying." I leaned forward on my knees and pulled a handkerchief out of my back pocket.

"I know she must have loved you very much," I said, "but she had to go away and leave you with other people. The way things turned out is that she left you with me."

Out on the lake people in boats were quietly casting their lines into the shadows. I remembered fishing on my own as a kid, and even younger going out with Mama, probably not being much help. I had a very clear memory of throwing a handful of rocks in the water and watching the fish dart away. And screaming my heart out. I wanted them, and knew of no reason why I shouldn't have them. When I was Turtle's age I had never had anyone or anything important taken from me.

I still hadn't. Maybe I hadn't started out with a whole lot, but pretty nearly all of it was still with me.

After a while I told Turtle, "You already know there's no such thing as promises. But I'll try as hard as I can to stay with you."

"Yes," Turtle said. She wiggled off my lap and returned to her dirt pile. She patted a handful of pine needles onto the mound. "Grow beans," she said.

"Do you want to leave your dolly here?" I asked.

"Yes."

Later that night I asked Esperanza and Estevan if they would be willing to do one more thing with me. For me, really. I explained that it was a favor, a very big one, and then I explained what it was.

"You don't have to say yes," I said. "I know it involves some risk for you, and if you don't feel like you can go through with it I'll understand. Don't answer now, because I want to be sure you've really thought about it. You can tell me in the morning."

Esperanza and Estevan didn't want to think about it. They told me, then and there, they wanted to do it.

SIXTEEN

Soundness of Mind and Freedom of Will

Mr. Jonas Wilford Armistead was a tall, white-haired man who seemed more comfortable with the notarizing part of his job than with the public. Even though he had been forewarned, when all of us came trooping into his office he seemed overwhelmed and showed a tendency to dither. He moved papers and pens and framed pictures from one side of his desk to the other and wouldn't sit down until all of us could be seated, which unfortunately didn't happen for quite a while because there weren't enough chairs. Mr. Armistead sent his secretary, Mrs. Cleary, next door to borrow a chair from the real-estate office of Mr. Wenn.

Mr. Armistead wore a complicated hearing aid that had ear parts, and black-and-white wires and a little silver box that had to be placed for maximum effectiveness on exactly the right spot on his desk, which he seemed unable to find. If he ever did, I thought I might suggest to him that he mark this special zone with paint as they do on a basketball court.

The silver box had tiny controls along one side, and Mr. Armistead also fiddled with these almost constantly, apparently without much success. Mrs. Cleary seemed during their working coexistence to have adjusted her volume accordingly. Even when she was talking to us, she practically shouted. It had an intimidating effect, especially on Esperanza.

But we all managed small talk while we waited. Which was all the more admirable when you consider that not one word any of us was saying was true, so far as I know. Estevan was an astonishingly good liar, going into great detail about the Oklahoma town where he and his wife had been living, and the various jobs he'd had. I talked about my plans to move to Arizona to live with my sister and her little boy. I think we were all amazed by the things that were popping out of our heads like corn.

Sister, indeed. I remembered begging my mother for a sister when I was very young. She'd said she was all for it, but that if I got one it would have to be arranged by means of a miracle. At the time I'd had no idea what she meant. Now I knew about celibacy.

Mrs. Cleary returned in due time, rolling a chair on its little wheels, and asked several questions about what forms would need to be typed up. We shuffled around again as we made room for Estevan and the new chair, and Mr. Armistead finally agreed to come down from his great height and roost like a long-legged stork on the chair behind his desk.

"It became necessary to make formal arrangements," Estevan explained, "because our friend is leaving the state."

Esperanza nodded.

"Mr. and Mrs. Two Two, do you understand that this is a permanent agreement?" He spoke very slowly, the way people often speak to not-very-bright children and foreigners, although I'm positive that Mr. Armistead had no inkling that the Two Two family came from any farther away than the Cherokee Nation.

They nodded again. Esperanza was holding Turtle tightly in her arms and beginning to get tears in her eyes. Already it was clear that, of the three of us, she was first in line for the Oscar nomination.

He went on, "After about six months a new birth certificate will be issued, and the old one destroyed. After that you cannot change your minds for any reason. This is a very serious decision."

"There wasn't any birth certificate issued," Mrs. Cleary shouted. "It was born on tribal lands."

"She," I said. "In a Plymouth," I added.

"We understand," Estevan said.

"I just want to make absolutely certain."

"We know Taylor very well," Estevan replied. "We know she will make a good mother to this child."

Even though they were practically standing on it, Mr. Armistead and Mrs. Cleary seemed to think of "tribal land" as some distant, vaguely civilized country. This, to them, explained everything including the fact that Hope, Steven, and Turtle had no identification other than a set of black-and-white souvenir pictures taken of the three of them at Lake o' the Cherokees. It was enough that I, a proven citizen with a Social Security card, was willing to swear on pain of I-don't-know-what (and sign documents to that effect) that they were all who they said they were.

By this point we had run out of small talk. I was over my initial nervousness, but without it I felt drained. Just sitting in that small, crowded office, trying to look the right way and say the right thing, seemed to take a great deal of energy. I couldn't imagine how we were all going to get through this.

"We love her, but we cannot take care for her," Esperanza said suddenly. Her accent was complicated by the fact that she was crying, but it didn't faze Mr. Armistead or Mrs. Cleary. Possibly they thought it was a Cherokee accent.

"We've talked it over," I said. I began to worry a little about what was going on here.

"We love her. Maybe someday we will have more children, but not now. Now is so hard. We move around so much, we have nothing, no home." Esperanza was sobbing. This was no act. Estevan handed her a handkerchief, and she held it to her face.

"Try, Ma?" Turtle said.

"That's right, Turtle," I said quietly. "She's crying."

Estevan reached over and lifted Turtle out of her arms. He stood her up, her small blue sneakers set firmly on his knees, and held her gently by the shoulders and looked into her eyes. "You must be a good girl. Remember. Good and strong, like your mother." I wondered which mother he meant, there were so many possibilities. I was touched to think he might mean me.

"Okay," Turtle said.

He handed her carefully back to Esperanza, who folded her arms around Turtle and held her against her chest, rocking back and forth for a very long time with her eyes squeezed shut. Tears drained down the shallow creases in her cheeks.

The rest of us watched. Mr. Armistead stopped fidgeting and Mrs. Cleary's hands on her papers went still. Here were a mother and her daughter, nothing less. A mother and child—in a world that could barely be bothered with mothers and children—who were going to be taken apart. Everybody believed it. Possibly Turtle believed it. I did.

Of all the many times when it seemed to be so, that was the only moment in which I really came close to losing Turtle. I couldn't have taken her from Esperanza. If she had asked, I couldn't have said no.

When she let go, letting Turtle sit gently back on her lap, Turtle had the sniffles.

Esperanza wiped Turtle's nose with Estevan's big handkerchief and kissed her on both cheeks. Then she unclasped the gold medallion of St. Christopher, guardian saint of refugees, and put it around Turtle's neck. Then she gave Turtle to me.

Esperanza told me, "We will know she is happy and growing with a good heart."

"Thank you," I said. There was nothing else I could say.

It took what seemed like an extremely long time to draw up a statement, which Mrs. Cleary shuttled off to type. She came back and was sent off twice more to make repairs. After several rounds of White-out we had managed to create an official document:

> We, the undersigned, Mr. Steven Tilpec Two Two and Mrs. Hope Roberta Two Two, being the sworn natural parents of April Turtle Two Two, do hereby grant custody of our only daughter to Ms. Taylor Marietta Greer, who will from this day forward become her sole guardian and parent.
>
> We do solemnly swear and testify to our soundness of mind and freedom of will.
>
> Signed before witnesses on this ——— day of ———, in the office of Jonas Wilford Armistead, Oklahoma City, Oklahoma.

Mrs. Cleary went off once again to Mr. Wenn's office, this time to borrow his secretary Miss Brindo to be a second witness to the signing. Miss Brindo, who appeared to have at least enough Cherokee in her to claim head rights, had on tight jeans and shiny red high heels, and snapped her gum. She had a complicated haircut that stood straight up on top, and something told me she led a life that was way too boring for her potential. I wished she could have known what she was really witnessing that morning.

In a way, I wish all of them could know, maybe twenty years later or so when it's long past doing anything about it. Mrs. Cleary's and Mr. Armistead's hair would have stood straight up too, to think what astonishing things could be made legal in a modest little office in the state of Oklahoma.

We shook hands all around, I got the rest of the adoption arrangements straightened out with Mr. Armistead, and we filed out, a strange new combination of friends and family. I could see the relief across Estevan's back and shoulders. He held Esperanza's hand. She was still drying tears but her face was changed. It shone like a polished thing, something old made new.

They both wore clean work shirts, light blue with faded elbows. Esperanza had on a worn denim skirt and flat loafers. I had asked them please not to wear their very best for this occasion, not their Immigration-fooling clothes. It had to look like Turtle was going to be better off with me. When they came out that morning dressed as refugees I had wanted to cry out, No! I was wrong. Don't sacrifice your pride for me. But this is how badly they wanted to make it work.

SEVENTEEN

Rhizobia

It had crossed my mind that Turtle might actually have recognized the cemetery her mother was buried in, and if so, I wondered whether I ought to take her back there to see it. But my concerns were soon laid to rest. We passed four cemeteries on the way to the Pottawatomie Presbyterian Church of St. Michael and All Angels, future home of Steven and Hope Two Two, and at each one of them Turtle called out, "Mama!"

There would come a time when she would just wave at the sight of passing gravestones and quietly say, "Bye bye."

Finding the church turned out to be a chase around Robin Hood's barn. Mattie's directions were to the old church. The congregation had since moved its home of worship plus its pastor and presumably its refugees into a new set of buildings several miles down the road. I was beginning to form the opinion that Oklahomans were as transient a bunch as the people back home who slept on grass-flecked bedrolls in Roosevelt Park.

The church was a cheery-looking place, freshly painted white with a purple front door and purple gutters. When Mattie used to talk about the Underground Railroad, by which she meant these churches and the people who carried refugees between them, it had always sounded like the dark of night. I'd never pictured old white Lincolns with soda pop spilled on the seats, and certainly not white clapboard churches with purple gutters.

Reverend and Mrs. Stone seemed greatly relieved to see us, since they had apparently expected us a day or two earlier, but no one made an issue of it. They helped carry things up a sidewalk bordered with a purple fringe of ageratums into the small house behind the parsonage. Meanwhile Estevan and I worked on getting possessions sorted out. Things had gotten greatly jumbled during the trip, and Turtle's stuff was everywhere. She was like a pack rat, taking possession of any item that struck her fancy (like Esperanza's hairbrush) and tucking another one into its place (like a nibbled cracker). Turtle herself was exhausted with the events of the day, or days, and was in the back seat sleeping the sleep of the dead, as Lou Ann would put it. Esperanza and Estevan had already said goodbye to her in a very real way back in Mr. Armistead's office, and didn't think there was any need to wake her up again. But I stood firm.

"It's happened too many times that people she loved were whisked away from her without any explanation. I want her to see you, and see this place, so she'll know we're leaving you here."

She woke reluctantly, and groggily accepted my explanation of what was happening. "Bye bye," she said, standing up on the seat and waving through the open back window.

I think we all felt the same exhaustion. There are times when it just isn't possible to say goodbye. I hugged Esperanza and shook hands with Reverend and Mrs. Stone in a kind of daze.

The day seemed too bright, too full of white clapboard and cheerful purple flowers, for me to be losing two good friends forever.

I was left with Estevan, who was checking under the back seat for the last time. I checked the trunk. "You ought to take some of this food," I said. "Turtle and I will never eat it all; it will just go to waste. At least the things there are whole jars of, like mustard and pickles." I bent over the cooler, stacking and unstacking the things that were swimming in melted ice in the bottom.

Estevan put his hand on my arm. "Taylor."

I straightened up. "What's going to happen to you here? What will you do?"

"Survive. That has always been our intention."

"But what kind of work will you find around here? I can't imagine they have Chinese restaurants, which is probably a good thing. Oh God," I put my knuckle in my mouth. "Shut me up."

Estevan smiled. "I would never pray for that."

"I'm just afraid for you. And for Esperanza. I'm sorry for saying this, it's probably a very nice place, but I can't stand to think of you stuck here forever."

"Don't think of us here forever. Think of us back in Guatemala with our families. Having another baby. When the world is different from now."

"When will that ever be," I said. "Never."

"Don't say that." He touched my cheek. I was afraid I was going to cry, or worse. That I would throw my arms around his ankles like some lady in a ridiculous old movie and refuse to let him go.

When tears did come to me it was a relief. That it was only tears. "Estevan, I know it doesn't do any good to say things like this, but I don't want to lose you. I've never lost anybody I loved, and I don't think I know how to." I looked away, down the flat, paved street. "I've never known anybody like you."

He took both my hands in his. "Nor I you, Taylor."

"Can you write? Would it be safe, I mean? You could use a fake return address or something."

"We can send word by way of Mattie. So you will know where we are and what happens to us."

"I wish that didn't have to be all."

"I know." His black pupils moved back and forth between my eyes.

"But it does, doesn't it? There's no way around the hurt, is there? You just have to live with it."

"Yes. I'm sorry."

"Estevan, do you understand what happened back there in that office, with Esperanza?"

"Yes."

"I keep thinking it was a kind of, what would you call it?"

"A catharsis."

"A catharsis," I said. "And she seems happy, honest to God, as happy as if she'd really found a safe place to leave Ismene behind. But she's believing in something that isn't true. Do you understand what I'm saying? It seems wrong, somehow."

"Mi'ija, in a world as wrong as this one, all we can do is to make things as right as we can." He put his hands on my shoulders and kissed me very, very sweetly, and then he turned around and walked into the house.

All four of us had buried someone we loved in Oklahoma.

I called Mama from a pay phone at a Shell station. I dug two handfuls of coins out of my jeans pockets, splayed them out on the metal shelf, and dialed. I was scared to death she would hang up on me. She had every right. I hadn't said boo to her for almost two months, not even to congratulate her on getting married. She'd written to say they'd had a real nice time at the wedding and that Harland was moving into our house. Up until the wedding he'd always lived in a so-called bachelor apartment, which means a bed plus hot plate plus roach motel in his sock drawer, in back of El-Jay's Paint and Body.

There was static in the line. "Mama, I'm sorry to bother you," I said. "I'm just outside of Oklahoma City so I thought I'd give you a ring. It's a lot closer than Arizona."

"Is that you? Bless your heart, it is you! I'll swan. Now weren't you sweet to call." She sounded so far away.

"So how's it going, Mama? How's married life treating you?"

She lowered her voice. "Something's wrong, isn't it?"

"Why would you think that?"

"Either you've got a bad cold or you've been crying. Your sound's all up in your head."

The tears started coming again, and I asked Mama to hang on just a minute. I had to put down the receiver to blow my nose. The one thing Lou Ann hadn't thought of was that I should have packed two dozen hankies.

When I got on the line again the operator was asking for more coins, so I dropped them in. Mama and I listened to the weird bonging song and didn't say anything to each other for a little bit.

"I just lost somebody I was in love with," I finally told her. "I just told him goodbye, and I'm never going to see him again."

"Well, what did you turn him loose for?" Mama wanted to know. "I never saw you turn loose of nothing you wanted."

"This is different, Mama. He wasn't mine to have."

She was quiet for a minute. We listened to the static playing up and down. It sounded like music from Mars.

"Mama, I feel like, I don't know what. Like I've died."

"I know. You feel like you'll never run into another one that's worth turning your head around for, but you will. You'll see."

"No, it's worse than that. I don't even care if I ever run into anybody else. I don't know if I even want to."

"Well, Taylor honey, that's the best way to be, is not on the lookout. That way you don't have to waste your time. Just let it slip up on you while you're going about your business."

"I don't think it will. I feel like I'm too old."

"Old my foot! Lordy, child, look at me. I'm so far over the hill I can't call the hogs to follow, and here I am running around getting married like a teenager. It's just as well you're not here, you'd have to tell everybody, Don't pay no mind that old fool, that's just my mother done got bit by the love bug at a elderly age."

I laughed. "You're not elderly," I said.

"It won't be as long as it has been."

"Mama, shush, don't even say that."

"Oh, don't you worry about me, I don't care if I drop over tomorrow. I'm having me a time."

"That's good, Mama. I'm glad, I really am."

"I've done quit cleaning houses. I take in some washing now and again to keep me out of trouble, but I'm getting about ready to join the Women's Garden Club instead. The only dirt I feel like scratching in nowdays is my own. They meet of a Thursday."

I couldn't believe it. Mama retired. "You know what's funny?" I said. "I just can't picture you without an iron or a mop or something like that in your hand."

"Oh, picture it, girl, it's a pretty sight. You remember Mrs. Wickentot? The one always wore high heels to the grocery and thought she was the cat's meow?"

"Yeah, I remember. Her kids never would give me the time of day. They called me the Cleaning Lady's Girl."

"Well you can put it to rest now, because I told her off good when I quit. I told her if I had the kind of trash she has in her closets, and the way she lets those boys run wild, what I found under their beds, I just wouldn't act so high and mighty, is what I told her."

"You told her that?"

"I did. And then some. All these years, you know, these ladies get to thinking they own you. That you wouldn't dare breathe a word for fear of getting fired. Now I think they're all scared to death I'm going to take out an ad in the paper."

I could just see it, right on the back page under the obituaries and deed-of-trust announcements. Or better yet, on the society page:

"Alice Jean Greer Elleston wishes to announce that Irma Ruebecker has fifty-two pints of molded elderberry jelly in her basement; Mae Richey's dishes would be carried off by the roaches if she didn't have hired help; and Minerva Wickentot's boys read porno magazines."

I couldn't stop laughing. "You ought to do it," I said. "It would be worth the thirty-five cents a word."

"Well, I probably won't. But it's good for a gal to have something like that up her sleeve, don't you think?" She chuckled. "It makes people respect you."

"Mama, you're really something. I don't know how the good Lord packed so much guts into one little person." The words were no sooner out of my mouth before I realized this was something she used to say to me. In high school, when I was having a rough time of it, she said it practically every other day.

"How's that youngun of yours?" Mama wanted to know. She never failed to ask.

"She's fine. She's asleep in the car right now or I'd put her on to say hi. Or peas and carrots, more likely. You never know what she's going to say."

"Well, she comes by that honest."

"Don't say that, Mama. That means it proves a baby's not a bastard. If it acts like you, it proves it's legitimate."

"I never thought about it that way."

"It's okay. I guess I'm just sensitive, you know, since she's not blood kin."

"I don't think blood's the only way kids come by things honest. Not even the main way. It's what you tell them, Taylor. If a person is bad, say, then it makes them feel better to tell their kids that they're even worse. And then that's just exactly what they'll grow up to be. You remember those Hardbines?"

"Yeah. Newt. I especially remember Newt."

"That boy never had a chance. He was just doing his best to be what everybody in Pittman said he was."

"Mama, you were always so good to me. I've been meaning to tell you that. You acted like I'd hung up the moon. Sometimes I couldn't believe you thought I was that good."

"But most of the time you believed it."

"Yeah. I guess most of the time I thought you were right."

The operator came on and asked for more money. My pile of change was thinning out. "We're just about done," I told her, but she said this was for the minutes that we'd already talked. I was out of quarters and had to use a whole slew of nickels.

"Guess what?" I said to Mama after the coins had dropped. "Here's the big news, Turtle's my real daughter. I adopted her."

"Did you? Now aren't you smart. How'd you do that?"

"Kind of by hook or crook. I'll tell you about it in a letter, it's too complicated for long distance. But it's all legal. I've got the papers to prove it."

"Lord have mercy. Married and a legal grandma all in the same summer. I can't wait to see her."

"We'll get back there one of these days," I said. "Not this trip, but we will. I promise."

"You better watch out, one of these days me and old Harland might just up and head for Arizona."

"I wish you would."

Neither of us wanted to hang up. We both said, "Bye," about three times.

"Mama," I said, "this is the last one. I'm hanging up now,

okay? Bye. And say hi to Harland for me too, okay? Tell him I said be good to you or I'll come whip his butt."

"I'll tell him."

Turtle and I had a whole afternoon to kill in Oklahoma City while we waited for some paperwork on the adoption to clear. After her nap she was raring to go. She talked up a storm, and wanted to play with Esperanza's medallion. I let her look at it in the side-view mirror.

"You have to keep it on," I told her. "That's St. Christopher, the guardian saint of refugees. I think you'd count. You're about as tempest-tossed as they come."

A tempest was a bad storm where things got banged around a lot. "Tempest-tossed" was from the poem on the Statue of Liberty that started out, "Give me your tired, your poor." Estevan could recite the whole poem. Considering how America had treated his kind, he must have thought this was the biggest joke ever to be carved in giant letters on stone.

I tried not to think about Estevan, but after a while decided it felt better to think about him than not to. And Turtle was good company. We cruised around in Mattie's Lincoln, a couple of free-wheeling females out on the town. Her favorite part was driving over the speed bumps at the Burger King.

During this time we had what I consider our second real conversation, the first having taken place at the foot of a pine tree at Lake o' the Cherokees. It went something like this:

"What do you want to do?"

"Okay."

"Are you hungry?"

"No."

"Well, where should we go, do you think? Anything in particular you want to see, as long as we're here in the big city?"

"Ma Woo-Ahn."

"Lou Ann's at home. We'll see her when we get home. And Edna and Virgie and Dwayne Ray and everybody."

"Waneway?"

"That's right."

"Ma Woo-Ahn?"

"That's right. Only let me tell you something. Starting right now, you've only got one Ma in the whole world. You know who that is?"

"Yes."

"Who?"

"Ma."

"That's right. That's me. You've got loads of friends. Lou Ann's your friend, and Edna and Mattie and all the others, and they all love you and take care of you sometimes. And Estevan and Esperanza were good friends too. I want you to remember them, okay?"

"Steban and Mespanza," she nodded gravely.

"Close enough," I said. "I know it's been confusing, there's been a lot of changes in the management. But from here on in I'm your Ma, and that means I love you the most. Forever. Do you understand what that means?"

"That beans?" She looked doubtful.

"You and me, we're sticking together. You're my Turtle."

"Urdle," she declared, pointing to herself.

"That's right. April Turtle Greer."

"Ableurdledear."

"Exactly."

On an impulse I called 1-800-THE LORD, from a public phone in the City Library where we'd come after Turtle decided she'd like to look at some books. I don't know what possessed me to do it. I'd been saving it up all this time, like Mama and our head rights, and now that I'd hit bottom and survived, I suppose I knew that I didn't really need any ace in the hole.

The line rang twice, three times, and then a recording came on. It told me that the Lord helps those that help themselves. Then it said that this was my golden opportunity to help myself and the entire Spiritual Body by making my generous contribution today to the Fountain of Faith missionary fund. If I would please hold the line an operator would be available momentarily to take my pledge. I held the line.

"Thank you for calling," she said. "Would you like to state your name and address and the amount of your pledge?"

"No pledge," I said. "I just wanted to let you know you've gotten me through some rough times. I always thought, 'If I really get desperate I can call 1-800-THE LORD.' I just wanted to tell you, you have been a Fountain of Faith."

She didn't know what to make of this. "So you don't wish to make a pledge at this time?"

"No," I said. "Do you wish to make a pledge to me at this time? Would you like to send me a hundred dollars, or a hot meal?"

She sounded irritated. "I can't do that, ma'am," she said.

"Okay, no problem," I said. "I don't need it, anyway. Especially now. I've got a whole trunkful of pickles and baloney."

"Ma'am, this is a very busy line. If you don't wish to make a pledge at this time."

"Look at it this way," I said. "We're even."

After I hung up I felt like singing and dancing through the wide, carpeted halls of the Oklahoma City Main Library. I once saw a movie where kids did cartwheels all over the library tables while Marian the librarian chased them around saying "Shhhh!" I felt just like one of those kids.

But instead Turtle and I snooped politely through the stacks. They didn't have *Old MacDonald Had an Apartment,* and as a matter of fact we soon became bored with the juvenile section and moved on to Reference. Some of these had good pictures. Turtle's favorite was the *Horticultural Encyclopedia.* It had pictures of vegetables and flowers that were far beyond both her vocabulary and mine. She sat on my lap and together we turned the big, shiny pages. She pointed out pictures of plants she liked, and I read about them. She even found a picture of bean trees.

"Well, you smart thing, I would have missed it altogether," I said. I would have, too. The picture was in black and white, and didn't look all that much like the ones back home in Roosevelt Park, but the caption said it was wisteria. I gave Turtle a squeeze. "What you are," I told her, "is a horticultural genius." I wouldn't have put it past her to say "horticulture" one of these days, a word I hadn't uttered myself until a few months ago.

Turtle was thrilled. She slapped the picture enthusiastically, causing the young man at the reference desk to look over his glasses at us. The book had to have been worth a hundred dollars at least, and it was very clean.

"Here, let's don't hit the book," I said. "I know it's exciting. Why don't you hit the table instead?"

She smacked the table while I read to her in a whisper about the life cycle of wisteria. It is a climbing ornamental vine found in temperate latitudes, and came originally from the Orient. It blooms in early spring, is pollinated by bees, and forms beanlike pods. Most of that we knew already. It actually is in the bean family, it turns out. Everything related to beans is called a legume.

But this is the most interesting part: wisteria vines, like other legumes, often thrive in poor soil, the book said. Their secret is something called rhizobia. These are microscopic bugs that live underground in little knots on the roots. They suck nitrogen gas right out of the soil and turn it into fertilizer for the plant.

The rhizobia are not actually part of the plant, they are separate creatures, but they always live with legumes: a kind of underground railroad moving secretly up and down the roots.

"It's like this," I told Turtle. "There's a whole invisible system for helping out the plant that you'd never guess was there." I loved this idea. "It's just the same as with people. The way Edna has Virgie, and Virgie has Edna, and Sandi has Kid Central Station, and everybody has Mattie. And on and on."

The wisteria vines on their own would just barely get by, is how I explained it to Turtle, but put them together with rhizobia and they make miracles.

At four o'clock we went to the Oklahoma County Courthouse to pick up the adoption papers. On Mr. Armistead's directions we found a big bright office where about twenty women sat typing out forms. All together they made quite a racket. The one who came to the front counter had round-muscled shoulders bulging under her pink cotton blazer and a half grown-out permanent in her straight Cherokee hair—a body trying to return to its natural state. She took our names and told us to have a seat, that it would be awhile. The waiting made me nervous, even though no one here looked important enough to stop what had already been set in motion. It was only a roomful of women with typewriters and African violets and pictures of their kids on their desks, doing as they were told. Still, I was afraid of sitting around looking anxious, as if one of them might catch sight of me fidgeting and cry out, "That's no adoptive mother, that's an impostor!" I could imagine them all then, scooting back their chairs and scurrying after me in their high-heeled pumps and tight skirts.

I needed to find something to do with myself. I asked if there was a telephone I could use for long distance. The muscular woman directed me to a pay phone out in the hall.

I dialed Lou Ann. It seemed to take an eternity for all the

right wires to connect, and when she finally did take the call she sounded even more nervous than I was, which was no help.

"It's okay, Lou Ann, everything's fine, I just called collect because I'm about out of quarters. But we'll have to keep it short or we'll run up the phone bill."

"Oh, hell's bells, Taylor, I don't even care." Lou Ann relaxed immediately once she knew we hadn't been mangled in a car crash. "I don't know how many times this week I've said I'd give a million dollars to talk to Taylor, so here's my chance. It just seems like everything in the world has happened. Where in the tarnation are you, anyway?"

"Oklahoma City. Headed home." I hesitated. "So what all's happened? You've decided to take Angel back? Or go up there and live in his yurdle, or whatever?"

"Angel? Heck no, not if you paid me. Listen, do you know what his mother told me? She said Angel just wants what he can't have. That I'd no sooner get up to Montana before he'd decide he'd had enough of me again. She said I was worth five or six of Angel."

"His own mother said that?"

"Can you believe it? Of course it was all in Spanish, I had to get it secondhand, but that was the general gist. And it makes sense, don't you think? Isn't there some saying about not throwing good loving after bad?"

"I think it's money they say that about. Good money after bad."

"Well, the same goes, is what I say. Oh shoot, can you hang on a second? Dwayne Ray's got something about ready to put in his mouth." I waited while she saved Dwayne Ray from his probably nineteen-thousandth brush with death. I loved Lou Ann.

Turtle was playing the game where you see how far you can get without touching the floor, walking only on the furniture. She was doing pretty well. There was a long row of old-fashioned wooden benches with spindle backs and armrests, lined up side by side down one wall of the hallway. For some reason it made me think of a chain gang—a hundred guys could sit on those benches, all handcuffed together. Or a huge family, I suppose, waiting for some important news. They could all hold hands.

"Okay, I'm back. So there's one more thing I have to tell you. Remember about the meteors? I called up Ramona Quiroz in San Diego, long distance. There wasn't any meteor shower. Not at all! Can you believe it? That was just the absolute last straw."

"Well, thank heavens," I said. It occurred to me that nobody else on earth could have understood what Lou Ann had just said.

"So that's the scoop, Angel's history. Now I'm seeing this guy from Red Hot Mama's by the name of Cameron John. Cameron's his first name and John's his last. Can you believe it?"

"I had a science teacher like that once," I said. "So does Red Hot Mama's give out a sex manual for the chile packers—how to do it without touching anything?"

"Taylor, I swear. He does tomatillos, and I just boss people now, as you very well know. Anyway I can't wait till you meet him, to see what you think. I know Mama would take one look and keel over dead—he's about seven feet tall and black as the ace of spades. But, Taylor, he is so sweet. My biggest problem is I keep feeling like I don't deserve anybody to be that nice to me. He invited me over for dinner and made this great something or other with rice and peanuts and I don't know what all. He used to be a Rastafarian."

"A what?"

"Rastafarian. It's a type of religion. And he's got this dog, a Doberman pinscher? Named Mister T, only Cameron didn't name it that, somebody gave it to him. It's got pierced ears, Taylor, I swear to God, with all these little gold rings. I can't believe I actually went out with this guy. I've gotten so brave hanging around you. Six months ago it would have scared the living daylights out of me just to have to walk by him on the street."

"Which, Cameron or Mister T?"

"Either one. And oh, I can't tell you, he was so good with Dwayne Ray. It just made me want to cry, or take a picture or something, to see this great big man playing with a little teeny pale white baby."

"So are you moving in with him, or what?" I tried my best to sound happy for her.

"What, me? No! Cameron's sweet as can be, but I'm real content with things the way they are now. To tell you the truth, I'm sure you're a lot easier to live with than him and Mister T."

"Oh. Well, I'm glad."

"Taylor, remember that time you were mad at me because you didn't want us to act like a family? That all we needed was a little dog named Spot? Well, don't get mad, but I told somebody that you and Turtle and Dwayne Ray were my family. Somebody at work said, 'Do you have family at home?' And I said, 'Sure,' without even thinking. I meant you all. Mainly I guess because we've been through hell and high water together. We know each other's good and bad sides, stuff nobody else knows."

It was hard for me to decide what to say.

"I don't mean till death do us part, or anything," she said. "But nothing on this earth's guaranteed, when you get right down to it, you know? I've been thinking about that. About how your kids aren't really *yours,* they're just these people that you try to keep an eye on, and hope you'll all grow up someday to like each other and still be in one piece. What I mean is, everything you ever get is really just on loan. Does that make sense?"

"Sure," I said. "Like library books. Sooner or later they've all got to go back into the night drop."

"Exactly. So what's the point worrying yourself sick about it. You'd just as well enjoy it while you've got it."

"I guess you could say we're family," I said. I watched Turtle climb over the armrests onto the last bench by the front door, which stood wide open to the street. She turned around and looked for me, and started making her way back.

There was silence on the other end of the line. "Lou Ann? You still there?" I asked.

"I can't stand the suspense, Taylor. Do you still have her?"

"Have who?"

"Turtle, for heaven's sake."

"Oh, sure. She's my legal daughter now."

"What!" Lou Ann shrieked. "You're kidding!"

"Nope. It's done, for all practical purposes. There's still some rigamarole in court for getting a birth certificate that takes about six months, but that's not too bad. It takes longer than that to make a kid from scratch, is how I look at it."

"I can't believe it. You found her mother? Or her aunt, or whatever it was?"

I looked down the hall. "I can't really talk here. We'll be home in two days at the outside, and I'll tell you everything then, okay? But it's going to take all night and a lot of junk food. Do you know what? I missed your salsa. The medium, though, not the firecracker style."

Lou Ann's breath came out like a slow leak in a tire. "Taylor, I was scared to death you'd come back without her."

We had cleared Oklahoma City and were out on the plain before sundown. It felt like old times, heading into the low western horizon. I let Turtle see the adoption certificate and she looked at it for a very long time, considering that there were no pictures on it.

"That means you're my kid," I explained, "and I'm your mother, and nobody can say it isn't so. I'll keep that paper for you till you're older, but it's yours. So you'll always know who you are."

She bobbed her head up and down like a hen, with her eyes fixed on something out the window that only she could see.

"You know where we're going now? We're going home."

She swung her heels against the seat. "Home, home, home, home," she sang.

The poor kid had spent so much of her life in a car, she probably felt more at home on the highway than anywhere else. "Do you remember home?" I asked her. "That house where we live with Lou Ann and Dwayne Ray? We'll be there before you know it."

But it didn't seem to matter to Turtle, she was happy where she was. The sky went from dust-color to gray and then cool black sparked with stars, and she was still wide awake. She watched the dark highway and entertained me with her vegetable-soup song, except that now there were people mixed in with the beans and potatoes: Dwayne Ray, Mattie, Esperanza, Lou Ann and all the rest.

And me. I was the main ingredient.

Animal Dreams

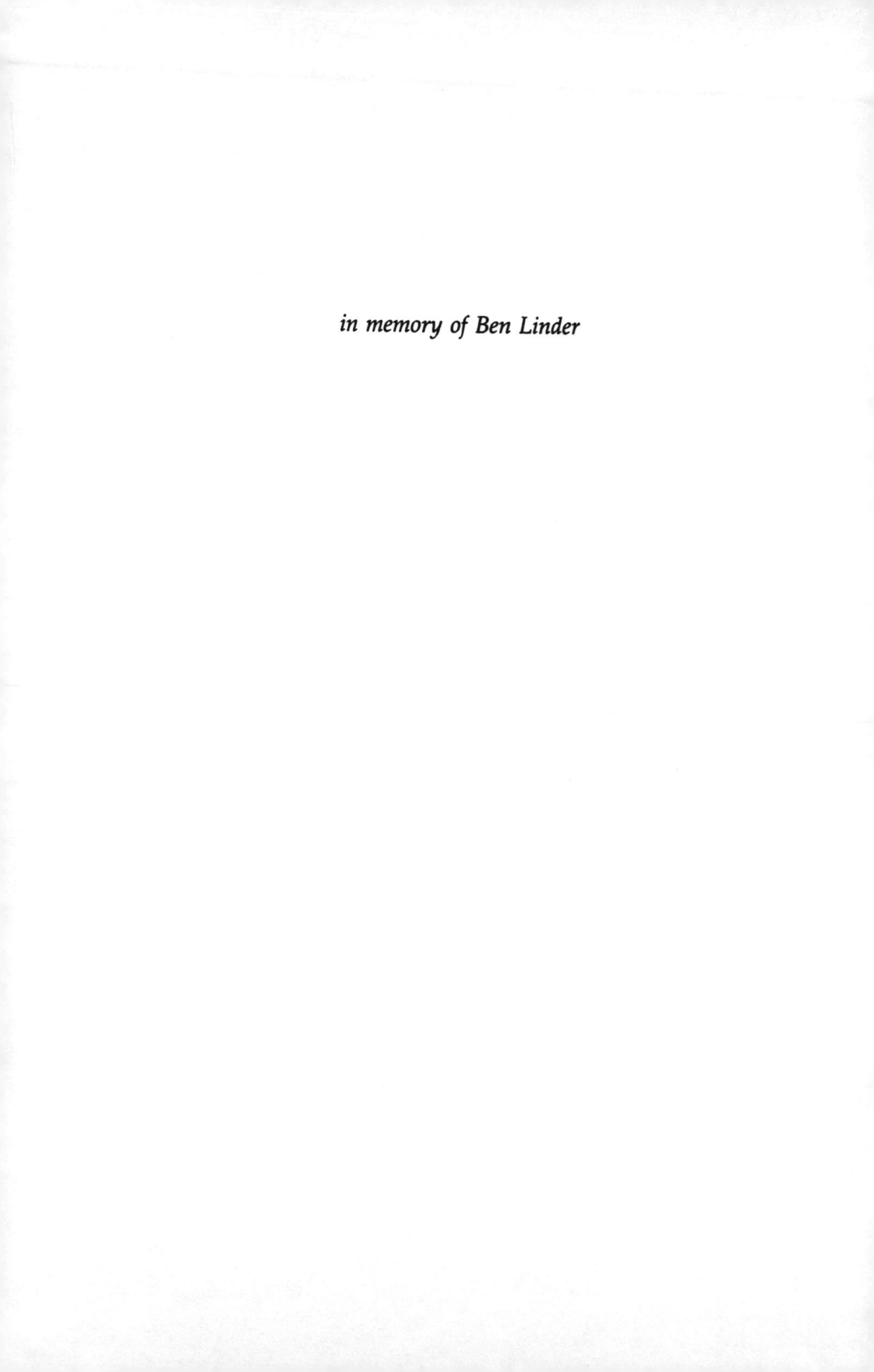

in memory of Ben Linder

CONTENTS

CONTENTS

AUTHOR'S NOTE

Grace, Arizona, and its railroad depot are imaginary, as is Santa Rosalia Pueblo, although it resembles the *Keresan* pueblos of northern New Mexico. Other places, and crises, in the book are actual.

I'm grateful for the example provided by many nonfictional volunteers from the United States who went to live and work for a new social order in Nicaragua during the decade following the 1979 revolution. Alongside the Nicaraguan people, they have made indelible contributions to that country, and to history.

For their support and contributions to this book I also owe a warm debt of thanks to my editor at Harper & Row, Janet Goldstein, my literary agent, Frances Goldin, and my remarkable family, especially Jessica Sampson (locomotive engineer extraordinaire), Wendell and Ginny Kingsolver, Joe Hoffmann, and Camille Hoffmann Kingsolver, who has attached me securely to this world.

HOMERO

1

THE NIGHT OF ALL SOULS

His two girls are curled together like animals whose habit is to sleep underground, in the smallest space possible. Cosima knows she's the older, even when she's unconscious: one of her arms lies over Halimeda's shoulder as if she intends to protect them both from their bad dreams. Dr. Homer Noline holds his breath, trying to see movement there in the darkness, the way he's watched pregnant women close their eyes and listen inside themselves trying to feel life.

A slice of white moon from the window divides their bodies deeply into light and shadow, but not one from the other. No light could show where one body ends and the other begins when they're sleeping like this. Maybe a mother's eye could tell, but that is the one possibility that can't be tried.

Halimeda's bed is still made. In the morning she'll rumple it so he'll believe she slept by herself, and then the girls will make it again. Their labors at deceiving him are as careful as surgery. But morning is worlds away now, it's still early night on the Day of All Souls. The two of them spent the whole day playing in the cemetery with neighbor children, Pocha and Juan Teobaldo and Cristobal and the twin babies, helping Viola Domingos build a bower of marigolds over the grave of a great-grandmother who is no part of this family.

For a long time he stands gripping the door frame, which is exactly the width of a newborn's skull and curves similarly against his palm. He watches his daughters, though there's nothing to watch, and thinks these words: "A great-grandmother who isn't their business." He decides this will be their last year for the cemetery and the Day of All Souls. There are too many skeletons down there. People count too long on the oblivion of children.

They're deep in the corpselike collapse that takes hold of children when they are exhausted, but still he won't risk going in to stand over the bed the way he once would have. He would see the usual things: unraveled braids and the scraped shins hidden from his punishing antiseptics. Tonight he would also see cheeks and eyelids stained bright yellow from marigold pollen. He's spent a lifetime noticing small details from a distance. From the doorway he smells the bitterness of crushed marigold petals on their skin.

There is a deeper draft of breath and they both move a little. Their long hair falls together across the sheet, the colors blending, the curled strands curving gently around the straight. He feels a constriction around his heart that isn't disease but pure simple pain, and he knows he would weep if he could. Not for the river he can't cross to reach his children, not for distance, but the opposite. For how close together these two are, and how much they have to lose. How much they've already lost in their lives to come.

COSIMA

2

HALLIE'S BONES

I am the sister who didn't go to war. I can only tell you my side of the story. Hallie is the one who went south, with her pickup truck and her crop-disease books and her heart dead set on a new world.

Who knows why people do what they do? I stood on a battleground once too, but it was forty years after the fighting was all over: northern France, in 1982, in a field where the farmers' plow blades kept turning up the skeletons of cows. They were the first casualties of the German occupation. In the sudden quiet after the evacuation the cows had died by the thousands in those pastures, slowly, lowing with pain from unmilked udders. But now the farmers who grew sugar beets in those fields were blessed, they said, by the bones. The soil was rich in calcium.

Three years later when my sister talked about leaving Tucson to work in the cotton fields around Chinandega, where farmers were getting ambushed while they walked home with their minds on dinner, all I could think of was France. Those long, flat fields of bone-fed green. Somehow we protect ourselves; it's the nearest I could come to imagining Nicaragua. Even though I know the bones in that ground aren't animal bones.

▼▼▼

She left in August after the last rain of the season. Summer storms in the desert are violent things, and clean, they leave you feeling like you have cried. Hallie had never left me before. It was always the other way around, since I'm three years older and have had to do things first. She would just be catching up when I'd go again, swimming farther out into life because I still hadn't found a rock to stand on. Never because I wanted to leave. Hallie and I were so attached, like keenly mismatched Siamese twins conjoined at the back of the mind. We parted again and again and still each time it felt like a medical risk, as if we were being liberated at some terrible cost: the price of a shared organ. We never stopped feeling that knife.

But she went. And true to the laws of family physics, the equal and opposite reaction, I was soon packed up too and headed northeast on a Greyhound bus. In our divergent ways, I believe we were both headed home. I was bound for Grace, Arizona, where Hallie and I were born and raised, and where our father still lived and was said to be losing his mind. It was a Sunday. I had a window seat, and in a Greyhound you're up high. You pass through the land like some rajah on an elephant looking down on your kingdom, which in this case was a scorched bristling landscape and the tops of a lot of cars. It wasn't all that different from my usual view of life, because I'm tall, like my father and Hallie. I don't look like who I am. They do, but I don't.

It was midmorning when I stepped down off the bus in Grace, and I didn't recognize it. Even in fourteen years it couldn't have changed much, though, so I knew it was just me. Grace is made of things that erode too slowly to be noticed: red granite canyon walls, orchards of sturdy old fruit trees past their prime, a shamelessly unpolluted sky. The houses were built in no big hurry back when labor was taken for granted, and now were in no big hurry to decay. Arthritic mesquite trees grew out of impossible crevices in the cliffs, looking as if they could adapt to life on Mars if need be.

I was the only passenger getting off. The short, imperious

bus driver opened the baggage door and made a show of dragging out luggage to get to mine, as if I were being difficult. A more accommodating woman, he implied, would be content with whatever bags happened to be right in front. Finally he slapped my two huge suitcases flat out in the dust. He slammed the doors and reclaimed his throne, causing the bus to bark like a dog, leaving a cloud of exhaust in the air, getting the last word, I suppose.

The view from here was orchards: pecan, plum, apple. The highway ran along the river, dividing the orchards like a long, crooked part in a leafy scalp. The trees filled the whole valley floor to the sides of the canyon. Confetti-colored houses perched on the slopes at its edges with their backs to the canyon wall. And up at the head of the canyon was the old Black Mountain copper mine. On the cliff overlooking the valley, the smelter's one brick smokestack pointed obscenely at heaven.

I dragged my bags to the edge of the street. Carlo, my lover of ten years, whom I seemed to have just left, would be sending a trunk from Tucson when he got around to it. I didn't own very much I cared about. I felt emptied-out and singing with echoes, unrecognizable to myself: that particular feeling like your own house on the day you move out. I missed Hallie. Carlo, too—for the lost possibilities. At the point I left, he and I were still sleeping together but that was all, just sleeping, with our backs touching. Sometimes Hallie would cough in the next room and I'd wake up to find my arm over his shoulder, my fingers touching his chest, but that's only because it takes your sleeping self years to catch up to where you really are. Pay attention to your dreams: when you go on a trip, in your dreams you will still be home. Then after you've come home you'll dream of where you were. It's a kind of jet lag of the consciousness.

Carlo loved Hallie. When he and I moved back to Tucson the three of us contrived a little household in a bad neighborhood, with jade plants on our front steps that kept getting stolen till Hallie thought to bolt down the pots. We played house to beat the band. Hallie and I made prickly-pear jelly, boiled and strained and poured blood-red into clean glass jars. We'd harvested the fruits from the physical therapy garden of the hospital where Carlo worked. A nun saw us out there with our grocery sack while she was walking an old man around the little race track, and Hallie and I just waved. We said we were living off the land.

Our home fell apart when she left. She was our center of gravity, the only one of us who saw life as a controllable project. Carlo was an orphan like me. We forgot about the jade plants, they went crisp as potato chips out on the porch, and Carlo withered as if he needed water also. Every man I'd ever loved had loved Hallie best and settled for me. It didn't bother me as much as you might think; I could understand it. I loved her too.

And now his life with the Noline women had run its course. He could go where he pleased. Carlo was a rolling stone: an emergency-room doctor, which gave him a kind of freedom almost unknown to the profession. You can always find work if you're willing to take up with a human body as soon as possible after one of life's traumas has left off with it. Carlo and I met in medical school, and in our years together he and I probably had more addresses than the Grace, Arizona, phone book. Along the way I'd landed a few presentable jobs, but in between I tended to drift, like a well-meaning visitor to this planet awaiting instructions. My career track had run straight down into the weedy lots on the rough side of town. It's the truth. For the last six months in Tucson I'd worked night shift at a 7-Eleven, selling beer and Alka-Seltzer to people who would have been better off home in bed. There wasn't a whole lot farther I could go. Now I was here.

A high-school friend, Emelina Domingos, had offered to meet my bus but I'd told her, No, don't bother, I'll make my own way. The plan was for me to live in the Domingos' guesthouse. Not with my father. My relationship with Doc Homer had always improved with distance, which is to say that mail was okay and short, badly connected phone calls were best. I thought I should still keep some miles between us, even though he was ill and conceivably dying. It was going to be touchy. He would be an unwilling candidate for rescue, and I was disaster in that department myself. But he had only two living relatives and the other one was behind the wheel of a Toyota pickup headed for

Nicaragua. I stood my suitcases side by side and sat on them for a minute to get my bearings. I think I was hoping Emelina might still show up.

There was no evidence of human life, or life that was *ongoing* in any obvious way. The one vehicle parked in front of the courthouse, a blue station wagon, had four flats and a bumper sticker stating "ONE DAY AT A TIME." I suspected it had been there in 1972, the year I finished high school, when I last climbed on a Greyhound and turned my back on Grace. There wasn't a soul on the street today and I thought of those movies in which a town is wiped clean of its inhabitants, for one reason or another—a nuclear holocaust, say, or a deadly mutant virus—leaving only a shell of consumer goods. The point, I think, is to make some statement about how we get carried away with all our trappings, but this wasn't the place to shoot a movie like that. Grace hadn't yet entered the era of parking meters, for example. There were iron rings mortared into the block wall of the courthouse where a person could tie a horse.

I tried to imagine Doc Homer coming downtown on horseback, looking silly, his tall, stiff spine bouncing up and down against his will. I erased the fantasy from my mind, feeling guilty. It was too late to be taking imaginary revenge on my father.

There wasn't much to Grace's commercial district. The window of the Hollywood Dress Shop leered from across the street, framing a ferocious display of polyester. The headless mannequins were dressed to the nines, with silver vinyl loafers and red nail polish. If I moved a little I could put my reflection there in the window with them: me in my Levi's and Billy Idol haircut. (I was the one with a head.) A friend of mine used to make bizarre collages like that—Nancy Reagan in mink among the slaves on an Egyptian mural; Malibu Barbie driving sled dogs in the Iditarod. She sold those things for good money.

The Hollywood Shop was flanked by Jonny's Breakfast (open all day) and the movie theater. Back behind these buildings ran the railroad tracks. On the other side of Jonny's were the State Line Bar and the Baptist Grocery. I tried to place myself inside these stores; I knew I'd been there. Directing Hallie through the grocery aisles on a Saturday, ticking off items from Doc Homer's list. Sitting in Jonny's afterward, hunched in a booth drinking forbidden Cokes, reverently eying the distant easy grace of the girls who had friends and mothers. But I couldn't see it. Those things didn't seem so much like actual memories as like things I might remember from a book I'd read more than once.

I had lied on the bus. I'd told the woman sitting next to me that I was a Canadian tourist and had never been to Grace. Sometimes I used to do that, tell tales on buses and airplanes—it passes the time. And people love you for it. They'll believe anything if you throw in enough detail. Once I spent a transatlantic flight telling a somber, attentive man about a medical procedure I'd helped develop in Paris, in which human cadavers could be injected with hormones to preserve their organs for transplant. I would be accepting a prestigious medical prize, the name of which I devised on the spot. The man seemed so impressed. He looked like my father.

I didn't do it anymore, I was more or less reformed. What I'd said that morning was the truest kind of lie, I guess, containing fear at its heart: I *was* a stranger to Grace. I'd stayed away fourteen years and in my gut I believe I was hoping that had changed: I would step off the bus and land smack in the middle of a sense of belonging. Ticker tape, apologies, the luxury of forgiveness, home at last. Grace would turn out to be the yardstick I'd been using to measure all other places, like the mysterious wornout photo that storybook orphans carry from place to place, never realizing till the end that it's really their home.

None of this happened. Grace looked like a language I didn't speak. And Emelina wasn't coming. I hefted up my suitcases and started to walk.

Oh Lord, the terror of beginnings. I dreaded having to see all the people who were going to say, "How long are you home for, honey?" Possibly they would know I'd come for the school year. We would all carry on as if this were the issue: the job. Not Doc Homer, who'd lately begun addressing his patients by the names of dead people. Since I really did need to come, I'd gotten myself hired to replace the high-school biology teacher who'd recently married and defected without warning. I had practically no teaching qualifications, I should add, and things like that get around. It's tough to break yourself as news to a town that already knows you. Grace formed its opinions of Hallie and me before we had permanent teeth. People here would remember our unreasonable height in seventh grade, and our unfortunate given names; our father actually named my sister Halimeda, which means "thinking of the sea," however reasonable a thing that might be to do in a desert. And my own name, Cosima, means something to the effect of "order in the cosmos" which is truly droll, given my employment history. I must have sensed the lack of cosmic order in my future, early on. Maneuvering for approval, I'd shortened it to Codi in the third grade, when Buffalo Bill and the Pony Express held favor with my would-be crowd.

Hallie was a more natural abbreviation, from the time she could walk people never called her anything but that, although *Halimeda* actually had some truth in it; she made you look for things beyond what you could see. I could imagine Doc Homer dreaming up these names, confident we'd both take noble courses. Suddenly I felt dragged down by emotions as I walked along, as if I'd swum out into a calm sea and encountered a bad undertow. I carried my suitcases toward the edge of town.

An old, densely planted pecan orchard stretched out from the edge of the courthouse square, and somewhere behind it lay Emelina's place. The reflected sky ran like a vein of silver in the irrigation ditch, but when I left the street and stepped under the canopy of trees it was dark. If you've never walked through an old orchard, you have to imagine this: it presents you with an optical illusion. You move through what looks like a hodgepodge thicket of trees, but then at intervals you find yourself at the center of long, maddeningly straight rows of trees, standing like soldiers at attention. There's a graveyard in northern France where all the dead boys from D-Day are buried. The white crosses reach from one horizon to the other. I remember looking it over and thinking it was a forest of graves. But the rows were like this, dizzying, diagonal, perfectly straight, so after all it wasn't a forest but an orchard of graves. Nothing to do with nature, unless you count human nature.

A bird scream rang out from the leaves and echoed up my spine with a shiver that ended in my scalp. I believe it was the first sound I'd heard since the gear grinding of the bus. I stopped to listen. Quiet. Then another bird answered from behind me, close by. It sounded like the throaty, exotic laughter of a foreigner—like a jungle bird. The peacocks. These orchards were full of peacocks, living more or less wild and at the mercy of coyotes but miraculously surviving in droves. There was a local legend, supposedly true, about how they got here a hundred years ago: the nine blue-eyed Gracela sisters came over from Spain to marry nine lucky miners in the gold camp, sight unseen. Back then these hills were run through with gold veins and drew a crowd of men who had too much money and too little love. The sisters were just children, and only agreed to come if they could bring their birds with them in the hold of the ship. Their legacy in Gracela Canyon was a population of blue-eyed, dark-haired descendants and a thousand wild peacocks. Their father stayed behind and got rich by proxy, for he'd literally sold his girls for a gold mine.

The branches were ringing with bird calls now. And I could hear kids laughing. A whole chorus of them screamed at once. Toward the far end of the orchard I could make out children's silhouettes jumping and dancing under the trees. It was dark in there for midday but I definitely saw kids: little girls in billowy dresses and boys in white shirts. I couldn't make out their game. The tallest boy had a stick and they were chasing something and flailing at it. I walked down the row toward them, towing my bigger suitcase like an anchor. I was traveling light in theory, but I'd dragged with me into Grace a substantial reference library. It had taken me a lot of nervous weeks to narrow down what books to bring. At the very last minute I'd thrown out Gray's *Anatomy* because Doc Homer would have it.

I stepped over the irrigation trenches, mindful of my Italian leather uppers. I'm picky about shoes, and there was no replacing these now. I smiled, thinking of the awful silver loafers in the Hollywood Shop. I envisioned my predecessor at the high school dressed like that, standing in front of a classroom of fifteen-year-olds, twisting her white chiffon scarf as she explained cell division. What would these kids make of me? My shoes were pointed and my, as the magazines say, personal style leaned toward apologetic punk. I'd never had a teacher who looked like me; probably there was a reason.

I stopped to massage my aching shoulder. There was something up there at the edge of the orchard all right, a bunch of kids, and something in the trees over their heads. I thought about skirting around the little gang to avoid spoiling their fun, or maybe, actually, because I was afraid. I tried to move quietly. Whatever it was they were chasing, they were going to get it.

I could see plainly then that it was a heavy-bodied peacock shuffling from side to side on a low branch. Apparently the creature was too dull-witted or terrorized to escape, or possibly already injured. The children pursued it ferociously, jumping up and pulling at its long tail feathers, ready to tear it to pieces. The boy with the stick hit hard against the belly and they all shrieked. He hit it again. I couldn't see the stick but I heard the sickening whack when it made contact.

I looked away. I'd arrived in Grace, arrived at that moment in my life, without knowing how to make the kind of choice that was called for here. I'm not the moral guardian in my family. Nobody, not my father, *no one* had jumped in to help when I was a child getting whacked by life, and on the meanest level of instinct I felt I had no favors to return. Especially to a bird. It was Hallie's end of my conscience that kept pinching me as I walked. I dropped my bags and walked a little faster, trying to think of some commanding thing to say. If they didn't stop soon the thing would be maimed or dead.

"Stop it!" I yelled. My heart was thumping. "You're killing that bird!"

The boy froze like a rabbit in headlights. The other kids, down on their knees, stared too. I'd arrested them in the act of grabbing fistfuls of bright paper and candy that sparkled on the ground. The mute peacock swung over their heads on a wire. Its fractured body hung in clay shards the size of plates, held together by a crepe-paper skin.

When I was ten I'd demolished a piñata exactly like this one, with blue paper wings and a long glossy tail of real feathers. At a birthday party. At some time or other every child in Grace had done the same.

After an impossible few seconds they went back to scrambling for their prize. Two older girls helped the smallest kids scoop candy into piles in their laps. A cluster of boys elbowed and slapped each other behind the girls' backs.

I felt disoriented and disgraced, a trespasser on family rites. I walked away from the little group of kids back toward the place in the center of the orchard where I must have left my suitcases. I wondered in what dim part of Grace I'd left my childhood.

HOMERO

3

THE FLOOD

The leaves shine like knife blades in the beam of his flashlight. The rain has slowed, but the arroyo is still a fierce river of mud and uprooted trees that won't crest until dawn. He is wet and chilled to his spine. The girls are lost. The sound of the flood makes his blood cold.

They wanted to gather prickly-pear fruits for jelly. They knew a storm was coming and they went anyway, while he was in his workroom. He follows the narrow animal path between thickets of thorn scrub along the bank, shining his light along the edge of the rising water. Acacias lean into the river with their branches waving wildly in the current, like mothers reaching in for lost babies. The girls ignore his cautions because they are willful children who believe nothing can harm them. Hallie is bad but Cosima is worse, pretty and stubborn as a wild horse but without an animal's instincts for self-preservation—and she's the older. She should have some sense.

He forces his body through the bank of oleanders near the house and turns back toward the riverbed to search the arroyo to the south. He has no idea which way they would have gone; they roam this desert like pocket mice. And everything in a desert is poisonous or thorned. Good Lord, he has already lost a wife, and did not think his heart would live beyond her. *Wished* it wouldn't. He slashes at the oleanders with the metal flashlight. He'd meant to cut these down when Cosima was born. One well-chewed leaf could bring on cardiac arrest in a child. He'd seen a case years ago, or was it later, after the girls left home? That blue girl?

Doc Homer sits up in his bed and stares at the orange pill bottles on the windowsill. There is light at the window. It's a Sunday morning in August. It is only a month ago he lost that blue girl. His own daughters are grown and living somewhere else, looking after themselves, but his heart is still pumping hard. His circulatory system believes they are still lost.

He turns his pillow and rests his head on it carefully because his brain gets jostled and things move around inside his head like olives in a jar of brine. Think about the flood. He is going south on the near side of the arroyo. He stops to look back upstream and his light finds them, by pure luck, on the opposite bank. Cosima's thin, waving arms shine like the crisscrossing blades of scissors. They are screaming but he only sees their mouths stretched open like the mouths of fledgling birds. Absolute expectation, Papa will save us. The road is washed out, and he has to think how else he will get to them. He realizes, stunned, that they have been huddled there for half a day. The road has been washed out that long.

How does he reach them? A boat? No, that wouldn't have been possible. He sits up again. He has no clear image of reaching them, no memory of their arms on his neck, he only hears them crying over the telephone. And then he understands painfully that he wasn't able to go to them. There is no memory because he wasn't there. He had to call Uda Dell on the other side of the arroyo. Her husband was alive then, and went down the bank on his mule to find them in a washed-open coyote burrow with seven pups the girls wanted to save.

"There were seven," she'd wailed over the telephone. "I could carry four but Hallie could only get one in each hand and we didn't want to leave the other one. He would have gotten drowned." Cosima is sobbing because in the end, after crouching for half a day in the small shelter of that gravel bank, waiting for the mother coyote to come back and save her children, they had to leave them. He hears Hallie shrieking in the background. They're both crying as if they are drowning themselves. Drowning pups.

When he gets them home they sit hugging each other on the davenport, wrapped in the black-and-red crocheted afghan. They won't stop shaking. They want to know if the baby coyotes died. If animals go to heaven. He has no answers. "We tried to put them in the paper bag we used for the prickle pears, but it fell all apart." The tears stream out until the afghan is wet and he thinks there will be no more fluid in them to run the blood cells through their veins. He makes them drink orange juice. God, why does a mortal man have children? It is senseless to love anything this much.

COSIMA

4

KILLING CHICKENS

Emelina's was a pleasant, ramshackle place with animals, an old plum orchard and five boys. When I walked up the drive with my suitcases they were preparing to kill roosters. Emelina's eyes and mouth drew wide and she looked briefly like a surprised fish. "Codi, this is *Sunday,* I thought you said *tomorrow.*"

"No, it was today, I'm here," I said apologetically. I was glad I hadn't waited any longer at the courthouse.

"Shoot, you look like a fifty-dollar bill. Where'd you get that haircut, Paris, France?" She gave me a hug and waved her hand at the driveway. "I'm sorry about this mess. We've just got the water boiled for the birds. Shoot."

I'd just witnessed what I'd thought was going to be the slaughter of a peacock, so I laughed, but this time it was real murder and mayhem. The drive was lined with pails, paper bags, and a tragically stained wooden block that had been used before. Emelina's twins, who were about ten, each held a fat white rooster by the feet. A younger brother was riding a tricycle precariously over the rocky ground. I put down my suitcases.

"Curty and Glen, look at you," I said. "And Mason. You guys are getting too big."

"Aunt Codi, look. If you hold them upside down they go to sleep," Glen said.

Curty said, "No, they get hypnotized."

"Well, either way it's a handy trick," I said. "You don't want them to see what's coming."

Emelina looked dismayed. "Codi, we don't have to do this now. What a god-awful thing to do in front of company."

"I'm not company. You're all set up, so do it. You can't go out of your way for me if I'm going to live here."

She rolled her eyes. "Go on back to the granny house then. John Tucker was supposed to sweep it out this morning before he went to his baseball practice but I'll fall over dead if he did it right now, instead of feeding the baby. I'll bet you fifteen dollars he's laying in the house watching the MTV."

John Tucker was Emelina's oldest, but I couldn't picture him old enough to feed the baby. I hadn't yet seen the baby, since he'd only arrived six months ago. But over the years Emelina and I had kept up. I'd taped her kids' school pictures to the woodwork of Carlo's and my many ill-furnished apartments. Sometimes repairmen would ask if they were my boys.

I went around to the side yard and pushed open a wire gate that wouldn't have kept out a determined hen. The guesthouse in the back faced the big ranch house across a huge brick courtyard that was wild and overrun with flowering vines. Every inch of space was taken up with fruit trees, painted flowerpots, and lawn chairs that looked like they'd been there since the last war. I could hear chickens clucking softly somewhere out of sight, and at the back of the courtyard a goat stretched its neck to get at a fig tree.

The guesthouse had a pink door flanked by pots of geraniums, whose crimson flowers stood out against the white walls like wine stains blooming on a tablecloth. Inside, the little house was whitewashed and immaculate. There were two brick-floored rooms: a living room and bedroom. The light pouring in the windows was stirred up by the motion of fig branches outside. The bed had a carved headboard, painted with red enamel, and a soft-looking woven spread. It was a fairytale bed. I wished I could fall down and sleep a hundred years in this little house with pale crisscrossing shadows on the walls.

I heard the goat moving around outside, munching loudly and bumping against the wall. I opened cupboards. Everything was spotless. The east window in the living room looked straight out onto the granite wall of the canyon a few yards away, a startling lack of view. Emelina's place was the last and highest on her street, backed up against the canyon. The floorboards of her front porch were on a level with her neighbors' roofs.

I took my time exploring. I savored the first minutes in a new home. Carlo would always go straight to unpacking boxes, looking for the sheets and coffeepot and swearing that we were going to get better organized, while I stepped stealthily over the bare floors, peeking around corners and into alluring doors, which generally turned out to be the broom closet. But there was that thrilling sense that, like a new lover, the place held attributes I had yet to discover. My favorite book as a child was *The Secret Garden*. It's embarrassing to think I'd merrily relocated again and again, accompanying Carlo to the ends of the earth, because of the lure of a possible garret or secret closet. But it might be true.

I tried out the two very old chairs in the living room. They had rose slipcovers and were comfortable. In a corner near the window was a beehive fireplace, and next to it, a clay vase of peacock feathers. Every home in Grace had one of those; it was a local feature. You could pick up half a dozen peacock feathers on any given day, in the orchards, as you went about your business. When the vase was full, you took them to one of the old women who made real-feather piñatas, and then you started your collection over. The practice had not been allowed in our house because Doc Homer said the feathers were crawling with bird mites; he dreaded to think what those old women's houses were harboring in the way of microorganisms. It became Hallie's and my joke. Whenever he unreasonably forbade us to do something, we'd look at each other and mouth the words "bird mites."

The bathroom and kitchen must have been added on about mid-century. The refrigerator looked prehistoric, but worked. It contained a loaf of fresh bread in a paper bag, some tomatoes and figs, a block of goat cheese, and a six-pack of Miller Lite.

Emelina's estimation of the bare essentials. I popped open a beer and went back around the house in time to witness the demise of the second rooster.

"Is it okay that there's a goat loose in the courtyard?" I asked Emelina.

"Shit! I'm going to tan John Tucker's hide. *John Tucker!*" she yelled. "Get your damn goat out of the garden, please, or we'll have him for dinner!"

There was a noise from inside and the back door slammed.

"You don't really want to watch this, Codi," she said. "But I guess you see a lot worse in your line of work."

I sat on the porch rail. I was no longer in the doctoring line of work. It's true I'd been educated to within an inch of my life, and had done well in medical school. My mistake was assuming medicine was a science like any other. If it's carburetors you know, you can fix cars, I reasoned; if it's arteries and tendons you fix people. For reasons that were unclear to me, I'd learned the science but couldn't work the miracle: I'd had a crisis while trying to deliver a baby. My problem turned out to be irreversible. Emelina knew all this. I was *here*, after all, with no more mission in life than I'd been born with years ago. The only real difference between then and now was wardrobe.

"Tell me if I can help," I said.

She ignored me. "Okay, watch your hands, Curty. Keep them way back." Emelina was small, but didn't give that impression. Her jeans had "Little Cowboy" stitched on the label, and undoubtedly belonged to one of her sons. Emelina and I graduated from high school the same year, 1972. Under my picture in the yearbook it said, "Will Go Far," and under Emelina's it said, "Lucky in Love." You could accept this as either prophecy or a bad joke. I'd gone halfway around the world, and now lived three-quarters of a mile from the high school. Emelina had married Juan Teobaldo Domingos the same June we graduated. Now J.T. worked for the railroad and, as I understood it, was out of town most of the time. She said it didn't bother her. Maybe that's as lucky as love gets.

Curty laid his hypnotized rooster on the block and held its

feet, keeping the rest of his body as far away as possible. It never regained consciousness. Emelina swung the axe over her shoulder and brought it down on the mark. The pink, muscular neck slipped out of the collar of feathers as if the two parts had been separately made. The boys hooted and chased after the body as it thrashed across the dirt. But I was fascinated by the head: the mouth opened and closed, silently, because the vocal cords were in the part that had been disconnected.

"That's the way, Curty," Emelina directed. "Don't get blood on your brother. Dip him all the way in. Now pluck him quick or he'll go stiff on you. Start with the wings, see how Glen's doing?" She wiped perspiration out of her eyes.

I was amazed by the muscle definition in her upper arms and her easy command of the axe. Her hands stayed surprisingly clean through the whole operation. She reminded me of Hallie, the way she could do things. Though of course Hallie would never decapitate anything.

"I can't believe you're watching this," she said when both boys were settled down to plucking feathers. She went inside and came out with a beer. She sat down next to me on the wide wooden rail, knocking the heels of her sneakers against the crossbar like a child. I was very conscious of my height. Sometimes I had an acute feeling that small women were better put together somehow, more in control of their bodies.

"You used to have a hissy fit when we'd go over to *Abuelita*'s and she'd be killing chickens," Emelina said. "Remember? Even when we were big, twelve or thirteen."

"No, that was Hallie. She's the one that had such a soft heart. We've always been real different that way. She'd cry if she stepped on a bug." I drained my beer. "She's still like that, except now she cries about bag ladies. I swear. She gives them quarters and then she wishes she'd given them a dollar."

I stared out at the treetops and the leaf-green gables of the roof on a house below us. The shingles were an odd, elaborate shape like the spade in a deck of cards. I wondered in what decade they'd stopped making shingles like that, and how this neighbor might repair the roof after a bad storm.

"You really do look great," Emelina said. "That's a terrific haircut, I mean it. You'll stand out in a crowd here till you get your first cut down at Beth's Butcher Shop."

I ran my fingers over my weedy scalp, feeling despair. I'd spent my whole childhood as an outsider to Grace. I was willing to march downtown and submit myself to butchery this minute if that would admit me to the club. I'd led such an adventurous life, geographically speaking, that people mistook me for an adventurer. They had no idea. I'd sell my soul and all my traveling shoes to *belong* some place.

"I always forget you have so much auburn. Doc Homer had the same coloring, didn't he? Sort of reddish before he went gray?" She fingered her own shoulder-length hair. "Speaking of him . . ."

"Speaking of him," I said.

"Have you talked to him?" She looked apprehensive. Emelina was my informant. When he started getting lost on his way home from the drugstore, she was the one person in Grace who thought to call me, rather than just draw him a map.

"I'll go up and see him tomorrow."

"And where's Hallie gone? You told me, but I forgot."

"Nicaragua," I said. "To save the crops. Cross between Johnny Appleseed and a freedom fighter."

Emelina laughed and I felt disloyal. I hadn't meant to sound glib. It was just hard to put Hallie into the context of regular life. "I guess it's really dangerous," I said. "But she's excited about it. She'll be happy." I was sure of this. Hallie didn't have my problem. She belonged wherever she was.

Emelina nodded. She watched the boys, who sat cross-legged on the driveway, transfixed by the importance of their task. They were dappled with blood and looked like they'd been through a strange war themselves—a children's war.

A scarlet bougainvillaea covered the front porch. In fact, it was so overgrown that the wood of the vine seemed to be supporting the structure over our heads. The breeze coming up the valley felt like a warm liquid against my arms and face. I held the sweaty beer can against my temple and watched the bougainvillaea arms swaying around us like seaweed under the ocean.

"No," Emelina said after a while. "I'm sure it was you that had a fit over the chickens. You'd start, and then Hallie would do it too. She always followed whatever you did."

"No. Hallie? We're chalk and cheese. Somebody ought to do a study on us, if they want to know how kids in the same family can turn out totally different. She was born with her own mind."

"Maybe she was, but she copied you like a picture," Emelina said. "She used to get so pissed off at me because I wouldn't go along with your boycott of *Abuelita*'s chicken and rice."

I didn't remember organizing boycotts. "Well, you're the witness here. Blood all over the driveway and I didn't faint."

"People change," she said. "Not everything stays with you all your life."

▼▼▼

I sat watching my suitcases for a good fifteen minutes, as if they might become inspired to unpack themselves, and then I went into the bedroom and lay down for just a minute, letting my shoes drop one at a time onto the brick floor. I tried to think how far Hallie might have gotten by now. Guatemala. Maybe farther. It was frightening to speculate on specifics; I'd been rationing my thoughts about her, but now I was exhausted and my mind ran its own course. I thought of Hallie at border crossings. Men in uniforms decorated with the macho jewelry of ammunition. No, not that far. I pulled her back to Tucson, where I'd seen her last and she was still safe.

She'd come by the 7-Eleven, all packed up, at the end of my graveyard shift. She knocked her knuckles on the plate glass to get my attention. I locked the cash drawer and took off. Sparrows were ruffling themselves in the sheets of fresh rain on the asphalt. As I walked her across the parking lot to her truck I could see just how we'd look to somebody, hanging on to each other by the elbows: like two swimmers in trouble, both of us equally likely to drown.

Or maybe only one of us was holding on for dear life. It was hard to believe I'd once been the one to strike out bravely for college, leaving Hallie crying in front of the Baptist Grocery. Now it seemed like I was the baby of the family, the one with no firm plans who's allowed to fiddle around forever keeping everyone young.

Hallie was headed for a war zone. She walked straight through the puddles, dragging me along, and I had to stretch out my legs and drench my shoes to keep up with her. When Hallie was intensely excited she had a wild-animal look to her that could stop people in their tracks. A vibration came from her skin, like a bell that has just been struck. Her hair was long and reckless, curling wildly in the humidity. Every part of my sister could stir rebellion. I was thinking that if anything happened to her I wouldn't survive. I couldn't see that there would be any method, or any point.

As long as I held Hallie's arm she would still be here, she wouldn't be climbing into the truck, turning the key, driving south through Arizona and Mexico and the perilous places farther on, wouldn't be stopped at a roadblock by men who might blandly shoot her in the head for being twenty-nine years old and alone and female, wearing blue jeans, carrying antihistamine pills in her glove compartment. It seemed like a chain of events I could hold back, there in the parking lot, with the bones of her elbow securely gripped in my hand.

Her little beat-up pickup looked impossibly loaded, like the tiny burros you see in postcards carrying elephant-sized burdens without complaint. I wasn't worried about the truck. I asked where she'd put her antihistamines. We knew of a photographer who'd been shot, ostensibly for running drugs, because he had a baby-food jar of aspirin and vitamin tablets in his camera bag.

Hallie said her pills were no place easy to find.

I put my head on her shoulder. "What if our houseplants die?"

"They won't," she said. Hallie knew I wanted easy answers.

I lifted my head again and she stared at me, thoughtfully. The sky had cleared. The early-morning light behind her head was orange, making her hair glow, and she looked like an angel.

She never had any idea how she looked to other people; she thought she was plain.

"If the flea beetles start getting at the ones on the porch," she said slowly, "dust them with Celite." Hallie worked for the Extension Service and answered the Garden Hotline, 626-BUGS. For a period of years ending on that day, garden pests were her life.

I hugged her with all the strength in my arms. "Hallie," I said, "could you please just change your mind now and not go?"

"You really love me, so you want me to stay here and keep the suburbs safe for geraniums."

"I know how I ought to feel," I said. "I just don't."

Her breath expanded her chest against my arms, and I thought of the way a tree will keep on growing after a fence is wired around its trunk. The unbelievable force of that expansion. And I let her go.

She started up her truck and waved from the corner, not a mournful gone-forever wave but a chin-up wave like you see in the World War II movies, where everybody is brave because they all believe in the same thing. I told myself because I had no other choice that Hallie would do all right. That we were both going to live.

I walked the six blocks home under dripping trees and a sun that was already too hot. Across the street I heard a woman say to her companion in an odd accent, "It's the *Desert* Museum. I had understood him to say the 'dessert museum,' and obviously I was expecting something quite different." I thought: this is how life is, ridiculous beyond comprehension. What I felt wasn't pain but a hollowness, like a drum with the skin stretched tight. It took me five minutes to get our front door open, because everything in Tucson with moving parts gets cantankerous in the rainy season. Hallie had meant to put graphite in the lock before she left.

A white balloon left over from her going-away party followed me from the living room into the kitchen. It was the size of a head, and had lost some helium so it hung at eye level, trailing its string along the floor like a tired old ghost. Static electricity drew it along behind me. I swatted it away from my head while I plundered the refrigerator. I found some red bell peppers that had been absurdly expensive at the health-food market, and washed one and ate it standing up in the kitchen. After that I found a paring knife and went to work on a cucumber. I didn't feel like cooking breakfast just for myself. Carlo was at the hospital and I had no idea when he was due back.

The phone rang and I jumped, I suppose because I felt guilty for standing in the kitchen eating costly vegetables. I was afraid it was going to be somebody with garden pests, but they'd already turned off the Garden Hotline. It was Hallie calling from a pay phone this side of the border to tell me she'd forgotten to graphite the lock.

"I knew you'd call about that." I was filled with a strange joy because she felt the same way I did: that we couldn't survive apart. I just stood still for a minute, giving Hallie's and my thoughts their last chance to run quietly over the wires, touching each other in secret signal as they passed, like a column of ants. You couldn't do that kind of thing at international rates.

"There's a library book, too," she said. "Those Baron Münchhausen stories. I found it in with my books when I was cleaning out my room."

"I know. I saw it. I'll take it back today."

"That book's got to be overdue, Codi. You were reading it in the car a month ago when we drove to Bisbee."

I took a bite out of the cucumber and chewed before answering. I wanted this phone call to last forever. I wanted to recall every book we'd ever read aloud together while driving. "You're right. It's overdue."

"Take it back and pay the fine, okay? Libraries are the one American institution you shouldn't rip off."

"Yes, ma'am," I said. "Miss Patty Hearst the Second." I heard her trying not to laugh. Hallie was intellectually subversive and actually owned a copy of Abbie Hoffman's *Steal This Book,* but by nature she was perversely honest. I'd seen her tape dimes to a broken parking meter.

"Apart from moral reasons, they'll cancel your card."

"I don't know why you think I'm such a library outlaw. I'm

all paid up over there." I munched on the cucumber. It wasn't that different from eating an outsize apple, say, or a peeled peach, and yet anyone looking in the window would judge me insane. "Don't worry about me, Hallie," I said finally. "Just worry about yourself."

"I'm not worried about myself. I'm the luckiest person alive."

It was an old joke, or an old truth, grown out of all the close shaves she'd walked away from. Bike wrecks, car wrecks, that kind of thing. I'd always been more or less a tragedy magnet, but Hallie was the opposite. One time she started out the door of the old science library at the university, and then turned around and went back in because she'd left her sunglasses by the microfiche machine, and two seconds later the marble façade fell off the front of the building. Just slid straight down and smashed, it looked like Beirut.

Hallie didn't believe she was invulnerable. She was never one of those daredevil types; she knew she could get hurt. What I think she meant was that she was lucky to be on her way to Nicaragua. It was the slowest thing to sink into my head, how happy she was. Happy to be leaving.

We'd had one time of perfect togetherness in our adult lives, the year when we were both in college in Tucson—her first year, my last—and living together for the first time away from Doc Homer. That winter I'd wanted to fail a subject just so I could hang back, stay there with her, the two of us walking around the drafty house in sweatshirts and wool socks and understanding each other precisely. Bringing each other cups of tea without having to ask. So I stayed on in Tucson for medical school, instead of going to Boston as I'd planned, and met Carlo in Parasitology. Hallie, around the same time, befriended some people who ran a safehouse for Central American refugees. After that we'd have strangers in our kitchen every time of night, kids scared senseless, people with all kinds of damage. Our life was never again idyllic.

I should have seen it coming. Once she and I had gone to see a documentary on the Abraham Lincoln Brigade, which was these Americans who volunteered without our government's blessing to fight against Franco and Hitler in the Spanish Civil

War. At that point in U.S. history fascism was only *maybe* wrong, whereas communism was *definitely*. When we came home from the movie Hallie cried. Not because of the people who gave up life and limb only to lose Spain to Franco, and not for the ones who came back and were harassed for the rest of their lives for being Reds. The tragedy for Hallie was that there might never be a cause worth risking everything for in our lifetime. She was nineteen years old then, and as she lay blowing her nose and sobbing on my bed she told me this. That there were no real causes left.

Now she had one—she was off to Nicaragua, a revolution of co-op farms and literacy crusades—and so I guess she *was* lucky. Few people know so clearly what they want. Most people can't even think what to hope for when they throw a penny in a fountain. Almost no one really gets the chance to alter the course of human events on purpose, in the exact way they wish for it to be altered.

I loved her for feeling so strongly about things. But I'd watched Doc Homer spend a lifetime ministering his solemn charity to the people of Grace and I'm not sure whose course was altered by that, other than Hallie's and mine, in a direction we grew to resent. It's true that I tried myself to go into medicine, which is considered a helping profession, but I did it for the lowest of motives. I did it to win love, and to prove myself capable. Not to move mountains. In my opinion, mountains don't move. They only look changed when you look down on them from a great height.

5

THE *SEMILLA BESADA*

I'd agreed to move into the guesthouse on the condition that I wasn't going to impose on Emelina's family life, but apparently her life was beyond imposition. She sent John Tucker over in the morning to fetch me for breakfast.

He stood tentatively outside my screen door, unsure of what to do with all his limbs. "Mom says she'll break your face if you don't come over for breakfast."

"Okay, sure," I said, following him back to the house. John Tucker was the most appealing kind of adolescent. I couldn't begin to picture the man he would soon become—armpits and arrogance, scratching the back of his neck, throwing a baseball. Out of the question. He was wearing a cap to cover what looked like an overly enthusiastic summer haircut.

"I know you don't have anything to eat over there yet," Emelina said. "Everything was closed, yesterday was Sunday. Today you can get on your feet. J.T. called from El Paso and said to be sure and give you a kiss." Emelina buttered a piece of toast and handed it to Mason, who was four going on five. "Glen, don't put jam on your brother. If you want to wear plum preserves today that's your nickel, but not Curtis's. Curty, honey, don't hit. John Tucker, help him with that, will you?"

"He called from El Paso?" I prompted. Conversations with a mother of five are an education in patience.

"Yeah, he's in Texas. He's got to stay for an investigation. So are you going to be able to stand living in that shack?"

"It's not a shack, Em. It's nice out there. I like it."

"Codi, honey, there was goats living in there at one time. And Grammy lived there too, before the goats. But she said she got the ague in her bones and she decided she had to move in upstairs." Grammy was J.T.'s mother, Viola Domingos.

"Mom, make Glen stop," Curtis said.

"Glen, for heaven's sakes, just eat that toast and put it out of its misery. The bus is going to be here in a minute and you don't even have your shoes on."

"No, but I know where they are," Glen declared.

"Well, go get them."

"School doesn't start till next week," I said, alarmed that I might be wrong. I was always having dreams like that.

"No, but they've got this summer thing for kids. They go up there to the river park and shoot each other with bows and arrows or something. Tomorrow's the last day. So you think you'll like it out there? We make enough noise over here to raise up the quick and the dead."

"It's fine. I used to live three blocks from a hospital ambulance entrance." I didn't add: with a man who reattached severed body parts for a living. I buttered my toast, holding my elbows in close and keeping an eye out for wayward jam knives. "So what kind of an investigation?"

"Oh, J.T.? He put sixteen cars on the ground outside El Paso. A derailment. Nobody got hurt. Oh shoot—John Tucker, honey, will you take the baby in the living room and watch him a minute? I can't hear myself think."

John Tucker took the baby from Emelina's lap and carried him under one arm into the next room. The baby waggled his arms and legs like a swimmer in green stretch pajamas.

"Okay. Mason, sweetie, put your feet up here on my lap and I'll tie your sneakers for you." Emelina took a gulp of coffee. "So they all had to give a urine sample—J.T., the fireman, the brakeman, and some other person, I can't remember who.

Maybe another engineer. It all had to happen within a half hour of the accident; the company made a very big deal out of that. J.T. says, here they were out in some cow pasture with sixteen boxcars of frozen mixed vegetables scattered from hell to breakfast, and all the damn supervisor cared about was making sure which person pissed in what jar."

The boys seemed unmoved by this off-color narrative. Having Emelina for a mother would neutralize the thrill of swear words.

"You know what, though," she said, looking startled. "Damn. We were just joking about drug tests, the day before yesterday. Grammy made a poppyseed cake for Curty's and Glen's birthday and J.T. said . . ."

"Mo-om."

"I'm sorry, Curtis, I forgot. He doesn't want us to call him Curty. Their actual birthday was yesterday."

I wanted to hear the rest of the derailment story, but this conversational flow was akin to freeway driving in L.A.; you don't back up. "Well, happy birthday," I said. "You boys get handsomer every time I see you, you know that?"

Curtis's ears turned red.

"You can say 'Thank you, ma'am,' can't you? Codi, they've all been asking me when you were going to get here till I thought they'd turn blue in the face, and now they're acting like they were raised outside in a pen with the dogs."

"That's okay." I felt a little intimidated myself. Even though I'd kept up with the family, it was inconceivable that in my absence from Grace Emelina could have produced this whole blue-eyed tribe of human beings.

"Mom, can I sleep out in the pen with Buster tonight?" Mason asked.

"No sir, you can't. So when we were eating that cake, J.T. was saying how he'd better not have an accident on the railroad, because poppyseeds show up some way on the drug test."

"That's true, they would." I reconsidered this. "He'd register positive for opiates. Poppyseeds are related to heroin. Is he going to be in trouble?"

"No, they know it wasn't his fault. It was a sun-kink or some darn thing with the rails. The drug test is just to cover their ass.

You know who else was on the train? The other engineer and the brakeman were both guys we went to school with, you might remember them. Roger Bristol and Loyd Peregrina. Loyd lived up at Whiteriver for a while but he's moved back."

I paid attention to my heart rate, to see if it would react in any way to this information. It didn't seem to.

"Aunt Codi, say something in Greece," Glen said.

"In Greek," Emelina corrected, giving me an apologetic look. "I already told them you looked like a fashion model and had lived overseas. They think you know David Bowie."

"Your mother exaggerates," I said.

Glen didn't seem too disappointed.

"So, Em, if I'm going to live here do I have to buy a pair of those silver loafers from the Hollywood Shop?"

She nodded seriously. "I'm pretty sure they won't let you teach down at the high school without them."

The school bus honked outside. "Okay, scoot," Emelina said. "Mason, give me a kiss."

The boys stampeded out the kitchen door, all legs, leaving the baby beached on Emelina's lap. His eyes roamed anxiously around the quiet kitchen, taking in the emptiness.

Emelina and I took each other in. All morning I'd felt the strange disjuncture that comes from reconnecting with your past. There's such a gulf between yourself and who you were then, but people speak to that other person and it answers; it's like having a stranger as a house guest in your skin.

"So what's new?" she asked.

"I don't know, everything. I don't think Grace has changed, but it feels different. There's a lot I don't remember."

Emelina smiled. "I know what you mean. Senility strikes." It was an odd thing to say; Doc Homer's exact problem was that his mind had begun to roam in alarming new pastures.

"I guess so," I said.

"Well, some things never change." She leaned forward and said in a low voice, "Grammy still collects figurines of Elvis."

I had to laugh. We'd known J.T.'s mother as children, of course—people here spent their childhoods tearing through the homes of their future in-laws—and I remembered her living room, which we used to call the Elvis Museum. She denied that the ones that were whiskey bottles were whiskey bottles. She'd always told us aftershave.

"So it's all over with Carlo? Or just a vacation?"

"I don't know. Over, I think. It's taken me all this time to figure out he's not going to tell me the secret to a meaningful life." I was serious. I'd loved Carlo best when he provided me with guidance.

"I used to think the ideal husband would be Doctor Kildare."

"Carlo's an emergency-room surgeon. A man that decides which way to sew a thumb back on would have a good hold on life, wouldn't you think? I just assumed it would rub off."

"Gross," Emelina remarked.

"I think it was his eyebrows. You know how he has those kind of arched, Italian eyebrows?"

"No, I never got to meet him. He was always at the hospital."

That was true. He was shy. He could face new flesh wounds each day at work, but he avoided actual people. "Well, he had this look," I said. "He always seemed right on the verge of saying something that would change your life. Even when he was asleep he looked like that."

"But he never did?"

"Nope. It was just his eyebrows."

I did miss him, or at least I missed being attached to someone in theory. Carlo had beautiful hands and a legendary sense of direction. Even when we were in Venice, where the tourist books advise you that "part of the Venice experience is wandering the narrow *strade* until you find yourself lost," we wandered but never got lost. The man had a compass needle in his cerebral cortex. And for all that, he'd still in the long run declined to be the guiding star I needed. Just as my father did. My father was dying on me.

Emelina collected the plates and cups. She stood up and tied on an apron over her bathrobe, miraculously keeping the baby situated on her hip throughout the operation.

"Well, you're no worse for the wear of five children in fourteen years," I said, and she laughed, probably not believing it. Emelina was noticeably pretty. That combination particular to

Grace, the pale blue eyes and black hair, never failed to be arresting, no matter how many versions of it you saw. The eyes were a genetic anomaly—in the first hours after birth, the really pure specimens of Grace's gene pool were supposed to have whitish, marblelike irises. I'd seen pictures. Doc Homer had written it up for the *American Journal of Genetics*, years ago.

"And John Tucker's a teenager," I said. "Are we that old?"

"I am. You're not." She started to clear the table with one hand. "Every minute in the presence of a child takes seven minutes off your life." I took the baby from her and she said, "Don't say I didn't warn you."

"They're your treasures, Em. You've got something to show for yourself."

"Oh, yeah. I know," she said.

The baby's name was Nicholas, but nobody called him anything but "the baby." I'd read somewhere that the brain organizes information in sets no larger than four—that's why Social Security and phone numbers are subdivided; possibly four children's names were the limit on parental memory. I sat in the rocker and settled nameless Nicholas on my lap, his head at my knees. My long thigh bones exactly accommodated his length.

Emelina scraped toast corners into a blue enamel pail and ran a sinkful of hot water. "I don't think I could stand to let Mason go off to kindergarten next year if it wasn't for the baby. It kills you to see them grow up. But I guess it would kill you quicker if they didn't."

"I remember you saying you were calling it quits after four."

"Famous last words."

While I watched her move around the kitchen, my fingers tingled with the pleasure of stroking the baby's fine black hair. It was longer by several inches than his big brother John Tucker's; someone had taken shears to that boy with a vengeance. Probably Emelina. A woman who beheaded her own chickens would cut her kids' hair herself.

Emelina washed and rinsed the plates and set them into the wire rack to drain. I sat feeling useless, though Nicholas seemed comfortable and was falling asleep on my lap. When that happens you feel them grow heavier, as if relaxation allowed them to be flooded with extra substance. A constriction ran across my lungs. I'd come close to having a baby of my own once, but I thought of it now so rarely that the notion of myself as a mother always caught me off guard.

In spite of the heat outside, Emelina's dishwater was fogging the window. A little collection of potted plants stood in a row on the windowsill. Prayer plants. I was struck with a sudden, forceful memory of Emelina's grandmother's house. Hallie and I called her *Abuelita* too, though of course she was no relation, and the old woman called us "the orphan girls," *huérfanas*. Nobody ever thought we could understand Spanish. The house had a stale, old-lady smell, but we loved her boxes of "pretties": cast-metal carts with broken wheels, lead soldiers, huge washers and carriage bolts, every species of unidentifiable metal part. Her dead husband was a blacksmith. There were also boxes of ancient dress-up clothes in satiny fabrics as brittle as paper. Our best playroom was the sunny alcove crammed with plants where we stalked lions through the parlor palms, dressed in our finery, more glamorous than Beryl Markham and the Baroness von Blixen could have managed to be in their dreams. We confronted real dangers in the form of rickety iron stands holding heavy, breakable pots and fragile plants. The African violets were furred like pets, and the prayer plants had leaves like an old woman's hands, red-veined on the back, that opened wide in the sun and folded primly together in the shade. *Abuelita* instructed us to sit and watch them, to try and catch them in the act of closing their leaves. Hallie always waited the longest, patient for enlightenment long after Emelina and I had returned to our rowdy diversions.

"You know, I'm so used to J.T. being gone," Emelina said, bringing me back. "I think he'd be underfoot if he were here. I'd give us about ten days, then I'd probably shoot him. Husband murder in Grace, oh boy." She seemed to be answering a question, however circumspectly, that I wasn't sure I'd asked.

"How long has he been on the railroad?"

"Just since the mine shut down, which was . . ." She frowned at the glass she was drying, decorated with white pigs in red bow ties. "Ten years, about."

"They used to always say they'd hire again up there when the price of copper went up."

"Well, you know, that's talk. Nobody's waiting around anymore. Now it's pecans and plums. And the railroad, thank God for that. I think we could live off the orchards if the boys didn't eat like horses and outgrow their shoes every ten days. Get this, now they're too fashion conscious to wear each other's hand-me-downs. Remember when boys didn't give a shit what they wore? We never should have got satellite TV." She turned around, drying her hands on her apron. "Is that rascal gone to sleep? Thanks, Codi. I'll take him upstairs and put him down for his nap." She lifted the baby onto her shoulder like a sack of valuable flour. "You got big plans for today?"

"I thought I'd make an excursion into the city," I said. "Check out the dry goods at the Baptist Grocery."

She laughed. "If you can wait awhile I'll go with you. Grammy can listen for the baby. She ought to be home pretty soon from her meeting." Emelina rolled her eyes as she left the kitchen. "Stitch and Bitch Club on Mondays, bright and early."

I stood at the window looking out at the grove of trees that ran the length of the canyon. Plum, pear, apple. And quince, I believe, though I couldn't identify a quince tree to save my life. I only remembered the word because of the way people here pronounced it—"queens"—with their Spanish-influenced vowels. In the distance I could make out white satellite dishes perched among the cacti on the red cliff—one to each house, like dogs. Well, that was something new. The sky was overcast. In the orchards on the other side of the river I could see men working among the trees. I remembered them beating the branches with long poles, bringing down scattered showers of pecans. Frailing, that was called. In the older orchards sometimes they had to climb up into the tallest trees to reach the upper branches with their poles. But it was too early in the year for that. Pecans didn't ripen till late fall.

Hallie and I had played in this house once or twice as children, when a pair of pigeon-toed girl cousins of J.T.'s had lived here. Now it belonged so securely to Emelina. It was hard to realize how fully life had gone on. Of course, it would. I could have stayed here, or gone away as I did, it made no difference to Grace.

I washed the baby's cup, running my finger around the inside rim. While the sun left the windowsill and moved on to other things, I noticed, the prayer plants had closed up when I wasn't watching. They stood in a self-satisfied row, keeping their thoughts to themselves.

▼▼▼

"You keep some of the dirt on them, and you just stuff them down in paper bags and keep them somewhere dark," said Lydia Galvez. "Do you have a root cellar?"

"No, uh-uh. We did, but the boys got into it and figured out how to cave it in some way," Emelina said.

"Well, you could put them anyplace dark. The bottom of a closet would do."

Lydia Galvez was the wife of John Tucker's little league coach. I'd been introduced. We'd discussed John Tucker, baseball, and Emelina's talent for producing boys. The whole town had been betting this last one would be a girl, Lydia Galvez told me. Now they were talking about dividing gladiolus bulbs.

"I've got some black," Lydia was saying. "Do you have any black? I could spare you some. They're not a *true* black, I'd really call it purple, but they're supposed to be important."

Emelina gave me a glance, so I knew she was trying to wind things up. Our whole afternoon had gone pretty much this way. Lydia, like everyone else, had no earthly notion of what to say to me, or I to them; I rarely even remembered who they were. But we were all polite, as if I were Emelina's lunatic maiden aunt.

I sat down on the wall in front of the courthouse and watched myself in the plate-glass window of Jonny's Breakfast, which was empty at this hour. My reflection stared back, looking more alone than anything I'd seen in my life. It occurred to me that I'd never drawn a breath here without Hallie. Not one I could be sure of. I was three when she was born. Before that I wasn't conscious of my place in the world, so it didn't matter.

Later, it mattered more than anything. Doc Homer drilled us

relentlessly on how we differed from our peers: in ambition, native ability, even physical constitution. The nearest thing to praise, from him, was "No one else in Grace knows *that!*" Or, "You are *Nolines*." We stood out like a pair of silos on a midwestern prairie. As far as I could see, being *Nolines* meant that we were impossibly long-limbed like our father and all the Noline relatives we never got to meet. He and mother came from a part of Illinois (this is a quote) where people were reasonable and tall.

The height, at least, wasn't lost on Hallie and me. We turned out to be six feet on average—Hallie one inch over, and I, one under. In high school they used to call us forty percent of a basketball team. We didn't play sports, but they still said that. Height isn't something you can have and just let be, like nice teeth or naturally curly hair. People have this idea you have to put it to use, playing basketball, for example, or observing the weather up there. If you are a girl, they feel a particular need to point your height out to you, as if you might not have noticed.

In fact, Hallie and I weren't forty percent of anything—we were all there was. The image in the mirror that proves you are still here. We had exactly one sister apiece. We grew up knowing the simple arithmetic of scarcity: A sister is more precious than an eye.

"You tell that daddy of yours I need a pill to get rid of my wrinkles," Lydia said loudly.

I made an effort to collect myself. "Okay."

I should have said, "You don't need any such thing," or something like that, but I didn't think fast enough. I wasn't managing this first day all that well. I had a lump in my throat and longed to get back to my cottage and draw the blinds. Grace was a memory minefield; just going into the Baptist Grocery with Emelina had charged me with emotions and a hopelessness I couldn't name. I'd finished my shopping in a few minutes, and while I waited for Emelina to provision her troops for the week I stood looking helplessly at the cans of vegetables and soup that all carried some secret mission. The grocery shelves seemed to have been stocked for the people of Grace with the care of a family fallout shelter. I was an outsider to this nurturing. When the cashier asked, "Do you need anything else?" I almost cried. I wanted to say, "I need everything you have."

▼▼▼

It was past midnight but a cold moon blazed in the window and I couldn't sleep. I lay on my back in the little painted bed in Emelina's cottage. I hated sleeping alone. As little as there was between Carlo and me, I'd adjusted to his breathing. All my life I'd shared a bed with somebody: first Hallie. Then in my first years at college I discovered an army of lovers who offered degrees of temporary insanity and short-term salvation. Then Carlo, who'd turned out to be more of the same. But companionable, still. Sleeping alone seemed unnatural to me, and pitiful, something done in hospitals or when you're contagious.

I'd finally reached that point of electric sleeplessness where I had to get up. I tucked my nightgown into my jeans and found my shoes out in the kitchen. I closed the door quietly and took a path that led away from the house, not down past other houses but straight out to the north, through Emelina's plum orchard and a grove of twisted, dead-looking apples. Every so often, peacocks called to each other across the valley. They had different cries: the shrill laugh, a guttural clucking—a whole animal language. Like roosters and children, on a full-moon night they would never settle down completely.

I wanted to find the road that led up the canyon to Doc Homer's. I wasn't ready to go there yet, but I had to make sure I knew the way. I couldn't ask Emelina for directions to my own childhood home; I didn't want her to know how badly dislocated I was. I'd always had trouble recalling certain specifics of childhood, but didn't realize until now that I couldn't even recognize them at point-blank range. The things I'd done with Hallie were clear, because we remembered so much for each other, I suppose, but why did I not know Mrs. Campbell in the grocery? Or Lydia Galvez, who rode our school bus and claimed to have loaned me her handkerchief after Simon Bolivar Jones chucked me on the head with his Etch-a-Sketch, on a dare. In fact, I felt like the victim of a head injury. I hoped that if I struck out now on faith I would feel my way to Doc Homer's, the way a water witcher closes her eyes and follows her dowsing rod to find a spring. But I didn't know. I could have lost the homing instinct completely.

I was on a road that looked promising, anyway. I could hear the river. (Why does sound travel farther at night?) I had my mother's death on my mind. One of my few plain childhood memories was of that day. I was not quite three, Hallie was newborn, and I'm told I couldn't possibly remember it because I wasn't there. The picture I have in my mind is nonetheless clear: two men in white pants handling the stretcher like a fragile, important package. The helicopter blade beating, sending out currents of air across the alfalfa field behind the hospital. This was up above the canyon, in the days when they grew crops up there. The flattened-down alfalfa plants showed their silvery undersides in patterns that looked like waves. The field became the ocean I'd seen in storybooks, here in the middle of the desert, like some miracle.

Then the rotor slowed and stopped, setting the people in the crowd to murmuring: What? Why? And then the door opened and the long white bundle of my mother came out again, carried differently now, no longer an urgent matter.

According to generally agreed-upon history, Hallie and I were home with a babysitter. This is my problem—I clearly remember things I haven't seen, sometimes things that never happened. And draw a blank on the things I've lived through. I told Doc Homer many times that I'd seen the helicopter, and I also once insisted, to the point of tears, that I remembered being on the ship with the nine Gracela sisters and their peacocks. For that one he forced me to sit in my room and read the *Encyclopaedia Britannica*. Novels were banned for a month; he said I needed to clear my mind of fictions. I made it to Volume 19, driven mostly by spite, but I still remembered that trip with the Gracelas. They were worried about whether the peacocks were getting enough air down in the hold of the ship.

I would concede now that all these things were fabrications based on stories I'd heard. Memory is a complicated thing, a relative to truth but not its twin. It was a fact that our mother had been terrified of flying. This part of our family history was well known in Grace. In her entire life she never left the ground. When her health deteriorated because of a failed kidney and a National Guard helicopter bore down from the sky to take her to Tucson, she'd explained to the men that she wasn't going to fly. When they ignored her, she just died before the helicopter could lift itself up out of the alfalfa. The big bird hovered for a minute, and went away hungry.

It wasn't her aversion to flight that was impressive; people in Grace didn't travel much by car, let alone by air. I think the moral of the tale, based on the way people told it, was the unsuspected force of my mother's will. "Who else would have married Doc Homer?" they seemed to be saying. And also, I suppose, "Who could have borne those unconforming girls?" People never said this directly, but when we were willful they would tell us, without fail: "You didn't suck that out of your thumb."

It made sense to me. I had no visual memory of a mother, and could not recall any events that included her, outside of the helicopter trip she declined to take. But I could remember a *sense* of her that was strong and ferociously loving. Almost a violence of love. It was the one thing I'd had, I suppose, that Hallie never knew. As the two of us grew up quietly in the dispassionate shadow of Doc Homer's care and feeding, I tried to preserve that motherly love as best I could, and pass it on. But I couldn't get it right. I was so young.

And somehow Hallie thrived anyway—the blossom of our family, like one of those miraculous fruit trees that taps into an invisible vein of nurture and bears radiant bushels of plums while the trees around it merely go on living. In Grace, in the old days, when people found one of those in their orchard they called it the *semilla besada*—the seed that got kissed. Sometimes you'd run across one that people had come to, and returned to, in hopes of a blessing. The branches would be festooned like a Christmas tree of family tokens: a baby sock, a pair of broken reading glasses, the window envelope of a pension check.

Hallie and I had a favorite *besada* in the old Domingos orchard, and one cold day on the way home from school we tucked wisps of our hair into its bark. Secretly. We'd hidden in the schoolyard to snip the ends off our braids and tie them up together with a pink thread unraveled from my coat button. If Doc Homer found out, he would construct some punishment to cure us of superstition. We agreed with him in principle—we were little scientists, born and bred. But children robbed of love will dwell on magic.

I stopped suddenly in the center of the road, in the moon's bright light, with shadow trickling downhill from my heels like the water witcher's wellspring finally struck open. I'd found the right path. The road angled up out of the orchards toward the top of the canyon. The steepness of the climb felt right. I would come back in daylight and go the rest of the way to Doc Homer's, past the old helicopter landing pad up in the alfalfa field. Those fields would surely be abandoned now, like half the cropland in Arizona, salted to death by years of bad irrigation. I didn't want to go up there now and see it all under moonlight, the white soil gleaming like a boneyard. It was too much.

I turned back down the road feeling the familiar, blunt pressure of old grief. Even the people who knew me well didn't know my years in Grace were peculiarly bracketed by death: I'd lost a mother and I'd lost a child.

6

THE MIRACLE

I was fifteen years old, two years younger than my own child would be now. I didn't think of it in those terms: losing a baby. At first it was nothing like a baby I held inside me, only a small impossible secret. Slowly it grew to a force as strong and untouchable as thunder. I would be loved absolutely. But even in the last months I never quite pictured the whole infant I might have someday held in my arms; that picture came later. The human fact of it was gone before I knew it. But evidently that word "lost" was somewhere in my mind because I've had thousands of dreams of losing—of literally misplacing—a baby.

In one of the dreams I run along the creek bank looking among the boulders. They are large and white, and the creek is flooded, just roaring, and I know I've left a baby out there. I thrash my way through mesquite thickets, stopping often to listen, hearing nothing but the roar of the water. I feel frantic until finally I see her in the middle of the water bobbing like a Cortland apple, little and red and bright. I wade in and pull her out and she lies naked there on the bank without so much as a surname, her umbilicus tied with a man's black shoelace such as my father might wear. I see her and think, "It's a miracle she's survived."

That thought is the truest part of the dream. Really there would be nothing new or surprising about a baby being born in secret and put into a creek. But to pull one out, that would be a surprise. A newborn has no fat yet; it wouldn't float. It would sink like a stone.

Loyd Peregrina was an Apache. He took me out four times. Our football team was called the Apaches, but Loyd was also a *real* Apache, and the kind of handsome you could see coming down the road like bad news. When he first asked me, I thought he'd made a mistake, or a joke, and I looked to see who was watching. Nobody was. Four Saturdays in a row, for exactly one lunar month: the odds of getting pregnant out of that were predictable, but I was unfathomably naïve. I was a motherless girl. I'd learned the words *puberty* and *menarche* from the *Encyclopaedia Britannica*. The rest I learned from girls in the schoolyard who weren't even talking to me when they said what they did.

Loyd wouldn't remember. For me it was the isolated remarkable event of a tenuous life but for Loyd—with his misspelled name and devil eyes—it was one in a hundred, he was a senior and ran around with everybody. Also he was such a drinker in those days that I was frankly surprised to hear he was still alive. He never knew what he'd spawned, much less when it died. Even Hallie didn't. It's the first time I understood that even with a sister I could be alone. At night I lay feeling my limbs, seeing what Hallie still saw, which was nothing near the truth, and I felt myself growing distant and stolid. I was the woman downtown buttoning her child's jacket, her teeth like a third hand clamped on a folded grocery list, as preoccupied as God. Someone important and similar to others. I was lured and terrified. I couldn't help but think sometimes of escape: the thing inside me turning to blood of its own accord, its bones liquefying, leaking out. And then one evening my savage wish was granted.

I never did tell Hallie. I kept quiet, first to protect her from the knowledge of terrible things, and later to protect myself from that rock-solid element she came to own. That moral advantage.

It divided me from the people I knew, then and later, but in broader human terms I don't pretend that it sets me apart in any great way. A miscarriage is a natural and common event. All told, probably more women have lost a child from this world than haven't. Most don't mention it, and they go on from day to day as if it hadn't happened, and so people imagine that a woman in this situation never really knew or loved what she had.

But ask her sometime: how old would your child be now? And she'll know.

7

POISON GROUND

Emelina was up with the chickens. I heard her out in the courtyard pulling honeysuckle vines away from the old brick barbecue pit. They came out with a peculiar zipping sound, like threads from a seam in rotten cloth. "You can see we haven't been festive for a while," she said. She was organizing what she called a "little fiesta" for the Saturday of Labor Day weekend. It was a family tradition; they roasted a whole goat. (Not John Tucker's.)

I found a broom and pitched in, sweeping up the pieces of a broken flowerpot I'd come to think of as part of the décor. Emelina asked, in the carefully offhand way a good mother would ask, if I'd been up to the school yet. I'd received numerous calls about a teacher's meeting.

"I know about the meeting, but I haven't gone up there yet," I confessed. School would begin the following Tuesday. I needed to get organized and see what kind of shape the labs were in, but I kept putting it off, on grounds of terror. I hadn't actually taught school before. When Emelina wrote me about the opening at Grace High School it had seemed sensible to apply. While Carlo slept I'd sat up in bed with my legal pad and a small reading light, feigning competence, attempting to organize the problem areas of my life into manageable categories: I had no real attachment to selling lottery tickets at 7-Eleven; Doc Homer was going off the deep end; Carlo was Carlo; Hallie would be leaving at summer's end, and without a destination for myself I'd be marooned. Grace was something. If I got this job I could spend ten months in Grace seeing about Doc Homer, possibly without his noticing. I reasoned that I wasn't qualified and didn't have a chance of being hired, and so I felt bold enough to apply.

They hired me. The state had some kind of emergency clause that in a pinch allowed people to teach without certification. And of course I did have a world of education in the life sciences. Also, I believe my last name had something to do with it. Nothing else I put down in my wobbly writing on that application could have impressed anyone too much.

I dumped the shards of the flowerpot into a plastic trash bag, making the satisfactory sound of demolition. I started in with Emelina on the honeysuckle vines. As we dragged them out she looped the long strands around her arm like strings of Christmas tree lights. "You excited about starting?" she asked.

"Nervous."

"Well hell, Codi, you're bound to be better than the last one. John Tucker says she was scared of her shadow. Some senior boys chased her into the teachers' lounge with a fetal pig."

Emelina's faith in me was heartening.

"Did I tell you J.T. called this morning?" she asked. "They're going to make it home for the fiesta. Him and Loyd. Do you remember Loyd?"

I yanked at a vine that was rooted right into the crumbling adobe. "Sure," I said.

"I didn't know if you would. I think you were the only girl in the whole high school that never fell for him."

It was humid and hot. I'd tied a bandana around my forehead and already it was soaking wet. The salt stung my eyes.

"I went out with Loyd a few times," I said.

"Did you? Him and J.T. are real good buddies. He's straightened out a lot. He's real sweet." She unburdened herself of the loops of vines, laying them in a pile, and stood up with her hands on her waist, arching her back. "Loyd, I mean." She laughed. "Not J.T. He's just the same as he always was."

I took off my bandana and wrung it out. The dark drops on

the hot brick dried up instantly, leaving behind a white lace of salt. Just like the irrigation water on the alfalfa. In just this way the fields get ruined, I thought to myself.

Emelina kicked tentatively at the brick barbecue pit. "You think this thing will stand up after we get the vines out of it?"

"I think they're what's holding it together," I said.

She cocked her head and looked at it thoughtfully. "Well, if it falls down we'll just have us a roasted-goat disaster. We'll just have to get extra beer."

▼▼▼

On the morning of the fiesta she sent John Tucker and me to town for last-minute supplies, including extra beer, although the barbecue pit showed every sign of standing through another Labor Day fiesta. I followed John Tucker down a path I didn't know, a short cut through a different orchard. "What kind of trees are those?" I asked John Tucker. The branches were heavy with what looked like small yellow-green pomegranates.

"Quince," he said, with a perfect short "i," not "queens." The Spanish-flavored accent of Old Grace was dying out, thanks to satellite TV, I suppose. I watched the back of his shorn head; the path was narrow and we walked single file. At thirteen he was my height, a head taller than Emelina. It must shift your liaison with a child when you have to look up to him.

I caught a glimpse of bright car windshield through the trees, and knew where we were. You could picture Grace as a house, with orchards for rooms. To map it of course you'd have to be a botanist. We left quince and entered pecan, where the ground was covered with tiny, immature nuts. "So what's happening with these orchards?" I asked, kicking at a slew of green pecans the size of peach pits. "I've been seeing this all over."

"Fruit drop."

John Tucker was already a man of few words.

The Baptist Grocery was nondenominational, but harked back to a time when everything in Grace, including grocery stores, was still segregated. This wasn't recent, but maybe a century ago. Here the Hispanic and Anglo bloodlines got very mixed up early on, starting with the arrival of the Gracela sisters. By the time people elsewhere were waking up to such ideas as busing, everyone in Grace had pretty much given up on claiming a superior pedigree. Nowadays the Baptist Grocery peddled frozen fish sticks to Protestant and Catholic alike.

John Tucker shopped like an automaton, counting out bags of chips and jars of salsa. Since he seemed interested in efficiency, not congeniality, I suggested we split up. I would go to the liquor store and meet him in front of the courthouse.

Drinking establishments had proliferated in Grace since my day. The mine had closed in the interim, of course; bars and economic duress are common fellow travelers. I passed the Horny Toad Saloon and the Little Dipper plus the one I remembered, the State Line, which was no more situated on the state line than the grocery was Baptist. New Mexico lay thirty miles to the east. I think the name referred to the days when Gracela County was dry and people had to drive to the border for beer.

Emelina had advised that I'd find the best price on beer at the Watering Hole, a package store. I located it on the corner of Main Street and the depot alley, which led down past the old movie theater to the railroad station. The theater had been remodeled into an exercise salon and video rental store called the Video Rodeo, with a huge hand-lettered sign in the window announcing "NINTENDOS NOWHERE." I stared for a good half minute before I made out that it meant "NOW HERE," not "NOWHERE." The calligrapher got cramped.

The Watering Hole was closed, with a sign on the door saying "BACK IN TEN," so I waited. The placard was lettered in the same hand as the "NINTENDOS" sign. Maybe one person actually ran all the stores in Grace from behind the scenes, like the Wizard of Oz, powerfully manipulating people through hand-lettered signs. It was hot and my mind was fraying at the edges. I wiped the sweat out of my eyes and massaged my prickly scalp, thinking I must look like a drowned hen, but maybe nobody would recognize me today. Living without a lover was beginning to produce in me the odd sense that I was invisible.

A pretty, old carob tree stood near the door of the liquor

store, throwing dappled shade on the sidewalk. I knew that its twisted, woody-looking pods could be crunched between the teeth and tasted like cocoa. I sat on a concrete block and leaned my back against the trunk. Apparently this was a frequent waiting spot. Fallen carob pods lay all around my feet. I picked one up, polished it on my T-shirt and bit down: the first sensation was sawdust, but then the splinters turned strongly bittersweet on my tongue, a nostalgic tang. I looked up into the leathery leaves. Hallie had told me carobs were dioecious, which means that male and female parts are possessed by separate individuals. In plain English, they're like us; it takes two to tango. This one was loaded with fruit, but there wasn't another carob tree in sight. I looked all the way down the main street and down toward the depot. No male carobs. I patted the trunk sympathetically.

The door of the Watering Hole was opened by a proprietor who looked as if she might not be legal drinking age herself. In fact this must have been the case because after she bagged and rang up my purchase she asked if I'd mind waiting while she went next door to the Video Rodeo and got her dad. He arrived shortly to accept my money and put it in the register. I suppose they switched off, since she probably wasn't old enough to rent out porno movies either. I recognized neither father nor daughter, and they didn't make a point of knowing or not knowing me: a relief. The daily work of remeeting people was overwhelming, and Emelina's party was going to be a whole lot more of the same.

I took my paper bags and headed across the street. A red pickup truck beeped its horn and startled me—I'd charged right across without looking. I froze up, like one of those ridiculous squirrels that darts one way and then the other and is doomed to end up a road kill. Except my life was in no danger here; he'd stopped. It was Loyd Peregrina, looking exactly like himself. If anything he looked younger than fifteen years ago. His arm was out the window and I hurried out of his way thinking it was a turn signal, that he was trying to turn right. It didn't occur to me till he'd gone on down the street that he was waving at me.

▼▼▼

I stayed in the shower forever trying to rinse the salt out of my scalp and skin. I had fantasies of not going to this thing, but Emelina would be hurt, and also my house sat in the middle of the party like a floral centerpiece. It would be hard to pretend not to be home. I put on the most minimal thing I owned, a white cotton dress, and sneaked out my front door.

It was like a high-school reunion. Everyone was boisterously friendly and dying to be filled in on the last decade and a half, which in my case was not that pretty a picture, and of course they asked about Hallie. Children ran underfoot like rebel cockroaches. Emelina, my guardian angel, kept setting me up in conversations before running off to clean up some mess the kids had gotten into or check on the goat.

J.T. came over and gave me a hug that lifted me off the ground—but that's J.T., plus a few beers. It really was nice to see him. "I hear you wrecked a train," I said.

"Wrecked her good," he said. J.T. was broad-shouldered and dark, with the kind of face that's made more handsome, not less, by the scars of teenage acne. We'd known each other since we were babies. His older sister Pocha was at the party, and his brothers Cristobal, Gus, and Arturo, all of whom had been our neighbors when Hallie and I were small. I remembered playing Dutchman's tag with them at the graveyard on All Souls' Days—it was always a huge family picnic up there—until Doc Homer decided the graveyard was off limits. (Bird mites no doubt.)

People were jammed into the courtyard belly to elbow and it soon got too noisy to talk. I stood near the edge of things, in the shade of an olive that was probably planted when the house was built, middle-aged as olives go. A band called the Sting Rays, featuring one of J.T.'s formerly pigeon-toed cousins, was belting out "Rosa Lee." I spotted Loyd across the way, but would have had to step on a hundred toes to get to him. He was leaning against the wall with his arms crossed, paying attention to a small woman in a strapless dress. Loyd looked like someone in a cigarette ad, except he wasn't smoking: white T-shirt, white smile, those models are always the picture of health. His hair was mink black, in a ponytail. And he had terrific arms. I hate to admit things like this, but in a certain frame of mind I am a sucker for good muscle definition.

A woman approached me suddenly from behind and shouted, "Codi Noline! God, honey, you look like a rock 'n' roll star."

In my sundress and dimestore thongs I looked no more like a rock 'n' roll star than Mother Teresa. "I'll take that as a compliment," I said. "I take them where I can get them nowadays."

"Lord, I know what you mean," she said. It was Trish Garcia, who was a cheerleader and clandestine smoker when I'd last known her. Now she smoked openly, had a raspy cough, and looked like a cartwheel was out of the question. "I heard Hallie's in South Africa."

I laughed. "Nicaragua."

"Well, what in the world's she doing there?"

In high school, Hallie and I were beneath Trish's stratum of normal conversation. I remembered every day of those years, no lapses there. Once in the bathroom I'd heard her call us the bean-pole sisters, and speculate that we wore hand-me-down underwear. I wondered how the rules had changed. Had I come up in the world, or Trish down? Or perhaps growing up meant we put our knives away and feigned ignorance of the damage. "She's teaching people how to grow crops without wrecking the soil," I said. "She has her master's in integrated pest management."

Trish looked indifferent, but she was working hard at being unimpressed, whereas before it came naturally. I took this as a good sign. "Well, I guess it pays good," she said.

"No, they're not really paying her, just living expenses is about all, I think. She's doing it just to do it. She wants to be part of a new society."

Trish stared. I pretended Hallie was there at the party somewhere, about to walk up behind me. "Six or seven years ago they threw out the dictator and gave all his land to the poor people," I said. "But they need a lot of help in the farming department now, because these soldiers keep attacking the poor farmers from across the border and burning up their crops."

Hallie would laugh at "farming department." She'd laugh at the whole scene, the education of Trish the Cheerleader. She would love me.

"The Communists," Trish said knowingly. "I heard about that. I heard they're thinking about sending the Marines down there to stop them from doing that."

"No, it's the other way around," I said patiently. "The Marines aren't rooting for the new society. The U.S. is paying the contras, the guys that attack the farmers." Hallie would not laugh now, she would be inflamed. She said we were a nation in love with forgetting the facts. She saved clippings that proved it. When Castro released those prisoners from Mariel: One day the headlines said we'd gotten him to free all these wonderful political prisoners. A month later when they were burning down halfway houses in Miami the papers castigated Fidel for exporting his hooligans and junkies.

Trish fiddled with her bra strap. "Hallie always would just up and do anything under the blue sky," she said.

"You're right," I told Trish. "I wish I were that brave. I'd be scared to death to be where she is."

"Well, you know, we can't all be the hero," she said, jutting her lower jaw to blow smoke up toward the olive branches. If I could have drawn blood, if I'd known how to do that with words instead of a needle, I would have. I wasn't sure what Hallie craved but I knew it wasn't glory.

"How's Doc Homer?" she asked.

I hadn't yet found the valor to go see him. I feared seeing him in failing condition. And still disapproving of me, on top of it. "Hard to say," I said.

I felt a tap on my shoulder and turned to see Loyd, grinning broadly. "Too good to speak to an Indian boy on Main Street?"

The tingle of a blush started behind my ears, and I ignored it. I'd learned since high school that in an emergency shyness can be disguised with a completely fake bravado. "You tried to run me down, Loyd! I ought to turn you in for reckless driving." I ran my fingers through my hair. "Actually, I didn't think you'd know who I was."

"Are you kidding? How many beautiful six-foot-tall women you think we've got in this town?"

"Five eleven," I corrected. "I'm the shorter of the bean-pole sisters." I felt suddenly drunk, though I wasn't, chemically speaking. Trish drifted off toward the barbecue pit.

He looked at me for a long time, just looked. Grinning. His left hand was fingering the tip of an olive branch and I expected him to snap it off but he didn't, he only took in its texture as someone might eat chocolate or inhale a cigarette.

"You want another beer?" he asked.

So that was going to be it, no filling in the last fifteen years. No constructing ourselves for each other—otherwise known as falling in love. "Think you can get over to that ice chest and back before this party is over?" I knew he wouldn't.

"In case I don't, I've got your phone number." He winked.

"Don't you worry. You'll be hearing from my lawyer."

I felt adrift and disappointed, though I hadn't held any conscious expectations of Loyd. I looked around at other faces, wondering if they all held secret disappointments for me. Doña Althea, the ancient woman we used to call the "Peacock Lady," was holding court in a lawn chair under the fig tree. She was the one who used to collect the feathers for piñatas. She looked today like she always had, dressed in black, fierce and miniature like a frightening breed of small dog. Even with her braided crown of silver hair she wasn't five feet tall. J.T.'s mother, Viola Domingos, and several other women sat in a group with her, fanning themselves in time to the music and drinking beer. J.T. and Loyd had apparently been commandeered into serving them food; the goat had been pronounced done. People were beginning to move toward the makeshift table, which I'd helped Emelina improvise from the doors to Mason's and the twins' rooms, covered with embroidered tablecloths compliments of the Stitch and Bitch Club. There was enough food to save an African nation. Potato salad, deviled eggs, *menudo,* tortillas and refried beans and a thousand kinds of dessert. I heard somebody say in a high-pitched voice, "*Tomato soup* in that cake? I wouldn't have guessed that for love nor money."

I wasn't in any hurry. I moved out of the way of the principal rush and stood near the gate to the side yard, near my little house. I noticed a dog lying very still and alert, just on the other side of the gate. It looked like an oversized coyote but it was definitely a domestic creature. It had a green bandana tied around its neck. This dog didn't belong to Emelina's household—I was pretty sure I knew all the family animals. It sat with its mouth slightly open and its ears cocked, staring steadily through the wire gate at the people inside.

"You thinking about crashing this party?" I asked the dog.

It glanced up at me for a second, with a patient look, then fixed its gaze back on the crowd. Or maybe on the roast goat.

"I'll bring you some of that, if you're willing to wait awhile," I said. "Nobody's going to miss one little bite."

The dog didn't respond to this promise.

All the old men had served themselves first and were settling down into a huddle of folding chairs near the front door of my cottage, holding their plates carefully horizontal above their knees. I started to move away, out of deference, but I noticed they were talking about fruit drop. I plainly heard one of them say the words, "poison ground." I stood four feet away and invisible, I suppose because they were men, and women talked to women. They asked questions of each other, to which they apparently already knew the answers.

"Do you know how much sulfuric they put in the river? He said the EPA give Black Mountain thirty days to shut down that leaching operation."

"Damn, man, that's *veneno*. How long you think we been putting that on our trees?"

"When did anybody ever tell the Mountain what to do?" The man who said this had a remarkably wrinkled brown face, like an Indian mummy I'd once seen in a roadside museum. "They'll pull some kind of strings," he said.

A man who sat with his back to me spoke up. "They won't fight the EPA. It's not worth it. They been saying for ten years that mine is dead. They're not hardly getting anything from that leaching operation."

Another man nodded at this, pointing his fork toward the head of the canyon. "Just enough to pay the taxes. That's all. They'll shut her down."

"You think so?" asked the one who reminded me of a mummy. "They're getting gold and moly out of them tailing piles. If they wasn't, they wouldn't keep running the acid through them. You boys know that damn company. They're not going to stop no leaching operation on account of our pecan trees." His voice trailed off and he was quiet for a minute, his callused fingers fooling with an unlit cigarette. I heard women's voices rising randomly over the din of the party, calling out instructions, reining in their kids. The party seemed like something underwater, a lost continent, and I felt profoundly sad though it wasn't my continent. I would go get a bite to eat, say something grateful to Emelina, and slip back into my house.

The man with his back to me said, "It's in Ray Pilar's apples and quince." He pronounced it "queens."

Another man, younger than the others, said, "It's going to kill every damn tree in this canyon. If I'm wrong, my friend, you can shoot me."

The man with the wrinkled face said, "If you're right, my friend, you might as well shoot yourself."

8

PICTURES

The dead mountain range of tailings on the lip of the mine had sat for decades, washed by rain, and still was barren as the Sahara. From a distance you might guess these piles of dirt to be fragile, like a sandcastle, but up close you'd see the pinkish soil corrugated with vertical ridges and eroded to a sheen, like rock. It would take a pickaxe to dent it.

It was high noon and I knew where I was. I bypassed the old mine road at the top of the canyon and stayed on the unmarked lane that people called, for reasons unknown to me, the Old Pony Road. All Grace's streets went by odd names that had mostly to do with picturesque forms of transportation: the Old and New Pony roads, the Goatleg, Dog-Cart Road, and the inexplicable Tortoise Road. Amazingly, most or all of these also had official, normal-sounding names like West Street and San Francisco Lane, which were plainly marked on painted aluminum street signs and totally ignored. Maybe somebody had just recently dreamed up these normal names and hammered up signs to improve the town's image.

From the canyon's crest I could see down into the isolated settlements at the north end of the valley, some abandoned, some buried in deep graves of mine tailings, through which, presumably, Black Mountain now ran quantities of sulfuric acid.

Far to the south lay open desert. The road I was on would pass through one more flock of little houses, all settled like hens into their gardens, before reaching Doc Homer's drafty two-story gray edifice.

I bypassed the main entrance of the hospital, the only one of the ghost town of Black Mountain buildings that was still in use. The hospital itself had finally closed—people had to leave Grace for a more equipped town if their problems were major—but Doc Homer's office in the basement could handle anything up to and including broken limbs. He wasn't working there today. I'd called him at home; I was expected.

"Cosima? *Cosima Noline!* I want you to look." A heavyset woman in a housedress and running shoes was standing at her mailbox, shouting at me. "Child, will you look. If you aren't the picture of your mother."

My mother was dead at my age. The woman put her arms around me. She was nobody I recognized.

"We've been so anxious to see you!" she said at a convincing decibel level. "Viola told us at sewing club you'd got in, and was staying down with her and J.T. and Emelina till you can help Doc get his place straightened out and move in up here with him. Oh, I know Doc's glad to have you back. He's been poorly, I don't expect he'd tell you but he is. They said when you was overseas you learned the cure they used on that actress in Paris, France. Bless your heart, you're a dear child." She paused, finally, taking in my face. "You don't remember me, do you?"

I waited, expecting help. It had been fourteen years, after all. But she offered no hints. "No, I'm sorry," I said. "I don't."

"Uda!" The woman said.

"Oh, Uda. I'm sorry." I still didn't have the foggiest idea who she was.

"I won't keep you, hon, but I want you to come for dinner soon as you can. I've baked Doc a squash pie I've been aiming to take up there. Hang on, I'll just run get it."

I waited while she hurried on her small feet up the path to the house and disappeared into the cave of honeysuckle that had swallowed her front porch. Uda returned directly with a covered pie tin that I accepted along with a bewildering kiss on both cheeks. I wondered how many people in Grace believed I'd flown in fresh from Paris with a cure for Alzheimer's.

▼▼▼

He'd told me two years ago. I had no idea if it was the confirmed truth or just his opinion, since Doc Homer made no distinction between the two. And if it was true, I still didn't know what to think. What we are talking about, basically, is self-diagnosed insanity and that gets complicated.

Carlo and I in fact weren't living in Paris (we never had), but in Minnesota; we'd already come back from Crete. Hallie had kept decently in touch with Doc Homer but I hadn't, and felt guilty, so I engineered a visit in Las Cruces. God knows how long he would have waited to tell me, otherwise. This meeting was not a plan he'd cooked up to give me the news, but my idea, sprung at the last minute. An accident of science, actually. Someone had recently spliced the glow gene from a glowworm into a tobacco plant, and the scientific world was buzzing over this useless but remarkable fact. All the top geneticists were meeting in New Mexico and my boss wanted me down there to take notes. I was working at a high-powered research lab; this was prior to my moving back to Tucson and falling into convenience-mart clerking. If I ever wrote down on paper my full employment history, I assure you it would look like the résumé of a schizophrenic.

And in my professional upswings I had more of what passes for confidence; it dawned on me that it's an easy bus ride over the state line from Grace to Las Cruces. I'd phone Doc Homer.

I was astonished when he agreed to come. "Barring unforeseen difficulties at the hospital," he'd said over the phone. I didn't know yet that the hospital had closed; that he sometimes forgot.

"You always say that." It was true, that was his standard disclaimer on every promise to Hallie or me, but it was uncharacteristic for me to tease him. Truthfully, after such an ice age, there was no such thing as characteristic. I tried out joking, more or less to see if it would work. "You'll say that at your own funeral, Pop," I'd said boldly into the receiver. Later, after he told me, I could have bitten my tongue off for that.

We met in the lobby of the Holiday Inn, just for a couple of drinks since he said he had to get back to Grace that night. The bar was done up in this madly cheerful south-of-the-border décor, with a blue tile fountain and silk bougainvillaeas climbing out of clay pots shaped like pigs. It was somebody's idea of what Old Mexico would look like if you didn't have to take poverty into account. The waitresses wore swishy miniskirts with ruffles in contrasting primary colors. In this setting my father told me he had a terminal disorder of the brain.

All I kept thinking was that he must be wrong. I doubted he'd had a CAT scan. The thing to do would be to check into the University Hospital in Tucson and get a neurological workup, to rule out other things, but I didn't try to talk him into it. The nature of my relationship with Doc Homer, which had eluded me over the phone, came back instantly when I saw him. There are all the small things you love and despise about a parent: the disappointed eyes, the mannerisms, the sound of the voice as much as the meaning of the words, that add up to that singular thing—the way you are both going to respond, whether you like it or not. It had settled heavily over our table and I could hardly breathe. I knew this man. He wouldn't seek out a second opinion to stack up against his own. He'd suffer his own doubts but never anyone else's. The waitress swished over and brought us fresh margaritas. The trickle of the fountain put me on edge, the way a running toilet will, or any sound of water going to waste. "What are you going to do?" I asked Doc Homer.

"I don't see a need to do anything special, for the time being. I'll make arrangements when the time comes."

My stomach was tight. I felt perversely annoyed with the smiling clay pigs. I touched my lips to the coarse salt on the rim of the margarita glass, and the crystals felt like sand in my mouth, or broken glass. I thought of walls I'd seen in Mexico—high brick *hacienda* walls topped with a crest of broken bottles imbedded in cement, to keep people on their correct sides of the fence. If they want to provide an authentic Mexican flavor they should have something like that in here, I thought.

"Nobody else knows," he said. "And I'd like for you not to mention it to your sister."

I stared at him. I knew it wouldn't matter what came next, whether I said "Okay," or "Why?" or "That's not fair," which is what I mainly felt. Dr. Homer Noline had stopped talking, there being nothing more to say, in his opinion. I imagined him going back to Grace on the bus and lying that night in his bed, tired but wide awake, recalling the events of his day and wondering what pathways of thought in his brain might be slipping off track. Trying to remember what vegetable he'd cooked for dinner or what tie he'd worn. He might be confronting these thoughts with fear, or only clinical interest. I really didn't know.

For the first time in my life then, and just for a few seconds, I was able to see Doc Homer as someone I felt sorry for. It was a turning point for me, one of those instants of freakishly clear sight when you understand that your parent might have taken entirely the wrong road in life, even if that road includes your own existence. I pitied Doc Homer for his slavish self-sufficiency. For standing Hallie and me in the kitchen and inspecting us like a general, not for crooked hems so much as for signs of the weakness of our age: the lipstick hidden in a book satchel, the smoldering wish to be like everyone else. Being like no one else, being alone, was the central ethic of his life. Mine too, to some extent, not by choice but by default. My father, the only real candidate for center of my universe, was content to sail his private sea and leave me on my own. I still held that against him. I hadn't thought before about how self-sufficiency could turn on you in old age or sickness. The captain was going down with his ship. He was just a man, becoming a child. It became possible for me to go back to Grace.

▼▼▼

I arrived at the house, nervous, ludicrously armed with Uda's squash pie. But he was in his darkroom. Not waiting. He called it his workroom, I think to try to legitimize his hobby to himself. Doc Homer made pictures. Specifically, he made photographs of things that didn't look like what they actually were. He had hundreds: clouds that looked like animals, landscapes that looked like clouds. They were pressed between slabs of cardboard, in closets. Only one was framed. The matting and framing were my present to him one Christmas when I was in high school, after I'd started making my own money. It had cost me a lot, and was a mistake. His hobby was a private thing, too frivolous in his opinion to be put on public display. I should have foreseen this, but didn't.

Nevertheless, he'd hung it in the kitchen, God only knows why because the man was far from sentimental, and there it still hung. It was the first thing I noticed when I knocked on the screen door and walked in. The photo was my favorite, a hand on a white table. And of course it wasn't a hand, but a clump of five saguaro cacti, oddly curved and bumpy, shot against a clear sky. All turned sideways. Odd as it seemed, this thing he did, there was a great deal of art to it.

I put the pie in the refrigerator and nosed around a little, telling myself it's what a good daughter would do. I pictured these good daughters—wifely and practical, wearing perms and loafers and Peter Pan collars. I didn't remotely look the part. As I crept around the house it felt to me like a great, sad, recently disclosed secret. The kitchen seemed smaller than when I was a girl, standing on a bucket to reach the sink, but that's natural. It was also crowded with odds and ends you wouldn't expect in a kitchen: a pair of Piper forceps, for example, washed with the day's dishes and sitting amongst them on the drainboard. This didn't signify any new eccentricity on his part. He'd always had a bizarre sense of utility. I could picture him using the forceps to deliver a head of cabbage from a pot of boiling water. Holding it up. Not in a show-off way, but proud he'd thought of it, as if he were part of a very small club of people who had the brains to put obstetrical instruments to use in the kitchen.

The rooms were cool and stale although it was hot outside. I stepped through the living room, over the old Turkish carpet, which looked malnourished, its bare white threads exposed like ribs. Doc Homer could afford better, I heard somebody say in my mind, a voice I couldn't identify. "All the money he's got up there." Which of course wasn't true, we never had much, that was just what people thought because we were standoffish.

Beyond the living room was the parlor where he used to see patients who'd come to the house, embarrassed, it seems to me now, at night when the office was closed. At present the parlor was shockingly cramped. The door to the outside porch was blocked by furniture I didn't remember: two sofas and something that looked like a cobbler's bench. Folded on a sofa was one thing I remembered well, a black crocheted afghan with red flowers. Hallie and I used to drag that thing around everywhere, our totem against disaster. It looked cleaner now than I'd ever seen it.

Magazines and journals were everywhere. His *American Journal of Genetics* was still organized chronologically on the shelf. That was his pet interest; they'd once published his article on the greatly inbred gene pool of Grace, with its marble-eyed babies. (He'd even rigged up a system for photographing the newborns' eyes, for documentation.) The trait first began showing up in the fifties, when third-cousin descendants of the Gracela sisters started marrying each other. Emelina would have been one of his subjects. You needed to get the gene from both sides; it was recessive. That's about what I knew. For me it was enough to understand that everyone in Grace was somehow related except us Nolines, the fish out of water. Our gene pool was back in Illinois.

Other magazines, many in number, were piled on the floor. I picked up a *Lancet:* 1977, my first year of med school. There was an important article on diabetes I remembered. Underneath, a recent *National Geographic.* There was no order at all. Though if I mentioned it he'd come up with some elaborate rationale before he'd admit to disorganization. South Sea Islands and Islets of Langerhans, I could see him saying, and not meaning it as a joke. The smell of mold was making my eyes water. I was inclined toward the stairs, to go up and see what kind of shape the bedrooms were in, but I didn't have the heart. It wasn't my house. I forced my hand to knock on the darkroom door.

"Open. I'm about to start printing."

I closed the door behind me. There was only a dim red light bulb. "Hi, Pop," I said.

He looked at me, unsurprised and not very much changed,

I could see as my eyes adjusted. I was prepared for frailty and incoherence but he was lucid and familiar. The same substantial hands and wrist bones, the straight nose and low, broad mouth—things I also have, without noticing much. He motioned for me to sit.

"So how are you these days?" I asked.

He ignored the question. We hadn't been together since the Holiday Inn lounge, two years ago, but from Doc Homer you didn't expect hugs and kisses. He was legendary in this regard. Hallie and I used to play a game we called "orphans" when we were with him in a crowd: "Who in this room is our true father or mother? Which is the one grownup here that loves us?" We'd watch for a sign—a solicitous glance, a compliment, someone who might even kneel down and straighten Hallie's hair ribbon, which we'd tugged out of alignment as bait. That person would never be Doc Homer. Proving to us, of course, that he wasn't the one grownup there who loved us.

I sat carefully on a cool file cabinet. He was adjusting black knobs on the enlarger, preparing to make a print. When he switched on the bulb an image appeared against the wall, in reverse: white trees, black sky, mottled foreground. I'd learned how to look at negatives many years before I read my first X-ray. He shrank the frame into focus, shut it off while he slid a rectangle of paper into place and set the timer, and then projected the picture again, burning it into the paper. In the center were two old men hunched on a stone wall, backs to the camera.

"They look like rocks," I said. "It's hard to see where the wall ends and the men start."

"Men who look like stones," said Doc Homer. His speech was more formal than most people's writing. Who else who would really say "stones"?

"Except for the hat," I said. "That hat's a giveaway."

"I'm taking it out." He held a small steel spatula into the beam of light and waved little circles over the area of the man's hat, as if he were rubbing it out, which is exactly what he was doing. Photographers call this "dodging," and the spatula was a "dodging tool," though in all probability this one was something used in gall-bladder surgery. When I was little I called it the Magic Wand.

The timer rang and he shut the projector off. I looked at his face in profile in the faint red light. Deep lines ran from his nose to the corners of his mouth. He didn't look well, but maybe he never had. He picked up the print by its edges.

"You haven't heard anything from Hallie, have you?"

He shook his head.

"You're sure you don't want me to tell her you've got, that you're sick? I'm sorry to bring this up, but it's hard to be the only one. I think she'd want to know."

He appeared not to have heard me. I knew he had. Doc Homer never argued, he just didn't participate in conversation that didn't please him.

"So did the man's hat go away?" I asked.

He slipped the paper into a dishpan of clear liquid. "We'll see." He seemed suddenly happy now, almost friendly, as he often did in here. The darkroom was the nearest I'd ever come to feeling like I had a dad. We stood without talking and watched a gray image grow on the paper like some fungus with a mind of its own. I thought about the complex chemistry of vision, remembering from medical school the textbook diagrams of an image projected through the eyeball, temporarily inscribed on the retina.

"I never thought about how printing a photograph duplicates eyesight," I said. "It's the same exact process in slow motion."

He nodded appreciatively and my heart warmed. I'd pleased him. "Probably there is no real invention in the modern world," he said. "Just a good deal of elaboration on nature." He lifted out the slick print and slipped it into a second tray, the fixer.

"The stone has no head," he pronounced, correctly; it looked like a rock wall with two extra rocks balanced on top. You'd think it was just a simple snapshot of what it looked like. His finest art defeated itself. God only knows what was the point, but it made him smile. When the timer rang again he took the photograph out and slid it into its final bath. He fished out several other prints and attached them with small clothespins to a wire. Then he dried his hands on a towel, one finger at a time. These gestures made me think of all the years he'd spent alone, doing his own dishes, his laundry.

I felt our visit drawing to a close, like a scientifically predicted death. We would go out into the light, find a little more to say, and then I'd go.

"There's a pie for you in the kitchen," I said. "From Uda. Who is she?"

"Uda Ruth Dell," he said, as though that explained it.

"I mean, what is she to me? Did I use to know her?"

"Not especially," said Doc Homer, still studying the photographs. "No better than you knew anyone else."

"She knows all about me, and then some," I said. "She probably knows what I had for lunch."

"You're in Grace," he said.

"Well, I was embarrassed because I couldn't remember her. She wasn't very helpful. She just stood there waiting for me to rack my brain and come up with her name. She sure knew me right off the bat."

Doc Homer didn't care for expressions like "right off the bat." He switched off the red light before opening the darkroom door, passing us through a moment of absolute darkness. He knew, but refused to accept, that I was afraid of the dark. The click and blackness plunged me into panic and I grabbed his upper arm. Surprisingly, he touched my knuckles lightly with his fingertips.

"You're in Grace," he said again, as if nothing had happened. "There is only one of you for all these people to be watching for. And so many of them for you."

▼▼▼

I'd lived all my life with a recurring nightmare. It would come to me in that drowsy twilight where sleep pulls on your mind with tempting music but is still preventable. When I let down my guard the dream would spring again, sending me back into weeks of insomnia. It had to do with losing my eyesight. It wasn't a complicated dream, like a movie, but a single, paralyzing freeze frame: there's a shattering pop, like glass breaking, and then I am blind.

Once, years ago on Crete, Carlo and I were driving on a badly rutted gravel road to get to a beach on the south of the island. A truck loaded with blood oranges kicked up a rock that broke the windshield in front of my face. I wasn't hurt, the rock only pocked the glass and spun out a spiderweb of cracks, but I spent the rest of the day in mute hysteria. Carlo never did know what was wrong. Any explanation I could think of sounded like superstition. My dream was very much more than a dream. It had so much living weight to it, such prescience, it felt like something that was someday bound to happen.

The insomnia, on the other hand, wasn't such a big problem as you might imagine. I worked around it. I read a lot. In med school I did my best studying while my classmates were in the throes of rapid eye movement. I still considered my night-prowling habits to be a kind of secret advantage I had over other people. I had the extra hours in my day that they were always wishing for.

Emelina would not understand this. The night before school started, she brought me warm milk.

"Don't worry about it," I said. She'd also brought out a blue embroidered tablecloth, which she shook out like a little sail and spread efficiently over my table. She felt the place needed more homey touches.

"You've got to have your sleep. They had a special on Nova about it. This man in Italy died from not sleeping for around eight months. Before he died he went crazy. He'd salute the doctors like he was in the army."

"Em, I'll live. That's too pretty, that tablecloth. Don't you need that?"

"Are you kidding? Since Grammy joined Stitch and Bitch she's been embroidering borders on the dish rags. What happens if you just lie in bed and count backward from ninety-nine? That's what I tell the boys to do when they can't settle down."

"Insomnia's different," I said. It was hard to explain this to people. "You know the light that comes on when you open the refrigerator door? Just imagine it stays on all the time, even after you close the door. That's what it's like in my head. The light stays on."

Emelina made herself comfortable in my other living-room chair. "You're like that Thoreau guy that lived at Walden Pond. Remember when we read that in Senior English? He only had two chairs. We need to get you some more stuff in here."

I was surprised that Henry Thoreau entered into Emelina's world view. "If I want company I can always go over to your house," I pointed out.

"That's the God's truth. I'm about ready to move out. Tonight Glen and Grammy got into it, oh boy, she says he's *impudent*. That's her all-time favorite word. Whenever Mason gets mad at somebody he yells 'You're impotent!' And people laugh, so we'll never get him to stop now."

I drank the milk. I could stand some mothering. I wondered if I'd had this in the back of my mind when I moved in here.

Emelina scrutinized my clean, white walls. "Codi, I hope you'll take this the right way, but I don't see how you can live in a place and have it feel like nobody lives there."

"I have things in here. My clothes, look in the closet. And books. Some of those books are very personal." This was true. Besides my *Field Guide to the Invertebrates* there were things Hallie had sent me over the years, and an old volume of American poetry—incomprehensibly, a graduation gift from Doc Homer.

"Your room was like this when we were in high school. I had posters of Paul Revere and the Raiders and dead corsages stuck in the mirror, every kind of junk. And when we'd go over to your house it was like a room somebody'd just moved out of."

"I'm neat," I said.

"It's not neat. It's *hyper* neat."

"Can you imagine what Doc Homer would have said if Paul Revere and the Raiders turned up in his home? Without an appointment?"

She laughed.

"Emelina, who's Uda Ruth Dell?"

"Well, you know her, she lives up by Doc Homer. She used to take care of you sometimes, I think. Her and that other woman that's dead now, I think her name was Naomi."

"She used to take care of us?" I'd been trying all day to place her. I couldn't believe I'd draw a complete blank on someone who'd been a fixture of my childhood.

"Sure. Uda's husband Eddie saved you and Hallie's life that time when you got stranded in a storm down by the crick."

"I don't have any idea what you're talking about."

"Yes you do. When you and Hallie almost drowned in that flood. You were just little."

"Well, how do you remember it, then? I don't."

"Everybody knew about that. It was a famous incident. You hid down in a coyote burrow and wouldn't come out and Eddie Dell found you and drug you out. You all stayed at Uda's. Doc Homer must have been working at the hospital or something."

"I don't remember anything about that."

Emelina looked at me peculiarly, as if she thought I might be pulling her leg. "It was a real big deal. There was a picture in the paper of you two and Eddie the big hero, and his mule."

"I guess I do remember," I said, but I didn't, and it bothered me that my childhood was everyone's property but my own.

"You know what you are, Codi? I don't know if there's a word for it, but it's the opposite of 'homemaker.' "

I laughed. She was still distressed by my blank walls. "There's a word. Home wrecker. But I'm not one."

"No I don't mean in the sense of home wrecker. I mean in the sense of home ignorer."

"Oh, that way," I said. I was playing dumb. I knew what she meant. My first boyfriend in college was a Buddhist, and even he had had more pictures on his wall than I did. It wasn't anything noble; I couldn't claim a disdain for worldly things. Hallie had once pointed out that I had more shoes than you'd find in a Central American schoolroom with class in session. What I failed at was the activity people call "nesting." For me, it never seemed like nesting season had arrived yet. Or I wasn't that kind of bird.

After Emelina left for the night, I wrote Hallie. I had a general-delivery address for her in Managua and I asked, the way we did when we were kids leaving notes for each other in secret hiding places, "Are you there yet? Are you reading this now?" I told her about the dead alfalfa fields around Gracela Canyon, which I thought would interest her professionally, and I told her Doc Homer seemed pretty much the same as ever, which was the truth. And I asked if she remembered the time we almost drowned in a coyote den.

9

THE BONES IN GOD'S BACKYARD

Grace High School, backdrop of the worst four years of my life, was as familiar as one of my bad dreams. Walking toward it up Prosper Street filled me with dread. The building itself had a lot of charm, though, which surprised me. As a child I'd paid no mind to the façade. It was a WPA-era building made of Gracela Canyon's red granite, with ornate egg-and-dart moldings on the white-painted eaves and woodwork over the doors. The school was actually built by the mining company, in its boom years, and with minerly instincts (or possibly just the proper tools) it was built right into the steep side of the canyon, sunk into rock. It was in an old part of town where the cobbled streets wrapped up and around behind the buildings, occasionally breaking into flights of steps and elsewhere so steep as to make motor vehicles pointless. The principal form of exercise in Grace was just getting from your house to wherever you needed to go.

The school had four floors, and each one had a street-level entrance. I'm pretty sure the building was in some record book on account of this. The main entrance was on the side, halfway up the hill: floor three. Carved into its granite arch was a grammatically suspect motto in Latin, CAUSAM MEAM COGNOSCO, which boys used to quote like pig latin or the inane "Indian" talk we heard in movies.

I checked into the principal's office, where his secretary, Anita, gave me a set of keys and an armload of official-looking papers and cheered me on. "There's a million forms there: grade forms, class roster, some new thing from the DES, and your CTA. It all has to be filled out."

"What, you mean I have to work for a living here? Somebody told me teaching high school was easy money." I looked through the stack of forms. "What about DOA? I may need one of those."

Anita looked at me oddly for half a second, then laughed. "We'll just call the coroner when they bring you in."

I smiled. Doc Homer was the coroner of Grace, and had been for the entirety of my life and then some. Obviously Anita didn't know who I was; she looked like a recent graduate herself. Anyone in high school now would have been a toddler when I left Grace. This filled me with hope. Walking those wainscoted halls, still painted the exact same shade of toothpaste green, made me shrink into my skin, and I had to keep reminding myself: None of them knows you as Doc Homer's misfit child. No one here has seen you in orthopedic shoes.

"The kids'll just love you," Anita said, surprising me. "They're not used to anybody so . . ." she paused, tapping a complete set of maroon fingernails on her metal desk and presumably fishing for a tactful adjective . . . "so *contemporary*."

I was wearing a dark green blazer, tight jeans, and purple cowboy boots. I ran a hand through my hair and wondered if I should have paid a call to the Hollywood Shop, after all. "Do you think I'm not enough of an authority figure? Will they revolt?" The teachers' meeting, two days prior, had been devoted primarily to theories of discipline.

Anita laughed. "No way. They know who turns in the grades."

I found the room where I would be teaching General Biology I and II, and made it through the homeroom period by taking attendance and appearing preoccupied. I'd finally paid my preparatory visit to the school a few days earlier, so I knew what to expect in the way of equipment: desks and chairs; some stone-topped lab benches with sinks and arched chrome faucets; an emergency shower; a long glass case containing butterflies and many other insects in ill repair; and a closet full of dissecting pans and arcane audiovisual aids. The quaint provisions led me to expect I'd be working in something like a museum, or a British movie. When the kids filled the room for first period, though, they gave it a different slant. So far in Grace I hadn't seen a lot of full-blown teenagers. I wasn't expecting skateboard haircuts.

The girls seemed to feel a little sorry for me as I stood up there brushing chalk dust off my blazer and explaining what I intended for us to do in the coming year. But the boys sat with their enormous high-top sneakers splayed out into the aisles, their arms crossed, and their bangs in their eyes, looking at me like exactly what I was—one of the last annoying things standing between them and certified adulthood.

"You can call me Codi," I said, though I'd been warned against this. "Ms. Noline sounds too weird. I went to this high school and had biology in this room, and I don't really feel that old. I guess to you that sounds like a joke. To you I'm the wicked old witch of Life Science."

This got a very slight rise out of the boys, not exactly a laugh. The girls looked embarrassed. A tall boy wearing a Motley Crüe T-shirt and what looked like a five-o'clock shadow on his scalp pulled a cigarette out of his pocket and thumped it against his knuckles.

"I was told we'd need an authority figure in the classroom, so I dug one up." I went to the closet and wheeled out a human skeleton. "This is Mrs. Josephine Nash."

I'd found her downstairs in a storage room filled with damaged field-hockey equipment and gym uniforms from the fifties. The skeleton was in pretty good shape; I'd only had to reattach one elbow with piano wire and duct tape (provided by the janitor). The name—along with an address in Franklin, Illinois—was written in fine, antique-looking letters on the flange of her pelvis. When I discovered her in the storage room I felt moved to dust her off and hang her up on the heavy cast-iron stand and wheel her up to my lab. I guess I was somewhat desperate for companionship.

"Miss," one of the boys said. "Miss Codi."

I tried not to smile. "Yes."

"That's Mr. Bad Bones." He enunciated the name in a way that made everybody laugh. "The seniors use him for the Halloween Dance."

"Well, not anymore," I said. Mrs. Nash was my compatriot from the Midwest; a possible relative, even. I could see her as somebody's mother, out pruning roses. "This isn't a toy," I said, my voice shaking slightly. "It's the articulated skeleton of a human being who was at one time, fairly recently, walking around alive. Her name was Josephine Nash and she lived in Illinois. And it's time she got some respect in her retirement."

I glared at them; teenagers are so attached to their immortality. "You never know where you're going to end up in this world, do you?" I asked.

Nineteen pairs of blank, mostly pale-blue eyes looked back at me. You could have heard a cigarette drop.

"Okay," I said. "Chapter one: Matter, Energy, Organization and Life."

▼▼▼

"I don't know if I'm going to live through this," I told Emelina, collapsing in her kitchen. Her kitchen chairs were *equipales* that took you in like a hug, which I needed. My first day had gone as smoothly as anybody could reasonably hope—no revolts, no crises major or minor. Still, I couldn't put a finger on what it was, but standing in front of a roomful of high school students seemed to use up a ferocious amount of energy. It made me think of those dancers in white boots and miniskirts who used to work bars in the sixties, trying desperately to entertain, flailing around like there was no tomorrow.

Emelina, Mason, the baby, and I were all exiled to the kitchen; Viola had taken over the living room with her friends for a special afternoon meeting of the Stitch and Bitch Club. They were preparing for their annual fundraising bazaar, and as a backdrop to our own conversation we could overhear the exchange of presumably vital information:

"Last year the Hospital Equipment Committee didn't make fifteen cents on them sachet cushions."

"Well, it's no wonder. They stunk."

"Lalo saw in a magazine where you can make airplanes out of cut beer cans. The propellers go around."

Emelina set a cup of tea in front of me. I picked it up and let the steam touch my eyelids, realizing that what I needed most at that moment was to lie in bed with someone who was fond of every inch of my skin.

"It must be weird, going back to that school," she said.

"Oh, sure. It is. I didn't let myself think too much about that part of the job. Till today."

Mason was on the floor, coloring, and Emelina was moving around the kitchen in an effortless frenzy, closing drawers with her hip, cooking dinner, and feeding the baby at the same time.

"Let me do that," I said, scooting myself over to the high chair and taking the cereal bowl from Emelina.

"Here, he makes a pretty fair mess, let me give you Grammy's apron," she said, tying around me a splendid example of Stitch and Bitch enterprise. The baby snapped up cereal as fast as I could spoon it in, wasting little on mess as far as I could see.

"You're having dinner with us tonight, right?"

"No, thanks," I said.

"Honestly, Codi, if you think one more mouth to feed is any trouble you're out of your mind. If I woke up one day and had six more kids I don't think I'd notice."

"No, Em, thanks, but I feel like resting in peace."

"You're not dead yet, hon."

From the living room we heard Viola raising her voice now in Spanish, saying something about peacocks: *pavones*. The other women answered in Spanish, and I could follow just enough to know that they'd moved rapidly onto the subject of fruit trees. Doña Althea sounded agitated. Her high-pitched voice was easy to recognize, exactly what you'd expect from a very small, strong-willed woman. Emelina raised her eyebrows as she looked under a pot lid. "Do you know the boys won't even speak Spanish to their Grammy?" she asked in a subdued voice.

I glanced at Mason, who was absorbed in his coloring book, though probably listening. "Is that a problem?"

"Oh, yeah. Viola's big on all the traditional stuff. She's real tight with Doña Althea. She wants us to raise the boys *puro,* speaking Spanish and knowing all the stories. Seems like it might be easier with girls, but these guys . . ." She shrugged her shoulders. "My parents were always so modern, you remember how Mom is, electric can openers all the way. I always felt like she wanted me to grow up *blonde,* you know? My dad told me she actually wanted to name me *Gidget!*"

I laughed. "No. He was pulling your leg."

"No, he wasn't. And poor Tucker was named after a car."

Tucker was a younger brother who'd died in infancy, before I ever knew the family. To tell the truth, I'd forgotten him, in spite of his name passed on to Emelina's first son.

The baby was sitting with his mouth opened unbelievably wide, waiting for my attention to return to his dinner. I poked in the next bite. A scattering of loud laughter like a rainstorm came from the other room, and all of us in the kitchen were quiet. This gang of old women staked out such a presence, we felt almost crowded out of the house. Mason actually gathered up his papers and started to go outside.

Emelina called him back. "Wait a minute, Mason, before you run off, come show Codi your hand. Codi, could you take a look at his hand? There's some kind of bump on it. Do you mind?"

"Why would I mind? Let's have a look." I felt uncomfortable, not because she'd asked, but with myself, playing doctor. I *was* a doctor, technically, which is to say I had the training, but it unnerved me to think people saw me in that role. Both Emelina and Mason were quiet while I examined his hand. I bent the wrist back and forth and felt the lump on the tendon. "It's a ganglion."

"Is that bad?" Emelina asked.

"No, it's not serious at all. Just a little bump. Usually they go away on their own. Does it hurt, Mason?"

He shook his head. "Only when he has chores to do," Emelina offered.

I put a kiss on my fingertips and rubbed it into his wrist. "There you go, Dr. Codi's special cure." As he ran off it occurred to me, with a certain self-punitive malice, that this was the extent of special curing I was licensed to dispense.

"So what's it like up there at the high school?" Emelina asked.

"Don't you keep feeling like Miss Lester's going to catch you smoking in the bathroom?"

"*I* never smoked in the bathroom," I said, scraping the bottom of the cereal bowl and wiping the baby's mouth with his bib. I'd never seen such efficient eating in my life.

"Oh that's right, Miss Goody Two-Shoes, I forgot. You didn't do things like that." Emelina smiled. She'd been at least as virtuous as I was in high school; the difference was she was popular. Virtue in a cheerleader is admirable, while in a wallflower it's gratuitous.

"Miss Goody Orthopedic-Shoes," I said.

She hooted. "*Why* on God's green earth did you and Hallie wear those shoes? I never did ask. I figured the polite thing was to just ignore them. Like when somebody has something hanging out of their nose."

"Thank you. We wore them because Doc Homer was obsessed with the bones of the foot."

"Kinky old Doc," she said, stabbing a wooden spoon into a pot of boiled potatoes.

"You have no idea. He used to sit us down and give us lectures on how women destroy their bodies through impractical footwear." I delivered his lecture, which Hallie and I used to ape behind his back: "Of the two hundred bones in the human body, more than a quarter are in the foot. It is a more complicated instrument that an automobile transmission, and it is treated with far less consideration."

Emelina was laughing. "Really, you have to give him credit. All my mom ever told me was 'Sit up straight! Don't get pregnant! And wear a slip!' "

"Doc Homer wasn't that great on pregnancy and underwear, but Lord knows the Noline girls were not going to have fallen arches."

"Where'd you get those god-awful things from? Not the Hollywood Shop, I know that."

"Mail order."

"No."

"Swear to God. Hallie and I used to burn the catalogues in the fireplace when they came but he'd still get those damn shoes.

For the sizing he'd draw around our feet on a piece of paper and then take all these different measurements. I expect I spent more time with Doc Homer getting my foot measured than any other thing."

Emelina found this hilarious. I know she thought I was exaggerating, but I wasn't. In a way we were grateful for the attention, but the shoes were so appalling. They affected our lives, the two of us differently. Hallie just gave up trying for image, while I went the route of caring too much. It was harder for me, being the first to break into junior high, then high school, in these shoes. I suffered first and therefore more.

"I'm positive that was the whole reason I hardly ever had any dates in high school," I told Emelina.

"That's ridiculous," she said. "The only reason boys didn't ask you out was because they thought you were too good for them. You were so smart, why would you want to run with a Grace boy? That's what they thought."

The meeting in the living room was beginning to break up. We lowered our voices automatically.

"No," I said solemnly. "It was the shoes. It's a known fact. The day I left Grace I bought a pair of gladiator sandals and my sex life picked right up."

▼▼▼

Emelina eventually remembered a letter for me she'd been carrying around a while. She'd stuck it in the diaper bag when she picked up the mail, and then forgotten it, so it suffered more in its last hundred yards of delivery than it had in its previous fifteen hundred miles. Of course, it was from Hallie.

I went home to read it, like a rat scurrying back to its hole with some edible prize. I settled into the living-room chair, polished my glasses, and scowled at the postmark: Chiapas, near Mexico's southern border, only days after she left. That was a disappointment, anything could have happened since then. I slit it open.

Codi dear,

I've been driving the way you're supposed to here, like a bat out of hell, the *wrong way* out of hell whenever that's possible. I'm getting the hang of outlawry. You'd be proud. I burned up the road till around La Cruz and then slowed down enough to enjoy the banana trees going by in a blur. The tropics are such a gaudy joke: people have to live with every other kind of poverty, but a fortune in *flowers,* growing out of every nook and cranny of anything. If you could just build an economy on flowers. I stayed in a house that had vanilla orchids growing out of the gutters and a banana tree coming up under the kitchen sink. I swear. There were some kind of little animals too, like mongooses. You would know what they are. I'm happy to be in a jungle again. You know me, I'm always cheered by the sight of houseplants growing wild and fifty feet tall. I keep thinking about 626-BUGS and all those sad ladies trying to grow zebrinas in an arid climate.

I wanted to take the coast highway as far as Nayarit, where it gets rugged, but I paid the price for that little adventure. (Doc Homer would say: I paid a dollar for my shiny dime.) I broke, not bent but flat out busted an axle in Tuxpan and spent two days waiting around while a man with a Fanta delivery truck and time on his hands brought in a new one from Guadalajara. The only hotel was a two-story pension with live band (euphemism) on weekends. I spent the time mostly sitting on my balcony watching pelicans dive-bomb the sea, and remembering our trip to San Blas. Remember those pelicans? If you'd been there, in Tuxpan, it would have been fun. I couldn't bring myself to do anything productive—there were people I could have talked to about crops and the refugee scene, but instead I spent one whole morning watching a man walk up the beach selling shrimp door to door. He had a pole over his shoulders, with the bucket of shrimp hung on one side and on the other side a plastic jug of water. Every time he sold a kilo of shrimp he'd pour out that much water and drink it, to balance the load. I watched him all the way down the bay and thought, *I want to be like that.* Not like the man selling shrimp. Like his *machine.* To give myself over to utility, with no waste.

But I was useless, lying around those two days. Saving my strength for what's ahead, I guess. I get more jumpy as I move south, like a compass needle or something. Saw an awful lot of dead cropland in the interior, and I know it will be worse in Nicaragua. War brings out the worst in production agriculture.

Tomorrow I cross the border, but it's hard to say where the border is, because this whole part of Chiapas where I am now is camps of

Guatemalans. This whole livelong day I drove horrible mountain roads in the rain and saw refugee camps, one after another like a dream. They say the Guatemalan army is on a new scorched-earth campaign, so people come running across the border with the clothes on their backs and their hearts in their throats and on a good day the Mexican cops don't bother them. On a bad day, they make them wake up the kids, take down their hammocks, and move into somebody else's district. It's a collective death. A whole land-based culture is being relocated out of its land—like a body trying to move out of its skin. Only the portable things survive. The women have their backstrap looms and woven clothes, like you see sometimes in import stores. All those brilliant colors in this hopeless place, it kills you.

Right this minute I'm sitting in the rain, waiting for the mail truck/water delivery (I keep expecting that same guy with his Fanta truck) and watching four barefoot kids around a cook fire. The one in charge is maybe six. She's sharpening cooking sticks while these damp black chickens strut around shaking themselves and the toddlers pull logs out and roll them to make sparks. I'm just on edge. You live your life in the States and you can't even picture something like this. It's easy to get used to the privilege of a safe life.

I know you're worrying but you don't have to, since we've established that I'm the luckiest person alive. Even though I don't feel like it. I'll write from Nica next. I'm sure I'll be happier once I'm put to some use. I miss you, Codi, write and make me feel better.

Love from your faithful adoring slave-for-life,

Hallie

The ending was an old joke: in our letters we used to try to outdo each other with ingratiating closures. The rest of the letter was pure Hallie. Even in a lethargic mood she noticed every vanilla orchid, every agony and ecstasy. Especially agony. She might as well not have had skin, where emotions were concerned. Other people's hurt ran right over into her flesh. For example: I'll flip through a newspaper and take note of the various disasters, and then Hallie will read the same paper and cry her eyes out. She'll feel like she has to *do* something about it. And me, if I want to do anything, it's to run hell for leather in the other direction. Maybe it's true what they say, that as long as you're nursing your own pain, whatever it is, you'll turn your back on others in the same boat. You'll want to believe the fix they're in is their own damn fault.

The strangest thing is that where pain seemed to have anesthetized me, it gave Hallie extra nerve endings. This haunts me. What we suffered in our lives we went through together, but somehow we came out different doors, on different ground levels.

▼▼▼

Friday night after the first week of school, the dog with the green bandana showed up again at the gate. I saw it when I came outside after my solitary supper to water the morning glories and potted geraniums on my front step. The heat seemed to wilt them right down to death's door, but water always brought them back. I could only wish for such resilience.

"Hi, buddy," I said to the dog. "No barbecues today. You're out of luck."

Thirty seconds later Loyd was standing at the door with a bottle of beer. "I told you I'd get back to you with this," he said, grinning. "I'm a man of my word."

"Well, okay," I said. "I guess you are." I wasn't sure how I felt about seeing him in my doorway, other than surprised. I pulled a couple of folding chairs onto the patio, where we could see the sunset. The sky was a bright, artificial-looking orange, a color you might expect to see in the Hollywood Shop. "Are you going to have one too, or do I drink this alone?" I asked him.

Loyd said he'd just take a soda because he was marked up and five times out. I was mystified by this information.

"I'm marked up on the call board at the depot," he explained. "To take a train out. Five times out means I'm fifth in line. I'll probably get called late tonight or early tomorrow morning."

"Oh," I said. "It sounded like baseball scores. The count is three and two and it's the bottom of the seventh."

Loyd laughed. "I guess it would sound like that. You get used to talking railroad talk like it was plain English. Around here that's about all everybody does, is railroad."

"That, and watch the fruit fall off their trees."

Loyd looked at me, surprised. "You know about that, do you?"

"Not very much," I said. I went into my house to get him a soda, picking my way over the rough bricks of the patio because I was barefoot. I will say this much for Doc Homer's career as a father: my arches are faultless.

When I came back out I sat down and handed over a Coke, letting Loyd fight with the easy-off twist cap himself. I had to use pliers on those things. It didn't give Loyd two seconds of trouble. He palmed it, then tipped his head back and drank about half the bottle. The things that aggravate me most in the world are the things men do without even knowing it.

"So is that your dog?" I asked.

"That's Jack. You met? Jack, this lady here is Codi Noline."

"We've met," I said. "I sneaked him some goat spare ribs the other day at the fiesta. I hope he's not on a special diet or anything."

"He's in love, is what he is, if you gave him a piece of that goat. That was one of Angel Pilar's yearling billy goats. Jack's had his eye on those spare ribs ever since last summer."

Jack looked at me, panting seriously. His tongue was purplish, and his eyes were very dark brown and lively. Sometimes when you look into an animal's eyes you see nothing, no sign of connection, just the flat stare of a wild creature. But Jack's eyes spoke worlds. I liked him.

"He looks like a coyote," I said.

"He is. Half. I'll tell you the story of his life sometime."

"I can't wait," I said, really meaning it, though it came out sounding a little sarcastic. Our chairs were close enough together so that I could have reached over and squeezed Loyd's hand, but I didn't do that.

"It was nice of you to come by," I said.

"So this was your first week of school, right? How's life with the juvenile delinquents of Grace?"

I was a little bit flattered that he knew about my job. But then everybody would. "I don't know," I said. "Pretty scary, I think. I'll keep you posted."

The sky had faded from orange to pale pink, and the courtyard was dusky under the fig trees. Every night as it got dark the vegetation around the house seemed to draw itself in closer, hugging the whitewashed walls, growing dense as a jungle.

Loyd touched my forearm lightly and pointed. On the cliff above the courtyard wall, a pair of coyotes trotted along a narrow animal path. Jack's ears stood up and rotated like tracking dishes as we watched them pass.

"You know what the Navajos call coyotes? God's dogs," Loyd said. His fingers were still resting on my forearm.

"Why's that?" I asked.

He took his hand back and cracked his knuckles behind his head. He leaned back in his chair, stretching out his legs. "I don't know. I guess because they run around burying bones in God's backyard."

Jack got up and went to the courtyard wall. He stood as still as a rock fence except for one back leg, which trembled, betraying all the contained force of whatever it was he wanted to do just then, but couldn't. After a minute he came back to Loyd's feet, turned his body in a tight circle two or three times, and lay down with a soft moan.

"Why do they do that? Turn in circles like that?" I asked. I'd never lived with a dog and was slightly infatuated with Jack.

"Beating down the tall grass to make a nice little nest," Loyd said. "Even if there's no tall grass."

"Well, I guess that make sense, from a dog's point of view."

"Sure it does." He bent forward to scratch Jack between the ears. "We take these good, smart animals and put them in a house and then wonder why they keep on doing the stuff that made them happy for a million years. A dog can't think that much about what he's doing, he just does what feels right."

We were both quiet for a while. "How do you know what the Navajos call coyotes? I thought you were Apache." I felt vaguely that it might be racist to discuss Loyd's breeding, but he didn't seem offended.

"I'm a lot of stuff," he said. "I'm a mongrel, like Jack. I was born up in Santa Rosalia Pueblo. My mama still lives up there. You ever been up there to Pueblo country?"

"No," I said.

"It's pretty country. You ought to go sometime. I lived up there when I was a little kid, me and my brother Leander. God, we ran wild all over that place."

"You have a brother? I never knew that."

"Twin," Loyd said. "He's dead."

Everybody's got a secret, I thought, and for the first time that evening I remembered the child of Loyd's that was unknown to him. It felt furtive and strange to hold it in mind in his presence, as if I were truly holding it, and he might see it.

A dust-colored peafowl hopped onto the courtyard wall and then into the fig, rustling the leaves and warning us off with a throaty, chirruping sound. She was awkward and heavy-bodied, no more flight-worthy than a helicopter.

"So you're Pueblo, and Apache, and Navajo," I said.

"My dad's Apache. We boys left Mama and came down to White Mountain to live with him, but it didn't work out. I ended up in Grace with my mama's sister. You knew my *tía* Sonia, right?"

"I don't think so. Is she still around?"

"No. She's gone back to Santa Rosalia. I need to go up there and see her and Mama one of these days."

It sounded like a strangely scattered family. I still wasn't clear on the Navajo connection.

"Can I use your phone?" he asked suddenly.

"Sure. It might be in use, it's Emelina's and J.T.'s phone. They just ran an extension out for me."

He looked toward the main house as he ducked into my front door. Emelina and J.T. were both home tonight, and Loyd seemed a little guilty about not going over to say hello. It would have been easy for him to come by on the pretense of visiting them, but he hadn't. I wondered if Loyd still had a reputation as a ladies' man. Though it was nothing to me, one way or the other. Jack raised his head and peered at me through the darkness, then got up and moved slightly closer to me. I stretched my leg and rubbed his back with my bare foot. His coat was a strange blend of textures: wiry on top and soft, almost downy underneath.

Hallie and I almost had a dog once, back when our Tucson house was on the underground railroad. Hallie had come home one night with a refugee woman and child and a little cinnamon dog. The mother had been tortured and her eyes offered out that flatness, like a zoo animal. But I remember the girl, in a short pink dress and corduroy pants, following that puppy under the bathroom sink and all over the house. I had no reason to believe, now, that any of the three was still living. The woman and her daughter were eventually arrested and sent back to tropical, lethal San Salvador. And we'd decided realistically that we didn't have room for a dog, so it went to the Humane Society. Terms like that, "Humane Society," are devised with people like me in mind, who don't care to dwell on what happens to the innocent.

Loyd came back out, being careful not to slam the decrepit screen door. "I'm next in line," he said. "Three guys ahead of me laid off to watch the Padres game. I better get home." Jack got up instantly and went to his side.

"Well, thanks," I said, still thinking of the cinnamon dog. I held up my bottle. "It's nice to see you again, Loyd."

He stood there grinning, the fingers of his right hand playing with Jack's nape. I didn't know quite how to finish off the evening. Loyd hesitated and then said, "I've got to drive up to Whiteriver, a week from Saturday. To see about something."

"Well, that sounds mysterious," I said.

"To see about some game birds. Anyway I thought you might like to get out of here for some fresh air. You want to go?"

I took a deep breath. "Sure," I said. I wasn't sure at all, but my mind had apparently made itself up. "Okay. I could use some fresh air."

Loyd gave a funny little nod, and went out through the gate. Jack disappeared behind him into the cactus jungle.

HOMERO

10

THE MASK

He is lying on his own examining table, resting his eyes. The telephone buzzes quietly but Mrs. Quintana, his receptionist, has given up the battle with insurance forms and gone home.

He places his long hands over his face, the fingertips lightly touching his forehead, thumbs resting on the maxillary bones beneath his eyes. His office in the hospital basement is cool even in this late September heat, and pleasant in winter as well. As practical and comforting as a cave. The lack of windows has never been a problem; artificial lighting is adequate. He has just examined his last patient of the day, a sixteen-year-old with six small gold rings piercing the cartilage of her left ear. She is expecting twins. They will be born small, and in trouble. There was no reason to tell her everything.

He imagines the procedure by which the tiny gold wires were inserted through flesh and spongy bone. It would have to be painful. He is mystified. Children devote slavish attention to these things, but can't be bothered with prophylactics.

He drifts between wakefulness and sleep, thinking of Codi. Her eyes are downturned and secretive, her heart clearly hardened against him already, to have done this. Her hair is in her eyes. She flips it sideways, chewing the inside of her lip and looking out the window when he talks to her. She'd wanted pierced ears at thirteen; he'd explained that self-mutilation was preposterous and archaic. Now they discuss shoes. He wants to ask, "Do you know what you have inside you? Does your sister know?" Hallie is young to understand reproductive matters but it's impossible that she wouldn't know, they're so much of a single mind, and he is outside of it completely. He has no idea what he can say.

She's in the fifth or sixth month, from the look of her, although Codi was always too thin and now is dangerously thin, and so skillful at disguising it with her clothes he can only tell by other signs. The deepened pigmentation under her eyes and across the bridge of her nose, for one thing, is identical to the mask of pregnancy Alice wore both times, first with Codi, then with Hallie. It stuns him. He feels a sharp pain in his spleen when he looks across the breakfast table each morning and sees this: his wife's face. The ghost of their happiest time returned to inhabit the miserable body of their child. He can't help feeling he has damaged them all, just by linking them together. His family is a web of women dead and alive, with himself at the center like a spider, driven by different instincts. He lies mute, hearing only in the tactile way that a spider hears, touching the threads of the web with long extended fingertips and listening. Listening for trapped life.

COSIMA

11

A RIVER ON THE MOON

Loyd and I didn't go to Whiteriver. He was called out on Friday for a seven-day stand on a switch engine in Lordsburg. He seemed disappointed and promised we'd go another time. Loyd didn't have much seniority on the railroad; he'd only moved back to Grace a few years earlier, and at Southern Pacific he was still getting what he called "bumped" a lot. It was hard to plan his time off.

I was somewhat relieved. I'd been unsure of what I was getting into, and had my doubts. Once I found out, I had more.

I'd asked J.T. what "game birds" were. He and I were out working in the old plum orchard one evening, pruning dead branches out of the trees. My job was mainly to stay out of the way of falling timber. It was a fair distance from the house, and Emelina had asked if I could go along to keep an eye on him. She wasn't the type to worry, but a man hanging from the treetops wielding a chainsaw is a nerve-racking sight, believe me. Even if he isn't your husband.

J.T. informed me that game birds were fighting cocks. He was taking a break just then, leaning on one hand against a tree trunk and drinking what seemed like gallons of water.

I was stunned. "You mean like cockfights."

J.T. smiled. "You been talking to Loyd?"

"He invited me to go with him up to Whiteriver. He said something about game birds, and . . ." I laughed at myself. "I don't know, I was thinking of something you'd eat. Cornish hens."

He laughed too. He offered me the jar of water and I drank from it before handing it back. I was surprised at the easy intimacy I felt with J.T. We hadn't been friends in high school—he was, after all, captain of the football team. Through no meanness on his part, but simply because of the natural laws of adolescent segregation, we might as well have gone to high school on different planets. Being neighbors again now brought back what we'd forgotten then: we had a relationship that dated back even before Emelina. We were next-door neighbors in toddlerhood. We'd played together before male and female had meaning.

He turned up the glass jar and drank it to the bottom, tensing the muscles in his jaw when he swallowed. J.T.'s whole body shone with sweat. I briefly imagined him naked, which disturbed me. I'd slept with someone's husband before—an Asian history professor in college—mistaking his marital status for something comforting and fatherly. But I was devoted to Emelina. No, that wouldn't happen.

It was early October, and still hot. Grace was supposed to have the perfect climate, like Camelot or Hawaii, and it's true that growing up here I could hardly remember an uncomfortable day, temperature-wise. Most of the homes had neither air-conditioning nor central heating, and didn't need them, but this fall had turned into hell warmed over. Down in the desert, in Tucson, every day was in the hundred-and-teens and the TV weathermen were reporting the string of broken records almost proudly, like scores in a new sport. In Grace no one kept track especially, but we suffered just the same.

J.T. knelt down to start the chainsaw again, but I spoke up before he could yank the cord. "I thought cockfighting was illegal."

"Most everywhere it is, but not in the state of Arizona. And up on the reservation they've got their own laws. Loyd's not a criminal, if that's what you're asking."

"I guess I don't know what I'm asking. I just can't see Loyd and cockfighting."

"His daddy was real big in the sport. He was kind of a legend up there in Apache country."

"So Loyd's got to keep up the tradition," I said, without sympathy. I knew Loyd's father was also a renowned drunk.

J.T. asked, "You an animal lover?"

"Not to extremes," I said. "I eat them." I thought of how unmoved I'd been watching Emelina chop off heads for our Sunday dinner, that first day in Grace. "But watching animals kill each other for sport," I said tentatively, "that's kind of an unsavory business, isn't it?" I looked toward the edge of the orchard. It was getting dark fast. Already I could see moonlight reflected in the irrigation ditches.

J.T. sat on his heels and looked straight up into the branches over our heads. "I don't know why I mess with these trees," he said. "They're sixty years old. They don't produce worth a damn anymore. I could cut them down and get a lot better out of this ground, not to mention the firewood. But my daddy gave me this orchard." He picked up the stone of a plum, weathered shiny white like a tooth, and rubbed it with his thumb. After a minute he raised his arm with a quick overhand snap and threw it toward the river. "Loyd's old man didn't have one damn thing to give him but cockfighting." J.T. looked at me. "I'm not crazy about it either, Codi. But you've got to know Loyd before you decide."

▼▼▼

I dropped the subject of cockfighting. Loyd had begun to come by fairly regularly in the evenings, which is to say regular for a railroad man: I'd see him three days in a row, and then not at all for a week. It reinforced the feeling that we were only casual acquaintances, meeting nearly by accident, and I tried to limit my expectations to the point where I paid no attention to how I looked in the evenings. Sometimes as I walked around the brick floors of my living room and bedroom I'd realize I was listening for the jingle of Jack's tags, and then I'd click on the radio.

When Loyd did show up we would drag our lawn chairs out for a view of the sun's parting shot at the canyon wall, and we'd talk about nothing in particular. For instance, he told me the story of Jack's life. Jack's mother was a coyote that Loyd took in when he was living up on the Apache reservation. She'd been crippled with buckshot in her shoulder, and had gone into heat. Loyd saw her one night skirting the arroyo behind his house, trying to get away from a pack of males. He got her attention with a low whistle, and then he left his front door open and went to bed; next morning, she was curled up under his cot.

I didn't question this. For one thing, he seemed to hold a power over females of all types. But truly Loyd had the most unself-conscious way of telling a story I'd ever heard, as if it didn't matter whether I was impressed or not, he was just going to give me the facts. It seemed as if he didn't care enough, one way or the other, to lie.

"I kept her shut up in the house for a week with my dad's old dog, Gunner. Gunner lost one of his back legs when he was a pup and he could get around real good, but he'd never in his life mounted a female. I thought she'd be safe with him."

This matter-of-fact talk about heat and mounting made me slightly edgy, or rather, edgy once-removed. I felt like I *ought* to be uneasy with Loyd, but I wasn't. To him it was life and death and dogs. Sometimes Loyd seemed about twelve.

"Well, Jack is here to tell the tale," I said. "So I guess she wasn't safe."

Loyd smiled. "Nope. Old Gunner had his one chance at love. He got into some poisoned coyote bait right after that. He died before the pups were born."

"How do you know they were his? She could have been pregnant already."

Loyd asked Jack, as politely as you'd ask a favor from a friend, to roll over. "See that?" Over Jack's heart was a white patch with a black crescent moon in its center. "That's Gunner's. There were seven pups, two black and five brown, and every one of them had that badge."

"How did you know which one to keep?"

He hesitated. "Dad decided," he said finally. "And Jack. Really I guess Jack's the one that decided."

They were nothing electrifying, these chats with Loyd in the dark, but they were a relief from my days at the high school, which were spent in a standoff just shy of open war. Occasionally Loyd took the tips of my fingers and rubbed them absent-mindedly between his own, the way he would surely stroke Jack, if Jack had fingers. The night of the story of Jack, he also kissed me before he left, and I was surprised by how I responded. Kissing Loyd was delicious, like some drug I wanted more of in spite of the Surgeon General's warning. Later on, when I slept, I had dreams of coyotes in heat.

I also saw Hallie. Her hair moved around her like something alive. "I've kissed a man who kills birds," I confessed, but she looked past me as if she didn't have a sister. Her eyes were pale as marbles. I woke up confused, too shaken to get up and turn on a light.

I'd dreamt of Carlo, too, on several occasions, for no good reason I could see. He'd written me a letter that was fairly medical and devoid of passion. He did miss me, though, and that sentiment brought comfort as I lay in my empty bed. It meant I was lonely by choice, or by difficult circumstances such as an ailing father; these things are supposed to feel better than being lonely because nobody wants you. Lately I'd started thinking about Carlo with a kind of romantic wistfulness, which I knew was bogus. The truth is, we'd essentially promised each other from the beginning that we wouldn't stay together. "No strings," we said, proving that we were mature medical students without spare time. The odd thing is that we did stay together, physically, and so I suppose falling out of love was our hearts' way of keeping the bargain. The end was always curled up there between us, like a sleeping cat, present even in our love-making.

Especially there. Carlo and I had gone to bed together for the first time one early dawn during our rotation in pediatric intensive care, after we'd worked all night trying to save a Papago baby brought in too late from the reservation. We'd gone straight from the dead baby to my apartment, my bed. There was hardly any talk that I remembered, we just held on to each other, joined, for as long as our bodies could stand it. I wanted anything that would stop that pain, and Carlo was strong medicine. Not happiness, nothing joyful, only medicine.

There was one other time of desperate, feverish connection that I particularly remembered. This was much later, when Carlo and I were living abroad. Carlo had been granted the opportunity to spend a year in an unbelievably remote clinic, halfway up the tallest mountain in central Crete.

The work was rugged, but in December we took a trip away from the village, to Venice. The clinic closed for some combination of clan ritual and Greek Orthodox holiday that practically evacuated the village. We set off for Italy feeling like truant school kids, drinking wine in tin cups on the train and reeling with the heady sense of getting away with something. Before that he'd scarcely managed an afternoon off, much less a week. Then Carlo came down with a cold on the overnight ferry to Brindisi, and by the time we reached Venice we were both burning up, our skin hot to the touch, like furnaces. Our bodies' internal combustion gave rise to an unquenchable craving for carbohydrates, and for each other, so we checked into the *Penzione Meraviglioso* and for a week ate plates of pasta and made a kind of sweaty, delirious love previously unknown to either of us, in a bed that was memorably soft and huge.

The *Penzione* looked out onto the cold, damp Grand Canal and a dim little plaza ominously named the Piazza of the Distraught Widows. (Distraught or Inconvenienced, it could translate either way.) The origin of this name was unknown to the elderly matron, who was born and raised in the building. She brought food up to us and was alternately scandalized by our appetites and worried for our well-being. She was of the opinion that in damp weather any illness at all would find its way to the lungs. She ventured to tell us we ought to see a doctor.

Carlo spoke Italian. His father had come to America on a steamer carrying cured leather and Chianti. He explained in grammatically imperfect but polite terms that we were both doctors. We could not be in better hands, he said. For my benefit, later, he'd translated the double entendre. By the end of the week, Carlo and the matron were bosom friends. In spite of his notorious shyness, whenever she brought us hot tea he would sit up in bed with a shirt on and give opinions on the infertility of her eldest daughter and the lung ailment of her son-in-law who worked in the glassblowing trade. I lay beside him, meanwhile, with the sheets pulled around my neck, feeling sinful and out of place, like a whore taken home to meet Mother. The matron didn't ask for my opinions, probably because she didn't believe I was actually a doctor. Which I wasn't, technically. I did some work at the clinic—rural Crete was not overly concerned about licensure—but to be completely honest, I was Carlo's paramour. I did the shopping. I learned the Greek words for oil and soap and bread.

I know that a woman's ambitions aren't supposed to fall and rise and veer off course this way, like some poor bird caught in a storm. All I can say is, at one of the many junctures in my life when I had to sink or swim, Crete was an island, a place to head for, new and far away. I had just dropped out of medicine in my first year of residency, a few months shy of becoming a licensed M.D. I'd discovered there was something serious, mainly a matter of nerve and perhaps empathy, that stood in my way. I learned all this while a baby was trying to be born feet first. I couldn't think how I was going to tell Doc Homer, and I'll admit I was attracted just then to the idea of putting an ocean between myself and that obelisk of disapproval. It also helped that Carlo really wanted me to go with him. But I had no mission beyond personal survival; it was nothing like Hallie's going to Nicaragua. Our village had its own kind of bleakness, the bones and stones of poverty, but the landscape was breathtaking. Our classmates were treating intestinal parasites in Niger and Haiti, black lung in Appalachia, while Carlo and I set broken legs on the steep slope of Mount Ida, mythical birthplace of Zeus. Poverty in a beautiful place seemed not so much oppressive as sublime. Basically it's the stuff of the world's great religions, I told myself, although I knew better.

▼▼▼

It was 100 degrees in the shade, and the burgeoning minds of Biology I and II took a field trip to the river; our putative goal was to get some samples of water to examine under the microscope. We were learning about the plant and animal kingdoms, starting right down at the bottom of the ladder with the protozoans and the blue-green algae. I could easily have collected a gallon of river water myself and brought it in, but the school had no air-conditioning and I'm not completely without a heart. I'd played it tough with the kids long enough to prove my point, if there was one, and I was tired of it. We all were.

I knew the trip to the river would turn into a party. I didn't try too hard to go against nature. The tall kid with the skinhead haircut, whose name was Raymo, was the first one to get wet up to his T-shirt. It took about ninety seconds. I only drew the line when boys started throwing in girls against their will.

"Okay, knock it off, scientists, Marta says she doesn't want to get wet," I said. Marta shot me a lipstick-red pout when they put her down, but she'd shrieked "No" and I felt there was a lesson to be learned here, all the way around.

"I've got a ton of sample bottles here, so let's get going." I sat a safe distance up the riverbank under an ash tree, labeling full bottles as they were brought to me. I'd suggested that they collect shallow and deep water, moving and stagnant, but they went far beyond this, collecting anything that moved. It was enough to make you believe in the hunting instinct. There was a low, grassy island in the middle of the riffle, and several kids were out there on their knees catching bugs and frogs. Raymo actually caught a six-inch perch with a net fashioned from his T-shirt. "Sooner or later I figure we'll get around to fish," he said. "A fish is an animal, right?"

"Right," I said, and let him dump it, along with the frogs, into a mop bucket we'd cajoled from the janitor. I don't know what teaching in a big-city school is like, but at Grace High we were flexible about interdepartmental appropriations.

Back in the lab, we rounded up all the creatures visible to the naked eye and made a home for them in an aquarium that had once held blue and orange Ping-Pong balls used for some mystical experiment in physics. Marta and two other cheerleaders disposed of the Ping-Pong balls and took over the terrarium project. They made a pond on one side for the fish, and an admirable mossy island on the other side, complete with a beach, and a cave they called the Motel Frog. They refused to deal directly with the clients, though. Raymo transferred the fish and frogs (with his bare hands) from the mop bucket.

The next day we got out the microscopes. The kids groaned, preferring to do experiments on the frogs. It's hard to get people interested in animals that have no discernible heads, tails, fins, or the like—and plants, forget it. There's no drama. You just don't have the skulking and stalking and gobbling up of innocent prey in the plant world. They don't even eat, except in the most passive sense. In college I knew a botany professor who always went around saying, "It takes a superior mind to appreciate a plant." Hallie and I were a case in point, I guess. We divided the world in half, right from childhood. I was the one who went in for the instant gratification, catching bright, quick butterflies, chloroforming them in a Mason jar and pinning them onto typewritten tags with their Latin names. Hallie's tastes were quieter; she had time to watch things grow. She transplanted wildflowers and showed an aptitude for gardening. At age ten she took over the responsibility of the Burpee's catalogue.

But now I was on my own in the Garden of Eden. I was expected to teach the entire living world to these kids. I would write Hallie and ask her advice on how to turn adolescents on to organisms that have no appreciable sex life. In the meantime we were doing protozoans, which I could handle. I drew huge, fantastic pictures in colored chalk of what we could expect to see in this river water: strands of Nostoc like strings of blue pearls; multi-tentacled hydras; rotifers barreling into each other like hyperactive kids. I demonstrated the correct way to put a drop of water on a glass slide, coverslip it, and focus the scope. The lab grew quiet with concentration.

They couldn't see anything. At first I was irritated but bit my tongue and focused a scope myself, prepared to see the teeming microscopic world of a dirty river. I found they were right, there was nothing. It gave me a strange panic to see that stillness under powerful magnification. Our water was dead. It might as well have come from a river on the moon.

▼▼▼

For homework I assigned my classes the task of being spies. They were to find out from their parents what the hell was going on with this river. The pH, which we tested, from some areas came in just a hair higher than battery acid. I couldn't believe the poisoning from the mine had gone this far. Protozoans are the early-warning system in the life of a river, like a canary in a mine. And this canary was dead. We took a closer look at Raymo's perch (named Mr. Bad Fish) and the frogs in the terrarium, which seemed in reasonably good health. But then, they'd been awfully easy to catch.

"It can't be legal," I lamented to Viola as we sat on the front porch with three of the boys and four grocery bags of snap beans. Emelina and John Tucker were in the kitchen canning as fast as we could snap. When it came to childbearing and gardening, Emelina seemed unable to walk the path of moderation.

"It's not legal," Viola said grumpily. "What difference does it make?"

We worked in silence for a while. The aluminum bowl between us rang like a bell when we threw our hard green beans against its sides. Mason hadn't managed to master the art of snap beans and had fallen asleep in the glider. The twins elbowed each other like irritable birds on a wire. Viola had been overseeing the boys in the garden most of the morning, and for once seemed tired. She was wearing lavender stretch pants, an embroidered blouse, and a baseball cap with the insignia of the Steelworkers' Union. J.T.'s father had worked in the smelter for forty years, from age eighteen until he died of lung cancer. The cap sat forward on Viola's head because her long hair was pinned in a thick circle at the back. According to Emelina, Viola felt the boys were losing touch with their past, but looking at her now I couldn't get a fix on what that past might be. I thought of the Elvis whiskey bottle collection up in her room. I didn't really know Viola the way I knew Emelina and J.T. and the kids. She was always skirting around the edges of rooms with her hands full, just ready to go somewhere, too busy to sit down and talk.

"They'll have to pay a fine if they don't stop polluting the river," I said cheerfully. "The EPA will shut them down if they don't clean it up." At Emelina's urging, I'd gone down to the courthouse and filed an affidavit with local authorities on the pH and biotic death of the river. I used the most scientific language I could muster, such as "biotic death" and "oxygen load." I'd written Hallie about it.

Viola said without looking up, "They're just going to divert the river."

"What?"

She bent over with a soft groan and took another double handful of beans out of the grocery bag between her legs, and set them into her apron. Curtis and Glen had stopped hitting each other for the moment and were having a race. It took them forever to snap any beans because they had to stop every two minutes to count who had done the most.

"Dam up the river," Viola said. "That's all they have to do to meet with the EPA laws. Dam it up and send it out Tortoise Canyon instead of down through here. The EPA just says they can't put it down here where people live."

"But then there would be *no* water for the orchards. That would be worse than the way it is now."

"That's right. But it's okey-dokey with the EPA. The men all had a town meeting about it yesterday, with this hot-shot guy from Phoenix. They sat and talked for about nine or ten hours and finally what he told them is if Black Mountain dams up the river, it's out of the jurisdiction of the Environmental Protection Agency." Viola reeled out the long words scornfully, as if she were glad to get them out of her mouth.

"That's impossible," I said. "There are water rights."

"Nobody around here's got water rights. All these families sold the water rights to the company in 1939, for twenty-five cents an acre. We all thought we were getting money for nothing. We had us a *fiesta*."

I stared at her. "So do you know for sure that's what they're going to do? Divert the river?"

She shrugged. "Who knows what anybody is going to do for sure? We could all die tomorrow. Only the Lord knows."

I wanted to shake her. I wished she would look me in the eye. "But this is what you've *heard* is going to happen?"

She nodded once, never taking her eyes off the snap beans that flew through her hands and rang freshly broken into the aluminum bowl.

I still couldn't believe it. "How could they do that?"

"With bulldozers," Viola said.

▼▼▼

Loyd and I made another date for Whiteriver, this time on a Sunday in October. The evening before, I went with Emelina to hear Chicken Scratch music at the outdoor restaurant run by Doña Althea's four daughters. The same traveling Waila bands had been coming over from the Papago reservation for decades, substituting sons for fathers so gradually that the music never changed. Emelina's normal taste ran to Country—Merle Haggard and Dolly Parton; but Waila was something special, she said, she was crazy about it. Her boys, enlightened by MTV, rolled their eyes. She took Mason and the baby with us because, as Emelina put it, they were too little to have a choice.

The restaurant was outdoors, in a walled courtyard that was a larger, more baroque version of Emelina's. Flowers bloomed everywhere out of pots shaped like pigs and squatty roosters, some of which had lost body parts, and two enormous old olive trees sparkled with tiny Christmas lights that evidently knew no season. Carved out here and there in the thick adobe wall were rounded niches that were home to weather-worn saints the size of a G.I. Joe; some, in fact, looked suspiciously like dolls in saints' clothing. In a corner, near where the band was setting up, stood a four-foot-tall, almost comically thin St. Francis of Assisi. He looked venerable and tired (also hungry), and was surrounded by a postmodern assortment of glazed ceramic and plastic birds.

The tables and chairs were of every imaginable type, following the same theme, and the flatware too—like snowflakes, no two alike. The effect was completely festive, in spite of Doña Althea's daughters. All four of them (who each had *Althea* lodged somewhere in her name) were over sixty, as thin as St. Francis but without his animal magnetism. They moved through the crowd with efficient scowls, taking orders and bringing out heavenly food from the little kitchen, all the while acting as though they couldn't quite understand why they'd agreed to go to all this trouble. You would think they'd have figured it out by now. It had been the most popular restaurant in town for half a century.

With tender, paternal attention the Alvaro Brothers unwrapped their musical instruments, which traveled in comfort, nestled in bright-blocked quilts. The men appeared to be three generations, rather than actual brothers. The elder Alvaro, dressed in cowboy boots and a formal Western shirt, cradled a gunmetal saxophone that reminded me of World War II planes. A middle-aged Alvaro with shoulder-length hair played accordion, and two boys in T-shirts played bass guitar and drums. The old sax player stepped up to the microphone. "We are the Alvaro Brothers," he said. "If we make too much noise, let us know."

It was the last time any of them smiled. From the instant they began to play, they stood motionless with their mouths turned down in concentration. Everybody else was dancing in their seats. Chicken Scratch music is Mexican-spiced Native American polka. It sounds like a wild, very happy, and slightly drunken wedding party, and it moves you up and down; you can't keep still. A line of older women in dark skirts and blouses, possibly Alvaro Sisters or Alvaro Wives, stood near the kitchen, swaying a little and tapping their feet. Several couples began to dance, and I could tell Emelina was itching to join them, but she held herself back. Mason showed no such restraint. He was out of his seat in no time, front and center, jumping in circles and running into people's legs. The younger people moved aside when the Papago women moved out from the wall and began to do the traditional six-step dance. They moved in a loose line, slightly bent over, shuffling over the gravel and sounding—if not looking—exactly like the scratching hens that give the music its name.

The place was packed. It took forever to get served and there were some mixed-up orders, and nobody cared. The music was so buoyant. One of the Althea sisters actually cracked a smile. After forty-five minutes the bass player plucked his lit cigarette from the bridge of his guitar and the Alvaros took a break.

Emelina told me she and J.T. had come here on their first date. They were fourteen. Viola had come too, but fortunately she spent the whole time in the kitchen advising Doña Althea on the *menudo,* Viola's specialty. J.T. was thus able to eat his whole meal with one hand on Emelina's knee, under the table.

"Just think," I said. "If you'd come on another night, the soup of the day would have been something else and you and J.T. might never have gotten married."

She smiled an odd little smile. "I don't think there's anybody else in this town I could have married but J.T. It was like we had each other's names printed on us when we were born."

"Seems like there's a lot of that in this town."

"Oh, yeah. And people do what their parents did. The father's a hoghead, the son's a hoghead."

I smiled. "What's a hoghead?"

"Locomotive engineer. I don't know why they call them that." She pecked her fingertips on the tabletop, watching the Papago women talking to the musicians.

For a while I'd believed that Emelina and J.T., with their congenial partnership and all those miles between them, were like Carlo and me, parallel lines that never quite touched. I was wrong. Two nights before when J.T. came home at 3 A.M. they made love in the moonlit courtyard, urgently, with some of their clothes on. My house was dark but I was awake, invisible in my kitchen. I felt abandoned. Emelina was nothing like me.

"It's dangerous," she said suddenly. "Shit, you can't think about it but it's hell, the railroad. Did you know Fenton Lee, in high school?"

"Sure."

"He was in a head-on wreck two years ago. Bringing his train out of the yard in El Paso, at night, and somebody else was coming in, lined for the same track. Nobody knows why. Maybe a signal failed. Southern Pacific says no. But J.T. says it happens."

"So Fenton was killed?" I remembered him plainly, in horn-rim glasses. He had blond bangs and a loud laugh.

"Yeah, it was real bad. They heard the crash all over the yard. The one engine climbed up the other one and sheared off the top. There wasn't a whole lot left."

I felt numb. A train wreck and Fenton dead in it were beyond what I was willing to imagine.

"You can jump off, when you see that coming," Emelina told me. "Fenton's brakeman and conductor jumped off, and the other crew did, but Fenton stayed on. I guess he didn't really believe it. I told J.T., 'If you ever see a headlight coming at you, don't you dare save the train. You get your butt out of there.' "

The band started up again and Emelina's mood quickly lifted. Our food arrived and Mason snapped back to the table. Emelina resettled the baby in the rickety high chair. "So you're going up to the rez with Loyd tomorrow," she said, her eyes twinkling. "This is getting serious. If I was your mother I'd tell you to wear garlic around your neck." She dipped the tip of her spoon into her refried beans and fed it to the baby. He took the spicy brown mush like manna from heaven. "But since I'm not your mother," she said soberly, "I'd advise you to wear nice-looking underwear."

She embarrassed me. "It's nothing serious," I said. "We're not exactly couple material, are we? Me and Loyd-with-one-L."

She looked up, surprised. "He can't help how his name's spelled." She paused a minute, studying me. "What, you think Loyd's dumb?"

Now I had embarrassed myself. "No, I don't think that. I just can't see myself with a guy that's into cockfighting."

I'm sure Emelina suspected this was nowhere near the whole truth. She was thinking I did hold Loyd's misspelled name against him, and a lot of other things. That I couldn't see myself with a roughneck Apache hoghead who was her husband's best friend. I felt myself blush. I was just like Doc Homer, raising himself and Hallie and me up to be untouched by Grace.

"I'll tell you something, honey," Emelina said, pausing her spoon midway enroute to the baby's open mouth. "Half the women in this town, and not just the single ones, would give up Sunday breakfast to go to Whiteriver in that little red truck."

"I know that," I said, paying attention to my enchiladas. I didn't know how to apologize to Emelina without owning up to something I wasn't sure I felt. Strictly speaking, I didn't think I was better than Loyd and half the women in Grace. I was amazed, in fact, by Loyd's interest in me. I also didn't think it would last very long.

Emelina directed her energies back to mothering. "Mason, honey, don't pull all that stuff out with your fingers," she shouted affectionately above the music, which had risen in pitch. "I know it's stringy. I'll cut it up for you." She reached across the table, expertly dissecting Mason's chicken burro.

For some reason I glanced up at the baby, whose eyes and mouth were wide. Something was severely wrong. He wasn't breathing. I knocked over my chair getting to him. I reached my finger into his throat and felt something, but couldn't dislodge it. He made a voiceless gag. I stood behind his chair and pulled him up by the armpits, folded him over my left arm, and gave him four quick whacks between the shoulder blades. Then I rolled him over so he was face up and wide-eyed but still head down; supporting his head with my right hand, I tucked two fingertips under his breastbone and poked hard. A small, hard, whole pinto bean shot out of his mouth like a bullet.

The whole operation took maybe thirty seconds. Emelina picked the bean up off the table and looked at me. Her face was ashen as the baby's.

"He was choking," I said dumbly, laying him carefully on the table. "That's the only way you can get something out of the windpipe when it's in that far."

He lay still for about half a minute, breathing but still looking gray, and then he coughed twice and began to scream. His face turned rosy purple. Several women from nearby tables had whipped the napkins off their laps and were crowding in close around us. The music stopped. Emelina stared at her son like he was something she hadn't ordered, set down on the table.

"It's okay to pick him up," I said. "He'll be sore in the ribs, but he's okay."

She held him against her shoulder. He was still shrieking,

and I don't think there was a person in the restaurant now who wasn't staring at us. At me, actually. Emelina looked up with enormous eyes, as if I were one of the saints in the wall: Our Lady of Blocked Windpipes. She wiped tears off her chin with the back of her hand.

"It's no big deal," I said.

It really wasn't. I'd just done what I knew how to do.

▼▼▼

Emelina begged me to sleep in the house with them that night, in case he stopped breathing again. There was no reason in the world for that to happen, and I told her so. But she was quietly beside herself. J.T. had left for El Paso that morning, for two weeks this time because of some mess about the derailment. Viola was out late at another so-called "emergency meeting" of her women's club. I think Emelina felt lonely, or vulnerable—afraid of the simple fact that life held possibilities she couldn't handle alone. It must have been a rare experience for Emelina, and I felt for her. While we were making up a bed for me in the baby's room, I stopped and hugged her. She held on to me like a child.

I knew better than to expect sleep. I lay curled on my side, listening in spite of myself to the baby's soft exhaled breaths, and I kept turning my mind away from the one thought that kept coming back to me, persistent as an unwanted lover's hand, that I'd saved a life.

I thought about Loyd instead. I knew nothing about where we were going tomorrow; I hadn't seen that country. My mind turned over various expectations, none of which I recognized as my own. Who did I think I was, and what did I want from an Apache cockfighter with a misspelled name? His body, yes. But I couldn't take that risk, and end up needing more.

At some time in my life I'd honestly hoped love would rescue me from the cold, drafty castle I lived in. But at another point, much earlier I think, I'd quietly begun to hope for nothing at all in the way of love, so as not to be disappointed. It works. It gets to be a habit.

A pack of coyotes set up a sudden racket near the house,

yipping and howling, so close by they sounded like they had us surrounded. When a hunting pack corners a rabbit they go into a blood frenzy, making human-sounding screams. The baby sighed and stirred in his crib. At seven months, he was just the size of a big jackrabbit—the same amount of meat. The back of my scalp and neck prickled. It's an involuntary muscle contraction that causes that, setting the hair follicles on edge; if we had manes they would bristle exactly like a growling dog's. We're animals. We're born like every other mammal and we live our whole lives around disguised animal thoughts. There's no sense pretending. Tomorrow, I thought, or the next day, or the day after that, I would have sex with Loyd Peregrina.

12

ANIMAL DREAMS

On Sunday morning I put on jeans, changed into a denim dress, then back into jeans again, feeling stupid. I can get into a mood where I annoy myself no end. At the moment when I got completely fed up and stopped caring, I had on jeans and a white cotton shirt and silver earrings, so that's what I wore. And yes, I'll admit it, nice underwear.

I waited on the porch and was relieved when Loyd pulled up before Emelina's household had roused. It was a little odd, living with a family that paid attention to my social life.

Jack stood up to greet me from the back of the pickup and I rubbed his ears. "I brought lunch," I told Loyd, sliding into the cab with a basket Emelina had helped pack the night before.

He smiled wonderfully. "That's mighty white of you."

I didn't know what to make of that. It was something people said, but usually when they said it both people were white.

I asked him to detour past the Post Office so I could check for mail. There was no regular mail delivery in Grace, probably on humanitarian grounds. A daily route up these stairstep streets would have put some postal employee into a cardiac high-risk category. Every family had a box at the P.O., which they could check daily or annually, as they pleased. Emelina leaned toward annual. I persuaded her to turn over the key to me; I was the only member of the household expecting mail.

The mailboxes were built right into the outside wall of the Post Office. I peeked through the little window of the Domingos family drawer and saw the striped margin of an airmail envelope.

"Hallie!" I called to Loyd, waving the envelope as I bounced back to the truck. He didn't seem to register. "My sister Hallie. In Nicaragua." I checked the postmark to make sure this was true, and it was. Mailed nearly three weeks ago. The stamps, two alike, were bright and beautiful, carrying across oceans and continents a childlike revolutionary hopefulness: a painting of a woman picking red coffee beans, and her baby strapped on her back. Hallie was in the fields of her dreams.

I ripped it open and read quickly. She'd arrived mid-September, was fine, got my letters, she spent a few days in Managua and then backtracked straight to the rural area near Chinandega. She'd expected (or feared) a little formality but they put her to work the day she arrived, wearing her one and only dress. "I'm in seventh heaven," she wrote, and I could see her hiking up that dress and striding across the plowed rows, leading a battery of stunned men. "This cotton's been getting sprayed to death and still eaten up with weevils. Cultivation practices are pitiful. I know exactly what to do. I think we'll get productivity up about 100 percent from last year. Can you imagine? You'd think it was Christmas, everybody's already talking about how the collective could use this prosperity: they could get a secondary-school teacher in here full time, or a good adult-ed program."

I got a vivid picture of Hallie's face and could hear her voice as I read. Her hair would be restrained in a red bandana, her face tense with concentration and her eyebrows knit at angles like accent marks. I could also recall her exact expression as she lay on our living-room sofa in Tucson with her long legs propped up, one hand pushing the hair up from her high forehead, while she calmly dispensed information over the Garden Hotline. I understood the full extent to which she'd been wasting her life on house plants.

The letter was short. She was living in a two-room house

with a widowed mother of four young children, who insisted that Hallie have one of the rooms to herself—a luxury that made Hallie uncomfortable. There was nothing to spare. The day she moved in, a request went out to the neighbors and somebody brought over a plate and a tin cup for her, and somebody else brought a fork. Both women had recently lost sons.

The territory she would have to cover, giving crop advice, was huge. She was issued a horse. There were problems with the roads, she said, that made jeeps a less desirable mode of transport for short trips: horses usually weren't heavy enough to trigger the land mines the Contras buried in the roads. The horse's name was *Sopa del Dia;* she was white with gray spots.

She signed it, "Your insane-with-love sister Hallie," with a P.S.:

> Re your question about botany: tell your students plants do everything animals do—give birth, grow, travel around (how do you think palm trees got to Hawaii?), have sex, etc. They just do it a lot slower. Bear this in mind: flowers are the sex organs of plants. Tell the boys to consider that when they're buying their dates corsages for the prom.

And a P.P.S.:

> Sure I remember when we almost drowned in a flood. Plain as day. God, Codi, don't you? We found those abandoned coyote pups, and the river was flooding, and you wanted to save them. You said we *had* to. I was chicken because Doc Homer would spank the shit out of us and I wanted to run for it, but you wouldn't let me.

"My sister's saving people's lives in Nicaragua," I told Loyd.

"She's a doctor? I thought she was a farmer."

"People can't live without crops. There's more than one way to skin a revolution."

He nodded.

I wanted him to know more than this about Hallie. That she was also a human being who did normal things. That she'd tried once, just as an example, to teach Carlo and me to break-dance.

She'd thrown her hair around like a prissy rock star and we died laughing. In wool socks on the hardwood floor she could moonwalk like Michael Jackson.

I kept folding and unfolding the letter. "She has to ride a horse, because there's land mines in the roads."

The cab of the truck shuddered every time we hit a pothole, but Loyd drove calmly, his mind far away, the way I imagined *he* might look riding a horse. I'd never seen him so relaxed. I looked back a few times to check on Jack, who seemed equally content. I presumed he'd walked around in circles a few times back there before curling up in his nest of imaginary tall grass.

"Is there anything you know of that you'd die for?" I asked Loyd.

He nodded without hesitation.

"What?"

He didn't answer right away. Then he said, "The land."

"What land?"

"Never mind. I can't explain it."

"The reservation? Like, defending your country?"

"No." He sounded disgusted. "Not property. I didn't say property."

"Oh."

We passed by another of Black Mountain's mines, abandoned for years, the buildings standing quiet as a shipwreck. The huge windows of the smelter were made of chicken-wire glass, but a lot of them were broken out anyway; inside loomed the dinosaur skeletons of old machinery. Next to the smelter were the concentrator and a hovel of shacks under rusting tin roofs. Beyond them lay more fallow alfalfa fields, their soil crusted white from all the years of slightly salty irrigation water. Hallie could have stayed right in Grace and done some good, but of course there was the question of relative desperation of need. Nobody was dying for lack of this alfalfa.

The edge of these fields was the southern border of the Apache reservation, just fifteen minutes north of Grace. I hadn't been there before, and was surprised it was that close.

"Are you kidding?" he asked. "Gracela Canyon used to be

in the reservation. The whites took that little section back after some guys hit gold down there."

"Is that true?"

"Look it up, Einstein. It's in the town records. They only gave the Apache this land in the first place because it looked like a piece of shit."

To some extent that must have been true: it was dead-looking country, though not as dead as the used-up cropland. It didn't look *murdered*. Here the gentle hills were pale brown grading to pink, sparsely covered with sage and fall-blooming wildflowers. Along the creekbeds were tall stands of cottonwoods. Their yellow leaves rained down. Every now and then we'd pass through clusters of homes that you couldn't exactly call towns, with long horse corrals strung between the houses. Red horses raised their heads and galloped along beside us for the short distance they'd been allotted, expertly turning aside just before they reached the ends of their corrals. Loyd waved at the people we passed, and they waved back.

"Do all those people know you?" I asked, incredulous.

"Nah. Just my truck."

Eventually we stopped in one of the settlements that was distinguished from the others by its size and the presence of a store. Rusting soft-drink signs nailed across the front porch marked it as a commercial establishment. Through the screen door I could see shadows of men in cowboy hats. Loyd pulled his parking brake, squeezed my hand, and held on to it for a second. "You want to come in?" he asked doubtfully. "It's only going to take me ten minutes."

"I know what this is about," I said. "J.T. told me you're into fighting cocks."

He nodded slightly.

"Well, is it okay for me to go in with you? Are women allowed?"

He laughed, then dropped my hand and flipped his index finger against my cheek. "Big old roosterfighting Indian boogeyman might get you."

"I'm a big girl," I said. I got out and followed him up the

wooden steps, but regretted it once we were inside. A short man leaning on the counter looked at Loyd and resettled his hat on his head, ignoring me completely. This wasn't going to be any of my business. I bought a lukewarm soft drink from the old guy behind the counter. He grasped it through his apron and screwed off the cap, leaving a broad asterisk of dust on the white cloth. The other men watched this gesture in silence.

"I'll be outside," I told Loyd.

I sat in a wooden rocker on the porch. Jack had lifted his head and cocked his ears but hadn't moved from the truck-bed.

Almost immediately I could hear Loyd raising his voice. "I told you I want Apodaca's line and not any of the others. I want gaffers. I'm not interested in knife birds."

The short man said, "Loyd, I'm telling you, you got to go up to Phoenix. They're getting goddamn tourists at those knife tourneys. It's a circus. You can get two hundred birds through there in a day."

"Don't tell me what I want. Do you have gaffers out there, or did I just waste a tank of gas?"

Their voices dropped lower again. I felt uncomfortable listening in, though I was fascinated and slightly appalled by the notion of "knife birds." It was encouraging that Loyd didn't want them, whatever they were. The words the men used were as mysterious as Loyd's railroad talk. He evidently spoke a lot of languages, not even counting Apache and Pueblo and Navajo.

Across the street from the store stood a substantial-looking whitewashed church—the only white building in an adobe town. It was shaped like the Alamo with a bell tower. The ground in front was planted with petunias, phlox, and marigolds: pink, purple, orange, in that order. One thing Hallie always said she loved about Indian reservations and Mexico was that there were no rules about color. She was right. It was really a splendid combination, now that I looked at it, but in some orderly country like Germany they'd probably arrest you for planting this in front of your house; in suburban Tucson they'd just avoid you. Keep their kids inside when you went out to weed.

People trailed out of the church in twos and threes, mostly

women, carrying out the same color scheme in their blouses and skirts. They all looked at me as they passed, not with hostility, but with the kind of curiosity you'd have if you noticed an odd plant had popped up in your garden: you wouldn't yank it out right away. You'd give it a few days to see what developed.

I could hear roosters cock-a-doodling somewhere, and I was curious. As I went down the steps an adobe-colored dog scooted out of my way and ran under the porch. The store, I discovered, had a deep back yard. The chain-link fence was overgrown with weedy vines, but I could still see in: it was a rooster garden in there. Roosters in small cubicles laid out in neat rows, one bird per cage. They strutted and turned in circles, eying each other as if each moment were new, as if they hadn't for all their natural lives been surrounded by these other birds. They had red faces and glossy black feathers that threw off iridescent flashes of color, like a hummingbird's throat. Beautiful. But the claustrophobic energy was tiring to watch.

I heard a door slam and I quickly went back around front. Loyd was ready to go, but not in the bad mood I expected. By the time we got to the edge of town he was smiling.

I offered him the last of my soda. "So, did you waste a tank of gas?"

He put his arm across the back of the seat, his thumb touching the nape of my neck, and shot me a sideways look. "No way."

We weren't headed back toward Grace. We drove north. There were no more towns, just reddish hills and a badly rutted road. "Was that Whiteriver?" I asked.

"No. This is what you'd call the Whiteriver metropolitan area."

"You used to live here? After you left your mother's pueblo?"

"Around here. We lived up at Ghost River. It's a little higher ground up there. It's nice, there's trees."

"You and your dad and . . ." I wanted to ask about his dead twin brother, but then again I didn't. Not today.

"And Jack," he said.

"Whatever happened to Jack's coyote mother?"

"After she had her litter, she left us. She went back to live in God's backyard."

I was quiet for a minute, taking in the hills. "And where are we headed now?"

He smiled. "Who wants to know?"

"A hometown girl, looking for some adventure."

"Well, then, we're headed for some adventure."

Loyd kept both hands on the wheel in the washed-out stretches, driving like a race-car driver—I don't mean fast, but skillfully, with that generous kind of concentration that seems easy as a reflex. We were gaining ground, getting higher, passing through intermittent stands of evergreens. In between were meadows, solidly carpeted in yellow flowers, punctuated by tall white poppies with silver leaves and tissue-paper petals. In the distance, the southern slopes of the mountainsides were dappled with yellow. We passed through another tiny enclave of houses and horse corrals. The people there would have been born into that life; I couldn't imagine it. For some reason I thought of Hallie's first letter—the babies playing around the cook fire, in the refugee camps. But this wasn't like that; it didn't look desperate, just lonely. It was hard to understand why a person would stay. Loyd hadn't. But then again, he wasn't born here. And yet he seemed drawn back, for reasons beyond fighting cocks.

The road smoothed out a bit and Loyd took his right hand off the wheel and laid it on my leg. For a little while he and I both pretended it wasn't there. Then I asked him, "What would these people around here say if they knew you had your hand on a white girl's thigh?"

He smiled. "They'd say I was a lucky son of a bitch."

He lifted the hand and ran his palm up the length of my arm, from my wrist to my shoulder, lightly, just stroking the hairs and not the skin. My nipples stood up and my scalp tingled and my whole body wanted that hand on it, everywhere at once. But he took it back and put it on the steering wheel, and I pitied myself for envying a steering wheel.

"You still haven't told me where we're going," I said.

He nodded at the road. "That's where we're going. We're almost there." After a minute he geared down into four-wheel drive and turned off the dirt road onto a side path, not really a road but a pair of tracks in the gravelly ground. If you hadn't known it was there, you'd never have seen it.

If we are going to see some more people about gaffers and knife birds, I thought, I'm going to have to sit and be still, be a white girl. No matter what, I'm going to have to stop thinking about kissing Loyd. I looked away from his face, out the window. There was nothing out there now but fields of yellow flowers, rocky red hills in the near distance, and off to the east very high mountains softly blackened around their tops by a pelt of pine forests. It would be cool up there now, even today. I pictured myself lying under the pines on a floor of brown needles. It was hard to keep Loyd out of the picture.

▼▼▼

"What *is* this?" I was out of the truck, entranced, before he'd even set the brake.

"Kinishba," Loyd said. "Prehistoric condos."

That's just about what it looked like. Out there in the middle of God's backyard, without a fence in sight, sat a long rectangular building made entirely of carefully set stone, no mortar. Dozens of small doors opened into it across the front.

"Can we go inside? Is it allowed?"

He hooked his elbow around my neck, like a friendly wrestler, as we walked toward the site. "It's allowed. I allow it."

"What, are you the landlord here?"

"Till somebody tells me I'm not."

He let me go and turned toward the truck, whistling once. Jack leaped in a high arc over the tailgate and streaked through the field of foot-tall grass, looking like the soul of happiness. He headed downhill toward what must have been a river; I could see cottonwoods. We were in higher country here, with more vegetation.

"That's a good dog," I said.

"Yep. That's a good dog."

The doors were no more than four feet high. I ducked through one into a small, rectangular room with a dust floor. It was cool as a cave, and quiet. The door was a square of bright light with the silhouette of Loyd coming through. Even inside the room, the ceiling was low, just inches above my head. I touched it. "People were short back then. Didn't eat their Wonder bread."

"They would've had to build a special room for you. You would have been their queen."

I laughed, though it struck me I'd been complimented. Was that how Loyd saw me? Not as a grain elevator on the prairie, but a queen? At the back of the room a door led into another room, which was darker, having no openings to the outside. Two more doors led out of that room—one to the side, and one up through the ceiling, which was made of thick, curved trunks of small trees. There was another whole set of rooms on top of this one.

"Can we go upstairs?"

He shook his head. "I wouldn't trust those beams. They're kind of old."

"How old?"

"Eight hundred years."

I looked at him. "Are you kidding?"

"Nope."

We went from room to room, changing directions in the dark until the compass points were entirely lost to me. It was a maze. Loyd said there were more than two hundred rooms—a village under one roof. The air smelled cold. I tried to imagine the place populated: stepping from room to room over sleeping couples, listening through all the noises of cooking and scolding and washing up for the sound of your own kids, who would know secret short cuts to their friends' apartments.

"The walls are thick," I observed.

"The walls are graveyards. When a baby died, they'd mortar its bones right into the wall. Or under the floor."

I shuddered. "Why?"

"So it would still be near the family," he said, seeming surprised I hadn't thought of this myself.

Without warning we came out into a bright courtyard in the center, surrounded by walls and doorways on all four sides. It was completely hidden from the outside—a little haven with a carpet of fine grass and an ancient ash tree. A treasure island. I was drawn to the shade. "We should've brought the picnic

he ash. The ground was cool. My
s gone; it seemed ghostly again.
se bones in the walls had been
the dry skittering of lizards.
said. He sat about two feet away
around his knees and looking at

ight hundred years ago?"
eblo. They had their act together

nning my eyes over the walls and
ones were mostly the same shape,
izes; there would be a row of large
e thinner rows, then a couple of
middle-sized rows. There was something familiar about the way they fit together. In a minute it came to me. They looked just like cells under a microscope.

"It doesn't even look like it was built," I said. "It's too beautiful. It looks like something alive that just *grew* here."

"That's the idea." Loyd seemed as pleased as if he'd built it himself.

"Of what? The idea of Pueblo architecture?"

"Yep. Don't be some kind of a big hero. No Washington Monuments. Just build something nice that Mother Earth will want to hold in her arms."

It was a pleasant thought. I also didn't mind the thought of being held in Loyd's arms, but he was making no moves in that direction. He was explaining the water system—they evidently had some sort of running water—and how they'd grown squash and corn on the hillside facing the river.

I reached over and ran a finger from his knee to his ankle. He looked up. "I'm talking too much, right?"

I shook my head. "No, keep talking."

"You sure?"

I hesitated. I hadn't expected to have to make the suggestion, and my stomach felt tight. "Yeah. Just, could you move over here and talk?"

His eyes brightened. I'd taken him by surprise. He leaned

over and I took his head in my hands and gave him the kiss I'd been thinking about for the last two hours. It lasted a good long while. He twisted his fingers gently through the hair at the base of my skull and held on tight, and my breath stopped while he laid down a track of small kisses from my earlobe to my collarbone. We lay back on the grass and I rolled against him, looking down into his eyes. They were dark brown, a color with depth to it, like stained glass. It was a little surprising to look at brown eyes after all the pale blues of Grace.

Just being held felt unbelievably good, the long drink I'd been dying for. For a second I hugged back as tightly as I could. Something inside his buttoned shirt pocket made a crackling, cellophane sound. I raised up a little and poked it with my finger. "If you've got a condom in your pocket, Loyd Peregrina, this is my lucky day."

He did. It was.

▼▼▼

By late afternoon the shade had moved, and we also had rolled over a few times in the grass, I suppose, traveling from our original spot. Anyway we were in the sun. We disconnected and I lay on my back, feeling the forbidden touch of sun on my nipples and eyelids.

Loyd lay with his head propped on his elbow, just looking at me again, the way he had on the day of Emelina's party. With a finger he traced concentric circles around my breasts, and triangles on my abdomen, as if warpainting me for some ceremonial mission. Whatever it might be, I felt up to the job. I knew when reason returned I'd be scared to death of feeling that good with another person, but my body was renewed. I felt like a patch of dry ground that had been rained on.

Jack had come into the courtyard and was sleeping in the shade, a little distance away. "He found his way in here without any trouble," I said. "You boys must come here a lot."

Loyd kissed my cheek and sat up and pulled on his jeans. "Yep, kind of a lot. Not as much as I'd like to."

I thought of the condom in his pocket, the presumption, and felt irritated. "Well it's a good seduction spot. It worked on me."

I found the rest of my clothes and concentrated on getting my shirt buttoned up. I'd lost an earring somewhere.

Loyd stared at me for a full half minute, and then lay back down, his hands clasped behind his head, looking straight up. "I don't mean that I *bring* people here. Nobody but me and Jack's ever been here before." He glanced at me, and then away again. "But I guess that's just what you expect me to say." He didn't say anything more for another minute, and then he said, "Shit."

"I'm sorry. I guess I believe you. I do believe you."

He was wounded. I suppose some sharp thing in me wanted to sting him, for making me need him now. After he'd once cut me to the edge of what a soul will bear. But that was senseless. Anybody would say that baby was my own fault, and he didn't even know about it. I looked at this grown-up Loyd and tried to make sense of him, seeing clearly that he was too sweet to survive around me. I would go to my grave expecting the weapon in the empty hand.

"Codi, I couldn't believe it when you said you'd come up here with me. I couldn't even believe I asked."

I sat forward, letting the point of my chin dig into my knee. "I can see what it means to you. I'm sorry for thinking what I did."

He spoke slowly. "I've been looking forward to this ever since Labor Day. Not because I thought we'd . . . Not for any one reason. I just wanted to come here with you."

I looked at him. It was the truth. I could think of nothing at all to say.

"I don't blame you if you're still pissed off at me for when we were in high school."

My heart lost its rhythm for a second. "What for?"

"For being a jerk."

"You remember that?"

I suppose it was an insulting question. He said, "I have a lot of reasons in my mind for the way I was, but they don't make much difference. I hurt a lot of people."

I looked at him carefully. "In what way exactly do you think you hurt me?"

He shrugged. "Well, maybe I didn't. Maybe you didn't care. But still, I could have been a lot nicer. We went out those couple of times, and then so long sucker, that's it. Loyd's a good-time boy, he don't call the same girl twice."

I breathed out. Nobody knew, so Loyd couldn't, but for one minute I'd been afraid. I didn't want him to know how much of a mark his careless love had made on my life. It would oblige him to one of two mean possibilities: compulsory kindness or a vanishing act. I leaned over and kissed him. "You're forgiven," I said. "Plain Jane forgives Mr. High School Honcho for being a red-blooded boy."

"Plain Jane my ass," he said, rolling me over on top of him and grabbing mine. "I like you a lot. A real, whole lot. You buy that?"

"I'll buy it. Just don't try to sell me no knife birds."

He looked straight into my eyes. "I'm serious, Codi."

"Okay," I said. "Sold." I laid my head on his chest and nearly went to sleep while he gently stroked my spine. I felt like a baby being coaxed, reluctantly, into dreamland. A few yards away, Jack was already there. His legs jerked helplessly, making him look vulnerable.

"I've lost an earring. You see it?"

"No. I'll help you look in a minute."

"What's Jack dreaming about?"

"Chasing rabbits," Loyd said.

"That's what everybody says, but I don't think all dogs dream about that. You watch a city dog that's never even heard of a rabbit—it'll do that same thing."

"How do you know they really dream?"

"They do. All mammals that have been tested have REM sleep, except spiny anteaters." I cringed after I said this. I sounded like Codi Noline, brain of the seventh grade, despised by her peers.

"Spiny anteaters?"

"Well, I'm sorry, but it's the truth. I read it in the encyclopedia one time."

"You are an amazing person."

He meant it, he wasn't making fun of me. His hand stopped

moving and came to rest on the small of my back. He was actually thinking about all this. Carlo wouldn't have paid the slightest attention to a conversation like this; he'd be thinking about whatever men think about, how much gas is left in the tank. Loyd asked, "What do you think animals dream about?"

"I don't know. Animal heaven." I laughed.

"I think they dream about whatever they do when they're awake. Jack chases rabbits, and city dogs chase, I don't know what. Meter readers."

"But that's kind of sad. Couldn't a dog have an imagination, like a person?"

"It's the same with people. There's nothing sad about it. People dream about what they do when they're awake. God, when I used to work for *Tía* sorting the pecans I'd go to bed and dream about pecans, pecans, pecans."

I studied his face. "Didn't you ever dream you could fly?"

"Not when I was sorting pecans all day."

"Really, though. Didn't you ever fly in your dreams?" Even I had done that, though not often.

"Only when I was real close to flying in real life," he said. "Your dreams, what you hope for and all that, it's not separate from your life. It grows right up out of it."

"So you think we all just have animal dreams. We can't think of anything to dream about except our ordinary lives."

He gently moved a lock of hair out of my eyes. "Only if you have an ordinary life. If you want sweet dreams, you've got to live a sweet life."

"Okay," I said, feeling happy. I was sure no other man I'd ever known would have concerned himself with what animals dream about. "I'm going to sleep now, and I'll give you a report." I settled my head back down on his chest. His heartbeat moved faintly against my ear as I looked out across the ground. I saw my silver earring gleaming in the grass.

HOMERO

13

CRYBABIES

His name is gone. He understands that this is his own fault. He took a pen to paper and changed it, canceled his ancestors, and now his grandchild—Codi's child—has been erased like something in writing too, rather than flesh and blood. He knows she's no longer carrying it. He's aware of the signs.

The red darkroom light burns like a dying sun, very old: red dwarfs, they call them when they reach that stage. He sometimes reads astronomy now, when he can't sleep. But at this moment, outside this sealed room, it's daytime. He considers carefully the time of day and of year, and his daughters' ages, a ritual he performs a dozen times daily to keep himself rooted in time. That was nearly twenty years ago, when Codi lost the baby. He has photographed the eyes of so many babies. He gets lost among years now, the way he used to lose track when he sat in the dark movie theater for too many hours. He has always loved the dark.

The liquid feels cool on his hands, though it's a chemical bath, not particularly good for the elasticity of human skin. He should use the Piper forceps from the kitchen, but he has misplaced them. He moves the photograph into the fixative and stares at the lines. And frowns. They are a precise copy of what the real world offered his camera, and nothing more: the branched shadow of a cane cholla falling across a square of pale, cracked ground. He found the image while walking in the arroyo, and immediately saw the illusion he could draw out of it: a river in the desert. He'd seen exactly this sight, in aerial view. It was years ago, in wartime—they had taken him in a small plane over the bombing range near Yuma; a soldier lay wounded out there and couldn't be moved. They flew the quickest route, over the Algodones dunes, a dead ocean of undulating sand. The pilot said it was harder to fly over dunes on a hot day than through a tornado; the plane shuddered until its rivets creaked. Then suddenly they were over the Colorado River agricultural plain. He marveled, feeling lucky as a spaceman. Surely no one had ever seen this amazing sight, a complex river fretted with canals cutting an unearthly path through the bone-dry land.

He can't remember the wounded soldier. He closes his eyes and tries, but he can't. Possibly some chest wound, a punctured lung? No, he can't bring the soldier back. But he remembers the vision of that water. He gently agitates the photograph in its stop bath, lost in technical possibilities. He knows there must be a way to transfigure this cactus shadow into that other vision, which no longer exists outside his mind. All his photographs begin in his memory. That is the point. He might be the only man on earth who can photograph the past.

He stops suddenly, feeling a presence outside the door.

"Codi?" He listens. "I'm printing, it will be a few more minutes. Codi, are you there?" He hears nothing. It's a Monday morning, she can't be here. She's teaching school. He drops the print into the fixer, annoyed, and goes back to the enlarger to try again. He should lock that door to guard against accidents. What a shock that would be to the girls, a locked door. They have always had rules about this; a closed door is a sacred thing. Privacy is respected. There is no call for bolted doors in the Noline household. But she still locked him out—she was in the bathroom that night for more than four hours. When he walked by he could see that the upper bolt was turned. She'd gone in right after dinner. There are rules about this.

"Codi?"

He listens again, but there is no sound at all.

He knocks. "I just want to know that you're all right."

"I'm all right."

She is crying softly. "I can hear that you're crying," he says. "Your sister is concerned. You could just tell us what's wrong."

"Nothing's wrong. I'm just a crybaby. You're always telling me I'm a crybaby, so you're right."

That isn't true, he doesn't use that word. He tells them they should try to be grown-up girls. But he hasn't needed to tell them that for years.

In another minute she calls out quietly, "Is Hallie out there? I need to talk to her."

Hallie is in her room, reading. She doesn't seem especially concerned; Codi has been so moody of late that Hallie leaves her alone. They don't argue but there is a new distance between them. A gulf. Codi crossed over into adolescence, leaving Hallie behind for the time being. They both seem lost. All three of them, really: a marooned family, shipwrecked on three separate islands. Before, when the girls were close, he worried about what would happen when they lost each other. Now they have.

"Hallie." He stands in the doorway to their room and repeats her name quietly. "Hallie." She is reading in poor light, ruining her eyes. She looks up, her eyes nearly marble-white under the small, high-intensity lamp above her bed.

"Your sister has asked for you. Can you please find out what she needs?"

She puts her open book face down on the bed and gets up without a word. The two of them confer through the bathroom door. He tries to hear their whispers from the kitchen. He sees that Codi is not letting her in.

"The black one. That old one that was mother's."

Hallie is gone for only a minute, then comes back. "I can't find it. I got your green jacket."

"No!" Codi says something else that he can't hear. He washes the cast-iron skillet and sets it on the stove on low heat, to drive out the moisture. He goes into the living room, where he can't see but can hear better. Hallie glances up as he walks past her in the hall, and she lowers her voice.

"Why do you have to have that exact sweater, Codi? Are you going outside? It's not even cold."

"Just bring me the black sweater. I mean it, Hallie, find it. It's in the bottom of one of my drawers."

After a long while Hallie comes back with it. He hears the bolt slide back, then lock again; the door was not open even for a full second. Hallie returns to her reading.

In another fifteen minutes he hears scrubbing. She is cleaning the floor. The toilet has flushed more than two dozen times. There are rules concerning all of these things.

Much later he watches without lamplight from the living room. The house is dark. Her curtain of hair falls as she leans out, looking down toward the kitchen. She comes out. The small bundle in her arms she carries in the curl of her upper body, her spine hunched like a dowager's, as if this black sweater weighed as much as herself. When he understands what she has, he puts his knuckle to his mouth to keep from making a sound. Quiet as a cat she has slipped out the kitchen door.

He follows her down to the arroyo. She takes the animal path that cuts steeply down the bank. Round volcanic boulders flank her, their surfaces glowing like skin in the moonlight. She is going down to the same dry river where they nearly drowned ten years ago, in the flood. This tributary carved out Tortoise Canyon; it would be the Tortoise River if it had a name, but it never runs. It did years ago when he was a boy, hiking these banks to escape his mother's pot-black kitchen, but now it does not run except during storms. The land around Grace is drying up.

He stands a hundred yards away from Codi, above her, in the shadow of cottonwood trees. She has reached the spot where the rock bank gives over to the gravel and silt of riverbed. Even in the semi-dark there is a clear demarcation where the vegetation changes. She stoops down into the low acacias and he can see nothing but her back to him, her bent spine through the sleeveless cotton blouse. It is a small white square, like a handkerchief. In better light he could photograph it and make it into that, or into a sheet on a clothesline. It's shaking just exactly that way, like a forgotten sheet left out in a windstorm. She stays kneeling there for a long time being whipped like that.

Then her head pushes up through the fringe of acacias and she moves toward him, her face shining beautifully with its own privacy of tears. He sees how deeply it would hurt her if she understood what he knows: that his observations have stolen the secrets she chose not to tell. She is a child with the dignity of an old woman. He moves back up through the cottonwoods and into the house, into his workroom. He can't know who she has buried down there but he can mark the place for her. At least he can do that. To save it from animals. Before he goes to bed he'll cover it with a pile of stones, the heaviest he can move.

He pretends for a long time to be busy in his workroom, periodically coming out to feign a need in the kitchen. Where has he put the Piper forceps? Codi is emptied out and exhausted and still stays up half the night doing homework. Six volumes of the *Britannica* lie open on the kitchen table; she states that she is doing a report on the marsupial mammals.

So many times he comes close to speaking, but the sentences take absurd forms in his mind: "I notice that you've been pregnant for the last six months. I meant to talk with you about this earlier." He would sell his soul to back up the time, but even if he could do that, could begin where he chose, he can't locate the point where it would have been safe to start. Not ten weeks ago, or ten years. If he has failed his daughters he's failed them uniformly. For their whole lives, since Alice died, they've been too far away to touch. It's as if she pulled them with her through a knothole halfway into the other world, and then at the last minute left them behind, two babies stranded together in this stone cold canyon.

He can't think of anything more to do in the kitchen, and she's still working. There are dark depressions under her eyes, like thumbprints on her white face. She tells him she has a headache, asks for aspirin, and he goes immediately to the closet where he keeps the medications. He stands for a long time staring at the bottles and thinking. Aspirin would increase the bleeding, if she's still hemorrhaging, which is likely from the look of her. But he would know if she were in danger, he tells himself. It was probably uncomplicated as stillbirths go; it would have been extremely small even at six months. She is so malnourished, he could have predicted toxemia, even placenta abruptio. He continues to stare into the closet, tapping a finger against his chin. He can't even give her Percodan—it contains aspirin. Demerol. That, for the pain, and something else for the cramping. What? He wishes he could give her a shot of Pitocin, but doesn't see how he can.

He returns to the kitchen and hands her the pills with a glass of water. Four pills, two yellow and two blue, when she's only asked for aspirin, but she swallows them without comment, one after another, without looking up from her books. This much she'll take from him. This is the full measure of love he is qualified to dispense.

▼▼▼

He bends down again over the developer bath, his face so near the chemicals that his eyes water. The picture slowly gives up its soul to him as it lies in the pan, like someone drowned at the bottom of a pool. It's still the same: plain shadows on dust. Damn. What he is trying for is the luminous quality that water has, even dark water seen from a distance. There is a surface on it he just can't draw out of these dry shadows.

He straightens up, his eyes still running, and pats his pockets for his handkerchief. He locates it finally in the wrong pocket and blows his nose. He has manipulated this photograph in every possible way, and none of it has yielded what he wants. He sees now that the problem isn't in the development; the initial conception was a mistake. He fails in the darkroom so seldom that it's hard for him to give up, but he does. For once he lets go of the need to work his will. He clicks off the old red dwarf and turns on the bright overhead light, and the unfixed prints lying in the bath all darken to black. It doesn't matter. The truth of that image can't be corrected.

COSIMA

14

DAY OF THE DEAD

On the last Monday of October Rita Cardenal made three announcements to the class: she was quitting school, this was her last day, and if anybody wanted her fetal pig they could have it, it was good as new.

We'd plowed right through the animal kingdom in record time, having had nothing to look at in the way of protozoans. We'd made a couple of trips back to the river and had given due attention to the amphibians and Mr. Bad Fish, whose glass home grew more elaborate with each field trip and was now called the Frog Club Med. There were fern palm trees and a mossy golf green, and the frogs obligingly did high-impact aerobics all over everything. Now we were up to exploring the inner mysteries of an unborn mammal, which had to be purchased mail order.

But Rita hadn't had the stomach to cut into hers, and I couldn't blame her, all things considered. She was expecting twins. She said she was dropping out because she felt too tired to get her homework done; I feared for these children's future.

Rita wore about half a dozen earrings in one ear and had a tough-cookie attitude, and I liked her. She'd been a good student. She seemed sorry to go but also resigned to her fate, in that uniquely teenage way of looking at life, as if the whole production were a thing inflicted on young people by some humorless committee of grownups with bad fashion sense. I was disappointed but unsurprised to lose Rita. I'd been watching her jeans get tight. The pregnancy dropout rate in Grace was way ahead of motor-vehicle accidents, as a teenage hazard. Rita was a statistic. On Tuesday I made my own announcement: we were doing an unscheduled unit on birth control.

The reaction in the ranks was equal parts embarrassment and amazement. You'd think I'd suggested orgies in study hall. There was some hysteria when I got to the visual aids. "Look, there's nothing funny about a condom," I said, pretending to be puzzled by their laughter. "It's a piece of equipment with a practical purpose, like a . . ." Only the most unfortunate analogies came to mind. Shower cap. Tea cozy. "Like a glove," I said, settling for the cliché. I turned from the blackboard and narrowed my eyes. "If you think this thing is funny, you should see the ridiculous-looking piece of equipment it fits over." The guys widened their eyes at each other but shut up. I was getting the hang of this.

"Miss," said Raymo. They'd never learned to call me Codi.

"What is it?"

"You're gonna get busted for this."

I finished my diagram, which looked somewhat more obscene than I would have liked. I brushed my chalk-dusty hands on my jeans and hopped up to sit on the tall lab bench that served as my desk. "I know some of your parents might not be too thrilled about this field of study," I said, thinking it over. "I didn't get permission from the school board. But I think we'd better take a chance. It's important."

"Okay then, tell us something we don't know," said Connie Muñoz, who had even more holes punched in her left ear than Rita. I wondered if this was some kind of secret promiscuity index.

"Shut up, Connie!" said Marta. (Pearl studs, one per earlobe.) "My dad would kill me if he thought I knew this stuff."

"What you *do* is between you and your dad," I said. "Or not. Whatever. But what you *know* is my business. Obviously you don't need to put everything you know into practice, just like you don't have to go spraying the fire extinguisher around because you know how to use it. But if your house is already on fire, kiddos, I don't want you burning down with it just because nobody ever taught you what was what."

Raymo shook his head slowly and said again, "Bus-ted." He drew the laugh he wanted.

"You know what, Raymo?" I asked, tapping a pencil thoughtfully against my teeth.

"What?"

"It doesn't matter a whole lot what the school board thinks." This dawned on me forcefully as I said it. I understood this power: telling off my boss at the 7-Eleven, for example, two days before I left Tucson. The invulnerability of the transient. "There's nobody else to teach this course," I said. "And I only have a one-year contract, which I wasn't planning on renewing anyway. I'm not even a real teacher. I've just got this provisional certification deal. So that's the way it is. We're studying the reproductive system of higher mammals. If I'm offending anybody's religion or moral turpitude here, I apologize, but please take notes anyway because you never know."

They were completely quiet, but toward the end of the day you really can't tell what that means. It could be awe or brain death, the symptoms are identical.

"Miss?" It was Barbara, a tall, thin, shy student (ears unpierced), whose posture tried always to atone for her height. She'd latched onto me early in the semester, as if she'd immediately sniffed out my own high-school persona. "You aren't coming back next year?"

"Nope," I said. "I'm outta here, just like a senior. Only difference between you and me is I don't get a diploma." I gave them an apologetic smile, meant for Barbara especially. "It's nothing personal. That's just my *modus operandi.*"

The kids blinked at this, no doubt wondering if it was a Latin name they needed to write down.

"Your *modus operandi* is the way you work," I said. "It's what you leave behind when you split the scene of a crime."

▼▼▼

At Grace High I taught Biology I, Biology II, two study halls, and I also pinch-hit an algebra class for a fellow teacher who was frequently absent on account of a tricky pregnancy. My favorite class was Biology II, my seniors—Raymo and Marta and Connie Muñoz and Barbara—but on that day I had a mission and didn't discriminate among souls. I gave everybody the lecture on baby prevention. Barbara, who was in my study hall and also in the algebra class, got to hear it three times, poor child, and I imagine she was the least in need.

It surprised me as much as the kids, this crusade, and I suspected my motives; what did I care if the whole class had twins? More likely I wanted to be sure of a terminal contract. After the last bell rang I erased the blackboard and stood for a minute sharing the quiet with the bones of my Illinois compatriot, Mrs. Josephine Nash. Our day was over. She gave me her silent, wide-jawed smile. Here was a resident of Grace who had never hurt me in childhood, didn't make me rack my memory for her name (she wore it on her pelvis), had thrown no spitballs at me nor asked for extra credit, and didn't suggest that I belonged in Paris, France, or a rock 'n' roll band.

From the back of the room I could hear the frogs clicking against the sides of their terrarium, constant as a clock: up and down, up and down, exposing soft white bellies. This time next year there would not even be fish or frogs in the river; these particular representatives of the animal kingdom were headed for extinction. Whoever taught this class would have to write Carolina Biological Supply and order those stiff preserved frogs that smell of formaldehyde, their little feet splayed like hands and their hearts exposed.

I stood over the terrarium and peered down into it from above, like a god. The fish hung motionless in its small lake. Droplets of condensation were forming on the underside of the glass top. Getting ready to rain in there. I'd grown fond of this miniature world, along with the kids, and had added my own touches: a clump of bright red toadstools that popped up in Emelina's courtyard, and a resurrection fern from the cliff behind my house. The terrarium was like a time capsule. I think everybody was trying to save little bits of Grace.

I slid the glass to one side, hating to disrupt the ecosystem but needing to feed the fish. The humid smells of mud and moss came up to meet my nose, and I thought of Hallie in the tropics. What would she do about these troubles if she were here? Well, stay, for one thing, whereas I wouldn't. I had come here with some sense of its being the end of the line, maybe in a positive way, but I found I had no claim on Grace. Seeing it as "home" was a hopeful construction, fake, like the terrarium. I'd deal with Doc Homer insofar as that was possible in one year, and then I'd rejoin Carlo, or think about another research job; I had no specifics in mind. My future was mapped in negatives. Next year I could be anywhere but here.

I'd told Hallie about my bold, ridiculous little deposition on the pH of the river, and a few days later I'd had to follow up with the news of the river's getting dammed—questions of pH being entirely academic. I felt humiliated. Eventually she wrote back to say: "Think of how we grew up. You can't live through something like that, and not take risks now. There's no getting around it." She was admonishing me, I guess. I should have more loyalty to my hometown. I wasn't brave; I was still trying to get around it. A good citizen of the nation in love with forgetting. I pelleted the surface of the water with goldfish flakes. In nature there are animals that fight and those that flee; I was a flighty beast. Hallie seemed to think I'd crossed over—she claimed I was the one who'd once wanted to dig in and fight to save the coyote pups. Emelina thought I'd been ringleader in campaigns to save stewing hens. In my years of clear recall there was no such picture. When Hallie and I lived in Tucson, in the time of the refugees, she would stay up all night rubbing the backs of people's hands and holding their shell-shocked babies. I couldn't. I would cross my arms over my chest and go to bed. Later, after my second year of med school, I'd been able to address their external wounds but no more than that.

The people of Grace would soon be refugees too, turned out from here like pennies from a pocket. Their history would dissolve as families made their separate ways to Tucson or Phoenix, where there were jobs. I tried to imagine Emelina's bunch in a tract house, her neighbors all keeping a nervous eye on the color coordination of her flowerbeds. And my wonderfully overconfident high-school kids being swallowed alive by city schools where they'd all learn to walk like Barbara, suffering for their small-town accents and inadequate toughness. It was easy to be tough enough in Grace.

Well, at least they'd know how to use condoms. I could give them that to carry through life. I settled the glass lid back over the terrarium and turned out the lights. I would be long gone before the ruination of Grace; I had a one-year contract. Now I'd made sure of it.

▼▼▼

Rita Cardenal called me up on the phone. She hesitated for a second before speaking. "I don't think your old man has all his tires on the road."

"It's possible." I sat down in my living-room chair and waited for her to go on.

"Did you tell him about me? About dropping out?"

"Rita, no. I wouldn't do that."

Silence. She didn't believe me. To Rita we were both authority figures—but at least she'd called. "My father and I aren't real close," I said. "I go up to see him every week, but we don't exactly talk." A pregnant teen could surely buy that.

"Well, then, he's got a slightly major problem."

"What did he do?"

"He just sorta went imbalanced. I went in for my five-month checkup? And he said the babies were too little, but he was all kind of normal and everything?" She paused. "And then all of a sudden he just loses it and gets all creeped and makes this major scenario. *Yelling* at me."

"What did he say?"

"Stuff. Like, that I had to eat better and he was going to make sure I did. He said he wasn't going to let me go *out of the house* till I shaped up. It was like he just totally went mental. He was using that tape measure thing to measure my stomach and then he just puts it down and there's tears in his eyes and he puts his hands on my shoulders and kind of pulls me against his chest. He goes, 'We have to talk about this. Do you have any idea what's inside of you?' I got creeped out."

I felt dizzy. There was a long pause.

"Miss? Codi?"

"Rita, I'm really sorry. What can I tell you? He's losing his mind. He's got a disease that makes him confused. I think he was really just trying to do his job, but he got mixed up about what was the appropriate way to talk to you."

"I heard that. That he had that disease where you go cuckoo and turn back into a baby."

"Well, that's not quite the way I'd put it, but it's true. Occasionally rumors are true."

"Is it true you're really a doctor?"

I looked out my east window at the wall of red rock that rose steeply behind the house. "No," I said. "That isn't true. Did he tell you that?"

"No." She paused. "Well, yeah. He said something a real long time ago, that you were in medical school or something. But not this last time. I heard it from somebody else, that you're a doctor and Doc Homer's dying and you're going to take over."

"Take over?"

"Take over being the doctor for Grace. They said you already saved that baby down at Doña Althea's restaurant."

"Oh, Jesus Christ."

"Look, people say stuff, okay?" Rita said. "This town is full of major mouths. It's just what I heard."

"I'm only here till the end of the school year, so you can tell whoever's spreading that gossip they're full of shit."

"Okay. Sor-ry."

I regretted snapping at Rita. "It's okay," I said. "It's not your fault. I'm not used to living in a place where everybody's into everybody else's business."

"It's the bottom level, isn't it? My mom found out I was pregnant from a lady that works at the bank. Mom goes, 'What is the date today?' and the lady goes, 'The fourteenth. Your daughter will be due around Valentine's Day, won't she? I had a baby on Valentine's Day.' " Rita paused for my opinion.

"Yeah," I said. "It's the bottom level."

"Uh-huh. Mom told me after that she had to tear up three checks in a row before she could make one out right. Like that was *my* fault."

▼▼▼

I set out to find Doc Homer the minute I hung up the phone, but it took me a long time to track him down, and my energy for drama kind of petered out. First I went to his office in the basement of the old hospital, up on the plateau—it was four o'clock on a Wednesday and he should have been there. But Mrs. Quintana said he'd gone downtown to check on old Mr. Moreno's oxygen machine because it was making a noise, and then he was going to stop at the grocery to pick up some pork chops. It had been half an hour so I figured I'd catch him if I skipped Mr. Moreno and went straight to the grocery, but I got there too late. The grocer, Mrs. Campbell, said he had come there *first*, having forgotten he needed to go to Mr. Moreno's. He'd stood for six or eight minutes in canned goods, as if lost, and then it came to him. Mrs. Campbell told me this with a sort of indulgent wink, as if he were Einstein or something and you could forgive it. He'd left for the Morenos' house, but first was going next door to the pharmacy to pick up Mr. Moreno's emphysema medication. I skipped the pharmacy and headed for the bright pink Moreno house, thinking I'd catch him as he came out and we could walk together back up the long hill, past the hospital, to his house. So the war on germs in Grace was being waged by a man who got lost in fruit cocktail. There was a clinic in Morse, just across the state line, and according to Mrs. Quintana a lot of people now drove over there. Disloyally, she had implied; she adored my father. She noted primly that they'd have problems with their state insurance forms.

On my way to the Morenos' I stopped at the P.O. There was a letter from Hallie, which I would save for later. I liked reading them alone, with time for filling in whatever she might leave out.

It turned out the Moreno visit had been unexpectedly brief, and he'd left already. The oxygen machine had stopped making noises all on its own. I walked back up the hill alone. By the time I finally did get to Doc Homer's kitchen his pork chops were cooked and he was just sitting down.

He looked surprised, almost pleased, his face turning up from the table, and he offered to put something on the stove for me but I told him I wasn't hungry. I sat down at my old place at the table where I'd passively refused food a thousand times before. But tonight it made me sad to watch him eat his solitary supper—he'd cooked one serving of an entire balanced meal, vegetables and everything. This amazed me. When Carlo went on his work binges at the hospital, I skipped meals notoriously; I was lucky if I hit all the food groups in four consecutive days. But I supposed Doc Homer had gotten the knack of solitude. For him it wasn't a waiting period, it was life.

"I hear you were kind of hard on Rita Cardenal," I said.

He flushed slightly. "Do you know her? She's expecting twins. She needs to take better care of herself."

"I know. She was one of my students till day before yesterday. She's a good kid."

"I'm sure she is," he said. "But she is rather hard to talk to. I wrote down a prescribed diet for her, which she wadded up and threw in the wastepaper basket before she left my office. She said she would eat what she pleased, since her life was already a totally creeped scenario. That is a quote."

I smiled. "Kids here have their own minds, I'm finding out. I hadn't really expected that."

"They do."

"My students talk like a cross between Huck Finn and a television set."

He seemed slightly amused. I knew I was avoiding the issue. I took a deep breath. "I think I've let things go too long. I should have talked to you a long time before now. I don't think you're doing too well, and I feel like I should be taking care of you, but I don't know how. We're the blind leading the blind here. All I know is it's up to me to do it."

"There is no problem, Codi. I'm taking an acridine derivative. Tacrine. It keeps the decline of mental functions in check."

"Tacrine *slows* the decline of mental functions, if you're lucky.

And it's experimental. I'm not stupid, I did a lot of reading in the medical library after you told me about this."

"No, you are not stupid. And I am fine."

"You always say you're fine."

"Because I always am."

"Look, I'm only here till next summer. We need to get things squared away. What are you going to do when you can't keep up your practice anymore? Do you think you're being fair?"

He cut up his cauliflower, running the knife between the tines of his fork. He dissected it into neat, identical-sized cubes, and did not answer me until he was completely finished. "I'll do what I've always planned to do. I'll retire."

"You're sixty-six," I said. "When do you plan to retire?"

"When I can no longer work carefully and capably."

"And who's going to be the judge of that?"

"I am."

I stared at him. "Well, I think there's some evidence that you're slipping in the careful and capable department." My heart was beating hard—I'd never come even close to saying something like that to him. I didn't wait for an answer. I got up and walked into the living room. It was the same, piles of junk everywhere. I was startled by something new: a dozen women's shoes from somewhere, arranged in a neat circle, toes pointed in. Superficial order imposed on chaos. It's exactly how I would have expected Doc Homer to lose his marbles. I felt dizzy and unsupported by my legs or Doc Homer's floor, and I sat down. I couldn't even tell Hallie this. She would come home.

The old red-and-black wool afghan, Hallie's and my comfort blanket in old times, was still folded tidily on the sofa. In the months I'd been here it hadn't been unfolded once, I was sure. I took the thick bundle of it into my arms and walked back into the kitchen and sat down, this time in Hallie's chair, the afghan pressed against my chest like a shield.

"I'm taking this, if you don't mind. I'll need it when it gets cooler."

"That's fine," he said.

I stared at him for another minute. "Do you know what people in Grace are saying?"

"That the moon is made of green cheese, I imagine." He got up and began to wash the dishes from his small meal. A large and a small skillet, a vegetable steamer, a saucepan, plate and glass, spoons and knives of various sizes, and the Piper forceps. Including the pot lids, around twenty separate utensils to cook and consume maybe eight ounces of food. I felt obsessive myself for counting it all up, but it seemed to be a symbol of something. The way he'd lived his life, doing everything in the manner he thought proper, whether it made sense or not.

"They're saying I'm a doctor," I said to his back. "That I've come here to save Grace." Hallie and I had already used up all the possible jokes on our town and Doc Homer: Saving Grace, Amazing Grace. Every one left a bitter taste in the mouth.

"And how do they propose that you're going to do that?"

"I don't know. However doctors usually perform their miracles."

"You know very well what doctors do. You finished four years of medical school and you nearly finished your internship. You were only two or three months away from being licensed to practice."

I touched my fingertip to some vagrant bread crumbs scattered across the table. Because his back was turned I had the courage to ask the question point blank. "How *severely* do you hold that against me? That I didn't make doctor?"

"Who is saying you didn't make it?"

"I'm saying it, right now. I don't have it in me, now or ever. Just the idea of me being a doctor is ridiculous. People depending on *me* in a life-or-death situation? Remember when I took Red Cross swimming lessons? I tried out the elbow-hold rescue on Ginny Galvez and we had a near-death experience."

He spoke without turning around. "How did you arrive at the conclusion that you could not be a doctor?"

For a minute I buried my face in the afghan, which smelled like a familiar animal. When I looked up again he was facing me, drying his hands on a dish towel, one finger at a time. "I would just like to know," he said.

"I couldn't make it through my rotation on OB-GYN. I was delivering a premature baby, which turned out also to be breach, and there was fetal distress, and the mother's pressure started to shoot up. I just walked away from it. I don't even remember exactly what I did, but I know I left her there. She could have died." I corrected myself. "They both could have died."

"You were only a first-year resident and it was a high-risk delivery. I'm sure there was someone on hand to back you up. Malpractice laws being what they are."

"That's not the point."

"You don't have to deliver babies to be a physician. I no longer deliver babies myself. There are a hundred specialties you could choose that have nothing to do with obstetrics."

"That *isn't* the point. People were looking to me for a decision, and I lost my nerve. You can't lose your nerve. You're the one that taught me that."

He looked me straight in the eye and said, "I lose my nerve a dozen times a day."

It was the last thing on earth I expected to hear. I felt as if I'd been robbed. I put my face back in the afghan and suddenly I started to cry. I have no idea where the tears came from, they just came from my eyes. I didn't want either one of us to admit helplessness here. I kept my face down for a long time, soaking the wool. When I finally glanced up he was putting something away in the refrigerator. In the dark kitchen, the brightly lit interior of the refrigerator was a whole, bright little foreign land of cheerful white boxes, stacked like condominiums. There must have been fifty tupperware containers in there: pies, cakes, casseroles. I thought of Uda's squash pie, and understood with surprise that all the women of Grace were taking care of Doc Homer. As a caretaker, I was superfluous.

He saw me looking at him. He stood with the refrigerator door half open, illuminating his face. "Codi, you could be a doctor if you wanted to do that. You learned the skills. Don't try to put the blame on something abstract like your nerve—you have to take responsibility. Is it something you want, or not?"

"I don't know."

He didn't move. I kept thinking he ought to close the refrigerator door. He'd always had a million rules about everything. Wasting electricity, for example.

"It's not," I finally said, for the first time.

"No?"

"No. I thought it would be an impressive thing to do. But I don't think it was a plan that really grew out of my life. I can't remember ever thinking it would be all that delightful to look down people's throats and into their nasty infected ears and their gall bladders."

"You're entitled to that opinion," he said. "That the human body is a temple of nastiness."

I held him steady in the eye and he smiled, ever so slightly. "You bet," I said. "People are a totally creeped scenario."

▼▼▼

The news from Hallie was brief and moderately alarming. There had been contra activity in her district, nobody hurt but four John Deere tractors burnt down to scorched metal hulls. She sounded sick about that. "A Deere is like a hunk of gold here. Because of the U.S. embargo we can't get parts, and the ones still running are Nicaragua's patron saints." She sounded completely, happily settled in, though, much more so than I was in Grace. She talked about waking up in the mornings: Roosters hopping up onto the windowsill. An army of little girls in polyester dresses out in the street with huge baskets on their heads, forging out on a hundred urgent missions. She was making good progress with some new cultivation methods; wished she knew more about diesel mechanics. A man named Julio, a literacy teacher from Matagalpa, had asked her out on a date. (She drew stars all around the word "date," making fun of herself.) They had busy schedules, so finally they met after work and rode together to a meeting in a church where Hallie delivered a lecture on pesticide safety. The church was full of gnats and kerosene smoke and little kids crawling around on a big piece of plastic, crying, impatient for their parents to take them home to bed. She and Julio had ridden over together on her horse, *Sopa del Dia,* and had a nice time going home.

▼▼▼

Sunday night was Halloween and Emelina's children took to the streets. Grace was at an interesting sociological moment: the teenagers inhaled MTV and all wanted to look like convicted felons, but at the same time, nobody here was worried yet about razor blades in apples.

Emelina volunteered me to go trick-or-treating with the four older boys while she stayed home to dispense bribes to the rest of the town's marauders; she felt a pagan holiday would do me good. I was only chaperone and crossing guard, not expected to go in costume. There was a state law against anyone over twelve wearing a mask or making direct requests at people's doors. The city fathers of Grace were independent to an extent: they ignored state law when they closed school on November 2 for the town's biggest holiday, the Day of All Souls. But to be on the safe side they were going along with the Halloween mask law. John Tucker was disappointed but tried not to show it. Emelina encouraged him to go with us anyway, more or less as a second chaperone. She was wonderful to watch. I guess I'd never really seen good mothering up close.

He agreed to go, dressed in J.T.'s black raincoat, with a quarter-inch of talcum powder on his face. Emelina ran deep eyeliner shadows under his eyes. It was convincing—he looked either sick or dead, depending on his position. Mason went as a bug, with grocery-bag wings and radio antennae strapped to his head with a yellow sweatband. He instructed Emelina to draw on bug fangs with her eyebrow pencil. I don't think Emelina ever actually wore makeup, she just kept it on hand for emergencies. The twins both were going as teenagers (i.e., convicted felons), but decided they needed fangs also.

We made a pretty good haul; in this fruit basket of a valley, I'd never seen such an orgy of sucrose. Jawbreakers and Gummi Bears multiplied in the kids' bags like the loaves and fishes. The twins pulled me along by both hands, and Mason gripped my leg when we crossed the street. We hit every house on the road that circled the canyon to the south—the longest possible route to the courthouse. John Tucker hung back in the shadows at the edges of yards, but I escorted the boys right up to the doorsteps, secretly enjoying these little peeks into people's bright living rooms. Our last stop was at the lemon-yellow home of Mrs. Nuñez, whom I knew to be an important figure in the Stitch and Bitch Club. I was beginning to learn my way around the matriarchy of Grace, a force unknown to me in childhood.

Old Mrs. Nuñez recognized the kids immediately, but for some reason mistook me for Emelina. I think she just didn't really look. She chattered at the boys as she dropped Hershey's kisses and bubble gum into their heavy grocery bags: "Oh, what an awful-looking bug you are. You get away from my house, you old *cucaracha*. And you ugly old twins, too. You're too scary." She kissed them all on the tops of their heads.

She stopped suddenly, holding her glasses and peering out at the pale apparition of John Tucker, who was hanging back around her shrubs as required by law. *"Cielo santo!"* she said, with real concern. "What's the matter with your brother?"

"He's thirteen," said Glen.

▼▼▼

All Souls' Day dawned cool, and the people of Grace put on their sweatshirts and gave thanks. The heat wave was broken. By half past eight the sun was well up and sweatshirts peeled off again, but it was still a perfect day. Every able-bodied person in Grace climbed the canyon roads to converge on the cemetery.

It was the bittersweet Mexican holiday, the Day of the Dead, democratic follow-up to the Catholic celebration of All Hallows. Some people had business with the saints on November 1, and so went to mass, but on November 2 *everybody* had business at the graveyard. The families traipsing slowly uphill resembled harvester ants, carrying every imaginable species of real and artificial flower: bulging grocery sacks of chrysanthemums and gladioli; tulips made from blue and pink Styrofoam egg cartons; long-stemmed silk roses bouncing in children's hands like magic wands; and unclassifiable creations out of fabric and colored paper and even the plastic rings from six-packs. The Stitch and Bitch Club had had four special meetings in a row.

When Hallie and I were very small we used to be allowed to

participate in this celebration, with J.T.'s family. I wondered if Viola remembered having us in tow. In my own mind it was all vague; what I remembered best was the marigolds. *Cempazuchiles,* the flowers of the dead. I asked Viola about them.

"They come on the truck," she answered cryptically.

"Do you remember when Hallie and I used to come up here with you?"

"Sure I do. You always ran all over the graves and messed up everything." Viola didn't pull her punches.

"Well, we were little," I said defensively. "Doc Homer made us quit coming after a while. I remember that. I remember him saying, 'Those great-grandmothers aren't any of your business.' "

"Well, he was the boss."

"Right. He was the boss."

Emelina and the four older boys were marching ahead, but I was pushing the stroller over gravel and Viola was over sixty, so we both had an excuse to lag. We were a harvester-ant clan ourselves, burdened not only with flowers but with food and beer and soft drinks and sundry paraphernalia. John Tucker was carrying a new, largish St. Joseph for Viola's husband's grave. J.T. was still in El Paso, and Loyd was on a switch engine in Yuma, but we didn't seem to need them all that much. It looked like a female holiday, what with the egg-carton flowers. A festival of women and children and old people and dead ancestors.

Viola stopped for breath, holding the bosom of her shiny black dress and looking down at the canyon. I waited with her, adjusting the red handkerchief Emelina had tied over Nicholas's bald head to shield it from sun. As he vibrated over the corduroy road the kerchief kept slipping down over his eyes, and he looked like a drunken pirate. I bent over and looked into his face, upside-down. He enlightened me with a wicked pirate smile.

It was a spectacular day. The roadside was lined with bright yellow plumes of rabbitbrush, apparently too common a flower for anyone to take to a grave, but I liked them. I would try to remember to pick some on my way back down, to stick into the clay ollas around my house; I was determined to prove to Emelina that I wasn't completely bereft of domestic instincts.

From where we stood we could look down on the whole of Grace plus the many small settlements that lay a little apart from the town, strung out along the length of Gracela Canyon and its tributaries, often inhabited by just a few families, some with their own tiny graveyards. These settlements were mostly abandoned now. A lot of them had been torn right up when Black Mountain chased a vein of copper under their floors; others had been buried; the company had an old habit of digging and dumping where it pleased. Grace's huge main cemetery was located on the opposite side of the canyon, as far as possible from the mine, for exactly that reason. Not even the graveyards were sacred.

At the upstream end of the canyon we could also see the beginnings of the dam that would divert the river out Tortoise Canyon. There had been a ridiculous photo in the local paper: the company president and a couple of managers at a groundbreaking ceremony, wearing ties, stepping delicately on shovels with their wing-tip shoes. These men had driven down from Phoenix for the morning, and would drive right back. They all had broad salesmen's smiles. They pretended the dam was some kind of community-improvement project, but from where Viola and I stood it looked like exactly what it was—a huge grave. Marigold-orange earth movers hunched guiltily on one corner of the scarred plot of ground.

"So what's going to happen?" I asked Viola.

"The Lord in heaven knows," she said.

I prodded. "Well, there was a meeting last night. Have you talked to anybody?"

"Oh, sure. The men on the council had another one of their big meetings about it and decided to have a lawsuit. A lawyer came up from Tucson to meet with Jimmy Soltovedas."

Jimmy was the mayor. The town council had nothing to do with Black Mountain anymore; Grace wasn't a company town in the classical sense, except for the fact that the company owned everything we walked on.

"What did the lawyer say?" In a moment of vanity I wondered if anyone had mentioned my affidavit. My line about "the approximate pH of battery acid" seemed like something a lawyer could gleefully quote.

"The lawyer said we might have grandfather rights to the water, and so we could have a class-action lawsuit to make the company give us back our river."

"How long will that take?"

She shrugged. "Maybe ten years."

"Ten *years?*"

"Right. In ten years we can all come back and water our dead trees."

"Did anybody go to the newspapers to get some publicity about this? It's ridiculous."

"Jimmy called the newspapers half a dozen times. I talked to Jimmy's wife. Nobody's interested in a dipshit little town like Grace. They could drop an atom bomb down on us here and it wouldn't make no news in the city. Unless it stirred up the weather over there and rained out a ball game or something."

"So it's a ten-year lawsuit." I didn't want to believe she was right, though her sources were always irreproachable. "Is that the only thing those guys can come up with against the Mountain?"

"Don't call that company the Mountain," she said curtly. "It makes it sound like something natural you can't ever move."

"I've heard the men call it that," I said.

Viola snorted like an old horse and started up the hill.

When we arrived, half a dozen elderly men were putting a fresh coat of white paint on the wrought-iron fence around the huge cemetery. Wrought iron was a theme here; there were iron crosses and wreaths, and over some of the graves there were actual little iron houses, with roofs. Through the ups and downs of Black Mountain's smelting plant, Grace had been home to a lot of out-of-work metalworkers.

Most families divided their time between the maternal and paternal lines, spending mornings on one set of graves and afternoons on the other. Emelina and the boys staked out the Domingos plot and set to work sweeping and straightening. One of the graves, a great-uncle of J.T.'s named Vigilancio Domingos, was completely bordered with ancient-looking tequila bottles, buried nose down. Mason and I spent half the morning gathering up the strays and resetting them all in the dirt, as straight as teeth. It was a remarkable aesthetic—I don't mean just Uncle Vigilancio, but the whole. Some graves had shrines with niches peopled by saints; some looked like botanical gardens of paper and silk; others had the initials of loved ones spelled out on the mound in white stones. The unifying principle was that the simplest thing was done with the greatest care. It was a comfort to see this attention lavished on the dead. In these families you would never stop being loved.

The marigold truck arrived at ten o'clock. Women swarmed down on it like bees, coming away with armloads of floral gold. There were many theories on the best way to put them to use, or to make them go farthest. Viola, who directed the Domingos family operations, was of the deconstructionist school. She had the boys tear the flowers up and lay the petals down over a grave, blanketing it like a monochrome mosaic.

John Tucker stayed at his work but the twins wandered and Mason disappeared altogether. Emelina wasn't worried. "He's refining his begging skills he learned on Halloween," she said, and was probably right. Grandmothers everywhere, who at lunch had set out extra plates for the dead, were now indiscriminately passing out the sweet remains of their picnics.

By mid-afternoon Emelina felt we should send out a search party, "before he eats so many cookies he busts." Viola volunteered, and I went with her, more or less as a tourist. I wanted to see what else there was in the line of beautified graves. We skirted Gonzalez and Castiliano and Jones, each family with its own style. Some were devotees of color or form, while others went for bulk. One grave, a boy who'd died young, was decorated with the better part of a Chevrolet. There were hundreds of holes drilled into the fishtail fenders, to hold flowers. It was beautiful, like a float in a parade.

The cemetery covered acres. To the west of us were collections of small neglected mounds whose stones bore the names of families that had died out. "Trubee," I read aloud, wandering toward the desert of the forgotten. "Alice, Anna, Marcus. Lomas: Hector, Esperanza, José, Angel, Carmela."

"Honey, we better get back to where people are," Viola cautioned, but I wandered on, as distracted in my way as Mason must have been, wherever he was.

"Nolina," I shouted. "Look, here's my long-lost relatives."

Viola looked at me oddly from her distance across the graves.

"I'm kidding," I said. We came from Illinois, as she well knew. "Here's my Aunt Raquel, my aunt . . . something Maria." Most of the graves were illegible, or so crudely marked there was nothing to read. Then I found one that stopped me dead.

"Viola. Here's a *Homero* Nolina."

"So it is," she said, not really looking. "Son of a gun."

I eyed her. "Do you know something about this?"

"What do you want me to tell you?"

"Who were the Nolinas?"

"Come on back away from there and I'll tell you."

I stood my ground.

"Honey, come on, let's leave these dead folks alone. Nobody put any plates of food out for them for a long, long time. They're not feeling so happy today."

"Okay, but you have to tell me."

She told me the Nolinas used to live up around Tortoise River, in the northern end of Gracela Canyon. There was a little settlement there that dispersed when the area was covered by mine tailings. The Nolinas had dug up what they could of the family graveyard and carried the bones a few miles to bury them up here. It wasn't all that long ago, she said. Around 1950.

"I don't know any Nolinas in Grace now," I said.

"No, they're about gone. They never did settle too good into Grace. The most of them went to Texas or somewhere, after their houses got tore up. They weren't . . ." She stopped and took off her shoe, cocking her stockinged foot against her plump ankle while she examined the inside of it, then put it back on. "The Nolinas weren't real accepted. They were kind of different all the way back. There was one of the Gracela sisters had auburn hair and a bad temper, and she married Conrado Nolina. They say that family went downhill."

"They were trash, is what you're telling me."

"No. Just different."

I followed behind her as she plodded along, dodging headstones. She was as intransigent, in her way, as Doc Homer. "So how come one of them has practically the same name as my father?"

"You better ask him that," she said. "It's his name."

At that moment something hit me from behind like a torpedo, tackling me around the knees. It was Mason.

"Where have you been, *pachuco?* Your mama was worried to death about you," Viola said. Mason had an enormous sucker ballooning under one cheek. He laughed, recognizing Viola's scoldings as a bald-faced lie.

"I was at a birthday party," he lied back.

It took a while to coax him back to the fold. There were an infinity of distractions: *Calaveras,* little skull-shaped candies for children to crack between their teeth. The promise of a chicken leg for a kiss. Little girls and boys played "makeup," standing on tiptoe with their eyes closed and their arms at their sides, fingers splayed in anticipation, while a grownup used a marigold as a powder puff, patting cheeks and eyelids with gold pollen. Golden children ran wild over a field of dead great-grandmothers and great-grandfathers, and the bones must have wanted to rise up and knock together and rattle with joy. I have never seen a town that gave so much—so much of what *counts*—to its children.

More than anything else I wished I belonged to one of these living, celebrated families, lush as plants, with bones in the ground for roots. I wanted pollen on my cheeks and one of those calcium ancestors to decorate as my own. Before we left at sunset I borrowed a marigold from Emelina's great-aunt Pocha, who wouldn't miss it. I ran back to lay it on Homero Nolina, just in case.

HOMERO

15

MISTAKES

He has to look at her for a long time before he trusts himself to speak. Who is this girl? His daughter Codi, but which Codi? He thinks.

"You look surprised."

"You startled me. I wasn't expecting anyone." He was doing Mr. Garrison's lab work, waiting for the centrifuge to spin down Mr. Garrison's blood cells, and when he looked up she was standing in the doorway. He detests surprises.

"Pop, I called five minutes ago, to see if you were here. I told you I was coming. I came straight here. I spent the day up at the graveyard."

She is leaning against the doorsill holding a bouquet of rabbitbrush and roadside weeds, showering the air with pollen like an old feather duster. She has on purple cowboy boots, which even now are damaging her arches.

"And now you are here," he says carefully.

"I found a surprise in the graveyard, a headstone with a name on it you might recognize. Yours. Almost yours."

"Perhaps I am dead."

She stares. "Do we have relatives from here?"

Uda Dell gave those to her, to both girls, for Christmas: the boots and straw cowboy hats and holsters with cap guns, so that they could run like banshees around the house pretending to fill each other with imaginary bullet holes. He took the guns away, for the preservation of their souls, and the boots on account of their arches. He let them keep the hats.

The minute hand on the wall clock jumps and the centrifuge slows to a stop, clicking suggestively, like the wheel of fortune. Without its mechanical whine the lab is very quiet. He looks up again and she is still there in her stocking feet and red straw cowboy hat, its dark cord knotted under her chin. She understands about the guns, but she wants the boots back. She has come on behalf of herself and her sister, she says. Her left foot in its white sock curls under. Why is it that only girls stand on the sides of their feet? As if they're afraid to plant themselves? Tears stream from her eyes.

He can't relinquish either the guns or the boots. He wishes he could do all these things differently, but he can't. He says, "I don't think we need to discuss this any further."

"Oh, come on, just tell me. Would it kill you to tell me?"

Startled, he looks again: she isn't in stockinged feet, she has boots on. She is much too tall. He is confused and becomes angry. He has a glass vial of blood in his hands. This is his office. She didn't need to sneak down here and startle him in his own doorway.

"I'm doing Mr. Garrison's hematocrit," he says. "I have a good bit more work to do."

She sighs loudly. She must be fourteen. In a year she will be sullen and furtively pregnant. Or has that passed too? He doesn't even look at her because there is too much there, and he's afraid. She is his first child, his favorite, every mistake he ever made.

COSIMA

16

BLEEDING HEARTS

At the first sign of winter the trees began to die. Leaves and aborted fruits fell in thick, brittle handfuls like the hair of a cancer patient. The abundance of sun and warmth, which we thought would never end, had led the trees on too, promising the impossible. But now the daylight grew thin and they showed no will to live. A dead sea of leaves drifted deep and undisturbed on the orchard floors. No children played there.

I spent a lot of time considering the mystery of my family tree. I didn't push the subject of the Nolinas, but I did ask people about my mother, whose leavings were scant. I'd grown up with only one sentence, repeated like a mantra: "It wasn't childbirth she died of, it was organ failure." I know this was meant to protect Hallie and me from guilt, but "organ failure," in its way, was equally unhelpful: a pronouncement that reminded me of those doubtfully groomed children in school whose report cards bore failing marks through every season, perennial as grass. "Organ failure" sounded like something our mother ought to be ashamed of, and us after her, *for* her, in death.

Viola dispensed with the organ-failure myth as easily as snapping a wishbone: "No, it was childbirth," she told me.

"But Hallie was born in June," I said. "She didn't die till later in the summer."

"It was a few weeks," Viola conceded. "Hallie gave her a real good round. She lost a lot of blood and after the birth she never got up again."

I was stunned by this news, and we walked in silence for a while. We were on our way to a special meeting of the Stitch and Bitch Club. To my surprise, I'd been invited as a guest scientist to talk about the pH of the river; needlework was not on the agenda.

Viola had on a brown cloth coat and what must have been her dead husband's hunting cap, earflaps down, the whole thing cocked forward to accommodate her thick, coiled bun. She stopped to pick up two stray peacock feathers, which she tucked into her coat pocket. One was perfect, with an iridescent blue eye bobbing at its tip. The other one had no eye.

"What did she look like?" I asked.

"Like you. Exactly like you, only smaller. She had real little hands and feet."

I looked down at my size 9's, defensively. "Not like Hallie?"

"Hallie always favored Doc more," Viola said.

I pondered this but couldn't see it—Hallie was so vital and Doc Homer looked drawn. But then what I saw really was their interiors, not their façades. Your own family resemblances are a frustrating code, most easily read by those who know you least.

"Well, I know she was pretty," I said. "Everybody says that. With a name like Alice how could you not be pretty?"

Viola made an odd sound, like unconsummated laughter.

"What?"

"He was the only one that ever called her Alice. Everybody else called her Althea. It means 'the truth.' "

"*Althea?* What, she was an honorary member of the Doña Althea family?"

Viola said nothing. I never knew what to make of her dark hints, but this one was wildly improbable. My impression was that she'd stayed an outsider, like the rest of us. Doc Homer had married my mother and come out here from Illinois after World War II, after he'd served in the army and finished his internship. Her maiden name was something like Carlisle. We never pressed him for more; when it came to our mother, Doc Homer seemed to be in an extended mourning period that lasted for our whole lives to date.

It made me curious, though. I had visions of trying again, of pinning his fragile shoulder blades against the wall of his basement office and forcing him to tell the whole truth about our family. As if Doc Homer's tongue could be forced.

Abruptly, Viola and I reached the American Legion hall. We walked into a noisy room bright with artificial light and I felt disoriented as to the decade. Women wearing cable-knit cardigans over thin housedresses crowded the hall with their talk, their large purses and imposing bosoms. When they saw Viola and me they began to come to some kind of order. Chairs were dragged, with much metallic howling, from conversational circles back into crooked rows. Many faces were familiar to me now from some encounter, such as old Mrs. Nuñez, who'd been so chatty when I took the boys to her house trick-or-treating, and others like Uda Dell I knew specifically. Doña Althea presided from an overstuffed chair at the front of the hall, but did not speak. Her face was as finely lined as the grain in maple wood, and about the same color. Her pale blue eyes blazed in the direction of the air over our heads. You could have taken her for a blind woman if you didn't know the truth, which was that Doña Althea's vision was sharp as a hawk's.

Norma Galvez, whose shellacked white hair was crowned with a navy bow that coordinated with her Steelworkers T-shirt, brought the meeting to order. It was a packed house. It took a while to achieve perfect quiet. Viola ushered me to a chair at the front table, hurried over to say hello to Doña Althea, and deposited the two feathers in a grocery bag of kindred feathers at the Doña's feet. Then she scurried back and took her seat by me.

"Viola brought a guest," announced Mrs. Galvez, accompanied by vigorous nodding from Viola. She'd removed her hunter's cap. "You all know Doc Homer's daughter Cosima. She's going to tell us about the contamination."

That was my introduction. I was expecting to hear all about myself and the situation, as is always done at meetings that go on too long. But she was through, and I was on. I stood a little shakily, thinking of Hallie, who felt at home giving a lecture in a church full of mosquitoes and kerosene smoke and squalling babies.

"I'm not an expert," I began. "Here's the chemistry of it. Black Mountain Mining has been running sulfuric acid, which is a clear, corrosive, water-miscible acid, through their tailing piles to recover extra copper. It combines to make copper sulfate, which is also known as 'blue vitriol.' People used to use it to kill rats and pond algae and about everything else you can name. There's a ton of it in your river. And there's straight sulfuric acid in there too. The EPA finally sent a report saying that kind of pollution is very dangerous, and they can't put it near people and orchards, so Black Mountain is building a dam to run the river out Tortoise Canyon. You know that part of the story. And the men on the town council are pushing for a lawsuit that will get some action in the twenty-first century." There was some snickering. I remembered my talk with Viola on the hill overlooking the dam construction site—her disgust. The Stitch and Bitch Club wasn't banking on the good old boys.

"I really don't know any way of helping out with your problem. All I can tell you is that you have a problem, and why, which I guess is what scientists are mainly good for." I paused to swallow. The room was a silent garden of blinking faces, expecting something from me.

"My students and I looked at the river water under microscopes, and the usual things that live in a river aren't there. Then we tested the pH of the river and found out it's very acidic. The EPA has tested it too, and they agree. But your trees knew all this way before we did. Watering them from the river is just like acid rain falling on them, if you've heard of that. The acid-rain problem here in the West comes mostly from mine smelters. It's the same acid, one way or the other. Sulfuric acid." I feared I was losing my grasp of the subject, but they were still listening.

"I don't think I can tell you anything helpful. But Viola said I should come anyway. If you have questions I'll try to answer them." I sat down.

A thin woman in cat's-eye glasses and a red dress stood up

and demanded, "You mean the fish and stuff is all killed? My husband claims they was catching croppies out of there a month or two ago."

"Well, no, the fish . . ."

"Stand up, honey, we can't hear you," said Miss Lorraine Colder, my fourth-grade teacher. She and Miss Elva Dann, who sat next to her, had lived together forever and resembled each other although they were no relation.

"Not the fish," I said. "They're still alive, but the smaller things that live in the water . . ." I considered how to phrase this, and started again. "Usually there's a whole world of microscopic things living in a river, and in the dirt, and the air. If you were in an airplane and flew over a city and looked down and saw *nothing* was moving, you'd know something was up. That's how you can tell if a river is healthy or not. You can't see them, but they're supposed to be there."

The woman in the red dress hugged her sweater around her. "Like bugs?"

"Kind of," I said.

Another woman said in Spanish that if the river water killed bugs, she'd better take some and sprinkle it around her son's house. There was a good bit of laughter.

"It won't kill cockroaches," I said. "Too bad. You could sell it for a fundraiser." They laughed again, though there were some surprised looks, and I was secretly satisfied. All my life here, people had spoken Spanish around me the way grownups spell around children.

The woman in the red dress was still standing. "What we want to know is, *is* the river poisoned for good? Would we be better off to let them run it out Tortoise Canyon?"

Every person in the room was looking at me. It dawned on me that they weren't conceiving of their situation as hopeless. What they wanted was not sympathy or advice, but information. "Well, no," I said. "The river could recover. It doesn't *start* here, it starts up on the Apache reservation, in the mountains where the snow melts. As long as that's pure, the water coming down here will be okay."

"So if you could stop Black Mountain from running the acid

through the tailing piles, then after a while the junk would get washed out?" inquired Mrs. Galvez. "Like flushing the john?"

"Exactly like that," I said.

Fifty women started talking at once. You'd think I'd commuted a death sentence. After a minute Doña Althea carefully pushed herself up from the arms of her chair and stood, waiting for quiet. In her black dress she rustled like an old crow. She gave a short speech in Spanish, the gist of which was that I'd told them what they needed to know, and now they had to figure out how to get the company to stop building the dam and stop polluting the river and go to hell.

I sat down, a bit stunned. My Spanish was passably good, thanks to the years of Hallie's refugees sleeping on my couch, but some of Doña Althea's more idiomatic swear words were new ones on me. Also, she referred to me as *la huérfana,* the orphan. They always called Hallie and me that. It seemed unkind.

"My husband used to be a crane operator when the mine was running," shouted a woman in the back row. "He would know how to fix up them bulldozers from hell to breakfast."

"My husband was a dynamite man," volunteered another woman. "That would be quicker."

"Excuse me, but your husbands won't put Chinese arithmetic past no bulldozers," said Viola. Mrs. Crane Operator and Mrs. Dynamite seemed unperturbed, but Viola added thoughtfully, "No offense. Mine would be just as lazy, except he's dead."

Mrs. Galvez nodded. "Well, that's the truth. My husband says the same thing, 'The *lawyers* will fix it up, honey.' If the men were any use they'd be here tonight instead of home watching the football game."

"What are you talking about, *football?*" asked Mrs. Dynamite. "*Muchacha,* didn't you hear? The *Miss America Pageant* is on tonight." She stood up. "Whose husbands was watching the Broncos game when you walked out of the house?"

There was a show of hands.

"Okay, ten seconds and . . ." she leaned forward, dropped her jaw, and bugged her eyes wide like a pair of fried eggs . . . "if you got remote control, *three* seconds."

"Sure, why do you think they hurried us all out of the house tonight?" a woman added from the front row. " 'Why, yes, honey, go on to your club. I'll be okay. I'll just eat me a TV dinner here and watch football.' Like hell. Football in a bathing suit."

"Okay, girls," said Mrs. Galvez, adjusting her hair and rapping the table with her high-heeled pump. "Like Doña Althea says, we got some darn good thinking to do tonight."

"I say we were on the right track with the dynamite," said Viola. There was general nodding.

The woman in the red dress stood again. "We don't know how to use the dynamite, though. And the men, they might be good men but they wouldn't do it. They'd be scared to, I think. Or they don't see no need. These men don't see how we got to do something *right now.* They think the trees can die and we can just go somewhere else, and as long as we fry up the bacon for them in the same old pan, they think it would be . . ." she faltered, hugging her elbows in earnest . . . "that it would be *home.*"

▼▼▼

On the way back Viola was quiet. She walked quickly, stopping only to pick up the feathers that littered the leafy orchard floor. The sudden cold snap that heralded the certainty of winter had caused the male peacocks to molt in unison. There being no hope of mating for months to come, they had shed their burdensome tails.

The meeting had ended in compromise: the Stitch and Bitch Club would officially sanction mass demonstrations against Black Mountain's leaching operation, to be held daily on the dam construction site, starting at 6 A.M. the following morning. Unofficially, the Stitch and Bitch Club would have no objection if a bulldozer met with premature demise.

Hallie wrote:

This morning I saw three children die. Pretty thirteen-year-old girls wearing dresses over their jeans. They were out in a woods near here, picking fruit, and a helicopter came over the trees and strafed them. We heard the shots. Fifteen minutes later an alert defense patrol shot the helicopter down, twenty miles north, and the pilot and another man in the helicopter were killed but one is alive. Codi, they're American citizens, active-duty National Guards. It's a helicopter from the U.S., guns, everything from Washington. Please watch the newspapers and tell me what they say about this. The girls were picking fruit. When they brought them into town, oh God. Do you know what it does to a human body to be cut apart from above, from the *sky?* We're defenseless from that direction, we aren't meant to have enemies attack us from above. The girls were alive, barely, and one of the mothers came running out and then turned away saying, "Thank you, Holy Mother, it's not my Alba." But it *was* Alba. Later when the families took the bodies into the church to wash them, I stayed with Alba's two younger sisters. They kept saying, "Alba braided our hair this morning. She can't be dead. See, she fixed our hair."

Codi, please tell me what you hear about this. I can't stand to think it could be the same amnesiac thing, big news for one day and then forgotten. Nobody here can eat or talk. There are dark stains all over the cement floor of the church. It's not a thing you forget.

She signed it, perversely, "The luckiest person alive."

I heard nothing. I listened to the radio, but there wasn't a word. Two days, nothing. Then, finally, there was one brief report about the American in the helicopter who was taken prisoner by the Nicaraguan government. He was an ex-mercenary running drugs, the radio said, no connection to us. He was shot down and taken prisoner, and that is all. No children had died in an orchard, no sisters, no mothers, no split skulls. And I'm sorry to say this, I knew it was a lie, but I was comforted.

▼▼▼

"Who came up with the idea that Indians are red?" I asked Loyd one morning. If I wasn't careful I could lose myself in this man. His color was like some wholesome form of bread, perfectly done. His forearm, which my head rested on, was sparsely covered with silky black hair.

He turned his head. His hair was perfectly straight, and touched his shoulders. "Old movies," he said. "Westerns."

We were in my bed very late on a Sunday morning. Loyd was a wonderful insomnia cure, good enough to bottle. That's what I'd written Hallie, whom I told everything now, even if my daily letters were comparatively trivial. "He's a cockfighter," I'd confessed, "but he's better than Sominex." When Loyd lay next to me I slept deep as a lake, untroubled by dreams. First I'd felt funny about his being here—exposing Emelina's children, and all that. But he didn't invite me to his place, saying mine was better. He liked to pull books down off my slim shelf and read parts aloud in bed, equally pleased with poetry or descriptions of dark-phase photosynthesis. It occurred to me that Emelina would have a good laugh over my delicacy concerning her children. She probably was daring them to look in the windows and bring back reports.

But the shades were drawn. "Old westerns were in black and white," I reminded him. "No red men."

"Well, there you go. If John Wayne had lived in the time of color TV, everybody would know what Indians look like."

"Right," I said, gently picking up Loyd's forearm and taking a taste. "Like that white guy in pancake makeup that played Tonto."

"Tonto who?"

"Tonto Schwarzenegger. Who do you think? Tonto. The Lone Ranger's secretary."

"I didn't grow up with a TV in the house." He withdrew his arm and rolled over on his stomach, forearms crossed under his chin. It looked like a defensive posture. "After we got plumbing in Santa Rosalia we all sat around and watched the toilet flush. Sounds like a joke, right? How many Indians does it take to flush a toilet."

"It's no big deal. Sorry. Forget it."

"No, it is a big deal." He stared at the painted headboard of my bed, rather than at me. "You think I'm a TV Indian. Tonto Schwarzenegger, dumb but cute."

I pulled up the covers. For a bedspread I'd been using the black-and-red crocheted afghan, Hallie's and my old comfort blanket. "And what is that supposed to mean?" I asked.

"Nothing. Forget it."

"If you said it, Loyd, you meant it."

"Okay, I did." He got up and began to put his clothes on. I reached over and caught his T-shirt when it was halfway over his head, and pulled him to me like a spider's breakfast. I kissed him through the T-shirt. He didn't kiss back. He pulled his head free of the shirt and looked at me, waiting.

"I don't know what you want from me," I said.

"I want more than I'm getting. More than sex."

"Well, maybe that's all I have to offer."

He still waited.

"Loyd, I'm just here till next June. You know that. I've never led you on."

"And where do you go after next June?"

"I don't know." I poked my fingers through the holes in the black-and-red afghan, a decades-old nervous habit. He held eye contact until I was uncomfortable.

"Who do you see yourself marrying, Codi?"

I could feel my pulse in my neck. It was a very odd question. "I don't."

"Yes, you do. But he'd have to be taller than you, smarter than you, more everything. A better job and more damn college degrees. You're like every other woman alive."

"Thanks very much," I said.

"Your height alone kind of limits the field."

"If that's supposed to be an insult, you're way off. I always wanted to be even taller than I am, taller than Hallie."

We sat not looking at each other for a minute. I took his hand and laid it, limp, against mine. It felt like a pancake or something. "This isn't about your deficiencies, Loyd. It's just me. I can't stay here. There's a poem by Robert Frost about this pitiful old hired hand who comes back home when he's run out of luck because he knows they won't kick him out. The poem says, 'Home is the place where, when you have to go there, They have to take you in.' " I stroked the tendons on the back of Loyd's hand. "I don't want to be seen as pitiful. I came here with a job to do, but I have places to go after this. I wish . . ." I turned my face toward the window so he wouldn't see tears.

"I'd like to find a place that feels like it *wants* to take me in. But this isn't it. At the end of the school year my time's up. If we get attached, you and me, then it's hard."

"That's your game, not mine, Codi." He got up and walked into the living-room to make his hourly call to the depot; he was expecting to be sent to El Paso soon. I was stunned that he would walk away from me when I needed to be taken in. Though I guess that's just what I'd asked him to do, walk away. His T-shirt was inside out, and he took it off and switched it around, still managing to keep the receiver cradled against his ear. He'd been put on hold. I watched him through the doorway and realized that the muscles in his back were taut with anger. I'd never seen Loyd mad, and was surprised he was capable of it.

I felt lost. I got up, throwing back the afghan and draping the flannel sheet around me like a sari, and went into the living room. The floor was cold. I shifted from one foot to the other, feeling vaguely like the Statue of Liberty. Jack on the front doorstep was scratching his neck vigorously, jingling his tags. That dog had the patience of Job.

"What's going on?" I asked, when Loyd hung up the phone.

"I'm five times out. Plenty of time for a fuck."

"That's not what I meant. Loyd, I don't think you're dumb."

"Just not anything worth changing your plans for."

I laughed. "As if I had plans."

He looked at me, his eyes searching back and forth between my two pupils as if he were trying to decide which door concealed the prize. "What would happen if you stayed here, Codi?"

"I would have the wrong haircut. Everybody would remind me that I don't quite belong. 'Oh, honey,' they'd say, 'you're still here? I heard you were on your way to Rio de Janeiro to have tea with Princess Grace.' And I'd say, 'No, I've grown up to be the new Doc Homer. I've moved into his house and I'm taking over his practice so I can save the town.' "

"Save us from what, Great White Mother?"

"Oh, shit, you guys can all just go to hell." I laughed, since the other choice was to cry. He took me in his arms and I crumpled against his chest like an armful of laundry. "This town was never kind to me," I said into his shirt. "I never even got asked out on dates. Except by you, and you were so drunk you didn't know better."

"You know what we used to call you in high school? Empress of the Universe."

"That's just what I mean! And you didn't care that the Empress of the Universe had to go home every night to a cold castle where the king stomped around saying hugs are for puppy dogs and we are housebroken."

Loyd seemed interested in this. "And then what?"

"Oh, nothing much. I'd hide in my room and cry because I had to wear orthopedic shoes and was unfit to live."

He turned my chin to face him. I hadn't noticed before that without shoes we were the same height. Proportioned differently—my legs were longer—but our chins punched in at the same altitude. "So, where you headed now, Empress?"

"God, Loyd, I don't know. I get lost a lot. I keep hoping some guy with 'Ron' or 'Andy' stitched on his pocket and a gas pump in his hand will step up and tell me where I'm headed."

His face developed slowly toward a grin. "I'll tell you. You're going with me to do something I'm real good at. The best."

I tried to figure this out. Behind his smile there was a look in his eyes that was profoundly earnest. It dawned on me. "Cockfights?"

There was no way I could say no.

▼▼▼

A fighting cock is an animal bred for strength and streamlined for combat. His wings are small, his legs strong, and when he's affronted his neck feathers puff into a fierce mane like a lion's. Individuality has been lost in the breeding lines; function is everything. To me each bird looked like any other. I couldn't tell them apart until they began dying differently.

The deaths are protracted. That was one thing I learned when I went to see Loyd excel in the profession to which he was born.

I'd had in mind that a cockfight would be an after-dark, furtive thing: men betting and drinking and sweating out the animal suspense under cover of night. But it was broad daylight. Loyd cut the wheel sharply, taking us off the road and up a gravel arroyo. He seemed to navigate the reservation by the same mysterious instincts that lead birds to Costa Rica and back home again unfailingly each year. We reached a thicket where a motley herd of pickup trucks were parked at odd angles, close together, like nervous horses ready to bolt. Loyd pulled his red truck into the herd. Beyond the trees was a dirt arena where roosters strutted around clearing their throats, barnyard-innocent.

Loyd steered me through the arena, his arm around my shoulders, greeting everybody. I saw no other women, but Loyd would have been welcome here if he'd shown up with a she-wolf. "Lot of people going to lose their shirts today," a man told him. "You got some damn good-looking birds." The man was handsome and thin, with a long ponytail tied up Navajo style. His name was Collie Bluestone. Loyd introduced us, seeming proud of me.

"Glad to meet you," I said. Collie's hand felt taut with energy. A chunk of turquoise on a leather thong rested on his collarbone, below the scar of an old tracheotomy.

"Collie's a cock mechanic," Loyd said. "We go back a ways."

I laughed. "You give them tune-ups before the fight?"

"No, after," Collie said. "I sew them up. So they live to fight another day."

"Oh. I thought it was to the death." I dragged a finger across my throat.

Collie smiled. "Out of every fight, one of them dies and one lives." He turned to Loyd. "How come the girls always forget about the one that lives?"

"Everybody loves a hero, I guess." Loyd winked at me.

"Nothing heroic about a dead bird," I pointed out.

The arena centered on a raked floor of reddish-brown dirt. Loyd maneuvered me through the men squatting and arguing at its perimeter to a dilapidated flank of wooden chairs where he deposited me. I felt nervous about being left alone, though the atmosphere was as innocuous as a picnic, minus women and food.

"I'll be back," he said, and vanished.

The place was thick with roosters but didn't smell like poultry, only of clean, sharp dust. I suppose the birds didn't stay around long enough to establish that kind of presence. Some men took seats near me, jarring me slightly; the chairs were all nailed together in long rows, the type used for parades. I spotted Loyd through the crowd. Everybody wanted to talk to him, cutting in like suitors at a dance. He was quite at home here, and relaxed: an important man who's beyond self-importance.

He returned to me just as a short, dark man in deeply worn plaid pants was marking out a chalk square in the dirt of the center pit. Betting flared around the fringes. An old man stabbed the stump of a missing forefinger at the crowd and shouted, angrily, "Seventy! Somebody call seventy!"

Loyd took my hand. "This is a gaff tournament," he explained quietly. "That means the birds have a little steel spur on the back of each leg. In the knife fights they get blades."

"So you have gaff birds and knife birds," I said. I'd been turning over this question since our trip to Kinishba.

"Right. They fight different. A knife fight is a cutting fight and it goes a lot faster. You never really get to see what a bird could do. The really game birds are gaff birds."

"I'll take your word for it," I said.

The first two fighters, men named Gustavo and Scratch, spoke to the man in plaid pants, who seemed in charge. Scratch appeared to have only one functional eye. Loyd said they were two of the best cockfighters on the reservation. The first position was an honor.

"The roosters don't look honored," I said. Actually they looked neither pleased nor displeased, but stalked in circles, accustomed to life on one square yard of turf. Their tail feathers ticked like weeds and one of them crowed nonstop, as if impatient. But impatience implies consciousness of time and a chicken is existential. I know that much about birds.

"How come you're not down there playing with your friends?" I asked Loyd.

"I've got people to train the birds, bring the birds, weigh in, all that. I handle. You'll see."

"*Train* the birds? How do you teach a bird to fight?"

"You don't, it's all instinct and breeding. You just train them not to freak out when they get in a crowd."

"I see. So you don't train, you handle," I said. "A handling man."

He pinched my thigh gently along the inside seam of my jeans. I'd been handled by Loyd quite a few times since Kinishba. The crowd quieted. Scratch and Gustavo squared off in the center of the pit, their charges cradled at thigh level, and they thrust their birds toward each other three times in a rhythm that was frankly sexual. Each time the men's hips rocked forward, the cocks dutifully bit each other's faces. Apparently the point was to contrive a fighting mood. Two minutes ago these birds were strutting around their own closed circuits, and if they looked away from each other even now they'd probably lose their train of thought and start scratching the dust for cracked corn.

But now they were primed, like cocked pistols. Their handlers set them down on opposite chalk lines and they shook themselves and inflated their pale ruffs. When the plaid-pants referee gave the word, the men let go. The birds ran at each other and jumped up, spurs aimed for the other bird's breast. They hopped over one another, fluttering their short wings, pecking each other's heads and drawing blood. After about thirty seconds the birds' spurs tangled and they lay helpless, literally locked in combat.

"Handle that!" the referee shouted.

The handlers moved in to pull them apart. They faced the birds off, waited for the count, and let them go at each other once more. Within another minute Scratch and Gustavo had to intervene again, this time because one bird had his spurs irretrievably embedded in the breast meat of his opponent. The handlers gently pulled them apart and started them again.

It takes a very long time for one bird or the other to die. Presumably they were dying of internal wounds and hemorrhage. Punctured lungs, for example, and literally bleeding hearts. Eventually they began to bleed from the mouths. At that point I could finally tell Scratch's bird from Gustavo's because it lay down in the dirt and wouldn't get up. Scratch had to place it on its feet and push it back in the direction of combat.

"Why don't they just declare the winner?" I whispered.

"There's rules."

It was a ridiculous answer, but correct. A death was required. It took thirty or forty minutes, and I guess the birds were showing their mettle, but it was hard to watch. The cocks were both exhausted and near death, no longer even faintly beautiful. Their blond breasts and ruffs were spotted with blood, stringy as unwashed hair. Collie Bluestone would have his work cut out for him here.

There seemed to be elaborate rules about how to keep things going after this point, when both birds really just wanted to sit with their beaks in the dirt. If one lay still, the other had no incentive to fight. I've studied a lot of biology; I quickly figured out that this industry was built around a bird's natural impulse for territorial defense, and that's where it broke down. No animal has reason to fight its own kind to the death. A rooster will defend his ground, but once that's established, he's done. After that he tends to walk around ignoring the bizarre surroundings and all the people who have next month's rent riding on him and he'll just act like a chicken—the animal that he is. The handlers had to keep taking the birds firmly in hand, squaring them off and trying to force the fight.

"This is making me sick," I told Loyd.

He looked at me with such surprise it angered me. Nobody could look at this picture and fail to see cruelty.

"I've seen little boys do this same exact thing," I said. "Take some pitiful animal and tease it and drag it back by the legs over and over again, trying to make it fight."

"The knife fights go a lot faster," he said.

"But you don't like knife fights. You like this. That's what you said."

He didn't answer. To avoid the birds I looked at the crowd, whose faces betrayed neither pain nor blood thirst but passive interest. It could have been any show at all, not two animals obliged to kill each other; it could have been TV. They were mostly old men in feed caps, or black felt cowboy hats if they were Apaches. I spotted a few families now, but knew if you asked these women about cockfighting they'd use the word *we*. "Oh, we love it," they'd say in cigarette-husky voices, meaning *he* does. A teenager in a black tank top, a greenish tattoo flowering across her broad back, hoisted a toddler onto her shoulder. She lit a cigarette and paid scant attention to the action in the pit, but her child took it in like a sponge.

Several people yelled loudly for Gustavo's bird. Then finally, without much warning, its opponent passed over from barely alive to dead. Without ceremony Scratch carried his limp loser out by its feet and tossed it into the back of a truck. Loyd Peregrina was called up next. A rooster was delivered into his arms, smooth as a loaf of bread, as he made his way down to the pit. This time I watched. I owed him that.

In the first fight I'd watched birds, but this time I watched Loyd, and soon understood that in this unapologetically brutal sport there was a vast tenderness between the handler and his bird. Loyd cradled his rooster in his arms, stroking and talking to it in a low, steady voice. At each handling call he caressed the bird's wings back into place, stroked its back, and licked the blood from its eyes. At the end, he blew his own breath into its mouth to inflate a punctured lung. He did this when the bird was nigh unto death and clearly unable to win. The physical relationship between Loyd and his rooster transcended winning or losing.

It lasted up to the moment of death, and not one second longer. I shivered as he tossed the feathered corpse, limp as cloth, into the back of the truck. The thought of Loyd's hands on me made the skin of my forearms recoil from my own touch.

▼▼▼

"What do they do with the dead birds?" I wanted to know.

"What?"

"What do they do with them? Does somebody eat them? *Arroz con pollo?"*

He laughed. "Not here. In Mexico I've heard they do."

I thought of Hallie and wondered if they had cockfights in Nicaragua. In the new, humane society that had already abolished capital punishment, I'd bet money they still had cockfights.

Loyd watched the road and executed a tricky turn. He was driving a little fast for gravel road and dusk, but driving well. I tried to picture Loyd driving a train, and came up with nothing.

No picture. No more than I could picture Fenton Lee in his head-on wreck.

"What do they do with them here?"

"Why, you hungry?"

"I'm asking a question."

"There's a dump, down that arroyo a ways. A big pit. They bury them in a mass grave. Tomb of the unknown chicken."

I ignored his joke. "I think I'd feel better about the whole thing if the chickens were getting eaten."

"The meat'd be tough," Loyd said, amused. He was in a good mood. He'd lost his first fight but had won four more after that—more than anyone else that day.

"It just seems like such a pathetic waste. All the time and effort that go into those chicken lives, from the hatched egg to the grave of the unknown chicken. Pretty pointless." I needed to make myself clear. "No, it's not pointless. It's pointed in a direction that makes me uncomfortable."

"Those roosters don't know what's happening to them. You think a fighting cock understands its life is pointless?"

"No, I think a fighting cock is stupider than a head of lettuce." I glanced at Loyd, hoping he'd be hurt by my assessment, but apparently he agreed. I wanted him to defend his roosters. It frightened me that he could connect so intensely with a bird and then, in a breath, disengage.

"It's a clean sport," he said. "It might be hard to understand, for an outsider, but it's something I grew up with. You don't see drunks, and the betting is just a very small part of it. The crowd is nicer than at a football game."

"I don't disagree with any of that."

"It's a skill you have in your hands. You can go anywhere, pick up any bird, even one that's not your own, a bird you've never seen before, and you can do this thing with it."

"Like playing the piano," I said.

"Like that," he said, without irony.

"I could see that you're good at it. Very good." I struggled to find my point, but could come up only with disturbing, disjointed images: A woman in the emergency room on my first night of residency, stabbed eighteen times by her lover. Curty and Glen sitting in the driveway dappled with rooster blood. Hallie in a jeep, hitting a land mine. Those three girls.

"Everything dies, Codi."

"Oh, great. Tell me something I don't know. My mother died when I was a three-year-old baby!" I had no idea where that came from. I looked out the window and wiped my eyes carefully with my sleeve. But the tears kept coming. For a long time I cried for those three teenage girls who were split apart from above while they picked fruit. For the first time I really believed in my heart it had happened. That someone could look down, aim a sight, pull a trigger. Feel nothing. Forget.

Loyd seemed at a loss. Finally he said gently, "I mean, animals die. They suffer in nature and they suffer in the barnyard. It's not like people. They weren't meant to live a good life and then go to heaven, or wherever we go."

As plainly as anything then, I remembered trying to save the coyotes from the flood. My ears filled with the roar of the flooded river and my nose with the strong stench of mud. I gripped the armrest of Loyd's truck to keep the memory from drowning my senses. I heard my own high voice commanding Hallie to stay with me. And then, later, asking Doc Homer, "Will they go to heaven?" I couldn't hear his answer, probably because he didn't have one. I hadn't wanted facts, I'd wanted salvation.

Carefully, so as not to lose anything, I brought myself back to the present and sat still, paying attention. "I'm not talking about chicken souls. I don't believe roosters have souls," I said slowly. "What I believe is that humans should have more heart than that. I can't feel good about people making a spectator sport out of puncture wounds and internal hemorrhage."

Loyd kept his eyes on the dark air above the road. Bugs swirled in the headlights like planets cut loose from their orbits, doomed to chaos. After a full half hour he said, "My brother Leander got killed by a drunk, about fifteen miles from here."

In another half hour he said, "I'll quit, Codi. I'm quitting right now."

17

PEACOCK LADIES AT THE CAFÉ GERTRUDE STEIN

"He's giving up *cockfighting* for you?" Emelina's eyes were so wide I could only think of Mrs. Dynamite's husband watching Miss America.

"I guess. We'll see if he stays on the wagon."

"Codi, that's so romantic. I don't think J.T. ever gave up a thing for me except cracking his knuckles."

"Well, that's something," I said.

"No, it doesn't even count, because I terrorized him out of it. I told him it would give him arthritis or something."

Emelina and I were eating chili dogs at a roadside diner on I-10. Loyd's pickup, which we'd borrowed for the trip, was parked where we could keep an eye on it. Piled high in the back, individually wrapped in dry-cleaner bags, were fifty peacock piñatas with genuine peacock tail feathers. We were headed for Tucson, prepared to hit the streets with the biggest fund-raising enterprise in the history of the Stitch and Bitch Club.

The project was Viola's brainchild, although she shared credit with Doña Althea, who had opened up her storehouse of feathers. They'd held two all-night assembly lines to turn out these masterpieces, and really outdid themselves. These were not the likes of the ordinary piñata, destined to meet its maker at the end of a blindfolded ten-year-old's baseball bat. They had glass-button eyes and feather crests and carefully curled indigo crepe-paper wings. These birds were headed for the city, and so was the Stitch and Bitch Club, *en masse,* by Greyhound. Our plan was to meet at the bus station and take it from there.

I was surprised when Viola asked if I'd come. She said they needed me, I knew the city; you'd think it was a jail break. But Loyd was doing switch-engine time in Lordsburg and it was Christmas break, so I had time on my hands. I begged Emelina to come too, and spend a few days in Tucson. I needed to walk on flat sidewalks, risk my neck in traffic, go see a movie, that kind of thing. J.T. could stay with the kids. He was home on thirty days' probation from the railroad, for the derailment that was officially not his fault. The railroad moves in mysterious ways.

Emelina hadn't gone anywhere without a child in thirteen years. Out of habit she packed a roll of paper towels in her purse. As we drove out of Grace she gasped for air, wide-eyed, like a hooked fish. "I can't believe I'm doing this," she kept saying. "Turn the truck around. I can't go."

I drove westward, ignoring my hostage. "What, you think J.T. doesn't know how to take care of his own sons?"

"No," she said, staring at the center line. "I'm afraid I'll come back and find him dead on the kitchen floor with a Conquerers of the Castle arrow stuck on his head and a fistful of Hostess Ding Dongs."

By the time we hit the interstate she'd decided it would work out. The boys could go to college on J.T.'s life insurance.

"Oh, they won't pay if it's murder," I said gravely.

She brightened a little. "I always forget. He's the one that wanted so many kids."

It was mid-December, fourteen shopping days till Christmas, and by afternoon it was clear and cold. Twenty-two women in winter coats and support hose took the streets of downtown Tucson by storm, in pairs, each cradling a papier-mâché piñata in her arms. No one who witnessed the event would soon forget it.

Emelina and I and the truck were more or less set up as headquarters. We parked in front of a chichi restaurant called the Café Gertrude Stein, for the sole reason that it sported an enormous green plastic torso out front and the women felt they could find their way back to this landmark. As soon as they sold their birds, they were to head back for more. Emelina and I held the fort, perched carefully in the midst of our pyramid of paper birds.

A man in a black fedora and glen plaid scarf came out of the café and gave us a startled look. We'd not been there when he went in. "How much?" he asked.

This had been a much-debated question; apparently the Greyhound driver had threatened to stop the bus if the Stitch-and-Bitchers didn't quit yelling about it. Ultimately we'd been instructed to try and get what we could.

"How bad do you want it?" asked Emelina, saucily crossing her legs. Monogamous as a goose, and a natural-born flirt.

A small crowd of homeless people had gathered on the other side of the street from where our truck was parked. It seems we were by a good margin the best entertainment of their day.

"Fifty dollars?" the man in the scarf asked.

Emelina and I looked at each other, cool as cukes. "They're made by hand," I said.

"Sixty?"

"Okay."

He handed us three twenties and Emelina forked over a plastic-wrapped bird. Its tail bobbed gently behind him as he made his way down the street. I mouthed the words, "Sixty dollars!" and we collapsed against each other.

"They're made by hand," Emelina said, eyebrows arched, in perfect imitation of an Empress of the Universe.

Miss Lorraine Colder and Miss Elva Dann came back to the truck almost immediately. They'd enlisted a bag lady named Jessie, who owned her own shopping cart. When Miss Lorraine explained the threat to the homes of Grace, Jessie cried for a little while and then rallied her wits. They were able to pack half a dozen piñatas into her cart, and the trio of women set out to sell them all in a single foray.

Norma Galvez, in the meantime, lost her partner at a crosswalk and had to be escorted back to the big green naked lady by a bicycle policeman named Officer Metz. In a conversation that lasted only five blocks she'd acquired an amazing number of facts about this man: for example, he had twin daughters born on Christmas Day, and wore a hernia belt. She told Emelina and me these things when she introduced him. Officer Metz was sympathetic, but did ask if the ladies had a vendor's permit. Mrs. Galvez, a quick thinker, explained that we weren't selling anything. We were soliciting donations to save our town. Each and every donor got a free peacock piñata. In the interest of public relations she gave him one to take home to his twins.

By five o'clock we were out of birds. As it turned out, Emelina and I didn't make the best sale of the day. While too many peacocks went for only ten or fifteen, Doña Althea haggled one elderly gentleman up to seventy-five dollars. When the transaction was completed, the Doña allowed him to kiss her hand.

By the time they were back in Grace on the last evening bus, I was later informed, the Stitch and Bitch Club had already laid plans to come back in ten days with five hundred peacock piñatas. There would be only two deviations from the original plan. First, each piñata would be accompanied by a written history of Grace and its heroic struggle against the Black Mountain Mining Company. To my shock I was elected, in absentia, to write this epic broadside and get it mimeographed at the school. (Miss Lorraine and Miss Elva had retired.) Second, the price would be fixed at sixty dollars. Some argued for seventy-five but the Doña overruled, pointing out that she couldn't be expected to kiss every damn cowboy in Tucson.

▼▼▼

Emelina and I let ourselves into my old house. Carlo was expecting us and had left the key under the usual brick. The neighborhood seemed even seedier than when I left. There was some demolition going on, with cheerfully nasty graffiti decorating the plywood construction barriers. Our old house with its bolted-down flowerpots stood eerily untouched, inside and out. Carlo had let all the plants finish dying, as expected, but beyond that he'd made no effort to make the place his own. He seemed to be living like a man in mourning, not wishing to disturb the traces of a deceased wife. Or wives.

"This is creepy, Carlo," I told him when he got home late that night from his ER shift. "Why haven't you moved things around? It looks like Hallie and I just walked out yesterday."

He shrugged. "What's to move around?"

Emelina had gone to bed, trying, I believe, to stay out of our way. She'd kept asking me if it wouldn't be awkward for us to stay with my "ex." It was hard for her to understand that Carlo and I were really "exes" right from the start. Having no claim on each other was the basis of our relationship.

I'd stayed up watching the news so I could see him when he got home. He slumped down next to me on the couch with a bag of potato chips.

"That your dinner?"

"You my mother?"

"I should hope not." On the news they were talking about an ordinance that banned charity Santas from collecting donations in shopping malls. The owner of a sporting-goods store was explaining that it took away business. Rows of hunting bows were lined up behind him like the delicately curved bones of a ribcage.

"You look exhausted," I told Carlo. He really did.

"I sewed a nose back on tonight. Cartilage and all."

"That'll take it out of you."

"So what's creepy about the way I'm living?" In his light-green hospital scrubs, Carlo looked paler and smaller than I remembered him. No visible muscles.

"It looks like you're living in limbo," I said. "Waiting for somebody else to move in here and cook a real meal for you and hang up pictures."

"You never did either of those things."

"I know. But it's different when there's *two* people living in a house with no pictures. It looks like you're just too busy having fun with each other to pay attention to the walls."

"I miss you. We did have fun."

"Not that much. You miss Hallie." Being here made me miss her too, more tangibly than in Grace. On these scarred wooden floors, Hallie had rolled up the rugs and attempted to teach us to moonwalk.

"How is she? Does she ever write you? I got one postcard, from Nogales."

"Yeah, we write. She's real busy." I didn't tell him we wrote a *lot*. We'd revived an intensity of correspondence we hadn't had since 1972, the year I escaped from Grace and Hallie came into a late puberty, both of us entirely on our own. This time she was over her head with joy and I with something like love or dread, but we still needed each other to make sure it was real. We had to live with an odd, two-week lag to our conversations. I'd be writing her about some small, thrilling victory at school, and she'd be addressing the blue funk I was in two weeks ago when I was getting my period. It didn't matter; we kept writing, knowing it would someday even out.

"How's your father?"

"Oh," I said, "deteriorating. Forgetting who I am. Maybe it's a blessing."

"Are you sleeping these days?"

"Yeah, I am, as a matter of fact," I said, evasively.

"You haven't had that eyeball dream?"

I'd never been able to explain this to Carlo's satisfaction. "It's not really an eyeball dream."

"What is it, then?"

"Just a sound, like popping glass, and then I'm blind. It's a very short dream. I'd rather not talk about it if you don't mind. I'm afraid I'll jinx myself."

"So you haven't been having it?"

"No, not for a while."

It was kind of him to be interested. He gently squeezed my shoulder in the palm of his hand, releasing the tightness in my deltoid muscle. Not that it applied to us anymore, but people who know a lot about anatomy make great lovers. "So you're getting along okay there?"

"As well as I get along anywhere," I said, and he laughed, probably believing I meant "As poorly as I get along anywhere."

"I've been giving some thought to Denver," he said. "Or Aspen."

"That would be a challenge. You could sew the faces back onto people who ski into trees."

"You want to come? We could ski into trees together."

"I don't know. I'm not really thinking too far ahead right now."

He took my feet into his lap and massaged my arches. He had the famous hands of a surgeon, there was no denying it, but I had no sexual interest in Carlo. I still had a slight hope he'd come up with the perfect plan for the two of us that would make me happy and fulfilled, but even that was fading.

"What else could a modern couple like ourselves do in Aspen?" I asked him. "Besides ski into trees, and try to spot movie stars snorting coke in hotel lounges? Aspen sounds kind of fast-lane."

"After Grace, it would be, yes."

"Don't make fun of my country of origin."

Carlo looked surprised. "I've never heard you defend it before."

"It was a joke."

"Well, what about Denver, then. Not so fast-lane."

"Denver's nice." I felt the familiar tug of a brand-new place that might, this time, turn out to be wonderful. And the familiar tug of Carlo wanting me to go with him. I'd seen Denver once. It had endless neighborhoods of sweet old brick houses with peaked roofs and lawns shaded by huge maples. It would be a heavenly place to walk a dog.

"Would you ever consider getting a dog, Carlo?"

"A dog?"

"They have four legs and say 'woof woof.' "

"Oh, right."

"I've met this wonderful dog, in Grace. He's half coyote and he'll sit for five hours in the back of a pickup truck waiting for you, just because he trusts you to come back."

"This sounds serious."

"He's a good dog." I realized I hadn't thought about Loyd all day, which I viewed as an accomplishment. This must be how it is to be alcoholic: setting little goals for yourself, proving you can live without it. When really, giving it all that thought only proves that you can't. My mood suddenly began to plummet; I'd felt elated all afternoon, but now I recognized the signs of a depression coming. If I timed it right, Hallie's letter addressing my *last* depression would arrive on target.

"Shoot, look at that!" Carlo dropped my feet and jumped to turn up the volume on the TV. "That's you!"

It was. I yelled for Emelina but the spot was over by the time she showed up in the doorway wearing one of J.T.'s shirts, looking stunned.

"You were on the news," Carlo explained excitedly. "They said something about the Peacock Ladies and then they said something about Southwestern folk art, and they showed you two standing up in the truck, and this old lady in a black dress . . ."

"Doña Althea," I said.

". . . holding up the piñata, and another lady and a cop . . ."

"Officer Metz."

". . . and I didn't hear anything else because we were yelling." He stopped suddenly, looking embarrassed by his enthusiasm. He and Emelina hadn't officially met.

"Oh. Carlo, Emelina. Emelina, Carlo. An old friend from a previous life."

I didn't say which one was the previous life, and which was the present. I didn't know.

Hallie, what I can never put a finger on is the *why* of you and me. Why did you turn out the way you did? You're my sister. We were baked in the same oven, with the same ingredients. Why does one cake rise and the other fall? I think about you on your horse, riding out to the fields in your gray wool socks and boots and your hair looking like the Breck Girl gone wild, setting off to make a new world. Life must be so easy when you have dreams.

I read in the paper that we'll be sending another 40 or 50 million to the contras, so they can strafe little girls and blow you up with your cotton crop. It hurts to know this; I could be a happier American if I didn't have a loved one sending me truth from the trenches. You're right, we're a nation of amnesiacs. I'm embarrassed. It's an inappropriately weak emotion. You risk everything, while I pay my taxes like everybody else and try not to recall the unpleasant odor of death.

My life is a pitiful, mechanical thing without a past, like a little wind-up car, ready to run in any direction somebody points me.

Today I thought I was a hero. We sold fifty peacock piñatas to raise money for the Stitch and Bitch Club, which will somehow save the town of Grace. But it's not my cause, I'm leaving. I have no idea how to save a town. I only came along today because it looked like a party and I was invited. Remember how we used to pray to get invited to birthday parties? And they only asked us because we were so grateful we'd do anything, stay late and help the mothers wash the cake pans. I'm still that girl, flattered to death if somebody wants me around.

Carlo asked me to go with him to Denver or possibly Aspen. Carlo's still Carlo. He wants to know why you haven't written. (I told him you're busy saving the world.) I almost think I *could* go to Denver. Carlo is safe because I don't really love him that much. If he stopped wanting me around one day, it wouldn't be so terrible. I wouldn't die.

Hallie, I realize how that sounds. I feel small and ridiculous and hemmed in on every side by the need to be safe. All I want is to be like you, to be brave, to walk into a country of chickens and land mines and call that home, and have it *be* home. How do you just charge ahead, always doing the right thing, even if you have to do it alone with people staring? I would have so many doubts—what if you lose that war? What then? If I had an ounce of your bravery I'd be set for life. You get up and look the world in the eye, shoo the livestock away from the windowsill, and decide what portion of the world needs to be saved today. You are like God. I get tired. Carlo says "Let's go to Denver," and what the heck, I'm ready to throw down the banner of the Stitch and Bitch Club and the republic for which it stands. Ready to go live in Denver and walk my dog.

I went out at dawn, alone, to mail my letter and prowl my old neighborhood. I kept trying to believe I felt good in this familiar haunt. I'd brought my city clothes: a short skirt and black tights and stiletto-heeled boots (the sight would have laid Doc Homer flat), and I walked downtown among strangers, smiling, anonymous as a goldfish. There was a newsstand four blocks down where I used to go for the *Times* or the Washington *Post,* which Hallie and Carlo would spread all over the living-room floor on Sunday mornings. Hallie would constantly ask us if she could interrupt for a second. "Listen to this," she'd say. She needed to read it all aloud, both the tragedies and the funnies.

I ducked into a coffee shop that had decent coffee and wonderful croissants. As I sat blowing into my cup I realized I was looking around to see who was there—a habit I must have picked up in Grace, where you looked at people because they were all identifiable.

A man at a table very close to my elbow kept looking at my legs. That's another thing you put up with when you're tall—men act like you've ordered those legs out of a catalogue. I crossed them finally and said, "See, look, I've got another one just like it."

He laughed. Amazingly, he wasn't embarrassed at all. I'd forgotten how the downtown scene could be—people cultivating weirdness like it was a disease or a career. He had a neatly trimmed beard and was extremely handsome. "How Emma Bovary," he said.

I smiled. "You seem to have lost your syntax. Perhaps you're in the wrong place. The Café Gertrude Stein is down the street."

"Well," he said. "Well well well. Perhaps you could provide me with some context. Do you have a name?"

"Cosima. It means Order in the Cosmos."

"Cosima, my love, I'm in desperate need of order. If you have the *New York Times* in your bag there, I'd be willing to marry you." I had the *New York Times*.

"I'm not in the habit of marrying strangers," I said. I was suddenly disgusted with what I was doing. I'd go anywhere Carlo wanted, I'd be a sport for my students in Grace, I'd even tried to be a doctor for Doc Homer, just as I'd humiliated myself in the old days to get invited to birthday parties. If I kept trying to be what everybody wanted, I'd soon be insipid enough to fit in everywhere. I grabbed my bag and stood up to go. I told the man, "You don't have the slightest idea who I am."

▼▼▼

The second night in Tucson I slept like a child, so drenched in sleep that when I woke up I didn't know where I was. For a minute I lay lost in the bed, trying slowly to attach the physical fact of myself to a name, a life, a room in a house within a larger place. It was a frightening moment, but nothing new to me, either. So rarely in my life did I truly surrender to sleep that it took an extra effort for me to pull myself out. It felt like slogging on my elbows up a riverbank.

Carlo wasn't in bed with me, of course; he'd skirted the awkward issue by saying he had a weird shift and might as well sleep on the sofa and not disturb anybody. But he'd had plenty of opportunities in the past to see me wake up confused. He always claimed there was something wrong with the electrical current in the temporal lobes of my brain. He said that explained why I couldn't remember parts of what I'd lived through, and remembered other parts that I hadn't. I was attracted to easy answers but mistrusted them too. Carlo's specialty was the nervous system; he tended to think all human difficulties were traceable to neural synapses gone haywire. And I feared—no, I knew—what was wrong with me was more complicated than what's wrong with a badly wired house.

Carlo was already gone but left a note, saying to think very seriously about Aspen. It sounded like a joke, put that way, but I folded the note and stuck it in my suitcase. Emelina was cheerful at breakfast. She'd sensed the previous day that my mood had turned black and blue, but she was intent on our having a vacation even if neither of our hearts was really in it. We'd gone to the movies and eaten at McDonald's, which by Grace standards is the high life. We ordered Happy Meals; she was collecting small plastic replicas of impossible-looking vehicles for her boys. We had enough now to go home.

On our way out of town she insisted that we stop at an obvious tourist trap called Colossal Cave. It was colossal by no means, but a cave. We stood a long time in the dim entry while the guide in a Smokey Bear hat made small talk, hoping for a bigger crowd. There were only seven or eight of us. It must be hard to give your whole spiel to a group that wouldn't even make a baseball team or a jury.

"So when's Loyd get home?"

"Friday," I said.

"That switch-engine deal gets long, doesn't it?"

"It never seems to bother you," I said, although I had an

acute memory of the night I'd glimpsed them making love in the courtyard.

"Mm," she said.

"Then again, Loyd might be making the whole thing up. He's probably got a sweetie in Lordsburg." Emelina looked startled. "I'm kidding," I said.

"Don't say stuff like that. Knock on wood." She thumped the side of her head.

"Well, it's occurred to me to wonder why Loyd wasn't married or anything when I came along. If he's such a hot item."

"He was."

"Married?"

"*No.* Seeing somebody, but not that serious. Definitely not married. He was once, awhile back, for a year or two, I think. No kids. He didn't tell you?"

"I never asked."

"Her name was Cissie. She didn't deserve him." Emelina peeled off her Dallas Cowboys sweatshirt (actually John Tucker's). It was cave temperature down there, only 55 degrees but much warmer than outside, where it was predicted to drop below freezing that night. A woman near us was wearing a mink coat.

"I wasn't about to leave it in the car," she said to us, without provocation.

Loyd had never mentioned even a large personal fact like a previous marriage, whereas this woman in mink felt compelled to explain herself to strangers. That's how it is: some people are content to wait till you ask, while others jump right in with the whole story. It must have to do with discomfort. Once while I was waiting to file off an airplane, a grandmother came down the aisle carrying a doll in one arm and a little boy in the other, and she actually took the time to explain to us all as she passed, "The doll is his sister's, she's up ahead." I could relate to the urge. I remembered all my tall tales to strangers on buses. I was explaining in my own way; making things up so there would be no discussion of what I was *really*.

At last our guide spoke some encouraging words and the little crowd followed him down into the cave. As he walked he told us about an outlaw who'd ducked in here to hide his loot, back in the days of Jesse James, and apparently had never come out. This was meant to give us a thrill of fear, but it seemed more likely that there was a back door somewhere and the bad guy got away with the money. That's how things go. I still believe Adolf Hitler is living in the South Pacific somewhere with sanded-off fingerprints and a new face, lying on a beach drinking mai-tais.

Emelina hadn't seen a cave before and was very impressed. There were delicate stalactites shaped like soda straws, and heavy, hooded stalagmites looming up from the cave floor. She kept pointing out formations that reminded her of a penis.

"You've only been away from home three days," I whispered.

"I didn't say it looked like *J.T.'s,*" she whispered back.

The sound of trickling water was everywhere, even over our heads. I shivered to think how many tons of rock and dirt were up there above us. I'd forgotten that caves were not my favorite thing.

The highlight of the tour was the Drapery Room, which was admittedly impressive in size. The guide pointed with his flashlight to various formations, which had names like Chief Cochise and The Drapes. The walls and ceiling glittered with crystallized moisture.

Then, for just a minute—they always have to do this—he turned off the lights. The darkness was absolute. I grabbed for Emelina's arm as the ceilings and walls came rushing up to my face. I felt choked by my own tongue. As I held on to Emelina and waited for the lights to come back on, I breathed slowly and tried to visualize the size of the room, the distance between myself and the roof that I knew was there. Instead I saw random images that didn't help: Emelina collecting the little fast-food cars for her boys; the man in the café who'd suggested I marry him. And then while we all still waited I understood that the terror of my recurring dream was not about losing just vision, but the whole of myself, whatever that was. What you lose in blindness is the space around you, the place where you are, and without that you might not exist. You could be nowhere at all.

18

GROUND ORIENTATION

Loyd and I were going to spend Christmas at Santa Rosalia Pueblo. Snow fell steadily as we drove north through the Apache reservation. It enclosed translucent desert trees in spherical white envelopes, giving them form and substance. It was surprising to look out over a landscape that normally seemed empty, and see a forest.

When I closed my eyes I saw papier-mâché peacocks. I'd been helping out on the piñata assembly lines. I'd had nightmares again and wasn't sleeping well; I figured I could be useful. We didn't turn out five hundred piñatas in ten days—that was a little ambitious—but we passed the halfway mark. The last fifty or so were the best by folk-art standards. By then we'd already used up every scrap of blue crepe paper from the attics and bureau drawers of Grace, and so had to be enterprising. Some women cut up denim jeans. Mrs. Nuñez made peacock wings out of the indigo-colored flyleaves of all twelve volumes of the *Compton's Children's Encyclopedia.* To be sure, there were no two alike.

I also sweat blood over my mimeographed broadside. I wasn't a writer except by default. Viola refused to help, saying I was the one that went to college so quit whining. I tried to include all the things that made Grace what it was: the sisters coming over with their peacocks; their blue-eyed descendants planting an Eden of orchards in the idyllic days before Black Mountain; the confetti-colored houses and stairstep streets—everything that would be lost to a poisoned river. All in one page. Viola wouldn't let me go longer, claiming nobody would read it. There was some argument over whether to put the note *inside* the piñata, like a message in a bottle. I said city people didn't buy art just to crack it open; I was respected as an expert on city people. So my modest History of Grace was rolled, bound in ribbon like a diploma, and inserted into each peacock's beak.

The second Tucson excursion filled two chartered buses. Some husbands and kids got into the act, and also my students. I declared it a class project. I told Raymo if he sold ten peacocks I'd give him a C+. But I didn't go. Loyd had asked for a week's layoff and we set out on the trip he'd been planning forever.

"Don't you have to stop somewhere and check on your roosters?" I asked. We were near Whiteriver.

"I don't have any roosters."

"You don't?" I was incredulous. I thought he'd just stop going to fights himself. "What, you sold them?"

"Collie Bluestone kind of took over the business."

"So you could get back into it if you wanted to."

"Nope. He's moved over to the Colorado River reservation. He's fighting them over at Ehrenberg."

This was a good bit more frightening than if Loyd had presented me with a diamond ring. "But I'm not . . . What if you and I don't work out, Loyd?"

He downshifted for a rutted stretch in the road. "No offense, Codi, but I didn't give up cockfighting to impress you. I did it because you were right."

"I was *right?*"

"About what you said."

"What did I say?"

He didn't answer. I vaguely remembered saying something about puncture wounds and internal hemorrhage. Making that a spectator sport. "I can't believe you'd do this thing all your life and then just quit one day after something I said. Maybe you were ready to give it up anyway."

"Maybe I was." We were both quiet for a while, passing through winter-killed fields of grass and sage. Two black horses grazed on bristly shrubs in a field with no apparent fences.

"You and your brother were twins, right?" I asked, apropos of nothing.

He nodded. "Identical. Twins are bad luck."

I laughed. "For the mother."

"No, in the pueblo. When twins are born people say there'll be a poor rainy season or grasshoppers or some darn thing. In the old days you had to let twins die."

"Both? You couldn't pick one and let the other one go?"

"Nope."

"I can't imagine the mother who'd do it," I said, though of course I could. I had probably starved my own child to death *in utero,* rather than risk known disaster.

"There's a Tewa story about a mother sneaking her twins out of the pueblo and leaving them with Spider Grandmother to raise."

"Yeah? See, if there was a story like that, people knew it was wrong to let them die."

"Knew it was hard. Not wrong, necessarily. When Leander and I were bad, our mother said she was like poor old Spider Grandmother, got stuck with the War Twins."

"Were you bad a lot?"

"Just twice as bad as a regular boy." He laughed. "People called us 'Twice as Bad.' Our sisters talked about us like we were just one boy. They'd say 'he went out riding,' or whatever. I think *we* thought we were one person. One boy in two skins."

"Hallie and I feel that way sometimes."

I could see clear crescents of water collecting on Loyd's lower eyelids. "You don't have to talk about this," I said.

"I don't ever talk about him. Sometimes I'll go a day or two without even thinking about him, and then I get scared I might forget he ever was."

I laid a hand on his gearshift arm. "You want me to drive?"

He stopped and turned off the engine. We sat watching snowflakes hit the windshield and turn into identical dots of water. Then he got out. I pulled on my mittens and followed him.

Outside the cab it was impossibly quiet. We'd climbed a little now, and were in forest. Snowflakes hissed against pine needles. Jack sat in the truckbed watching Loyd carefully, exhaling voiceless clouds of steam.

"I ever tell you how I came to keep Jack?" Loyd asked.

I thought about it. "No. You told me how you took in his mother and she had pups. You didn't say how you picked Jack."

"He picked us." Loyd was leaning against the truck with his arms crossed over his chest. He looked cold. "Dad meant to drown the whole litter. He put them in an empty cement bag and tied the top real good and drove down to the river and pitched them in. He didn't know what he was doing; he was drunk as seven thousand dollars, I imagine. On the way back he picked me up from work and I said, 'Dad, here's one of the pups in the back of the truck.' He was hiding down in a box of pipe T-joints. Dad's old truck was a junkyard on wheels; you could find anything in the world back there. So I says to Dad, 'Where's the rest of them?' " Loyd's voice caught, and he waited a second, wiping his eyes. "I don't know what I'm getting all broke up for. God knows what I would have done with seven mongrel coyote pups."

God knows what I'd have done with a baby at sixteen, I thought. It's not the practical side of things that breaks us up. I leaned on the truck beside him and took his left hand between my mittened palms. It felt like a cold bottle. "So what happened? Why did you lose Leander?"

"Why?" He looked up at the sky. "Because we left the Pueblo. We were like the War Twins, I guess. A lot for our mother to handle. Our sisters were all older and having their own babies by that time. And people thought boys should go out in the world some. Be with our dad. He'd been down at Whiteriver more or less as long as we could remember. If we'd stayed up there in Santa Rosalia it would have worked out, but we came down here and Leander just ran into trouble. We didn't have anybody looking after us. Dad couldn't look after himself."

"Doesn't sound like it," I said.

"Everybody always talked like Leander died of drinking, but he wasn't but fifteen. Not old enough to sit down and order a beer. Everybody forgets that, that he was just a kid. We drank some, but I don't think he was drinking the night he died. There was a fight in a bar."

"What did he die of, then?"

"Puncture wounds. Internal hemorrhage."

▼▼▼

I drove through the pine forest, thinking off and on of Hallie, mindful of the slick road. Loyd was quiet, but took the wheel again when we descended into the Navajo reservation. He pointed out areas that were overgrazed. "It seems as big as the whole world, but it's still a reservation," he said. "There's fences, and a sheep can't cross them."

As dusk took us the landscape changed to an eerie, flat desert overseen by godheads of red sandstone. We were out of the snow now. The hills were striped with pinks and reds that deepened as we drove north and the sun drove west. It was dark when we left the highway and made our way down a bumpy road into the mouth of Canyon de Chelly. We passed several signs proclaiming the canyon bottom to be Navajo tribal land, where only authorized persons were admitted. The third sign, sternly luminous in the headlights, said, "Third and Final Warning."

"Are we *allowed* in here?" I asked.

"Stick with me. I can get you into all the best places."

Down in the canyon we bumped over rough road for an hour, following the course of a shallow river. There was no moon that I could see, and I lost any sense of direction I might have had while we still had sun. I was exhausted but also for the first time in weeks I felt sleepiness, that rare, delicious liqueur, soaking into my body like blotter paper. I almost fell asleep sitting up. My head bobbed as we crossed and recrossed the frozen river and climbed its uneven banks. Finally we stopped, and slept in the truckbed, cuddled like twin mummies inside a thick wrapping of blankets. We turned our bodies carefully and held each other to keep warm. Outside the blankets, our lips and noses were like chipped flint striking sparks in the frozen air.

"No fair, you've got Jack on your side," I murmured.

"Jack, other side, boy," Loyd commanded. Jack stood up and walked over the cocoon that contained us, stepping carefully on our chests. He turned around a few times in the wedge of space behind me, then dropped down with a groan and snuggled against my back. Within minutes I could feel the extra heat and I fell into heaven-sent unconsciousness.

In the morning, a sugar coating of snow had fallen, lightly covering the rocks. Ahead of us the canyon forked into two; from the riverbed a red rock spire rose a thousand feet into the air. Low clouds, or high fog, brushed its top. I held my breath. Looking up at a rock like that gave me the heady sensation of heights. He'd parked so this would be the first thing I saw: Spider Rock.

The canyon walls rose straight up on either side of us, ranging from sunset orange to deep rust, mottled with purple. The sandstone had been carved by ice ages and polished by desert eons of sandpaper winds. The place did not so much inspire religion as it seemed to be religion itself.

I was dressed in an instant and walking around awestruck like a kid, my head bent all the way back. "It doesn't look like a spider," I said, of the rock. "It looks like a steeple."

"It's named for Spider Woman. She lived up there a long time ago. One day she lassoed two Navajo ladies with her web and pulled them up there and taught them how to weave rugs."

The thought of standing on top of that rock, let alone trying to learn anything up there, made me shiver. "Is that the same Spider Grandmother who raised the twins?"

I expected Loyd to be impressed by my memory, but he just nodded. "That's a Pueblo story and this is a Navajo story, but it's the same Spider Woman. Everybody kind of agrees on the important stuff."

I shaded my eyes and looked up the canyon. Its narrows gave window views into its wider places. Giant buttresses of rock extended from the canyon walls, like ships, complete with knobbly figureheads standing on their prows. Some of the figureheads had been stranded, eroded away from the mother rock, and stood alone as sculptured spires. Where the canyon grew narrower the rock buttresses alternated like baffles, so the river had to run a slalom course around them. So did we. The truck crunched over icy shoals and passed through crystal tunnels of icy cottonwood branches. We passed a round hogan with a shingled roof and a line of smoke rising from its chimney pipe. A horse wandered nearby, nosing among the frozen leaves.

Several times Loyd stopped to point out ancient pictures cut in the rock. They tended to be in clusters, as if seeking refuge from loneliness in that great mineral expanse. There were antelope, snakes, and ducks in a line like a carnival shooting gallery. And humans: oddly turtle-shaped, with their arms out and fingers splayed as if in surrender or utter surprise. The petroglyphs added in recent centuries showed more svelte, self-assured men riding horses. The march of human progress seemed mainly a matter of getting over that initial shock of being here.

Eventually we stopped in a protected alcove of rock, where no snow had fallen. The walls sloped inward over our heads, and long dark marks like rust stains ran parallel down the cliff face at crazy angles. When I looked straight up I lost my sense of gravity. The ground under my boots was dry red sand, soft and fine, weathered down from the stone. If the river rose to here, the mud would be red. Loyd held my shoulders and directed my eyes to the opposite wall, a third of the way up. Facing the morning sun was a village built into the cliff. It was like Kinishba, the same multistory apartments and unbelievably careful masonry. The walls were shaped to fit the curved hole in the cliff, and the building blocks were cut from the same red rock that served as their foundation. I thought of what Loyd had told me about Pueblo architecture, whose object was to build a structure the earth could embrace. This looked more than embraced. It reminded me of cliff-swallow nests, or mud-dauber nests, or crystal gardens sprung from their own matrix: the perfect constructions of nature.

"Prehistoric condos," I said.

Loyd nodded. "Same people, but a lot older. They were here when Columbus's folks were still rubbing two sticks together."

"How in the world did they get *up* there?"

Loyd pointed out a crack that zigzagged up from the talus

slope to the ledge where the village perched. In places the crevice wasn't more than two inches deep. "They were pretty good rock climbers," he said. Loyd's forte was understatement.

There wasn't a sound except for the occasional, echoing pop of a small falling rock. "What were they scared of?" I asked quietly.

"I don't know. Maybe they weren't scared. Maybe they liked the view."

The doors were built so you'd have to step high to get out. Obviously, for the sake of the children. "Gives you the willies, doesn't it? The thought of raising kids in a place where the front yard ends in a two-hundred-foot drop?"

"No worse than raising up kids where the front yard ends in a freeway."

"You're right," I said. "No worse than that. And quieter. Less carbon monoxide."

"So you do think about that sometimes," Loyd said.

"About what?"

"Being a mother."

I glanced at him and considered several possible answers. "All the time," and "never" seemed equally true. Sometimes I wanted to say, "You had your chance, Loyd, we had our baby and it's dead." But I didn't. That was my past, not his.

"Sure, I think about it," I said, needing to relieve the pressure in my chest. "I think about hotwiring a Porsche and driving to Mexico, too."

He laughed. "Only one of the two is legal, I'm told."

I wanted to try and climb up into the cliff village, but Loyd explained that we'd crack our skulls, plus you weren't supposed to mess with the antiquities.

"I thought you broke all the rules," I said, as we climbed back into the truck and headed farther up the canyon.

He looked surprised. "What rules have I broken?"

"Authorized Navajo personnel only, for starters. We're not even supposed to be down here."

"We're authorized guests of Maxine Shorty of the Streams Come Together clan."

"Does she live here?"

"Not now. Almost everybody drives their sheep out and spends the winter up top, but the farms are down here. Leander and I spent almost every summer here till we were thirteen."

"You did? Doing what?"

"Working. I'll show you."

"Who's Maxine Shorty?"

"My aunt. I'd like you to meet her but she's down visiting at Window Rock for the holiday."

Loyd was full of surprises. "I'll never get your family straight. How'd you get a Navajo aunt? Are Navajos and Pueblos all one big tribe or something?"

Loyd laughed rather hysterically. It occurred to me that this redneck Apache former cockfighter must find me, at times, an outstanding bonehead. "The Pueblo people were always here," he explained patiently. "They're still building houses just like this—the Rio Grande Pueblos, Zuñi, Hopi Mesa. Not in the cliffs anymore, but otherwise just the same. They're about the only Indians that haven't been moved off their own place into somebody else's."

"And the Navajo?"

"Navajos and Apaches are a bunch that came down from Canada, not that long ago. A few hundred years, maybe. Looking for someplace warmer."

"And this is now Navajo tribal land, because?"

"Because the U.S. Government officially gave it to them. Wasn't that nice? Too bad they didn't give them the Golden Gate Bridge, too."

The truck crunched over frozen sand. "So the Pueblo are homebodies, and the Navajo and Apache are wanderers."

"You could look at it that way, I guess."

"What are you?"

"Pueblo." There was no hesitation."What are you?"

"I have no idea. My mother came from someplace in Illinois, and Doc Homer won't own up to being from anywhere. I can't remember half of what happened to me before I was fifteen. I guess I'm nothing. The Nothing Tribe."

"Homebody tribe or wanderer tribe?"

I laughed. "Emelina called me a 'homewrecker' one time. Or no, what did she say? A 'home ignorer.' "

He didn't respond to that.

"So how'd you get a Navajo aunt?" I asked again.

"The usual way. My mother's brother married her. Pueblo men have to marry out of the clan, and sometimes they go off the pueblo. The land down here stays with the women. So my uncle came here."

Maxine Shorty's farm, which she inherited from her mother and would pass on to her daughters, was a triangle bordered by the river and the walls of a short side canyon. We parked by the line of cottonwoods near the river and walked over the icy stubble of a cornfield. A sad scarecrow stood guard. It occurred to me that the barrenness of a winter farm was deceptive; everything was there, it was still fertile, just as surely as trees held their identity in the shape and swell of their bare winter twigs.

"Has it changed much?"

I meant it as a joke, I saw nothing that *could* have changed, but Loyd looked around carefully. "Those little weedy cottonwoods have grown up along the stream. And there's a big boulder on that slope, you see the one with dark stripes? That used to be up there." He pointed to a place in the canyon wall, visible only to himself, from which the boulder had fallen. Most men, I thought, aren't this familiar with the furniture in their homes.

"So what did you do here?"

"Worked our butts off. Weeded, picked corn, grew beans and watermelons. And had to carry a lot of water in the bad years."

"Were those peach trees here?" I asked. A weathered orchard occupied the steep upper section of land.

"They're older than my aunt. The peach trees go way back. They were planting orchards down here three hundred years ago."

"A canyon of fruit. Like Grace."

He inspected the trees carefully, one at a time: the bases of the branches, the trunks, the ends of twigs. I didn't know what he was looking for, and didn't ask. It seemed like family business. On this land Loyd seemed like a family man.

"And did the people that lived up in the cliffs grow corn and beans too?"

"That's right."

"So how come this canyon's stayed productive for a thousand and some-odd years, and we can't even live in Grace for one century without screwing it up?"

It was mostly a rhetorical question but Loyd considered it for a long time as he led me along a path up the talus slope to the back of the box canyon.

"I know the answer to that," he said finally. "But I can't put it in words. I'll have to show you. Not here. Later on."

I felt sadly let down, though it was closer to an actual promise of revelation than I'd gotten in nine years of watching Carlo's eyebrows. I could wait for "later on."

At the top of the slope was another ancient dwelling, this one mainly just ruined walls. The floor plan was clear. It interested me that the doors all lined up, I suppose to admit light to the interior.

"I found a whole clay pot in here one time," Loyd said. "It's in my mother's house." He lowered his voice. "Don't tell any Navajos, they'll throw Mama in jail."

"You brought it back to her at the end of one summer, right? As a present. And she still treasures it."

He smiled a little shyly. The image of a ten-year-old Loyd brought the threat of tears to my eyes. I'd spent my life watching mother-child rituals from outside the window.

"So you played in here when you were little?"

"Oh, yeah. This used to be me and Leander's fort."

"Cowboys and Indians?"

He laughed. "Good Indians and bad Indians."

"Which were you?"

"Nobody can be good all the time. Or bad all the time. We took turns."

He led me over a couple of tumbledown walls to the base of the cliff, and knelt down. I looked where he pointed. Set carefully among an assortment of old petroglyphs were two modern ones: the outlined left hands of two small boys, just touching, perfectly matched.

▼▼▼

We crossed the high desert from Chinle to Ship Rock, New Mexico, and on to the Jemez Mountains. Wind battered the windows and we warmed our hands at the heater vents and talked about everything under the sun. Loyd talked about his marriage to Cissie Ramon, which he said was noisy and short. Cissie was crazy about rooster fighting, men, and unusual colors of nail polish, like green. He'd thought she was exotic, but she was just wild; there was a difference. She ran out on him.

He was a good deal more interested in talking about working in his aunt's pecan orchards, in Grace. This aunt was his mother's sister, Sonia. She married a Pueblo man from her village but moved with him to Grace when Black Mountain drafted Native American men into the mines during World War II. Sonia and her husband planted fruit trees there thinking the war would last at least twenty years, and when it didn't they felt they ought to stay on in Grace anyway, for the sake of the orchards.

It was a different story from farming in Canyon de Chelly, Loyd said. Sonia had started out as a tenant picker, before buying her own pecan orchard, and she learned harvesting the modern way. Usually the harvest started in October and ran till Thanksgiving. To get the nuts off the trees, they used a machine called a tree shaker.

"I remember guys hitting the branches with sticks, when I was a kid," I said.

"Nah, we were high-tech. After the tree shaker comes the harvester, which is this big thing with a vacuum-scooper that you drive along between the rows. It scoops up everything and blows the sticks and leaves out the back, and the pecans and rocks fall down into this cage at the bottom. More junk falls out the slots as it rolls around, and the hulls fall off, and the idea is you end up with mostly pecans. But really you end up with pecans and pecan-sized dirt clods and pecan-sized rocks."

"So did you get to drive the big machines?"

"Nope. Mostly I got to pick rocks and dirt clods off the conveyor. I think that was the best job I ever had. The hardest, but the best, because I grew up on it. Stopped thinking about myself all the time and started thinking about something else, even if it was just damn pecans."

I took it from Loyd's use of the singular pronoun that Leander was dead by this time. Slowly I was patching together Loyd's life, and it was not the poor little gypsy story I'd imagined. I suppose I'd wanted to see him as a fellow orphan. But everywhere he'd been, he'd been with family.

"How long will Grace last without the river?" I asked.

"Two or three years, maybe. The old orchards will go longer because their roots are deeper." He glanced at me. "You know I have an orchard?"

"No. In Grace?"

"Yep. Not the pecans, those belong to my cousins, but Tía Sonia's leaving me the peach orchard. The fruit trees were always my job, keeping the birds and squirrels off the fruit."

"How do you do that?"

"Well, the main way is by killing them."

I laughed.

"What's funny?"

"I don't know." I stared out the windshield. In the distance, Ship Rock floated like a ghost vessel on the snowy plain. "So you now have a dying orchard to call your own. Your Aunt Sonia's moved back to Santa Rosalia, right?"

"Right. But the orchard's not mine till I have kids."

"That doesn't seem fair."

"No, it makes sense. When you have a family, you need trees." He paused, carefully, it seemed to me, and redirected the conversation. "What job did you grow up on?"

I thought this over. "Maybe I haven't had it yet."

He smiled. "You went to medical school, right? And almost finished. That can't be too easy."

"When it stopped being easy, I quit."

"What were you doing in Tucson, then, before you came to Grace?"

"You don't want to know. Cashier in a 7-Eleven."

"Shoot. And I thought you were too good to go out with a locomotive engineer. What about before that?"

"You don't want to know."

"Yes, I do."

"Well, I did medical research at the Mayo Clinic in Minnesota."

"Damn! Really?"

"Yep. I was living up there two years ago when I first found out Doc Homer was sick."

"And before that?"

I rolled my head back and looked at the roof of the car. "You *really* don't want to know."

"You were President of the United States."

"Guess again."

"You hotwired Porsches."

I laughed. "The biggest thing I ever stole was a frozen lobster, for my boyfriend's birthday. I was working in frozen foods and I think I actually wanted to get fired. Doesn't that sound stupid?"

"Yes, it sounds stupid. So that came before Mayo Clinic?"

"That, and a bunch of different odd little things. A few piddly research jobs in between. Believe me, I never put everything on the same résumé."

"And what's the one you never mention? The one you're trying not to tell me about."

"For a few years in there I lived overseas."

"No kidding. Did you fly? Shoot, I'd love to go someplace in an airplane."

"Flying's okay," I said. In truth, flying terrified me. It's the one thing I knew I had in common with my mother, who'd flat-out refused, there at the end. In my own life I handled it by means of steadfast denial. I'd flown over the Atlantic Ocean twice without even checking to see if there really was a flotation device under my seat; flotation seemed beside the point. Oh, I flew like a bird.

"So, okay, what were you doing overseas?"

I glanced at him. "I was my boyfriend Carlo's girlfriend. On the island of Crete."

He seemed amused. "What, you mean you cleaned house and made cookies?"

"Kind of. Sometimes I'd help out in the clinic. One time I set the broken leg of a sheep. But mostly I was a housewife."

"So you'd, what, go shopping in a bikini?"

I laughed. "It really was not that kind of island. You know where it is, right? In between Greece and Egypt. The women wear black wool dresses and crucifixes the size of a hood ornament. Getting the picture?"

He nodded.

"The main baby present for a boy is a silver knife, which they present in this ceremony where the godparents list all the enemies of the family going back to around Adam and Eve."

"You liked it that much, huh?"

I took my coat off. It was finally warming up. "Well, it was interesting. It was someplace to go. It was like going to another century, actually. But I felt like a complete outsider." I closed my eyes, fighting an old ache.

"How do you mean?"

"I'm pretty good at languages but I never could get the hang of fitting in. Not anywhere, but especially not there."

"Why do you think you don't fit in? Give me an example."

It was plain that I'd always been an oddity in Grace, so he must have meant how was I an oddity in Crete. "Well, my first day there I marched into the bakery and asked for a *psoli*. The word for a loaf of bread is *psomi*. A *psoli* is a penis."

Loyd laughed. "Anybody could make a mistake like that."

"Not more than once, I promise you."

"Well, you were foreign. People expect you to say a few dumb things."

"Oh, every day I did something wrong. They had complicated rules about who could talk to who and what you could say and who said it first. Like, there were all these things you were supposed to do to avoid the Evil Eye."

"How do you do that?" he asked. Loyd was full of curiosity.

"You wear this little amulet that looks like a blue eyeball. But the main thing is, you never *ever* mention anything you're proud of. It's this horrible social error to give somebody a compliment, because you're attracting the attention of the Evil Eye. So you say everything backward. When two mothers pass each other on the road carrying their babies, one says to the other, 'Ugly baby!' And the other one says, 'Yours also!' "

Loyd laughed a wonderful, loud laugh that made me think of Fenton Lee, in high school. Who'd died in the train wreck.

"I swear to God it's true."

"I believe you. It's just funny how people are. People in Grace do that too, in a way. You give them a compliment and they'll say, 'Oh, no, that's just something I've had a long time.' We're all scared to be too happy about what we've got, for fear somebody'll notice and take it away." He reached over and stroked the underside of my arm, from the elbow up. "Like you, Codi. You're exactly like that. Scared to claim anything you love."

"Am I?" I was willing to believe whatever he said. Talking with Loyd was like talking to myself, only more honest. Emelina was always asking me what it was like to live overseas, and I knew she would love the penis story, but I'd never told her much about Crete. I was afraid of her seeing me as more of an outsider in Grace than I already was. But Loyd didn't make those judgments. I could have told Loyd I'd lived on Neptune, and he'd say, "Uh-huh? What was it like, was it cold?"

▼▼▼

In the Jemez Mountains we drove up the slope of what looked like a huge old volcano. A fluted core of granite jutted from its mouth, and twisted black ridges of old lava flows ran like varicose veins down its sides. The snow was deep and the road icy. We crept along, then stopped. Loyd got out of the truck and started down the bank toward a frozen creek that cut between the road and the steep mountainside.

"Are you nuts?" I inquired.

"Come on." He waved energetically.

"Why should I follow you down there?" I demanded, following as fast as I could.

"It's a surprise."

It was near sunset, near or below freezing, and Loyd wasn't

even wearing his jacket. I slipped several times behind him and then we both slid flat-out down the hill on our backs. We were sledding, not on snow but on an exposed hillside of bizarre, rounded gravel. I picked up a handful in my mitten and tossed it in the air. It was porous and weightless like Styrofoam popcorn. "What is this stuff?" I asked, but Loyd was already crossing a log over the frozen creek. I scrambled behind him up the forested slope on the other side. I picked my way between rocks, grabbing roots and tree trunks to pull myself up. Halfway up I had to stop, hugging a pine trunk and panting. The cold air cut my lungs, and I blinked hard against the sensation that the water in my eyes might freeze over.

"It's the altitude," I whined. Loyd grabbed my hand and pulled me gently uphill. Suddenly we were following the course of an odd unfrozen stream with lush plants thriving alongside it, their leaves glossy green against the snow. I'd never seen anything like this in nature, only in the sort of paintings that show improbable and dreamlike things. Loyd, who had gotten ahead of me again, was now taking off his shirt. I wondered if perhaps I was, after all, in one of my strange dreams, and whether I would soon be looking under the foliage beside the stream for my lost baby.

I climbed over the top of a boulder and there stood Loyd, naked, smiling, an apparition bathed in steam. He slid into the blue pool at the base of the boulder. I touched the steaming water and it blessedly scalded my fingertips. I undressed more quickly than I probably have in my life, before or since, and immersed myself up to my eyes.

The sun set. Venus opened her eye on the horizon. From where we sat we could see the Jemez range and the valley floor fifty miles to the south, its buttes and mesas still lit by a distant sun. When our bodies turned red we stood up briefly among the snow-covered boulders, shouting, and the steam rose off our uplifted arms like smokestacks.

Loyd asked, "So, am I nuts?"

I stretched my legs along the sandy bottom of the pool until my toes found his. The heat relaxed every muscle and sinew and reflex in my body, and most of the ones in my head. This kind of happiness was sure to attract the attention of the Evil Eye. "Have you got any more surprises?" I asked. "Or is this the last one?"

"I've got some more."

He scooted over and lifted me off the sand, supporting my floating body with both hands under the small of my back. "I don't give them away all at once, though," he said. "Only a half dozen a year."

I counted on my fingers: Kinishba. Spider Rock, the Cliff house, and Maxine Shorty's farm. And this, volcanic hot springs. I didn't know whether to count the cockfights or not. That he could give up cockfights, I'd have to count that. "So I've used up my half-dozen already," I said.

He lifted me slightly out of the water and kissed my ribs, one at a time. "If you're only staying around for a year. That's the rules."

"That's bribery."

"Whatever it takes." He kissed my navel and the damp hill over my pubic bone.

The front of my body was very cold and the back was very hot. Somewhere in the middle, near my heart, I was just right. I opened my eyes and saw constellations whose names were their own business. "Were you ever in love with my sister?" I asked.

He looked at me oddly.

"It's just a joke. Every man I've ever been with, it seems like, was really in love with Hallie."

"I can't picture your sister. She's shorter than you, right?"

I ducked my chin a little, immersing my smile. Right then I could have signed on for life.

▼▼▼

The day we left Grace, there had been four airmail letters in the P.O. box. Lately Hallie's letters sometimes came in bunches, owing to the accumulated pauses in postal service between Chinandega and Grace. But I saved them and read only one per day. It supported the pleasant, false notion that she was available to me all the time and would always be there tomorrow.

The fourth day of our trip was Christmas Eve. In the morning as we drove down from Jemez, before we arrived in Santa Rosalia, I laid out all four letters on the dash in order of postmark and spent one last hour with my sister.

I reread the old ones before opening the fourth one. Hallie's week had gone wildly up and down. On Tuesday she was nigh unto manic because the government had had a successful national meeting on the pesticide problem. Central America was becoming a toilet bowl of agricultural chemicals, she said, because of war-strained farming economies and dumping from the First World. In the seventies, when Nicaragua was run by the U.S. Marines and Somoza, it was the world's number-one consumer of DDT. But it seemed the new Nicaragua (*our* government, she called it) planned to take responsibility for its poisons. She also mentioned that her friend Julio was back in Chinandega after a stint of literacy work near the Atlantic coast. I couldn't read anything between the lines.

On Wednesday, a child was rushed in from the village of San Manuel to the Chinandega clinic in critical condition because someone had stored paraquat in a Coke bottle.

On Thursday she was grimly happy. Five contras were making a secret sabotage raid on a hydroelectric plant, somewhere to the east, and were surprised by some armed farmers who took them captive. The culprits had passed through town in the back of an open Jeep, slit-eyed with dishonor, on their way to trial in Managua. Wouldn't it be something, she mused, if that Jeep hit one of the contra road mines? But there was the driver to consider, and even if there hadn't been, it wasn't something she could wish for. She said, "You can't let your heart go bad like that, like sour milk. There's always the chance you'll want to use it later."

I wondered at what point I'd given up on later and let mine go sour. I didn't know, although Hallie might. I reread each of the three letters with fascination but also the same dissatisfaction I'd had on the morning I'd opened it. It was all just *things happening,* and selfishly, I wanted Hallie. Even if she didn't speak to me directly, I wanted her to speak.

I tore open the last envelope and was hit full in the face with what I wanted. It was four pages long, in a cursive enlarged by rage. When God wants to punish you, as Isak Dinesen declared, He answers your prayers.

I am like *God*, Codi? Like GOD? Give me a break. If I get another letter that mentions SAVING THE WORLD, I am sending you, by return mail, a letter bomb. Codi, please. I've got things to do.

You say you're not a moral person. What a copout. Sometime, when I wasn't looking, something happened to make you think you were bad. What, did Miss Colder give you a bad mark on your report card? You think you're no good, so you can't do good things. Jesus, Codi, how long are you going to keep limping around on that crutch? It's the other way around, it's what you *do* that makes you who you are.

I'm sorry to be blunt. I've had a bad week. I am trying to explain, and I wish you were here so I could tell you this right now, I am trying to explain to you that I'm not here to *save* anybody or any thing. It's not some perfect ideal we're working toward that keeps us going. You ask, what if we lose this war? Well, we could. By invasion, or even in the next election. People are very tired. I don't expect to see perfection before I die. Lord, if I did I would have stuck my head in the oven back in Tucson, after hearing the stories of some of those refugees. What keeps you going isn't some fine destination but just the road you're on, and the fact that you know how to drive. You keep your eyes open, you see this damned-to-hell world you got born into, and you ask yourself, "What life can I live that will let me breathe in & out and love somebody or something and not run off screaming into the woods?" I didn't look down from some high rock and choose cotton fields in Nicaragua. These cotton fields chose me.

The contras that were through here yesterday got sent to a prison farm where they'll plant vegetables, learn to read and write if they don't know how, learn to repair CB radios, and get a week-long vacation with their families every year. They'll probably get amnesty in five. There's hardly ever a repeat offender.

That kid from San Manuel died.

Your sister, Hallie

"What's new with Hallie?" Loyd asked.

"Nothing."

I folded the pages back into the envelope as neatly as I could, trying to leave its creases undisturbed, but my fingers had gone numb and blind. With tears in my eyes I watched whatever lay to the south of us, the land we were driving down into, but I have no memory of it. I was getting a dim comprehension of the difference between Hallie and me. It wasn't a matter of courage or dreams, but something a whole lot simpler. A pilot would call it ground orientation. I'd spent a long time circling above the clouds, looking for life, while Hallie was living it.

19

THE BREAD GIRL

Five miles outside of Santa Rosalia Pueblo, Loyd stopped the truck, pulled off his cowboy boots, and put on moccasins. Shortly we were going to have to get out and walk through snow.

"Saving your boots?" I asked.

He ignored me. Those particular boots looked as though they'd hitchhiked to hell and back without getting a single ride.

"Me and Leander used to come home at the end of the summer wearing cowboy boots and Mama would have a fit. And cowboy hats. She'd grab off our hats and swat us with them and say, 'Ahh! You look like Navajos!' "

I'd never seen Loyd wear a hat of any kind, now that I thought about it. His story brought back a memory, vague and incomplete, of cowboy boots and a hat I'd had myself, as a child. I could just recall the sheen of lacquered straw, and a terrible sadness.

"You see it yet?"

I squinted toward the south, but saw only snow-covered hills dotted with dark, spherical juniper bushes. The horizon was punctuated with bleak mesas whose rock shoulders stood exposed to the cold. "See what?"

"Where we're going to sleep tonight."

"I hope not."

A few minutes later he asked again. I saw mesas and scalped hills with rocky outcroppings on their tops. I saw juniper trees, and snow. "Is this an eye test?" I asked.

We were practically inside Santa Rosalia Pueblo before I saw it. The village was built on a mesa and blended perfectly with the landscape, constructed of the same stones as the outcroppings that topped all the other, empty mesas. Horses and broad-faced cattle looked up at us from their pens as Loyd's red truck, the newest-looking thing within a hundred miles, rolled up the dirt track into town.

It was a village of weathered rectangles, some stacked stepwise in twos and threes, the houses all blending into one another around a central plaza. The stone walls were covered with adobe plaster, smooth and appealing as mud pies: a beautiful brown town. The color brown, I realized, is anything but nondescript. It comes in as many hues as there are colors of earth, which is commonly presumed infinite.

We left the truck in the company of other pickups and station wagons at the edge of town, and walked up into the narrow streets. In his moccasins Loyd walked with a softer, less aggressive gait. Jack stayed close to his left knee. There wasn't a soul out, but lines of smoke drifted from chimneys and the big adobe beehive ovens that squatted in every third or fourth backyard. A black dog pawed at the edge of a frozen puddle. The ladders that connected one rooftop to the next were drifted lightly with snow. One house had a basketball hoop nailed to the end beams. Front curtains everywhere glowed with warm interior light, though it was still early afternoon, and strings of bright red chilies hung by the front doors.

Loyd's mother's house had a green door. The front window was crowded with artificial flowers and ceramic animals. Loyd's oldest sister, Birdie, met us at the door. The two of them spoke rapidly in a language that sounded like song, as if the pitch might be as important as the syllable. Birdie had a perm, and wore a large turquoise necklace over her flowered blouse. She stopped talking to Loyd just long enough to touch my arm and say, "He still has that dog, don't he?" and "Come get warm." We followed her into the kitchen, where Loyd's mother enveloped him with a hug, then tugged his ponytail and lightly boxed his ears.

"What's she saying?" I asked Birdie.

"She's saying he looks like a Navajo."

The kitchen smelled of cedar smoke. Inez Peregrina was cooking a goose, among other things. She wore a large dress composed of about six different cotton fabrics, florals and plaids, somehow colorfully harmonic. The frames of her glasses were large and owlish. Her gray hair was trimmed in bangs and a pageboy over her ears, but long in back, twisted into a heavy, complicated coil and tied with red cloth. Her hands were noticeably large. I wanted her to hug me too, but she only smiled and touched my cheek when Loyd introduced us. She continued talking to him in a steady, musical downpour, to which he was attentive.

Birdie disappeared and soon returned at the head of a flock of women, and I was introduced, but the conversation between Inez and Loyd went on, uninterrupted. One at a time, each of the other women held out both hands to me, which I took, trying to appear gracious while I struggled to get their positions straight. They were Loyd's sisters; a niece; his Aunt Sonia, who had lived in Grace during the war and after; and someone Loyd called his "navel mother." I couldn't discern the generations. Aunt Sonia spoke to me in Spanish and poured cups of coffee for Loyd and me from a huge tin pot on the wood-fired stove. There were also a propane stove and the adobe oven in the backyard, and all three were in use.

I felt spectacularly out of place. For one thing, I stood a foot taller than any other woman in the room; we don't even have to get into matters of wardrobe. But I was also fascinated to watch Loyd being his mother's son, his sisters' brother, the apple of the family eye. The only remaining boy. The sisters asked him in calm, uninflected English about the drive and the length of our stay and whether he'd seen Aunt Maxine, who evidently had a heart condition. Aunt Sonia asked several specific questions about people in Grace, some of whom I knew better than Loyd because of my Stitch and Bitch association, but I was reluctant to speak. She and the sisters drifted away to other tasks, and Inez still hadn't stopped talking.

"Is it okay if I look around?" I asked Loyd.

"You can dance on the table if you want to, you're the guest," he said, grabbing me around the waist.

"I don't want to dance on the table."

He held on to me for just a minute, asking Inez in English what she thought of me. I passed a hand through my hair, thankful that it had had time to grow out from Billy Idol to a more or less regulation Mary Martin.

Inez smiled and said something, running the ladle in her right hand up and down an imaginary line. I looked at Loyd for translation.

"She says I'm lucky to have gotten such a big, strong girl. She thinks I'm lazy."

"Tell her I don't put up with lazy men. I make them pull their weight."

He told her and she laughed, giving me the hug I'd coveted.

The frosted windowpanes looked out onto the cold plain and dish-shaped, empty cornfields that lay to the south, but the kitchen was smoky and warm. The open pantry behind Inez was stocked with jars of dry yellow corn, cans of Spam, and fruit cocktail. (No orchards here, evidently.) And hominy. In Grace it was golden jars of home-canned peach halves that sat smug on kitchen shelves. Here it was puffy white hominy, jar after jar of it, hominy enough for an army.

The kitchen was at the end of a big room that contained a long wooden table, a sofa, numerous small chests, and many, many photos. A radio in another room played Hank Williams. I moved around the living room, idly looking out the windows and examining photographs. There was one of Inez and a man I presumed to be Loyd's father standing together in formal dress: he in silver-buttoned moccasins and a royal blue velvet shirt, Inez in turquoise bracelets and a silver squash-blossom necklace over her dark ceremonial dress. Her legs looked like white birch stumps in their buckskin leggings, and the woven blanket folded across her shoulders seemed to weigh her down. She looked much older than she must have actually been.

Most of the available tabletops were populated by little ceramic animals of the pastel, cute variety. Loyd had told me Inez made the best pottery in the Pueblo, but evidently it was made for Anglo collectors, not for home use. I did find in a china cabinet a display of extraordinary black-and-white pots, their glazed surfaces covered with microscopically fine geometric designs. Some of the pots were slightly less well made, maybe some of the proud early efforts of Inez's daughters. A crude, dark bowl with a chipped rim sat in the cabinet's central place of honor, and I stared at it, puzzled, until I realized this was Loyd's pot, the one he'd found in the ruins. Loyd's offering from Canyon de Chelly.

I peeked into the next room. Charlie Rich was singing from the radio now, and Birdie hummed "Behind Closed Doors" while she bent over an electric sewing machine. Its small light glowed on her face. A baby slept on a flat, fur-lined cradle board that hung like a swing on ropes from the ceiling. On every fifth arc of the swing, Birdie reached up without looking and gave it a push. She noticed me standing in the doorway and inclined her head toward the end of the room, where an iron bed stood behind a drawn-open curtain of blankets. "You can put things there. That's for you and Loyd."

"Thanks," I said. "Who's the little one?"

"My daughter's girl. Hester."

"How old?"

"Three weeks."

"Does your daughter live here too?"

Birdie pulled her cloth from the machine and shook her head slightly while she broke the thread with her teeth. "She goes to boarding school in Albuquerque."

I returned to exploring the living room. I was stunned to run across a small framed photo of two little Loyds, identical, sitting astride very different horses. Behind them was a backdrop of dry hills and a brown water tank. Loyd and Leander, nine years old, looking as if they owned the world. Until I saw that picture

I hadn't really heard a word he'd told me about losing his brother. You can't know somebody, I thought, till you've followed him home.

▼▼▼

That evening Inez's house filled with relatives for the feast. Cousins and uncles and aunts showed up, stamping the snow off their moccasins, bringing covered dishes and their own chairs. All the older women had their hair cut in the same style as Inez's, with short flaps over the ears and the heavy chignon in the back, and they wore silver necklaces and elaborate turquoise rings that shielded their knuckles. The teenage girls wore jeans and about everything else you'd expect on a teenage girl, except makeup. One of them nursed a baby at the table, under her T-shirt.

Loyd and I shared one chair; apparently we were the official lovebirds of this fiesta. He spent a lot of time telling me what I was eating. There were, just to begin with, five different kinds of *posole,* a hominy soup with duck or pork and chilies and coriander. Of the twenty or so different dishes I recognized only lime jello, cut into cubes. I gave up trying to classify things by species and just ate. To everyone's polite amusement, my favorite was the bread, which was cooked in enormous, nearly spherical loaves, two dozen at a time, in the adobe ovens outside. It had a hard brown crust and a heavenly, steaming interior, and tasted like love. I ate half a loaf by myself, believing no one would notice. Later, in bed, Loyd told me they were all calling me the Bread Girl.

Our bed was small, but after three nights in the truck it felt deliciously soft. I cuddled against Loyd. "What's a navel mother?" I asked, drowsy with warmth and a half loaf of bread.

"She's like a special aunt. She's the one that cuts the cord when you're born, and helps your mother get up out of bed when she's ready. They count that as your birthday—the day your mother gets up."

"Not the day you were born?"

"Not the day you came out. They count the mother getting better as all part of the birth."

"Hallie doesn't have a birthday, then," I said. "After she was born, our mother never got up. She got real sick, and then a helicopter tried to come get her and she died. All without ever putting her slippers on."

"Then Hallie never finished getting born," Loyd said. He kissed the top of my head.

I was aware of the sleeping sounds of Inez and Hester on the other side of the makeshift curtain. I asked, "Is it okay that we're sleeping together?"

Loyd quietly laughed at me. "It's okay with me. Is it okay with you?"

"I mean with your family."

"They're not hung up about it. Mama wanted to know if you're my woman."

"Meaning what?"

"As opposed to woman of the week, I guess."

"Woman of the year," I said.

In the morning snow had fallen, as deep as five or six quilts. The windows were round blue tunnels to the light, like the mouths of caves. Loyd got up and went outside, where, at dawn, Inez and Birdie were already involved with the day's industry. He was sent back to bed with a whole fresh loaf of bread.

▼▼▼

"How did your dad meet her?" I asked. Loyd and I were sitting on the roof of Inez's house now, facing south, waiting for ceremonies to begin in the plaza.

"At a dance over in Laguna. In the summertime. It was a corn dance. Everybody says she was a knockout when she was young. A real good dancer."

"I think she's a knockout now."

"He grew up over at Jicarilla."

"Where's that?"

"Not too far from here. It's another Apache reservation. Everybody goes to everybody's dances. We used to go over to the Navajo powwows in the fall."

Today, on Christmas Day in Santa Rosalia, there were supposed to be dances from morning till night. Half the town seemed to be preparing to dance, while the other half were busy getting good seats. I had no idea what to expect. Anxious-looking little boys clutching feather crowns and fox pelts ran across the corners of the plaza bent low, as if this would make them invisible. Earlier in the day these same little boys had run in boisterous gangs from house to house banging on doors and begging for warm crusts torn from the morning loaves. A wholesome version of trick-or-treat. Give these kids one Halloween in Grace, I thought, and they'd never be content with complex carbohydrates.

"So he married your mother," I said. "And came here."

"The women are kind of the center of things up here. The man goes to the wife's place."

"But he didn't stay."

"I never really knew Dad that well. He was already gone when he was still here, if you know what I mean. I don't know what it was that hurt him. I know he grew up at a boarding school and never had much family and he couldn't keep to the old ways. Or didn't know them. I don't know. It was real hard for him here."

I let the subject go. As the twig is bent, so grows the tree, Doc Homer used to say, referring mostly to the bone structure of the feet but it applied to moral life as well. And who knew how the kinks happened; they just did. I ought to know. As Hallie had bluntly pointed out in her letter, I'd marked myself early on as a bad risk, undeserving of love and incapable of benevolence. It wasn't because of a bad grade on a report card, as she'd supposed. It ran deeper than that. I'd lost what there was to lose: first my mother and then my baby. Nothing you love will stay. Hallie could call that attitude a crutch, but she didn't know, she hadn't loved and lost so deeply. As Loyd said, she'd never been born—not into life as I knew it. Hallie could still risk everything.

Loyd and I dangled our feet over the side of the roof, looking out over the plaza and beyond, to where the plaza ended suddenly, perforce, by the drop of a sheer cliff. I could only see this precipice as a threat, and wonder how toddlers lived to the age of reason without toddling over it, but many little feather-bedecked children were running along its edge as if it were nothing more than the end of a yard.

I heard a drum and a brief burst of what sounded like sleigh bells. Then nothing. If anything ever did happen, we'd have a good view. We'd climbed a ladder to get where we were. Jack had given a long, dejected look up the rungs as if he might consider the climb, if he weren't so dignified. Now he lay curled at the bottom keeping watch. Old wooden ladders and aluminum extension ladders were propped everywhere; second- and third-story roofs served as patios. All around the plaza, legs hung like fringe over the sides of buildings. I spotted Inez and some other relatives across the way. Inez's owlish glasses were the type that turn dark outdoors; two huge black disks hid her round face as she sat, hands folded, inscrutable as a lifeguard.

Not far from us in a sheltered corner of the roof was a wire pen full of geese and turkeys muttering the subdued prayers of the doomed. "Does your mama know you were a cockfighter?" I asked Loyd.

"No." He hesitated. "She knew Dad did it, and that he took Leander and me to the fights when we were little, but she didn't care for him doing that. She never knew I went on with it. And you better not tell her."

"I'm gonna tell," I said, poking him in the ribs. "I'm going to look up in my *Keres*–English dictionary, 'Your son is a dirty low-down rooster fighter.' "

Loyd looked pained. Pleasing his mother was nothing to joke about. He'd given up cockfighting for Inez, not for me, I now understood. I'd just been the cricket in his ear. But that wasn't insignificant, I decided. I could settle for that. I looked down at the plaza, whose quilt of fresh snow remained a virginal white, unmarred by tracks. This seemed miraculous, considering the huge number of people crowded around its edges—a good two hundred or more. People must have come from outside the Pueblo. Jicarilla Apaches looking for knockout wives.

"How come those houses over there near the edge of the cliff are falling down?" I asked. Their adobe plaster had cracked off, revealing the same artful masonry as Kinishba, in a state of collapse.

"Because they're old," Loyd said.

"Thank you. I mean, why doesn't somebody fix them up? You guys are the experts, you've been building houses for nine hundred years."

"Not necessarily in the same place. This village was in seven other places before they built it up here."

"So when something gets old they just let it fall down?"

"Sometimes. Someday you'll get old and fall down."

"Thanks for reminding me." I shaded my eyes, looking to the east. Something was happening near the kiva, which was a building with a ladder poking out through a hatch in its roof. Loyd had suggested I shouldn't show too much interest in it.

"The greatest honor you can give a house is to let it fall back down into the ground," he said. "That's where everything comes from in the first place."

I looked at him, surprised. "But then you've lost your house."

"Not if you know how to build another one. All those great pueblos like at Kinishba—people lived in them awhile, and then they'd move on. Just leave them standing. Maybe go to a place with better water, or something."

"I thought they were homebodies."

Loyd rubbed his hand thoughtfully over my palm. Finally he said, "The important thing isn't the house. It's the ability to make it. You carry that in your brain and in your hands, wherever you go. Anglos are like turtles, if they go someplace they have to carry the whole house along in their damn Winnesotas."

I smiled. "Winnebagos. They're named after an Indian tribe." It occurred to me too late that Loyd already knew both these things. For months, I think, I'd been missing his jokes. Empress of the Universe, instructing the heathen.

"We're like coyotes," he said. "Get to a good place, turn around three times in the grass, and you're home. Once you know how, you can always do that, no matter what. You won't forget."

I thought of Inez's copious knickknacks and suspected Loyd was idealizing a bit. But I liked the ideal. The thought of Hallie's last letter still stung me but I tried to think abstractly about what she wanted to tell me: about keeping on the road because you know how to drive. That morality is not a large, constructed *thing* you have or have not, but simply a capacity. Something you carry with you in your brain and in your hands.

I'd come on this trip knowing I still had to leave Loyd in June, that Grace wouldn't keep me, but maybe I was just keeping to the road. I felt guilt slip out of me like a stone. "It's a nice thought," I told him. "I guess I'll probably carry something away with me when I leave Grace."

He looked at me carefully, started to speak, then stopped. And then did speak. "It's one thing to carry your life wherever you go. Another thing to always go looking for it somewhere else."

I didn't respond to that. I blinked hard and tried to look unconcerned, but the guilt nudged back along with the sharp glass edge of my own rationalization, recognized for what it was. I wasn't keeping to any road, I was running, forgetting what lay behind and always looking ahead for the perfect home, where trains never wrecked and hearts never broke, where no one you loved ever died. Loyd was a trap I could still walk out of.

I listened to the sad geese in their pen, and realized the crowd was quiet. The snowy plaza was marked with a single line of tracks: in the center of the white square stood a tall young woman in a black dress that hung from one shoulder. Her other shoulder was bare. Her waist, her upper arms and wrists, and her buckskin moccasins were all decorated with garlands of colored yarn, fur, and sleigh bells; at the crest of her head was a tuft of white eagle down. The sun shone purposefully on her hair. It was cut like Inez's, but hung loose to her waist, swaying as she moved slightly from one leg to the other, her feet barely leaving the ground. She looked graceful and cold.

The sound of drums and then the drummers themselves emerged from the kiva. The four old men took their position at the edge of the plaza and propped their huge drums on their knees without missing a beat. They began a soft chant. A second line of men with blankets draped over their shoulders climbed down from the kiva, also singing, and took their places behind the old drummers.

Then deer arrived, from everywhere. They were men and

boys with black shirts and leggings, white kilts, and deer antlers. Their human features disappeared behind a horizontal band of black paint across the eyes. They moved like deer. They held long sticks in front of them, imitating the deer's cautious, long-legged grace, and they moved their heads anxiously to the side: listening, listening. Sniffing the wind. The woman in black stepped forward shaking her gourd rattle, and they followed her. They *became* deer. They looked exactly as deer would look if you surprised them in a secret rite in the forest, moving in unison, following the irresistible hiss of a maiden's gourd rattle.

I was entranced. More people climbed down out of the kiva. Some were dressed and armed as bow hunters who stalked the deer with patience. One man, who didn't seem to have any realistic function in the drama, was nearly naked and bizarrely painted. His body was ringed with black and white horizontal stripes, he had black rings painted around his eyes and mouth, and his hair was pulled up into a pair of corn-tassel horns. He bounced around like a hysteric, possibly in the interest of keeping warm.

"Who's the striped guy?" I asked Loyd.

"Koshari," he said. "A kachina. He has to do with fertility. His home's in the East."

This struck me as humorous. "The East, as in New York? Area Code 212?"

"The East as in where the sun rises."

"That's all part of his job description?"

"All the kachinas have whole histories and families and live in one of the important places."

"I thought a kachina was a little doll."

"That's right."

"And also a person dressed up?"

"Yep. And a spirit."

"A spirit with a family and a mailing address."

"That's right. When the person dresses up a certain way, the spirit comes into him. And into the doll, if it's made right."

"Okay," I said.

"What?"

"Nothing, just okay. I understand."

He smiled at me sideways. "You think it sounds voodoo?"

"All right, I'm narrow-minded. It sounds kind of voodoo."

We both paid attention to the dancers for a while. I needed to keep a little distance from Loyd.

"Anglos put little dolls of Santa Claus around their houses at Christmas," Loyd said without looking at me.

"Yeah, but it's just a little doll."

"And does it have a wife?"

"Yes," I conceded. "A wife and elves. And they live at the North Pole."

"And sometimes one guy will dress up like Santa Claus. And everybody acts a certain way when he comes around. All happy and generous."

I'd never been put in a position to defend Santa Claus. I'd never even *believed* in Santa Claus. "That's just because he stands for the spirit of Christmas," I said.

"Exactly." Loyd seemed very pleased with himself.

One of the hunters had drawn his bow and shot an invisible arrow into a deer. It gave an anguished shiver, and then the other hunters lifted its limp carcass onto their shoulders.

"I've seen Jesus kachinas too," Loyd said. "I've seen them hanging all over people's houses in Grace."

Now there was a thought to ponder.

Koshari must also have been the spirit of nuisance, or a good belly laugh. The other deer dancers still followed the maiden, ignoring the hunters and their own fallen brother, but Koshari clowned and cut between them, getting in their way and generally interfering with their solemnity. But when one of the youngest dancers lost his antlers, Koshari picked up the headdress and carefully reattached it by its buckskin laces. The boy kept dancing, eyes front, paying no attention to the hobgoblin who was putting his costume back together.

At some later point, I noticed, Koshari had acquired a new-looking straw cowboy hat, which he cocked ridiculously on one of his horns. I had a feeling it wasn't the Navajo he was aping here. He walked duck-footed with a John Wayne swagger and was using a length of two-by-four as a gun. He knelt and fired repeatedly at the dancing deer, grandly falling over backward each time. Later he stalked them, trailing his gun in the snow and tripping over it with admirably practiced body comedy.

The deer eventually retreated to the cliff, and the plaza filled with two lines of new dancers—a row of black-clad women and a row of men in white kilts—whose bodies beat a loud rhythm as they walked. Their chests were crisscrossed with lines of seashell bells. The two rows of dancers faced one another and stamped their feet, shaking the bells, crowding the air above the plaza with a loud, hollow clicking like summer insects. The men wore crowns of eagle feathers and the women wore spectacular wooden headdresses painted with stylized clouds and slanting blue lines of rain and green blades of corn. This was the corn dance, officially a summer prayer but danced at every important occasion, Loyd said, because you couldn't pray it often enough.

"Most of the dances have to do with rain," he said. "Here, that's what everything hangs on."

Santa Claus kachinas and the beauty of the spectacle notwithstanding, I still felt outside of it. "So you make this deal with the gods. You do these dances and they'll send rain and good crops and the whole works? And nothing bad will ever happen. Right." Prayer had always struck me as more or less a glorified attempt at a business transaction. A rain dance even more so.

I thought I might finally have offended Loyd past the point of no return, like stealing the lobster from frozen foods that time, to get myself fired. But Loyd was just thinking. After a minute he said, "No, it's not like that. It's not making a deal, bad things can still happen, but you want to try not to *cause* them to happen. It has to do with keeping things in balance."

"In balance."

"Really, it's like the spirits have made a deal with *us*."

"And what is the deal?" I asked.

"We're on our own. The spirits have been good enough to let us live here and use the utilities, and we're saying: We know how nice you're being. We appreciate the rain, we appreciate the sun, we appreciate the deer we took. Sorry if we messed up anything. You've gone to a lot of trouble, and we'll try to be good guests."

"Like a note you'd send somebody after you stayed in their house?"

"Exactly like that. 'Thanks for letting me sleep on your couch. I took some beer out of the refrigerator, and I broke a coffee cup. Sorry, I hope it wasn't your favorite one.' "

I laughed because I understood "in balance." I would have called it "keeping the peace," or maybe "remembering your place," but I liked it. "It's a good idea," I said. "Especially since we're still here sleeping on God's couch. We're permanent houseguests."

"Yep, we are. Better remember how to put everything back how we found it."

It was a new angle on religion, for me. I felt a little embarrassed for my blunt interrogation. And the more I thought about it, even more embarrassed for my bluntly utilitarian culture. "The way they tell it to us Anglos, God put the earth here for us to use, westward-ho. Like a special little playground."

Loyd said, "Well, that explains a lot."

It explained a hell of a lot. I said quietly, because the dancers' bells were quieting down, "But where do you go when you've pissed in every corner of your playground?" I looked down at Koshari, who had ditched his cowboy hat and gun and seemed to be negotiating with Jack.

I remembered Loyd one time saying he'd die for the land. And I'd thought he meant patriotism. I'd had no idea. I wondered what he saw when he looked at the Black Mountain mine: the pile of dead tailings, a mountain cannibalizing its own guts and soon to destroy the living trees and home lives of Grace. It was such an American story, it was hardly even interesting. After showing me his secret hot springs, Loyd had told me the Jemez Mountains were being mined savagely for pumice, the odd Styrofoam-like gravel I'd thrown into the air in handfuls. Pumice was required for the manufacture of so-called distressed denim jeans.

To people who think of themselves as God's houseguests, American enterprise must seem arrogant beyond belief. Or stupid. A nation of amnesiacs, proceeding as if there were no other day but today. Assuming the land could also forget what had been done to it.

▾▾▾

Our Koshari friend had somehow bought off Jack and taken away the ladder that was Loyd's and my only way down. He was standing down there clowning now, pantomiming a smooching couple and talking at great length, playing to the crowd, which was laughing. At one point they all applauded. Loyd was plainly embarrassed.

"What's he saying?" I asked.

"I'll tell you in a minute."

When Koshari had gone to another part of the plaza and people had stopped staring, I pressed Loyd again.

"He said now we'll have to stay up here together a long time."

"He talked for five minutes, Loyd. I know he said more than that."

"Yeah. He said by the time the snow melts, we'll . . . Basically he said in the spring there'd have to be a wedding."

I made a face. "And people *liked* that idea? Of you marrying me? They were clapping."

"You're not . . ."

He stopped, because a kind man in the crowd had come over to replace our ladder.

"You're not the Ugly Duck, you know," Loyd said, once the man had gone.

"They don't even know me. I'm an outsider."

"I'm an outsider too," he said. "They probably know my mother likes you."

"How would they know that?"

"Word gets around."

"I mean, how does *she* know that? I can't even talk to her."

"Do you like her?"

"Yeah. I do."

"How do you know?"

"I like her hugs. She makes good bread."

"Well, maybe that's why she likes you. You like her bread."
It was hard to stay mad at Loyd.

▼▼▼

The corn dancers had remarkable stamina. Sometimes they danced in two facing lines, their whole axis rotating around the plaza like a wheel. At other times the women's line moved into and through the men's and then they broke into pairs, the men leading, practically prancing, while the women held their eyes on the ground with such concentration as to render it fertile. I would have believed a thunderclap just then, and a summer rainstorm. They danced on and on. The women's moccasined feet and thickly wrapped legs moved only a fraction of an inch with each step, but the restrained action of that step must have cost more effort than jumping jacks. They did it, and did it, and did it until early afternoon.

The corn dance was followed by an eagle dance, which seemed to involve all the young children in the village and a few older, more skillful dancers. Each one was dressed in a dark shirt and leggings, a white embroidered kilt, and a hood of white eagle down, complete with eyes and a hooked beak. Running from fingertip to fingertip across their backs, they had eagle-feather wings. The youngsters trembled with concentration as they crouched low, then rose in unison, raising their wings and soaring in convincing eaglelike fashion.

It seemed slightly less reverent than the previous dances, more akin to the childhood phenomenon of the dance recital, but Loyd said this was also a prayer. Every dance is a prayer. The eagle carries people's thoughts to the spirits in the sky. Animal messengers for the small, human hope. As they danced, the children's lips moved constantly in silent recitation.

"Watch," Loyd said. "One will go toward the east." One did. It was one of the older, more reliable dancers. He glided with outstretched wings to the edge of the plaza and past it, down the central street toward the eastern end of the village. Loyd explained that he was carrying the mothers' concerns for all the boys in the armed service.

Koshari was now solemnly busy among the children, who

needed a good deal of prompting and putting-together of costume parts. At several points he left the dancers and made his way around the crowd taking requests for special blessings, special worries. I asked Loyd to get his attention.

"For my sister," I said, and Loyd translated. "She's in the south. A long way to the south."

Near the end of the dance, one small eagle arched his wings and ran all the way to the southern end of the plaza. The wind lifted his feathers as he paused on the edge of the precipice and for just a second I was sure he would have to fall, or fly.

HOMERO

20

THE SCREAM

The kettle is about to boil, and the telephone rings. He dries his hands slowly and goes to answer it, expecting Mandy Navarrete's fourth child. Christmas Day, a long silent day, will end now with a long unpleasant night. There was a time when deliveries excited him; during the gene-pool study he looked forward to those infant eyes, and setting up his camera and lights. But there is nothing to study now. Mandy Navarrete is all muscles and resistance, a woman who delivers in her own time. Her grandmother Concepcion Navarrete was his first-grade teacher. She was similarly muscular, and disapproved of his family.

He lifts the receiver slowly on the fourth or fifth ring. The voice speaks in hurried Spanish but he answers in English because he knows they can understand. He hasn't spoken Spanish since the day he married Alice. "There is plenty of time," he says. "I know this process. We don't need to be in a panic."

He hears silence, static, several different voices and questions and then the same voice again, emphatically repeating its word: *Secuestrada*. Kidnapped.

"Who is this?"

He listens. The voice is very distant and often breaks. It is a woman, a friend of his daughter. He tries to understand which daughter they mean. *Secuestrada*. Codi has been away for several days but this voice is saying "Hollie." Someone is keeping her. She was in the field alone, with her horse, when they came to blow up the building where she has chemicals for the crop. He understands none of this and lets it sift past him like pollen, like his life. There are many more words in his life than he would like, most of the time.

Hollie, the woman insists, as if she is trying to wake him from sleep. Are you the father? *El padre de Hollie Nolina?* We are very much afraid.

We are very much afraid.

In the first grade she hit a boy and they kept her after school. The boy's name was Simon Bolivar Jones. He was angry at her and had called her vicious names because she climbed to the top of the tall slide the wrong way, up the slide and not the steps, and stood up there and danced, shouting, her hands outstretched. No boy could do it.

"You should let her come home. She hasn't done anything wrong. She's being punished for an act of bravery." He isn't sure whether he has just spoken in Spanish or English.

Sí, the voice answers after a moment. *Claro que sí.*

"Where is she?"

No estamos seguros. We think they must have taken her into Honduras, where they're camped. A large patrol has gone to look for her. Thirty people, more than half of them from the village where she lives. There were more who wanted to go. Even an eight-year-old boy. Hallie has many friends.

Even an eight-year-old boy. Thirty people.

The words are so much fine dust suspended in the air before him, in the long, trapezoidal block of sunlight from the window. He examines the dust. He sees the word "Hallie." It was Codi who stood up and danced on the slide.

"You should let her come home," he says again. He can remember precisely the muscular line of Mrs. Navarrete's disapproving jaw. "Let my daughter come home now."

The voice rejects this statement, says nothing.

He touches the corner of his eye and is surprised to find moisture on his fingertips. He stares at an iron coal bucket beside the fireplace, trying to recall its history, how it came to him. He thinks, for no reason, that this iron coal bucket could save his life, if only he could remember. He remembers instead that he no longer delivers babies, the telephone call could not possibly be Mandy Navarrete. It is a woman from another country, who knows his daughter. He is trying hard not to look at the dust in the air but the sun has illuminated each particle so that it glows. Each word burns.

"Is there something I can do?" he asks finally. "I know she has friends in the Ministry of Agriculture. Do they know?"

"Everyone knows. Our Ministry of Agriculture, your Ministry of Agriculture." There is a pause. "You understand that this occurs every day. We're a nation of bereaved families. The only difference this time is that it happens to be an American. It happens to be Hallie." The voice weakens again, and he waits, and it goes on. "We sent a telegram to your President and the NBC. We think if they are embarrassed enough by their contras, they could do something."

If they are embarrassed enough.

"Wait. Let me take down the number where you are. So I can call you tomorrow."

"I'm in the office of a church in Managua. Nobody here knows anything. You can call the Ministry of Agriculture if you want. Or your President. He is the responsible party."

He understands that she is being as helpful as she can. She is a kind, tired voice. He doesn't want her to hang up, because then his life will begin. There is a pause while she talks to someone else who is there with her, and then she returns to him and says, "I'm sorry."

"Is there anything more? Besides waiting?"

"I'm sorry. There is nothing."

Carefully he puts down the receiver and looks at the air in front of the window in this empty room. The dust. He listens inside himself for a long time before he understands that it's the teakettle that is screaming.

COSIMA

21

THE TISSUE OF HEARTS

Hallie was somebody's prisoner. Whether my eyes were open or closed, I saw her with a white cloth tied tightly over her mouth. That's the only image that would ever come.

If she couldn't scream, I did. I was in every way unreasonable, especially with the kids at school. Even at the time, I was lucid enough to be thankful that Rita had dropped out. One member of my family had already yelled at her; she didn't have to know that neither one of us had all our tires on the road.

The students had tried to be cooperative. They went to Tucson to assist the Stitch and Bitch Club, as I'd requested, and found the city to be a superb adventure. They discovered a video arcade; Raymo sweet-talked more than ten young women into buying piñatas; there were rumors that Connie Muñoz gave Hector Jones a hand job in the back seat of the bus on the way home. What did I expect? They were teenagers. I knew that, but still I screamed at them because Black Mountain was poisoning their mother's milk and all they cared about was sex and a passing grade.

I had rational intentions. I talked about evapotranspiration and rain forests and oxygen in the biosphere, how everything was connected. The last virgin timber cleared and milled to make way for a continent of landfills choking on old newspapers. It was a poetic lecture. Marta made the mistake of asking me how much of this poetry was going to be on the test.

I glowered. "Your life is the test. If you flunk this one, you die."

The whole front row looked stunned. Their pens stopped moving.

"What you people learn for a test you forget the next day. That's bullshit. That's a waste of your brains and my time. If I can't teach you something you'll remember, then I haven't even been here this year." I crossed my arms and glared at them. "You kids think this pollution shit is not your problem, right? Somebody will clean up the mess. It's not your fault. Well, your attitude stinks. You're as guilty as anybody. Do you, or do you not, think the world was put here for you to use?"

Nobody was fool enough to answer. I observed during the long silence that half the kids in the room were wearing stone-washed jeans. I yanked up Hector Jones by the arm and made an example of him. I have to admit I disliked Hector partially for unfair reasons: his father was a former hoodlum named Simon Bolivar Jones who'd been noticeably unkind to me in school.

"Stand up here," I said. "Show everybody your jeans. Nice, right? Turn around. Nice ass, Hector. Wonderful jeans. They were half worn out before you bought them, right?" I smacked Hector lightly on the butt and let him sit down.

"You know how they make those? They wash them in a big machine with this special kind of gravel they get out of volcanic mountains. The prettiest mountains you ever saw in your life. But they're fragile, like a big pile of sugar. Levi Strauss or whoever goes in there with bulldozers and chainsaws and cuts down the trees and rips the mountainside to hell, so that all us lucky Americans can wear jeans that look like somebody threw them in the garbage before we got them."

"Trees grow back," Raymo said. Raymo was a brave young man.

"Excuse me?"

He cupped his hands around his mouth and spoke as if I were his deaf grandmother: "Trees . . . grow . . . back."

I cupped my hands around my mouth and said, just as loudly, "Not if the whole . . . damn . . . mountain is gone, they don't."

"Well, there's other mountains."

"Sure, there's some other mountains," I said, feeling that I might explode if I weren't careful. "If you got hit by a truck, Raymo, I guess your ma would say, 'Well, I have some other kids.' "

About half the class thought that was funny. The other half was probably trying to figure out how to get out of my classroom alive.

I stared them down, ticking like a bomb. "Sure. Trees grow back. Even a whole rain forest could grow back, in a couple hundred years, maybe. But who's going to make it happen? If you had to pay the real price for those jeans—the cost and the time and the work of bringing that mountain back to life instead of leaving it dead—those pretty jeans would have cost you a hundred dollars."

I felt strangely high. Furious and articulate. "Think about the gas you put in a car," I said. "The real cost. Not just pumping it out of the ground and refining it and shipping it, but also cleaning up the oil spills and all the junk that goes into the air when it gets burned. That's part of what it costs, but you're not paying it. Gas ought to be twenty dollars a gallon, so you're getting a real good deal. But soon the bill comes due, and we pay it, or we eat dirt. The ultimate MasterCharge."

I can't swear they were listening, but they were watching me carefully. Thirty-six blue eyes ticked back and forth as I paced the floor in front of my desk.

"If Grace gets poisoned, if all these trees die and this land goes to hell, you'll just go somewhere else, right? Like the great pioneers, Lewis and Clark. Well, guess what, kiddos, the wilderness is used up." I walked around my little square of floor like a trapped cat. "People can forget, and forget, and forget, but the land has a memory. The lakes and the rivers are still hanging on to the DDT and every other insult we ever gave them. Lake Superior is a superior cesspool. The fish have cancer. The ocean is getting used up. The damn *air* is getting used up."

I pointed at the ceiling, meaning to indicate the sky. "You know what's up there? Ozone. It's this stuff in the atmosphere that acts like an umbrella."

I stopped and reconsidered this effete analogy. Teenagers who won't use condoms aren't impressed by the need for an umbrella. I surveyed the class thoughtfully and demanded, "Whose Dad or Mom ever worked in the smelter?"

About half the hands went up, reluctantly.

"You know what they did up there, right? One way or another they were around thousand-degree hot metal. You ever see them dressed for work? They wore coveralls like Mr. Neil Armstrong walking on the moon, and a big shield over their faces, right?"

They nodded, relieved, I suppose, that I wasn't going to single them out for humiliation. I sat on the desk and crossed my arms. "Imagine that's you, working up there with that hot metal in your face. Now, somebody rips that mask off you while you're working. Goodbye face. Goodbye nose and eyelids, beauty queens. You're dead."

They might well have been dead, for all the sound they made.

"That's what the ozone layer does for us, boys and girls, it's a big face shield in the sky." I was skipping a few steps here, but not really exaggerating the consequences. Not at all. I attempted to lower my voice and sound faintly reasonable. "And it's slipping away from us. There's a big hole in it over the South Pole. When you use a spray can you make that hole bigger. There's something in most aerosol cans and refrigerators and air conditioners, called chlorofluorocarbons, that neutralizes the ozone. Factories are still making tons of it, right now."

I suspect "chlorofluorocarbons" was the largest word ever spoken within the walls of Grace High, and I'm fairly sure also that nobody forgot it for at least the rest of the day.

After the bell rang, Connie Muñoz eyed me and said, "Miss, I seen you wear stone-washed jeans to school sometimes." The other kids were already out of there like bats out of hell.

"You're right," I said. "I didn't know about the mountains when I bought them. Just like Hector didn't, and you didn't."

"Yeah?" She chewed her gum and held me under a neutral,

military sort of gaze. I'd publicly humiliated her new boyfriend; this would require some diplomacy.

"I've been learning a lot of this stuff just lately," I told her. "I'm not saying I'm not part of the problem."

"So how come you're so mad at us, Miss?"

I felt conscious of my height, and embarrassed. "Connie, I don't really know. Because I'm guilty too, I guess. And now I'm trying to fix it all at once."

A hint of life came into her eyes. "Don't sweat it," she said. "I think it's cool that you cuss and stuff when you're mad. Everybody was paying attention. What you said was right, these guys just think when they use something up there's always going to be more."

"I shouldn't have cussed," I said. "I'm supposed to be setting an example. And I shouldn't have picked on Hector the way I did."

She laughed and cracked her gum. "Hector Jones is a dick-head."

▼▼▼

I had dinner at Doc Homer's house. I'd done so every night since I got back from Santa Rosalia and found out Hallie had been kidnapped. If I badgered him enough, I kept thinking, he would have something more to tell me. But he couldn't remember anything. If I'd ever doubted Hallie was his favorite, there was no question about it now—I'd never seen him so affected by any event in our lives. He still functioned, cooked for himself and went to work, but it was only an obstinate ritual; he was a mess. I'd found some of his medication bottles in a cache in the living room, inside an old iron coal bucket. There was no way to know whether he was taking them. Half the time he talked to me as if I were six years old.

"Who was the person you spoke with on the phone?" I asked again. "Was she somebody in the government? There's got to be somebody we can call." I cautiously eyed the plate he set down in front of me. Doc Homer had prepared liver with steamed apples and yellow squash. In certain restaurants things like this passed for *haute cuisine,* I knew, but here it passed for weird. It was getting to where he'd combine anything he found in his refrigerator. I'd started shopping for him, lest he get down to refried beans and ice cream.

"She suggested that we call the President of the United States," he said.

I set my fork down on the table. He'd said this quite a number of times before. "I think I *will* call the President." I moved my chair back from the table. It was an idle threat; I'd probably just get a polite recording. But I knew Doc Homer wouldn't want what he would consider an absurd long-distance call on his bill.

"I understand you have a boyfriend," he said, cutting his liver and apples into small pieces.

"What do they think will happen? Did this person you talked to sound real worried? Or did she say this was a routine kind of thing? Sometimes they'll just take a foreign hostage to get attention and then they'll let them go the next day. She's probably back at her house already." I knew this was unlikely. The contras, as I understood it, didn't need attention. They were fully supported by the richest sugar daddy in the modern world.

"He drinks, Codi. He will take advantage of you."

I stared at Doc Homer for a long time. "Not anymore," I said. "He doesn't drink anymore. And he couldn't take advantage of me if he wanted to. I'm as sweet and innocent as the Berlin Wall. Your concern is approximately two decades too late."

"My concern is for your welfare."

"Your concern." I picked up slices of apple and ate them with my fingers, to annoy him. "I'm going to have to go down there. I can get a bus to Tucson tonight and a plane to Managua and be there tomorrow." I doubted it was this easy.

The teakettle boiled and he jumped up. He seemed edgy. He got out the filter paper and slowly set up the drip machine for coffee, carefully positioning each part of the apparatus as if it were some important experiment in organic chemistry.

"I told you it wasn't a good idea," he said, pouring boiling water into the funnel. I waited for some further clue. He could be evaluating any mistake I'd made since age three.

"What idea is that?" I prompted, since he didn't go on.

"Loyd Peregrina."

We both watched the water pass through the dark grounds, absorbing their color and substance. He'd never mentioned Loyd's name before; I was surprised he knew it. I wondered whether Doc Homer had a whole other life in his head, in which he dispensed kind, fatherly advice. This gulf—between what Doc Homer believed himself to be and what he was—brought out the worst in me, or the most blunt. "Don't worry about Loyd Peregrina," I said. "I can't get hurt now. I'm leaving him this time. It's just a short-term thing."

"He won't elevate your life."

"Damn it, you don't know the first thing about my life. What's to elevate? I'm a medical-school dropout who works graveyard shifts in quick-marts."

"You left the profession by choice. We've established that."

"Okay, so I walked out the door with my eyes open. What did I choose instead? What am I good at? Name one thing."

He balked. I knew he would. Doc Homer wasn't fluent in the language of compliments.

"I have no career, no kids, not even a place I consider home. Basically I'm a bag lady with an education."

"That's a preposterous assessment."

"How would you know? You don't really see me, you just see what you want. You take pictures of people and turn them into rock walls."

"That is not what I do. I begin with a picture in my head, from the past. I try to duplicate it from the images I have at hand."

This was a new one. "I don't believe I give a damn about the images you have at hand." I lowered my voice. The quickest way to lose points with Doc Homer was to lose control. I said, "You always just wanted Hallie and me to be above everybody in Grace."

"You *were* above your peers."

I snorted at that. "I was as trashy as Connie Muñoz and Rita Cardenal, without half their guts or one-tenth of their sex appeal. I was ugly and embarrassed to be alive."

Doc Homer had a strange way of actually getting quieter when he raised his voice. "My daughters were not trash," he said.

I looked him square in the eye. "I got pregnant when I was fifteen."

"I know. I watched you bury the baby in the riverbed."

I felt an odd flush in my neck and face. For about a minute we both listened to the dripping of the coffeepot. Then I said, "Why do you lie about everything?"

"I've never told you anything but the truth."

"You've never told me anything, period. You said you and mother came from Illinois. But you came from here. You've got a whole family lying up there in the damn graveyard."

"We did come here from Illinois. I was stationed there, and went to medical school there. We moved back here after the war."

"What kind of war had people stationed in Illinois?" I asked absurdly, close to tears. "I'm sorry, but in history class they never told us about the Midwestern Front."

"Alice's family despised me."

I stopped, remembering how Viola had averted her eyes and said, "that family went downhill," the day I discovered Homero Nolina up in the cemetery. The red-haired Gracela sister with the temper, who married Conrado Nolina and produced a legacy of trash—that was my father's family. What he believed he came from, and what we still were. Auburn-haired and angry, living in exile in our own town. There wasn't enough air in the kitchen for me to breathe, and get all this in.

"So you, what, ran off to the army. Got yourself educated on the G.I. Bill, and then came back here as the mighty prodigal doctor with his beautiful new wife, and acted like nobody could touch you."

I watched him closely, but could read nothing. I couldn't even *see* him, really; I had no idea how he'd look to a stranger. Old? Sick? Mean-spirited? He poured coffee into two mugs and gave the larger one to me.

"Thank you," I said.

"You're welcome."

"Why did you come back here? If it was so important to you to start over, you could have gone anywhere. You could have stayed back there in Illinois."

Doc Homer sat down opposite me. He clenched and unclenched his left hand, then spread it flat on the table and examined it abstractly, as if it were a patient. I looked at the framed photograph on the wall over his head: his portrait of a hand that wasn't a hand, but five cacti with invisible spines.

"Why do you suppose the poets talk about hearts?" he asked me suddenly. "When they discuss emotional damage? The tissue of hearts is tough as a shoe. Did you ever sew up a heart?"

I shook my head. "No, but I've watched. I know what you mean." The walls of a heart are thick and strong, and the surgeons use heavy needles. It takes a good bit of strength, but it pulls together neatly. As much as anything it's like binding a book.

"The seat of human emotion should be the liver," Doc Homer said. "That would be an appropriate metaphor: we don't hold love in our hearts, we hold it in our livers."

I understand exactly. Once in ER I saw a woman who'd been stabbed everywhere, most severely in the liver. It's an organ with the consistency of layer upon layer of wet Kleenex. Every attempt at repair just opens new holes that tear and bleed. You try to close the wound with fresh wounds, and you try and you try and you don't give up until there's nothing left.

▼▼▼

For Christmas, Loyd had given me an Apache burden basket. It was exquisitely woven, striped with the colors of dried grass, and around its open mouth hung tin bells on leather thongs that made whispery, tinkling sounds. It wasn't much bigger than a teacup. The night he gave it to me in Santa Rosalia I felt it would easily hold all my burdens, forever. Now it hung on the wall over my bed, and at night I looked at it and wept for my own stupidity in trusting that life could be kind.

I apologized to my classes. I couldn't see trying to maintain the recommended authoritative distance; I told them my sister had been kidnapped and that I was scared to death. I told them everything seemed very serious to me now, including things like the ozone layer. The kids were extremely quiet. I don't think any adult had ever apologized to them before. From the storeroom we got down a pre–World War II map that showed all the world's climatic zones, and we found Nicaragua, Honduras, Costa Rica, El Salvador. The shapes and names of many nations had changed during the lifetime of that map, but not the climatic zones. We talked more calmly about the rain forest and the manner in which fast-food chains were cutting it down to make hamburger farms. We talked about poor countries and rich countries and DDT in the food chain, and the various ways our garbage comes home to us. The memory of the land. My students understood these things perfectly well. There is nothing boring about the prospect of extinction.

On Friday I took the day off to make phone calls. Hallie had left me a list of emergency telephone numbers, mostly speculative, and I called them all. It took the whole morning. I got nowhere with the State Department and the U.S. Department of Agriculture, and ended up with the Nicaraguan Ministry of Agriculture. Viola helped me contend with the impenetrable Spanish of international operators. Emelina sat on my other side holding my hand, wringing the fingers, apparently forgetting that it wasn't hers. Mason and the baby sat on the floor in front of us, silent, wondering as children always must wonder in a crisis what terrible thing they had done to wreck the world.

We learned nothing useful. They were sure now that Hallie had been taken across the border into Honduras, probably to a camp where many other prisoners were held. It was a well-outfitted camp; they had Sony radios and high-quality C-rations. It made me smile, a little, to think Hallie might be eating C-rations I'd dutifully paid for with my taxes. Dinner was on me. So were the land mines.

I spoke with a dozen secretaries of this and that and finally with the Minister of Agriculture himself. He knew Hallie. He talked for a long time about what an extraordinary person she was; it made me suspicious that she was dead, and I started crying. Viola took the phone and translated until I was fit to talk again. The Minister promised me she wasn't dead. He would call me the minute they knew anything at all. He was fairly sure the contras took her by mistake, not knowing she was an American citizen, and now were probably confused as to how to release her without generating too much bad publicity. He asked, had I called the President of the United States?

In the meantime, Hallie's letters still came to the Post Office box. I knew she had mailed them before she was kidnapped, but their appearance frightened me. They looked postmarked and cheerful and real, but they were ghosts, mocking what I'd believed was a solid connection between us. I'd staked my heart on that connection. If I could still get letters like this when Hallie was gone or in trouble, what had I ever really had?

I didn't read them. I saved them. I would open them all once I'd heard her voice on the phone. I wouldn't be fooled again.

▼▼▼

At some point between Christmas and mid-January, Grace became famous. The several hundred piñatas planted in Tucson had grown into great, branching trees of human interest, which bore fruit in the form of articles with names like "This Art's Not for Breaking" and "What Piñatas!" in slick magazines all over the Southwest. The Stitch and Bitch Club's efforts in papier-mâché became a hot decorator item in gentrified adobe neighborhoods like the one in Tucson that Hallie used to call Barrio Volvo.

It was the birds that caused the stir, but because it was there, people were also reading my urgent one-page plea for the life of Grace. Where Mayor Jimmy Soltovedas's repeated calls to the press had failed, Stitch and Bitch succeeded: our story became known. Hardly a day passed without some earnest reporter calling up to get a statement from Norma Galvez. The club designated her the media spokeswoman; Doña Althea was more colorful, but given to unprintable remarks. Ditto for Viola, who was even more unprintable because she spoke English.

But when a scout crew from CBS News came to town, they wanted the Doña. They sat in on a meeting at the American Legion hall and zeroed in on the Stitch and Bitch figurehead with her authority and charm and all she represented in the way of local color. They got some of the meeting on tape, but made an appointment to come back on Saturday with a crew to interview the Doña in her home. Norma Galvez would be (for safety's sake) her interpreter. By the time Saturday morning came, when CBS rolled into town in their equipment Jeeps like Jesus into Jerusalem on Palm Sunday, the whole town was anticipating the visit of what Viola had been calling "the B.S. News."

There were about fifty of us packed into Doña Althea's living room, just there to watch. The Doña looked as she always looked: tiny, imperious, dressed in black, with her long white braid pinned around her head like a crown. As a concession to the cameras she clutched an embroidered shawl around her shoulders.

She refused to close the restaurant, though, and it was lunchtime, so there were still comings and goings and much banging of pots. Cecil, the sound man, had to run his equipment off the outlet in the kitchen, since it was the only part of the house that had been wired in the twentieth century. "Ladies, we're just going to have to be cozy in here," he said, turning sideways and scooting between two Althea sisters to reach the plug.

"Son of a," he said, when one of the sisters tripped over his cord and unplugged it for the third or fourth time. The Althea in question stopped in her tracks and looked for a minute as if she might deck him, but decided to serve her customers instead. She was so burdened with plates it's lucky Cecil didn't get *menudo* in his amps.

The director of the crew had the Doña sit in a carved chair that normally stood in her bedroom and held the TV. Two men carried it out, sat her down in it, and arranged vases of peacock feathers at her feet. "Just cross your ankles," the director told her. Norma translated, and the Doña complied, scowling fiercely. She looked like a Frida Kahlo painting. "Okay," he said, wiping sweat off his forehead. He was a heavy man, dressed in Italian shoes and a Mexican wedding shirt, though his mood was not remotely festive. "Okay," he repeated. "Let's go."

There was a camera on the interviewer and two cameras were on Doña Althea: bright, hot lights everywhere. A crew member dabbed the interviewer's nose and forehead with a powder puff, eyed the Doña once, and backed off. The interviewer introduced himself as Malcolm Hunt. He seemed young and wore an outfit that suggested designer-label big-game hunting or possibly Central American revolutions. He probably meant well. He carefully explained to Doña Althea that they would edit the tape later, using only the best parts. If she wanted to go back and repeat anything, she could do that. He suggested that she ignore the cameras and just speak naturally to him. Norma Galvez translated all this. The Doña squinted at the lights, fixed her scornful gaze on a point just above the kitchen door, and shouted all her answers in that direction. Cecil took it personally and slinked around behind the steam table.

Mr. Hunt began. "Doña Althea, how long have you lived in this canyon?"

"Desde antes que tú cagabas en tus pañales!"

Norma Galvez shifted a little in her chair and said, "Ah, since before your mother was changing your diapers." The Doña scowled at Norma briefly, and one of the Altheas laughed from the kitchen.

Mr. Hunt smiled and looked concerned. "When did your family come to this country?"

The Doña said something to the effect that her family had been on this land before the Gringos took over and started calling it America. The prospectors came and mined out the damn gold, and the Black Mountain company mined out the damn copper, and then they fired all the men and sent them home to plant trees, and now, naturally, they were pissing in the river and poisoning the orchards.

Mrs. Galvez paused. "A long time ago," she said.

Mr. Hunt lost his composure for the first time. He made an odd, guttural noise and looked at Mrs. Galvez, who spread her hands.

"You want an exact translation?"

"Please."

She gave it to him.

It wasn't the afternoon anybody had expected. Malcolm Hunt

kept adjusting his posture and his eyebrows and appearing to start the whole interview over, framing new questions that sounded like opening lines.

"The Black Mountain Mining Company is polluting—and now actually diverting—the river that has been the lifeblood of this town for centuries. Why is this happening?"

"Because they're a greedy bunch of goat fuckers" (Mrs. Galvez said "so-and-sos") "and they got what they wanted from this canyon and now they have to squeeze it by the balls before they let go."

"They're actually damming the river to avoid paying fines to the Environmental Protection Agency, isn't that right? Because the river is so polluted with acid?"

The Doña waited for Norma's translation, then nodded sharply.

"What do you think could stop the dam from being built, at this point?"

"*Dinamita.*"

Mr. Hunt appeared reluctant to follow this line of questioning to its conclusion. "In a desperate attempt to save your town," he said, trying another new tack, "you and the other ladies of Grace have made hundreds of piñatas. Do you really think a piñata can stop a multinational corporation?"

"Probably not."

"Then why go to all the trouble?"

"What do you think we should do?"

She had him there; Malcolm Hunt looked stumped. He looked from Norma to the Doña and back to Norma. "Well," he said, "most people write their congressmen."

"*No sé.* We don't write such good letters. I don't think we have any congressman out here anyway, do we? We have a mayor, Jimmy Soltovedas. But I don't think we have any *congressman.*" She pronounced the word in English, making it stand out from the rest of her speech like a curse or a totally new concept. "*Si hay,*" she went on, "If we do, I haven't seen him. Probably he doesn't give a shit. And also we don't know how to use dynamite. What we know how to do is make nice things out of paper. Flowers, piñatas, *cascarones.* And we sew things. That's what we ladies here do."

I smiled, thinking of Jack following old habits, turning around three times on the kitchen floor and lying down to dream of a nest in the grass.

"But why peacocks, what's the history?" Malcolm persisted, after hearing the fully translated explanation. "Tell me about the peacocks."

"What do you want to know about peacocks?" the Doña asked, giving him a blank look. The full Spanish name for peacock is *pavo real,* "royal turkey," but Mrs. Galvez let that one slip by.

"How did they get here?"

Doña Althea lifted her head, adjusted her shawl, leaned back and put her hands on her knees, which were spread wide apart under her black skirt. *"Hace cien años,"* she began. "More than one hundred years ago, my mother and her eight sisters came to this valley from Spain to bring light and happiness to the poor miners, who had no wives. They were the nine Gracela sisters: Althea, Renata, Hilaria, Carina, Julietta, Ursolina, Violetta, Camila, and Estrella."

She pronounced the names musically and slowly, drawing out the syllables and rolling the r's. They were the names of fairy princesses, but the story, in her high, sustained voice, was Biblical. It was the Genesis of Grace. And of Hallie and me. Our father's own grandmother—mother of Homero Nolina up in the graveyard—was one of those princesses: the red-haired, feisty one. I could picture her barefoot, her hair curly like Hallie's and coming loose from its knot. I saw her standing in the open front door of her house, shaking a soup spoon at her sisters' arrogant children who came to tease her own. Perhaps she was Ursolina, the little bear.

When Hallie and I were little I used to make up endless stories of where we came from, to lull her to sleep. She would steal into my bed after Doc Homer was asleep, and I would hold her, trying to protect her from the wind that blows on the heads of orphans and isolates them from the living, shouting children who have inherited the earth. "We came from Zanzibar," I would whisper with my mouth against her hair. "We came from Ireland. Our mother was a queen. The Queen of Potatoes."

I could never know the truth of my mother, but there was another story now. Another side. I closed my eyes and listened to Doña Althea with the joy of a child. I don't know what they heard on the CBS news. I heard a bedtime story thirty years late.

22

ENDANGERED PLACES

It rained and rained in Gracela Canyon. February passed behind a mask of clouds. It seemed like either the end of the world or the beginning.

The orchards, whose black branch tips had been inspected throughout the winter for latent signs of life, suddenly bloomed, all at once: pears, plums, apples, quince, their normal staggered cycle compressed by the odd weather into a single nuptial burst. Through my classroom window I watched drenched blossoms falling like wet snow.

Water, in Grace, is an all-or-nothing proposition, like happiness. When you have rain you have more than enough, just as when you're happy and in love and content with your life you can't remember how you ever could have felt cheated by fate. And vice versa. I knew, abstractly, that I'd been happy, but now that I was in pain again, that happiness was untouchable. It was a garish color picture of a place I had not been. Memory runs along deep, fixed channels in the brain, like electricity along its conduits; only a cataclysm can make the electrons rear up in shock and slide over into another channel. The human mind seems doomed to believe, as simply as a rooster believes, that where we are *now* is the only possibility.

But it isn't. In spite of the promise of plenty that dripped from the rooftops and gushed down Gracela Canyon's ravines throughout February, the winter rains would soon dry up. Then there would not be another drop until July. During those brittle months the taste and smell of rain would be lost to us, beyond the recollection even of children and the deepest root tips of trees. That is the way of the seasons in a desert place. Only the river ran continuously. The river was Grace's memory of water.

▼▼▼

We heard nothing from Hallie. First I tried to tell myself she was already out of danger. In the past, the two-week delay of her letters had caused me to keep a distrustful eye on Hallie, like a star so many light years away it could have exploded long ago while we still watched its false shine. Now I tried the reverse psychology: we would hear, soon, that she'd been safe while we worried.

But we didn't, and I gave over to panic. I began to call Managua every week. The Minister of Agriculture, whose secretary now knew me by voice, said there wasn't any reason for me to fly down to Nicaragua; there was nothing I could do there but wait, which—he implied—I was doing badly enough where I was. He really was not unkind, just frustrated, like any of us. He pointed out that Hallie was an exceptional person, to those of us who loved her, but not an exceptional case—the contras made daily forays across the border to attack workers in their fields, sometimes even schoolchildren. Thousands of civilians had died. "If you came here," he said, "you would see." Every home had a framed photograph on a table that stood for a fresh empty space in the family, he said. Teachers and community workers were particularly at risk.

He said I might try making Hallie's status known to the general public in the United States. It could pressure her captors to show restraint; or, he warned me frankly, it could do the opposite.

I knew nothing else to do, so I wrote letters. Emelina helped. We papered her kitchen table with letters in progress. I drafted mine on stationery from the Grace High School principal's office, but the letterhead intimidated Emelina, who preferred lined paper from her kids' loose-leaf notebooks. Viola put a request to the Stitch and Bitch Club, and after that we had volunteers in Emelina's kitchen for nightly letter-writing sessions. I dictated the main ideas and then they all got the hang of it. I looked up who had voted for sending the guns, and who had voted against, and either way we tried to work it in. I expect we sent out more than a thousand letters. When we lost track of which congressmen we'd written, we wrote them again. We wrote radio stations and any other public entity we believed might be reading its mail. Sometimes I stopped and laid my head on my arms. Emelina would massage the back of my neck and say nothing, because we both suspected words were beside the point.

There may have been publicity we never knew about. We didn't get the *New York Times* in Grace. I do know there was a short piece in the Tucson morning paper, in the "Money" section, of all things, right next to an article about how to reduce your mortgage with twice-monthly payments. There was a small, smiling photo of Hallie, who was identified as a former employee of the University Extension Service. The reporter had called up the Minister of Agriculture as I'd suggested, and said that he "alleged" she had been kidnapped by agitators based in Honduras. This was followed by a much longer quote from a state senator who said the Nicaraguan civil war was a tragedy, and that the United States was doing its best to bring democracy to the region, and that no U.S. citizen could go there without expecting to be caught in crossfire.

The reporter, believing I would be pleased, sent me the clipping along with a note wishing my family all the best. The breadth of his ignorance made me feel hopeless, as I've sometimes felt in dreams, when the muscles dissolve and escape is impossible. I wept uncontrollably all day. At school I asked my students to read *Silent Spring* for an hour while I put my head down on my desk and cried. They were subdued. I suspected people in Grace of walking around me on tiptoe now, the way a town might avert its eyes when its resident crazy lady hikes up her skirt and scratches an itch and swears at the blackbirds watching from a telephone wire.

I stopped going to Doc Homer's for dinner. We were in the

worst position to comfort one another. I guessed he could go on about his routine—that had always been the core of his resilience—but I don't think I'd slept a single night since she'd been taken, and I was reaching an abnormal state of exhaustion. I fought off hallucinations. Late one night Hallie appeared in my bedroom doorway, very small, looking up at me. With those same eyes she used to ask without words to crawl into my bed.

"Hallie, I'm trying so hard. But I don't know how to save you."

She turned on stocking feet and walked back into the dark.

I got up and rifled my desk drawers till I found the newspaper clipping with her picture. I looked at it hard, trying to convince myself that Hallie wasn't a child. I had the black-and-red afghan bundled around me but I felt chilled and hard as a frozen branch. My hands shook. I tucked the clipping into an envelope and wrote a note to the President of the United States, begging him please just to look at her. "This is my only sister," I told him. "I'm coming to understand responsibility. You gave those men a righteous flag to wave and you gave them guns. If she dies, what will you tell me?" I licked the envelope and sealed it. I knew the address by heart.

We began to get letters back, to the effect that the matter would certainly bear investigation. They weren't form letters, each one was typed by a different secretary, but they all said the same thing. It surprised me to see how a meaningless phrase repeated again and again begins to resemble truth.

▼▼▼

In the middle of that gray month Emelina's youngest son learned to walk. I was alone with him when it happened. The sun had come out briefly as I walked home from school, and the baby and I were both anxious to be outdoors. Emelina asked if I could just not let him eat any real big bugs, and I promised to keep an eye out. I settled with a book in the courtyard, which was radiant with sudden sunlight. The flowers were beaten down, their bent-over heads bejeweled with diamond droplets like earrings on sad, rich widows.

For quite a while now Nicholas had been cruising the perimeters of his world, walking confidently from house to tree to lawn chair to wall, so long as he had something to hold on to. Sometimes what he touched was nothing more than apparent security. Today I watched the back of his red overalls with interest as he cruised along a patch of damp, tall four-o'clocks, lightly touching their leaves. He had no idea how little support they offered.

He spotted a hummingbird. It buzzed around the red tubes of a potted penstemon that stood by itself in the center of the courtyard. His eyes followed the bird as it darted up and down, a high-strung gem; Nicholas wanted it. For a long time he frowned at the brick path that lay between himself and the bird, and then he let go of the wall. He took one step and then more, buoyed up by some impossible anti-gravity. After two steps the hummingbird was gone, but Nicholas still headed for the air it had occupied, his hands grasping at vapor. It was as if an invisible balloon floated above him, tied to his overall strap, dragging him along from above. He swayed and swaggered, stabbing one toe at a time down at the ground, pivoting on the ball of one foot, and then suddenly the string was cut and down he bumped on his well-padded bottom. He looked at me and screamed.

"You're walking," I told Nicholas. "I promise you it gets easier. The rest of life doesn't, but this really does."

I stayed out there with my book for the rest of the afternoon, surreptitiously watching as he tried it over and over. He was completely undeterred by failure. The motivation packed in that small body was a miracle to see. I wished I could bottle that passion for accomplishment and squeeze out some of the elixir, a drop at a time, on my high school students. They would move mountains.

▼▼▼

The Stitch and Bitch Club was now wealthy beyond historic measure. On the heels of the blockbuster piñata sale came a steady flow of donations from the outside. Loulou Campbell, the treasurer, had always kept the club's funds in a coffee can in the back of the Baptist Grocery where she worked. But when the volume of cash filled twelve baby-formula cans she grew nervous. Loulou opened an account at the bank and turned the passbook over to Doña Althea, whose years as a top-notch restaurateur had made her somewhat more comfortable with affluence.

The cash languished in its vault while the women pondered its meaning. Having sent their peacocks out into the world like Noah's dove over the flood, they waited for the world to inspire their next move.

Inspiration came in the guise of an art dealer from Tucson. His name was Sean Rideheart, and he was a funny, charming little man who understood people as well as he understood beauty. The spectacular popularity of the Grace piñatas (some had been resold for as much as five hundred dollars) moved him to make a pilgrimage to the source. Mr. Rideheart was already an expert and he became a connoisseur; before he ever set foot in Grace he could already recognize the works of several individual piñata makers. Of particular value were those made by Mrs. Nuñez, who had been so resourceful with her *Compton's Children's Encyclopedia*. He wanted to know this town better.

I met him on his third visit, when he came to meet Viola. There was no school that day—I believe it was the birthday of a President—and I was staring at clouds. Emelina didn't bother me on my bad days; I was allowed to do nothing, not even pretend to feel better, which I recognized as a rare act of human kindness and I appreciated. I spent the morning sitting on Emelina's front porch, watching our neighbor, whose roof was on the same level with our floorboards. We were having another brief break in the rain, as if the clouds had called a time-out to muster their resources. Our neighbor Mr. Pye was taking advantage of the moment to climb up and inspect his roof.

"Got a few leaks," he called out in a friendly way. I waved back, unsure of how to answer. I watched the top of his engineer's cap bob down the ladder out of sight, and shortly thereafter, appear again. Mr. Pye negotiated the ladder with one hand while balancing a small, old-looking cardboard box against his hip. It made me think of the surprises coming out of the kiva at Santa Rosalia Pueblo. Mr. Pye knelt near his chimney pipe and opened the box like a birthday present, carefully lifting out some shingles. They were green, and shaped like the ace of spades—an exact match to the ones on his roof, only a little brighter. Grass-green rather than the green of old bronze. I remembered once, months ago, looking at that roof of antique shingles and assuming them to be irreplaceable.

Curiosity overcame my lassitude. "How'd you match those shingles?" I called out.

He looked at me, puzzled.

"Where'd you get the new shingles? They're a perfect match."

He examined the shingles in his hands, as if noticing this for the first time, and then called back, "Well, they ought to be, they're all from the same lot. I bought two hundred extras when I put this roof on."

"When was that?" I asked.

He looked up at the clouds. I don't know whether he was divining the weather or the past. "Right after the war," he said. "That would have been forty-six."

Just then Mr. Rideheart came walking up the road under a navy blue umbrella. Maybe it was still raining down the way, where he'd just come from. He walked directly to the front porch where I sat, jauntily hopped up the steps, stomped his feet delicately a few times as if to knock off mud (though his shoes were immaculate), and extended his hand to me. I'd expected to spend the day in numb, depressed solitude, and now I felt uncomfortably honored to sit at the end of Mr. Rideheart's long line of effort—like a princess in a tale of impossible tasks. Although I was fairly sure he hadn't come all this way looking for me.

"Sean Rideheart," he said. He had white eyebrows and bright green eyes; an appealing face.

"Codi Noline." I shook his hand. "I've heard about you. You're the piñata collector."

He laughed. "I've been called many things in my time, but that's a first. I'm looking for Viola Domingos." At my invitation he sat down in the only other chair on the porch, wicker, of doubtful character.

"She's not here," I said. "Nobody's home today. Viola and the kids have gone down to the church. They're having some kind of a big party down there today, painting the saints."

"Painting the saints?" Mr. Rideheart extracted a largish blue handkerchief from the pocket of his tweed jacket and cleaned his wire-rimmed glasses with extraordinary care. I watched for a long time, mesmerized, until he glanced up at me.

"The statues of saints, in the church," I explained. "I guess they have to get freshened up every so often, like anybody else. The women paint the saints and the kids paint each other."

He replaced his glasses and observed the rooftops and treetops that led stepwise down the hill. Mr. Pye had his back to us now. He was industriously tacking down shingles he'd secured for this purpose ten years before Hallie was born.

"Quite a place," Mr. Rideheart said, finally. "How long have you lived here?"

It wasn't an easy question to answer. "I was born here," I said slowly. "But right now I'm just on an extended visit. My time's up soon."

He sighed, looking out over the white path of blossoming treetops that led up toward the dam. "Ah, well, yes," he said, "isn't everybody's. More's the pity."

▼▼▼

At first the Stitch and Bitch was divided in its opinion of Mr. Rideheart. While he was graciously received into the kitchens of half the club members, where he drank tea and stroked his white mustache and listened in earnest while the piñata artists discussed their methodologies, the other half (led by Doña Althea) suspected him of being the southwestern equivalent of a carpetbagger.

But for once the Doña judged wrong. His intentions were noble, and ultimately providential. When the club assembled in March for its monthly meeting in the American Legion hall, Mr. Rideheart was the guest speaker. He was supposed to lecture on folk art, which he did, but mostly he talked about Grace. He told these women what they had always known: that their town had a spirit and disposition completely apart from its economic identity as an outpost of the Black Mountain Mining Company. During the last century while men labored underground to rob the canyon of its wealth, the women up above had been paying it back in kind. They'd paid with embroidery and peacocks and fruit trees and piñatas and children. Mr. Rideheart suggested that he had never known of a place quite like Gracela Canyon, and that it could, and *should,* be declared a historic preserve. There existed a thing called the National Register of Historic Places. The landmarks on this list, he said, were protected from the onslaught of industry, as if they were endangered species. He allowed that it wasn't perfect; listing on the register would provide "a measure of protection from demolition or other negative impact," he said. "In other words, a man can still shoot an elephant, even though it has been declared endangered, and the elephant will still be dead. But the man will come out looking like a very nasty guy."

"But really it's not our houses that are going to get endangered by the poison and the dam," Norma Galvez pointed out. "It's the trees."

Mr. Rideheart replied, "Your trees are also historic."

He knew all the ins and outs of becoming a historic place. He explained where to begin, and where to go after that, to see that the river would run clean and unobstructed. There was a fair amount of bureaucracy involved, but the process was reasonably speedy. "Considering the amount of publicity that has already been brought to bear," he said, gesturing toward the window, or possibly the invisible airwaves of CBS, "I think it could be done in less than two years."

He said we would need to document everything, to prove the age and architectural character of the community. "All the photocopying, photography, and so forth can be expensive. Sometimes communities apply for block grants."

After a brief silence Viola said, succinctly, "We don't need any block grants. We're rich." And that was that.

▼▼▼

At some point during the spring I got a letter from Carlo. He'd finally made plans: he was going to Telluride. The clutch had gone out on our old Renault and he'd junked it—he hoped I wasn't attached. He was thinking of getting a motorcycle, unless I was coming to Telluride, in which case we'd get another car.

I was in such a state, running on so little sleep and such dead nerve endings, I didn't know what to think. I knew I'd have to make plans soon. And I was touched that he still took me into account when he made his move, as if we were family. But I felt nothing when I read his words; maybe it was just the same nothing there had always been between us. The words seemed to be coming from a very great distance, with the same strange, compressed tone as a satellite phone call. I looked carefully at each sentence and then waited for it to register. All I could really get clearly was the name of the town, with its resonant syllables: Telluride. It sounded like a command.

▼▼▼

I'd become estranged from Loyd after our trip. Of course, because of Hallie. I felt guilty for being away when the call came. Loyd and I had been laughing and making love for all those days while the news was laid out like a corpse in Doc Homer's house. I didn't even call him the night we got back into town. We hadn't wanted the vacation to end, so we just went straight to Loyd's house and spent the night. Surprisingly, I'd never slept in his bed. Loyd's house was entirely his own: a mobile home set up against the cliff of upper Gracela Canyon on a masonry foundation he'd built slowly himself, over the years. Through his efforts the stonework had gradually grown up over the metal shell, so that now it was pretty much a rectangular stone house, overgrown with honeysuckle vines.

Leafless for winter, the honeysuckles made a lace curtain over the bedroom window. Their shadows left faint tracings on the walls, which I watched all through the bright, moonlit hours of that first night home. Loyd held on to me tightly in his sleep. I couldn't find sleep myself, but I was happy.

The next morning he left at dawn for a seven-day stand in Yuma, and I walked down to have breakfast at Emelina's. But of course as things turned out I didn't eat—not that day or the next. By the time Loyd got back from Yuma I was too far gone to be touched.

▼▼▼

It was Uda Dell on the phone, telling me Doc Homer had gone to Tucson for a CAT scan. She called it a "skin the cat."

I sat up in bed, cradling the phone and pulling the red-and-black afghan around me; school was out for the spring break, so my life had lost what little sense of order daily work could still impose. "When did he go?" I asked. "Just this morning?" What I wanted to ask her was "Why did he tell you, and not me?" But I guess I knew the answer to that.

"No, honey, he went yesterday. He took the bus." Uda seemed industrious on her end of the phone, even as she spoke. Every few seconds she paused and I could hear a high ascending sound like cloth ripping.

"Did he tell you how long he'd be gone?"

There was another rip, then Uda's voice. "Honey, he didn't tell me a thing about it. I don't think he wanted anybody to know. You know Doc. He don't want anybody to make a fuss. [Rip . . .] But he come over and asked me to look after the house. If you or anybody was to come looking for him, he said just tell them he'd gone to Tucson for the weekend to get some medical supplies. [Rip . . .] Now, I knew that didn't sound right. I never heard of him doing that before, and you'd think whatever we all got along without for forty years we could get along without till the Judgment, don't you think? [Rip . . .] So I said, 'Doc, are you pulling my sleeve, there's something up, ain't it,' and he said there was more to it, he was going to get tested for his Alsizer's and get a Cat Skin Test done on him."

"Oh, well, that's good," I said. It was a challenge to follow this trail of reason. I could perfectly picture Uda: her large face, the cheeks tightly packed and shiny like a plum. I rubbed the top of my head and looked at the clock, with astonishment. I'd fallen asleep around 4 A.M. and slept an unprecedented seven hours.

"So, honey, what I'm calling you for is [Rip . . .] I've been itching to get into that house and clean. I know he hasn't been up to it, and I don't mean any offense, Lord knows I think the world of Doc, but I expect he needs somebody to get up there and clean. And I was thinking now'd be a good time but I didn't feel right about just going in. I've had the key all this time, ever since I used to keep you girls. He never did want the key back." She paused. "But I thought I better call and see what you said."

The key was more or less a symbolic matter. He didn't lock his front door. Nobody in Grace did. "I think the cleaning's a good idea. But I also think he'd be mad." I hesitated, uncertain of my loyalties. Outside my window I could see John Tucker in the courtyard with a tape measure. He appeared to be measuring the hundred-year-old beams that supported the roof of the back porch. I knew what it was about—the Historic Register. I had a brainstorm.

"Uda, let me go up there with you. I've got to go through the attic and dig up some old documents on the house and the land for the historic preserve thing. I've been meaning to do it, and you could help me. We could tell him you were helping me look through stuff, and that we just got carried away and beat the rugs and mopped the bathroom while we were at it. If he even notices."

Uda undertook the conspiracy with the relish of a criminal. I agreed to meet her at Doc Homer's in half an hour.

▼▼▼

The attic was pleasantly chilly and smelled of pine. Decades of summer heat had forced droplets of resin out of the rough floorboards, which in cooler weather hardened to little amber marbles that scattered in all directions as we shifted trunks and cardboard boxes. The afternoon is fixed in my memory with the sharp smell of resin and that particular amber rattle, like the sound of ball bearings rolling around in a box. It's surprising how much of memory is built around things unnoticed at the time.

I was amazed by what we found. Doc Homer's disease had manifested itself mostly downstairs; up here, our past was untouched by chaos. Stacked boxes of Hallie's and my old clothes, school papers, photo albums, and all kinds of other detritus stood in neat rows, labeled chronologically and by content. I felt overwhelmed by so much material evidence of our family's past. I couldn't think why he'd kept it. He was so practical. What conceivable use did he foresee for a box marked "ALICE, MATERNITY," for example? But you don't ask questions of an attic. Museums are their own justification.

"Look," I said to Uda, tipping up a cardboard box so she could see inside: some thirty pairs of black orthopedic shoes stacked from small to large, toes up, neat as eggs in a crate. There was a little more variety than I'd remembered. Two pairs were rather dapper little saddle oxfords, black and maroon. Another year—I vaguely did remember this—we'd been allowed to order them in charcoal suède.

Uda had a full-front apron over her old trousers and a print blouse, and she looked prepared for anything. Her lavender hoop earrings matched her wedgies, and she'd tied a red handkerchief over her hair. I was tempted to ask what she'd been ripping up this morning. She bent over beside me and picked out one of the smallest shoes, cradling it like an orphaned bird. "Law, he was so careful about you girls and your feet. I remember thinking, Oh, mercy, when those girls get big enough to want heels there's going to be the Devil to pay."

I laughed. "He wasn't just careful. He was obsessed."

Uda looked down at me. "He just wanted awful bad for you kids to be good girls," she said. "It's hard for a man by himself, honey. You don't know how hard. He worried himself to death. A lot of people, you know, would just let their kids run ever which way."

She stopped, cocking her head a little, staring at the shoe in her hand. "One year for Christmas I gave the two of you little cowboy outfits, with guns, and you just loved them, but he had to take away the guns. He didn't want you killing, even pretend. I felt awful that I'd done that, once I thought about it. He was right."

As she talked, I remembered the whole story: the cowboy outfits and the guns. Hallie and I had tried to claim moral high ground, saying he was taking away what belonged to us. He stood in front of the window, his thin face turned to the light, speaking to the world outside: "I will not have the neighbors arming my children like mercenaries." I'd looked up "mercenaries" in the dictionary, later, and felt ashamed. I explained the ethics of armament to Hallie.

"How long did you take care of us?" I asked Uda.

"Oh, I expect close to ten years all in all. Till you was about fourteen and Hallie was eleven. You remember that. You'd come up after school and we'd play Old Maid or you'd play swinging statues out in the yard. We had us a time. And I'd come up here at night when he had to go tend a baby or something. Sometimes of an evening you'd run off with the Domingos kids without telling me where you'd gone to." She laughed. "I liked to skinned you alive a couple of times. You girls was a couple of live potatoes. She was bad and you was worse."

I remembered her arms when they were thinner; a younger Uda. And I remembered standing at a kitchen counter, on a stool, patting out my own handprints in floured dough while she wove strips of piecrust, pale and thin as flayed skin, over and under to make a perfect pie top. I was experiencing a flash flood of memories. I feared I might drown in them. My skull was so crowded with images it hurt.

"He raised you to be good girls," she said again. She reached over and squeezed my upper arm before returning the shoe to its box.

I didn't know what to tell her we were looking for, for the historical project—anything documenting the age of the house would be helpful, and more generally, old photographs of any kind. Uda seemed content to poke into boxes at random, but I tried to ground myself by reading labels: "CROCKERY AND FLATWARE." "GARDEN RECORDS." One bore the mystic title "ELECTRICITY." I looked inside: socket hardware, lamp cord, the reflector from a heat lamp, a pair of rubber gloves.

I couldn't resist getting sidetracked by one marked, "ARTWORK, H., AGE 3–6." The subjects of Hallie's crayon drawings were mainly the two of us, stick sisters holding hands, or else just me, my orangeish hair radiating from my head like a storm of solar flares. There was not one figure anywhere representing Doc Homer. I wondered if he'd noticed. But he must have. He was the one who'd picked up each drawing, rescued it from destruction, and finally labeled the box. The invisible archivist of our lives.

Out of curiosity I tracked down the corresponding box called "ARTWORK, C." As I'd expected, it was full of family portraits. Big sister, little sister, father, mother, a cockeyed roof over our heads and above that an omnipresent yellow sun. It didn't resemble anyone's reality but mine, but there it was. Or maybe it wasn't so much a matter of reality as of expectation—what I felt the world owed me. I held two of our drawings side by side and concluded that there was no puzzle as to why we were different. Hallie and I had grown up in different families.

"Here's pictures," Uda reported suddenly. There was a whole aisle of boxes marked "PHOTOGRAPHS," with inscrutable suffixes. I picked up one marked "PHOTOGRAPHS, AM JOUR GEN" and found it surprisingly light, so I carried it over to the east window and sat down on a steamer trunk, settling the box on my lap before opening it. Inside were stacks of ancient eight-by-tens, their brown edges curled like autumn leaves. Each one was a photograph of a newborn baby with a startled-looking face and marble-white eyes. I leafed through them, one after another, awestruck by the oddity of these children. Of course I knew about the eyes, an anomaly of pigmentation that was genetic proof of Gracela heritage on both sides. But I'd never seen them. They tended to darken just hours after birth, and in modern times a person can easily go through life, in Grace or anywhere, without seeing a newborn.

On top of the stack of photos was a handwritten page with the heading: "Notes on Methodology." The ink had faded to brown. This would all be for his genetics paper: Doc Homer's careful notations on how he'd set up the camera, the distance, the amount of light. Apparently he'd rigged some set-up that used powerful flashbulbs, the old-fashioned kind that popped once and then were used up. It was before the days of modern electronics.

All those babies. How they must have screamed, one second

after he shot them in the name of science. Or in the name of his own desire to set himself apart. What could be more arrogant than to come back and do a scientific study of your own townspeople, like so many natives in Borneo? I looked through the photos again and kept coming back to one that had an arresting familiarity. The eyes looked back as if they knew me. I stared at the baby for a long time.

It was *me*.

"You were a doll baby," Uda said. She was looking down over my shoulder.

"That's me? Are you sure?"

She took the stack and shuffled through it like a card trick. She produced another photo. "There's Hallie. You didn't look a thing alike when you were born." To her the eyes were commonplace, not a feature to connect us, but they were the only feature I could see. To me, we looked identical.

I held the two photographs up to the light, mystified. The eyes were unearthly. We were two babies not of this world. Just like every other one in the stack of photos; two more babies of Grace. He was doing exactly the opposite of setting himself apart. He was proving we belonged here, were as pure as anybody in Grace. Both sides. *Our mother's name was Althea. Her family despised him.*

"We're *puro,*" I said out loud. And then I dropped the photographs because I heard the broken-glass pop of the flash and went blind. I heard myself make an odd little whimper.

Then Uda appeared in my field of vision, moving away. "Codi, hon, I'm going on downstairs and beat the rugs or something. I'll try not to scare up too much dust."

23

THE SOULS OF BEASTS

"Hallie, I'm going to die."

"I'm Codi."

"I'm dying."

"Well, I know. We all are, more or less." After a lifetime on the emotional austerity plan, my father and I were caving in to melodrama. When I put my hand on his hand it lay dead on the sheet. It was the diagnosis that killed him. Sometimes that's how it happens.

"Where is Hallie?"

"Please don't ask me that again. We don't know where she is. Don't worry about her right now, okay? We can't do anything."

He looked at me accusingly. "You shouldn't have stood on the slide. I defended you on principle, but it was dangerous."

How do people live with loved ones after their minds have fallen into anarchy? I rejected his ruined monologues every day, still expecting order to emerge victorious in Doc Homer's universe. I can remember once seeing a monument somewhere in the desert north of Tucson, commemorating a dedicated but ill-informed platoon of men who died in a Civil War battle six months after Lee had surrendered at Appomattox. That's exactly who I was—a soldier of the lost cause, still rooting for my father's recovery. Pain reaches the heart with electrical speed, but *truth* moves to the heart as slowly as a glacier.

He'd gone off the Tacrine, his experimental drug; the doctors in Tucson found his liver was wrecked from it. Now his mind scuttled around like a crab, heading always for the dark corners. People with this disease can linger on for six or seven years, I'd read, and on average they do. But Doc Homer wouldn't.

"Do you want something to eat? Uda brought over this thing made out of crackers and walnuts and apples. It looks like one of your concoctions."

"No, thank you."

His bedroom was the largest upstairs room, with dark green walls and a high white ceiling and dormer windows across the west side. As children, Hallie and I rarely came into this room; it held an aura of importance and secrecy, the two things that most attract and frighten children. But for two days now I'd been taking care of Doc Homer here, and when I stopped to notice, I found myself the most commanding presence in the room. I felt long-legged and entitled, and strode around in my boots, adjusting curtains and moving furniture to suit myself. I'd tried to close the blinds, but he wanted them open. He insisted on the light, so I let it be.

I'd been keeping a restless vigil by his bed throughout the late afternoon, watching for signs of a lucid moment. I'd about decided it wasn't coming. I pulled my chair closer and squeezed his hand hard in an effort to make him pay attention. "Pop, I want to talk to you about Mother."

"Her kidneys were weak, and we knew it was a possibility. She had already had one episode of renal failure with the first pregnancy. She knew the risk."

I didn't really try to absorb this information. "Her name was Althea. How was she related to Doña Althea?"

"No relation." The answer, quick and firm.

"*What* relation? I know she came from here. I found some things in the attic. What was she, a great-niece?"

"What things in the attic?"

"Cousin?" I crossed my arms like the obstinate child I was.

No answer.

"Granddaughter?"

His face changed. *"Malcriado."*

"Doña Althea's family didn't want you to marry her, right?"

He let out a short, bitter little laugh unlike any sound I'd ever heard him make. "We were *Nolinas.*" Just the way he said it told me plenty.

"And you married her anyway. You eloped." I leaned forward and touched his forehead, something I'd never done. It felt cool and thin-skinned, like a vegetable. "That's so romantic. Don't you know that's what all of us would like to think our parents did? You didn't have to hide something like that from us."

"You understand nothing." He seemed very lucid. At times I suspected him of feigning his confusion, or at least using it to his advantage.

"That's probably true," I said, withdrawing my hand.

"We were a bad family. Try to understand. We learned it in school along with the multiplication tables and the fact that beasts have no souls. I could accept the verdict, or I could prove it wrong."

"You did that. You proved it wrong."

In the slanted afternoon light his eyes were a cloudy blue and his skin was translucent. He looked up at the ceiling and I had a disturbing view of his eyes in profile. "I proved nothing," he said. "I became a man with no history. No guardian angels. I turned out to be a brute beast after all. I didn't redeem my family, I buried it and then I built my grand house on top of the grave. I changed my name."

"You still have plenty of guardian angels."

"I don't think anybody in this town remembers that I'm a Nolina."

"No, you're wrong about that, they do remember. I think people are sorry. And they love you. Look at your refrigerator."

He gave me an odd, embittered look. How could he not know this was true? "Refrigerators don't preserve love," he said.

"The hell they don't. Yours does. The women in this town

bake you casseroles and pies like the world was going to end."

He made a slight sound by breathing out of his nose. He seemed strangely like a child.

"They probably can't forgive themselves for the past," I said. "Mother died before they could get everything straightened out. And then you kind of took your phone off the hook, emotion-wise."

He looked away from me again. "We aren't from here, we came from the outside. That is our myth and every person in Grace believes it, because they want to. They don't want to see a Nolina when they look at me. They want a man they can trust with their children's ear infections. And I am that man. If you change the present enough, history will bend to accommodate it."

"No. I'm pretty sure you're wrong about that. What's true is true, no matter how many ways you deny it."

He closed his eyes for a while. I'd never seen him frail or impaired. All the time I'd been his daughter, he'd never been sick.

"How long are you going to stay in bed?" I asked softly, in case he was falling asleep.

"I'm exhausted."

"I know. But after you rest, you might want to get up for a while. I can warm up some soup."

He didn't open his eyes. "Do you think Hallie is coming back?"

"I don't know what to think. We have to think yes, don't we?"

"You're the advocate of ordained truth. Are you telling me now that we can *will* Hallie back to safety?"

"No. I don't guess we can. We just have to wait."

It was the first honest conversation we'd had about Hallie. It took us both by surprise. We were quiet for a long time then, but I knew he wasn't sleeping. I could see his eyes working back and forth under his eyelids, as if he were reading his own thoughts. I wondered what his thoughts looked like, in his clear moments and in his confusion. I very much wished to know him.

"Pop?"

He slowly opened his eyes and looked at the ceiling.

"Did you really see me bury the baby?"

He looked at me.

"Why didn't we ever talk?"

He sighed. "You get beyond a point."

"You could have just given me a hug or something."

He turned away from me. His short, gray hair stood up in whorls on the back of his head. He said, "It's Friday, isn't it? Mrs. Nuñez's lab work is due back today. Can you pull her chart?"

"Okay, sleep now," I said, reaching over to pat his shoulder. "But after a while I want you to get up and get dressed. Today or tomorrow, whenever you're feeling up to it."

"I feel fine."

"Okay. When you're feeling better, I want you to take me to the place where I buried it. I can remember a lot of that night. Cleaning up the bathroom, and that old black sweater of Mother's, some things like that. But I can't remember the place."

He didn't promise. I think he'd forgotten again who I was. We were comically out of synchrony—a family vaudeville routine. Whatever one of us found, the other lost.

▼▼▼

I received a letter from the school board. It was early April, a long time after I'd stopped my hopeful excursions to the Post Office box and had given the key back to Emelina, so this letter appeared on my table among the breakfast dishes while I was at school. I saw it the minute I walked in, but tried to ignore it for the longest time. I carefully went around to the other side of the table and dropped a heavy pile of tests and began to grade them, trying not to see it. "A predator is a big guy that eats little guys," wrote Raymo. "A herbivore is your wussy vegetarian. In other words, lunch meat." She'd wedged it between the coffee cup and a bottle of aspirin. Did she think it would be bad news? I gave in and tore it open.

I can't really say what sort of news it was. Surprising news. It was notification that my contract was going to be renewed for the next year. The term wasn't over, but the school board recognized my circumstances as unusual and wanted to give me ample notice; they were eager for me to return in the fall. My temporary teaching certificate could easily be extended, especially if I had intentions of working toward certification. It was a personal letter written on behalf of the entire board and signed by someone I knew of but had never met, a Mr. Leacock. His letter cited my popularity with the students and commended me for my "innovative presentation" and "spirited development of a relevant curriculum." It didn't mention contraception or Mrs. Josephine Nash or the ozone layer. I wondered how much they really knew; it made me nervous. I kept looking sideways at that word "spirited." After knocking myself out to be accepted, I'd finally flown off the handle in a seditious direction, and won a gold star. "We are all aware of the difficulties of engaging teenagers in a vital course of academic instruction," wrote Mr. Leacock. Someone apparently felt I'd succeeded in this endeavor. I was going to be named something like teacher of the year. Teachers and kids all voted, secret ballot.

I was stunned. I stuck the letter into the pocket of my corduroy jumper and went out for a walk. I tramped quickly down the hill past Mr. Pye's green roof and Mrs. Nuñez, who sat in a rocker on her front porch, leaning precariously forward out of her chair, trying to nail a fast-moving spider with the rubber tip of her cane. She lifted the cane and stabbed the air sociably as I passed by; I waved back. I wondered about the lab work Doc Homer had mentioned in his delirium. Was she really waiting for someone far away to examine her cells or her blood and pronounce a verdict? Or was this history, a sentence she was already serving?

In town, the 4-H Club had set up a display of rabbits and fancy chickens in cages in front of the courthouse. A little county fair was planned for Easter weekend. The rabbits were of an odd-looking breed but all exactly alike, fancily marked with black-tipped ears and paws and a gorget under the throat, and it occurred to me how much simpler life would be if people were like that, all identically marked. If I were not the wrong breed. I corrected an old habit of thought: both my parents were born in Grace, and their parents before them. Possibly Doc Homer was right—I'd believed otherwise for so long it had become true; I was an outsider not only by belief but by flesh and bone.

Children knelt by the cages and talked to the rabbits in high voices, poking in sprigs of new grass from the courthouse lawn. Some shoppers had strayed over from their errands across the street. Mary Lopez, a middle-aged woman I knew from Stitch and Bitch, waved at me. She was there with her mother, a very short, broad woman with a long black braid down her back. The old woman leaned over the rabbit cages like a child. Mary rested a hand on the back of her mother's neck, a slight gesture that twisted my heart. I turned up the road toward Loyd's house. I knew he was home, or would be shortly. He was on a fairly regular schedule these days, running the Amtrak to Tucson and back. We stayed in touch.

The air had a fresh muddy edge, the smell of spring. I had several choices of route, and on a whim I took a less familiar road. I found myself walking through a neighborhood that wanted to pull me into it: the dirt shade of salt cedars, the dogs that barked without getting up. A woman and her husband argued congenially while they picked grapefruits off the tree in their back yard. The fruits rustled solidly into grocery bags while the woman talked in a low, steady voice and the man answered, on and on, a cycle of gentle irritation and love that would never be finished.

"Gee, you're pretty. Are you the new schoolteacher?"

I turned around, startled by a man on a moped. I'd never laid eyes on him before, but I was completely charmed by his line. I felt like Miss Kitty in *Gunsmoke.*

"Well, yes," I said.

"You want a ride? There's a wicked pair of brindle bulldogs up at the corner."

"Okay." I gathered my skirt and straddled the back of his bike. We buzzed smoothly uphill past the putative wicked bulldogs, who lay with their manifold chins on their paws.

"My son Ricky's in one of your classes. He says you give them a pretty good round."

"They give me one, too," I said.

He laughed. "You're Doc Homer's girl, aren't you?"

"That's right. Homer Nolina of the white trash Nolinas. He married his second cousin for mad love." I'd been lying to strangers all my life, and no wonder. Here was the truth and it sounded like a B-grade fairy tale. But I wanted to know if Doc Homer was right—if everyone had forgotten.

"I never heard that," my driver said. "I just heard she was dead."

"She's dead all right. But she was born and grew up right here. You're around the same age I am, you wouldn't remember her, but it's the truth. Her family thought unkindly of my daddy, so they ran off for a while and he put on an attitude."

He laughed at that, but said, "You oughtn't to talk bad about a man like him."

"Oh, I know. Doc Homer's inclined to be useful. But I swear it looks to me like he's been running his whole life on vengeful spite."

"I got me an old Ford that runs on something like that."

Ten seconds later he let me off at the base of the path up to Loyd's house. Loyd was sitting outside, drinking coffee under the huge mesquite that shaded his front yard. He was just out of the shower, wearing only a pair of soft gray sweatpants. His damp hair lay loose on his shoulders. He looked very happy to see me but also unsurprised; typical, maddening Loyd. Jack betrayed excitement in his thumping tail, but Loyd made no sudden movements. He let me come to him, bend over to kiss him, sit down in the chair beside him. I was oddly conscious of his skill with animals.

"You want coffee?"

"No thanks."

He sat looking at me, smiling, waiting.

"Guess what," I said finally, handing him the letter. He read it, grinning broadly.

"It doesn't mean anything," I said. "I still can't stay."

"It does mean something. It means they want you, whether you stay or not. It means you're real good at what you do."

I took the letter back and looked at it, not at the words but the object itself. "I guess you're right," I said. "I don't think anybody ever told me that before. Not in a letter. I guess that's something."

"Sure it is."

"I was thinking of it as just one more choice I'd have to make. A complication."

"Life's a complication."

"Sure," I said. "Death is probably a piece of cake by comparison."

We looked at each other for a while. "So tell me about your day, honey," I finally said. We both laughed at that.

"Another buck in the bank, doll."

"Is that it? Do you like driving trains? You never talk about it."

"You really want to hear about it?"

"I think so."

"Okay. Yeah, I like driving trains. Today I went out on a dog catch."

"Not the Amtrak?"

"No. A special mission."

"You had to catch a dog?"

"A dog catch is when you go out to bring in a train after the crew's died on the main line."

"The whole crew died?" I was visited by the unwelcome thought of Fenton Lee in his sheared-off engine, after the head-on collision. I knew this couldn't be what Loyd meant.

He smiled. "Died on the hours-of-service law. They'd worked a full twelve hours but there were holdups somewhere and they still hadn't gotten to a tie-up point. You can't work more than twelve hours straight because you'd be tired and it would be dangerous; it's federal law. So you just stop where you are, and wait for a relief crew."

"Good thing airline pilots don't do that," I said.

"I bet they go to sleep at the wheel more than we do, too." Loyd said.

"So you went out and caught the dog."

"Me and another engineer and a conductor and a brakeman all deadheaded out to Dragoon to pick up the train. The dead crew came back to Grace in a car."

"And you, what, took the train on into Tucson?"

"Yep."

"So what does that mean, what do you do exactly? Is there a steering wheel?"

He laughed. "No. You adjust throttles, you set brakes, you watch signals. You use your head. Today I had to use my head. I was the lead engineer and it was a real heavy train, over ten thousand tons. There were two helper engines coupled at the rear of the train."

"Ten thousand tons?"

He nodded. "A little better than a mile and a half long."

"And you're in the front engine, and there's two engines pushing on the back?"

"Yep. The hard part was topping over Dragoon. That's a real long hill, a long descending grade from Dragoon to the Benson bridge, and there's a siding you sometimes have to pull into there, at twenty-five miles an hour. But the train is so damn heavy it wants to take off on you down that hill. I've messed up on that hill a bunch of times before. Just between you and me, one time I went flying through there at sixty, hoping to God there was nobody coming on the main line. I never could have gotten into the siding track."

"I guess there was nobody coming."

"No. But today there was, and I got us in safe and sound. Today I did it exactly right." He smiled at me over his coffee cup.

"So tell me about it."

"Well, we topped over the hill way below the speed limit, and when I got about half the train over the hill I set a minimum amount of air brakes. Then I waited for it to take hold. The brakes take hold all along the train, in every car, front to back. And then I just watched the speedometer keep coming up."

"You're still speeding up? Even after you've set the brake?"

"You've got six thousand tons and a mile of train coming down the hill behind you. What do you think it's going to do?"

Doc Homer used to pose puzzles like this to Hallie and me, to develop our cognitive skills. "But you've also got some-odd thousand tons still coming *up* the hill behind you."

"That's right. A little less coming up, and a little more coming down, every minute. That's the tricky part. That's the Zen of Southern Pacific."

I was extremely impressed.

"On a normal train you'd be real leery of setting the brake while half your train's still coming up the hill. The rear would start pulling backward and you'd break in two."

"Oh," I said. "So then you'd have two trains."

"Then you'd have a nice long vacation without a paycheck."

"Oh."

"But I had helper engines that could push on me from the back, so I was pretty sure we wouldn't break in two. I radioed my helper engineer back there to keep pushing up the hill at full throttle, that's throttle eight, and then cut it back to throttle one when he topped over."

"So he was pushing and you were braking at the same time."

"Yep. Setting the brake early enough, that was the part I never got before. It kind of goes against what you think's right."

"Nobody can just tell you how to do that hill?"

"No, because every train's different on every hill. Every single run is a brand-new job. You have to learn the feel of it."

"So you can't necessarily do the same thing next time?"

"Not exactly the same thing, no. But on this train the minimum set worked perfect. And then I worked the throttle to maintain forty miles an hour. I came down the hill through Sybil and Fenner, the last siding before the Benson bridge. I got a flashing yellow after Sybil so I knew we'd probably have to go into Fenner. Then we went by a yellow, and the next signal was a diverging approach, a red over yellow, and I had to be down to twenty-five at that signal so we could get into the siding. Sure enough, there was a train on the main line headed east."

"What if you'd been going sixty, like last time?"

He winked. "I wouldn't be getting any nice letters telling me how good I am at my job."

"Seriously. What if you saw a headlight coming at you in the dark?"

"You heard about Fenton Lee, then, did you?"

"What would you do?"

Loyd looked at me. "Jump off."

"Yeah?"

"Oh, yeah. I did it one time already, when I was a fireman. The engineer hit a siding too fast and that sucker looked like it was going off the track. I was out of there like buckshot. I got a big old bruise on my butt, and the guys laughed at me because they didn't derail. I don't care. There's things worth risking your life for, but a hunk of metal's not one of them."

I watched him drink his coffee. In the hot sun his hair had dried to its normal glossy, animal black. The mesquite leaves cast feathery shadows all over his face and the muscular slope of his chest. The sight of his bare feet stirred me oddly. I badly wanted to take him inside to bed.

"Well. But you *are* real good at your job," I said.

"I'm getting there."

"I guess I never knew there was so much to it."

He set down his cup and crossed his arms. "Pretty good for an Injun boy, huh?"

"You could have told me more about it."

He smiled. "Codi, did anybody ever tell you a damn thing you didn't want to know?"

I stalled, avoiding the question. "If I told you I wanted to go to bed with you right now, would you think I only loved you for your mind?"

His eyes sparkled. "I think I could overlook it."

▼▼▼

That night I lay in Loyd's arms and cried. Since the day I spent with Uda in the attic, wishes and anger had backed up in me, and now they rushed out, rocketing my mind around on a wild track toward emptiness. I told Loyd about the photographs and unrelated things, old things, like making pies with Uda Dell. "I have all these memories I couldn't get hold of before, but it doesn't make me feel any better," I said.

"What kind of memories?"

"Everything. Really, my whole childhood. Most of it I had no idea was there. And most of it's happy. But Loyd, it's like the tape broke when I was fifteen, and my life started over then.

The life I'd been living before that was so different—I don't know how to say this, but I just couldn't touch that happiness anymore, I'd changed so much. That was some other little bright-eyed, righteous girl parading around trying to rescue drowning coyotes and save chickens from the stewpot. A dumb little kid who thought the sun had a smiley face on it."

"And what happened when she was fifteen?"

I withdrew from Loyd's arms. Had I set him up to ask? I lay looking at the wall, considering whether I could tell him. If I only had two more months in Grace, it wasn't long enough. "I can't explain it," I said. "I guess it finally hit me that nobody was going to take care of me."

"In high school you were doing a pretty good job of taking care of yourself."

"That's what it looked like. It probably looks like that now, too."

Loyd took me back onto his shoulder, which felt hard like a cradleboard under my head. He stroked my cheek. "You still have all the family you grew up with. Hallie's somewhere out there. She'll come back. And Doc's still here."

"Neither one of them is *here.*"

"Codi, for everybody that's gone away, there's somebody that's come to you. Emelina thinks you're her long-lost sister. You know what she told me? She wants you there in that little house forever. She said if I let you leave Grace she'll bust my butt. She loves you to death."

"So this is all a conspiracy, I said."

"Yeah. Emelina bribed me to fall in love with you." He laughed and kissed my hair. "Honey, there's not that much money in the world."

I didn't wish to be comforted. "You can't replace people you love with other people." I said. "They're not like old shoes or something."

"No. But you can trust that you're not going to run out of people to love."

"I don't think I can trust life that far. I lost my mother. You don't know what that's like."

"No, I don't."

"You don't have any idea what the whole story is, Loyd. You don't know everybody I've lost."

He gathered me into his arms and we didn't talk anymore, but in my chest I could still feel a small, hard knot of anger and I held on to it. It was my wings. My exit to safety.

▼▼▼

Finally I read all of Hallie's letters. There were half a dozen I'd never opened, the ones that came after. I knew she'd mailed them before she was kidnapped—I could read the postmarks—but I still held the hope that there might be some clue in there that would help bring her back. Once I opened the letters that hope would be gone.

But I was past a certain point now, like Loyd's train going over the hill. The momentum of wanting to hear Hallie, even for a few minutes, was growing heavier than anything I might have had to lose. More than ever in my life I needed to ask her what to do, how to live without guarantees, without safety.

So I read the letters, and there were no clues. Only the ordinary, heartbreaking details of war and rural life and the slow progress of hope.

I'd forgotten that her last letter, which I'd read on the trip to Santa Rosalia, was a tirade. I had to get it out and read it again to remember, and the sting was gone. "If I get another letter that mentions SAVING THE WORLD, I am sending you, by return mail, a letter bomb." (Had I really used those words? But I knew I had, more than once.) "I don't expect to see perfection before I die. What keeps you going isn't some fine destination but just the road you're on, and the fact that you know how to drive." Two hours after she'd mailed that, she had written a pained apology that reached me now, a lifetime later. Any one moment could be like this, I thought. A continental divide.

> Codi [she wrote], I'm sorry, I didn't say it right. I'm touchy about being worshiped. I'm afraid of becoming Doc Homer Junior, standing on a monument of charity and handing down my blessings, making sure everybody knows where we all stand. I don't *feel* like I'm doing that, but it's the thing you fear most that walks beside

you all the time. I don't want you of all people to see me that way. I'm not Saving Nicaragua, I'm doing the only thing I can live with under the circumstances. The circumstances being that in Tucson I was dying among the garden pests. Working with refugees, and also subsidizing the war that was killing them. I had to get out.

By virtue of our citizenship we're on one side of this war or the other. I chose sides. And I know that we could lose. I've never seen people suffer so much for an ideal. They're sick to death of the embargo and the war. They could say Uncle, vote for something else, just to stop this bludgeoning. And you know what? I don't even consider that, it's not the point.

You're thinking of revolution as a great all-or-nothing. I think of it as one more morning in a muggy cotton field, checking the undersides of leaves to see what's been there, figuring out what to do that won't clear a path for worse problems next week. Right now that's what I do. You ask why I'm not afraid of loving and losing, and that's my answer. Wars and elections are both too big and too small to matter in the long run. The daily work—that goes on, it adds up. It goes into the ground, into crops, into children's bellies and their bright eyes. Good things don't get lost.

Codi, here's what I've decided: the very least you can do in your life is to figure out what you hope for. And the most you can do is live inside that hope. Not admire it from a distance but live right in it, under its roof. What I want is so simple I almost can't say it: elementary kindness. Enough to eat, enough to go around. The possibility that kids might one day grow up to be neither the destroyers nor the destroyed. That's about it. Right now I'm living in that hope, running down its hallway and touching the walls on both sides.

I can't tell you how good it feels. I wish you knew. I wish you'd stop beating yourself up for being selfish, and really *be* selfish, Codi. You're like a mother or something. I wish you knew how to squander yourself.

I sat with this letter for a long time trying to understand what peace she was asking me to make.

The others were impersonal, full of description and the usual manic-depressive mélange of experience. The weather had been too dry. A shipment of Yugoslav tractors had come in and they were working out well. "The Deeres were better," she lamented, "but you have to run them like glass hammers, they can be dry-docked for lack of a bolt. The U.S. refuses to trade with us and then makes secret, niggling lists of what we get from the Eastern bloc. The embargo having slipped their minds, apparently."

In another letter she said they heard gunfire almost every night. "People talk about the second reconstruction. They mean after the U.S. invades. We get up every day and scan the horizon for holocaust." In this same letter she talked about her young trainees and the joy of seeing a new idea take root in a mind; I knew the moment. When Raymo grasped DNA, his countenance was touched with light. We'd shared something.

I stayed up most of the night rereading letters, all the way back to the first one from the Guatemalan border, where she saw women running from the army carrying babies and back-strap looms. And earlier, on the beach, where she'd watched a man sell shrimp from a bucket that was counterweighted with a plastic jug of drinking water. He drank as he went along, to keep the load balanced. The purity of direct necessity.

But the letters ended, finite as a book or a life, and I had no choice but to keep coming back to the last one, scrutinizing it for a sign of goodbye. It wasn't there. It was a description of the children's Christmas Eve pageant, three or four words about Julio, and a self-effacing story of how she'd broken her plate that morning at breakfast. Of course it was a disaster; there was only one anything per person in the house. She was mad at herself for being careless, but the neighbor women rounded up a new plate. They made a joke of its being tin, unbreakable.

Nothing else. The closest thing to prescience had come a few days earlier, in a pensive pared-down note that said: "Sometimes I still have American dreams. I mean literally. I see microwave ovens and exercise machines and grocery-store shelves with thirty brands of shampoo, and I look at these things oddly, in my dream. I stand and I think, 'What is all this for? What is the hunger that drives this need?' I think it's fear. Codi, I hope you won't be hurt by this but I don't think I'll ever be going back. I don't think I can."

▼▼▼

I had my own nightmare again, but this time I understood that it wasn't blindness. It was a flash bulb in my father's camera. Even from inside the dream I knew that, and I didn't wake myself when I heard the glass pop. I took the risk of staying where I was, and went on dreaming. What I saw next was an infant face that wasn't my own but my child's, lit in the flash. Then I saw her whole body in moonlight. She was a seventeen-year-old girl, naked and long-limbed, walking up the path toward our house. I stood in the kitchen and watched her through the screen door as she came up the path from the river. For a second she disappeared in the inky shadows under the cottonwoods and I felt completely afraid, but then she emerged again in the light. Her skin glowed white.

I thought: "If she tries to walk through this screen door into Doc Homer's kitchen, she'll evaporate. She can't come in here." So I ran outside and gathered her up, a ridiculous bundle of long arms and legs. I carried her back through the cottonwood grove and down the path, away from the house. Over our heads was a chalky full moon with cloud rubbed across it, like something incompletely erased. I was hunched over and stumbling and I started to run along the dry riverbed, absurdly burdened with this long-legged child as big as myself. I didn't talk or look at her, I just carried her along.

Hallie followed me down the path. I didn't see her come, but I heard her voice right behind me.

"Codi, stop. She's too heavy. You can put her down now."

I clamped her weight against my chest. "No I can't, she'll fall."

"Let her go. She won't fall."

"I can't."

Hallie urged gently, "Let her go. Let go. She'll rise."

And then I woke up with empty arms.

24

THE LUCKIEST PERSON ALIVE

The call came sometime before dawn.

While I brushed my teeth I watched the mirror closely and became aware of my skull: of the fact that my teeth were rooted in bone, and that my jawbones and all the other bones lay just under the surface of what I could see. I wondered how I could have missed noticing, before, all those bones. I was a skeleton with flesh and clothes and thoughts. We believe there is such a safe distance between the living and the dead. I recalled how I'd used Mrs. Josephine Nash to shock my students into paying attention, on the first day of school. I'd thought I understood something they didn't, about death. That it was understandable.

I was still at the mirror when Loyd came. I saw him appear behind me. First he wasn't there, and then he was. He was going to drive me to Tucson. I had to go to the Mexican consulate to get a registered letter and some papers, and then I would sign some other papers from the Nicaraguan government. Of course, there was no Nicaraguan consulate. It was the Minister of Agriculture who called. We had become something like friends, though we would probably not speak again now. Or perhaps we would. I'd heard of people united by disaster keeping track for years afterward, holding reunions. I thought of boat people.

Business executives stranded overnight in elevators. How would they celebrate? What specific moments would they recall for each other? My thoughts kept straying onto random paths like these, hoping to get lost in a thicket.

The Minister said there would be a package coming later. Not her body, but a parcel of personal things, some books and journals. Her plate and cup, her clothes, those items were distributed to neighbors. The body would stay there. She had requested of somebody, at some point, that she be buried in Nicaragua if that ever had to happen. She said Nicaragua could use the fertilizer.

What was the last thing she said to me in person? How did she look? Why can't I remember?

"Loyd," the face in the mirror said. "What do I do now?"

"Put on your shoes."

"Okay."

The sun was just coming up as we drove away from Grace. The world looked inhospitable.

"I should have gone down there," I said.

"And done what?"

We drove past an old junkyard outside of town. I'd never noticed it before, though it must have been there since before I was born. A man stood on the bonnet of a rusted car, shading his eyes, looking down into the ravine.

"On the phone they said her hands were tied," I told Loyd. "He said they found her that way. But I can't believe that. It doesn't sound right to me that she would let anybody just tie her up and then shoot her in the head."

"Maybe they made a mistake," he said. "Maybe it didn't happen exactly that way."

"I know my sister. I think she would get away somehow," I said.

"Wait for the letter. That'll tell everything."

"Maybe they made a mistake," I repeated. "Maybe so."

Within an hour the daylight had overcome its early bleakness. Now it looked like any normal, slightly overcast day. The normalcy made me angry, but it was a weak kind of anger that held no pleasure.

"If I'd told her about Doc Homer back in December, how bad he was, she would have come home."

"You can't make this your fault."

"But she would have come home"

"Codi," Loyd said, looking at me and not finishing. His face held such pain I didn't want to see it. Finally he said, "You could probably think of a hundred little things that would have made this turn out different. But you'd be wrong. A life like your sister's isn't some little pony you can turn around any way you want. It's a train. Once it gets going it's heavier than heaven and hell put together and it runs on its own track."

I didn't say anything to that. Loyd barely even remembered meeting my sister. How could he know what her life meant?

On the interstate we passed the site of a bad accident. You could see it coming: the cop cars and ambulances all huddled around, lights flashing importantly, making their scene. As we came closer we had to slow down; one lane was blocked by a trailer rig with a smashed front end. Out in the median, at an angle that bore no relation to the direction of traffic, sat a white convertible with its frame bent violently into a V-shape.

When we passed it I saw that it wasn't a convertible after all; the top had been sheared off, and lay on the other side of the road. An arc of glass and chrome crossed the highway like a glittering river littered with flotsam and jetsam: a pair of sunglasses, a bright vinyl bag, a paperback book. At the trail's end was the pile of steel. I'd never seen such a badly wrecked car.

"Doesn't look like anybody walked away from that one," Loyd said.

I thought of Hallie walking out of the library that time, years ago, then remembering her sunglasses and turning back just before the marble façade fell down. She could just as well have died then. It made no difference now.

The luckiest person alive.

The ambulance pulled out right behind us, its warning lights alternating like crazy winking eyes. We quickly left it behind, though, and we weren't speeding by any means. Loyd saw me watching the ambulance and glanced up at the rear-view mirror. "They're not in much of a rush, are they?"

Just then, while we watched, the lights stopped flashing. I understood that I had just seen someone die. No reason to hurry anymore. My limbs flooded with despair and I didn't see how I was going to survive. I kept imagining what that little white car must have looked like half an hour ago, and the driver, some young woman listening to the radio, checking her hair in the mirror, preoccupied with this afternoon or tonight or whatever small errand had taken her out.

"Why does a person even get up in the morning?" I asked Loyd. "You have breakfast, you floss your teeth so you'll have healthy gums in your old age, and then you get in your car and drive down I-10 and die. Life is so stupid I can't stand it."

"Hallie knew exactly what she was doing. There wasn't anything stupid about her life."

I practically shouted at Loyd, "I'm not crying about Hallie right now. I'm crying about that person that just died in the ambulance."

He was quiet.

"Loyd, I don't know what I'm going to do." I was afraid the muscles in my chest might tear themselves apart. I thought senselessly of Doc Homer's discussion of liver tissue and heart tissue. As if it mattered what part of your body was the seat of emotion, all of it could be torn up, it was just flesh. Doc Homer didn't even know about this yet. I'd called, and we talked, and it was clear he didn't know what I was telling him. He talked about Hallie being kept after school. Maybe he never would understand, maybe his mind would just keep wandering down other happy trails. Loyd handed me his handkerchief and I tried to blow my nose.

"What would she want you to do?"

"*She* would be crying for a person in a damn ambulance that she didn't even know. Not *me*."

I saw lightning erupt in the dark clouds behind the Catalina Mountains. It was an impossible time of year for a lightning storm. I'd seen photographs of lightning frozen in its terrible splendor, ripping like a knife down the curtains of the sky. They say that to take those pictures you just open your camera on a dark night, in a storm, and if you're lucky you get a wonderful picture. You have no control.

"Hallie isn't dead," I said. "This is a dream." I laid my head back against the headrest and cried with my knucklebones against my mouth. Tears ran down to my collarbone and soaked my shirt and still I didn't wake up.

25

FLIGHT

Getting on the bus was the easiest thing in the world. I only took what I could carry. Emelina would send my trunk to Telluride.

I noticed the junkyard again on the way out of town. They should have had a sign there: Welcome to Grace. Farewell to Grace. Dead grass poked up through the rusted husks of big old cars that hunched on the ground like elephants, the great dying beasts of the African plain. It was early June, soon after the end of school. The land was matchstick-dry and I felt the same way, just that brittle, as if no amount of rain could saturate my outer layers and touch my core. I was a hard seed beyond germination. I would do fine in Telluride. Carlo had lined up a job for me as a model in a summer fine-arts school. I would sit still for solid hours while people tried for my skin tones.

Uda Dell and Mrs. Quintana, Doc's assistant for twenty-one years, were going to take shifts with Doc Homer. His office was closed for good, and everybody now drove over to New Mexico to be healed. There were no thunderclaps when it happened; all this time we'd thought he was indispensable. Uda and Mrs. Quintana revered him. I couldn't picture them feeding him, buttoning up his shirt, but I knew they would do those things. Somehow reverence can fashion itself into kindness, in a way that love sometimes can't. When I went up there to tell him goodbye, he was eating a soft-boiled egg and said he couldn't tarry, he was in a hurry to get to the hospital.

I bobbed along with the motion of the Greyhound bus, leaning with the curves. When I relaxed enough I could feel like a small chunk of rock in outer space, perceiving no gravitational pull from any direction: not from where I was going, nor where I had been. Not Carlo, not Loyd, not Doc Homer. Not Hallie, who did not exist.

"Where do you think people go when they die?" Loyd asked, the day before I left. He was on his way out to take a westbound into Tucson; the next day he would fetch home the Amtrak. We stood in my front door, unwilling to go in or out, like awkward beginners trying to end a date. Except it wasn't a beginners' conversation.

"Nowhere," I said. "I think when people die they're just dead."

"Not heaven?"

I looked up at the sky. It looked quite empty. "No."

"The Pueblo story is that everybody started out underground. People and animals, everything. And then the badger dug a hole and let everybody out. They climbed out the hole and from then on they lived on top of the ground. When they die they go back under."

I thought of the kivas, the ladders, and the thousand mud walls of Santa Rosalia. I could hear the dry rattle of the corn dancers' shell bells: the exact sound of locusts rising up from the grass. I understood that Loyd was one of the most blessed people I knew.

"I always try to think of it that way," he said, after a minute. "He had a big adventure up here, and then went home."

Leander, he would mean. My spleen started to ache when I thought of Hallie fertilizing the tropics. Thinking about how much she loved stupid banana trees and orchids. I said, "I have this idea that if I don't stay here and cry for Hallie, then there's no family to absorb the loss. Nobody that remembers."

"And that's what you want? For Hallie to be forgotten?"

I couldn't have said what I meant. "No. I just don't want to be the one that's left behind to hurt this much. I want to be gone already. If you're dead when somebody stabs you, you don't feel it."

"Leaving won't make you dead. You'll just be alive in a different place."

"This place has Hallie in it. When I lived here, I was half her and half me."

"Going away won't change how you feel."

"I won't know that till I'm gone, will I?"

He picked up my hand and examined it as if it were a foreign object, which was just how it looked to me. He was wearing a green corduroy shirt with the sleeves rolled to the elbows, and I felt I could look at that shirt for as long as Loyd might choose to stand in my door. There were all those small ridges, the greenness, the nap of the cloth. If I kept my focus minute enough I could remain in the world, knowledgeable and serene.

"Anyway you're wrong," he said. "There's family here to absorb the loss."

"Doc Homer, Loyd, he's . . . I don't think he understands she's gone."

"I wasn't talking about Doc Homer."

I shifted my field of vision to include the lower part of Loyd's face and the blunt dark ends of his hair. A whole person seemed an impossible thing to take in all at once. How had I lived so long and presumed so much?

"I'm sorry about everything, Loyd."

"Listen, I know how this is. You don't think you'll live past it. And you don't, really. The person you were is gone. But the half of you that's still alive wakes up one day and takes over again."

"Why should I look forward to that?"

He turned my hand over. "I can't answer that."

"Well, I'm sorry, Loyd."

"I'm sorry too."

"Well. You've got to go to work." I avoided his eyes.

Loyd took my face in one hand and put the other hand on

the small of my back and he kissed me for a long time. His mouth felt cool as green corduroy, a simple thing I could understand. We began the kiss standing up, and when we finished we were sitting on the step.

"You have to go," I said again. That was the last thing, my last words for Loyd.

When he and Jack were gone I stood for a long time looking out at the rambling jungle of the courtyard. A hummingbird, possibly the same one that had inspired Nicholas to learn to walk, was hovering at the red funnels of the trumpet vine climbing my wall. I watched the bird move stiffly up and down over an invisible path, pausing, then moving left, then up again and back, covering the vertical plane with such purpose it might have been following a map.

I felt Emelina's presence. She stood in her kitchen door, shading her eyes, watching me. I waved, but she didn't wave back. Her face was drawn tight with mute, unarmed rage; it must have been the worst thing she was capable of aiming at a friend. She didn't know my tricks, that you could just buckle up your tough old heart and hit the road. My course must have been as indecipherable to her as the hummingbird's. We are all just here, Emelina, I wanted to say. Following our maps, surviving as we know how.

The kitchen door closed quietly and I understood that it was her kindest goodbye. The sun was strangely bright on the whitewashed wall and the hummingbird hung in the air, frozen inside its moment. A photograph of the present tense.

▼▼▼

All morning on my last day people came pecking softly at my door like mice. A legion of mice bearing gifts. It was mostly women from the Stitch and Bitch. No one else was as succinct as Emelina. They wanted to know what I would be doing, where I would live. I mentioned the art school, but wasn't specific.

"We sure do love you, hon," said Uda Dell. "I packed you a lunch. There's yellow banana peppers in there from the garden. They're not as big as some years but they've got a right smart bite. Stay another year," she added.

"Do you have a good winter coat?" Norma Galvez asked me. "It snows up there. You'd just as well stay here."

In their eyes my life should have been simple, purely a matter of love and the right wardrobe. It was as if I had fifty mothers.

In the last hour before I left I had to go through Emelina's kitchen to retrieve a pair of jeans from the laundry room. John Tucker was folding laundry. He told me Emelina was lying down upstairs with a bad headache.

"You got a baseball game today?" I asked.

"Yeah."

"Sorry I won't be around to see you win."

He smiled. In a year I'd watched him grow into his elbows and lose the better part of his shyness. His voice was beginning to crack. "Mom's really going to miss you. She'll be a witch for the next month. She'll make us clean out the chicken pens and stuff."

"It's all my fault," I said, grabbing a runaway corner of a sheet and helping him fold it. "You guys can send me hate mail in Telluride."

He laughed. "Okay."

"If it gets too bad you can run away from home. Come up and see me. We'll go skiing."

He hoisted his laundry basket and headed for the stairs.

When I came back out through the kitchen Viola was there at the table, lying in wait like a predator.

"Sit down," she said. "Save your shoes."

I was lunch meat. I sat down.

"Boy oh boy, kiddo," she said.

"What does that mean? That I should stay here?"

"Sure you should."

"Well," I said.

"But nobody ever could tell you a darn thing."

"That's what I hear."

"I been wanting to tell you something."

"I know Emelina's pissed off at me."

She snorted. "If you don't know that already you're not going to hear it from me."

"Oh." I thought about what else she might have to reveal to

me. "I know about my mother," I said. "I know she came from here, that she was a cousin or something to Doña Althea. And that she and Doc Homer ran off."

Viola smiled a little. "Son of a gun. He told you?"

"More or less."

She adjusted the coil of hair on the back of her head, reclaiming its territory with the planting of a few long bobby pins. "Well, that's not what I was wanting to tell you."

We sat looking at each other for a good while. Her T-shirt said I WAS DEEP DISHED AT MAMA LENARDA'S. I had no idea where it might have come from.

"I'm not supposed to tell you," she added.

"Says who?"

"Says me. Doc Homer would shoot me if he found out."

"I don't think there's much danger, Viola."

"Well, but it's the principles."

Now I was curious. "So, did you sit me down here to tell me something or not?"

She hesitated, shifting her weight forward onto her elbows on the table. "I was looking after you girls the day your mama died."

"You kept us at home?"

She nodded. "I was supposed to."

"But you didn't."

"I thought you had the right to say bye to your mama, like anybody else. To tell her, *'Vaya con Dios.'* Anybody else had no business up there, they just went to watch the show, but you had business and you was not allowed to go. Hallie was just born, she didn't know anything anyway so I left her with Uda Dell."

"And you took me up to the field to see the helicopter come down."

Viola leaned back in her chair. "I'm not saying I did, and I'm not saying I didn't."

"What are you saying?"

"Just that you had a right. That's all. Now, skedaddle. *Que le vaya bien.*"

▼▼▼

The Greyhound was mostly empty, a dry gourd rolling across the desert, occasionally spilling out a seed or two in an inhospitable outpost: Bowie, Willcox, Benson. It was 110 degrees down there, not something people would travel through unless they were desperate to be elsewhere.

As things had turned out, Grace was not going to dry up. The women of the Stitch and Bitch had won back the river. A vice-president of the Black Mountain Mining Company called a press conference in Phoenix to announce that after seventy years of productive and congenial relations with the people of Gracela Canyon, the mine operation there was closing up shop. It was a matter of the leaching operation's being no longer profitable, he said. The dam would be deconstructed. Naturally, if any harm had been incurred, all necessary reparations would be made to the people of Grace. He made no mention of the historic registry petition that had been filed one week earlier. So mountains could be moved. Now I knew.

When my bus paused in Willcox a woman climbed aboard and chose to sit by me, rather than take her chances on something worse that might come along, I guess. She wore an ample white jogging suit and had an odd, metallic hair color. I spent the next fifty miles in fear of a conversation I wasn't in the mood for, but she just kept scowling at a gardening magazine.

Then suddenly she held out her magazine as if it had offended her. "That kills me, how people can grow four o'clocks like that," she said, whacking the page with the back of her plump hand.

I glanced over at the unbelievable floral displays in her magazine. I could relate to her frustration. You just knew they trucked in those flowers from a climate-controlled greenhouse somewhere and arranged them on the lawn, right before snapping the photo.

"I'm Alice Kimball," the woman explained. "I get the worst slugs."

Alice. Would my mother be wearing tepid jogging suits now,

if her organs had not failed her? I tried to smile. "Where do you get them?"

"In my four o'clocks. That's what I'm trying to tell you, I can't grow a four o'clock to save my life. The leaves get so full of holes they just look pitiful. And they get in the lawn, too. My husband says he hears them out there eating up his grass. What can you do?"

"I'm not the right person to ask," I said. "My sister could sure tell you, though. She got a degree in Integrated Pest Management. She used to answer the Garden Hotline in Tucson, 626-BUGS."

Mrs. Kimball brightened as if I'd offered her a peppermint. "I've called that before. They have the nicest little girl on that line, she'll tell you anything you want to know."

"That was my sister you talked to. Hallie Noline." I was amazed by the coincidence, but then again probably half of Tucson had turned to Hallie for advice. And half of Nicaragua. "That was part of her job," I said. "She did that for six years."

Mrs. Kimball looked around at the neighboring seats as if Hallie might turn up for consultation. "Well, do you mean she's quit? I just thought the world of her."

"Yep, she quit. She left the country."

"Left the *country?*"

"She went to Nicaragua." Everybody in this country should know her name, I thought. During the Iran hostage crisis they had a special symbol on the newscasts: a blindfolded man, and the number of days. A schoolchild glancing up from a comic book would know that this story was about *them.* But a nation gloats on the hostility of its enemies, whereas Hallie had proved the malevolence of some men we supplied with machine guns. Hallie was a skeleton in the civic closet.

Some people knew. I'd gotten a card from a nun in Minneapolis who had known Hallie. She was one of several thousand people who had gone down to Nicaragua for just a week or two, she said. They helped pick coffee, or if they had training they did other helpful things. The idea was just to be there in the danger zone, so that if the U.S. should attack, it would have to attack some of its own citizens. This nun, Sister Sabina Martin, had helped give vaccinations. She met Hallie at the clinic in Chinandega the day Hallie brought in a child who'd drunk paraquat from a Coke bottle. Sister Martin and Hallie sat with the child the whole day, and she said that although I might not think it possible, she felt she'd come to know Hallie well during that time. In some circumstances, she said, an afternoon can be a whole life.

"Oh, well," Mrs. Kimball said, after quite a while. "You must miss her."

"I will, when it really sinks in. She hasn't been gone that long."

"I know what you're going through," said Mrs. Kimball. "I lost my sister in 1965."

I hadn't told her Hallie was dead. Mrs. Kimball had seized the subject of death all on her own. "I'm sorry," I said, not really wanting to be encouraging, but you couldn't just ignore it, either.

"She's been dead all this time of an aneurysm and there are still days when I think, 'Oh, wait till I tell Phoebe about that!' Before I realize. I always think it's harder to believe they're gone when it's sudden."

"My sister," I said, and then stopped, afraid of the lie I was about to tell. I was going to say, "isn't dead." I heard an old voice in my head, the teller of tales: I am a cello player running away from home. We are from Zanzibar, we're from Ireland, our mother is the Queen of Potatoes. I was through constructing myself for other people. I didn't say anything.

Several seats ahead of us, a teenage couple had begun necking enthusiastically. You couldn't blame these kids, the scenery was boring and would drive you to anything, but they made me feel hopelessly alone.

"Well," Alice said, apparently remembering it was garden pests we'd agreed to talk about. "What would *you* do for the slugs?"

"I really don't know, I'm not that good with plants." I considered the problem for a while. "I think what Hallie used to do was put out beer for them, in little tin cans. The slugs are attracted to it and they fall in, or something. I know that sounds crazy but I'm pretty sure it's right."

"Well." She stared at me thoughtfully. "My husband and I aren't drinkers, but I guess I could go out and get some beer for the slugs. Do you know what brand?"

"I don't think it matters. I'd get whatever's on sale."

"All right, I'll do that," said Mrs. Kimball. She opened her magazine again to the incendiary four o'clocks, but then closed it right back up, holding the place with her finger. "You ought to try to keep in touch with your sister," she told me. "Young people think nothing will ever happen. You should treasure your family while you have it."

"Well, really I don't have it," I said, resentful of her assumptions. "It's gone. My mother died when I was little and my father will probably be dead before the year's out, and my baby died, and now my sister is dead too. Maybe I'm not as young as you think."

Mrs. Kimball looked stunned. "Your sister? The one on the phone?"

"She got killed by the contras. The ones down there that we send all the money to. I think you probably heard about it."

She looked uneasy. "I don't know. I might have."

"It made the news in Tucson, at least for a day. You just forgot. That's the great American disease, we forget. We watch the disasters parade by on TV, and every time we say: 'Forget it. This is somebody else's problem.' "

I suppose I was going, as Rita Cardenal would say, mental. I didn't look at Mrs. Kimball but I could see her magazine drift slowly to her lap. I looked at the bright garden on the magazine cover and felt strangely calm. "They kidnapped her one morning in a cotton field," I said. "They kept her as a prisoner for weeks and weeks, and we kept hoping, but then they moved everybody to another camp and some of the prisoners they shot. Eight of them. Hallie and seven men. All of the men were teachers. They tied their hands behind them and shot them in the head and left their bodies all sitting in a line at the side of a road, in a forest, right near the border. All facing south."

I felt a hard knot in my chest because this was the one image I saw most clearly. I still do. My voice sounded like a voice that would come from some other person's throat, someone who had a dead sister and could speak of such things. "The man that found them was driving up from Estelí, coming along the road, and at first when he saw them all sitting there he thought, 'Oh, that's too many. I can't give them all a ride, they won't fit in my truck.' "

Mrs. Kimball and I didn't speak again after that. I looked out the window. Far to the south, low cone shapes pushed up against the flat, bright sky. Those distant mountains were probably in Mexico, I knew, though borders in this barren land seemed beside the point. I heard Mrs. Kimball turn a page of her magazine. We'd been silent for over an hour before she first spoke up about the four o'clocks, but the silence was much more noticeable now, after we'd broken it with our little conversation. Awareness is everything. Hallie once pointed out to me that people worry a lot more about the eternity *after* their deaths than the eternity that happened before they were born. But it's the same amount of infinity, rolling out in all directions from where we stand.

▼▼▼

My airplane was said to be bound for Denver, but it sat on the runway for a very long time. I had a window seat and could watch other planes lift their noses one after another and plow their way up an invisible road into the sky. I wasn't impatient. Normally at this point in a flight my heart would pound and my mouth would go to cotton, but today my viscera were still. It didn't matter especially if we burned in a fiery crash.

I thought maybe the air traffic controllers were trying to decide whether we were worth the trouble; we were only a small, twin-engine plane, incompletely filled. A few seats ahead of me a mother coached her preschooler, who was already crying because he knew his ears would hurt when we went up. This was not the first leg of their trip.

"You swallow, honey. Just remember to swallow, that makes your ears feel better. And yawn."

"I can't yawn."

"Sure you can." She demonstrated, her voice stretching wide over the yawn: "Think about being real, real sleepy." People yawned all the way back to the smoking section, so strong was the power of motherly suggestion. I felt overcome with sadness.

The aisle seat of my row was occupied by a teenager, and the empty seat between us was filling up with her overflow paraphernalia. She threw down a hairbrush and a curling iron—whack! whack!—and pulled a substantial mirror out of a makeup case the size of my carry-on luggage. She began applying careful stripes of pastel eye shadow. When she blinked, her eyelids waved like a pair of foreign flags.

"Give it a rest, Brenda," said the man sitting across the aisle. "You're not going to see your boyfriend for ten whole days. Why not take this wonderful opportunity to let your face get some fresh air?"

Brenda ignored this advice, staring with deep absorption into her makeup mirror while her parents in B and C beamed her the Evil Eye. The mother was wearing a polka-dot jumpsuit with coordinated polka-dot earrings, all a little too eager-looking even for the first day of vacation. The man had on sunny golf pants that clashed with his disposition. It was hard to ignore them, but Brenda was practiced. She glanced serenely at her left wrist, which bore three separate watches with plastic bands in the same three shades as her eye shadow. Her hair looked as if each strand had been individually lacquered and tortured into position. No matter how you might feel about the aesthetic, you had to admire the effort. Most people put less into their jobs.

"Brenda, honey, please pay attention when your father is talking to you," said the woman in the polka dots. "Could you please just try? Listening to you and your father bicker for a week and a half is not my idea of a vacation."

"You should have left me at home," Brenda said quietly, staring directly ahead. " 'Honey, I think we forgot something. Did I leave the iron on? No, we forgot Brenda.' " She shot me a glance, and I think I smiled a little. I couldn't help being on Brenda's side here. In my term as a schoolteacher I'd gained sympathy for adolescence. If I had to take a trip with those two I'd probably paint my face blue for spite.

The plane jerked a little and then began to roll creakily down the runway, gathering speed. We were taking off without a warning announcement of any kind. "Flight attendants prepare for takeoff" came out in a single scrambled burst over the intercom, and the women in pumps and dark suits ran as if from an air-raid siren. I closed my eyes and laid my head back, trying to hold on to my visceral indifference, but it fell right away. My heart had caught up with me. I heard the little boy chattering to his mother and I yawned nervously. So much of life is animal instinct: desire and yawning and fear and the will to live. We left the earth and climbed steeply into the void.

My habit was to count seconds during the lift-off, with my mind on news stories that ran along the lines of "crashed into a meadow only seconds after takeoff . . ." Somewhere I'd gotten the idea it took seven minutes to get past imminent peril. I counted to sixty, and started over. We'd been airborne for maybe three or four minutes when our pilot's deep Texan voice came over the intercom. "Folks, I apologize for the delay in taking off today. We had trouble getting one of these cantankerous old engines started up."

The announcement startled my eyes open. I looked at Brenda, who widened her eyes comically. "Great," she said.

"It's nice to know you're riding the friendly skies in a bucket of bolts."

Brenda laughed. "Like my boyfriend's car."

"I think we'd be safer in your boyfriend's car."

"Not in their opinion," she said, inclining her head across the aisle.

I closed my eyes again. I tried to relax, but couldn't help listening to every change of pitch in the engine noise. They sounded wrong. Suddenly I confided in Brenda, "I hate to fly. You know? It scares me to death."

I hadn't admitted this aloud before, and was surprised to hear it come out so naturally. The truth needs so little rehearsal. Brenda reached over and patted my hand.

"Folks, this is Captain Sampson. I'm sorry to report that we've lost that engine again."

Against my will I glanced out at the wing to see if anything had actually fallen off. My heart beat hard and out of synch with itself and I felt I might die of fright. I let the fingertips of my right hand lie across my left wrist, tracking the off-rhythm of my aimless heart. If I were really dying, I wanted to be the first to know.

After another minute, during which I imagined Captain Sampson and his copilot trying everything, his paternal drawl crackled on again. "We could probably make it to Stapleton on one engine," he said, "but we'll play it safe. We're going to turn around and head back into Tucson to see if they'll let us have some new equipment."

I hated the sound of the word "equipment." I had visions of men in coveralls running out to strap a spare engine onto the wing. If we made it back to the airport at all. Suddenly we banked so steeply my stomach turned. I must have looked pale, because Brenda reached over and squeezed my hand again.

"Try to think about something relaxing," she said. "Think about kissing your boyfriend."

"That's *relaxing?*"

She smiled. "No. But it takes your mind off."

She was right; it did, for a second or two. I thought of Loyd's last kiss on my doorstep in Grace. But it also made my chest ache, further distracting my heart from the task at hand. Nausea pressed on the back of my throat. I closed my eyes, but vertigo is an internal distress; shutting out the world does nothing to help. The plane took another steep bank.

We were in an unnatural position, vertical in the air and slipping down, with nothing to support us.

When we finally leveled out again I opened my eyes. We were skimming low over Tucson and I was comforted—irrationally I know—by the nearness of things. Clusters of houses huddled together as if for reassurance, and in between them lay broad spans of flesh-colored desert. The freckled ground was threaded with thin, branched lines of creeks, like veins in the back of a hand. It looked as if there were water in the creeks, although I knew better. At this time of year they were bone-dry rivers of sand.

The rush of adrenalin had rinsed me clean. I looked hard out the window and understood suddenly that what I saw was full of color. A watercolor wash of summer light lay on the Catalina

Mountains. The end of a depression is that clear: it's as if you have been living underwater, but never realized it until you came up for air. I hadn't seen color since I lost Hallie. I thought hard, trying to remember; it seemed unbelievable, but there was none. Almost none. Loyd's green corduroy shirt, and the red flowers and the hummingbird against the brightly lit wall, the moment Emelina said goodbye. And that was all. Before that, the last thing I clearly remembered in color was Santa Rosalia in its infinite shades of brown.

I laughed at myself for carrying my mother's phobic blood in my veins. And for telling Alice Kimball how to cure slugs. Practicing all this family business without a license. It seemed extraordinary and accidental that I was alive. I felt crowded with all the sensory messages that make up life, as opposed to survival, and I recognized this as something close to joy. As we slipped down over the city every building and back lot was beautifully distinct. I forgot about my heart, left it to look after itself. We passed south of downtown, over the railyard, where the boxcars stood in line looking sweet and mismatched like a child's toy put together with no eye for color coordination. Just past the railyard was a school where a double row of corn-colored school buses were parked in a ring, exactly like one of those cheap Indian necklaces made for tourists. Bright backyard swimming pools gleamed like turquoise nuggets. The land stretched out under me the way a lover would, hiding nothing, offering up every endearing southwestern cliché, and I wanted to get down there and kiss the dirt.

I made a bargain with my mother. If I got to the ground in one piece, I wasn't leaving it again.

▼▼▼

The Amtrak didn't depart until three-thirty; I made it with time to spare. The station clerk wouldn't sell me a ticket to my destination, saying it wasn't a passenger stop. I argued. I knew the train stopped there for a crew change. Finally I realized he could sell me a ticket for anywhere at all on the eastbound line, it didn't matter. I knew where I was getting off.

We pulled out of the station and I hugged myself, cradled in the wide reclining seat, letting the rails rock me like a baby. The car smelled like smoke and old leather. I lay sideways in the seat, facing the window, my legs curled under me. Tucson, Arizona, passed slowly enough to nod at, take notice of, and then let go. At a steady, measured pace these things were revealed to me: the backs of brickyards, the backs of barrios, a large outdoor factory where Mexican women painted tiles. We passed buildings whose high walls, empty of windows, were spray-painted with huge secrets seen by no one but the travelers of the Southern Pacific. And then came the broad, open desert—mile after mile of it. I understood the appeal of train travel. You couldn't help knowing where you'd been.

At some point I fell asleep, and at some point I woke up again. I felt I'd been on that train for the whole of my life. We approached Grace from a direction that was new to me. We didn't go by the junkyard. There was a tunnel through the granite cliffs and we entered it fast—the dark rock wall magnifying the rocketing clamor of tons of forward motion—and then, quiet and sudden, out into the bright light again. I blinked against the overexposed world. By the time my eyes adjusted we were right downtown behind the old jailhouse, pulling the sighing brakes, slowing down. We came gliding under the long wooden porch of the depot. The sun glinted on its pleated tin roof, and I noticed a carob tree there with a trunk the size of a rain barrel. It must be the male—the mate to the one up by the liquor store. The one I'd been looking for.

The conductor looked a little surprised when I pulled my bag off the rack and hopped down onto the concrete apron of the depot.

"This isn't anywhere, sweetheart," he said, looking down at me from the doorway. He was a very old, very dark-skinned man whose uniform looked as if it could hold up its shoulders without him.

"I know," I said.

"You can't get back on," he warned. "Ten minutes for a crew change, and then we're headed out for El Paso."

"I know. I don't want to get back on. I live here."

"Well, how do you do," he said. He stepped back into the

car and waved at me through the window. His gloved hand fluttered like a dove.

A hundred yards up the line I saw the fireman climb down the ladder from the engine. It was someone I'd gone to school with—Roger Bristol. Loyd tossed down Roger's grip and his own, one at a time, and then swung himself easily down the ladder as if he were born for this work. He talked briefly with two other men—the oncoming crew, I guessed. They would speak in their magical language of dog catchers and sun kinks and the ones that had died on the line, picking up trains from the dead and moving on. They parted ways and the new crew climbed into the engine. The other two men walked toward the depot carrying their grips and lunch buckets: one short and stocky, the other taller, broad-shouldered, with his hair in a ponytail. The people you love always look perfectly proportioned from a distance.

Shortly the train began to move again, very slowly, the speed of a living creature. You could still run and catch it. Loyd and Roger kept walking toward me without seeing me. Standing there watching him, knowing what he didn't, I had so much power and none at all. I was on the outside, in a different dimension. I'd lived there always.

Then he stopped dead, just for a second. I'll remember that. The train moved and Roger moved but Loyd stood still.

He caught up to me in an instant, with a twinkle in his eye and his bag slung over his shoulder like a ready traveler.

"Thanks for the ride," I said.

He put one arm around my neck and gave me the kind of kiss no fool would walk away from twice.

26

THE FIFTY MOTHERS

For several days I kept coming back to this: we had no body. I wanted to have a funeral for Hallie, but I was at a loss. I knew the remains should not have been important, but in a funeral the body gives the grieving a place to focus their eyes. We sit facing it, bear it on our shoulders, follow it down the road in procession and finally long to follow it into the ground. The body would have provided an agenda and told me what to do, in lieu of Hallie, who was gone.

I went to look for something else that in my mind stood for her: the *semilla besada,* one of the supernaturally blessed trees that in the old days were festooned like Christmas trees with the symbols of people's hopes. We could hold a funeral there, outside, under the leaves. I wanted to find the exact plum tree where we'd hidden a lock of our intertwined hair. I knew the orchard but couldn't find the tree. Either it was gone, or it was no longer exceptional. Maybe the trees all around it had stretched their taproots and found the same nurturing vein.

It was June, a week before Hallie's thirtieth birthday. The canopies were in full green, each one as brilliant as a halo. The blossoms had dropped and left behind incipient fruits swelling three and four to a cluster, not yet pruned by nature or by hand. Every tree in every orchard looked blessed. So we had the funeral there, in the old Domingos plum orchard.

I'd asked people to bring something that reminded them of Hallie. I spread the black-and-red afghan on the ground and we stood around that. Instead of decorating a tree with our hopes for the future, we decorated a blanket with icons from the past. All the women from Stitch and Bitch were there. And J.T. and Emelina, of course, and Loyd. All of my students, as well. Doc Homer didn't make it. He didn't go very far out of his house these days, or very far out of his head.

It was awkward getting started. I remembered the last time I'd hugged her, thinking I could hold on and stop our lives right there. I took some breaths. "Hallie asked to be buried in Nicaragua," I said. "She wanted that. To enrich the soil of a jungle. But I wanted something here too." I stopped, because it sounded to me like small talk. Words only cover the experience of living. I looked around at the unpretentious faces like slices of bread, all the black dresses, the dark shoes, and I looked up at the bright leaves lit from above. It was a brilliant, hot day and I didn't feel at all like crying. The black dresses made me think of Greece. Nothing seemed quite real.

Several peacocks had gathered in the trees behind our heads, keeping their distance, but curious, probably hoping for food. A peacock wouldn't know the difference between a picnic and a funeral. The outward signs were similar.

"Do you think we should sing?" I asked.

"Yes," said Emelina. "We ought to sing."

"What?" I couldn't think of any particular song that Hallie liked, except some silly things from our teenage years. "Mother and Child Reunion" and "Maggie May." I thought of Hallie moonwalking to "Thriller," and then I thought abstractly about never seeing her again, what that really meant. In the back of my mind I was still wondering when she would come home. I couldn't concentrate. Someone suggested "Let the Circle Be Unbroken," so we sang that, and then we sang "De Colores" because everybody knew it. Norma Galvez's husband Cassandro played the guitar.

Then it was quiet again. People shifted slightly on their feet, the same motion repeated many times throughout the crowd, like the dancers at Santa Rosalia. Except unconscious, and unrehearsed. I pulled some letters out of my pocket and read parts of them that Emelina had helped me pick out. I read what Hallie said about not wanting to save the world, that you didn't choose your road for the reward at the end, but for the way it felt as you went along. And I read some things she'd said about nations forgetting. Refusing to sell tractor parts, then wondering why people would turn to Yugoslavia for tractors. I was aware that my reading might seem a little rambling, but I felt there was some logic to it, and people were tolerant. Truly, I think they would have listened to me all day. It occurred to me that such patience might be the better part of love.

I read a quote she'd written me that seemed important, a thing said by Father Fernando Cardenal, who was in charge of the literacy crusade: "You learn to read so you can identify the reality in which you live, so that you can become a protagonist of history rather than a spectator." I waited a minute, while a peacock screamed. Then I read some words of Hallie's: "The very least you can do in your life is to figure out what you hope for. And the most . . ."

Another peacock suddenly howled nearby. I saw Emelina's twins craning their necks, trying to spot it. I went on:

"And the most you can do is live inside that hope. What I want is so simple I almost can't say it: elementary kindness. Enough to eat, enough to go around. The possibility that kids might one day grow up to be neither the destroyers nor the destroyed."

I finished by reading the letter from Sister Sabina Martin. She said thousands of people joined us in mourning Hallie. "I know that doesn't make your grief any smaller," she wrote. "But I believe it makes Hallie's presence larger. Certainly, she won't be forgotten."

Several peafowl had hopped to the ground and were making insistent, guttural noises, impatient for food. I saw Glen and Curtis sneak off into the trees in pursuit of a peacock they'd never catch.

"This is what I brought." I knelt by the afghan and set down a pair of Hallie's small black shoes, about second-grade size. They could have been mine, it was impossible to tell, but I said they were Hallie's. I put them in the center of the red-and-black crocheted blanket. "I brought these because they just reminded me of growing up with Hallie. We had to wear these ugly shoes. It was just one of the important things we did together. I don't know. We felt kind of alone sometimes." I stood up and looked at the trees through the curtain of water in my eyes.

Viola laid down some marigolds. She had on her polyester, the funeral dress for all seasons, and she was perspiring; broad damp spots underlined her bosom. "Whenever I think of you kids I think of the *cempazuchiles* and being up at the graveyard for All Souls'. You were always a very big help."

I looked at Viola. She stared back, rubbing the bridge of her nose. There was the faintest light of a smile.

Several women had things they claimed we'd left in their houses when we played there as children: a doll with unpleasant glass eyes and a gruesomely pockmarked head where its hair had come out; a largish plastic horse; a metal hen that, when you pushed her down on her feet, made a metallic cluck and laid a small marble egg. Also a pink sweater, size 6X. Mrs. Nuñez swore it was Hallie's. "It was behind the refrigerator. I didn't find it till last year when the refrigerator give out and we had to call the man to move it out and get us a new one in there. The dust, I hate to tell you! And there was this little sweater of Halimeda Noline's. She used to set up there on top of the refrigerator, because I told her she couldn't drink beer till she was as tall as her daddy."

This was the truth, dead center. I remembered her up there huddled among the Mason jars and bright cracker boxes. I stared at the freshly laundered pink sweater lying with outstretched arms and thought about how small Hallie had been at one time. Miss Colder and Miss Dann were just then displaying an ancient-looking picture book, but there was a roaring in my ears and I lost track of what they were saying. I believe it was the physical manifestation of unbearable grief. But you learn in these situations that all griefs are bearable. Loyd was standing on one side of me, and Emelina on the other, and whenever I thought I might fall or just cease to exist, the pressure of their shoulders held me there.

I could hear people's words, but my vision was jarred by showers of blue sparks. Or the world went out of focus. And at other times I could see but couldn't hear. Doña Althea clumped forward with her cane and set down a miniature, perfectly made peacock piñata. It perched there on the pile of childhood things, its small eyes glittering and its tail feathers perfectly trimmed. It was an exquisite piece of art that could have made it into Mr. Rideheart's gallery, but it was for Hallie. I tried to listen to what she was saying. She said, "I made one like this for both of you girls, for your *cumpleaños* when you were ten."

To my surprise, this was also true. I remembered every toy, every birthday party, each one of these fifty mothers who'd been standing at the edges of my childhood, ready to make whatever contribution was needed at the time.

"*Gracias, Abuelita,*" I said softly to Doña Althea as she clumped away.

She didn't look at me, but she heard me say it and she didn't deny that she was my relative. Her small head crowned with its great white braid nodded a little. No hugs or confessions of love. We were all a little stiff, I understood that. Family constellations are fixed things. They don't change just because you've learned the names of the stars.

Uda Dell went last. "I brought this bouquet of zinnias because every spring Hallie helped me dig my zinnia bed." She laid down the homely, particolored bouquet, and added, "I crocheted that afghan, too."

"You did?"

She looked at me, surprised. "Right after your mommy died. Well, I don't guess you'd remember."

"This blanket got us through a lot of tough times," I said. I was feeling a little more steady on my feet. I folded in the corners and drew it all up into a bundle against my chest. About everything Hallie and I had ever done was with us there in the Domingos orchard. Everything we'd been I was now.

"Thank you," I said, to everybody.

I turned my back and headed alone with my bundle up the Old Pony Road to Doc Homer's house.

HOMERO

27

HUMAN REMAINS

There are women in every room of this house, he thinks: Mrs. Quintana upstairs, and now there is Codi, standing in the kitchen with her baby. Her arms and chest clutch the black wool bundle and it weighs her down like something old, made of stone. The weight makes him want to turn away. He thinks, This is the fossil record of our lives.

"I'm going to bury this. Do you want to help me?" She looks up at him and tears stream down. The grief on her face is fresh as pollen.

"You already buried it."

"No, no, no!" she screams, and slams the screen door behind her. He follows her down the path but she doesn't go down to the riverbed this time, she turns and goes right around the house into the backyard. When he catches up, a little breathless, she is standing with her boots on the ground like rooted stalks. Standing beside the old plot where Hallie used to grow a garden. A few old artichoke bushes have gone thistly and wild around its perimeter. Codi drops the knotted bundle and goes to the tool shed to retrieve a shovel. She comes back and digs hard into the ground. It hasn't been disturbed for many years.

"Are you sure this is a good place?" he asks.

Without speaking, she steps on the shovel and its tip bites

into the sandy soil again and again, lifting, digging, and lifting out a deep, square hole.

"You might want to have a garden here again someday. When this house is yours."

The shovel stops suddenly. "Did you know I'm staying?" She looks at him.

He looks back, waiting.

"I told Loyd about the baby. Yesterday I took him down there to the riverbed where you showed me. I can remember every minute of that night. You gave me some pills, didn't you? You really did want to help." She looks up at the sky, using gravity and the small, twin dams of her eyelids to hold in tears. "So Loyd knows about that now. He's sad. I didn't think about that part—that he would be sad. I was thinking the baby was just mine."

"It wasn't just yours."

"I know." She wipes her cheeks with the back of her hand, leaving a faint dark smudge under each eye. She looks at him very oddly. "We might have another one. Loyd and I. I don't know. There's time to see."

"Yes."

"Did you know I'm a good science teacher? The kids and the teachers all voted. They say I'm spirited. How do you like that?"

"It's what I would expect."

"I'm teaching them how to have a cultural memory." She looks at her hands, and laughs, but looks sad. "I want them to be custodians of the earth," she says.

He also looks at her hands. They remind him of something. Whose hands?

"You really can't approve of me staying, can you?" she demands, suddenly angry. "You raised me to turn my back on this place. That worked for you, but the difference is you *knew* it was really your home. You knew you had one. So you had a choice."

"That's all very well and good," he says, "but you still might want a garden. These artichoke bushes still produce. Every summer they bloom as if their hearts depended on it. Never mind that there was nobody taking in the harvest." He takes the tip of a silvery leaf between his fingers. It looks knifelike, but is yielding and soft.

She looks at him for quite a long time, smiling, and then she looks down at the bundle. "It's all right to bury this here," she says. "There are no human remains."

No human remains. No. Human. Remains. The three words chime in his head like large, old bells, three descending notes that ring and ring, speeding up in tempo until they clang against one another.

"How true," he says finally.

She shaves out the edges of the hole so it is neat and square, and then drops the bundle in. She throws a handful of dirt on top of it and stands there looking down.

"We're a pair of scarred old souls, aren't we, Codi?"

"I don't know what we are. I'm trying to figure out what I hope for."

"It's a most dangerous thing, hope."

Her eyes flash with something bright. Love or anger. But she doesn't speak.

"Hope involves giving a great deal of yourself away," he tells her.

"That's a pitiful excuse."

"Oh, it's pitiful all right, but there you have it. It's hard to give much away when you're the subject of widespread disapproval and your heart is leaking from puncture wounds."

"That's true. We got punctured pretty bad. But we still gave the world a lot, Pop. We gave it Hallie."

"We did. We surely did."

She begins shoveling dirt back into the grave. He thinks about the fact that all these particles of dirt have now been rearranged. No fixed strata. Alice was the gardener. When she has finished she moves to his side and he takes her elbow. They stand side by side in their small garden of sand and buried children. The bones in his wife's arm are as thin as whistles. "Do you have any idea how much I love you?" he asks her.

She stares at him, then squeezes his hand. "Hallie was a protagonist of history," she says.

"She wanted to save the world."

"No, Pop, that's not true. She wanted to save herself. Just like we all do."

He looks at the tall, living daughter his wife has suddenly become. He is no longer angry about these changes. "Save herself from what?"

"From despair. From the feeling of being useless. I've about decided that's the main thing that separates happy people from the other people: the feeling that you're a practical item, with a use, like a sweater or a socket wrench."

He asks, "Are we the other people?" He is curious.

"You're not useless. You gave yourself to this town for forty years. Scarred soul or not."

"Yes. But I gave for the wrong reasons. As you have pointed out."

She laughs. "I did, didn't I? Damn!" She pulls at the end of a silver artichoke leaf. "I was scared to death I was going to grow up to be just like you." She looks at him, and laughs again. She says: "God, I could never be just like you."

They are standing in the garden, in a dwarf forest of artichokes. She has just dug a hole and buried God knows what and now has made a confession of either contempt or admiration. He waits to see what will happen next.

"Maybe the reason you gave yourself to this town doesn't matter that much. Maybe what matters is just that you did it. Maybe that makes you a good man. You know what Loyd told me one time?"

"No."

"He thinks people's dreams are made out of what they do all day. The same way a dog that runs after rabbits will dream of rabbits. It's what you do that makes your soul, not the other way around."

It's what you do that makes your soul. Standing opposite him, staring down into the grave, he sees two sad little girls in cowboy hats. Is this what he has done? "I don't think you should be here," he says to them.

The elder daughter looks up, her pale eyes steady. "But we are here, Papa."

"Yes, you are."

"Why don't you want us?"

"Oh, God, I do." He kneels down and takes them both in his arms and pulls them against his chest. He understands for the first time in his life that love weighs nothing. Oh God, his girls are as light as birds.

COSIMA

28

DAY OF ALL SOULS

Gracela Canyon, if you strip it down to the enduring things, is a great, granite bowl of air. It's a wonderful echo chamber. Voices of women and children in the cemetery reached Viola and me from all the way across the canyon, rising on invisible air currents with the ravens and the spirits of all those old bones being tended by their children. It was getting on toward late afternoon, and we walked slowly. Viola had spent the morning supervising family operations, and said she was tired. But she'd promised that any day I asked her she would take me to the place where we watched my mother go. I chose that particular day in 1989, the end of a decade, the Day of All Souls, when we were all up decorating the graves. I don't know why.

I'd finished sweeping off my father and the other Nolinas and had decked them out with little bunches of marigolds at their heads and feet. It was something like tucking children into bed. I was their historian and their guardian angel. I never found Ursolina, the little bear. I imagine she's somewhere closer to the mine, where the earth has been shifted too many times to bear witness to what it has buried in it. The rest of the family, for all the times they'd had to be exhumed, had stayed together surprisingly well.

I knelt all morning in the dirt, laying out a border of creek rocks around Doc Homer. He'd been gone more than two years, but it took me awhile to decide on this. Emelina's boys had hauled the rocks up there for me. When we took them out of the water and piled them into the wheelbarrow they lost their luster, all drying to the same whitish color of dust, and I was afraid after all that work they would be the wrong thing, but they were fine. Uniform and shipshape, washed smooth by the abrasion of natural forces. I laid them end to end around the dirt mound, knocking them together and working them back and forth a little to find a natural fit. As I worked I thought of the masonry walls of Kinishba, with the bones of children inside.

When I stood back finally and dusted my chapped hands against my jeans, I saw I'd achieved nothing so fine as Kinishba, but had marked out a clear boundary, anyway. He would like it. I'd brought some order to his cosmos finally.

I squinted into the sun. Across the tops of about a hundred gravestones and many people I saw Viola in her black dress, standing on a little rise, her gray hair wandering from its knot. She pressed one hand to the small of her back while Mason and Nicholas danced in front of her with their hands full of candy, begging for something, wearing her out. Nicholas was three and a half; John Tucker was talking about quitting school to be a hoghead for Southern Pacific. I thought: "I can't wait forever." So I went and asked her right then and she said fine, after lunch we would go. "I'm about done here," she'd said, cracking the sugar skull of a *calavera* between her molars. "They can figure out which end of the flowers to put in water without me."

We took the quickest road down into town, then cut across the hill behind the high school and through the splendid canopies hung with fruit that the Stitch and Bitch Club had won back from Black Mountain Mining. From there we headed up the Old Pony Road toward the abandoned mine. The tops of the flat tailing mounds were dimpled with rain-catching basins and I'd noticed that sprigs of rabbitbrush were starting to grow up there.

The road was steep. No route out of Grace was an easy climb. Twice I had to ask Viola to let me catch my breath. I held a fist to my breastbone, panting hard, a little embarrassed by my infirmity but also a little pleased by the external proof of what was still mostly an internal condition. I was pregnant.

"I feel like I don't have any energy. I come home from school and sleep till Loyd wakes me up for dinner, and then I go back to bed." This new relationship with sleep was a miracle to me.

"Oh, yeah," she said. "All your get-up-and-do-it goes to the baby. Right from the start you know who's gonna be the boss."

Those first few weeks are an unearthly season. From the outside you remain so ordinary, no one can tell from looking that you have experienced an earthquake of the soul. You've been torn asunder, invested with an ancient, incomprehensible magic. It's the one thing we never quite get over: that we contain our own future.

I'd written this to Hallie in the pages of a bound notebook that would never be torn out or mailed. These letters stayed with me. I told her: it feels like somebody's moved in. It's a shock. You find you're not the center of the universe, suddenly it's all flipped over, you have it in you to be a parent. You're not all that concerned any more with being someone's child. It helps you forgive things.

We reached the crest of the canyon where the white salt crust of the old alfalfa fields began. Dead for two decades, the earth was long and white and cracked, like a huge porcelain platter dropped from the heavens. But now the rabbitbrush was beginning to grow here too, topped with brushy gold flowers, growing like a renegade crop in the long, straight troughs of the old irrigation ditches.

A wind was picking up from the south, and Viola and I could smell rain. High storm clouds with full sails and a cargo of hail made their way in a hurry across the sky. Viola's hair blew around her face as she walked. I asked, "Did you know her kidneys had failed her once before, when she was pregnant with me?"

"Sure," Viola said. "She was real sick both times."

"But she went ahead and had Hallie anyway."

"You don't think about it that much. You just go on and have your kids."

I wanted to believe my mother had thought about it. That

Hallie was her last considered act of love—an act with unforeseen consequences, some of them just now coming into flower in the soil of another country. I said, "I always knew I was up here that day. I can remember seeing the helicopter."

"You remember that?"

"I thought I did. But people told me I hadn't, so I'd about decided I'd made it up."

Viola took my hand. I could feel the soft flesh and the hard wedding band in her grip. "No, if you remember something, then it's true," she said. "In the long run, that's what you've got."

I knew the place when we came to it. We were right there already.

This is what I remember: Viola is holding my hand. We're at the edge of the field, far from other people. We stand looking out into the middle of that ocean of alfalfa. I can see my mother there, a small white bundle with nothing left, and I can see that it isn't a tragedy we're watching, really. Just a finished life. The helicopter is already in the air and it stays where it is, a clear round bubble with no destination, sending out circular waves of wind that beat down the alfalfa. People duck down, afraid, as if they're being visited by a plague or a god. Their hair is blowing. Then the helicopter tilts a little and the glass body catches the sun. For an instant it hangs above us, empty and bright, and then it rises like a soul.

Pigs in Heaven

FOR CAMILLE

ACKNOWLEDGMENTS

This book germinated under the warm encouragement of friends in the Cherokee Nation, especially Ron Watkins, Nancy Raincrow Pigeon, and Loretta Rapien. Regina Peace, Toby Robles, Carol Locust, and Donna Goldsmith patiently helped me understand the letter and spirit of the Indian Child Welfare Act. Joe Hoffmann, Georgia Pope, Frances Goldin, Sydelle Kramer, and Janet Goldstein helped the story find its way through the woods. Camille Kingsolver gave me five-year-old insights and reasons to keep writing.

The legal dispute described in *Pigs in Heaven* is not based on a single case history, but was constructed from the materials of existing law and historical fact, insofar as I understand them. The specifics of legal process vary among tribes. Other people would tell this story differently, and none of them would be wrong.

SPRING

AFS

QUEEN OF NOTHING

WOMEN ON THEIR OWN run in Alice's family. This dawns on her with the unkindness of a heart attack and she sits up in bed to get a closer look at her thoughts, which have collected above her in the dark.

It's early morning, April, windless, unreasonably hot even at this sun-forsaken hour. Alice is sixty-one. Her husband, Harland, is sleeping like a brick and snoring. To all appearances they're a satisfied couple sliding home free into their golden years, but Alice knows that's not how it's going to go. She married him two years ago for love, or so she thought, and he's a good enough man but a devotee of household silence. His idea of marriage is to spray WD-40 on anything that squeaks. Even on the nights when he turns over and holds her, Harland has no words for Alice—nothing to contradict all the years she lay alone, feeling the cold seep through her like cave air, turning her breasts to limestone from the inside out. This marriage has failed to warm her. The quiet only subsides when Harland sleeps and his tonsils make up for lost time. She can't stand the sight of him there on his back, driving his hogs to market. She's about to let herself out the door.

She leaves the bed quietly and switches on the lamp in the living room, where his Naugahyde recliner confronts her, smug as a catcher's mitt, with a long, deep impression of Harland running down its center. On weekends he watches cable TV with perfect vigilance, as if he's afraid he'll miss the end of the world—though he doesn't bother with CNN, which, if the world did end, is where the taped footage would run. Harland prefers the Home Shopping Channel because he can follow it with the sound turned off.

She has an edgy sense of being watched because of his collection of antique headlights, which stare from the china cabinet. Harland runs El-Jay's Paint and Body and his junk is taking over her house. She hardly has the energy to claim it back. Old people might marry gracefully once in a while, but their houses rarely do. She snaps on the light in the kitchen and shades her eyes against the bright light and all those ready appliances.

Her impulse is to call Taylor, her daughter. Taylor is taller than Alice now and pretty and living far away, in Tucson. Alice wants to warn her that a defect runs in the family, like flat feet or diabetes: they're all in danger of ending up alone by their own stubborn choice. The ugly kitchen clock says four-fifteen. No time-zone differences could make that into a reasonable hour in Tucson; Taylor would answer with her heart pounding, wanting to know who'd dropped dead. Alice rubs the back of her head, where her cropped gray hair lies flat in several wrong directions, prickly with sweat and sleeplessness. The cluttered kitchen irritates her. The Formica countertop is patterned with pink and black loops like rubber bands lying against each other, getting on her nerves, all cocked and ready to spring like hail across the kitchen. Alice wonders if other women in the middle of the night have begun to resent their Formica. She stares hard at the telephone on the counter, wishing it would ring. She needs some proof that she isn't the last woman left on earth, the surviving queen of nothing. The clock gulps softly, eating seconds whole while she waits; she receives no proof.

She stands on a chair and rummages in the cupboard over the refrigerator for a bottle of Jim Beam that's been in the house since before she married Harland. There are Mason jars up there she ought to get rid of. In her time Alice has canned tomatoes enough for a hundred bomb shelters, but now she couldn't care less, nobody does. If they drop the bomb now, the world will end without the benefit of tomato aspic. She climbs down and pours half an inch of Jim Beam into a Bengals mug that came free with a tank of gas. Alice would just as soon get her teeth cleaned as watch the Bengals. That's the price of staying around when your heart's not in it, she thinks. You get to be cheerleader for a sport you never chose. She unlatches the screen door and steps barefoot onto the porch.

The sky is a perfect black. A leftover smile of moon hides in the bottom branches of the sugar maple, teasing her to smile back. The air isn't any cooler outside the house, but being outdoors in her sheer nightgown arouses Alice with the possibility of freedom. She could walk away from this house carrying nothing. How those glass eyeballs in the china cabinet would blink, to see her go. She leans back in the porch swing, missing the squeak of its chains that once sang her baby to sleep, but which have been oppressed into silence now by Harland's WD-40. Putting her nose deep into the mug of bourbon, she draws in sweet, caustic fumes, just as she used to inhale tobacco smoke until Taylor made her quit.

She raised a daughter in this house and planted all the flowers in the yard, but that's nothing to hold her here. Flowers you can get tired of. In the record heat of this particular Kentucky spring the peonies have blown open their globes a month ahead of Memorial Day. Their face-powder scent reminds her of old women she knew in childhood, and the graveyard. She stops swinging a minute to listen: a huffling sound is coming from the garden. Hester Biddle's pigs. Hester lives a short walk down the road and has taken up raising Vietnamese miniature potbellied pigs for a new lease on life after her stroke. She claims they're worth two thousand per pig, but Alice can't imagine on what market. They're ugly as sin and run away for a hobby, to root in Alice's peony beds. "Go on home," Alice says in a persuasive voice. The pigs look up.

"I mean it," she says, rising from the porch swing, her hands on her hips. "I'm not above turning you all into bacon."

In the dim light from the kitchen their eyes glow red. Pigs are turning out to be the family curse: Alice's mother, a tall, fierce woman named Minerva Stamper, ran a hog farm alone for fifty years. Alice picks up an empty flowerpot from the porch step and throws it at the pigs. The darkness absorbs it. She throws a dirt clod and a pair of pruning shears, which also vanish. Then a medium-sized aluminum bowl. Harland ordered the Cornucopia Of Bowls from the shopping channel for their wedding anniversary, so now their home has a bowl for every purpose. She picks up another one and gives it a fling. She'll have to pick them up in the morning, in front of God and the Biddles, but she wants those pigs out of her life. She finds a galvanized watering can and lifts herself on the balls of her feet, testing her calves. Alice is in good shape, despite her age; when she concentrates she can still find all her muscles from the inside. When her first husband left her the house fell apart but she and her daughter held up well, she thinks, everything considered.

She heaves the watering can but can't tell where it's gone. It lands with a ding—possibly it struck a member of the Cornucopia. The red pig eyes don't even blink. Alice feels defeated. She returns to the porch to collect her losses.

She's not walking away from here. Who would take her in? She knows most of the well-to-do women in town, from cleaning their houses all the years she was raising Taylor, but their respect for Alice is based on what she could tell the world about their basements. On Fridays, Alice plays poker with Fay Richey and Lee Shanks—cheerful, husky-voiced women who smoke a lot and are so thankful to still be married, if she left Harland they'd treat her like she had a virus. Minerva and the hog farm are both gone, of course, the one simply dead and buried, the other sold to pay its own debts. It depresses Alice deeply to think how people's lives and all other enterprises, like life insurance, can last long enough to cancel themselves out.

A mockingbird lands on the tip of a volunteer mulberry that has grown up through the hedge. Flapping to stay balanced, he makes the long branch bob and sway like a carnival ride. His little profile flails against a horizon the color of rising dough. In the few minutes it took Alice to make an accounting of her life, dawn was delivered to this address and the automatic spotlight on Biddles' barn winked off. No matter what kind of night you're having, morning always wins.

The mockingbird springs off his mulberry branch into darkness and then materializes up on the roof, crowing to this section of the county that her TV antenna is his and his alone. Something about the male outlook, Alice thinks, you have got to appreciate. She stands with her arms crossed against her chest and observes the dark universe of the garden, which is twinkling now with aluminum meteorites. She hears the pigs again. It's no wonder they like to come here; they get terrified down at Biddles' when Henry uses more machinery than he needs. Yesterday he was using the hay mower to cut his front yard, which is typical. The poor things are just looking for a home, like the Boat People. She has a soft spot for refugees and decides to let them stay. It will aggravate Hester, who claims that every time they eat Alice's peonies they come home with diarrhea.

The neighborhood tomcat, all muscle and slide, is creeping along the top of the trellis where Alice's sweet peas have spent themselves all spring. She's seen him up there before, getting high on the night perfume, or imagining the taste of mockingbird. The garden Alice wishes she could abandon is crowded with bird music and border disputes and other people's hungry animals. She feels like the queen of some pitiful, festive land.

Welcome to Heaven.

For the first time in years she thinks of Sugar Boss: her family tie. Sugar is a second cousin and the most famous citizen of Heaven, Oklahoma. Alice has her picture put away in the scrapbook with Taylor's high school diploma and whatever else there is in the way of family papers. It's an old picture cut out of *Life* magazine, summer of '55. Sugar posed for a photographer with a pop bottle raised to her lips and a crown of daisies in her hair, leaning against the WELCOME TO HEAVEN sign, and was seen all over everywhere in the advertisement. Alice saw her at the grocery checkout and couldn't believe her eyes. She sent a letter, needing no more address than "Sugar Marie Boss, Heaven, Okla.," and it got there, even though by then she was no longer technically a Boss but a Hornbuckle. Sugar wrote back.

They'd spent their last years of childhood together on the farm during the Depression, along with dozens of other people who showed up at Minerva's door once they'd run out of everything but relatives. Of all the cousins, Alice and Sugar were closest, born a mere month apart. At nine they could pass for twelve and got jobs at the mattress factory, where it was all young girls, sewing up the ticking and stuffing in feathers. Their arms grew muscled and the down stuck on their hair, making them look like duck girls. Those times made bonds among people. The clotheslines ran from house to house and the wash ran between families like the same drab flag repeated over and over, uniting them all in the nation of washtubs and rough knuckles. There was love in that life, a kind of solid hope. Children ran heedless under the flapping laundry in a nation of their own. But it's Alice's impression that most of them grew up with hungry hearts, feeling sure that one day they would run out of everything again.

After their chance reconnection, she and Sugar shared their memories in long letters pressed into fat envelopes, but once they'd finished with the past, neither one had it in her to sustain the correspondence. Alice suspects Sugar's life never reached the same elevation again; in her letters there was mention of daughters prone to pregnancy. Alice pictures a rattletrap house and flowerbeds gone to jimson weed.

But Sugar once put Heaven on the map, and that has to carry some weight still. Alice stretches her legs into the pale orange morning that is taking hold around her, and it dawns on her with a strange shock that she is still the same person she was as a nine-year-old. Even her body is mostly unchanged. Her breasts are of a small, sound architecture and her waist is limber and strong; she feels like one of those California buildings designed for an earthquake. As surely as her organs are in the right places, she feels Sugar is still there in Heaven. She could write her today. She's kept feelings for Sugar, her long-lost relative who came home to her one day in the checkout line. Something like that is as bad or as good as a telephone ringing in the night: either way, you're not as alone as you think.

2

A MEAN EYE

"LOOK UP, TURTLE. ANGELS."

Taylor stoops to her daughter's eye level and points up at the giant granite angels guarding the entrance to the Hoover Dam: a straight-backed team, eyes on the horizon, their dark, polished arms raised toward the sky.

"They look like Danny," Turtle observes.

"Biceps to die for," Taylor agrees. Danny, their garbage man, is a body builder on his days off.

"What do angels need muscles for?"

Taylor laughs at the thought of some saint having to tote around the overfilled garbage bags of heaven. "They made this back in the thirties," she says. "Ask Grandma about the Depression sometime. Nobody could get a job, so they had this WPA thing where people made bridges and sidewalks and statues that look like they could sweat."

"Let's take a picture." Turtle's tone warns off argument; she means Taylor will stand under the angels and *she* will take the photo. Taylor stands where she's placed and prepares to smile for as long as it takes. Turtle concentrates through the rectangular eye, her black eyebrows stranded above it in her high forehead. Turtle's photos tend to come out fairly hopeless in terms of composition: cut-off legs or all sky, or sometimes something Taylor never even saw at the time. When the pictures come back from the drugstore she often gets the feeling she's gone on someone else's vacation. She watches Turtle's snub-nosed sneakers and deliberately planted legs, wondering where all that persistence comes from and where it will go. Since she found Turtle in her car and adopted her three years ago, she has had many moments of not believing she's Turtle's mother. This child is the miracle Taylor wouldn't have let in the door if it had knocked. But that's what miracles are, she supposes. The things nobody saw coming.

Her eyes wander while Turtle fiddles. The sun is hot, hot. Taylor twists her dark hair up off her neck.

"Mom!"

"Sorry." She drops her arms to her sides, carefully, like a dancer, and tries to move nothing but her eyes. A man in a wheelchair rolls toward them and winks. He's noticeably handsome from the waist up, with WPA arms. He moves fast, his dark mane flying, and turns his chair smoothly before the angels' marble pedestal. If she strains her peripheral vision Taylor can read the marble slab: it's a monument to the men who died building the dam. It doesn't say who they were, in particular. Another panel across the way lists the names of all the directors of the dam project, but this one says only that many who labored here found their final rest. There is a fairly disturbing bronze plaque showing men in work clothes calmly slipping underwater. "Poor guys," she says aloud. "Tomb of the unknown concrete pourer."

"Working for fifty cents an hour," the wheelchair man says. "A bunch of them were Navajo boys from the reservation."

"Really?"

"Oh, yeah." He smiles in a one-sided way that suggests he knows his way around big rip-offs like this, a fancy low-paying job that bought these Navajo boys a piece of the farm.

The shutter clicks, releasing Taylor. She stretches the muscles in her face.

"Are you the trip photographer?" he asks Turtle.

Turtle presses her face into her mother's stomach. "She's shy," Taylor says. "Like most major artists."

"Want me to take one of the two of you?"

"Sure. One to send Grandma." Taylor hands him the camera and he does the job, requiring only seconds.

"You two on a world tour?" he asks.

"A small world tour. We're trying to see the Grand Canyon all the way around. Yesterday we made it from Tucson to the Bright Angel overlook." Taylor doesn't say that they got manic on junk food in the car, or that when they jumped out at the overlook exactly at sunset, Turtle took one look down and wet her pants. Taylor couldn't blame her. It's a lot to take in.

"I'm on a tour of monuments to the unlucky." He nods at the marble slab.

Taylor is curious about his hobby but decides not to push it. They leave him to the angels and head for the museum. "Do not sit on wail," Turtle says, stopping to point at the wall. She's learning to read, in kindergarten and the world at large.

"On wall," Taylor says. "Do not sit on wall."

The warning is stenciled along a waist-high parapet that runs across the top of the dam, but the words are mostly obscured by the legs of all the people sitting on the wall. Turtle looks up at her mother with the beautiful bewilderment children wear on their faces till the day they wake up knowing everything.

"Words mean different things to different people," Taylor explains. "You could read it as 'Don't sit on the wall.' But other people, like Jax for instance, would think it means 'Go ahead and break your neck, but don't say we didn't warn you.'"

"I wish Jax was here," Turtle says solemnly. Jax is Taylor's boyfriend, a keyboard player in a band called the Irascible Babies. Taylor sometimes feels she could take Jax or leave him, but it's true he's an asset on trips. He sings in the car and is good at making up boredom games for Turtle.

"I know," Taylor says. "But he'd just want to sit on the wall. You'd have to read him his rights."

For Taylor, looking over the edge is enough, hundreds of feet down that curved, white wing of concrete to the canyon bottom. The boulders below look tiny and distant like a dream of your own death. She grips her daughter's arm so protectively the child might later have marks. Turtle says nothing. She's been marked in life by a great many things, and Taylor's odd brand of maternal love is by far the kindest among them.

Turtle's cotton shorts with one red leg and one white one flap like a pair of signal flags as she walks, though what message she's sending is beyond Taylor's guess. Her thin, dark limbs and anxious eyebrows give her a pleading look, like a child in the magazine ads that tell how your twenty cents a day can give little Maria or Omar a real chance at life. Taylor has wondered if Turtle will ever outgrow the poster-child look. She would give years off her own life to know the story of Turtle's first three, in eastern Oklahoma, where she's presumed to have been born. Her grip on Turtle is redundant, since Turtle always has a fist clamped onto Taylor's hand or sleeve. They cross through the chaotic traffic to the museum.

Inside, old photos line the walls, showing great expanses of scaffolded concrete and bushy-browed men in overalls standing inside huge turbines. The tourists are being shuffled into a small theater. Turtle tugs her in for the show, but Taylor regrets it as soon as the projector rolls. The film describes the amazing achievement of a dam that tamed the Colorado River. In the old days it ran wild, flooding out everyone downstream, burying their crops in mud. "There was only one solution—the dam!" exclaims the narrator, who reminds Taylor of a boy in a high school play, drumming up self-importance to conquer embarrassment. Mr. Hoover's engineers prevailed in the end, providing Arizona with irrigation and L.A. with electricity and the Mexicans with the leftover salty trickle.

"Another solution is they didn't need to grow their cotton right on the riverbank," Taylor points out.

"Mom!" hisses Turtle. At home Turtle whines when Taylor talks back to the TV. Jax sides with Turtle on the television subject, citing the importance of fantasy. Taylor sides with her mother, who claims over the phone that TV has supernatural powers over her husband. "Just don't believe everything on there is true," Taylor warns often, but she knows this war is a lost cause in general. As far as her daughter is concerned, Mutant Ninja Turtles live in the sewers and that is that.

Outside the museum, a foil gum wrapper skates along the sidewalk on a surprise gust of wind. A herd of paper cups and soda straws rolls eastward in unison. Lucky Buster sits on the ramparts of the Hoover Dam, trying to figure out how to save the day. People will throw anything in the world on the ground, or even in the water. Like pennies. They end up down there with the catfish. There could be a million dollars at the bottom of the lake right now, but everybody thinks there's just one red cent—the one they threw.

Lucky sits very still. He has his eye on a bright red soda-pop can. His friend Otis is an engineer for the Southern Pacific, and he's warned Lucky about pop cans. They catch the sun just right and they'll look like a red signal flare on the tracks. When you see that, you've got to stop the whole train, and then it turns out it's just a pop can. Bad news.

The people are all up above him. One girl is looking. Her round face like a sweet brown pie can see him over the wall. He waves, but she bobs behind the mother and they go away. Nobody else is looking. He could go down there now. The water is too close, though, and scares him: water is black, blue, pink, every color. It gets in your eyes there's so much light. He looks away at the nicer camel hump desert. Now: *go.*

Lucky drops down and scoots along the gray wall that runs along the edge. One side is water, fish-colored; on the other side you fall into the hole. He is as careful as the circus girls in silver bathing suits on TV, walking on wires. One foot, another foot.

A white bird with scabbed yellow feet lands in front of Lucky. "Ssss," he says to the bird, shaking his hands at it. The bird walks away fast, one spread foot and then the other one. Lucky is two steps away from the pop can. Now one step away. Now he's got it.

The bird turns its head and looks straight at Lucky with a mean eye.

The sun has dropped into the Nevada hills and rung up a sunset the color of cherries and lemons. Turtle and Taylor take one last stroll across Mr.

Hoover's concrete dream. Turtle is holding on so tightly that Taylor's knuckles ache. Their hypochondriac friend Lou Ann has warned Taylor about arthritis, but this snap-jawed grip is a principle of their relationship; it won Turtle a nickname, and then a mother. She hasn't deliberately let go of Taylor since they met.

The water in the shadow of the dam is musky green and captivating to Turtle. She yanks on Taylor's fingers to point out huge catfish moving in moss-colored darkness. Taylor doesn't really look. She's trying to take in the whole of Lake Mead, the great depth and weight of water that formerly ran free and made life miserable for the downstream farmers. It stretches far back into the brown hills, but there is no vegetation along the water's edge, just one surface meeting another, a counterfeit lake in the desert that can't claim its own shoreline. In the distance someone is riding a kind of small water vehicle that seems pesty and loud for its size, like a mosquito.

Storm clouds with high pompadours have congregated on the western horizon, offering the hope of cooler weather, but only the hope. The Dodge when they get back to it is firecracker hot and stinks of melted plastic upholstery. Taylor opens both front doors and tries to fan cooler air onto the seat. The ice-cream cone she bought Turtle was a mistake, she sees, but she's not an overly meticulous parent. She's had to learn motherhood on a wing and a prayer in the last three years, and right now her main philosophy is that everything truly important is washable. She hands Turtle a fistful of fast-food napkins from the glove compartment, but has to keep her eyes on the road once they get going. The Dodge Corona drives like a barge and the road is narrow and crooked, as bad as the roads she grew up risking her neck on in Kentucky.

Eventually they level out on the Nevada plain, which looks clinically dead. Behind them the lake stretches out its long green fingers, begging the sky for something, probably rain.

Turtle asks, "How will he get out?"

"Will who get out?"

"That man."

"Which man is that, sweetheart?" Turtle isn't a big talker; she didn't complete a sentence until she was four, and even now it can take days to get the whole story. "Is this something you saw on TV?" Taylor prompts. "Like the Ninja Turtles?"

"No." She looks mournfully at the waffled corpse of her ice cream cone. "He picked up a pop can and fell down the hole by the water."

Taylor narrows her eyes at the road. "At the dam? You saw somebody fall?"

"Yes."

"Where people were sitting, on that wall?"

"No, the other side. The water side."

Taylor takes a breath to find her patience. "That man out on the lake, riding around on that boat thing?"

"No," Turtle says. "The man that fell in the hole by the water."

Taylor can make no sense of this. "It wasn't on TV?"

"No!"

They're both quiet. They pass a casino where a giant illuminated billboard advertises the idea of cashing your paycheck and turning it into slot-machine tokens.

Turtle asks, "How will he get out?"

"Honey, I really don't know what you mean. You saw somebody fall down a hole by the dam. But not into the water?"

"Not the water. The big hole. He didn't cry."

Taylor realizes what she could mean, and rejects the possibility, but for the half second between those two thoughts her heart drops. There was a round spillway where the water could bypass the dam during floods. "You don't mean that spillway, do you? The big hole between the water and the parking lot?"

"Yes." Turtle's black eyes are luminous. "I don't think he can get out."

"There was a big high fence around that." Taylor has slowed to about fifteen miles an hour. She ignores the line of traffic behind her, although the drivers are making noise, impatient to get to Las Vegas and throw away their money.

"Turtle, are you telling me the absolute truth?"

Before she can manage an answer, Taylor U-turns the Dodge, furious at herself. She'll never ask Turtle that question again.

* * *

Hoover's guardian angels are in the dark now. The place is abandoned. They bang on the locked museum doors and Taylor cups her hands to see inside, but it is deserted. A huge blueprint of the dam shows elevators, maintenance towers, and on each side a long spillway looping like a stretched intestine under the dam to the river below. Taylor's own gut feels tight. "They've gone home," she tells Turtle, who won't stop banging the door. "Come on. Show me where he fell."

Turtle is willing to substitute one course of action for another. The legs of her shorts whip against each other as they cross to the Arizona side, where she dripped a trail of ice cream an hour before. "There," she says, pointing down.

Taylor examines the throat of the spillway: a rectangular concrete funnel, maybe fifty feet across, whose lower end narrows into a large round hole.

Dots of car lights twist down the mountain, looking lonely. Out over the lake, bats dip and flutter after mosquitoes. Taylor looks at the dark gullet. "Head first, or feet first?"

Turtle ponders this. "He was walking on there." Her finger projects a line down the retaining wall between lake and spillway. "He picked up a pop can. Then he fell down. Sideways first." Her hand burrows into her shorts pocket, frightened of its own revelations.

Taylor squeezes the other hand. "Don't worry. He's one lucky sucker that you've got such sharp eyes. Did you see him go all the way into the hole?"

Turtle nods.

Taylor feels weak-kneed, as she did looking over the parapet wall. The hardest thing about motherhood, she thinks, is that you can never again be the baby of your family, not even for ten seconds. She tries to sound steady. "Should we yell? Think he might hear us?"

Turtle nods.

Taylor screams: "Anybody in there? Hey!" They listen to the passive response of two million tons of concrete.

Taylor leans farther over the rail and makes a splay-fingered megaphone with her hands, to show Turtle this is fun, and will work. "Hey! Youuu! Hello down there, can you hear me? Heyy! Got two dimes for a nickel? Whooo! Hello!"

From far away over the lake comes the high buzz of a motorboat. Nothing else. Turtle cries without making a sound.

She feels for her mother's fingers, the one sure thing. They are standing in the dark. Taylor makes the round moon of flashlight go all over the policeman in the chair but he doesn't wake up. Behind the metal house are machines with long animal necks, and they are sleeping too.

"Hey, mister," Taylor says, louder. The light slides up his brown shirt and brights out a square name badge. Then his eyes. He wakes up and goes for his gun.

"What the fuck?"

"Excuse me, Mister Decker, but don't shoot us, okay? My daughter here is six and we're real defenseless."

Turtle makes herself feel her mother's hand. The man gets up and switches on a world of light. A motor sings and cries in the metal house. "What the hell you after?"

"We'd like to report an emergency, okay? Somebody fell into the dam. Into the spillway."

Mister Decker stares while all his dreams run away.

"He had on a dark shirt, and a green bandana around his head." Taylor looks down, and Turtle touches her hair.

"And long hair. Dark brown."

"Intoxicated?"

"We don't know. It's not somebody we know, we're just reporting it."

Mister Decker fixes his crotch. "When?"

"Around sunset."

"And you decided to come tell me about it in the middle of the night."

"There's nobody at the museum. It took us forever to find anybody."

"It's fucking Easter Sunday tomorrow. You want a parade?"

"Well, I'm sorry you got stuck on a dog shift, but we're trying to report a human life in danger here."

"Sumbitch."

Taylor clicks her flashlight on and off. "You ever think about a new line of work?"

Mister Decker goes into the shed and makes a phone call. When he comes back out he asks, "Any more I.D. on this guy? How old?"

Taylor asks Turtle, "How old was he?"

Turtle looks inside her forehead. "Big."

"Like, a big kid? Or my age? Or older than me."

"Bigger than a kid. Maybe like you."

Mister Decker's whole body slumps suddenly, like a sack with nothing in it. "Are you telling me you personally didn't see the incident occur?"

"My daughter saw the incident occur."

"*She* saw it." He looks. "You believe in Santa Claus, honey?"

Turtle finds her mother with the front of her face and doesn't say. Inside her mother she feels the air rising up.

"Sir, you're intimidating your witness here. She saw what she says she saw. My daughter doesn't miss much. When your boss gets here she could tell him how hilarious you looked when we found you up here snoring on your shift. So you want to take some happy pills and try acting a little nicer to us, or what?"

Hugo Alvarez, Decker's boss, looks them over. His office is the kind of no-frills arrangement that goes out of its way to prove the Park Service isn't wasting taxpayers' money. Taylor makes herself sit still in the orange plastic chair while Mr. Alvarez takes down the facts. "Your daughter doesn't look a thing like you," he notes.

She's used to this. Strangers stare at the two of them with that inquiring-minds-want-to-know look, wondering if maybe they've seen that child on a milk carton somewhere. "She's adopted," Taylor says flatly.

"Mexican-American?"

"Indian. Cherokee."

Mr. Alvarez writes this down on his notepad; apparently it's one of the facts.

"The guy might be banged up," Taylor points out. "Could we speed this up at all?"

Mr. Alvarez has a dark fringe around his bald head, and the eyes of an indifferent hound. He states with no apparent emotion, "There's an eight-foot security fence around the spillway."

"We don't know how he got over the fence," Taylor says, trying to match his tone. The fluorescent lights seem abusive at this hour, and she squints, trying to remember the hillside near the dam. "Maybe he came the other way, down the mountain. Or off the lake."

"We have security personnel watching that area like hawks."

"No offense, but we spent the better part of this night looking for one of your hawks."

"It's a holiday weekend."

"Happy Easter," Taylor says. "Let's go hunt some eggs."

Alvarez sighs. "I know you mean well, miss, but it doesn't sound very probable. Somebody else would have seen it. We can't justify calling out a rescue on this unless we have a witness."

"We have a witness. My daughter is the witness."

Alvarez rubs his nose with his pen and decides not to add anything to his log of facts.

"She's never told a lie in her life," Taylor adds.

"Frankly," he says, "I haven't heard her say anything."

"She doesn't talk much. If you leave out all the bullshit in life, there's not that much left to say, is there?"

Alvarez looks at Decker again and carefully winds his watch. Taylor gets up and walks to the door and back, reining in a real need to kick a chair leg with her cowboy boot. "Do you want *me* to lie? Do you want me to say I saw it too? If you write that down on your report, then can you call a rescue party?"

"Just tell me what happened. Just the truth."

"Just the truth is: a man fell down the spillway of your wonderful dam, today, right around sunset. My daughter saw him go in, and it would give her a better impression of the human race if you'd act like you give a damn. Because if he dies in there he's going to be just truly dead."

* * *

On Sunday, after a few hours of cramped nightmares on the seat of the Dodge, Taylor and Turtle find the head grounds janitor in the employee parking lot coming onto his shift. Taylor likes the looks of his truck: a '59 Ford, cherry. Maybe he'll be the one to listen. She works in the automotive business and has noticed that people who take care of old things usually have some patience.

"Down the spillway?" he asks. "Can't be. We got a fence around that. I saw a guy go right over the top once, down there." Taylor shudders, thinking of that long free-fall. "Middle of the day," he says. "Accident. Your suicides, they mostly hop off at night. Scrambled eggs in the morning."

Taylor is woozy from lack of sleep and could live without the scrambled-egg report. "This guy was about my age. Long hair. He had on overalls and, what else? A bandana."

"A green bandana?" The janitor's face comes on like someone threw a switch behind it. "Tied around his head, like this? And hair like this?" He chops his hand to his shoulder.

Taylor and Turtle nod.

"Oh, hell, that's Lucky Buster." He heads for the spillway.

They follow him. "You *know* this guy?" Taylor asks.

"Retarded guy. Oh, hell. I can't believe this. When?"

"Last night. You know him?"

"He's been hanging around here a couple weeks. I can't believe this. He was driving me crazy. He's a little kid in his mind, you know what I mean? He has this thing about litter."

Taylor yells, "Wait up!" Turtle is dragging on her fingers like a water skier. "What thing about litter?"

"He's nuts. Two or three times I caught him climbing around places a damn mountain goat should not be climbing around. Trying to pick up soda cans, would you believe. Oh, hell. Lucky Buster."

He stops at the spillway and they all look down, at nothing. The janitor is trying hard to catch his breath. "Oh, hell."

At ten o'clock Monday morning, six volunteers from the North Las Vegas Spelunking Club, plus one paramedic with rock-climbing experience, emerge from the spillway on the Arizona side. It took all night to assemble this team, and they have been down in the hole for hours more. Taylor and Turtle are front row in the crowd that is pushing quilt-cheeked against the security fence. Guards shout through bullhorns for the crowd to disperse, attracting more new arrivals.

The rescuers look like miners, blacked with grit. The rope that connects them waist to waist went down at dawn in yellow coils, but now is coming up black. Only the clinking buckles of their climbing gear catch the sun.

The stretcher comes out of the hole as a long, stiff oval, like a loaf shoved from the oven. Lucky Buster is wrapped in rubber rescue blankets and strapped down tightly from forehead to ankles with black canvas straps, so he bulges in sections. He can't stop blinking his eyes. That crowd on the fence is the brightest thing he has ever seen.

3

THE TRUE STORIES

TEN O'CLOCK IN KENTUCKY: THE sun has barely started thinking about Arizona. She can't call yet. Alice has been cleaning out her kitchen cabinets since dawn. She saw something on the early-morning news that disturbed her and she needs to talk to Taylor. Time zones are a mean trick, she feels, surely invented by someone whose family all lived under one roof.

Cardboard boxes crowd the linoleum floor like little barges bristling with their cargo: pots and pans, Mason jars, oven mitts, steak knives, more stuff than Alice can imagine she ever needed. The mood she's in, she's ready to turn out the cookstove. She doubts Harland would notice if she stopped cooking altogether. When she met him he was heating up unopened cans of Campbell's soup in a big pot of water every night. It amazed her to see the cans rolling around like logs in the boiling water. "Don't they bust?" she asked him, and he shyly put his hand on hers and allowed as how sometimes they did. His idea of a home-cooked meal is when you open the can first and pour it in a saucepan. Alice has been wasting her talents.

With aggressive strokes of her cleaning rag she reaches back into a high cabinet, feeling her Bermuda shorts slide up her thighs where the veins have turned a helpless blue. She's exposing herself to no one at the moment, but still feels embarrassed that her circulatory system has to start showing this way. Getting old is just a matter of getting easier to see through, until all your failing insides are in plain view and everyone's business. Even the ads aimed at old people are embarrassing: bathroom talk. You're expected to pull yourself inside-out like a sleeve and go public with your hemorrhoids.

It's hard for Alice to picture the portion of her life that still lies ahead. Her friend Lee Shanks saw a religious call-in show about turning your life around through Creative Imaging, and Lee has been trying ever since to image a new Honda Accord. But when Alice closes her eyes she sees, at the moment, Mason jars. She knows that no woman with varicose veins and a brain in her head would walk away from a decent husband, but she's going to anyway. Aloneness is her inheritance, like the deep heartline that breaks into match sticks across her palm. The Stamper women might sometimes think they're getting somewhere, nailing themselves down to kin, but some mystery always cuts them loose from people in the long run. Her mother used to tromp around the farm with her eyes on the sky as if some sign up there said: FREEDOM AND HAPPINESS THIS WAY, AT THE END OF THE LONELY ROAD.

Alice never wanted to be like her. She married young and misguided but with every intention of staying with her first husband, Foster Greer. She met him in a juke joint at the edge of the woods by the Old Miss slaughter pen, and on that very first night he danced her out to the parking lot and told her he was going to take her away from that smell. Between the hog farm and the slaughter pen Alice had lived her whole life within a perimeter of stench, and didn't know what he meant. It amazed her to discover that air, on its own, was empty of odor. She breathed through her nose again and again like an addict high on a new drug, and in the narrow parting of a highway cut through cypress swamps they drove all the way to New Orleans before breakfast. Even now Alice can feel in her skin the memory of that crazy adventure: speeding through the alligator bayous at midnight, feeling alive and lucky, as if there were only one man and one woman on earth this night and they were the ones chosen.

As a husband, though, Foster wore his adventures thin. He made a career of what he called "fresh starts," which meant getting fired from one house-framing job after another and consoling himself with Old Grand-Dad. Anything that's worth doing, he told Alice, is worth starting over right in a new town. And then he told her she was too much fun, as if it were her fault he could never settle down. He made Alice promise she would never try anything cute like getting pregnant, and she didn't, for nearly ten years. It wasn't so easy in those days; it was an endeavor. When it finally did happen, she'd known Foster long enough to know a good trade when she saw one, him for a baby. He had given her fresh air, but that's not such a gift that you have to stay grateful your whole life long. When he moved on from Pittman, Alice and the baby stayed.

She'd believed that motherhood done fiercely and well would end her family's jinx of solitude; Alice threw herself into belief in her daughter as frankly as Minerva had devoted herself to hogs. But kids don't stay with you if you do it right. It's one job where, the better you are, the more surely you won't be needed in the long run. She looks at the clock again: seven-thirty in Tucson. She picks up the phone and dials.

A baritone voice says, "Yo."

That would be Jax. Alice feels ridiculous. What she saw on TV was not about Taylor and Turtle. They are probably still in bed. "Oh, well, hi," she says. "It's me, Alice."

"Hey, pretty Alice. How's your life?"

"It'll do," she says. She never knows what she ought to say to Jax. She hasn't met him and finds him hard to picture. For one thing, he plays in a rock and roll band. He comes from New Orleans, and according to Taylor he is tall and lanky and wears a little gold earring, but his voice sounds like Clark Gable in *Gone With the Wind.*

"Your daughter has fled the premises," Jax reports. "She took the second generation and went to see the Grand Canyon. How do you like that?"

"Then it's true!" Alice shouts, startling herself.

Jax isn't rattled. "True blue. They abandoned me here to talk things over with the door hinges." He adds, "Then what's true?"

Alice is completely confused. If something had happened to them, Jax would know. "Nothing," she says. "Some darn thing I saw on TV. Harland had the news on and they had somebody falling over the Hoover Dam, and I could have swore there was Taylor Greer talking to the camera, just for a second."

"If Taylor fell off the Hoover Dam, she wouldn't be talking to the camera," Jax points out.

"Well, no, she wouldn't, so I got worried that it was Turtle that had fell off."

"Couldn't be," Jax says in his gentleman's drawl. "She would never let Turtle fall off anything larger than a washing machine. And if she did, she'd be on the phone to you before the kid hit bottom."

Alice is disturbed by the image but feels fairly sure Jax is right. "I kept hoping they'd show it again, but Harland's gone over to Home Shopping now and there's no coming back from that."

"Could be they're at the Hoover Dam," Jax says thoughtfully. "She doesn't always keep me up to date."

"They both did go, then? She took Turtle out of school?"

"School is out for Easter break. They thought they'd go have a religious experience with sedimentary rock."

"You should have gone with them. That ought to be something, that Grand Canyon."

"Oh, believe me, I wanted to. But my band got a gig in a bar called the Filth Encounter, and you can't miss something like that."

Alice finds herself calming down, listening to Jax. He always sounds so relaxed she wonders sometimes about his vital signs. "Well, that's good they went," she says mournfully. "That little girl's already way ahead of me. I've never even got down to see the new Toyota plant at Georgetown yet."

"Is everything okay?" Jax asks.

Alice touches her eyes. Half the time he comes across like he was raised on Venus, but his voice is wonderfully deep and slow, something she could use around the house. "Well, not really," she says. "I'm a mess. Just crazy enough to think I was seeing my own daughter on TV." She pauses, wondering how she can confess her troubles to someone she's never met. It's midmorning in an empty kitchen: the territory of lonely-hearts call-in shows and radio preachers for the desperate. She tells him, "I guess I'm leaving Harland."

"Hey, that happens. You never did like him much."

"I did so. At first." She drops her voice. "Not to live with, but I thought he'd improve. Under the influence of good cooking."

"You can't rehabilitate a man who collects light bulbs."

"No, it's headlights."

"Headlights. Is that actually true?"

"Off old cars. Any old car parts really, as long as they don't make any noise. You should see my living room. I feel like I've died and gone to the junkyard."

"Well, come live with us. Taylor leaves all her car parts at work. We need you, Alice. Taylor hates to cook, and I'm criminal at it."

"There's no hanging crimes you can do in the kitchen," Alice says. "I give a man extra points just for trying."

"Your daughter doesn't give a man extra points just for anything."

Alice has to laugh. "That's a fact."

"She says I cook like a caveman."

"Well, forever more." Alice laughs harder. Clark Gable with a gold earring and stooped shoulders and a club. "What does that mean?"

"No finesse, apparently."

"Well, I couldn't move in with Taylor. I've told her that fifty times. I'd be in your way." Alice has never lived in a city and knows she couldn't. What could she ever say to people who pay money to go hear a band called the Irritated Babies? Alice doesn't even drive a car, although few people know this, since she walks with an attitude of preferring the exercise.

"I don't think Taylor loves me anymore," Jax says. "I think she's got her eye on Danny, our garbage man."

"Oh, go on."

"You haven't seen this guy. He can lift four Glad Bags in each hand."

"Well, I'm sure you've got your good points too. Does she treat you decent?"

"She does."

"You're in good shape, then. Don't worry, you'd know. If Taylor don't like somebody, she'll paint the barn with it."

Jax laughs. "She does wish you'd come visit," he says.

"I will." Alice has tears in her eyes.

"I do too," he says, "I wish you would come. I need to meet this Alice. When Taylor says she wants you to live with us, I'm thinking to myself, this is ultra. Everybody else I know is in a twelve-step program to get over their dysfunctional childhoods."

"Well, it's my fault that she don't give men the extra points. I think I turned her against men. Not on purpose. It's kind of a hex. My mama ran that hog farm by herself for fifty years, and that's what started it."

"You have a hog farm in your maternal line? I'm envious. I wish I'd spent my childhood rocked in the bosom of swine."

"Well, it wasn't all that wonderful. My mother was a Stamper. She was too big and had too much on her mind to answer to 'Mother,' so I called her Minerva, just the same as the neighbors and the creditors and the traveling slaughter hands did. She'd always say, 'Mister, if you ain't brung it with you, you won't find it here.' And that was the truth. She had hogs by the score but nothing much to offer her fellow man, other than ham."

"Well," says Jax. "Ham is something."

"No, but she'd never let a man get close enough to see the whites of her eyes. And look at me, just the same, chasing off husbands like that Elizabeth Taylor. I've been thinking I raised Taylor to stand too far on her own side of the plank. She adopted the baby before she had a boyfriend of any kind, and it seemed like that just proved out the family trend. I think we could go on for thirteen generations without no men coming around to speak of. Just maybe to do some plumbing once in a while."

"Is this the Surgeon General's warning?"

"Oh, Jax, honey, I don't know what I'm saying. I'm a lonely old woman cleaning my kitchen cupboards to entertain myself. You kids are happy and I'm just full of beans."

"No, you stand by your stories. Whatever gets you through."

"I better let you go. Tell Taylor to send pictures of the baby. The last one I have is the one from Christmas and she's looking at that Santa Claus like he's Lee Harvey Oswald. I could live with something better than that setting on my TV."

"Message registered. She'll be back Sunday. I'll tell her you called, Alice."

"Okay, hon. Thanks."

She's sad when Jax hangs up, but relieved that Taylor and Turtle aren't dead or in trouble. She hates television, and not just because her husband has left her for one; she hates it on principle. It's like the boy who cried wolf, spreading crazy ideas faster than you can find out what's really up. If people won't talk to each other, they shouldn't count on strangers in suits and makeup to give them the straight dope.

She crosses the kitchen, stepping high over boxes of spatulas and nested mixing bowls. It looks like an estate sale, and really Alice does feel as though someone has died. She just can't think who. Out in the den, the voice of a perky young woman is talking up some kitchen gadget that will mix bread dough and slice onions and even make milk shakes. "Don't lose this chance, call now," the woman says meaningfully, and in her mind Alice dares Harland to go ahead and order it for their anniversary. She will make him an onion milk shake and hit the road.

4

LUCKY BUSTER LIVES

LUCKY AND TURTLE ARE ASLEEP in the backseat: Taylor can make out their separate snores, soprano and bass. She scrapes the dial of the car radio across miles of West Arizona static and clicks it off again. Suspended before her in the rearview mirror is an oblong view of Lucky's head rolled back on the seat, and now that it's safe to stare, she does. His long, clean hair falls like a girl's across his face, but his pale throat shows sandpaper stubble and a big Adam's apple. He's thirty-eight years old; they are a woman, man, and child in this car, like any family on the highway headed out on an errand of hope or dread. But Taylor can't see him as a man. The idea unsettles her.

From the moment of his rescue he has begged them not to tell his mother what happened. Angie Buster runs a diner in Sand Dune, Arizona, and over the phone sounded tired. Lucky has no idea that she has spoken with Taylor, or that she watched his body come out of the hole again and again on the TV news. Computer graphics turned the Hoover Dam inside-out for America, showing a red toy image of Lucky moving jerkily down into the spillway and lodging there like the protagonist of a dark-humored video game. Only Lucky and Turtle, perpetrators of the miracle, still believe they've witnessed a secret.

It was Turtle's idea to drive him home once the doctors had bandaged his sprained ankle and held him for observation. Turtle is a TV heroine now, so police officers and even doctors pay attention to her. One reporter said that Turtle's and Lucky's destinies were linked now; that according to Chinese belief, if you save someone's life you're responsible for that person forever. Taylor wonders if he was making this up. Why would you owe them more than what you'd already provided? It sounds like the slightly off-base logic you sometimes get in a fortune cookie.

She turns the car south on Arizona 93 and picks up a signal on the radio. An oldies station, they're calling it, though it's playing the Beatles. If Beatles are oldie now, where does that leave Perry Como, she wonders, and all those girl groups with their broken-heart songs and bulletproof hair? As nearly as she remembers, Taylor was in kindergarten when the Beatles first hit it big, but they persisted into her adolescence, shedding the missionary suits and skinny ties in favor of LSD and little round sunglasses. She can't identify the song but it's one of their later ones, with that odd sound they developed toward the end—as if their voices are coming from inside a metal pipe.

What did he think about for a day and a half down there? Taylor can't bring herself to imagine. Now, with his fingernails scrubbed, his red checked shirt cleaned and respectfully pressed in the hospital laundry, what he's been through seems impossible. The doctors presumed he never lost consciousness, unless he slept. From the looks of him now, he didn't, or not much.

She came so close to driving away that night. Worn down by the uniforms and beard stubble and patronizing looks, it would have been such a small thing to get back in the car and go on to Nevada. She shivers.

The Beatles give up the ghost and Elton John takes over, his honky-tonk piano chords bouncing into "Crocodile Rock." This one Taylor remembers from dances on the bleached wood floor of the Pittman High gym, with some boy or other who never could live up to her sense of celebration on those occasions. They were always too busy trying to jam a hand between two of your buttons somewhere. The song is about that exact war, and it excited the girls as much as the boys to hear it because you knew how Suzy felt when she wore her dresses—as the song says—tight. Like something no boy could ever touch. Taylor liked Elton John, his oversized glasses and preposterous shoes, laughing at himself—such a far cry from other rock stars with long limp hair and closed eyes and heads rolled back to the sounds of their own acid chords, going for the crucifixion look.

Music is all different now: Jax belongs to neither breed, the Jesuses or the Elton Johns. Now they don't just laugh at themselves but also their audience and the universe in general. Jax's wide-eyed, skinny band members wear black jeans and shirts made of torn newspapers. Irascible Babies, pleading ignorance, just wishing they could suckle forever at the breast of a pulsing sound wave.

Jax is a problem in Taylor's life, though she would never say that aloud. She feels disloyal for thinking it, even. He's the first boyfriend she's ever had who is actually funnier than he thinks he is. He is nice to Turtle to the point that it's nearly embarrassing. Jax is so laid-back it took Taylor months to figure out what was going on here: that he's crazy in love with her. Possibly that's the problem. Jax's adoration is like the gift of a huge, scuffling white rabbit held up at arm's length for her to take. Or a European vacation. Something you can never give back.

She turns southwest at the little noncity of Kingman, back toward the Colorado River or what's left of it after all those dams, a tributary robbed blind and fighting hard to make the border. Mountains rise low and purple behind the river like doctor's-office art. She'll follow the river south through Lake Havasu City, where some rich person, she has heard, actually bought the London Bridge and shipped it over block by block to stand lonely in the desert. Eventually they'll reach Sand Dune, where Angie Buster awaits her son. Taylor can call Jax from there and tell him about the new twist on their vacation.

She's not keeping close track of the radio: now it's Otis Redding singing "Dock of the Bay." This one always chokes her up. You can picture poor Otis looking out over the water, the terrible sadness in his voice suggesting he already knows he's going to end up frozen in a Wisconsin lake

Taylor follows Angie to a table near the dust-frosted window pane. Angie's hair is dyed such a dark black that she has a slightly purple scalp, like some of Jax's backup singers. She turns around suddenly and tells Taylor in a quieter voice, "I owe you for this. You just don't know, that boy means the whole world to me."

Taylor is startled by the tears in Angie's eyes and can only think to say, "Thank you." For no physical reason Taylor can work out, Angie reminds her of her own mother. It must be nothing more than the force of her love. Angie goes to retrieve Turtle and Lucky from the photographer and deliver them both to the table. Lucky looks ecstatic, and surprisingly so does Turtle.

"Everybody's real proud of you," Taylor tells her.

"I know. I saved my friend Buster." She swings her feet against the legs of her chair. Lucky reaches out and strokes Turtle's shoulder twice. Taylor thinks of the reporter's fortune-cookie prediction that Turtle's life has been changed forever.

Angie doesn't take any orders, she just brings food. Lucky leans so eagerly over his mashed potatoes that Taylor has to look away. This must be what people dislike about the retarded: they get straight down to the animal business of life, revealing it for what it is. Taylor admits to herself how hungry she is.

Angie brings over a customer named Collie Bluestone. "He's a real good rooster fighter," Angie says by way of introduction.

"No," he says modestly, sitting down. "I don't fight them. I sew them up afterward."

Taylor is intrigued by the man's mystifying profession and the scar on his neck. He's handsome in the same way Jax is, thin and knuckly. On men it works, it can be sexy. "I used to go to cockfights," she tells him. "Well, once I did. In somebody's barn, in Kentucky. On a blind date."

Collie makes an odd noise, a sort of a hiss, but he is smiling so it's apparently not a threat. "I hope your date turned out better than the chicken's."

"Not a whole lot better, but thanks. It's not too legal back there. Is it legal here? Or just kind of a hobby?"

"The fights aren't up here," he says. "They're down by the Crit reservation. That's where I live. I just come up here ever so often to check on Angie."

Taylor speculates on the relationship of Angie Buster and Collie Bluestone, and wonders briefly if Collie is Angie's chicken supplier, but decides not to ask. Turtle is eating as if she hadn't been fed since the change of seasons. Taylor is positive they had breakfast. "What kind of Indian is Crit?" she asks Collie. "I never heard of them."

Collie makes the same noise again. "C-R-I-T, it stands for Colorado River Indian Tribes, which there aren't none. It's a fake tribe made out of whoever got left out when they carved up the territory. It's like if they called everybody in a prison 'the Leavenworth family.' "

"Oh. Sorry I asked."

"Well, everybody's got to live someplace, right? There's some Hopi, Navajo, Mojave."

"And everybody gets along okay?"

"We marry each other, but we don't get along."

Angie arrives again with more food and men. She introduces the men but Taylor doesn't catch their names, only their hands to shake as they sit down. One of them wears a dog-colored cowboy hat and keeps putting his arm around Angie's waist. "Did you see that London Bridge up at Lake Havasu?" he asks.

Lucky pipes up suddenly with his cover story. "Mom, I accidentally walked on the railroad tracks to Havasu."

Angie and all the men throw their mouths open and laugh. Lucky joins in, enjoying his own joke, since that's what it turned out to be. Angie wipes her eyes and it gets very quiet.

"We didn't stop this morning to look at the bridge," Taylor says. "I've heard about it, though. Some guy really did buy it and bring it over here?"

Lucky quietly sings, "London bridges falling down."

"Some fat cat," says the man in the cowboy hat. "And here's the thing. After he bought it, he decided he had to get it cleaned. He said it cost more to clean it than to buy it."

"I had a jacket like that one time," Taylor says, feeling a certain pressure to keep the conversation going.

"Set down," cowboy hat tells Angie. Ordering people around seems to be the m.o. of Angie's Diner. "Tell them about the time Lucky run off with the Hell's Angels."

"He didn't run off with them, either." Angie crosses her arms and doesn't sit.

"I want to hear about the mules that kidnapped him in Mexico." Taylor looks uneasily at Lucky, after she's said this, but he is beaming. This is his element. The window illuminates his face, raising the color of his eyes to a gas-flame blue.

"Oh, honey, that was unbelievable," Angie says. "They told him they was going to shoot him." Taylor tries to imagine stubborn four-legged animals with guns, until Angie explains that mules are men who have something to do with drug running. "If you're anywheres near Mexico and someone shoots you for no apparent reason," she says knowledgeably, "they're a mule."

Taylor is relieved to be home in one piece. She and Jax sit up in bed with his tape of They Might Be Giants turned down low, so they'll hear when Turtle has fallen asleep in the next room. Turtle talks herself to sleep nearly every night in a quiet language no one can understand. Over the years, Taylor and Alice have had many long-distance phone calls about motherhood. Alice told her not to worry when Turtle was three and still didn't talk, or later, when she did talk but would say only the names of vegetables in long, strange lists. Alice still says there's nothing to worry about, and she has always been right before. She says Turtle is talking over the day with her personal angels.

They hear Turtle sigh and begin to hum a low, tedious song. Then they hear the clunk of her comfort object, a flashlight she calls Mary, which she has slept with since the day she found it years ago in Taylor's employer's truck.

"I missed you," Taylor tells Jax. "Compared to what I've been through lately, you seem normal."

He kisses her hair, which smells like a thunderstorm, and her shoulder, which smells like beach rocks. He tells her, "Sex will get you through times with no money better than money will get you through times with no sex."

"The thing I really missed was your jokes."

"I missed your cognitive skills," he says. "And your syntax. Honestly, that's all. Not your body. I *despise* your body." He drawls on purpose, sounding more southern than he needs to, though he can't match the hard-soft angular music of her Kentucky hills.

"Well, that's sure a load off my mind," she says, laughing, shuddering her dark hair off her shoulders without self-consciousness. She's the first woman he's ever known who doesn't give a damn how she looks, or is completely happy with the way she looks, which amounts to the same thing. Usually women are aware of complex formulas regarding how long the legs should be in relation to the waist in relation to the eyelashes—a mathematics indecipherable to men but strangely crucial to women. Taylor apparently never took the class. He wishes he could have been there when she was born, to watch the whole process of Taylor. He lies across the bed with his head in her lap, but when he realizes she's looking at his profile, turns his face away. Although he rarely sees it himself, he knows his profile is unusual and even startles people: there's no indentation at all between his forehead and the bridge of his nose. Taylor says he looks like an Egyptian Pharaoh, which is exactly what she would say, with no apologies for never having seen any actual Egyptian art. Taylor behaves as if what she believes, and what she is, should be enough for anyone.

She's not the first woman on earth to insist on his good looks; that's not why he is in love with her. Jax has broad shoulders and hands that apparently suggest possibilities. He's proud that he can reach an octave and a half on a piano like Franz Liszt; his one gift is largeness. When his band performs, women tend to give him articles of their clothing with telephone numbers inked on the elastic.

"You think she's asleep?"

Taylor shakes her head. "Not yet. She's having trouble relaxing. I learned a lot about her breathing on this trip."

"You're picking up certain character traits from your friend Lou Ann."

Lou Ann Ruiz, who is like a second mother to Turtle, tends toward an obsession with health and safety. But to her credit, Jax allows, Lou Ann is making bold changes in her life: she recently got a job at an exercise salon called Fat Chance and now wears Lycra outfits in color combinations that seem dangerous, like the poisonous frogs that inhabit the Amazon.

"Is now a good time to tell you about the phone calls?"

"What phone calls?" Taylor asks, through a heartfelt yawn.

"The approximately four thousand calls that have come in since you achieved national prominence on Monday."

"Oh, right."

"You think I'm kidding." Jax gets out of bed and rifles through the mess of music and lyrics on his desk. Sometimes, in his nightmares, everything on this desk sings at once. He comes back with a legal pad and his horn-rimmed glasses, and reads.

"Lou Ann: wants to know if you took Dramamine for Turtle because she threw up that time in the car. Lou Ann again: to tell you never mind, it was *her* son that threw up in the car."

"Lou Ann often called me before I was famous." Taylor presses her mouth against her kneecap. Sometimes when she's concentrating on something else she seems to be kissing her own knees, or the backs of her hands. Jax has tried it out in private, to see how it feels to love oneself unconsciously.

"Okay," he says, "I'm skipping all the Lou Anns." He runs his finger down the page. "Charla Rand from the *Phoenix Gazette*. Marsh Levin from the *Arizona Daily Star*. Larry Rice, photographer from the *Star*. Helga Carter from the *Fresno Bee*."

"The what? I don't believe this. What do they want?"

"The story of the year. A suspense-movie plot with endearing characters, a famous tourist landmark and a happy ending."

"Shit. Is that all of them?"

"Almost. There are five more pages."

"Skip over the *Queen Bee News* exetera."

"Check. Skip the *Queen Bee News* and the Lou Anns." He turns a couple of pages and then flips back. "Oh, your mother. She called before I'd started writing everything down. She thought she saw you on the news."

"In *Kentucky*? That can't be."

"Well, basketball season's over."

"Lord, it must have scared the bejesus out of her."

"Don't worry, I'm very good in crisis situations. I told her she was hallucinating. Then after I heard, I called her back and told her you and Turtle pulled through without a scratch."

"It's not like *we* fell down any holes."

"She won't completely believe that till she hears from you."

Taylor smiles. "I'll call her in the morning."

"She wants a new picture of Turtle. Her theory is that in the one you sent Santa Claus looks like Sirhan Sirhan."

"No, like Lee Harvey Oswald."

He looks at her, takes off his glasses and throws the notepad on the floor. "How did you know that?"

"I lived with her twenty years. I know what she'd say."

"You two ought to be in the *National Enquirer.* TELEPATHIC MOTHER-DAUGHTER DUO RECEIVE MESSAGES THROUGH FILLINGS."

"We're just close."

"*Perversering* mother-daughter duo."

"Would you please shut up? You're jealous of everything, even my mother."

"Did you and Turtle really persevere perversely?"

"I'm going to be sorry I let you keep a scrapbook."

"It's great material. Oh, and another news flash also: She's leaving her husband."

Taylor stares at Jax. "Who? My mother is leaving Harland? Where's she going? Is she coming here?"

"You didn't get the message through your fillings?"

"She's *leaving* him? Where's she going?"

"I don't know." He closes his eyes. "Not here. She sounded a little sad."

"I have to call her right now."

She shoves his head off her lap, but Jax catches her around the waist and pulls her back onto the bed. "It's two in the morning there, sweet thing. Let her sleep."

"Damn it. I *hate* time zones. Why can't they just make it the same time everywhere at once?"

"Because if they did, somewhere on earth some poor musicians would have to sleep at night and go to work in daylight."

Taylor relaxes a little against Jax, who puts his arms around her. He spreads his hands across the bony marimba of her ribs, wishing for the music they hold. "Are you in love with our garbage man?" he asks.

"Danny! Oh, pew, his truck smells like compost city."

"Uh huh. So you're saying you *would* be in love with him, if his truck smelled better."

"Jax, why do you do this?"

"I'm thinking you'll leave me, now that you're famous."

"A world-famous employee of a car-parts store."

"You're the manager. Don't sell yourself short. You don't need me."

She strokes his kneecap, which is angular and hard as a box terrapin. "Jax, honey, I never did," she says.

"I know."

"Or Danny, or Bruce Springsteen, or the man in the moon. It's nothing personal."

"I know. It's because of your mother's guiding myth."

"What's that?"

"That the women in your family need men only as a remedy for minor plumbing irritations."

"Well, maybe that's true. And I'm here in your bed anyway, how about that," she says. It is, technically, his bed; she got rid of hers in a yard sale when she and Turtle moved into Jax's tiny house at the edge of town. She tips her head back until it rests against his chin. "So will you shut up about my leaving you, and is that all the big news you have for this evening?"

"I'll show you big news," he says, delicately biting the nape of her neck. He lifts her breasts, which fit perfectly into his hands, though he knows this is no promise that he gets to keep them. A million things you can't have will fit in a human hand. He lets her go, gently. "No, that's not all. There's something else, but we can talk about it tomorrow."

Taylor's pulse jumps. "What?"

"Really, you do not want to hear about it now."

"Don't tell me what I want."

"Okay. Oprah Winfrey called."

She laughs, relieved. "Did she? I've been neglecting her and I feel awful about it."

"It's not a joke. Oprah Winfrey called. Not *Oprah,* but one of her producers, or researchers or something. They're doing a show called 'Children Who Have Saved Lives.' "

"Would you please save the hooha for your screaming fans?" She settles back against his chest.

"I agree with you, it's one of the weirder things I've heard of. They want you and Turtle to come to Chicago."

It dawns on Taylor that Jax is not making up Oprah Winfrey. "Why would we want to go to Chicago?"

"It's a happening town. You could show Turtle the Museum of Science and Industry. Since she got short-sheeted on the Grand Canyon."

"What would I say on national TV?"

"Most of the time you strike me as having no shortage. What would you *like* to say on national TV?"

"Would they let me say *anything?*"

"Well, it's not Geraldo."

"I'm serious. Could I say what I wanted to, do you think?"

"She'd probably want you to stick to the general theme of children who have saved lives."

"That's a very weird subject," Taylor points out. "How many could there be?"

"The Chinese say if you save somebody's life you're responsible for them forever."

"Somebody else told me that! I thought he was making it up. Do you think Turtle's life is changed forever?"

"Could be," Jax admits. "Not necessarily for the worse."

"I liked her the way she was."

They are quiet for a long time with their eyes looking down, listening.

Taylor says quietly, "You know what I keep going back to? Nobody believed her. They took one look at this skinny Indian kid and said, 'Well, ma'am, we don't actually have a witness.' "

"But you believed her. And Lucky Buster lives."

"I had to, Jax, I'm her mother. That part is nothing."

They both listen again. Turtle has stopped conversing with the angels.

5

THE SECRET OF TV

TAYLOR IS GETTING A LONG, hard look at someone's bald spot. He has reclined his seat to a point where he's closer than a dinner plate, maybe twelve inches from her face. The top of his head is covered with fine, almost invisible fur that lies flattened in a complicated pattern, like a little prairie swept by a tornado. It reminds Taylor of a theory Jax once told her about, that humans evolved from some sort of water ape and spent the dawn of civilization in a swamp. Streamlined hair patterns are supposed to be the proof, but Taylor wonders as she stares, Does that mean we moved through the water headfirst? Could be. Kids move through the world that way, running into things with the tops of their heads. This man has a scar up there, no doubt forgotten through the decades until now that it's lost its cover.

The pilot comes on the intercom again. He's a chatty one; right after takeoff he introduced himself as "your captain," and Turtle's eyes grew wide. She asked Taylor if he only had one hand. Now, after mulling it over the whole afternoon, it dawns on Taylor that the only captain Turtle knows about so far is Captain Hook. She may never get on a plane again without envisioning a pirate at the helm.

Captain Hook now explains they are passing over the Mississippi River, and that if he can do anything to make the passengers more comfortable they should just let him know. Frankly, although she doubts the captain can help her out here, Taylor doesn't feel comfortable being intimate with a stranger's hair loss. She doesn't even know the top of Jax's head this well. She's looked at it, but not for three and a half hours.

Turtle is finally sleeping. She seems to be coming down with a cold, and really needed a nap, but was so excited she sat for hours with her face pressed hard against the window. When the window turned icy cold, even when there was nothing to see but a vast, frosted field of clouds spread over a continent, rutted evenly as if it had been plowed, Turtle still stared. Everybody else on the plane is behaving as though they are simply sitting in chairs a little too close together, but Turtle is a child in a winged tin box seven miles above Planet Earth.

Taylor hasn't flown before either, and for the first few hours she felt the same excitement. Especially when they were taking off, and before, buckling up, watching the stewardess show how to put on a yellow oxygen mask without messing up your hair. And before that, leaving the airport: walking behind Turtle down the sloping hallway to the door of the plane, stepping across from solid ground to something unknown, furtively checking the rivets around the door, but what can you do? She has no choice but to follow her daughter into this new life she's claimed from a fortune cookie.

Chicago is tall on one side of the freeway, open sky on the other, because of the lake. Taylor never thought of Chicago as a beach town, but there they are, hundreds of people in swimsuits throwing Frisbees into the wind. It's the first week of June. She and Turtle are cruising down the freeway in a long white limousine with smoked-glass windows and baby blue velvet upholstery. As they speed away from the airport, people in other cars turn their heads to try and get a look inside this vehicle of mystery. The driver calls them both "Miss," as if they are the types to travel everywhere by limo.

It occurs to Taylor that this would be quite the line of work, driving Oprah Winfrey guests around: some would be royalty and some would be famous murderers or men with a wife in every state, and if you're only the driver you'd never know which was which. You'd have to play it safe and treat them all politely.

"This is the best-planned city in the nation," the driver explains. Turtle is glued to the window, still. "It all burned down in the great fire of October 8, 1871. Everything went. Two hundred million dollars of property damage. So they had the opportunity of starting it over from the ground up."

"I've heard of that fire," Taylor says. "I heard it was started by a cow."

"No, that is not true, that is a myth. The Great Chicago Fire was not started by a cow." He hesitates a little, and Taylor realizes she's blown their cover; bringing up the subject of livestock has put them more on the criminal than the royalty side of the fence.

"Well, it makes a good story," she says. She doesn't care if he thinks she and Turtle are serial killers. He still has to take them to their hotel.

For all this city's famous planning, the traffic is horrible. As soon as they turn away from the lake toward the tall glass buildings, they are mired in a flock of honking cars. The driver has evidently finished with the glories of his city. Once in a while as they sit there he hits the horn with his fist.

Turtle sneezes. She's got a cold, there's no getting around it. Taylor hands her a tissue out of her pocket. "How're you feeling, Toots?"

"Fine," she says, blowing her nose carefully, still looking out the window. Turtle almost never complains. Taylor is well aware of how unusual this is. If all you knew about kids came from watching the sitcoms, she thinks, you would never guess there were children on earth like Turtle.

"Mom, look." She pulls on Taylor's finger and points at a City of Chicago garbage truck, which is stalled next to them in the traffic jam. A fancy gold seal painted on the side gives it an air of magnificence. The driver smiles down at them from his perch on high. Then he raises one eyebrow and winks.

"Why'd he do that?"

"He thinks you're cute," Taylor says, "and he likes my legs. Also he probably thinks we're rich."

"But we're not, are we?"

"Nope, we're not."

"He gets to drive a better truck than Danny's."

"Definitely."

Taylor is wearing a skirt—something she's not accustomed to, but Lou Ann insisted on loaning her a nice beige suit for Oprah Winfrey. She claimed it was against some regulation to wear jeans on television. Jax got a good laugh out of that, but to his credit, he is nicer to Lou Ann than most guys would be.

Taylor gets a nervous stomach when she thinks about the taping tomorrow morning. She suspects these shows are just a way of making a spectacle out of bad things that happen to people. But Turtle really wanted to do it. She'd never understood before that actual people could appear on television. She seems to have a vague idea they will meet the Ninja Turtles.

The garbage guy is still looking. He has curly hair and a terrific smile. Taylor crosses her legs and raises her hand just a little. If he can really see in, he'll take it as a wave.

He does. He makes a small motion with his chin, indicating that she and Turtle should abandon their limo in favor of his garbage truck. Taylor gives it some thought, but decides to go ahead with Oprah.

"It's an adorable outfit," the wardrobe woman tells Taylor, "but I'm just suggesting something a little more feminine. We have this little jumper from wardrobe, see? The color would look absolutely super on the set."

Lou Ann can have the last laugh now: Oprah Winfrey's people don't want Turtle to wear her overalls on television. The overalls are brand new, bright green, perfectly decent. "That dress is ten sizes too big for Turtle," Taylor says.

"Doesn't matter. We just pin it in back, see? Nobody sees the back. That's the secret of TV—you only have to worry about what shows up front, your back can be a mess. And we'll put this bow in her hair, okay, sweetheart? She'll look super."

"She'll look younger," Taylor says. "If that's what you're going for. She'll look like a baby doll that saved somebody's life."

The woman crosses her arms and frowns. Her short, black hair looks wet and oiled, like a sea otter. The comb rakes through it stay perfectly in place. "It's going to be difficult," she says. "We'd have to run her mike wire up from the back."

"You can manage," Taylor says, knowing this can't be the problem. Men wear pants on television every day of the week. The other guests are not being harassed about wardrobe concerns. Taylor met them all in the hotel lobby this morning while they waited for the limos. There's a Cub Scout who flagged down help when his scoutmaster collapsed on their tenderfoot survival hike; a fourth-grader who saved her sister from a pit-bull attack by hitting it with a dog dish and the whole Barbie Dream Date ensemble, including the convertible; and an eleven-year-old who drove the car home when her baby-sitter passed out from multiple bee stings in a city park. Taylor feels, frankly, that the eleven-year-old showed bad judgment all around, and the other two probably just acted without thinking. Turtle is the youngest and has the best story. She doesn't see why they need to blow it out of proportion by dressing her up like Barbie's baby sister.

The small green room where they are waiting is crowded and tense. Turtle fidgets, and the wardrobe woman hovers, her raised eyebrows still pushing the question.

"What do you want to wear?" Taylor asks Turtle.

Turtle hugs herself. "This," she says.

Taylor smiles at the sea-otter woman. "Looks like she's made up her mind."

The woman pushes the purple jumper against Turtle's front, looking at Taylor. "I really think, look, don't you? It's so much more of a visual."

"My daughter said no, thank you." Turtle recoils from the bunched fabric, and Taylor narrows her eyes at the woman, who seems nevertheless to be holding her ground. A makeup man comes over at a trot. He's wearing the laced-up, tassely loafers that people call "boating shoes," even though most of them will never lay leather to a boat. Taylor wonders why everyone here seems dressed for some kind of sport—the secretaries in leggings, the camera crew in running shoes, all bustling around frowning, with nothing the least bit sporty on their agendas. It's as if they're expecting at any minute a sudden announcement: Vacation starts *now.*

"You have wonderful cheekbones, dear," the makeup man tells Taylor, and he lobs her in the face with a powder puff.

6

THIEVES OF CHILDREN

ANNAWAKE FOURKILLER LOOKS UP FROM her law briefs, startled. "Could you turn that up?"

The secretary, Jinny, automatically reaches to turn down the volume on the little TV at the end of her desk.

"No, up, please." Annawake stares with her head cocked. Her black hair is cropped so close to the nap it stands up like an exotic pelt, and her broad mouth has the complicated curves of a foreign punctuation mark, making it anyone's guess whether she's smiling or not. Jinny shrinks behind her glasses, wondering if Annawake is making a joke and she's not getting it. "It's just Oprah Winfrey," she says.

"I know. I want to hear this."

Jinny shrugs. "Okay." She stretches one blue-jeaned leg out behind her for balance as she reaches across hills of papers for the volume knob, then slumps back down to her typewriter. Mr.

Turnbo is out of the office for the afternoon so it's just the two of them, and Jinny is unsure of her relationship with Annawake. Jinny has worked here longer—she started as Franklin Turnbo's secretary-receptionist when she graduated from high school last year; Annawake only finished law school out in Phoenix a month ago, and has come back home to Oklahoma to intern here on an Indian Lawyer Training grant. Mr. Turnbo has never minded if Jinny's little TV talked quietly on the desk, as long as she gets everything typed. She's not wrapped up in the soaps, she just likes Oprah and Sally Jessy and sometimes *General Hospital*. Annawake doesn't say she minds, either, but she makes faces at Sally Jessy and calls her the blonde Puerto Rican, which makes Jinny feel guilty for perming her hair. For trying to look *yonega*, as her grandma says.

Through the front window she sees a line of dusty cars and pickup trucks pulling out of the parking lot of Cherokee Nation headquarters, heading back up the highway toward Kenwood and Locust Grove; the afternoon session of Tribal Court is over. Mr. Turnbo will be back soon and she's still behind on her work, but that's not Oprah Winfrey's fault.

"That little kid in the overalls?" Annawake asks. She is staring with her chin on her hand. "I heard somebody say she was adopted."

"Yeah. Before the first commercial Oprah introduced them as being somebody and her adopted daughter Turtle."

"Cherokee," Annawake says. "I'll bet you a Coke."

"Uhn-uh," Jinny says, "Navajo, I bet. They're from Arizona. She looks exactly like my brother's girlfriend's little girl, out in Albuquerque."

"Where in Arizona, did they say?"

"Tucson."

Annawake eyes the TV as if it had just called her a name. Jinny finds Annawake completely fascinating: she dresses like she doesn't give a hoot, in jeans and moccasins and white shirts from J. C. Penney's men's department, and she totes around a backpack held together by gray duct tape instead of a briefcase, but she has that fashion-model mouth with a deep indentation in the center of her upper lip that's hard to stop staring at. Men must want to kiss her every minute, Jinny thinks. When the perky music comes up and Oprah fades out to another commercial, Annawake takes off her glasses and rubs her eyes. "Tired," she says. "You too?"

"Yeah. Grandma's mad at my brother Woody for quitting school. Nobody's been getting much sleep at our house, except Woody. He took his bed out in the yard."

"Robert Grass didn't call yet?"

"Robert Grass! That turkey. Not since the drive-in two weeks ago."

"He will," Annawake says. "My brother Dellon knows him from the construction site over on Muskogee highway. He said Robert Grass is talking *osda* about his new girlfriend."

"Maybe she's nobody I know."

"If she's not you, you would have heard about it. Tahlequah's not that big."

"That's the truth. The whole *Nation's* not that big. Somebody all the way over to Salisaw told Grandma she'd seen me in a truck with the weediest Grass ever to come up."

Annawake smiles. "There's no getting away from the people that love you." She slides her glasses back on and takes the pencil from behind her ear to mark up the page she's reading. Jinny thinks: *You don't even know. Nobody would gossip about you, they all adore you too much, plus you have no noticeable habits other than working.* She blows a puff of air through her bangs and flips to a new page of the Arkansas River Gravel Claim. Why anyone cares this much about river gravel is beyond Jinny Redcrow.

"This Oprah show is about kids that saved people's lives," she offers Annawake as an afterthought, wondering if there's a legal angle she has missed. Annawake and Mr. Turnbo are always speaking to each other in a language Jinny types but can't read.

"Mmm-hm," Annawake says, not looking up. She's ignoring the sexy-sounding commercial and doing the smile-frown thing she does when she is reading. Annawake is known for being a super brain. Jinny went to Tahlequah High School seven years after her, and the teachers were still talking about Annawake Fourkiller like some comet that only hits Oklahoma once per century. Once at a stomp dance the chief gave her as an example of a good life path. He didn't embarrass the family by singling out her name, though of course everybody knows who he meant. But Annawake acts like *she* hasn't figured it out yet. She lives with one of her sisters-in-law in a bad little house on Blue Springs Street, and she ducks her head into the files when the good-looking guys come in making noise about their land-use papers, and she's even nice enough to ask about stupid Robert Grass. The only real problem with her is her hair is strange. She used to have long Pocahontas hair—Jinny has seen pictures in the yearbook: valedictorian, jock, president of Cherokee Pride club, nicknamed "Wide Awake Annawake"—but she cut it all off when she went away to law school. Now it's spiky and short like Jinny's little brothers', more Sinead O'Connor than Cherokee Pride. She doesn't see how Annawake can go pointing her finger at Sally Jessy Raphael.

"Can I put Arkansas River on the floor?" Annawake asks suddenly. Oprah is back, and Annawake is scooting some papers around to make room for herself on the edge of Jinny's desk.

"You can put Arkansas River in the river," Jinny says. Annawake laughs, and Jinny feels guilty for thinking bad-hair thoughts. Actually, Jinny thinks, if she had Annawake's bone structure she'd cut her hair off too, or do *something* different.

"So what's the story on that little kid?"

There are four kids: a show-off boy in a scout uniform who keeps patting the hand of his huge father; two tall, skinny white girls in braces who could be sisters; and the Indian girl in overalls.

"That white girl with her is the mom. The adopted mom."

The mother is young-looking and pretty, dressed in a nice beige suit but swinging her crossed leg like it's not her business to act like Nancy Reagan. She is telling the story of how her little girl saw a man fall down a hole in the Hoover Dam.

Annawake makes a face of pain. "Give me a break. She made up that Hoover Dam to get on the show."

"No, that was on the news. You were out there in Phoenix when it happened, didn't you see it on TV?"

"Really? Maybe. I can't think of it if I did. In law school I missed all the news that was legally uncomplicated."

"Oprah has people that check your story," Jinny says, a little defensive. She spends almost every afternoon with Oprah, and feels she can be trusted.

"You think it's true?"

Jinny shrugs. "Listen. You can tell." The woman explains that she herself didn't see the man fall down the hole, only Turtle did. For two whole days no one else believed it, but she did, and they kept trying to get help.

"*National Enquirer* for sure," Annawake says. "She read it in the grocery store."

Oprah is talking to the mother now, whose name is something Taylor. "I can see there's a wonderful bond between you and your daughter. Can't you see it?" Oprah turns around, her loose rayon jacket swirling, and the studio audience says Yes, they can. She asks, "You adopted her when she was how old, two?"

"Probably she was three," the mother says. "We don't know for sure. She was abused and hadn't been growing right before I got her. It was kind of an unusual situation. Somebody just gave her to me."

"Gave her to you?"

"Left her in my car."

Oprah makes one of her funny big-eyed faces at the camera. "You all hear that?" she asks in a deeper, down-home voice. "*Check your car* before you drive out of the parking lot."

Annawake looks at Jinny with raised eyebrows, and asks the TV set, "Where?"

"I'd just stopped for a cup of coffee," the mother says, and seems a little surprised when the audience laughs. *No way is she making this story up,* Jinny thinks. "I was on a trip across the country. I'd just left home and was headed out West. The funny part about it is, all the time I was growing up in Kentucky my main goal was to not get pregnant. All my girlfriends had these babies up to their ears."

"But that wasn't going to happen to you," says Oprah.

"No, ma'am."

"And your first day out, somebody gives you a baby."

"Second day out," she says, and the audience laughs again. With Annawake watching, Jinny feels slightly embarrassed about the low laugh threshold of Oprah's studio audience.

"You could have walked away. Why did you take her?" Oprah asks in a caring way.

"Seeing as how it's against the law," Annawake adds.

"Which law?" Jinny asks, surprised.

"Indian Child Welfare Act. You can't adopt an Indian kid without tribal permission."

Franklin Turnbo has come in and hung up his jacket. Annawake motions him over, still concentrating on the black-and-white screen. The three of them watch the mother push her hair out of her eyes, thinking. She seems unaware that she's on TV—unlike the Cub Scout, who keeps bobbing on the edge of his chair and raising his hand as if he knows the answer.

"I felt like I *had* to take her," the mother finally answers. "This woman just plunked her down on the seat of my car and looked at me and said, 'Take her.' I said, 'Where do you want me to take her?' I thought she needed a ride somewhere."

Finally the audience is completely quiet.

"Take who?" Franklin Turnbo asks.

"That Cherokee kid," Annawake says, nodding at the screen. The mother looks down at the little girl and then back at Oprah. "The woman told me Turtle's mother was dead, and that somebody had been hurting Turtle. She was the dead mother's sister, and it looked like somebody'd been hurting her too. Then she got in this truck with no lights, and drove off. It was the middle of the night. At the time I felt like there was nothing else in the world I could do but take the baby. I'd been driving forty-eight hours. I guess my judgment was impaired."

The audience laughs, uneasily. The little girl is staring at Oprah and clutching a fistful of her mother's skirt. The mother carefully moves the child's hand into one of hers. "The next summer I went back and legally adopted her."

"Can't be," says Annawake. "Not legally."

Oprah asks, "Where did all this happen?"

"Oklahoma, Indian country. Turtle's Cherokee."

Annawake bangs the desk like a judge, bringing the court to order.

The sky has gone dishwater gray. There could be rain on this west wind, Annawake thinks. But it's Third Saturday, stomp-dance night, and old people love to tell you that rain always holds back till the dancing is over. They're mostly right. She parks her truck, gathers up her bouquet of blue and white papers from the office, and wonders briefly what ought to be done about the aluminum siding that is buckling on the north side of the house. With two free fingers she forks up the handlebars of a tricycle from the front walk and parks it out of harm's way on the porch.

"*Siyo,*" she says, latching the screen door to keep kids in and dogs out. Her brother and sister-in-law are kneeling on the kitchen floor and return her greeting without looking up. They must be on speaking terms this week: they're hammering the legs back onto the old pine dining table, and it's not easy to take on a project like that without communicating.

Annawake watches the two of them, united for once as they both concentrate on keeping the table leg on straight while Dellon drives the nail. His thick braid swings like a bell rope as he hammers, and their heads almost touch. "Got her?" he asks, and Millie nods, her crinkled perm softly brushing Dellon's shining black crown. They were married less than a year and have been divorced for five, but it hasn't interfered with their rate of producing children. When the table leg is secure, Millie rolls sideways and takes hold of the lip of the sink. Annawake takes her other hand and pulls her up.

"Seems like you take one month longer with every baby," Dellon says, and Annawake laughs because it's true: the first was premature, the second right on time, the third one three weeks late, and this one seems to have staked Millie's ample territory for its homestead.

"Don't say that out loud, he'll hear you." Millie leans over her stomach and tells it, "You're coming out of there this weekend, you hear? If you go any longer past due you're walking home from the hospital yourself."

Annawake gets a soda out of the refrigerator and sits in a chair, moccasins together, facing the upside-down table. "Is this thing going to live?"

"It'll never walk again," Dellon says, squatting on his heels. He shrugs his braid back over the great round loaf of his shoulder and gives the table leg a couple of trial knocks with the hammer. He grins up at his little sister. "You scalp the cowboys today?"

"I did my best."

"Don't make fun of Annawake's job, Dell," Millie says, turning her back on them, running water into a big aluminum kettle. The sun shining through her shocked hair reveals the perfect globe of her skull.

"I never make fun of Annawake. She'd beat me up."

"Dad, let's go." Baby Dellon, who is almost six and hates to be called Baby Dellon, runs into the kitchen with a football helmet on.

Dellon stands up and puts a hammerlock on Annawake's neck from behind. "When you getting married, beautiful?" he asks.

"When Gabe says he'll come to my wedding." She feels Dellon's body slump against her back, and she realizes she said what she did just to feel that slack sadness in another person. She's the only one who will still say their brother Gabriel's name.

"Leave her alone," Millie says, shifting her heavy kettle onto the stove. "Getting married's not what it's cranked up to be. What time you bringing Baby Dellon back?"

"Tomorrow noon, if we're not too hungover."

"I'm going to kill you one of these days."

"I'm not Baby Dellon, I'm Batman," says Baby Dellon, and they are out the door.

"I'm going to kill him one of these days."

"He's a good dad," Annawake says, setting the table back on its feet, wondering if it might give itself a dignified shake and walk off, like a turtle. "He won't be drinking at a stomp dance. He wouldn't even get into the stomp grounds if he was."

Millie laughs. "Did you ever hear what happened on our first date?"

"You went to a stomp dance."

"That's how Dellon tells it. If I told you the real story he'd shoot me." Millie leans against the counter, smiling. Her bunched print skirt hangs down from her waist like a dust ruffle on a bed. She brushes crimped wires of hair from her eyes, and Annawake knows she's going to tell the story.

"We were up in the mountains and it was hot, and Dellon wanted to have a beer. I knew there was the dance that night so I wasn't going to drink, but he did anyway. We had a fight, and later on we both went to the dance, but not together. I was in the inside circle wearing the turtle shells, so here comes Dellon, dancing right in the next circle, trying to get my eye. Next thing I hear him say, 'Uh-oh, here comes the fuzz.' Ledger tapped him on the shoulder and he had to leave. He'd just had one beer, but Ledger knew. He can spot it a mile away."

"Tell me about it. I lived through most of my teenage years under Uncle Ledger's eagle eye."

"But you had nothing to worry about, you were Miss Perfect," Millie says, wagging her stirring spoon at Annawake.

"Well, of course. I never had a chance." Annawake knocks back her soda.

"You had to make up for your wild brothers," Millie says, grinning. "I should have known right there and then not to marry him."

A Mason jar on the counter at Millie's elbow is crammed with daisies and wild phlox the kids have picked by the road somewhere; Annawake reaches for the jar and sets it in the exact center of the table. "I think he wishes you'd trust him more with the kids."

"I trust him. But you still have to tell him what to do."

Millie's youngest, Annie, all big dark eyes and belly, stands naked in the doorway. Annawake jumps up from her chair. "Whoah, let's get a diaper on you, baby doll, before we get puddles."

"It's okay, I decided to get her started on potty training today. Figured it's easier to let her run around that way. Put her out in the yard every hour, like a pup."

"Millie!"

"I'm kidding. Annie, go show Annawake your potty."

Annie disappears.

"You're not going back to the office, are you? On Third Saturday?"

Annawake sighs. "I'm thinking about it. There's this wild goose I'm chasing down. An illegal adoption."

"Forget it. Whatever it is will keep."

"I don't know."

Annie reappears in the door with a stuffed bear twice her size. "Pa-pa," she says.

"You better learn the difference between a teddy bear and a potty seat," Millie says. "Your time's about up as baby of the family."

Annie drops the bear on its head and climbs onto Annawake's lap.

Annawake laces her fingers together over the child's naked belly, which has the rubbery firmness of a hard-boiled egg. "Dellon hates it when I bring up Gabe," she tells Millie's back.

"I don't think Dell was ever as close to him as you are. You're his twin. Dell was half grown before you two were born."

"They're still brothers."

"Mm," she says. She dumps a package of macaroni into the pot of boiling water. "But now he's got his own kids to worry about."

"What difference does that make?"

Millie rocks her body to the table and carefully sits down. "None, that's not what it is. He hates it when you bring up Gabe, because he's the oldest and he thinks he should have done something to keep the family from getting torn up."

Annawake looks at Millie's tired face. The skin under her eyes looks bruised, the way it gets with every pregnancy. The things people go through for love. "It's not his fault, what happened."

"Not yours, either, Annawake, and look at you. I think it's great you went to law school and everything. But you don't ever stop."

The egg of Annie slides through Annawake's hold and vanishes again.

"I'm not blaming myself for Gabe."

"If you say so. Seems to me like all of you do. Like you're all married to him, some way."

They both listen to the small, steady sounds of children in other parts of the house. Annie comes back to the kitchen again, this time dragging her white potty seat. "Bear," she says.

"What would you do," Annawake asks Millie, "if you found out somebody was trying to take a Cherokee kid out of the Nation?"

"It's a whole different thing, asking me that now. You were little when they took Gabriel. I'm not little."

"That's what I mean. If it happened right now, what would you do?"

Millie pulls a bedraggled daisy out of the Mason jar and twirls its stem between her thumb and fingers. "It can't happen now. That's what we've got people like you for, isn't it? To watch out for the kids."

Annawake feels the weight of this confidence exactly as if Millie had lovingly sat down upon her chest.

* * *

Tahlequah is a town that might as well roll up its sidewalks at sunset. Annawake knows what night life there is—the stray dogs stealthily marking streetside oaks, and the bootleg liquor houses where music from parked cars stakes an otherworldly claim on the night air. She's walked these streets after dark since high school, pacing the length of her loneliness, Annawake the perfectly admired untouchable. Tonight she has nearly finished her circular route home. Her restlessness had no destination until just now, when she thought of a shoebox of old things she stashed in Millie's carport shed years ago, before she left for Phoenix. The box seemed empty at the time; the only thing of any value at all was the gold locket her mother used to wear for luck. But tonight she could use the company of family secrets. She turns up Blue Spring Street, finding her way by moonlight.

The back shed has a metal door that complains when she scrapes it open. She snaps the chain of the overhead bulb at the same moment a thin slice of white cat, an antishadow, slips past her legs. "Hi, little ugly," she tells it. The cat skits away and turns its head far sideways like a bird to look at Annawake. It's been hanging around for a week or two—Millie even put out a can of tuna for it, and now the can is empty but the cat has nothing to show for it, still just ears and bones. Annawake feels guilty for getting its hopes up. In the pocket of her backpack she finds half a hard peanut candy bar degenerating to sand. "Come on," she says, holding out the candy on her flat palm. The cat watches her with its head oddly tipped; it might be blind in one eye. It makes no move to come to her, but when she sets the candy bar on the doorsill the cat makes a predatory leap, holding the candy down with its paws, making cracking sounds as it jerks its tiny head up and down, laboring over the peanuts. It's pitiful food for a carnivore. With one finger Annawake tentatively strokes its back. The cat allows this, but its little back is nothing. A hammock of fur slung between shoulder blades.

She finds her shoebox wedged under a pile of Millie's baby equipment waiting to make its comeback. Annawake sits cross-legged on the floor with the box on her lap, sorting its treasures with her slender fingers. She finds the locket and works the catch gently to open it. Inside is a photograph of her mother and father in front of the old brick Cherokee County courthouse on the day they married. Her mother's hair is blowing across her eyes, and she looks worried. She's already carrying the beginnings of a boy whose name will be Soldier, who will die before he's old enough to fight back.

Annawake closes the locket and tucks it into her pocket. She doesn't want to jinx it, but she seriously doubts its power. Her mother was wearing it the day she met her husband and thereafter believed in it so thoroughly she wouldn't go anywhere important—not to a baptism or a funeral or even the landlord's to borrow another month—without it. It's difficult, though, for Annawake to picture the more luckless version of that life.

She wishes her mother had left her something that held more promise for blessing her decisions: a beaded medicine pouch with oak leaves inside, or ash from a ceremonial fire. But there's no chance; all the ceremony is on her father's side of the family. Her mother would have called anything of that nature a piece of junk. Annawake smiles a little, hearing her mother's profound Okie accent say "*a pace of ju-unk.*" Bonnie Fourkiller was a die-trying acculturated Cherokee, like most of her generation, who chose the Indian Baptist Church over stomp dances and never wore moccasins in her life. She owned one pair of nylons at a time, throughout her lifetime, each folded carefully into the same piece of tissue paper that had harbored all its forebears.

Annawake leafs through other mementoes in the box. A photo of Redbird, her dog, taken in front of their house in Kenwood. Several other shots of her Uncle Ledger's shantyboat on Tenkiller Lake, where she and her four brothers lived out most summers until they were old enough for more productive employment. She finds a picture of herself and Gabe on the wide porch of the shantyboat, wearing baggy cut-off jeans and dumb-kid smiles, and there goes all their ragged laundry strung from the porch posts to the willow trees. The lard buckets were strung up high on poles, out of reach of the notorious thieving armies of raccoons that ran the riverbanks at night. Uncle Ledger claimed the raccoons would steal anything, even a child, but Annawake could never see the point in that. Children were the one thing you could always have plenty of. She'd had no idea.

She and Gabriel passed the months on Ledger's shantyboat with their hearts in their throats, dreading the end of summer. Gabe, her roommate in the before-life, who followed her out the birth door and right through childhood. Sweet Gabe, who was stolen from the family and can't find his way home. She holds the photo as close as her eyes will focus, and drinks the frightening liquor of memory: an A-frame of twins leaning on themselves, elbows around each other's necks. When Annawake runs she can feel the stitch in her side where the invisible wound closed over, the place where they tore him out. How would it have been to go through high school with Gabe? To walk into adulthood? To have had that permanent date, instead of being the Only. The perfect lonely heart. Two hearts, they became, separated by the Texas Panhandle and a great plain of want.

She turns the photos facedown and glances through other things. Letters from her brothers and Uncle Ledger, a photo of someone's new baby. And the family inheritance: a very old book of medicine incantations written by her grandfather in the curly Cherokee alphabet Annawake wishes she could read. She still speaks Cherokee in her dreams sometimes, but never learned to write it. By the time she was six, they only taught English in school.

With her fingertips she delicately unfolds another old document and is surprised to recognize a fragile, creased magazine ad, black and white, showing a smiling young woman wearing a halo of flowers and holding up a soft drink under the sign outside their town. WELCOME TO HEAVEN, the sign in the ad declared, so everybody in America could laugh at the notion of finding heaven in eastern Oklahoma, she supposes. The ad is older than Annawake—the woman was a friend of her mother's, Sugar Hornbuckle. The picture made her famous for a time.

The cat is back at the door, staring in.

"No, you go on now. I'm not a reliable source."

She puts the photographs away. She should have taken these things to school with her. In that air-conditioned universe of mute law books she was terrified that she might someday fail to recognize her own life. You can't just go through life feeding cats, pretending you're not one of the needy yourself. Annawake has spent years becoming schooled in injustices and knows every one by name, but is still afraid she could forget the face.

7

A WORLD OF FREE BREAKFAST

THE WORDS ON THE PAGE in front of Franklin Turnbo have disappeared. He stares at the front door of his office and sees a little forest of African violets there, leafy and leggy and growing out of their pots, heading for the light as if they intend to walk once they get out there. A bright yellow eye blinks in the center of each purple flower. The front office space where Jinny and Annawake work is overgrown with plants as healthy as children: a huge rubber tree slouches at ceiling level like a too-tall girl, and something with small leaves spreads itself flat-handed against the storefront window. Jinny brings them in and tends them, Franklin supposes. He feels sure he's never seen the plants before this moment, although he could have been hanging his hat and coat on the rubber tree for months, for all he knows. As usual, the place is being taken over benignly by women, without his notice.

The front door jingles and Pollie Turnbo brushes past the violets. She comes into her husband's office cubicle and sets a basket on his desk. "I made bean bread, it's still warm," she says, breathless as if she herself were fresh from the oven.

Franklin never makes it home for dinner on Monday nights, though their ritual is that he pretends he'll try, and she pretends she just happened to be passing by his office with food in hand. He stands up to kiss Pollie. Her hair is coming loose at the back of her neck and her eyes are bright, in a hurry. She looks like the African violets. Franklin wishes Pollie would stay and talk, but she won't.

"I have to get out there and keep the boys from running under cars," she says, as if the boys had a plan to do that.

He looks into the basket after she's gone. Bean bread, pork chops, much more than he can eat. Pollie misses him these days; he is working too much, and it's her way to try to make up for every loss with food. She still cooks all the old-fashioned things that take more time than most women have had for decades. She learned from her mother, a full-blooded Cherokee, who grew up around Kenwood and never learned English. Franklin's mother is full-blood too, but his father is white, and Franklin grew up in Muskogee. His mother served time in the kitchen only at Christmas and when it was her turn for the PTA bake sales. Franklin never gave two thoughts to being Cherokee until he began to study Native American Law—like many his age, he's a born-again Indian. He laughs at this. Annawake would like him better if he had that title on a little plaque on his desk.

Thinking of Annawake brings the return of his dread. He leans out his door and asks her to come into his office. Franklin already knows what she is going to do, but has to make the show of talking her out of it.

"Would you like something to eat? Pollie makes this bread."

Annawake shakes her head. "Thanks, Jinny just brought me a Big Mac, and like a fool I ate it. I should have waited."

"No baby at your house yet?"

Annawake smiles and shakes her head. "We think it's waiting for a new administration."

She breaks off a slice of bean bread anyway, and Franklin uses the silence to wrestle his doubts. The AILTP is paying her to work in his office and learn from him, but he feels like an ungenuine article—a new car put together from the parts of a lot of old ones and given a fresh coat of paint. A born-again Indian lawyer. Annawake learned about truth from her old uncle, who, Franklin has heard, comes from a medicine family and lives on a houseboat on Tenkiller and shoots squirrel with a blowgun.

Franklin opens his mouth for a long time before talking, and then starts slowly, the way he would get into ice water if he had to.

"This case you've opened. You have to have something on a birth parent," he tells her.

Annawake slaps crumbs off her hands and leans forward, her eyes alive. "Okay, but look. In the case of Mississippi Band of Choctaw *versus* Holyfield, the mother voluntarily gave her children to the white couple. The children had never even lived on the reservation. And the Supreme Court *still* voided that adoption." Annawake apparently has learned enough white-lawyer ways to leap into ice water without flinching.

"And how does that apply here? In that case, both birth parents were known and involved."

She lifts her chin a little. Annawake always enunciates her words as if she can taste each one and there is nothing else left to eat. "The birth mother gave the children up, but her choice was overruled."

"Meaning?"

"It shows the spirit of the law. The Indian Child Welfare Act is supposed to protect the interests of the Indian community in keeping its children. It's not supposed to be defeatable by the actions of individual tribe members."

Franklin waits until there is a question, and Annawake finds it. "So why do we need a birth parent?"

"The Supreme Court recognized that the tribal court had exclusive jurisdiction over that adoption, you're right," he says, correcting her as tactfully as a knife touching up a pencil point. The Holyfield decision was handed down just weeks ago, and Annawake appears to have memorized it. "But if I'm remembering it right, that birth mother was domiciled on the Choctaw reservation, making the child a tribe member. In this case, we have no idea whether this child falls under our jurisdiction. You don't have a domiciled parent or an enrolled parent because you don't have a parent."

"I have a mystery parent. Two of them. The transfer of custody was witnessed by a notary in Oklahoma City, who had no business with this kind of placement. The parents are listed as Steven and Hope Two-Two, allegedly Cherokees but not enrolled, also not enrolled Social Security–paying citizens of the U.S.A."

Franklin's eyebrows rise. "You found all that?"

"It was Jinny Redcrow's big moment. She got to call up Oprah Winfrey on official business. The researchers were pretty helpful with i.d. and background. And the United States government is always eager to be of assistance, naturally."

He doesn't smile. "You still don't have anything that makes it officially our business."

Annawake touches her fingertips together, making a little fish basket of her hands, and looks into it. Sometimes she mentions her spirit guide, a thing Franklin Turnbo can only half understand. She is so quick she seems guided by racehorses or the fox that runs ahead of the dogs.

"You heard the mother on TV, right? Her story was that on her way out to Arizona she picked up this baby, who is obviously Native American, in Cherokee territory, from the sister of its dead mother. But in the official records we have consent-to-adoption forms filed by two living parents with invented names. I'd say it's incumbent on the mother to prove it's *not* our business."

"You seem angry," he says.

She looks surprised, then says, "Well, yeah. Maybe. All the housewives watching TV last Friday saw that our kids can be picked up as souvenirs."

"Like your brother was."

Her eyes don't register any change. She says only, "I'm asking you if we could make a case for vacating an improperly conducted adoption."

"And then what?"

"And then we could work with Cherokee Nation Child Welfare Services to find a proper placement."

"Are you getting ahead of yourself?"

"Okay, or to evaluate the existing placement, first. But that should all be the tribe's decision. That baby should never have been taken out."

Franklin Turnbo leans back in his chair and sighs like a punctured air mattress. Annawake respectfully waits for him to run out of air.

"Annawake, I admire your energy. I wish I had it. But we have child-welfare problems filed in this office that could keep us all busy till I personally am old and gray. And then there are the land-use disputes and civil rights cases and the divorces and the drunks and the disorderlies. And all the people trying to hold on to what little there is left."

Annawake makes a basket with her hands again, and waits for the question.

"You've gone to school, and now you've come back to fight for your tribe. Who's going to do this work if you're riding your white horse around, gathering up lost children?"

"Don't you think there's a hole in somebody's heart because that child is gone? Did you *ever* hear of a Cherokee child that nobody cared about?"

"But somebody cares about her now, too. That mother who found her."

Annawake's eyes register a cloud of doubt, but she asks, "Finders keepers? Is that fair?"

"Not for wallets. Maybe for kids."

"You and I could have been lost children. I very nearly was. What would you be, without the tribe?"

Franklin, avoiding her eyes, looks out his office window, which reveals the highway to Muskogee. Along with the sound of tanker trucks there is the crazy music of a meadowlark on a telephone wire. Franklin has a powerful, physical memory of the time he ran out of gas on I-40 at age nineteen, a mixed-up kid playing hooky from university, driving home to see his mother. He coasted into a Chevron station laughing at his good luck. It took him a minute to realize the place was boarded up, the nozzles padlocked to the pumps. All around him were fields of oil derricks, and he was on empty. But the fields were so beautiful, and a meadowlark above him on the wire was singing its head off, and Franklin still couldn't stop laughing at his good luck.

She asks, "What did you mean when you said, trying to hang on to what little there is left? You think we're that pitiful?"

Franklin is embarrassed, and reaches for his meadowlark: the memory, at least, of right-mindedness. "I used to feel about this place the way you do," he says. "That the Nation is spiritually indestructible, because the birds in the woods don't care who owns the title to the land. And you're right, belonging to this tribe gave me a reason to stop chasing girls and show up for Judicial Process classes. But I've been a lawyer so long now I mainly just see how people fight and things get used up."

Annawake stares at him, and Franklin wishes she were less beautiful. A treacherous thought, for many different reasons. "It's such a terrible long shot," he says. "There may be nothing at all, no relatives, no proof."

"I know," Annawake says gently, the same way Pollie would, the way women talk to men: I know, honey. Relax.

"You'll probably lose what you put into it," he tells her. "I want to give you free rein, but it's also my business to look after the investments of time in this office."

"The Native American Law conference starts on the fifteenth, so I have to be in Tucson anyway, to give my paper. That's where she lives, Tucson. I can just go by and talk to the mother, see what her story is. No big investment."

"No matter what her story is, a lot of hearts are involved."

"I know," Annawake says again, but this is one thing Franklin doesn't believe she can truly know. She isn't a mother.

"Can you tell me why you're sure this is the best thing?"

She presses her curved lips together, thinking. "In law school I slept in the library pretty often. There was a couch in the women's lounge. After I pass my bar exams they're probably going to put up a plaque there. The Annawake Fourkiller Couch."

Franklin smiles. He finds he can picture it.

"People thought my life was so bleak. And I guess it was, so far from home, hearing the ambulances run by all night to the hospital, somebody cracked up or beat up or old and dumped out by their family, and laws jumping up and down in my head. But I always dreamed about the water in Tenkiller. All those perch down there you could catch, any time, you know? A world of free breakfast, waiting to help get you into another day. I've never been without that. Have you?"

"No," he admits. Whether or not he knew it, he was always Cherokee.

The fish were down there, for him as much as for Annawake.

"Who's going to tell that little girl who she is?"

Franklin wants to say, "She will have other things," but he can't know this for certain. Franklin wears a Seiko watch and looks as Cherokee as Will Rogers or Elvis Presley or the eighty thousand mixed-blood members of his Nation, yet he knows he isn't white because he can't think of one single generalization about white people that he knows to be true. He can think of half a dozen about Cherokees: They're good to their mothers. They know what's planted in their yards. They give money to their relatives, whether or not they're going to use it wisely. He rotates his chair a little. On his desk is an ugly little duck-shaped paper-clip holder his kids gave him as a present. He told Annawake once that it was his spirit guide. She didn't laugh.

"Okay," he says finally, "I trust your judgment on where to go with this."

Annawake's mouth moves into its most irresistible presentation, the strange upside-down grin. Her eyes are laughing, not at him, but at something. Crazy chances. "Thanks, boss," she says, standing up, touching his desk. "While I'm in Arizona I'll see if I can find me a big white horse."

8

A MORE PERFECT UNION

TAYLOR SITS ON THE FRONT porch steps, hugging her knees, glowering at the indifferent apricot tree. It's an old knotty thing planted long ago when the house was new, and rarely bears anymore. But this summer it has hit on some prolific internal cycle to bring the neighborhood a bonanza of apricots—and birds.

"If they'd all get together and eat the fruit off one side of the tree, I wouldn't grudge them," she tells Lou Ann. "But they just peck a little hole in each one and wreck it."

Lou Ann looks mournful in spite of her outfit of lime-green Lycra. In ten minutes she has to go lead the Saturday-morning Phenomenal Abdominals class at Fat Chance. She's come over to Taylor's porch to wait for her ride. "I thought Jax was going to make a scarecrow," she says.

"He did." Taylor points at a cardboard cutout of a great horned owl in the top of the tree. It has realistic eyes and a good deal of feather detail, but is hard to recognize because of all the finches perched on it.

"Poor Turtle," says Lou Ann, sadly.

"This kills me. Have you ever seen her make a fuss before over something to eat, *ever,* before this? And now all of a sudden she loves apricots. But she won't eat one if it's got a hole pecked in it."

"I don't blame her, Taylor. Who wants to eat after a bird? There's probably bird diseases."

Cicadas scream brightly from the thorn scrub around the house. It's a shimmering day, headed for a hundred degrees. Taylor picks up a rock and throws it through the center of the apricot tree, raising a small commotion of brown feathers. They immediately settle again. The birds turn their heads sideways, wet beaks shining, bead eyes fixed on Taylor. Then they return to the duty of gorging themselves.

"Granny Logan used to say she was going to take my school picture and set it out in the cornfield to scare the crows."

"Your Granny Logan ought to be shot," Taylor suggests.

"Too late, she's dead." Lou Ann puts her hands behind her neck and knocks off a few quick sit-ups on the floor of the porch. Her curtain of bobbed blond hair flaps against the lime-colored sweatband. "I should get Cameron ... to come over here and ... stand under the tree," she puffs between sit-ups. "That'd scare them off."

Cameron John is Lou Ann's recurring boyfriend, and it's a fact that he is scary in several ways. He has dreadlocks down to his waist, for example, and a Doberman pinscher with gold earrings in one of its ears. But Taylor expects the birds would perceive Cameron's true nature and flock to him like St. Francis of Assisi. She can picture his dreadlocks covered with sparrows. She tosses another rock just as her neighbor, Mr. Gundelsberger, comes out of his house across the way. The rock lands near his feet. He stops short with his heels together, looks at the rock in an exaggerated way, then pulls his handkerchief out of the pocket of his gray flannel pants and waves it over his head.

"Peace," he shouts at Taylor. "No more the war."

"It's a war against the birds, Mr. G.," Taylor says. "They're winning."

He comes over and stands directly under the tree, shading his eyes and peering up into the branches. "Ach," he says. "What you need is a rahdio in the tree."

"A rodeo?" Lou Ann asks, incredulous. Her ex-husband was a rodeo rider. She could picture him roping birds, he was that small-minded.

"No, a *rahdio.*" Mr. Gundelsberger holds his fist against his ear with one finger pointed up. "Transistor."

"A radio!" Lou Ann and Taylor say at the same time. Taylor asks, "Really?"

"Rock and roll," Mr. Gundelsberger says, nodding firmly. "You try it, you will see. Rock and roll will keep da birds off da peach."

Lou Ann grabs her bag and sprints down the stone steps in her waffle-soled cross trainers. She waves at Taylor as she and Mr. Gundelsberger pull out of the drive in his Volvo. He often gives her a ride downtown, since his jeweler's shop is only two blocks from Fat Chance.

Mr. G. moved in just a few months ago. His daughter, a locally famous artist who goes by the name of Gundi, has for years owned this whole little colony of falling-down stone houses in the desert at the edge of town. In bygone days it was a ranch; the gravel drive that leads uphill from the main road is still marked with an iron archway that reads RANCHO COPO. The first time Jax brought her out here, they sat on his roof and he told Taylor a wild tale about fertility rites and naming the ranch Copo to get the cows to copulate. Since then she's discovered it means "Ranch of the Snowflake," which frankly makes less sense than cow copulation. But it's an enviable place to live. Taylor heard of it even before she met Jax. People get on waiting lists to move out here, once they've been approved by Gundi.

Gundi lives in the big hilltop house, where she displays her huge abstract paintings on the stone walls of what was once the ranch hands' dining hall. All the other houses are small and strange: some have no heating or cooling; one has an outdoor bathroom. Jax's is tiny but has a weird stone tower on its southern end. The places rent for almost nothing. Taylor has noticed that a lot of the people who live here are musicians, or have Ph.D.s in odd things.

Before Rancho Copo, Taylor and Turtle lived downtown in a more conventional rundown house with Lou Ann and her baby. Lou Ann took them in when they first arrived in Tucson, and Taylor still feels a debt. She wouldn't move in with Jax until Gundi had also approved Lou Ann as Rancho Copo material.

Taylor goes in the house and rummages through the studio Jax has created in his bell tower. He says the acoustics are Christian. There isn't a lot of floor space, but the shelves on the four narrow walls go all the way up. She drags the ladder from wall to wall, certain that in all this mess of electronics he must have a transistor radio, but she can't find one. She brings down a portable tape player instead, and one of Jax's demo tapes. She's decided to try out the Irascible Babies on a new audience.

Annawake bumps up the long gravel drive in her rented car until she's stopped by the sight of a woman in a tree. She can't be sure from the legs that it's the same woman she saw on Oprah Winfrey, but the address seems right so she parks and gets out. The ground is covered with spoiled fruits and hard pits that hurt the soles of her feet through her moccasins. She shouts into the branches, "Hello, I'm looking for Taylor Greer."

"You've found her, and she's up a tree." Taylor is using a rope to attach a boom box to an upper limb. "You just stay right there. To tell you the truth I prefer the ground."

A thunderous bass line begins to pound through the leaves. Annawake watches the woman's sneakers step down the cross-hatched ladder of limbs, then hang for a second, then drop. At ground level she's a few inches shorter than Annawake and maybe a few years younger, with long brown hair and unsuspicious eyes. She slaps the thighs of her jeans a few times, looks at the palm of her right hand, and extends it.

"Annawake Fourkiller," Annawake says, shaking Taylor's hand. "I'm from Oklahoma, in town for a professional meeting. You've got some pretty country out here."

Taylor smiles at the mountains, which at this hour of the morning look genuinely purple. "Isn't it? Before I came here I didn't expect so many trees. The only difference between here and anywhere else is that here everything's got thorns."

"Tough life in the desert, I guess. Be prickly or be eaten."

Taylor has to raise her voice now to compete with Jax, who is singing loudly from the treetops. "You want to talk? Come in and I'll shut the door so we can hear ourselves think."

Annawake follows Taylor inside, through a narrow stone hallway that barely accommodates an upright piano, which they squeeze past into the kitchen. The walls there are cool slant faces of slate. Annawake sits at a wooden table, whose legs are painted four different colors; she thinks of Millie and Dell fixing the table at home, and the new baby ruling the roost now. Taylor is putting water on for coffee.

"So, what did you kill four of, if I may ask?"

Annawake smiles. This is the woman she saw on TV—she recognizes the confidence. "It's a pretty common Cherokee surname."

"Yeah? Is there a story?"

"The story is, when my great-great-grandfather first encountered English-speaking people, that's the name he got. He had four kids, so he'd carved four notches in his rifle barrel—it was something they did back then. Out of pride, I guess, or maybe to help remind them how much game to bring home every day. But the white guys took it to mean he'd shot four men." Annawake glances at Taylor. "I guess Grandpa never set them straight."

Taylor smiles, catching the slender, almost dangerous thing that has passed between them. She clatters coffee mugs and pours black grounds into the filter. "Your accent makes me homesick. I know it's Okie, but to me it doesn't sound that far off from Kentucky."

"I was just thinking that," Annawake says. "You sound like home to me. Almost. There's a difference but I can't name it."

Taylor stands by the stove and for a while neither woman speaks. Taylor takes in Annawake's appearance: her black brush of hair all seems to radiate out from a single point, the widow's peak in her forehead. Her skin is a beautiful pottery color you want to touch, like Turtle's. She's wearing a maroon cotton shirt with blue satin ribbons stitched on the yoke and shoulder seams. Taylor fiddles with the gas burner. They listen to a long guitar riff and Jax's voice coming from outside:

"Big boys ... play games. Their toys ... follow me home. Big boys play games, big bang, you're gone ..."

Annawake raises an eyebrow.

"That's my boyfriend's band." Taylor looks out the window. "Hey, it's working. No birds."

"Is this some kind of experiment?"

Taylor laughs. "You must think I'm cracked. I'm trying to keep the birds out of the apricot tree. My little girl likes apricots more than anything living or dead, and she's the kind of kid that just doesn't ask for much. I've been going out of my head trying to think how to get the birds out of the fruit."

"My grandma planted mulberry trees next to her peach trees. The birds liked the mulberries better. They'd sit in the mulberry and laugh, thinking they were getting away with something good, and leave all the peaches for us."

"No kidding," Taylor says. "Wish I'd thought of that twenty years ago."

"Your daughter. That's Turtle, the apricot lover?"

"That's right."

After another long minute of quiet, the teakettle begins to rattle. Taylor lifts it and pours hissing water into the coffee grounds. "She's not here at the moment. She'll be real surprised when she comes back and sees those birds gone." Taylor smiles down at the counter in a way that surprises Annawake because it is almost timid. Private. It passes, and Taylor looks back at Annawake. "Jax took her and a neighbor kid to see these two new rhinoceroses they got in at the zoo. He and Turtle are trying to write a song about endangered species."

"What's the story of that name?"

"What, Turtle? Well, not as good as yours. It's just a nickname more or less, because of her personality. Turtle is ... well, she holds on. From the time she was little she'd just grab me and not let go. In Kentucky where I grew up, people used to say if a snapping turtle gets hold of you it won't let go till it thunders. Do you take cream or anything?"

"Black, please."

"That's the story," she says, serving Annawake and sitting down opposite. "There's not much about us that hasn't been in the papers already. To tell you the truth, I think we're storied out. No offense, but we're hoping to just get back to normal."

Annawake shakes her head slightly.

"You're a reporter, right? I just assumed you saw us on TV. You said you're here for some kind of a journalist convention?"

Annawake holds her coffee mug in both hands and takes a sip. "I'm sorry, I've misled you," she says carefully, one phrase at a time. "I did see you on television, but I'm not a reporter. I'm an attorney. I'm in town for a Native American Law conference."

"A lawyer? I never would have guessed a lawyer."

"Well, thanks, I guess. I work in an office that does a lot of work for the Cherokee Nation. That's what I want to talk with you about. Turtle's adoption might not be valid."

Taylor's cup stops an inch from her lips, and for nearly half a minute she does not appear to breathe. Then she puts down the cup. "I've been through all this already. The social worker said I needed adoption papers, so I went to Oklahoma City and I got papers. If you want to see, I'll go get them."

"I've already looked at the records. That's the problem, it wasn't done right. There's a law that gives tribes the final say over custody of our own children. It's called the Indian Child Welfare Act. Congress passed it in 1978 because so many Indian kids were being separated from their families and put into non-Indian homes."

"I don't understand what that has to do with me."

"It's nothing against you personally, but the law is crucial. What we've been through is a wholesale removal."

"Well, that's the past."

"This is not General Custer. I'm talking about as recently as the seventies, when you and I were in high school. A third of all our kids were still being taken from their families and adopted into white homes. One out of *three.*"

Taylor's eyes are strangely enlarged. "My home doesn't have anything to do with your tragedy," she says. She gets up and stands at the window, looking out.

"I don't mean to scare you," Annawake says quietly. "But I want you to have some background on the problem. We need to make sure our laws are respected."

Taylor turns around and faces Annawake, her hair wheeling. "I didn't take Turtle from any family, she was dumped on me. *Dumped.* She'd already lost her family, and she'd been hurt in ways I can't even start to tell you without crying. Sexual ways. Your people let her fall through the crack and she was in bad trouble. She couldn't talk, she didn't walk, she had the personality of—I don't know what. A bruised apple. Nobody wanted her." Taylor's hands are shaking. She crosses her arms in front of her chest and slumps forward a little in the manner of a woman heavily pregnant.

Annawake sits still.

"And now that she's a cute little adorable child and gets famous and goes on television, now you want her back."

"This has nothing to do with Turtle being on television. Except that it brought her to our attention." Annawake looks away and thinks about her tone. Lawyer words will not win any cases in this kitchen. She is not so far from Oklahoma. "Please don't panic. I'm only telling you that your adoption papers may not be valid because you didn't get approval from the tribe. You need that. It might be a good idea to get it."

"And what if they won't give it?"

Annawake can't think of the right answer to that question.

Taylor demands, "How can you possibly think this is in Turtle's best interest?"

"How can you think it's good for a tribe to lose its children!" Annawake is startled by her own anger—she has shot without aiming first. Taylor is shaking her head back and forth, back and forth.

"I'm sorry, I can't understand you. Turtle is my daughter. If you walked in here and asked me to cut off my hand for a good cause, I might think about it. But you don't get Turtle."

"There's the child's best interest and the tribe's best interest, and I'm trying to think of both things."

"Horseshit." Taylor turns away, facing the window.

Annawake speaks gently to her back. "Turtle is Cherokee. She needs to know that."

"She knows it."

"Does she know what it means? Do *you?* I'll bet she sees Indians on TV and thinks: *How.* Bows and arrows. That isn't what we are. We have a written language as subtle as Chinese. We had the first free public school system in the world, did you know that? We have a constitution and laws."

"Fine," Taylor says, her eyes wandering over the front yard but catching on nothing. *We have a constitution too,* she thinks, *and it is supposed to prevent terrible unfairness,* but all she can remember is a string of words she memorized in eighth grade. "We the people," she says out loud. She walks over to the sink and picks up a soup ladle, then puts it back down. The voice outside sings, "*I can't feel it. You know they're stealing it from me.*"

Annawake feels an afterimage of her niece's egg belly under her hands. "I'm sure you're a good mother," she says. "I can tell that."

"How can you tell? You march in here, you ..." Taylor falters, waving a hand in the air. "You don't know the first thing about us."

"You're right, I'm assuming. You seem to care about her a lot. But she needs her tribe, too. There are a lot of things she'll need growing up that you can't give her."

"Like what?"

"Where she comes from, who she is. Big things. And little things, like milk, for instance. I'll bet she won't drink milk."

Taylor picks up the ladle again and bangs it against the metal sink, hard, then puts it down again. "You've got some Goddamn balls, telling me who my kid is. I'd like to know where you were three years ago when she was on death's front stoop."

"I was in law school, trying to learn how to make things better for my nation."

"We the people, creating a more perfect union."

Annawake offers no response.

"This here is my nation and I'm asking you to leave it."

Annawake stands up. "I'm sorry this hasn't been a more friendly meeting of minds. I hoped it would be. I'd still like to see Turtle." She leaves her card on the table, a small white rectangle embossed with red letters and the seal of the Cherokee Nation. "I think it would be good for her to talk about her heritage."

Taylor says nothing.

"Okay. Well, I'm in town till Monday. I'd like to meet her. Should I come back tomorrow maybe? After dinner?"

Taylor closes her eyes.

"Thanks for the coffee."

Taylor walks to the front door, holds it open, and watches the visitor pick her way through the fallen fruit in the yard. Annawake finds the keys in her pocket and stands for a second with her hand on the car door.

Taylor shouts, "She loves milk. We buy it by the gallon."

Annawake's rental is a low-slung blue Chrysler that gives her some trouble backing out. It wobbles and crunches its way down the rutted drive, headed back toward town.

Taylor stands on the porch, arms crossed, witnessing the retreat. The words "a more friendly meeting of minds" are smacking like angry pent-up bees against the inside of her head.

High overhead in the apricot branches the taped music has reached its end, and gone quiet. One by one the birds emerge from the desert and come back to claim their tree.

9

THE PIGS IN HEAVEN

UNCLE LEDGER WOULD SAY, "ONCE you have ridden a horse, you should know what a horse is." So it bothers Annawake that when she stands for the second time in front of the little rock house where Turtle stays she sees things she could swear were not there before. An odd stone tower at the end of the pitched roof, for instance, the kind of thing the white people in storybooks would hold prisoners in, or crazy aunts.

Of course, last time she was nervous. And watching a woman up a tree. Now there is only a skinny man in black jeans sitting on the porch steps. He's staring at his hands, which seem to be dozing on his knees, a pair of colossal, torpid spiders.

"Hi," Annawake tries. She stands with her own hands in her pockets, waiting for some kind of offer. "I'm Annawake," she adds.

"Oh, believe me, I know that." He seems to be rousing himself from his thoughts, very slowly, with a lot of effort, as if coming out of hibernation. "Where are my manners?" he says finally in a voice deep with despair, or the South. "Sit down here on this dirty old porch."

The stone step is broad and slumped like the gateway to some ancient wonder of the world. When she sits, it bleeds coolness into her thighs, a feeling of dampness. "Are you the musician?"

"Jax," he says, nodding a couple of times, as if barely convinced that this is his actual name.

"I heard your work yesterday. From that tree."

"It terrified the birds, I hear. I think I've found my market." Jax picks up a green apricot the size of a golf ball and flings it toward the cardboard owl in the treetops. It misses by a generous margin.

"Maybe. I liked your music all right," she says. She throws an apricot and hits the owl with a loud pop, causing it to shudder and list on its branch.

"Jesus," he says. Jax throws again, this time aiming for the trunk, and nicks the side. Annawake follows quickly, hitting the spot where his shot bounced off.

He looks at her sideways. With his dark brows and glint of gold earring, he resembles a pirate. "Is this one of those visitations? Are you about to reveal the meaning of my life?"

Annawake doesn't feel she ought to laugh. "I used to be kind of good at this throwing game we have, *sgwalesdi*. It's just a coincidence, I'm not that good at everything."

"If you are, I don't want to hear about it."

"I don't know the meaning of your life."

"Good. Because I'm not ready to hear it. Takes the fun away, you know? Like when you're reading a good book and somebody says, 'Oh, that's a great one, did he get hit by the train yet?' "

Annawake smiles. She's noticed that the house is truly run-down by social-service standards, worse than some things she's seen in the Cherokee Nation, and accepts that this could be used to her advantage. Toward the west, the desert rises up to meet the splintered rock peaks of the Tucson Mountains. Annawake shades her eyes to look at the descending sun. It's an effort for her not to shove the conversation forward. "I can see why you'd want to live out here," she says. "Out of the city."

"Oh, well, that's a very sad story. I got kicked out of the city of Tucson. They have an ordinance against Irascible Babies."

"Who?"

"My band. We all used to live together in a chicken house, downtown. But by some estimates we were too loud."

"Why would they have a chicken house downtown?"

"It wasn't, anymore. They'd closed it down because of the smell. I'm telling you, it's a very intolerant town."

This boyfriend is nothing that Annawake planned on. She's surprised to find him so serene and obliging, though she knows she may be mistaken. He may simply be in a coma. "Jacks is short for Jackson?"

"No, with an X." He makes a cross with his marvelously long index fingers. "Short for nothing. My mother was one of the best-known alcoholics in the French Quarter of New Orleans. I was named after a venerated brand of beer."

"You're named after Jax Beer?"

He nods morosely. "Somewhere in this world I have a sister named Hurricane. I'm telling you the God's honest truth."

"You don't know where she is?"

"Mother nor sister. If they are even on this earth."

"Damn. I used to think all you needed was white skin to have an easy life," Annawake says.

"I used to wish I was an Indian. I shaved my head one time and wore beads and made everybody call me Soaring Elk."

Annawake looks at him, and this time she does laugh. "You're not a Soaring Elk."

Jax studies his sneakers. "I could use a more meaningful name, though, don't you think? Something athletic. Maybe Red Ball Jets."

For a minute they regard their four shoes lined up on the step. Jax's trashed-out hightops look oversized and tragic, whereas Annawake's moccasins are perfect: stitched suede, the burnished red of iron-oxide soils in Oklahoma.

"Cool moccasins," Jax observes. "They look brand new."

"They are. I have to buy them out here. Nobody in Oklahoma wears moccasins anymore."

"No?"

She shakes her head. "The ones they sell to tourists at the Cherokee Heritage Center are made by this hippie in Albuquerque."

Jax sighs. "What is this world coming to?"

Suddenly, noticeably, the failing sunlight turns golden and benevolent. The cacti lit from behind glow with halos of golden fur, and Jax's and Annawake's faces and limbs seem similarly blessed. After a minute the light changes again, to flat dusk.

"They're gone, aren't they?" Annawake finally asks.

"Yep."

"How gone?"

Jax ponders the question. "She packed all Turtle's clothes. All of her books. She picked about two hundred green apricots and laid them out on the shelf behind the backseat hoping they'd ripen. When they pulled out of here it looked like the Joads."

Annawake has to think awhile to place the Joads, and then remembers *The Grapes of Wrath,* from high school English. White people fleeing the dust bowl of Oklahoma, ending up as fruit pickers in California. They think they had it bad. The Cherokees got marched out of their homelands *into* Oklahoma.

"No forwarding address, I guess."

Jax smiles.

"She manages an automotive place downtown, right? For a woman named Mattie, who must be a friend because she couldn't come to the phone when I called. You're lucky to have a mechanic in the family."

"Good work, Sherlock, only, A, even if Taylor were a mechanic she'd probably tell me to fix my own car. And B, she's not one. It used to be mainly a tire store, but Taylor hates tires so when they branched into auto parts Mattie let her take over the muffler and fanbelt side of the enterprise."

"I guess she had vacation time saved up."

"Nobody down there exactly punches a clock," Jax says. "It's a nice outfit. Kind of sixties Amish. They take in strays."

"Like Turtle?"

"Like Central American refugees. Could I remind you that you are the engineer of my recent wrecked life? Is this an official interrogation?"

"I'm sorry. No. I can get the information some other way, if you'd like me to go now and leave you alone."

"Left alone is exactly what I have been," Jax says. He's quiet long enough for Annawake to hear air moving around them.

"Mattie loves Taylor like a son," he says suddenly. "So you're going to end up talking to the air compressors down there. Don't waste your time."

"But you can't tell me where she's gone, I don't suppose."

"You suppose correctly."

They both watch as the sun touches the mountains. The horizon is softly indented as if the landscape had been worn down right there, like the low spot in the center of an old marble step, by the repeated tread of sunset. The red ball collapses, then silently hemorrhages into the surrounding clouds.

"I may get phone calls now and again, to let me know they're all right. But there is no forwarding address."

"Well, thanks for being honest," Annawake says.

Jax laces his fingers behind his head and cracks some junction of his bones with a resounding pop. "I do a lot of wicked things to my body, but I never perjure it."

"Wise choice," she says. "Only we're not in court."

"So are they really in trouble? Is this going to be a James Dean kind of situation where the Cherokee Nation chases them down to the riverbank and shines the lights in their eyes and finally they surrender?"

Annawake says, "No."

"Could I have that in writing?"

"You haven't told me anything, but you've been very nice about it, so I'll be honest with you. The Cherokee Nation isn't pursuing this case, I am. The thing is full of holes. I don't know how we can prove Turtle is Cherokee, unless some relatives come forward on the Nation. And even if that happens, I'm not positive the tribe's Child Welfare Department would take her from Taylor. Or even if they *should.*"

"What does the law say?"

"The law says we can take her. There have been kids who were with adoptive parents five, ten years, that the Indian Child Welfare Act has brought back to their tribe, because the adoptions were illegal."

"Wow. That's radioactive."

"It's hard for someone outside of our culture to understand, I guess. To see anything more sacred than Mom and Dad and little red baby makes three."

"What do you see?"

Annawake hesitates. "First choice? I'd rather have seen her go into a Cherokee home, with relatives, that's always the best thing. But we can't always get first choice. And now that she's been taken out, it's way complicated. My boss thinks I'm on the warpath. Annawake Crazy Horse."

"Are you?"

"Well, sure. Taylor should have gotten permission from the tribe. And Turtle should have connections with her people. She should know ..." Annawake pauses, corrects her aim. "There are ways of letting her know about who she is. My position is essentially neutral. I have information Taylor could use."

"Neutral snootral. You know that thing they say about getting between a mother bear and her cub? Annie dear, *you* might think you're just out picking blueberries, but that's highly irrelevant to Mama Bear."

"I accept your point."

A small breeze seems to come right up out of the ground, stirring the tree branches in every direction. Voices drift down from the large stone house on the hill, fragments of laughter, and a chorus of bird chatter rises from the mesquite thicket. Annawake listens to the bird music, identifying some of its individual parts: the monotonous croon of a dove, a woodpecker's laugh, and stitched through it all, the intermittent shriek of crickets. She stops listening so closely then, preferring the whole song to any of its solo voices.

Jax slaps his knee abruptly. "Damn this," he says.

"I agree."

"You don't know the half of it, listen. Taylor is the woman my mama used to tell me to save myself for. I swear, I kind of wish I had. You ever feel that way about a person?"

"Not one person, no," Annawake says. She doesn't have to think about it.

"Well, then, maybe you can't understand what I'm going through. If I went in and played it on the piano, you'd understand. You'd say, This Jax, boy, I think he going to lie down here and die if that woman stays away past the fourth of July."

The clouds in the western sky are still lit brightly on their undersides like the yellowy-silver bellies of fish, but overhead some stars are out. "There you go," Jax tells Annawake. "That's Venus, the goddess of love. Don't ask me why she comes out at eight o'clock when people are still washing their supper dishes."

"Prime time," Annawake says. Listening to Jax encourages free association.

"You bet."

"You know the thing that first really got my attention about this case?"

Jax says, "The sheer awesome height of Hoover Dam."

"No, I missed that part of the show, believe it or not. What got me interested is that her story doesn't square up. On TV she said Turtle was a foundling, more or less. That some Cherokee woman handed her this kid in a coffee shop. But the records show two parents who voluntarily gave Turtle up."

"Did anyone ever tell you that you, personally, are beautiful beyond the speed of light?"

She stares at Jax for a minute, then laughs. "In those words, no."

"Just wondering. Could I kiss you?"

"Is this a diversionary tactic?"

"Yes, more or less. Although I'd probably have a good time."

"Your heart's not in it, Jax. Nice try, though."

"Thank you."

"So apparently, from what I've found out, the story of the foundling in the coffee shop is the true one. Strange but true. They fixed up that adoption, didn't they?"

"Righty-o."

"Why?"

"Well, you know. You need papers in this big old world. Some social worker here in Tucson figured out that legalwise Taylor's goose was cooked, finding the birth parents was hopeless. So she put her onto some official in Okie City that apparently is not obsessed with the long arm of the law. Taylor went back there with two friends that posed as Turtle's parents."

"So Steven and Hope Two Two are a fraud."

Jax runs a hand through his ragged hair. "You'd already figured that out, don't play Little Bo Peep. But you'll never find Steven and Hope; they were Guatemalans without papers and they've disappeared into America the beautiful. And the guy that approved the adoption, he was old, Taylor says. He's probably retired. There couldn't be a whole lot of brownie points involved in nailing him now."

She understands suddenly what Jax is doing, and admires it: he is neither obliging nor comatose, he's protecting the people he loves. He has learned much more from her than she from him. She feels some lawyerly chagrin. "I'm not necessarily looking to nail people," she says.

"You're a good shot, Ms. Fourkiller. Maybe you should just make sure you're not loaded."

"I want to do the best thing for the most people."

"She loves Turtle, that's one thing you should know. She would jump off Hoover Dam herself for that kid, headfirst. Me, the great Jax, she *enjoys*, but Turtle she loves. She didn't exactly have to meditate before she walked out of here. It was no contest." He looks at her, his eyes luminous and hard, and then back at the mountains. For the first time Annawake notices his strange profile: a perfectly straight line from his forehead to the end of his nose. She finds it beautiful and disturbing. She clamps her hands tightly between her knees, shivering a little. The temperature has dropped unbelievably, as it will when the desert loses the sun.

Jax stands up and goes inside and stays for quite a while. She's uncertain whether this signifies the end of the interview. She hears a few dramatic nose blows, and then she can hear him singing quietly: "Be careful what you take, Anna Wake, be careful what you break." She decides that if he starts playing the piano she will leave, but he comes back out with his fingers hooked into the mouths of two slim brown bottles of beer.

"Here," he says. "Let's have a party. Kennedy and Khrushchev drink to a better world." He sits beside her, very close, and she can feel his body heat through her jeans. Strangely, she feels comforted rather than threatened, as if Jax were one of her brothers. Possibly it's because she has only heard her brothers, and no other man before now, confess to her his absolute love for some other woman.

Jax leans back on one elbow and begins pointing out constellations: Ursa Major, which Annawake has known since she could walk, and the Pleiades.

"The what?"

"Pleiades. Seven sisters."

She takes a long pull on her beer and squints at the sky. "You people must have better eyes than we do. In Cherokee there are only six. The Six Bad Boys. *Anitsutsa.*"

"*Anitsutsa?*"

"Yeah. Or *disihgwa,* the pigs. The Six Pigs in Heaven."

"Excuse me but you're making this up."

"No. There's a story about these six boys that wouldn't do their work. Wouldn't work in the corn, wouldn't fix their mothers' roofs, wouldn't do the ceremony chores—there's always stuff to be done at the ceremonial grounds, getting firewood and repairing shelters and things like that. They weren't what you'd call civic-minded."

"And they got turned into pigs."

"Now wait, don't jump ahead. It's their fault, they turned themselves into pigs. See, all they wanted to do, ever, was play ball and have fun. All day long. So their mothers got fed up. They got together one day and gathered up all the boys' *sgwalesdi* balls. It's a little leather ball about like this." Annawake holds up a green apricot. "With hair inside. Animal hair, human, whatever. And they put all the balls in the stewpot. They cooked them."

"Yum, yum," says Jax.

She throws the apricot, carefully aiming at nothing. "Okay. So the boys come home for lunch after playing around all morning, and their mothers say, 'Here's your soup!' They plop those soggy old cooked balls down on their plates. So the boys get mad. They say, 'Forget it, only a pig would eat this,' and they rush down to the ceremonial grounds and start running around and around the ball court, asking the spirits to listen, yelling that their mothers are treating them like pigs. And the spirits listened, I guess.

They figured, 'Well, a mother knows best,' and they turned the boys into pigs. They ran faster and faster till they were just a blur. Their little hooves left the ground and they rose up into the sky, and there they are."

"Holy crow," Jax says. "Your mom tell you that, when you wouldn't make your bed?"

"My Uncle Ledger," she says. "There's a lot of different versions of all the stories, according to what mood you're in. But you're right, that's the general idea. The Pigs, and also Uktena, this big snake with horns—those are the Cherokee boogeymen. I was always very civic-minded when I lived with my uncle."

"So that's your guiding myth. Do right by your people or you'll be a pig in heaven."

Annawake thinks this over. "Yes. I had a hundred and one childhood myths, and they all added up more or less to 'Do right by your people.' Is that so bad?"

"Myths are myths. They're good if they work for you, and bad if they don't."

"What are yours?"

"Oh, you know, I heard the usual American thing. If you're industrious and have clean thoughts you will grow up to be vice president of Motorola."

"Do right by yourself."

Jax finishes the last half of his beer in one swallow. She watches his Adam's apple with amazement. "You think Taylor's being selfish," he states.

Annawake hesitates. There are so many answers to that question. "Selfish is a loaded word," she says. "I've been off the reservation, I know the story. There's this kind of moral argument for doing what's best for yourself."

Jax puts his hands together under his chin and rolls his eyes toward heaven. "Honor the temple, for the Lord hast housed thy soul within. Buy that temple a foot massage and a Rolex watch."

"I think it would be hard to do anything else. Your culture is one long advertisement for how to treat yourself to the life you really deserve. Whether you actually deserve it or not."

"True," he says. "We all ought to be turned into pigs."

Annawake's mouth forms a tight, upside-down smile. "Some of my best friends are white people."

Jax goes limp, as if he's been shot.

"We just have different values," she says. "Some people say religion is finding yourself, and some people say it's losing yourself in a crowd."

Jax revives. "You can do that? Lose yourself?"

"Oh, sure. At the dances."

"Dancing?"

"Not like *American Bandstand,* not recreational dancing, it's ceremonial. A group thing. It's church, for us."

"I say po-tay-toes, and you say po-tah-toes." Jax lies flat on his back and balances his empty bottle on his stomach. It tilts a little when he breathes or talks. "And never the Twain shall meet, because he's dead." He laughs crazily and the bottle rolls off and clinks down the stone steps, but doesn't break. He sits up. "You're being kind of *anisnitsa* yourself, you know."

"Anti-*what?*"

"Anisnitsa. Isn't that what you said, for pig?"

"Sihgwa."

"Whatever. You're being one. In your own fashion."

"I'm trying to see both sides."

"You can't," Jax says. "And Taylor can't. It's impossible. Your definitions of 'good' are not in the same dictionary. There is no point of intersection in this dialogue."

"Surely you don't think it's *good* for the tribe to lose its children? Or for Turtle to lose us? She's entitled to her legacy."

"Her legacy at the moment may be green apricots for dinner."

"What a thought. Did they have someplace to go?"

Jax doesn't answer.

"It's not a trick question."

"Well, then, yes. The answer is yes. Right now they are someplace."

"Please tell her I'm sorry if I'm the cause of this."

"*If* you're the cause of this?"

"You have to believe this much, the last thing I want is to put Turtle through more dislocation."

Jax reaches down carefully and sets the beer bottle on its head. "Dislocation," he says.

"You're the only connection between Turtle and me at this point, and," she waits for him to meet her eyes, "and I need that connection."

"Don't look at me, Mama Bear," says Jax. "I'm just picking blueberries."

10

THE HORSES

"TURTLE, DRINK YOUR MILK."

Turtle's plate is a boneyard of grilled-cheese sandwich crusts. She picks up her full glass and drinks, holding a steady sidelong eye on Taylor. As soon as Taylor looks away, she sets down her glass.

Angie Buster's diner is deserted. At four o'clock Angie declared that not even the starving Armenians would come out for a meal in this weather, and she went home to take a nap. Taylor and Turtle and Pinky the bulldog sit near the front window watching long knives of rain attack the ground at a hard slant. The first storm of the summer has blown in from Mexico, arousing the dust and dampening the Virgin of Guadalupe outside, causing her yellow bows to drop off one by one. Lucky is missing in action again. Angie isn't worried; it has only been half a day, and she says she can feel in her bones when it's going to be a long one. Her bones say this one isn't.

Angie owns not only the diner, it turns out, but also the adjacent Casa Suerte motor inn, which Taylor understood as "Casa

Sweater" over the phone. According to Angie, *suerte* means "good luck"; she bought it ten years ago when the state finally persuaded Lucky's father to catch up on his child support. The idea of this place as someone's good fortune depresses Taylor. The low brick units of the motor inn surround a doubtful patch of grass, an empty swimming pool, and one palm tree that escaped the short, trashy stage only to find itself leggy and ridiculous above the telephone wires. Each unit has a single metal chair outside its door, suggesting a concept of neighborliness, but the place seems short on neighbors. Taylor has seen only one other person around, an old woman with frightened-looking hair. She is grateful to have somewhere to hide out while she considers their next move, but being here is only slightly better than being nowhere.

"So what do you want to do now?" she asks Turtle.

"Go home."

"I know. But we can't. We're on vacation for a while."

Turtle bites her lips between her teeth, then releases them. She picks up her fork and idly begins poking things with it: her plate, the tablecloth, her hair. The bulldog watches with mild interest. Taylor frowns unconsciously, fearing slightly for Turtle's eyes, but she bites down on the impulse to tell her to put the fork down. Turtle will only go so far, she's found. Not to the point of self-damage.

From their table Taylor can see the glossy slabs of laminated newspaper hanging in the entrance to the diner: articles from the *Phoenix Republic*, the *San Francisco Chronicle*, even the *Washington Post*, all concerning the great adventure of Lucky and Turtle. It's no comfort to Taylor that people in San Francisco and Washington, D.C., are aware of Angie's diner.

"Let's watch TV," Turtle suggests.

"Sure, we can go watch TV. Pinky will cook and wait tables if the starving Armenians come in. Right, Pink?"

The dog wags its rear end with its ghost of bobbed tail, and Turtle smiles, her first all day. Taylor feels relieved for that, at least, as they shove the door open and run across the wet courtyard.

* * *

Sideways rain stings Turtle's eyes and arms. She tried to see in the pool as they hurried by but there is no blue in there, only a big mud-color shape of a thumbprint growing on the bottom. Lucky Buster said he could swim, before, and now Lucky Buster is gone. Her mother is trying to fit the key in the door of their room. The scaredy white-hair woman comes toward them holding a little roof of newspaper over her head.

"Have you seen the horses?" she wants to know.

"No," Taylor says. The key is on a wood card like Popsicle sticks. When it slips out of Taylor's hand it goes away on the water down the sidewalk.

"Well, they were here," the woman says. "Can you give me a present?"

Turtle catches the float-away key and gives it back. "What kind of present?" Taylor asks. She tries to make the lock open, but her hands are shaky like they were the day Turtle and Jax and Dwayne Ray came home from the rhinoceros zoo and they had to put everything in a suitcase.

"The horses! Didn't you see them?"

"I'm sorry," Taylor says.

Turtle doesn't want to see a horse's clomping feet. Everyone here is afraid. Turtle feels the old place coming, with him and no light and you can't get air.

"Oh, you're sorry. I'm sure you are." The woman runs away with her feet in flip-flops splatting the ground with little steps. The door gives in and they fall inside, where the room smells safe and nose-stinging like clean bathrooms. She finds Taylor's cold hand and knows they will stay right here.

Turtle clicks on the television and stands a few inches from the screen, punching the channel button, sorting through the brazen images. She settles on a documentary about repairing a cathedral, and climbs onto the bed. Taylor isn't sure what the appeal is, but she accepts Turtle's choice. The narrator is describing the chemicals they have to use on the ancient walls; meanwhile, a man in a little wooden swing moves up and down the high steeple in his system of ropes, like a spider, but not so graceful. A male spider with a bucket seat and chemicals.

"Where do you think Lucky Buster is now?" Turtle asks.

Taylor has stripped down to her bra and begins pulling off Turtle's wet clothes. "Oh, I think he's at a friend's house chewing banana bubble gum and eating all kinds of junk Angie won't let him have."

"Like me and Jax do when you're at work?"

"Ha, ha." Gently she pushes a dry shirt over Turtle's damp head, which smells like baby shampoo, and pulls her arms through the holes.

The cooler unit in the window thumps doggedly, overworked but useless in the damp heat. Taylor is suddenly irritated with the prickly weight of her hair; it reminds her of Jax breathing on her neck. She yanks it over her shoulder and begins corralling it into a braid.

"Why do we have to have this vacation?" Turtle asks.

Taylor feels gooseflesh rise on the skin of her bare arms. "Well, because we can't be hanging around at home right now."

"Why?"

Taylor examines the end of her rope of hair, trying to look unconcerned. It would be so simple to lie: Jax decided to paint the whole house purple. "Do you remember when I took you to Oklahoma that time to get your adoption papers?"

Turtle nods, and Taylor doesn't doubt that she remembers. Sometimes she will mention events from years ago. Taylor finds it miraculous and disturbing that Turtle can find words for things she witnessed before she could talk.

"We had to go on that trip because the social workers said we needed those papers so you could stay with me. And this is something like that. We need to go on another trip, to make sure we can stay together."

"A trip to where?"

"Well, that's the part I don't know yet. Someplace lucky. Where do you think we should go?"

"Sesame Street."

"Good idea," Taylor says.

Now the television is showing the paintings inside the church. There is a sad, long-faced Jesus made up of small squares and triangles, as if he were glass, and had been smashed and reassembled. Taylor rolls over on her stomach and nuzzles Turtle's neck. Her spirit is revived by the exact unchanging smell of Turtle: shampoo, sweat, and something nutty and sweet, like peanut butter. She blows against her brown cheek, making a loud noise, then gives her a kiss. "This church is getting depressing," she says. "Could we watch something with a little more story line?"

Turtle gets up and changes the station to a movie.

"Thanks, pal."

The movie is about a big, tough, angry wife who is trying to ruin the life of her rabbity husband, who ran off with a rich romance writer. Nothing about the movie seems realistic to Taylor, but Turtle asks her not to talk to the TV, so she tries. They both like the mean wife the best. She does spectacularly horrible things, and they laugh. Taylor also likes the Indian actor who plays the rich lady's smug, smart-alecky butler. The lady keeps snapping, "Garcia, take care of it this instant!" and Garcia keeps rolling his eyes and walking away.

In the last few days Taylor has been noticing images of Indians everywhere: the Indian-chief profile on a Pontiac. The innocent-looking girl on the corn-oil margarine. The hook-nosed cartoon mascot of the Cleveland Indians, who played in Tucson. Taylor wonders what Annawake meant when she said Turtle should be in touch with her Indian side. Maybe that doesn't mean feathers, but if not, then what? Taylor is supposedly part Indian herself; Alice used to talk about some Cherokee great-grandmother way in the back of the closet, but everybody and his brother has one of those, even Elvis Presley did. Where do you draw the line? Maybe being an Indian isn't any one thing, any more than being white is one thing. What mascot would they use for a team called the Cleveland White People?

The movie has become a commercial without Taylor's notice: she realizes now that the dancing women lifting drinks from a tray have nothing to do with Garcia the Indian butler. Taylor doesn't care for her own train of thought. She could end up like the woman outside, running around in the rain, asking people, "Have you seen the Indians?"

Just as Angie's bones predicted, Lucky returned with the end of the rainstorm. He was at his friend Otis's, working on model trains. "Next time use your brain and call me, will you, Otis?" she scolds when he drops Lucky off at the diner.

"My phone went out," Otis says.

"My butt," Angie replies.

Otis is very old and bald, with bad posture and big splay feet in white sneakers. She orders him inside for a piece of pie, and he obeys. Like everyone else around, he seems to turn into a child in the presence of Angie. Taylor marvels at this talent of hers, like one of the superpowers a cartoon character could possess: the hypersonic mother-ray.

Taylor is helping Angie put away the soggy yellow bows from the Virgin of Guadalupe. The storm has left them floating in a puddle around her feet like bedraggled water lilies. "Do you put these up every time he disappears?"

"Well, it's kind of a signal to the town, to be on the lookout," Angie says. "So if anybody sees him wandering they'll send him on home."

Angie pronounces "wandering" like "wondering," and before her meaning dawns on Taylor, she is stumped on what it is that Lucky would be wondering about. He seems to have little room for doubt in his life. She can see him inside now, talking excitedly to Turtle. Turtle looks rapt. Taylor envies Lucky's assurance, and Turtle's state of grace: to be able to see neither forward nor backward right now, to see Lucky as a friend, just that. Not an instrument of fate.

The phone rings and Angie goes in to get it, but returns immediately. "It's for you."

Taylor's heart thumps hard when she picks up the receiver; she can't think what news there might be that isn't bad.

"Are we not the species of critical thinkers?" the telephone inquires.

"Jax!"

"Oh, big surprise. Nobody else on Planet Earth knows where you are."

"I hope. Have you heard from her? Did she come back?"

"She walks in beauty like the night." He pauses. "Are you jealous?"

"No. What did she say?"

"That the Seven Sisters are actually the Six Pigs in Heaven."

"The what?"

"Seven Sisters, the constellation. They're actually six juvenile males who got turned into pigs because of being selfish and not community-minded."

"I swear I never can follow you, Jax. What did she say really?"

"That she's really on your side."

"Right. What else?"

"She says she's on the warpath. Can you picture that woman galloping over the hill on an Appaloosa? Too divine."

Taylor can picture it. She looks out the window and sees Otis filling up his car at the minimart across the street. "Does she know I've left town?"

"Yes. And her aim is true. She can hit a cardboard owl between the eyes at fifty paces."

"Meaning what, Jax?"

"This woman is smarter than your average box of rocks. Before she came here she'd already talked to people down at Mattie's, and she'd figured out everything about the fake adoption. She might figure out where you are—returned to the scene. First she'll try Oprah, then Lucky Buster."

"You really think that? Is she still in Arizona?"

"No. She flew back to Oklahoma this morning."

"How can you be sure?"

"I can't, as a matter of fact. She could be over eating kugel with Mr. Gundelsberger at this moment."

"Shoot, Jax, I'm scared. We've got to get out of here. But I don't know where. I can't even go home, Mama's moving out on Harland. Turtle wants to go to Sesame Street."

Jax laughs. "Good idea."

"I think we've had enough of TV land." Taylor rolls her head from side to side, relaxing her neck, trying to stave off panic. Turtle is watching from the corner of the diner. "How's everything back at the ranch? How's Lou Ann? And Mr. G.?"

"Lou Ann is Lou Ann. Mr. G. is a troubled individual. He has to leave his shades down at all hours so he won't see his voluptuous daughter exploring the desert in her natural state."

"Gundi's started her nature walks again? She's amazing. I'd be scared of getting snakebit in a personal area."

"Gundi has no personal areas. She's painting a series of nude self-portraits with different cactus configurations."

"Well, be nice to her anyway. She's your landlady."

"Landperson, please. Don't worry, she's not going to kick me out. I'm one of her favorite boys this week. This morning she was taking a very special interest in the cactus configurations outside my studio window. Turtle would have gotten an education."

"Well, pay the rent anyway, it's due this week, okay? Being handsome will only carry you so far in life."

"Would you say that I'm actually handsome? I mean, in those words?"

"Listen, Jax, do you feed Turtle junk food when I'm at work?"

"We experiment. Peanut butter and green bean sandwiches. Nothing hard core."

"She misses you."

"I miss you both. I'm radioactive with despair."

Taylor knows he wants her to say she loves him, but she can't. Not under pressure. It feels a little empty and desperate to her, like when husbands send wives into the store to pick out their own birthday gifts.

"Well, look," he says finally. "Don't even tell me where you're going next, because maybe Miss Jaxkiller will come back and seduce me, and I'll tell all."

"I'm thinking we'll head north," Taylor says. "I'm so nervous right now I can't think right. I'll call you from somewhere outside the state."

"Have you slept with another man yet?"

"Jax! Good Lord, it's only been forty-eight hours."

"So you're saying you need more time."

"Thanks for calling. You're really making my day here."

"I'm sorry. It's just, this is harder than it looks. You pack up your unripe fruit and drive out of here and you're gone."

"We didn't leave *you*, Jax."

"I know."

"We'll be back. This will be all right."

"Make me believe."

"You'll see." Taylor hangs up, wishing she had Angie's power to make the entire world sit down for milk and cookies.

* * *

"For an adventure you have to have rations," Taylor insists. She's in the grocery, trying to get Turtle interested in food. She made the mistake of panicking, hurrying Turtle away from Lucky and into the car after Jax's phone call, and now Turtle has gone deep inside herself. In situations where other children have tantrums, Turtle does some strange opposite of tantrum.

"Look, these pears are three pounds for a dollar. You can tell they're ripe because they smell like pear. We'll eat these until the apricots turn ripe."

Turtle sits backward in the shopping basket with her eyes fixed on Taylor's shirt buttons. This is the Turtle of years ago; for months after Taylor found her, Turtle gazed out at the world from what seemed like an empty house. But all through those mute seasons Taylor talked and talked to Turtle, and she does it again now, to keep her fear at bay. People in the store look at her and then look closely, for ten seconds too long, at this child too big to be sitting in a shopping basket. Taylor doesn't care.

"Okay, listen up because I'm going to give you a valuable lesson on how to pick the best checkout clerk when you're in a hurry. Okay? As a general rule I say go for the oldest. Somebody that went to school in the days when you still learned arithmetic."

"I know arithmetic," Turtle points out quietly, without expression. "I know how to add."

"That's true," Taylor says, trying not to leap at this. "But that's because you come from a privileged home. I taught you how to add when you were four years old. Right? What's three plus seven?"

Turtle recedes again, giving no hint that she has heard. Exactly as in the old days before she spoke, Turtle seems to be concentrating hard on some taste at the back of her mouth. Or a secret sound, a tuning fork struck inside her head.

Taylor considers the checkout options: three female teenagers with identical sticky-looking hairdos, and a middle-aged Hispanic man with a huge mustache. Taylor heads her cart toward the mustache. While they wait she scans the tabloids by the register, half expecting to see news of herself and Turtle on the run. She was right about the cashier: their line moves twice as fast as the others and promptly the store has expelled them into the parking lot. When she loads in the groceries and slams the trunk, apricots go flying.

"Those damn things!" she says, and Turtle's mouth hints at a smile. Taylor lifts her with some effort out of the basket and sets her down beside the car. She stands motionless, a stuffed child skin, while Taylor returns the cart. Taylor has been swearing at the apricots since they left Tucson, and Turtle has found it funny: the fruits roll around noisily on the shelf behind the backseat and bobble forward like a gang of little ducks at every hard stop. There are green apricots in the ashtray, on the seat, on the floor. Taylor is pretty sure they were a bad idea. Instead of turning yellow, most of them seem to be hardening and shrinking like little mummy heads.

She lifts Turtle into the front seat and she scoots across and buckles up mechanically, letting Taylor in after her. "Will you look at this?" Taylor reaches down and fishes an apricot from under the clutch. Pretending to be furious, she throws it hard out the window, then ducks her head when it hits another car. Turtle giggles, and Taylor sees then that she is back, there is someone home behind her eyes. "So what we're going to do now," she says calmly, touching the tears out of her own eyes, "is we have to look for a sign. Something to tell us where to go."

"There," Turtle says, pointing at a billboard.

"That says to go buy snakeskin boots at Robby's Western Wear Outlet. You think we should buy snakeskin boots?"

"No!" Turtle says, pulling her head back hard against the seat, tucking her chin down and shaking her whole body with the negative.

"Okay, look for something else."

"There," Turtle says after a minute, pointing at an envelope stuck under the windshield wiper.

"Shoot, how can they give you a ticket in the parking lot of a damn grocery store?" Taylor opens the door at a stop sign and reaches around to grab it. "I'm sorry to set a bad moral example for you, Turtle, but if this is a ticket I'm throwing it away. I didn't do anything wrong, plus they'll never find us anyway." She hands it to Turtle and accelerates.

Turtle takes a very long time to tear open the envelope.

"What's it say? 'Citation' starts with C-I-T, it means a ticket."

"It says: Dear Cad Die ..."

"Dear cad die?"

"C-A-D-D-I-E."

"Caddie. Let me see that."

"I can read it," Turtle says. "It's not too long."

"Okay." Taylor concentrates on being patient and not hitting pedestrians. People in Sand Dune don't seem in tune with the concept of traffic lights.

"Dear Caddie. I am sorry I did-n't see you at miggets ..."

"Miggets?" Taylor glances over at Turtle, who is holding the paper very close to her face. "That's okay, keep going."

"At miggets like I pro, pro-my-sed."

"Like I promised."

"Like I promised. Here is the S 50."

"S 50?" To Taylor it sounds like a fighter plane.

"The S is crossed out."

"A line through it?" Taylor considers. "Here is the 50? Oh, a dollar sign, here is the *fifty dollars?* Look in the envelope, is there anything else in there?"

Turtle looks. "Yes." She hands over two twenties and a ten.

"What else does it say? Is there a name at the bottom?" Taylor can't wait any longer, and reaches for the note:

> Dear Caddie, I'm sorry I didn't see you at Midget's like I promised. Here's the $50. Now we're even and I'll beat the pants off you next time, right, Toots? Love, Hoops.

It reminds Taylor of the mysterious ads in the newspaper's personal section: "Hoops, I'll never forget the fried clams at B.B.O.G., Your Toots." It stands to reason that the kind of person who would waste money on those ads would leave fifty dollars on the wrong car.

"Who's Caddie?" Turtle wants to know.

"Somebody else with a big white car. Some guy named Hoops owed her money, and didn't want to face her in person."

"Why did he give it to us?"

"Because we're lucky."

"Was that the sign telling us where to go?" Turtle asks.

"I guess. It's a sign our luck has turned. Money's walking to us on its own two feet. I guess we ought to go to Las Vegas."

"What's Las Vegas?"

"A place where people go to try their luck."

Turtle considers this. "Try to do what with it?"

"Try to get more money with it," Taylor says.

"Do we want more money?"

"It's not so much we want it. We just have to have it."

"Why?"

"Why?" Taylor frowns and tilts the rearview mirror to get the setting sun out of her eyes. "Good question. Because nobody around here will give us anything, except by accident. Food or gas or what all we need. We've got to buy it with money."

"Even if we really need something, they won't give it to us?"

"Nope. There's no free lunch."

"But they'll give us money in Las Vegas?"

"That's the tale they tell."

Even a joke has some weight and takes up space, and when introduced into a vacuum, acquires its own gravity. Taylor is thinking about her high school physics teacher, Hughes Walter, and what he might say about her present situation. To amuse herself on long drives she often puts together improbable combinations of the people she's met in her life, and imagines what they would say to each other: Her mother and Angie Buster. Lou Ann's mean, prudish grandmother and Jax. Better yet: Jax and the woman looking for the horses.

They are driving toward Las Vegas because it's the only suggestion anyone has made so far, besides Sesame Street, and when introduced into a vacuum the idea acquired gravity. They're approaching the Hoover Dam now. Maybe it's what Jax said, that they've been drawn back to the scene of the crime. Whether she is the one who made off with the goods, or was robbed, she doesn't know yet. Taylor would just as soon skip the dam, but the only way out of this corner of the state is to cross the Hoover or get wet. Turtle is sitting up, looking excited.

"We're going to see those angels again," she says, her first words in more than thirty miles.

"Yep."

"Can we stop?"

"And do what?"

"Go see that hole."

Taylor is quiet.

"Can we?"

"Why do you want to do that?"

"I want to throw something at it."

"You do? What for?"

Turtle looks out the window and speaks so quietly Taylor can barely hear. "Because I hate it."

Taylor feels her face go hot, then cold, as her blood strangely reverses its tide. Turtle understands everything that has happened. There is no state of grace.

"Yeah, okay. We can do that."

Taylor parks the car very near the spillway. Since the dramatic rescue, they've added a new fence on the mountainside and pinkish floodlights in the parking lot. It feels bright as day when they get out, but deserted and wrongly colored, like some other planet with a fading sun. They both stand with their hands in their pockets, looking down.

"What can we throw?" Turtle asks.

Taylor thinks. "We have some empty pop cans in the car. But I hate to throw trash. It doesn't seem right."

"Rocks?" Turtle suggests, but the parking lot has been resurfaced and there aren't any rocks. The Hoover Dam people have really gone all out.

"Green apricots!" Taylor says suddenly, and Turtle laughs out loud, a chuck-willow watery giggle. They clamber into the backseat and scoop up armloads of the mummified fruits.

"This one's for Lucky Buster," Taylor shouts, casting the first one, and they hear it: ponk, ponk, ricocheting down the bottomless tunnel.

"Here's for Boy Scouts that have saved lives, and that stupid purple dress they tried to make you wear on TV. And for Annawake Fourkiller wherever she is." Handfuls of fruit rain down the hole.

"Lucky, Lucky, Lucky, Lucky," Turtle chants, throwing her missiles slowly like precious ammunition. While the two of them, mother and child, stand shouting down the hole, a fine rain begins to fall on the desert.

* * *

Afterward, Turtle seems spent. She lies across the front seat with her head on Taylor's right thigh and her tennis shoes wagging idly together and apart near the passenger door. The low greenish lights of the dashboard are reflected in her eyes as she looks out at the empty space of her own thoughts. Beside her face Turtle cradles Mary, her square utility flashlight. It's the type that people take deer hunting, large and dark green, said to float if dropped in water. She never turns it on; Turtle doesn't even particularly care whether it has batteries, but she needs it, this much is clear. To Taylor it seems as incomprehensible as needing to sleep with a shoebox, and just as unpleasant—sometimes in the night she hears its hollow corners clunk against Turtle's skull. But anyone who's tried to take Mary away has found that Turtle is capable of a high-pitched animal scream.

Taylor squints through the windshield wipers. She's driving toward the blaze of lights she knows has to be Las Vegas, but she can barely see the sides of the road. The storm moving north from Mexico has caught up to them again.

Turtle shifts in her lap and looks up at Taylor. "Am I going to have to go away from you?"

Taylor takes a slow breath. "How could that happen? You're my Turtle, right?"

The wipers slap, slap. "I'm your Turtle, right."

Taylor takes a hand off the wheel to stroke Turtle's cheek. "And once a turtle bites you, it doesn't let go, does it?"

"Not till it thunders."

Turtle seems cramped, and arches her back, pushing herself around with her feet. When she finally settles, she has crawled out of her seat belt and curled most of her body into Taylor's lap with her head against Mary. With one hand she reaches up and clenches a fist around the end of Taylor's braided hair, exactly as she used to do in the days before she had any other language. Outside, the blind rain comes down and Taylor and Turtle flinch when the hooves of thunder trample the roof of the car.

SUMMER

AY

11

SOMEONE THE SIZE OF GOD

CASH STILLWATER LOOKS UP FROM his work and sees a splash of white birds like water thrown at the sky. They stay up there diving in circles through the long evening light, changing shape all together as they fly narrow-bodied against the sun and then wheel away, turning their bright triangular backs.

Cash had only glanced up to rest his eyes but there were the birds, shining outside his window. His eyes fill with tears he can't understand as he follows their northward path to the dark backdrop of the Tetons, then back again to some place he can't see behind the Jackson Hole fire station. They make their circle again and again, flaunting their animal joy. He counts the birds without knowing it, sorting the shifting group into rows of odd and even, like beads. In the daytime Cash works at a health-food store putting tourists' slender purchases into paper bags, but in the evenings he makes bead jewelry. His lady friend Rose

Levesque, who works at the Cheyenne Trading Post, takes in the things he's made, pretending to the owner that she did it herself. Cash learned beadwork without really knowing it, simply because his mother and sisters, and then his daughters, were doing it at the kitchen table all his life. Before his wife died and the family went to pieces and he drove his truck to Wyoming, he raised up two girls on the Cherokee Nation. He never imagined after they were grown he would have to do another delicate thing with his hands, this time to pay the rent. But since he started putting beads on his needle each night, his eye never stops counting rows: pine trees on the mountainsides, boards in a fence, kernels on the ear of corn as he drops it into the kettle. He can't stop the habit, it satisfies the ache in the back of his brain, as if it might fill in his life's terrible gaps. His mind is lining things up, making jewelry for someone the size of God.

Rose walks in his door without knocking and announces loudly, "Nineteen silver quills down the hatch, did I tell you?" She plumps herself down at his kitchen table.

"Down whose hatch?" Cash wants to know, watching his needle. The backs of his hands remind him of paper burning in the fireplace, the moment the taut membrane goes slack into a thousand wrinkles, just before it withers to ash and air. He wonders if you get used to waking up old.

"Willie Levesque's big old, ugly, hungover hatch, that's whose." Rose lights a cigarette and drags on it with an inward sigh. Willie is Rose's oldest boy, who is half her age, nineteen, and twice as big. "I had them in an aspirin bottle in the kitchen. In the *kitchen*, for God's sake, it's not like they were in the medicine cabinet."

Cash glances at Rose, who is peevishly brushing ash off her blouse. Because she is shorter and heavier than she feels she ought to be, she clacks through her entire life in scuffed high heels, worn with tight jeans and shiny blouses buttoned a little too low. You can tell at thirty paces she's trying too hard.

"Didn't he look what he was taking?" he asks her.

"No. He said they went down funny, though. Like fillings." Cash works his needle and Rose smokes inside another comma of silence, then says, "The *silver* ones, wouldn't you know. Twenty dollars' worth. I'm about ready to take it out of his hide. Why couldn't he have eat up some fake turquoise?"

Rose brings Cash the supplies for making jewelry, pretending she is taking them home herself, but her boss, Mr. Crittenden, holds her accountable for every bead. In the morning he puts on his jeweler's glasses and counts the beads in every piece she's brought in, to make sure they're all there. It must be hard work, this business of mistrust.

"Those quills ought to pass on through without much trouble," he tells Rose. "My girls used to swallow pennies and all kinds of things, you'd be surprised. They always turned up. You could tell Willie to give them back when he's done."

"Maybe I'll do that," Rose says. "Hand them over to Mr. Crittenden in a little paper sack." Cash can tell she is smiling; he knows Rose's voice, its plump amusement and thinned-out resentments, because so often he is looking at something else while she speaks to him.

He met her, or rather saw her first, in the window of the Trading Post. He made a habit of pecking on the glass and winking at her each day on his way to work, which apparently won her heart, since she says she feels like a plastic dummy up there on display. Mr. Crittenden makes her sit at a little antique schoolroom desk in the bay-window storefront, where tourists can behold a genuine Indian hunched over her beadwork, squinting in the bad glare. Presumably they will be impressed or moved by pity to come inside.

Rose's beadwork is unimpressive, close up. She's nothing close to a full-blooded Indian, that's her excuse, but she could learn the more complicated patterns Cash does, if she cared to. It's a skill you acquire, like tuning an engine. The things you have to be an Indian to know, in Cash's experience—how to stretch two chickens and a ham over sixty relatives, for example—are items of no interest in the tourist trade.

He gets up to take his bread out of the oven and start dinner. Cash has discovered cooking in his old age, since moving away from his sisters and aunts, and according to Rose he acts like he invented the concept. She doesn't seem to mind eating what he cooks, though—she's here more nights than she's not. While she smokes at the kitchen table, Cash unpacks the things he brought home from the Health Corral, lining them up: six crimson bell peppers, five white potatoes, six orange carrots. He imagines putting all these colors on a needle, and wishes his life were really as bright as this instant.

"Looky here, girl," he says, waving a bell pepper at Rose.

"Cash, you watch out," she says. The pepper is deformed, with something like testicles. Cash gets to bring home produce that is too organic even for the health-food crowd. In his tiny apartment behind this tourist town's back, Cash feeds on stews of bell peppers with genitals and carrots with arms and legs.

He spreads newspapers on the table and sits to peel his potatoes. He feels comforted by the slip-slip-slip of his peeler and the potatoes piling up like clean dry stones. "Somebody come in the store today and told me how to get rich," he says.

"Well, from what I hear you've gotten rich fifty times over, except for the money part," Rose says.

"No, now listen. In the store we sell these shampoos they make with ho-hoba. It's this natural business the girls want now. A fellow come in today and says he's all set up down in Arizona to grow ho-hoba beans on his farm. They'll just grow in the dirt desert, they don't need nothing but a poor patch of ground and some sunshine. I'll bet you can buy you a piece of that land for nothing."

"Why would somebody sell it for nothing if they could get rich growing shampoo beans on it?"

"It takes five years before the plants start to bear, that's the hitch. Young people don't have that much patience."

"And old people don't have that much time."

"I've got my whole retirement ahead of me. And I know how to make things grow. It could work out good."

"Like the silver foxes did," Rose says, slicing him carelessly. In January, before the tourist jobs opened up, Cash skinned foxes. With frozen fingers he tore the delicate membranes that held pelt to flesh, earning his own pair to breed. It seems like a dream to him now, that he believed he could find or borrow a farm of his own. He was thinking he was still on the Nation, where relatives will always move over to give you a place at the table.

"Johnny Cash Stillwater," Rose says, shaking her head, blowing smoke in a great upward plume like a whale. She speaks to him as if she's known him her whole life long instead of two months. "I don't think you've ever gotten over being your mama's favorite."

Cash only lets Rose hurt him this way because he knows she is right. As a young man he turned his name around in honor of his mother's favorite singer. Now he's working as a fifty-nine-year-old bag boy at the Health Corral; his immediate superior there is an eighteen-year-old named Tracey who pops the rubber bands on her braces while she runs the register. And still Cash acts like luck is on his side, he's just one step away from being a cowboy.

Rose says suddenly, "They're going to shoot a bunch of pigeons that's come into town."

"Who is?"

"I don't know. A fellow from town council, Tom Blanny, came in the Trading Post today and told Mr. Crittenden about it."

Cash knows Tom Blanny; he comes into the Health Corral to buy cigarettes made of lettuce leaves or God knows what, for people who wish they didn't smoke.

"Tom said they're causing a problem because they don't belong here and they get pesty. They flock together too much and fly around and roost in people's trees."

Cash looks up, surprised. "I saw those birds tonight. I could see them out this window right here." His heart beats a little hard, as if Rose had discovered still another secret she could use to hurt him. But her concern is Town Council men and information, not an unnamable resentment against some shining creatures whose togetherness is so perfect it makes you lonely. Cash attends to peeling his potatoes.

"Tom says they could crowd out the natural birds if they last out the winter. A pigeon isn't a natural bird, it's lived in cities so long, it's like a weed bird."

"Well, aren't they natural anywhere?" He knows that in Jackson Hole people are very big on natural.

"New York City," she says, laughing. Rose has been around. "There's nothing left there for them to crowd out," she says.

Slip-slip-slip goes the peeler. Cash doesn't feel like saying anything else.

"What's eating on you, Cash? You thinking about going back to Oklahoma?"

"Naw."

"What's the weather like there now?"

"Hot, like it ought to be in summer. This place never heats up good. We're going to be snowed under here again before you know it. I wasn't cut out for six feet of snow."

"Nobody is, really. Even up in Idaho." Rose fluffs her hair. "You'd think they'd be used to it by now, but I remember when I was a kid, people going just crazy in the wintertime. Wives shooting their husbands, propping them up on a mop handle, and shooting them again."

Cash is quiet, leaving Rose to muse over murdered husbands.

"Well, go on back, then," she says. "If the weather's not suiting you good."

They have had this argument before. It isn't even an argument, Cash realizes, but Rose's way of finding out his plans without appearing to care too much. "Nothing to go back for," he says. "My family's all dead."

"Your daughter's not."

"Might as well be."

"Well then, what about your other daughter, the one that died—how about her baby?"

When Cash first knew Rose, she made herself so comfortable in his bed that he felt safe telling her family stories. Now he regrets it. "She's gone," he says.

"A baby ain't made with disappearing ink, Cash."

"You read about it in the papers ever day," he tells her, but he knows this is a lie. A mother might drive her car into the river on purpose, but still there will be a basket of outstretched hands underneath her children, or should be. It's the one thought in Cash's mind that never lights and folds its wings.

"I waited my whole life away down there in the Nation," he tells Rose. "Where nobody is nothing but poor. When my wife died, seem like I'd been waiting out something that wasn't coming. At least in Jackson Hole people have something."

"You and me don't have any of it."

"No, but we're right next door to it," he says, standing up to throw vegetables into hot water. "Maybe some of it will fall off the tree."

At one o'clock exactly, Rose whips off the patterned headscarf she has to wear in the window and scoops little cascades of clicking beads back into their plastic vials, careful to let none escape onto the plank floor. Mr. Crittenden allows Rose to go to lunch with Cash if they go late, after what he imagines to be the noontime rush. The truth is there is no rush, just a slow, steady dribble. Jackson Hole has a hundred Indian trading posts, and most of them have better gimmicks than a tired mother of teenagers in the front window ruining her eyes.

Rose wants to walk across town to the Sizzler for the salad bar, but Cash warns against it; a storm is cooking in the south. They stay close by at McDonald's just in case, taking the shortcut through the little flowered strip park on Main. While Rose talks and Cash doesn't listen, his mind counts pansies and ageratum: yellow, yellow, purple, purple, a beautiful, cast-off beaded belt of flowers stretched along the highway collecting dirt.

"Foof," Rose says. "I don't see how it has any business being this muggy." While they wait for traffic she reaches back to adjust something in the heel of her shoe. Rose is thirty-eight, the age his daughter Alma would be now if she had lived, and Cash realizes he treats Rose more like a daughter than a lady friend, cautioning about getting caught in the rain, clucking his tongue over the escapades of her boys. He wonders what she sees in him. Cash at least doesn't drink, or eat beads, but he knows he's getting old in a way that's hard to live with. It was a purely crazy thing for him to want to move up here two years ago. Oklahoma Cherokees never leave Oklahoma. Most don't even move two hickory trees away from the house where they were born.

In line at McDonald's, he notices men looking at Rose. Not a lot, not for long, but they look. Cash they don't even see; he is an old Indian man no one would remember having just walked by. Not just because of three generations of tragedy in his family—even without cancer and suicide and a lost grandchild, those generations would have come to pass; he would have gotten old.

"Just french fries and a chef salad today, hon, I'm on a diet," Rose says, flirting with the teenager at the register.

Cash misses his wife with a blank pain in his chest, and he misses his sisters and cousins, who have known him since he was a strong, good-looking boy. Everyone back there remembers, or if they are too young, they've been told. The old ones get to hang on the sweet, perfect past. Cash was the best at climbing trees; his sister Letty won the story bees. The woman who married Letty's husband's brother, a beauty named Sugar, was spotted one time drinking a root beer and had her picture in *Life* magazine. They all know. Now she has thin hair and a humped back but she's still Sugar, she gets to walk around Heaven, Oklahoma, with everybody thinking she's pretty and special. Which she is. That's the trouble with moving away from family, he realizes. You lose your youth entirely, you have only the small tired baggage that is carried within the body.

It shouldn't matter so much to Cash. He still has most of what he started with: a talent for schemes and friendship, and all of his hair. No one can ever hold a thing against Cash, except his restlessness. For thirty years, whenever Cash started talking like a white man, his wife would put extra food on his plate and turn her back tenderly and a little abruptly. After she got sick, Cash came untethered somehow, decided they needed to ride horses and see the Rocky Mountains. She died the year after they claimed she was cured: the doctor found no more cancer in her, and she only wanted to sit down and breathe out slowly and watch her grandbaby grow, but Cash danced her around the kitchen and swore he would show her the world. She told him television was a bad influence. Probably she was right. Like those white birds he's been seeing outside the window, it flashes its wings and promises whatever you want, even before you knew you wanted it.

Rose has nabbed a spot for them in the crowded restaurant and clears a huge mess from the table; the previous people were probably foreigners who didn't know the McDonald's custom of dumping your own burger wrappers. "It's party time in Jackson, ain't it?" Rose asks over the din, plumping down in her chair.

Cash nods. For nine months he trudged out on sidewalks dangerous with glassy shards of ice, the dirty snow piled deep and hopeless as a whole winter's worth of laundry. Now, for five or six weeks, the laundry is done. The streets swarm with people who will take their sunny raft trips and green-meadow pictures and spend the rest of their lives claiming Jackson Hole as one of the places they know.

The couple at the next table are speaking some language. The woman has on little green cloth slippers that you'd think would have fallen apart long before they made it halfway to anywhere from overseas. Cash knows these women; they come into the store and go crazy over anything herbal, then they march straight over to the Trading Post and buy Cash's earrings, Rose tells him, three pairs at a time. The Indian look is evidently big in Europe, where they don't have any Indians. They ask Rose personal questions, thinking she is something exotic. The Americans are different, they edge around Rose in the store, not looking, as if her clothes were terribly stained and she didn't know. Sometimes they'll come close and snap a picture. Cash has witnessed this, and he has to hand it to her for the way she sits still, holding her tongue for once. The customers pile up their purchases by the register, dropping in one minute what it takes Cash three weeks to earn.

"That guy mopping the floor has one cute butt," Rose states, fluffing her layers of dyed-black hair. "I feel like dropping a spoon or something just to see him pick it up."

"Rose, you have to decide if I'm your boyfriend or your daddy. I can't do both."

She flashes her eyes at him. "You know how much I love you, honey."

Cash doesn't add anything to that. He is grateful that McDonald's doesn't give out spoons.

"Just think," she says, "we could be in Paris, France or Hong Kong. They have McDonald's in every country in the world."

"That's what I hear," Cash says, but he doesn't feel like he's in Paris, France, he feels like he's in McDonald's.

"You seem depressed," Rose observes, and Cash wonders if that's what he is, after all. He thinks of the way you press dough down with your fist: take a big, round hopeful swelling and punch the rise right out of it. Yes, he thinks. Depressed.

* * *

Cash is off work at last. For the last ten minutes of his shift a couple stood in line arguing over whether or not to buy some expensive peaches. Cash stood silently by, wishing they would take their marriage someplace else, but Tracey rolled her eyes in a way that could not be missed, and still the couple paid no attention. The man's T-shirt said THINK ONLY OF SURFING. It amazes Cash what people will advertise, as if convictions mean so little they can put on a new one each morning after a shower.

The birds come every day now, mysteriously increasing their numbers overnight. Cash can see them right now as he walks down Main toward the Trading Post to pick up Rose. She has repeated to him the theory that pigeons are migrating here from Salt Lake City, to escape the falcons that are nesting on the ledges of tall buildings there. The balance of nature is upside-down, Cash thinks: the predators are moving to the cities and city birds taking over the land where the buffalo roam. He finds he mistrusts the pigeons. One minute they flash their silver underwings all together, all one color, and the next, their white backs, changing from moment to moment like a card trick.

This evening Mr. Crittenden wants to talk with him, a fact Cash dreads. He finally noticed that the beadwork Rose does in the store is nothing near the quality of what she brings in. Rose hedged, fearing she'd lose her job, but finally confessed it was made by her Cherokee friend. Mr. Crittenden wasn't angry, it turns out, but wants to meet Cash to ask about his methods. Cash has been in the store more than fifty times, but Mr. Crittenden never wanted to meet him before now.

"Foof, it's muggy," says Rose when he walks into the store. "I wish that rain would get here and get over with. It's not the heat gets me, it's the humanity."

Cash smiles. "That's the whole truth."

"Mr. Big Shot stepped out. He'll be back in a minute."

The cluster of tin bells over the door jingles behind Cash, but it's a customer, a tall, thin man wearing sandals and gray-speckled socks. He nods at Rose, who is at the register.

"Take a look around," she tells him with a broad smile Cash understands, and dislikes. "Does it look like that storm is coming in? We need some rain. We haven't had rain in a long time." Cash grins. He likes Rose better now because she is speaking to Cash in code, saying, "This one is going to look at everything in the entire store, and then buy some postcards." When she asks, "You folks drive a long ways?" she's predicting a big buy. "Front case is all marked down, rock bottom" means "All the jewelry in Jackson won't help this homely soul."

Cash stands near the window, looking out. He doesn't see the white birds but he knows they're up there still, moving in their rich, lazy wheel above it all, showing off, taking their freedom for granted. They aren't real birds like the ones he hunted in childhood, whose eggs he shimmied trees to snatch, birds who catch insects and build nests and feed their young. These are tourist birds. Like his own restless dreams that circle with no place to land.

The man in sandals leaves finally, without even buying a postcard. "Yep, long drought," Cash says, and Rose laughs. The tin bells jingle again, and they look up to see the white cockaded head of Mr. Crittenden. They stop talking, but the quiet that has come in with him is heavier than an absence of talk. He acknowledges Cash, then stands for a minute with his hands resting on the glass jewelry case, his thin elbows angled out. He always wears a white shirt and black bolo tie. Rose is curious about whether he is married; Cash says, just look at the pressed shirts he wears to work, but Rose maintains he could afford to send them to the laundry, which is true. She's heard a rumor that he owns his own airport somewhere, and another rumor that he has cancer. Neither of them believes the cancer story. If he planned on dying anytime soon, why would he spend so much of his time counting beads?

He nods at Cash again, and with a tight throat Cash follows him into the office, a small room crammed with ledgers and anthropology books and strange pets. Mr. Crittenden has seven or eight shrieking birds back there, and a python in a jewelry case half filled with dry sand. Rose warned Cash about the snake; she has to come in here to get her paychecks under its cool eye. The air chokes him with bird smells and loneliness. Mr. Crittenden gets down two large books that smell of dust. When he opens them, their insides are slick as white glass.

"This is very old beadwork," he tells Cash. He slowly turns the pages of black-and-white photographs. "Do you recognize the patterns?"

Cash does, some of them, but is afraid to admit to much, so he only nods or shakes his head at the photographs. While Mr. Crittenden turns the pages, a nervous gray bird in a cage near the window makes clicking sounds and picks at its neck as if it has a skin disease. Occasionally it raises its head and screams, and then the rest of the room rings with whistles and the scratch of dry feet on thin metal bars. Cash holds his air inside him for as long as he can between breaths.

"This whole world of knowledge is being lost," Mr. Crittenden says, touching the page of his book as if he can feel the patterns. He leans his white head into the space between them, his blue eyes feverish, pink-edged.

"Are the men the artists in your tribe?" he asks.

Cash tries not to smile. "No, the women just let me pick it up a little."

"Do your daughters know how to do this kind of work?"

"They do it," Cash tells him, and it's true, they did, before Alma landed upside-down in the river and Sue landed in the hospital for the third or fourth time with a broken cheekbone and a few other presents from her boyfriend. But even before all the sadness, they didn't do beadwork in the picture-perfect way Mr. Crittenden surely imagines. Cash's daughters and nieces have perms and belong to Weight Watchers. If they make up a pair of earrings from time to time, it happens while they're on the phone with each other, laughing their deep smokers' laughs, criticizing their husbands' friends. Cash was never entirely in on the conversation, but still, that is the world he's sad to have lost.

Mr. Crittenden sees Cash staring at the window. "That's a gray-tailed cockatoo. They used to be terrible pests in Australia. Wheat farmers shot them by the thousands. Now there aren't a great many of her kind left."

But Cash had been thinking how sad it was there was not even a plant on the windowsill in here. Not one green thing that can sit in the sun and be quiet.

The humidity rises all week. Friday afternoon feels weighted and endless, like the end of a life. By six, Cash feels desperate. He is back at the Trading Post again, waiting for Rose to finish up. Maybe they will go to a movie. Something to take his mind away from here for two hours. But Mr.

Crittenden still hasn't come in to lock up and dole out his beads.

"When was he in last?"

Rose thinks. "Didn't he come at lunchtime?"

"No, we just went."

"That's right."

Cash stands in the bay window, looking up at the birds he despises, wheeling in a tight, anxious circle. Tonight they seem to be looking for something—their own lost wishes. New York City, maybe. He smiles to himself.

"His door's open," Rose says.

"Maybe we should close it up and go."

"Maybe we should go find where he keeps all the money."

"Rose, I swear. Just close the door. I don't know how you listen to them parakeets all day, they would drive me insane." He watches the gathering storm. *Man, you're already crazy, no driving needed,* he thinks, just as Rose shouts: a tremulous, rising "Whooo?"

Cash's shoulders tighten and he turns. "What is it?"

"He's in here."

Cash wonders instantly if Mr. Crittenden has been listening to their talk, to Rose's gossip. Her joke about taking his money! He tries to remember what other wild thing she might have said that could lose her job for her.

"Cash," Rose says, her face white, her voice once again a rising note, and then he understands what it is. Mr. Crittenden has not heard a thing.

Cash stays up late working on a beaded belt. He is tired, but can't imagine sleeping. He and Rose spent a long time repeating the details to each other, as if they'd been shipwrecked in some new place where only this event existed: the police said suicide, no question, he'd taken prescription sleeping pills and left his account books organized. There is a wife, it turns out; she lives in Rock Springs and probably had nothing to do with his shirts. Her instructions over the phone were to keep the store open for the rest of the season, if possible. A management company in town will see that Rose gets paid. Cash doubts that she will have the nerve to go back. The whole time the police were there she clutched her bosom and breathed as if she'd run a mile in those high heels.

Cash wants to know things Rose hadn't even considered: who will come get the animals, for example? He doesn't favor the idea of her working under the same roof as a starving snake. And how long was Mr. Crittenden dead in there? He can't get his mind's eye to stop staring at Mr. Crittenden blue at the mouth and fingertips, frozen in his last slump while three men turned him through the doors like furniture and carried him out of the store. Did he kill himself in the middle of the night, or at dawn? Cash wanted every single how and what, in order to muffle the sound of "Why?"

Rose has taken the Valium the doctor gave her and gone to untroubled sleep in Cash's bed, leaving Cash alone with the bare light bulb and the wall calendar from Wickiup Hauling. The month of July shows families on a yellow river raft. They have cameras and bright-colored clothes and expressions of surprise, each mouth like a slack little rip in the face: they're coming into white water. He recognizes his own innocence, before he came up here. Now he knows enough about shining promises to wonder who sat by the river all day slapping mosquitoes to get this picture, and what he got paid for it. His knuckles ache because of the changing weather, and twice tonight he has lost plastic beads into the orange linoleum, which is curled up and cracked in places as if volcanoes planned to erupt from under his floor. "Let them go," he whispers aloud, but the habit of holding on to every small, bright bit of color is hard to forget.

When he finally goes to bed he still doesn't rest, but has a dream about his dead wife. She is standing in the kitchen of their little crooked house in the woods, cutting up a hen for soup.

"How come you won't turn around and face me?" he asks.

"You turned loose of family," she says. "I have to turn my back on you."

"Why even talk to me, then?" he asks.

"I'm cooking for you, aren't I?"

"Yes. But I'm afraid you hate me."

"Why would I cook for you, then?"

"I don't know," he says.

"Pay attention to who takes care of you."

She stirs the huge pot on the stove. Turning in the bubbling surface,

Cash can see a dry tuft of Mr. Crittenden's white hair. His wife is very large. There is no roof on the kitchen, only a forest clearing and legs like trees. Her head looks like carved stone against the sky, a head he can't precisely recognize. It could as easily be his mother, or his daughter. "There's a hundred ways to love someone," her voice tells Cash. "All that matters is that you stay here in the same room."

He wakes with his chest so full it might burst. He wonders whether he has had a heart attack, or is simply dying of loneliness. "I have to go back," he tells Rose, not caring that she is asleep, and will not hear.

The summer rains in the Rockies come all the way up from Mexico. Or so Cash has often told himself, in an effort to make himself believe he's leading an exciting life. But Mexico or no, the rain is terrible for tourism, the Health Corral has been empty all day. Tracey sits at the checkout counter reading the gossip magazines, asking Cash whether he believes a woman could actually give birth to triplets with three different fathers. Cash thinks of his own wild daughters, and doesn't doubt it.

Rose wasn't afraid to go back to work. At lunchtime she reported it was the same over there, no business. She claims the news has gotten around and nobody wants to come into a store where a man took his life. Cash knows better: people around here would come in hunting bargains, hoping for a suicide sale. It's the weather causing the slowdown. Vacationers expect perfect happiness, perfect weather, and if they don't meet it here they'll drive on toward Missoula or wherever else they imagine they will find it. Young people, like Rose, one eye always on the road out of town.

When Cash hears the first shots, he feels strangely exhilarated. He'd thought maybe they would call off the bird shoot because of the rain, but the boom of gunfire comes again, rattling the plate-glass store front. He leaves his post at the checkout and presses himself near the window, waiting. "They're shooting those pigeons today," he tells Tracey.

"I read about that in the paper. That's gross, isn't it? They can't just let some poor little birds alone?"

"They're weed birds," Cash says. "They want to live here but they can't. That's why they keep going around and around up there."

He feels another boom, and the subtle aftershock. His whole body vibrates with the plate glass. Suddenly the birds are there in the sky, not circling in their perfect wheel but scattered in every direction by twos and threes, turning in flighty panic. On their own. He thinks of the place a world away from here where he climbed trees with no greater longing in his chest than to find a nest full of eggs. Cash can see his own face in the plate glass, empty with relief, as the shot birds fold their wings and vanish one by one, finding the ground at last.

12

THE TWILIGHT ZONE OF HUMANITY

ALL THREE GENERATIONS OF ALICE'S family have been lifted into the air for the first time this summer: first Turtle and Taylor flew to Chicago and back, and now the first leg of Alice's own flight is coming in for a landing. Alice feels this shows an unusual degree of togetherness. Her plane scoots under the clouds, revealing the Mississippi River and St. Louis far below. A huge metal arch on the riverbank stands higher than any building, put there for no purpose Alice can envision. As useful as spitting off a bridge, but people do such things, to prove they were here on earth for a time. The descending plane sweeps over the largest graveyard Alice has seen so far. Her neighbor in the window seat has spent the flight hunched in silence, and now remarks: "Well, that's some welcome."

"I can see the point of it," Alice says, determined to disagree cordially with this cheerless woman. "If you have to make so much noise, you'd just as well pester the dead as the living."

"We won't have far to be carried if we don't make it," the woman says dryly. She has a surprisingly small head, and auburn hair that looks artificial, and for the whole trip from Lexington she has been wearing an aggrieved little face as if her shoes are on the wrong feet. Alice is dismayed. She'd expected everyone else on the plane to be experienced travelers from big cities slouched back in their seats, snapping open their papers to the Money section. But here she is as usual, bearing up those around her. To change the subject from graveyards she asks, "Is St. Louie the end of the road for you?"

The woman nods faintly, as if the effort might be incompatible with her hairstyle.

"I stay on till the next stop, Las Vegas," Alice reports. "I've got a daughter and a little grandbaby out there that have fell on hard times."

The woman perks up slightly. "She divorcing?"

"Oh, no," Alice says, "my daughter's never been married. She found the little girl in her car one time and adopted her. She's independent as a hog on ice."

The woman turns back to the window and its outstanding display of graves.

"Somebody just left the baby in her car and said 'So long, sucker!' What could she do?" Alice reaches for the pictures in her purse. "It turned out all right, though; that little girl is a pistol. Whoever left her off had no eye for good material."

Alice flatters herself that she knows how to get a conversation going, but for this woman it's the subject of divorce and graveyards or nothing; she snaps the window shade down and closes her eyes. Alice leaves the pictures of Turtle in her wallet, dreading the picture in her mind's eye: an old woman talking to herself. She offers a peppermint LifeSaver to the man across the aisle but it's the same story over there, he barely shakes his head. They are a planeload of people ignoring each other. Alice has spent her life in small towns and is new to this form of politeness, in which people sit for all practical purposes on top of one another in a public place and behave like upholstery.

She can't remember when she was ever around so many people at one time that she didn't know. They look strange: one is shrunken-looking with overblown masses of curly hair; another is hulky and bald, the head too big for the body; another has the troublesome artificial look girls get from earrings, glasses, a glint of braces, too many metal things around the face. It's as if these people were all produced by different manufacturers who couldn't agree on a basic design. Alice saves this up to tell Taylor when she gets to Las Vegas. Whenever she used to mention to Harland anything more than life's broadest details, he thought she was cracked. But Taylor will know what she means.

Alice takes off her glasses and lays her hands on her face, feeling her eyes like worried, wet marbles under the lids. Taylor in trouble is not something Alice knows how to think about. Everything she's done before now, however crazy-quilted it might have seemed, always ended up with the corners square. The first time Taylor took a step, she walked right out the door of the Pittman P.O. Alice was at the counter buying stamps and asking the postmistress, Renata Hay, when her baby was due; Taylor was eleven months old and hung on the hem of Alice's coat until she felt she'd grown a heavy tail back there. Suddenly a grand round of applause went up among the old men waiting for their Social Security checks, and Alice turned in time to see her baby headed out into the street. Old Yancey Todd held the door for her like a gentleman.

Some people would say a headfirst child like that was bound to wind up headfirst in the mop bucket. Alice doesn't think so. In her heart, she knows her daughter would have looked both ways before she went out to play in East Main. Or Yancey would have flagged down the cars. When you're given a brilliant child, you polish her and let her shine. The universe makes allowances. When Taylor called from a phone booth in Las Vegas with her soul broken in twenty pieces, Alice felt deeply betrayed. The universe has let them down.

The seat-belt sign dings on, and Alice opens her eyes. A stewardess is coming slowly down the aisle taking people's plastic cups away, like a patient mother removing toys her babies might try to swallow. Alice watches, marveling at the outfit: under her navy blazer she wears a buttoned white shirt and a paisley silk tie with, even, a fine gold chain fastened across it. How long it must have taken her to get it all just right, in spite of her busy life. Alice is a passenger in need of comfort and she takes some from this: the touching effort some people put into just getting dressed in the morning, believing a little gold chain fastened over a silk tie will somehow make a difference.

Taylor and Alice tower over Turtle, holding on to each other with heads together and legs apart, leaning like a crooked teepee. They stand that way for a long time in the airport while people walk around them without looking, desiring only to make their connections. Alice's empty white sweater sleeves hang from her shoulders. Turtle pushes her head against Taylor and holds the hem of her shirt, since there isn't anything else. She met her Grandma Alice once before but that time nobody was crying.

"Mama, I haven't been like this, I swear," Taylor says. "I didn't fall to pieces till just this minute."

Alice rubs her back in a circle. "You go ahead and fall apart. That's what I'm here for." Turtle watches the hand with big knuckles move up and down her mother's back, and waits for something to fall. After a while they move apart. Taylor tries to carry everything Alice has.

"What'd you put in this suitcase?" she asks. "Rocks? Harland's headlights?"

"I'll Harland's headlights you," Alice says, laughing, smacking Taylor on the bottom.

She comes down to Turtle with a hug. She smells like chewing gum and Kleenex and sweaters. Turtle thinks: this is the telephone Grandma. She is nice and this is how she looks.

"Turtle, you can carry this carry-on bag for Grandma, okay?" Taylor stoops to put the strap over Turtle's shoulder. "I can't believe how strong you are. Look, Mom, doesn't she walk like a queen? I swear I didn't teach her that. It's a natural talent, she has perfect posture."

Turtle leans against the weight of the bag and puts each heel and toe on the long blue line in the carpet.

Alice blows her nose again. "Did you all eat? I'm starved. I had roasted peanuts for lunch."

"We had apricots for lunch," Turtle says, and her mother starts crying again. It's the crying that looks like laughing from the back, but isn't. The most bad thing would be if her mother goes away and the bad place comes. Turtle wishes she could put the words she said back in her mouth and eat them. They would taste bright and sour, like dimes. She feels the door of her back teeth closing. There are forty or a hundred people in the airport so she makes sure to follow the blue jean legs and the white grandma sandals. Their heads are big and too far away like dinosaurs. The talking comes out like round bubbles. When they go outside the sun hurts a little, as much as water hurts when it runs out hot on your hands.

"Turtle, Turtle, Turtle," someone is saying. "It's okay, Mama, I told you about." All the cars are shiny animals under water. They can't get air.

Somewhere else in the old place was that shine of angels or stars too close, the underwater, shoes on the floor and no light and a man's voice across your mouth and you can't get air. A woman crying.

A woman turned on a flashlight and moved her arms that were like fish arms, and her mouth opened and closed.

"We can eat at the coffee shop," her mother's voice is saying. The bubbles break open and Turtle hears each one of those words come out. So much time has passed that it might be another day, or the same day but dark. It isn't dark. They are in the car, moving. The front seat is far away. A boy on a bicycle goes by, the gold bicycle lifting its front wheel off the sidewalk again and again like a scared horse. The boy has a yellow shirt and blond hair in his eyes, laughing, not afraid. His feet move faster than he is going. Turtle kneels on the seat and looks back, watching this one boy and bicycle that look the right way, until they are gone. She sits down again.

"The good news is you can get a hotel room in this town for eleven dollars a night. If you stay in a junky place with a casino downstairs. I guess they figure on getting your money by other means."

"They done got yours," Grandma says.

"A hundred and ten dollars. I could shoot myself."

Turtle sees her hands, and thinks: *These are my hands.*

"That's if you would have stopped when you got to the top. That's not what you started out with."

"No, we started with fifty."

"So that's all you lost, really."

"Why didn't I stop?"

"Because you were speculating. If you could get a hundred and ten out of fifty, why couldn't you make a thousand out of a hundred and ten."

"Stupid."

"Stupid as every other soul in this town, honey. Look at those neon lights, and tell me who you think is paying the electric bill."

"We were feeling lucky."

"That's who's paying it. Mister and Missus I was feeling lucky."

"We found the fifty dollars on the car windshield. Turtle found it." She looks back in the driving mirror and smiles. Her face around her eyes is red and white. "It felt like maybe that money was charmed." She laughs the way that means nothing is really funny: tssh, pushing out air, shaking her head. "I still can't believe a person could put two hundred quarters in a slot machine one right after another and not win *anything.*"

Grandma laughs. "You've got a hair of your daddy in you. Foster was a gambler."

Turtle says, "Mama, do you have a daddy?" But they don't hear, the words only walked inside her ears. The back-teeth door is still closed. When her six-year molars came in, they felt like a pocketful of small rocks squeaking and rubbing.

"A better one than me, I hope."

"Lord, no, he wasn't worth a toot as a gambler. If there was a storm coming in he'd bet you it was going to stay dry, just to put spice in his day. One time he bet a man he could outrun his dog."

"What kind of a dog was it?"

"I don't know, but it left Foster at the starting post. If the dog had lapped up as much Old Grand-Dad as Foster had, Foster might of had a chance."

Turtle opens her mouth wide and says, "Mama, do you have an old granddad?" In the front seat they both laugh out loud. True laughing, not pushed air. They have heads on their bodies, laughing mouths, and hands; they look the right way again. Turtle has hands also. She lies down and hugs herself.

"Look at us. Three crazy girls in the city of lonely hearts." Taylor squeezes Alice's hand on top of the table. The hotel is called the Delta Queen Casino, and the coffee shop is decorated in a con-artist theme: on the wall are large framed photos of Clark Gable as Rhett in *Gone With the Wind,* and Paul Newman in *The Sting.* The red plastic chairs look like someone got them in a bad trade. The background music is a chorus of high steady dings, the sound of coins in slot machines, which reach Taylor like repeated small slaps in the face. She can't believe she was a fool just like every other fool. The one thing she's always hoped for is to stand out of the crowd. She grits her teeth at the TV screen over the bar, which is blinking out colorful letters and numbers so that the people who don't want to waste any time can play video Keno while they eat.

Alice is making conversation with Turtle. "Do you hate it when old ladies make a big fuss and tell you you've grown two feet?"

Turtle shakes her head.

"Well, you have." She bends her gray head close to Turtle's and speaks seriously, without condescension. "You're a big long-legged *girl* now, not a baby anymore." Taylor watches the cards of her own childhood played out at the table. Alice always knows what you need. Being near her mother makes Taylor aware of all her inside parts, cradled soft things like the livers in supermarket chickens.

"Taylor says you know how to write your name." Alice fishes in her huge purse for a pen, and turns a napkin on the table in front of Turtle. "Can you show me?"

Turtle shakes her head again.

"Doesn't matter. You still know how, right? If you need to sign a check or something, then we know we can count on you. No sense wasting a signature on a napkin."

She leaves the pen on the table. From the casino someone's voice shouts out "*Ho*-ly," followed by the chattering rain of quarters into the jackpot bucket. Taylor is afraid she's going to cry again and send Turtle into a tail-spin, so she keeps her face behind the plastic menu. "What do you want for dinner, Turtle?" she asks. "A glass of milk and what else?"

Turtle shrugs. Taylor can see the gesture without even looking.

"Grilled cheese?"

"Okay."

Taylor looks over the top of the daily special and tells Alice, "You get kind of hypnotized, sitting there listening to the quarters ding. Then you start thinking, 'It's been this long, my number's got to be *almost* up.' And then you put your hand in your pocket and pull out a gum wrapper."

Alice holds on to her hand.

At a table nearby, a wife and husband are having a fight. They have on matching outfits, jeans and fringed shirts that cowboys might wear, or people in a cowboy-related industry. The woman has colorless flippy hair molded together with hairspray so that it all comes along when she turns her head. The man looks very old. "Five hundred dollars," he keeps saying, again and again, like the talking change machines out in the casino that will turn your paper cash into silver dollars. The woman says different things each time, including "Like hell" and "You don't know your butthole from the road to China." Suddenly she stands up and starts hitting him on the side of the head with her purse. Her stiff hair wags excitedly. The man bends his head down and accepts the blows as if he has known all this time they were coming, like pie for dessert. Taylor is relieved that Turtle has her back to this event.

"I don't know what I would have done if you hadn't said you'd drop everything and come," she tells Alice. "I swear I was at the end of my tree."

"Well, it was good timing," Alice says. "I'd run out of marriage and I needed a project. Have you heard any more about," she moves her eyes slowly toward Turtle and back.

"It's okay to talk about it, Mama. Turtle knows. I called Jax last night and he said there was nothing new."

They both look at Turtle, who has put the menu very close to her face and is quietly reciting the names of different foods.

The woman who was hitting her husband sits down for a breather. She drags heavily on her cigarette, as if her only possible oxygen must come through that less than ideal source.

"This is the twilight zone of humanity," Taylor announces. "That's what Jax would say right now: 'We have arrived at the twilight zone of humanity. Let us bow our heads in a moment of silent prayer.' "

"I believe he's making you turn cynical," Alice says. She adds, "That waitress over there has been staring at us like a stuck pig."

"I know. I hope she's getting her eyes full."

Turtle twists in her seat to look at the staring waitress.

"How's that Jax treating you, anyway?" Alice asks.

"Oh, he treats me good. Too good. I don't deserve him."

"You hush. You know better than that."

Taylor smiles. With her left hand, the one that isn't holding Alice's, she puts down the menu and rubs the bone behind her left ear. "Yeah, I know better."

"I picture him as looking exactly like that." Alice points to the photo of Rhett Butler.

Taylor laughs out loud. "Oh, that's Jax to perfection. If you leave out the hair, the face, the body and the mustache."

"Well, that's how he talks, anyway. Like a southern gentleman. Except for some of the wild things he comes up with. He's real entertaining over the phone."

"I'm glad you think so. He keeps asking me if I'm truly in love with our garbage man. He's a lot more insecure than Rhett Butler."

"If you're having trouble sticking with him, that's my fault. I didn't bring you up with men as a consideration. I think single runs in our family."

"It's nothing you did wrong, Mama, I never missed having a dad. Plus I don't think your theory holds water. My friend Lou Ann grew up without her dad, and she feels like if she doesn't have a man in the house she's not worth taking up shelf space."

"Well, you're solid gold, honey, don't let that slip your mind. You deserve the King of France."

"Maybe that's my problem then. Jax is definitely not the King of France."

The staring waitress walks toward them. When she gets to the table she stands staring while three glasses of ice water sweat it out in her hands. She is tanned and blonde, her hair in a tight ponytail, almost aggressively pretty; the jawbones and cheekbones push up hard under her skin as if something in her might burst. Finally she says, "Oprah Winfrey, right?"

Alice makes a surprised smile with raised eyebrows and her tongue against her lips. Taylor waits a second before saying, "Is that the whole question?"

"I saw you on Oprah Winfrey, right? The show where the Barbie Dream Convertible was used to save a young girl's life? I have it on tape. It's you, right?"

"Kind of."

She thunks down the glasses of water with conviction. "I knew it! When you came in I saw you sit down over here in my station and I'm like, 'It's them, it's them!' and the other girls go, 'You're nuts,' but it is. I knew it was."

She extracts a pencil and pad from the pocket of her low-cut uniform, a short, red showboat outfit with frills. She stands gazing at them some more. Up close, Taylor decides, she looks slightly apart from the mainstream of the human race; she has hair of an unnatural color, pure yellow, and little curled bangs, and blue eye makeup that exceeds the size of her actual eyes. Her figure is the kind you notice even if you're not all that interested in women's great figures.

"I think we're ready to order now," Taylor says.

"Okay."

"A glass of milk, two Cokes, three grilled cheeses."

The waitress doesn't write anything.

Taylor asks, "You have that Oprah Winfrey show on *tape?* That's amazing."

"I have probably the largest personal collection of Barbie-related items in the entire world. There's this Barbie Hall of Fame Museum down in Palo Alto, California, right? And I've been there ten times so I know everything they have, all the original ones that cost, like, one thousand dollars to buy, in the original box. I don't have those. But I've got videotapes and stuff they don't have in Palo Alto. I'm like, why not? You know? Didn't they even think of it? I have autographs, even. That kid that hit the dog with the Dream Convertible and saved a young girl's life, is she a friend of yours?"

"No," Taylor says.

"After I saw that show I got the idea of an ensemble called the Barbie Rescue Team, with an ambulance, where she's dressed up as a paramedic, you know? A little white skirt with a tiny slit, and an emergency bag with those blood-pressure things? It could come with a teeny bulldog to inflict the wounds. I wrote Mattel about it, I'm like, 'Guys, this would be so cute,' but I haven't seen them come out with it yet."

Taylor and Alice look at each other. Turtle rubs her nose. The waitress blinks, exactly twice. "So a milk, two Cokes, three grilled cheese, anything else?"

"No, I changed my order," says Alice. "I want the turkey open-face special. I've gotten hungrier while we were setting here waiting to order."

"Sorry!" the waitress says, and heads for the kitchen fast on her red wedgie heels.

"Well, shut my mouth," Alice says. "I had no idea I belonged to such a world-famous family."

"Mama, that's not normal. Nobody ever recognizes us from that show. Do they, Turtle?"

Turtle shakes her head.

"The waiters here are just weird. The one this morning was a comedian; he kept telling us knock-knock jokes about the Manson family."

"Well," Alice says, "why else would somebody live here? They're looking for a career as nightclub acts, and hashing tables till they get the big break."

"Yeah, but this one takes the prize. She's accepted Barbie as her personal savior."

Alice spits out her ice water on her lap, and Taylor feels like something special again. She still can make Alice laugh.

13

THE CHURCH OF RISK AND HOPE

CHECKOUT TIME AT THE DELTA Queen Casino is eleven o'clock; at 11:17, Alice is having a difference of opinion with the manager. "All we want is to grab a bite of lunch and we'll be out of your hair in a jiffy," she explains. Huck Finn and Tom Sawyer, pictured from some old movie, grin from the wall behind the desk.

The manager has fat, pale hands decorated with long black hairs, and a gold watch that looks painful on his wrist. "You're welcome to stay in your room another hour, ladies, but I'm going to have to charge you the full day's rate."

"For seventeen minutes. Because people are banging down your door to get in here and you're turning them away," Alice says, staring him down. The place looks deserted, maybe even shut down on account of hygienic difficulties. The brown edges of coffee stains on the manager's desk blotter remind Alice of a map of the world that Columbus might have used. The front door has cardboard taped where some panes of glass should be, causing the sign to read oddly: "A QUEEN SINO HOTEL." The casino shows no sign of life at this hour. Apparently the Las Vegas lifestyle involves gambling till dawn, then remaining passed out through the heat of the day. Only a few lone hangers-on sit stubbornly at their video poker machines.

"Okay," Alice declares, looking him in the eye, "we're gone. Our room's empty. We left the key up there in the ashtray and walked out at ten fifty-nine." She crosses her arms, daring him to jog upstairs and see if she's telling the truth. His craggy eyebrows are collecting sweat under her gaze. He belongs to that species of men who are so spherical in the trunk you have to wonder what holds their pants up. There's no chance in this world Alice is going to lose her gamble. After they pay, Taylor can run up, pack their things, and come down by the fire exit.

"I'll meet you at the pancake house across the street," Alice whispers to Taylor as she takes Turtle and heads for the front door. Taylor reads her mind perfectly. They are Tom Sawyer and Huck Finn.

"Vegas ain't what it used to be," Alice tells Turtle as they wait outside to cross the street. "I was here before, I drove out here one time with your mama's wild daddy. But it's all different with these video games. People dragging downstairs in house slippers and sitting at a machine all day. Back then it was pigs in clover."

"What's pigs in clover?"

"Rich people that don't know how to behave. Ladies in high heels smoking, and gentlemen drinking too much and pinching their bottoms." The pedestrian light blinks WALK, a woman in leather shorts on a motorcycle runs the red light, and then they cross. Turtle is holding Alice's hand in a way that reminds her of an arthritis flare-up.

In truth, Alice thinks Las Vegas was far more interesting the last time. She remembers people crowded around a green felt table, each one bringing a different story and a different need to that smoky room, joined together in a moment of risk and hope. In a way it was like church, with more interesting clothes.

Now there is hardly a green felt table to be seen; Las Vegas is just a giant video arcade. Blackjack, poker, whatever you want, you play it on a machine. Last night they went down to Caesar's Palace just for fun, and in the giant casino five hundred people sat expressionless and completely alone, slumped at their machines, dropping in tokens. From what Alice can see, Americans now prefer to lose their money in private.

The Queen Bee's House of Pancakes is sunny and clean, at least, and puts her in a better mood. Each table has three different kinds of honey in a cloverleaf-shaped container, and the busy-bee waitresses wear antennae headbands with bobbling yellow balls on long springs. Alice and Turtle sit at a booth by the window, where Turtle's head is crowned with light. Alice writes words on her napkin for Turtle to read, discovering that she is confident with three-letter words, and likes rhymes. Turtle ducks her head and giggles at the sentence, "I let my pet get wet." Her skin is brown velvet against her white T-shirt, and her soft bangs divide on her forehead when she shakes her head, making long upside-down Vs.

"What a con job," Taylor declares, out of breath, suddenly sliding into the booth beside Turtle. "I had to set off the fire alarm to get out the back door. That guy's going to put our picture up in the lobby." Taylor sits back, closes her eyes and tilts her head against the high seatback. Her long hair slides behind her shoulders like a curtain drawn open. She exhales loudly, sounding happy. "Mama, it's hot as fire out there already. We're going to roast, driving out of here." She's wearing a pale pink T-shirt, Alice notes—a color Taylor used to make a point of hating. She always had to wear outspoken things, red, purple, orange, sometimes all at once. Alice realizes something important about her daughter at this moment: that she's genuinely a mother. She has changed in this way that motherhood changes you, so that you forget you ever had time for small things like despising the color pink.

Alice is filled with satisfaction, sitting with her daughter and granddaughter in a booth where three varieties of honey glow in the sun. Taylor's skin is much lighter than Turtle's but her hair is nearly as dark, and they share something physical, a beautiful way of holding still when they're not moving. Alice reminds herself that it's not in the blood, they've learned this from each other.

"Oh, my God!" Taylor almost shouts suddenly, staring, but Alice can't see what she's seeing.

"What?"

"America's number-one teenage fashion doll."

It's the waitress from last night, sitting on a stool at the counter. Her red uniform looks slept-in, and her makeup looks as if she's given birth to a child since it was applied. "Good Lord," Alice whispers. Turtle is trying to see too. Taylor waves, with limited enthusiasm.

"We ought to invite her to join us, don't you think?" Alice asks. Clearly the child is in some kind of fix.

Taylor rolls her eyes. "And hear more about the one point two million pairs of shoes that have been sold for Barbie's personal use?"

Alice hesitates, but is overcome by mothering drives. "But look at her."

"Okay, sure." Taylor motions her over, and she appears instantly, with bright eyes and a smile sunk into her desperate face.

"Set down, hon," Alice says. "No offense, but you look like you've been drug through a knothole."

"No, I lost my job at the Delta Queen." She scoots in and reaches for a paper napkin to blow her nose, then delicately works at her eyes. Alice finds a mirror in her purse, which is a mistake. The poor child takes a look and starts bawling.

The pancake house waitress appears just then with their paper place mats and a pot of coffee. Her antennae bob quietly over her gray curls as she stands for a moment appraising her chances of getting them to place an order. She looks at Alice's eyes and says, "I'll come back."

Turtle stares at their new friend, the disheveled waitress. Taylor looks down, studying her place mat, a line-drawing map of the Southwest noting features of interest and Queen Bee's Houses of Pancakes in four states. They all seem to radiate out from Salt Lake City, the mother hive.

"I'm Alice," Alice says finally, pouring everyone coffee. "I'm the mother and grandmother of these two famous girls."

The waitress rallies quickly. "I'm Barbie. No last name, I had it legally changed. I sign it like this, with the little trademark sign after it." She picks up Alice's ballpoint pen and writes a cheerfully looped, upward-slanting "Barbie TM" on Turtle's napkin, directly beneath "I let my pet get wet."

"Well, that's real unique," says Alice.

"I was born in 1959, exactly the same year that the first Barbie was developed and marketed by Mattel. Don't you think that's like too coincidental? The woman that invented her named the doll after her own daughter Barbara, and guess what. My name at birth was Barbara." She looks wide-eyed around the table and blinks. Her eyelashes have remained amazingly long in spite of the disaster that's occurred on the rest of her face.

"How'd you get fired?" Taylor inquires, trying for common ground.

"The manager said I spent too much time talking to you guys. He said I was ignoring the other people in my quadrant. That's what he says, *your quadrant,* okay, like he's the designer of the space module."

"Well, that couple near us was having a bad fight," Alice says helpfully. "I don't think they wanted to be served."

"I know." Barbie makes her mouth into a specific pout. "The poopy old manager says some stupid thing to me every single day. And the other waitrons don't help, they take his side. They say I tell people too much about my hobby. This is, like, so stressful for me, that choice of words. Barbie is not a hobby, do you understand what I mean?"

Alice, Taylor, and Turtle say nothing, but she has their complete attention.

"This is a *career* for me, okay? I've changed my name, and I have worked so hard getting the wardrobe, I have thirteen complete ensembles and a lot of the mix-and-match parts. To fit me, I mean, that I can wear. They have to be made special, or you can put things together from St. Vincent de Paul's and the Goodwill, but it's extremely creative. I study the originals very carefully. I think somebody ought to appreciate a person's career goals, don't you?"

Alice says, "Were you thinking maybe you could be Barbie in a nightclub act?"

Barbie dips a fresh napkin into her water glass and goes at her eyes again. "I haven't totally thought out all the details, but something like that. I did the Barbie birthday party at a shopping center in Bakersfield. I was only nineteen at the time and they paid me two hundred dollars. But there's only so many opportunities in Bakersfield, so I thought being a waitron at, like, a casino in Las Vegas, you know? You're bound to meet somebody in high places. Life is full of surprises, right?"

Alice thinks of the sad outfit at the Delta Queen and can't imagine the depths of this poor girl's delusion. She is ready to adopt her on the spot. Their waitress sneaks back tentatively on her crepe soles, and looks relieved when they all order the breakfast special.

"There's a very exciting development coming out this fall," Barbie says, looking back and forth between Taylor and Turtle. "Mattel is launching its new line of ethnic Barbies. Hispanic and African-American."

Alice realizes with an indignant shock that Barbie has been scrutinizing their skin color. Taylor is stirring her coffee and seems not to have noticed. "Here, Turtle, you can color your placemat," Taylor suggests.

"I saw pictures of them," Barbie continues, leaning forward confessionally. "I have access to some very exclusive advance information on this. They appear to be identical to the original model except I think maybe they used plastic from darker dye lots. Also the hair is very special."

"Turtle has a Rastafarian Barbie," Taylor says. "Talk about special hair. She has blond dreadlocks."

Barbie goes blank. "I thought I knew every model on the market."

"This one isn't on the market. It's been rolling under the bed too long with the dust bunnies."

Alice turns to Barbie. "Hon, what you need is a cold washcloth and ten minutes in the ladies' room. Why don't you take my hankie and put yourself together before the pancakes come."

"Oh, thank you so much," Barbie says, taking Alice's handkerchief and rising as if there's a book on her head.

Taylor puts up her hand, knowing what's coming. "Mama, I know I wasn't nice, but she's a kook." She glances at Turtle, who is using Alice's ballpoint carefully to blacken the entire state of Nevada.

"A kook in need of kindness."

"She's thirty years old!"

"Well, you will be too here in a minute. And I guess you've never been caught with your head stuck out on a limb."

Taylor drinks her coffee. "I don't see what we can do for her."

"What are we going to do for any of us?" Alice asks. "Get out of here, to start with. This town feels like poison. Everybody's so busy looking out for number one they'll run over you in the crosswalk. We ought to head for California or Yellowstone Park. Someplace wholesome."

"You think we should offer her a ride out of town?"

"I do. If she's ready to give up on meeting a movie star producer in the Delta Queen."

"That's a big If, Mama. We'd have to try to deprogram her like they did those Moonies."

"If she stops being perky for ten seconds, we'll know we're making headway."

"What's Moonies?" Turtle asks. "Moon people?"

"No, earth people," Taylor says. "People that got stuck thinking too much about one thing."

"Oh," Turtle responds. "Like Barbie."

The pancakes arrive, along with Barbie, surprisingly repaired except for the crumpled uniform. They eat in silence. Alice wonders how much makeup this woman carries on her person at any given time. She decides to let Taylor make the move, if she wants to take on an extra passenger. It's her car, after all, and her life that's gone to hell in a handbasket.

"Drink your milk, please, Turtle," Taylor says.

Turtle's dark eyes go to her grandmother's, then back to Taylor. She picks up the big white glass like some unwanted child of her own.

After several minutes Taylor asks, "So um, what are your plans now?"

"I could really use a shower," Barbie says. "Sheesh. But here's the thing, I live in the Delta Queen, and I'm just like totally not interested in going back in there at this moment in time."

"I meant, for the longer term."

"You mean later today? Or tomorrow? Holy smokes, I don't know. Get another job, I guess."

"Do you have any other prospects? Because if you ask me, this whole city looks like more of the same."

Barbie looks out the window and narrows her eyes, momentarily making a face unlike any ever seen on a teenage fashion doll. "Shit," she says, "I hate this town."

Taylor cuts Turtle's pancakes into small triangles, and smiles at her mother.

* * *

After breakfast they find the car where Taylor has hidden it, in the alley behind the Delta Queen.

"I'll just run upstairs and get my stuff and be down in ten seconds," Barbie says.

"Don't tell the manager you're with us," Alice warns.

"I'm not telling him poop," she replies.

"Mama, this is crazy," Taylor says when she's gone. "We don't know one thing about her except she's an obvious nut case. She could be a serial killer."

"You reckon she'll stab us with her eyebrow pencil?"

Taylor smiles, though she's trying to be serious. "The next town, that's all, Mama. I know you're the world's number-one soft heart, but you've been in Pittman all these years, and the world's changed. Don't you watch 'America's Most Wanted'? It's not safe to pick up hitchhikers."

"We're kind of responsible, though," Alice says. "She got fired for talking to us."

"I'm sure she talks to everybody about Barbie till their ears drop off."

"Yeah, but you and Turtle were a special case. She'd seen you on an Oprah Winfrey show devoted almost entirely to Barbie." Alice blinks her eyes twice.

"Mama, you kill me. I can't fight with you." She looks at her little mother, ready to hit the road in her white shell blouse and lavender pants.

"Well, what else are we going to do, just run off and leave her flat?"

"*Flat* she's in no danger of," Taylor says.

Alice is puzzled for a minute, then laughs. "You think those are real?"

"I dare you to ask."

They both watch the back door of the Delta Queen. Turtle is already in the center of the backseat, her usual post, prepared for whatever comes next.

"Are we going to fit all thirteen of her mix-and-match ensembles into the car?" Taylor asks.

"We'll see."

"It's just to the state line, right? Maybe she'll have better luck in Lake Tahoe. Maybe Ken lives there."

"We'll see," Alice repeats.

Barbie takes more than ten seconds, but less than half an hour. She appears, dressed in a traveling ensemble that includes white gloves and a hat. The rest of her outfits fill only two suitcases and a hatbox, and fit easily into the Dodge's huge trunk. While Taylor reorganizes their things in the back of the car, Barbie clutches her square black purse possessively and seems nervous. She yawns and stretches in the way people really don't do in real life. "I am so tired!" she exclaims. "Can I take a snooze in the backseat?"

Turtle nods, her whole body moving with her head, and moves far to one side of the seat to let Barbie lie down. Alice gets in front and heaves the door shut. It weighs about as much as she does. Taylor seems relaxed in the driver's seat, even without a specific destination.

From a highway overpass Alice gets a glimpse of the desert that lies around them. "Mercy, look what we've got to drive through now," she says. "A whole lot of nothing."

Taylor nods. "I think that's why Las Vegas is the way it is. It's kind of like the only trash can for a hundred miles, so all the garbage winds up in it."

"Imagine if you really lived here. I mean born and raised." They've left the city and are speeding through the suburbs now, row after row of square brick houses with yards that aren't even trying. No flowers, barely a bush. At the corner of a deathly quiet intersection, two tough little sunburnt girls have set up a lemonade stand. They aren't having a great day. A series of descending prices have been marked out on their cardboard sign. Now it says, LEMONADE: WHATEVER YOU CAN PAY.

"Look at that," Taylor says. "Socialism has arrived at the outskirts of Las Vegas."

Alice replies, "Lord, let us pray that it's so."

14

FIAT

"WE ARE COMING TO THE FINISH LINE of the human race," Jax says in the key of D, trying it out. "If you want to see who wins, then don't be in first place." Not very satisfying, but he writes it down anyway on the back of an envelope, which happens to be a telephone bill he hasn't had time to open yet.

Jax is writing the song in Gundi's Fiat. The car doesn't have a steering column at the moment, and is parked in what the neighborhood kids call the Retarded Desert, since this piece of land lies between Rancho Copo and a former halfway house for retarded adults. Jax has already written a song called "The Retarded Desert," so he isn't concerned about that right now. Like many musicians and other people who have tried out singing in different locales, he feels his voice expresses its best qualities inside a small car. Jax doesn't have a car of any size, so he borrows Gundi's. The windows have to be rolled up for acoustical reasons, and since it's July, Jax is sweating a good deal. His skin reminds him of porpoises. He rolls down the window for a breather. Above his house he can see a hawk with white underwings, riding air currents. It has been there for hours. The sparrows in the apricot tree have achieved perfect stillness, waiting for death, each one hoping to outlast its small feathered neighbor.

Turtle should be here now. She likes to sit in Gundi's Fiat with him in all seasons except summer, and often contributes verses. Jax feels that children below the age of, say, driving are more lyrical than adults.

He misses Taylor too, badly. She's been gone twelve days, with no homecoming party in sight. Taylor's and Jax's arrangement, sex-wise, is indefinite: Taylor said if Jax felt like being with someone else, that was okay with her, because it was going to be a long haul. "It's not like we're married," Taylor told him, and Jax felt the small green tree that had been growing up in the center of their bed suddenly chopped back to the root. He doesn't feel fine about Taylor's being with someone else. He wants her to get his name tattooed on her person, or have his baby. Or both. Jax would like his own baby. He and Turtle could take it to the park, where they go to observe duck habits. He would wear one of those corduroy zipper cocoons with the baby wiggling inside, waiting for metamorphosis. He likes the idea of himself as father moth.

Someone is coming toward him in a hurry through the Retarded Desert; it's Gundi, his landlady and owner of the Fiat. She has clothes on today. She moves fearlessly among her intimate friends, the cacti, and waves a small green slip of paper toward him. He doesn't get out of the car, but puts down his portable keyboard and sits with his elbow out the window, like a driver waiting for a long line of traffic to pass.

"A registered letter for you, Jax," Gundi says in her purple silk voice with its foreign, deeply emphasized r's. She hands him the green slip, but he is still listening to the dark carved valleys of her r's: "A registered letter for you." If his name were Robert, the sentence would have been musically perfect.

"This is a letter?" he asks eventually.

She laughs, a purple silk laugh. "You have to sign that. Come, Bill is waiting. He says he can't give the letter to anyone but you. It must be very important."

Jax totes his keyboard and follows her "vurry im*pohr*tant" back over Gundi's invisible path of safety through the desert. She moves snakishly, her blonde hair strumming the ridges of her shoulder blades. She's wearing leather sandals of the type worn by practitioners of yoga and pacifism, though the rest of her outfit is more aggressive: something in the line of a black brassiere, he can't get the full picture from behind, and a skirt made up of many long, satisfactorily transparent scarves.

Bill the mailman stands patiently in his blue shorts on the entry patio of Gundi's stone house. He has left a large pile of letters and catalogs in the little grotto by her door, where all residents of Rancho Copo come to collect their mail. The stone grotto was formerly a shrine, but Gundi removed the Virgin long ago and put in one of her own sculptures, a bright-colored dancing dog with a parrot in its mouth.

"Mr. Jax Thibodeaux?" the mailman asks.

"I am he." If Jax had a hat on, he could take it off and bow.

"Can you show some form of identification?"

Gundi says, "Oh, yes, of course, this is Jax," waving lazily to make everything agreeable, and the letter is left in Jax's hand. Gundi kisses Bill, who is not particularly young, on the cheek before he goes. Being European in origin, Gundi kisses everyone, probably even the exterminators who show up from time to time to rid her foundations of termites.

"Well, Jax, *come in,* you have to share your mystery."

The letter is from Oklahoma, on stationery belonging to the Cherokee Nation. Jax doesn't care to read the letter in front of Gundi's black brassiere, but he follows her into the cave of her entry hall, and then into the light of her sun-struck studio. The rest of the odd little houses of Rancho Copo are falling down by degrees, but Gundi has done a lot of remodeling here in the main house. The windows across the west wall reach all the way to the high ceiling, framing a dramatic view of the mountains.

"Sit here," she commands, pointing to the turquoise cushions of the long window seat. Jax puts down his keyboard and sits at one end of the window seat, his back resting against the deep windowsill, his legs stretched out on the turquoise cushions. He holds the letter at arm's length, looks at Gundi, and drops it on the knees of his jeans.

"It's bad news, I'll share that much of my mystery without further ado." He crosses his arms.

Gundi rests her weight on one sandal, a little uncertainly. "Then I will leave you and go make a pot of raspberry tea. When I come back you have to tell me what is so important and terrible that you have to prove with identification you're Mr. Jax Thibodeaux." She pronounces it correctly, "Tee-ba-doe," the first person in years to do so, but Jax tries not to be too grateful; it may just be an accident on Gundi's part, a result of being foreign-born.

When she's gone, he slits one end of the envelope and sees the same seal on the letter inside, Cherokee Nation, an eight-pointed star inside a wreath of leaves.

Dear Jax,

I'm glad I met you in Tucson. I feel you're a person with careful thoughts and a kind spirit. I want to tell you frankly that I'm worried about Turtle. I've spoken with Andy Rainbelt, a social psychiatrist who works with Cherokee children, and he authorized me to write on behalf of our Social Welfare Department. It's premature to take legal action yet, he says, but it's extremely important for Taylor to be in contact with the Nation; there are things she needs to know. I trust you'll get this information to her.

It's difficult, I know, for non-Native people to understand the value of belonging to a tribe, but I know you care about problems Turtle will face on her own. I appeal to you on those grounds. Adopted Native kids always have problems in adolescence when they're raised without an Indian identity. They've gone to school with white kids, sat down to dinner every night with white parents and siblings, and created themselves in the image of the family mirror. If you ask them what they think about Indians, they'll recall Westerns on TV or doing Hiawatha as a school play. They think Indians are history.

If these kids could stay forever inside the protection of the adoptive family, they'd be fine. But when they reach high school there's enormous pressure against dating white peers. They hear ugly names connected with their racial identity. If you think this kind of prejudice among teenagers is a thing of the past, think again. What these kids find is that they have no sense of themselves as Native Americans, but live in a society that won't let them go on being white, either. Not past childhood.

My boss thinks I'm crazy to pursue this case, but I have to tell you some-

thing. I used to have a brother named Gabriel. We grew up wearing each other's jeans and keeping each other's secrets and taking turns when our uncle asked, "Who made this mischief?" Gabe was my ayehli, *my other wing. When I was ten, our mother was hospitalized with alcoholism and other problems. Social workers disposed of our family: my older brothers went with Dad, who did construction in Adair County. I stayed with my Uncle Ledger. And Gabe was adopted by a family in Texas. No one has ever told me why it was done this way. I assume they thought my dad could handle grown, income-earning sons, but not Gabe and me. As for Gabe, probably the social workers knew a couple who wanted a little boy—something as simple as that. He wrote me letters on fringe-edged paper torn out of his ring-bound school notebooks. I still have them. Texas was hot and smelled like fish. His new parents told him not to say he was Indian at school, or they would treat him like a Mexican. He asked me, "Is it bad to be Mexican?"*

They put him into the Mexican classrooms anyway; his parents were bigots of the most innocent kind, never realizing that skin color talks louder than any kid's words. He failed in school because the teachers spoke to him in Spanish, which he didn't understand. The Mexican kids beat him up because he didn't wear baggy black pants and walk with his hands in his pockets. When we were thirteen he wrote to tell me his new Mom had closed the bedroom door and sat on the foot of his bed and said quietly he was letting his new family down.

When he was fifteen, he was accessory to an armed robbery in Corpus Christi. Now I only know where he is when he's in prison.

You said, the night we met, that I was only capable of seeing one side of things. I've thought about that. I understand attachments between mothers and their children. But if you're right, if I have no choice here but to be a bird of prey, tearing flesh to keep my own alive, it's because I understand attachments. That's the kind of hawk I am—I've lost my other wing.

I wonder what you are giving Turtle now that she can keep. Soon she's going to hear from someone that she isn't white. Some boy will show her that third-grade joke, the Land O' Lakes Margarine squaw with a flap cut in her chest, the breasts drawn in behind the flap, and ask her, "Where does butter come from?" On the night of the junior prom, Turtle will need to understand why no white boy's parents are happy to take her picture on their son's arm.

What does she have that will see her through this into a peaceful womanhood? As a citizen of Turtle's nation, as the sister of Gabriel Fourkiller, I want you to understand why she can't belong to you.

Yours sincerely,
Annawake Fourkiller

15

COMMUNION

"IT'S NOT SUCH A HARD name, Teebadoe," Gundi says. "It's Cajun, right? A bayou name." The turquoise cushions are on the floor around them, and Jax's head is in her lap. The raspberry tea is gone; they are past that stage of the consolation.

"My daddy was an alligator," Jax tells her, enjoying the pity. "He only bit once."

"What do people usually say, when they get your name wrong?"

"Thimble Dukes."

"And your girlfriend, what does she say?"

"She says, 'Jax, honey, get your butt in here please and pick up your socks.' " He rests his long hands on his face and rubs his eye sockets deeply.

Gundi strokes Jax's hair. "I'm very sorry for this strange disaster that has entered your life."

"I'm sorry too." Jax sits up, putting a few inches of turquoise cushion between himself and Gundi. She talks like a nineteenth-century romance novel with twentieth-century intentions. "I'm sorry Taylor and Turtle are living in a Dodge Corona. That part I know is a disaster. The rest I'm not sure about." He picks up his cup and cradles its warmth in his palms. They're drinking saki. Gundi believes in drinking warm things on warm days. The afternoon sun through the west windows is finally losing some of its hostility, but Jax's skin remains salty from his session in Gundi's Fiat. She commented on his taste, earlier, when she put a teacup in his hands and kissed his forehead.

"What if this Fourkiller is right?" he asks. "Just as an exercise in giving equal consideration to out-there points of view. What if the best thing for Turtle is to go back?"

"You mean go back permanently?"

"I think that's what *she* means."

"Isn't there another path?" Gundi asks. She says *pahth,* and moves her head in a large, lazy loop so that her light hair slides out of her eyes. Her earrings are made of beads that glitter like small metallic sparks. "The *I Ching* advises the moderate path," she says.

"Unfortunately, skin color doesn't come in 'moderate.' It comes in 'white' and 'other.' "

"I don't know about this. When I was a girl in Germany we read a little story in school about the Hopi, and I wanted to grow up to be an Indian. I think that's why I came here to Arizona, because of unconscious desires. I wanted my paintings to be touched by the primeval spirits of the land."

On the wall behind her, facing Jax, is a full-length portrait of nude Gundi with a saguaro. She stands in profile, her arms outstretched, so close to the cactus that her chin and other parts of her body appear to be recklessly touching its spines. The painting is more realistic than those in her previous series, which represented the moods of water. It will sell for more money, too.

"Do you think people like you and me can understand the value of belonging to a tribe?"

She looks at him, tilting her head. "Of course. We all long for connection."

"What do you want most in the world?" he asks.

"For my paintings to be extraordinary and great," she says without hesitation.

"And you write your name on every one."

"Well, I paint it on there. With a fine brush. Yes. Does that make me a bad person?"

"It makes you a solo flyer. Charles Lindbergh aiming for France. Not a group migration of geese."

"But I don't make paintings for myself, they are for other people. For the world. I want them to bring the world something more than its ordinary light."

"But you also want it known that Gundi made that light."

"Well, I want to get paid for my paintings, sure."

"Okay," Jax says, stretching his limbs. "Say I'm a genial millionaire and I will pay you a stellar salary to live on Rancho Copo and paint the great paintings, and donate them benevolently to the universe. Then you wouldn't sign them?"

"I think I would, still."

"Why?"

"Because I would want people to know this was the work of Gundi, and it didn't fall out of the sky."

"Gundi alone, apart from all other paintbrush-friendly members of the breed."

"Well, what about you, Jax? Would you perform your music with a ... with a grocery sack over your head?"

"I have, as a matter of fact. As a courtesy to my listening public."

She inclines her head again, smiling. Her beaded earrings struggle in the air like small hooked fish. "Would you like to take a bath?" she asks him. "I have a Japanese tub, four feet deep, you float in it."

"I don't float. I sink like a Cadillac."

Gundi laughs. "No, really, it's totally relaxing. I've used it almost every day since the workmen finished it." Jax can imagine Gundi kissing each one of these workmen on the day they departed. She stands up, and he finds himself once again following the irresistible gravity of a woman.

The room with the Japanese tub is the deep slick blue of a starless night, entirely tiled except for a tall window that opens onto a westward exposure of empty desert. Gundi sheds her clothes, which seemed only provisional anyway, so it isn't a big step. Jax follows her example while her back is turned, as she adjusts the steaming water. They sit on opposite sides, waiting for the deep, square hole between them to fill.

Jax with clothes on looks impossibly thin, but without them he is something else, articulated limbs, long and fine without excess. Exactly like his hands. Gundi glances at his legs stretched on the dark blue tile while she attends to the water. The gleaming faucet grows too hot to touch, and she winds her hair around it to protect her hands when she needs to adjust it. She is wearing only earrings and a fine gold chain around her left ankle.

"It's a lot of water," Jax says, looking out the window at dry mesquites and one lone saguaro, its arms raised in surprise or invocation. "Don't you feel guilty, with all those thirsty plants staring in at you?"

Gundi shrugs. "They are plants." She sits across from him, facing him with the full ammunition of her body, her back very straight. A square, steaming lake is rising between them. "We don't really belong in this desert, you and I," she says. "When we have used up all the water and have to leave, the plants and snakes will be happy to get rid of us."

"What about your unconscious Hopi desires?"

"Sometimes I feel I belong to this place. Other times I feel it is only tolerating me with a curled-up lip."

Jax curls his lip. "Did you see how much H_2O the blonde puts in that tub?" he asks in a cactus voice.

Gundi laughs. "You should write a song with all this angst."

"I think I was. Before you and Bill the Mailman impeded my progress."

They both watch the surface of the water, pummeled by the incoming stream but still glossy and intact.

Jax asks, "How do you claim your position as a citizen of the human race?"

"I don't know," she says apologetically. "Register to vote?"

"But how can you belong to a tribe, and be your own person, at the same time? You can't. If you're verifiably one, you're not the other."

"Can't you alternate? Be an individual most of the time, and merge with others once in a while?"

"That's how I see it," Jax says. "I'm a white boy, with no tribal aptitudes.

My natural state is solitary, and for recreation I turn to church or drugs or biting the heads off chickens or wherever one goes to experience sublime communion."

"The only people I know who experience sublime communion all the time are yogis and heroin addicts." Gundi tests the water with the ball of one foot. "Do you think it's possible to live without wanting to put your name on your paintings? To belong to a group so securely you don't need to rise above it?"

"As I understand it, that's the policy Turtle is being offered."

"It sounds very romantic," she says. "But when I went to the Navajo reservation to buy jewelry, I saw people living in falling-down mud houses with television antennas and bottles stacked by the door."

"And that's the whole story, poverty? Nothing else more important could be stacked behind those doors?"

Gundi is quiet. The clasp of her ankle bracelet winks in the slanted light.

"I think it was bad strategy for them to jump bail," Jax says.

"Bail? Taylor was arrested?"

"Not legally. Morally. She felt accused, and was too freaked out to stand trial, and now they're fugitives. It makes it look like she's in the wrong."

"Why did she go, then?"

"For the reason mothers throw themselves in front of traffic or gunfire to save their offspring. It's not an answerable question."

Gundi places both her feet on the surface of the water and looks at them for a long time. "I don't have children," she says finally. "I suppose I don't know that kind of love."

"I suppose I don't either. To put yourself second, every time, no questions asked? Sounds like holy communion."

Gundi turns off the water and eases herself, a pale crocodile, over the dark bank of tile. "You are supposed to be relaxing. Come into the water, I know a type of massage for bodies floating in the water."

Jax laughs. "The problem is, as I told you, I don't float."

"Of course you do. Every living human body floats."

"Theoretically it's possible that I'm dead," he says. "You decide." He slides onto the scalding water, inhaling slowly. He begins gradually to sink, first his feet and legs, then the rest of him. He empties his lungs and refills them just before his face slides under the surface.

"All right, you don't float," Gundi says, reaching under his arms and pulling him up, dripping and laughing. His hair lies close to his skull and his forehead is gleaming. "You're extremely dense, for a human."

"So I'm told," he says. Droplets of water collect in his eyelashes. Gundi lightly touches them with her fingertips, stroking downward from his face to his neck and then his chest. His nipples are hard. His mouth and hers exchange a gentle pressure and their tongues salute each other, blind sea creatures without armor, touching one another's soft surfaces with hopeful recognition.

Jax slides around behind her, holding her against him, burying his face against the nape of her neck. Her hair is a soft veil around her, still dry except for the ends, hundreds of small dark points like watercolor brushes, ready to paint the world with more than its ordinary light. Jax explores her strong, slick belly with his hands, thinking for the second time in a day of porpoises. But then he turns her around to him, cupping her jawbone gently in one hand and placing his other on the small of her back, yielding to the urge that humans have, alone among all animals, to copulate face to face. At least for the first time. At least with an unknown member of the tribe.

16

MAROONED

"SEX-MAD MOM, FIFTY-FIVE, elopes with daughter's prom date," Alice reports.

Barbie, who has already been laughing to the point of makeup damage, collapses in the backseat. Turtle asks, "What's a prongdate?"

"Mama, don't even get started on that one," Taylor warns.

Alice turns to the inner pages of her tabloid. "Here you go, an educational story from nature. The cassowary of Australia is a bird that has been known to kill humans. Eight feet tall, it attacks by leaping in the air and slashing its victim with razor-sharp toenails."

"Mama, that's not exactly educational," Taylor says, frowning into the freeway glare.

Alice reads on, carefully pronouncing all the syllables. "They are kept as pets and form a part of the economy of certain aboriginal cultures as payment for brides."

"What a deal," Taylor says. "I'll trade you my daughter for an eight-foot bird with razor-sharp toenails." Instantly the words "trade you my daughter" seize up in her stomach. She moves the rearview mirror to find Turtle, who has grown dangerously silent in her nest of stuffed toys and dog-eared books. Taylor has been having panic-stricken dreams of misplacing Turtle.

"I want to hear about the sex-mad mom," Barbie whines. "Practically that exact same thing happened to me when I was in eighth grade. My mom flirted with my boyfriend Ryan till he was like, 'Excuse me, I don't even want to come to your house.' I was so depressed I stopped using hair spray for three weeks."

Taylor snaps the mirror back into driving position. "Okay, read the sex-mad mom," she concedes, since it may be the only hope of fending off another Barbie story. This morning they have already heard about the new ecological Animal Lovin' Barbie, and the mystery of the transvestite Ken, who turned up factory-sealed in a Tampa toy store wearing a lace apron and miniskirt. They have also learned that a Barbie doll's measurements translated to the human figure are 36-18-33, which are Barbie's own measurements except she's still a few inches away from the 18. Taylor asked if Eco-Barbie was biodegradable.

"Here we go," Alice pipes up cheerfully, doing her best to keep the peace. She has been reading tabloids aloud since Tonopah. "What an adventure. Three men were marooned on their overturned charter boat off the coast of Florida and drifted without food for thirty-seven days before rescue."

Taylor shivers. "They must have been ready to eat each other."

"Oh, *gag* me," from the backseat.

"Taylor, hush," Alice says. "They probably played alphabet games."

"Right."

She reads ahead silently, and a worried expression clots her forehead. "Well, they didn't eat each other. But it's not very nice. They kind of ganged up on the one they didn't like. Oh, dear. They used him for bait."

The air in the car becomes quiet. The only sound is the sticky hiss of tires on the road, coming in through the vents. The women take in this sound as if their lives depended on it.

Alice says abruptly, "Francis the runaway pig on the lam in Canada. Francis the pig broke out of a slaughterhouse in Red Deer, Alberta, jumped a yard-high fence, sneaked through a sausage factory and pushed open the back door with his snout. The butcher chased but lost him." She skims ahead for the good parts. "... took up residence in a large park. Was once seen fighting off coyotes. Case became nationally known when Francis, grown lean and powerful, evaded professional trackers for six weeks.

Finally he was hit with a tranquilizer dart, but ran for miles and escaped into the bush. Schoolchildren across the nation contributed money to the butcher, asking that his life be spared. Psychologists explain the support for Francis by comparing him to Jesse James or Pretty Boy Floyd."

"Way to go, Francis," Taylor says.

"Who's for lunch?" asks Barbie.

"Francis the pig."

"Oh, gross, Taylor. Who *wants* lunch, I mean."

Taylor has the eerie feeling that the cracked brown desert moonscape outside the car will go on forever. That only the four of them are alive. She checks her watch and informs Barbie that it's only eleven o'clock.

"Well, tell that to my *tummy.* It's like, 'Feed me, okay, I'm starved.'"

Alice gives Taylor a meaningful glance over her newspaper. Taylor asks, "Turtle, do you have to pee?"

Turtle nods.

"Okay. Next exit we'll stop."

"Oh, shoot, it has a sad ending," Alice says. "He was finally installed in his own St. Francis Park. But one of the tranquilizer darts had pierced his intestines and he developed per-i-tone-something or other." Alice adjusts her glasses. "And died. Vets called it a strange twist of fate."

"Mama, this is depressing, all your stories have morbid endings. You're as bad as Lou Ann. She always thinks Dwayne Ray's going to catch perito-something or other at day care."

"They're not my stories," Alice says, raising the palm of her hand toward Taylor, as if taking a vow. "I'm just reading you the printed word."

Taylor wishes with all her might that someone else was in the driver's seat of this car. Even Jax. She's visited with a sudden memory of Jax standing with her in the grocery, leaning down to kiss the top of her head. A gesture that is all give and no take.

"Excuse me," Barbie says to Alice, leaning forward over the seat. "I'm in this awkward situation so I'll just go ahead and say it. I don't know your name. Taylor introduced you as her mom, but it's not like I can call you *Mom.*"

"Alice Greer," Alice says.

"Greer?" Taylor asks.

"I never did like Harland's last name a bit. It never sat right."

"Are you newly divorced, Alice?" Barbie asks, sounding exactly like a talk-show host.

"Well, I didn't get the papers yet, but it's over with. All over but the shouting."

"Didn't sound to me like there was ever much shouting," Taylor says.

"Oh, no. It's just an expression. I don't know what it would take to get Harland to let out a holler. He wouldn't even fart out loud. There was days I'd walk by him in his chair in front of his everloving TV set and I'd think, 'Well, now, what if Harland was to die on me? I wouldn't even know it till the fumes started coming off him.' "

"Oh, *gag* me," says Barbie.

Don't tempt me, Taylor thinks. She eases into the right lane and takes an exit marked Gabbs. They have spent the morning climbing out of Death Valley, but escaping from that particular death comes only by degree, it seems. The territory still looks empty. Only the square-headed good samaritans of gas-station signs loom above the dead fields.

"We're like Francis Pig," Turtle announces suddenly. "We're runaways."

"That's right, we're heroes. But nobody's going to shoot us with tranquilizers," Alice promises.

"Or take up a collection to install us in our own park," Taylor adds.

"Do you think we could find a place with milk shakes? I would die totally for a shake right now."

Taylor is not too distressed by the idea of Barbie dying totally. Last night she hinted strongly that they should go their separate ways in the morning, but so far Barbie has absorbed hints with the sensitivity of a fire hydrant. And Alice does nothing to discourage her. They pull in at an interstate diner and Barbie leads the way across the parking lot. She's wearing a pink-and-yellow flounced miniskirt over a baby-blue leotard and tights, with a silver-studded pink fringed jacket and pink high-heeled cowboy boots. Her boots make deep scraping sounds on the asphalt and her short skirt swings like a bell.

The diner has gingham curtains at the windows and a surplus of artificial flowers; Barbie fits right in with her Western ensemble. Her purse is at odds, though: she has been clutching the same square black bag against herself like a stomach ache since they left the Delta Queen. She even took it with her into the bathroom when she showered, in their motel room in Tonopah. It looks heavy.

"What do you think she's got in there?" Taylor asks, once Barbie has downed two burgers and a strawberry shake and excused herself to visit the so-called little girls' room.

"Makeup," Alice says.

"Pennies," Turtle says. "I heard it jingle."

"All I can say is she eats enough for Ken too," Alice observes. "I'd like to know how she hangs on to her 36-18-33."

"She acts like that purse is her baby kangaroo," Taylor says. "Why would you have to take your purse to the bathroom every single time?"

"She has a relationship with the bathroom, don't she? Every time she eats something, up she has to get to the little girls'."

Taylor is relieved to feel that she and Alice are on the same side again, united in their mistrust of Barbie. Turtle takes the pen Alice offers and writes her name four times on her napkin: twice from left to right, and twice in reverse.

"I'd like to get a look in that purse. I bet she's on drugs."

"Makeup," Alice says confidently.

"Could be," Taylor concedes. "She has to fix herself up so much from crying. She seems nervous ever since we left Las Vegas. Maybe she's depressed that things didn't pan out at the Delta Queen."

"Well, she can't be that depressed," Alice points out. "She hasn't quit using hair spray yet."

"No, she hasn't. I think we've got our own personal Eco-Barbie hole in the ozone following us across Nevada. We'd better look out where we park it."

Behind Gundi's bed are tall windows standing open to let in the clear yellow scent of creosote bushes and whatever bird or long-legged animal might be passing by. Gundi props her head on one elbow. Lit from behind, her hair is like golden mosquito netting. To distract himself, Jax imagines a country where people sleep under such a thing, to protect themselves from tiny golden mosquitoes carrying a blissful golden strain of malaria. He sings with his eyes closed.

She strokes the center of his chest. "You have a problem, don't you?"

"I do." Jax opens his eyes briefly, then closes them again.

"Tell me."

"Do you want to know everybody's problems as much as you want to know mine?" he asks.

"No," she says. "I'm selective. You have interesting problems. Bill the mailman has hives." She waits. "Well?"

"My situation here is something like being Catholic, which I was at one time. It takes a lot of the fun out of the moment of sin when you know you're going to have to confess it later."

Gundi stares. "What we have been doing all week you have to confess to a priest?"

"No. To Taylor."

Gundi draws the sheet up to her shoulders. "Why?"

"Because I can't lie to her."

"You think she tells you everything?"

"She tells me everything. Believe me."

Gundi's eyes grow wider still. "You have to tell her the *whole* thing? Details?"

"Just the general plot line, I think. Boy meets girl in Japanese tub, et cetera."

Gundi sits up to light a cigarette. She shakes out the match with annoyance, inhales, and crosses her arms over her sarong of white sheet. "Well, maybe she won't ask."

"Yes, by George, that's it. Next time she asks me what I've been up to, this will be one of the tiny little boring things I'll just leave out: Rucker broke his E string during rehearsal, naturally she doesn't want to hear about that, and I mopped the bathroom floor, I had blistering sex with Gundi, I mopped the bathroom floor again."

"A lot of mopping you have been doing."

"Jax mops till he drops." Flat on his back, arms at his sides, he looks as if he may not float even on a mattress.

"Who does it hurt if you don't tell her?"

He sits up, facing Gundi. "Then I know something she doesn't. I've got this robin's egg in my hand. Sky blue, you see it?" He cups his hand and they both look at it and Gundi can see the blue egg plainly.

"Do I give it to her, or do I not?" Jax asks, watching his hand. "Maybe she'll cook it, maybe she will throw it at me, who knows?" He moves his hand carefully behind his back, palm upward, so slowly she can see the ropes of tendon in his wrist roll over one another.

"So I keep it in my hand, right here. And every day when I talk to Taylor, and when I lie in bed with Taylor, it's here in my hand, and I'm thinking, If I forget for one minute then we'll roll over on this thing, uh-oh, big mess. Until that happens, I'm holding it and I can feel the shell of it as thin as the shell on your teeth. I'm choosing what Taylor knows and what she doesn't. I have the power. I will be the nervous yet powerful guy in the know, and she will be the fool."

They both watch the trail of smoke from Gundi's cigarette. It broadens into the room like a genie.

"And if she's a fool," Jax says, "then how can I worship the ground she walks on?"

"Which at the moment you are doing?"

"Which at the moment I am doing. I'm being a bad boy, but bad boys can still confess and beg for penance."

Gundi blows smoke, dispersing the apparition. "You talk about Taylor as if she is the Notre Dame Cathedral."

"She is. And the Statue of Liberty and Abbey Road and the best burrito of your life. Didn't you know?"

"I don't think so." Gundi jabs out her cigarette in the china-red bowl by the bed and gets up.

"Hey, whoa, Miss Kitty. I broke the rules, didn't I?"

"What rules would those be?" Gundi throws open her lacquered armoire and begins putting on more clothes than she has been seen in anytime this year.

"Rules like, when you're in bed with somebody, even if it's just a roll in the snow, you tell the woman you're with that she is the Snow Queen of your Heart." He folds his hands primly over his penis. "I apologize."

"I don't need you to lie to me, Jax. We both know this is nothing."

Jax lies back with his hands behind his head, trying on the feeling of "this is nothing." He finds it surprisingly painless.

"Thank you, Jax. I need to paint now. Why don't you go mop some floors."

"Yes, ma'am," he says, making no immediate move from her bed.

"And, your rent is past due."

"Tyrant," he says, and steps out her bedroom window with his clothes in his hands.

17

TREASURE

IN THEIR MOTEL ROOM OUTSIDE Carson City, Barbie stands between the two double beds in her white silk pajamas, stubbornly brushing her hair one hundred strokes.

"We could rent another room if you want to pay for it," Taylor says. "Otherwise, we have to share." She is using a more patient voice than she would normally use with a person her own age. Like Lucky Buster, Barbie doesn't strike all the right chords as a true adult. Taylor wonders if this is some new national trend like a crop disease. Failure to mature. Taylor matured at age nine, she feels, on a day she remembers: a Saturday when Alice was cleaning for Mrs. Wickentot. One of the little Wickentot boys told his friend as they came in the house, "You don't have to talk to her, that's the cleaning lady's girl." Taylor presses her spine against the imitation wood headboard of the motel bed, still dressed in her T-shirt and jeans. She is thin and leggy like Barbie, but feels like a member of an entirely different species, one that wears canvas sneakers with holes in the toes instead of fluffy slippers with small heels.

"I'll share a bed with Turtle," Barbie says, and goes back to her hair-brushing project, frowning intensely.

The four of them have taken one room, as they did the night before in Tonopah, but the sleeping arrangements are awkward this time. The manager here claims he can't bring in an extra cot because of fire regulations, so they have to share two beds. Barbie feels the most appropriate thing is for herself to share with Turtle, and for Taylor and Alice to take the other bed, but Turtle will have none of it. She's sitting on Taylor's legs with a hank of Taylor's hair wound around one fist like the leash of a wayfaring dog.

"Don't worry, hon, I won't bite," Alice says, clicking off the bedside light and rolling to the far edge. "I'll probably be up most of the night anyway. I don't sleep that good since I went through the change of life."

Barbie sits, bangs her hairbrush down next to her black purse on the night table, and takes off her mules, leaving them crouched like Pekingese littermates on the carpet. Wordlessly she pulls up the covers.

"Goodnight," Taylor says. Turtle lets go of Taylor's hair and happily begins to get ready for bed.

Barbie reaches for her black purse, stuffs it under her pillow, and resettles her head with several irritated heaves. By the time Taylor and Turtle are curled under their own blanket, she is snoring demurely.

Taylor feels pressure on her shoulder and confuses it inside her dream of being chased in a strange landscape, a city where it rains and rains and streets rise suddenly into walls. In a corner against dark buildings, a cluster of horses look at her, muscles twitching inside the cloth of their damp shoulders. The pressure comes again, and she hears Alice whisper, "Shhh."

"What?" The horses, gone. Where is Turtle?

"Shhh. Come here. You've got to see this."

Taylor slowly reassembles her memory of this room. She carefully moves Turtle's hand, which feels like a rubber glove tightly packed with flour, from her own arm. "Christ, Mama, what?" she whispers.

She can see nothing but the small outline of Alice moving toward the bathroom. She follows, and Alice closes the door behind them. She clicks on

Turtle's flashlight and Taylor sees silver moons, silver edges and circles. Silver dollars. Hundreds of them, in the silk-lined cave of Barbie's black purse.

"Holy shit. Buried treasure."

"Shhh." Alice turns off the flashlight and they sit on the cold tile in total darkness.

"Mama, I told you it wasn't makeup."

"Where do you think a gal comes by about a thousand dollars in silver coin?"

Taylor grabs Alice, what turns out to be her arm in its pajama sleeve. "She stole it from the casino."

"We don't know that."

"Okay, where'd she get it?"

Alice speaks reluctantly. "I've been studying on that for a couple of hours. So far I haven't come up with a story I feel real positive about."

"No wonder she came out of that hotel like a bat out of hell!" Taylor squeaks in a high whisper, "Okay, everybody, I've got my Bank Robbin' Barbie ensemble on, let's go!"

"Hush!"

"Mama, what do we do?"

"Call the police, I reckon."

"No way. And get them on our case?"

"Taylor, the *police* aren't after you."

"No, but we'd have to identify ourselves. It would get in the news. Believe me, I know how that one goes. Me and Turtle and Francis the Pig are out of the hero business."

"Well, we can leave her here, then."

"Mama, you were the one that said we had to bring her. She's a pain in the butt, but still. We can't just dump her in the middle of Death Valley. That would be like those guys marooned on that fishing boat."

"It wouldn't be just dumping her, she's got *coins*. She wouldn't have no trouble getting her way in a phone booth."

Taylor smiles in the dark. "That hotel manager must be having a conniption. He was a creep. *You* lied to him, Mama. Right in front of your own grandchild."

Alice laughs. "I did lie. Like a rug."

"It's gambling money, anyway. It was wrongfully come by in the first place. It wasn't really his."

"Whose was it, then? And how come you're on her side now? Ten hours ago you were ready to dump her off at a rest stop with no facilities."

Taylor can't answer the question. She reaches out in the dark and, as if guided, her fingers touch cold silver. "That money belonged to the hard-luck cases of Vegas," she says. "Part of it's mine."

Even in the Carson City *laundromat* there are slot machines lined up on the wall to laugh at Taylor. "We've got to get out of this state," she says bitterly.

"Every laundromat's a gambling parlor," Alice says, making herself at home among the white-elephant appliances. "You drop your quarters in and hope maybe this time the spin cycle will work."

"We should have brought some extra change from you-know-who." Taylor glances at Turtle, who is building a tower of bright orange detergent empties. Barbie claimed her clothes were clean, and elected to sleep in. She asked if they would do just a couple of things for her, which turned out to be bikini underwear and a pair of purple Spandex pants.

"How do you think she's planning on spending her loot?" Alice asks, holding a pair of Turtle's jeans under her chin and pulling a pink sock out of each leg. She throws the socks in with the whites. "I notice she hasn't offered to pick up the tab for anything yet."

"Don't you think that'd be a little suspicious, Mama? Plunking down Long John Silver's booty bag on the check-in desk and counting out thirty dollars in coin?"

A heavy young woman comes into the laundry with a jumbo box of clothes and three brown-skinned, orange-haired children. The oldest sticks out his arms and begins barnstorming around the machines. He knocks over Turtle's tower and careers away, making burning-engine noises. Turtle begins rebuilding without a word.

"Maybe we should stop at a bank and let her trade in her change for paper money," Taylor suggests. "She's going to get a hernia hauling around all that precious metal."

Alice stares. "I'll swan, Taylor. You talk like you're still going to let her ride with us."

Taylor fiddles with the unrolling hem of one of Turtle's T-shirts. "I kind of respect her now. This robbery thing adds a whole new dimension to her personality."

"Well, it's your car. If you want to use it for transporting the criminal element." Alice begins sorting a dark load. "Have you given any thought to where we're going to end up? We can't just drive and read dumb newspapers till the cows come home."

"Mama, don't you think I know that?" Taylor feels her whole self shaken by this small, continuing antagonism with her mother. Her mouth turns down at the corners as she tears open a detergent box and shakes its green-smelling contents into the machine. "How am I supposed to know? I jumped in the car with Turtle because I was scared to death and it seemed like the safest way to go. That's all I can tell you. I got started rolling down this hill, but I don't know why or how far."

"Don't you sometimes think you ought to just go talk to this Six-shooter woman, see if she'll listen to reason?"

"Fourkiller. No, Mama, I don't. Because what if she won't?"

Alice leans her hip against the washer and looks kindly at her daughter. "I know, hon. No mother that ever loved her child is going to argue with you."

Taylor feels an ocean of relief. She busies her hands with clothes. "I don't know how far we should go. I was thinking California maybe, some little town where you and me and Turtle could find a place to rent. I'm smart enough to know how to keep us from starving, I can find work. And in two or three months this thing will pass over and we can go back home."

Alice holds Barbie's stretch pants against herself, and laughs. She has hardly an ounce of extra on her frame, but against that purple Spandex outline she looks like a stout tree trunk. Taylor holds them against her own body, which is lean but nothing close to Barbie's hourglass. She tosses the pants in with their jeans. "I'll have to cross off fashion model as a career option. I've put on weight since I got Turtle." She laughs at herself. "And I wasn't even pregnant. I don't know what it is. I guess just observing regular mealtimes for Turtle's benefit."

"Taylor, I can't believe my ears. Look at you, slim as a grass snake. You're perfect."

At the light, clattering sound of cardboard boxes, they both turn and see that the orange-haired boy has leveled Turtle's tower again. His mother pays no mind; her doughy breasts in a stretched T-shirt tremble with concentration as she loads one machine after another with crumpled jeans. As the boy zooms away, Turtle keeps her eye on him for a long time. Finally she starts again from the bottom.

"Well, Mama, perfect I may be, but I *have* put on weight. Hanging around Miss America in her leotards makes you notice yourself."

"Taylor, I never heard you run yourself down before. You'd just as well jump off a bridge than to start in like that." Alice closes a machine lid and sighs. "When I was in my thirties I had these little square hips left over from being pregnant and I just hated it. I kept thinking, 'All those years before, I had a perfect glamour-girl body, and I didn't spend one minute appreciating it because I thought my nose had a bump in it.' And now that I'm old, my shoulder hurts and I don't sleep good and my knuckles swell up, and I think, 'All those years in my thirties and forties I had a body where everything worked perfect. And I didn't spend one minute appreciating it because I thought I had square hips.' "

Taylor smiles. "I take your point."

Turtle has made a new tower, bright and precarious by the window, nearly as tall as she is. She stands beside it with her fingers tense at her sides, following the boy around the room with her eyes like a person with a fly swatter and a killing intention. He wheels around the end of a row of washers and starts toward her. Turtle waits till his fingertips are almost in reach of the tower before she scoops both arms wide and knocks it down herself, sending the boxes flying.

Jax's voice on the phone is empty of humor. The voice by itself scares Taylor, let alone what he is reading to her, a letter from Annawake Fourkiller. She can't concentrate at all.

"... premature to take any legal action yet," he says, and Taylor is distracted by her memories of confronting social workers before Turtle's adoption—confident young women in offices who wouldn't believe in a child named Turtle without a birth certificate, any more than they believed in fairies.

"What does she have that will see her through this into a peaceful womanhood?" Jax asks, but it isn't Jax asking, it's Annawake Fourkiller, who sat in the kitchen drinking coffee less than two weeks ago, when Taylor's world was still intact. Her mind fathoms random images of Turtle, the mean, dark eyes of that boy in the laundromat when Turtle sent boxes flying into his face.

Jax reads, "... she can't belong to you. Yours sincerely, Annawake Fourkiller."

Taylor is quiet for a long time, watching her mother and her daughter through the scratched glass of the telephone booth. They're working off steam in a playground across the highway while Taylor makes her call and Barbie attends to her cuticles. Turtle is in the swing, and Alice is trying to teach her how to pump. Turtle does the right moves, pulling back on the chains and kicking out her legs, but she does them at the wrong time and the swing goes nowhere. There are things the mind can learn but the body will only do when the time is right.

"What else, Jax? Is there anything more?" Taylor asks. Behind the phone booth is a gas station and, some distance away, a middle-aged man with longish hair leaning on his red sports car, apparently waiting to use the phone. Taylor doesn't care that he's waiting. Probably he stayed out all night gambling and is thinking up some excuse to tell his wife.

"Any more to the letter? No."

"I wish I could read it. I can't tell if I'm hearing it right. What does it mean?"

"I think this letter is about Gabriel Fourkiller, the boy who got lost."

"But the Social Welfare Department thing, that part about legal action. Does that mean I have to talk to the guy or else?"

"Taylor, sweetheart, I don't think so, but I don't know. You decide."

"I can't think straight."

Turtle has finally gotten herself going in an acute zigzag. Alice catches the chains and straightens her out a little. Tall pines shade the playground area, and the park beyond them is empty save for a heavenly field of green grass, probably the envy of every cow forced to graze in the state of Nevada.

"I took your suggestion, I'm working on the song about the Twilight Zone of Humanity," Jax says, trying for cheerful but sounding like he's trying.

"Jax, did you pay the rent yet?"

There is a pause. "In services rendered."

"What's that supposed to mean?"

"It means I have to tell you something."

Taylor watches Turtle jump out of the swing and run for the slide. She seems, physically, happy. "You know what, hang on, I'm going to go get Mama. I want you to read that letter to her. She'll know what it means."

"Taylor, I'm crazy in love with you," Jax says, but Taylor has dropped four more quarters in the slot and dashed across the highway, leaving the phone dangling.

Taylor sits in one of the swings; Barbie has gotten out of the car, stretched conspicuously, and ambled across the road to come and sit in the other swing. Turtle is collecting pop tops out of the dust and carefully bending the tab of each one into the ring of the next, making a chain. She says it's a necklace for Mary. Probably the most beloved utility flashlight of all times, Mary already possesses a baby bottle and some doll clothes, which naturally don't fit all that well. Taylor has offered to buy her a real doll, but Turtle is offended by the suggestion. She has accumulated yards of pop-top necklace by now and is dragging it behind her, looking like an escapee from a chain gang. Alice has been on the phone a long time.

Barbie's skirt has lost some of its flounce. Her poodle bangs flip up and down as she rocks in the swing. Taylor finds herself looking at this woman a lot, trying to find the hidden casino robber in the picture.

"What time is it? You guys are like, E.T. phone home on this vacation. Why does your mother have to talk to your boyfriend? If my mother ever talked that long to my boyfriend, then for sure I'd know she had the hots for him. No offense. I mean, Alice doesn't seem like the type."

Taylor sits quietly for a while under the rain of Barbie's chatter. Then she says, "I don't know how to bring this up, but Mama and Turtle and I are not on vacation, and you've got something besides blusher in your purse."

Barbie looks at the black pocketbook in her lap, as if it had suddenly been flung there from an asteroid belt, then back to Taylor. "How do you know what's in my purse?"

"We looked. We invaded your privacy when you were asleep last night."

"Snoops." Barbie kicks out her pink boots and drifts in the swing.

"I was just curious why you always had to take it to the bathroom with you. If you'd left it sitting in front of my nose, believe me, I wouldn't have had the slightest desire to look in your purse."

"So? Okay, so I've got money in there."

The man with the red sports car sits on the front fender and crosses his arms, impatient to make his call.

"Money from the casino," Taylor says.

"Yeah. From the silver-dollar machine. Stupid Wallace kept the key in the cash register. At the better establishments they keep all the machine keys in a safe."

Taylor is startled that Barbie makes no effort to lie. "Well, that's between you and Wallace," she says. "I personally don't care that you ripped him off, but I'm not interested in being chased by the police."

"Wally would never call the cops." Barbie narrows her eyes at the highway. "They'd check his gaming odds and send him directly do not pass go to San Quentin."

Taylor understands that where Barbie is concerned she has no idea what she's dealing with. But she finds she prefers this to her previous assumption, which was that Barbie had cotton candy for brains. "Well, here's *my* true confession," Taylor says. "I don't want the police around because Turtle and I are hiding from somebody. Not the police exactly. Somebody that might get custody of Turtle."

"Oh, your ex-husband? I've seen that on *America's Most Wanted.*"

"No. It's complicated." Taylor wonders if child-custody disputes really do make it onto *America's Most Wanted.*

"Well, whatever," Barbie says. "Ask me no questions I'll tell you no lies."

Alice has come out of the phone booth. Taylor looks up and sees her standing by the road with her hands dangling at her sides and tears streaming down her face. She looks like she's been hit by something. Two cars in succession slow down to look.

"Could you stay here a minute and keep an eye on Turtle?" Taylor asks, setting off at a jog. By the time she's crossed the highway, Alice is in the car. Taylor gets in on the driver's side.

"I could take the bus from Reno," Alice says, staring forward, though her line of sight seems unable to pass through the windshield.

"Take the bus to where? We have the car."

"I can stay with my cousin Sugar. Somebody ought to go talk to them, Taylor. I understand why you ran when they yelled fire, but I think there's another way to handle this."

"Mama, I'm not giving up Turtle."

"I think all they're saying is they need to talk to you, to tell you there's another side to it." Alice speaks low, and Taylor feels shut out.

"I already talked to her. She wants to take Turtle."

"Maybe not. She's just touchy on the subject, on account of her brother." Alice looks out at the sky. "That poor little boy," she croons, hugging herself, as if she's had a dream.

"What little boy?"

"The one they took away."

"Jesus, Mama, whose side are you on here?"

Alice turns to Taylor and hugs her. "Yours. I'm with you and Turtle to the crack of doom, hon. You know that."

They sit rocking back and forth by the highway while Taylor holds on to Alice, trying to understand the bad news. Through the car window she can plainly see the man leaning on the red car, who suddenly brightens at the sight of a woman who must be his wife, coming from the service station. They hail each other with words in a strange language. Taylor is startled. This ordinary man in jeans, whose thoughts she believed she knew, opens his mouth and becomes a foreigner. It occurs to her that this one thing about people you can never understand well enough: how entirely inside themselves they are.

18

NATURAL SYSTEMS

ALONG THE HIGHWAY THE CORNFIELDS lie newly flayed, mile after mile, their green skin pulled back to reveal Oklahoma's flesh of orange velvet dirt. The uncultivated hills nearby show off a new summer wardrobe of wildflowers. The massed reds flecked with gold are Indian blanket; Cash recalls this name with pleasure, like a precious possession lost and retrieved. He fixes the radio on the sweet, torn voice of George Jones and breathes deeply of the air near home.

A woman in the Oklahoma Welcome Station told him that schoolkids take up collections of pennies to buy the wildflower seeds. Cash had thought wildflowers just grew. He considers this now as he drives, and decides maybe they just *tell* the kids they use their money for wildflowers. So the little ones can look out the car window and think they did all that with their pennies.

Cash hums along with George, who is gloating about putting a gold ring on the right left hand this time. He thinks briefly of Rose, back in Jackson Hole, admiring the rear ends of boys in

McDonald's; he wonders how quickly she'll forget about his tired, flat hind end altogether. He doesn't much care. He is headed back to the home he never should have left, and right now he feels the possibility of fresh love for his own life. When he stopped for the restroom at the welcome station, he gazed at the educational display of the seven different types of barbed-wire and felt he could leap over all seven in one bound.

As he nears the Arkansas River and Cherokee country, the fields give way to trees and there are more varieties of living things, it seems: scissortail birds snipping over the meadows catching bugs, and big-headed kingfishers sitting on high lines overlooking the river. He drives into the outskirts of Tahlequah, through the motel strip along the Muskogee Highway and then into the older, pretty part of town. The old brick courthouse and the seminary building and all the old oaks haven't changed. The main road leads him out again, into the woods.

At a bend in the road outside Locust Grove, Cash is moved by the sight of a little field with a heartbreaking hedgerow of wild pink roses and one small, sweet hickory in the center, left standing because the Cherokee man or woman who plowed that field wouldn't cut down a hickory. He keeps an eye out, afraid to miss one single sight as he makes his way. Crowds of black-eyed susans stand up to be counted, and five beagles sit side by side in someone's yard, reverent as a choir, blessing his overdue return.

Annawake is first aware of a rectangle of brightness framing the window shade, then the pile of quilts arguing on her bed: wild geese, double wedding ring, trip around the world, stitched by three different aunts who quarreled, when they were alive, about which pattern was best. And there is something under the quilts, a lump, stealing along like a mole beneath the garden. Annawake reaches behind her head, pulls herself to a half situp, and conks the lump with a pillow. It flattens and giggles. She pulls out a naked Annie.

"I found a rat in my bed. What am I going to do with this rat?" She covers Annie's face with kisses. When she exhausts her affectionate assault, Annie lies on her back next to Annawake and sucks her thumb with a contented, arrogant air.

"You got kicked out of Millie's bed, didn't you."

Annie nods.

"That's because there's another baby now. You've moved up in the world. Now you get to be a big sister. Doesn't that sound fun?"

Annie shakes her head.

"I don't blame you. Who needs it?" Annawake lies on her back too. They both look for a while at the ceiling, which is decorated with a few unwelcome suggestions of mildew. Before Annawake finished law school and moved back to Tahlequah, Millie doubled up the kids into the front room, mounted a convulsing stepladder and scrubbed this room to within an inch of its life. But there has been rain since then, and the roof is older than anyone living under it.

Dellon pokes his head in the door. "There she is. The escaped prisoner." He comes in with Annie's clothes, and Annie uses her sturdy legs to scoot herself under the quilts again.

"Hey, Dell," Annawake says. She sits up, clasping her arms around her blanketed knees. "Watch out, the prisoner's lawyer is present."

Dellon sits on the foot of the bed holding Annie's small red sneakers like baby birds in his large hands. Dellon's long hair is loose, his T-shirt looks like what grasshoppers do to crops, and his beefy shoulders seem slumped this morning with the weight of fatherhood. He narrows his eyes at Annawake. "Hey, that's my shirt. I've been looking for that one."

Annawake looks down innocently at the maroon flannel she's been sleeping in. "The color's good on me, don't you think?" She cocks her profile.

"Why don't you get a boyfriend, so you can steal *his* clothes?"

"Good idea. I knew there was some reason women sought out the company of men."

"Listen, I was supposed to have the kids out of here by ten o'clock. Millie has to take the baby over to Claremore for his shots or something."

"Christ, what time is it? Are you telling me I slept past ten o'clock?"

"Yeah, I think they're going to make it a national holiday. National Annawake Slept Past Ten O'clock Day."

"Look, I'll stay here with the kids. It's not even worth going into the office now."

"You're not going into the office? On a Saturday morning? Definitely a national holiday." He half stands and reaches behind the aged lace curtain to snap up the shade.

Annawake shades her eyes from the light. "Get out of here," she tells him affectionately. "Annie and I need our beauty sleep." She flips the pillow behind her head and lies back down. The lump of Annie wildly animates the double wedding rings in the region of Annawake's knees.

"Okay," Dellon says. "I'm taking Baby Dellon and Raymond over to my house. You've got this one." He stands up and gently swats Annie through the quilts with her red shoes. "The naked savage. Teach her some girl stuff, will you, like how to wear clothes?"

"See you later, Dell."

"Oh, listen. Did Millie tell you about the hog fry?"

Annawake sits up. "Another one? I'm going to get fat this summer. Who's this one for?"

"Cash Stillwater, just moved back from somewhere. It's down at Letty Hornbuckle's over in Heaven."

"Miss Letty, the one that used to run everybody's business in the grade-school cafeteria? I haven't seen her since I got breasts."

"You have breasts? Let me see."

Annawake makes a frightening face at her brother.

"So, you coming?"

"Cash Stillwater," she repeats. "I think I went to school with his son, who was it, Jesse Stillwater? Real tall?"

"No, Jesse is Cash and Letty's youngest brother. I think there was eleven or twelve of them. Cash had a daughter—remember that Alma, she drove herself into the river a few years ago?"

"Oh, yeah. Off that bridge."

"They're some kin to Johnetta Hornbuckle that drives the school bus. There's Johnetta and Quatie. She married Earl Mellowbug."

"Quatie." Annawake thinks. "That's right. Her mother was Mama's girlfriend. Remember her, the beauty queen? Mama kept that picture of her that was in a magazine. I still have that thing somewhere."

"I'll be back around six to pick you up. Unless you get a better date."

"We'll be here, Dell. You're the best I'm ever going to do."

Annawake smiles, watching the bear shape of her brother duck out through the doorway. Annie has made no progress with female apparel in the meantime, but has fallen back to sleep. Annawake smooths the layers of covers, remembering from her childhood the noisy aunts who made those three quilts: they lived in one house, and could never agree on anything in this world except that love is eternal.

On the stone floor of Jax's studio Lou Ann sits cross-legged, nervously tapping the toes of her athletic shoes while Jax frowns at his new amplifier rig. He picks up a yellow electrical cord and examines it closely. "Do you think this should be plugged into something?"

"Don't ask me. Do I look like Mozart?"

"No," Jax says. Today he doesn't have the energy even to laugh at Lou Ann.

"Dwayne Ray, honey, don't mess with Jax's stuff."

Dwayne Ray, a resolute child with disorganized mud-colored hair, is pulling an assortment of bamboo flutes out of a milk crate and laying them end to end.

"I'm making a space shovel," he explains.

"No problem," Jax says. "Take them out in the hall. You can line up the whole star fleet out there."

Dwayne Ray happily drags the crate out the door. In the hallway he begins to accompany his industry with Indy 500 sounds. Lou Ann simply stares at Jax. He finds a socket for the yellow plug and then glances up, feeling her eyes.

"Jax, you never let him *touch* those before. You would have cut his little pecker off if he'd tried to use your music stuff for toys."

Jax returns to his wires. "So, I'm feeling generous. Your male line has escaped dismemberment."

Lou Ann's blue eyes are wide. "Jax, honey, I miss her too, but you have got to get a grip."

He puts down his pliers and really looks at Lou Ann. The sun from the high east window lights her upturned face and her electric blue leggings and the bag of tangerines she brought over, and Jax wishes merely to weep. All this color and worry focused on his welfare, and it's going to waste. He sits down next to her.

"Do you know," he says, curling his long fingers through Lou Ann's, "all her earthly clothing fit into two drawers in the bureau. Can you believe God made a woman like that? And she saw fit to live with me?"

"Gosh, Jax, I could never be your girlfriend," Lou Ann says, sounding hurt. "I'd get disqualified just on the basis of shoes alone."

"I love you anyway. But you've got to let me wallow in my misery. This is not a situation that can be resolved through Welcome Wagon technology." He leans sideways and gives her a kiss of dismissal.

Lou Ann stands up and, with one last worried look, leaves him. She steps over the electrical cords as if they might be napping snakes. In the hall she collects Dwayne Ray and the flutes. Jax hears the sounds of their internal wooden emptiness as she piles them back into their crate. He stands up again, facing the window, realizing how clearly these days he can hear the emptiness inside things. He lets his hands walk around on the keyboard, which is powerless, its internal circles of current still interrupted somewhere by an imperceptible fault line. It makes no sound at all as his fingers modulate their laments in one key after another.

Jax feels entirely separate from his hands as he looks out the window. His eyes follow the golden, drawn-out shape of what he finally understands to be a coyote circling the trunk of a palo verde tree. His hands go still. The coyote's belly hangs low with incipient pups or with milk, it's impossible to tell which, because she keeps herself low in the brush.

Suddenly with violent effort she leaps into the tree and falls back, bouncing a little on her forelegs, with a nest of sticks in her mouth. A dove flies off in the same instant, startled as a heartbeat. The coyote crouches at the base of the tree and consumes the eggs in ugly, snapping gulps. She stands a moment licking her mouth, then creeps away.

Jax is crying. He feels deeply confused about whom he should blame for his losses. The predator seems to be doing only what she has to do. In natural systems there is no guilt or virtue, only success or failure, measured by survival and nothing more. Time is the judge. If you manage to pass on what you have to the next generation, then what you did was right.

19

CHEWING BONES

ALICE DIALS DIRECTORY ASSISTANCE FROM a motel room in Sacramento, in pursuit of Hornbuckles.

"You can't find a Robert? No, wait," she commands the operator, shifting the receiver to her better ear. "It's Roland, I think. Roland Hornbuckle. Look up that one." She waits, rolling her eyes across the room to Taylor, who returns a less irritated, more troubled version of her own expression. Alice has never gotten over the initial shock of seeing her own facial features plastered across another human being, with plans of their own.

"You worrying about Turtle?"

Taylor nods.

"What's her problem?"

"She found out you were leaving. She hates when anybody leaves her. I just went in there and found all our shoes and Barbie's slippers in the toilet. Now she's lying in the tub."

"I'll talk to her," Alice says. "I'll tell her it's just so I can try and make them let you and her stay together."

"I already told her that. It doesn't matter if you have a logical reason."

"Well, then, try Rocky Hornbuckle," Alice tells the operator. She whispers to Taylor, "Has she got her flashlight in there? I don't mean to worry you, but Harland's sister got killed listening to 'Jesus Loves You This Morning' on the radio in her bathtub."

"Oh, don't worry, there's no water. She just gets in with her clothes on and pulls a blanket over her head and says she's buried."

Alice says in a louder voice, "No? Okay, listen. Just give me every Hornbuckle you've got in Heaven, Oklahoma."

Taylor gets up to examine Barbie's slippers, which are drying out badly in front of the air-conditioner unit. "Boy, is she going to be pissed off when she sees these. They look like drowned guinea pigs."

"Where'd she go?"

"Who, Barbie? Out to get more Cheese Doritos, I think."

Alice begins writing hurriedly, trying to keep up. She hangs up and waves her list at Taylor. "Eight Hornbuckles with telephones. One of them's got to be Sugar, right? Maybe she remarried."

"Well, then, her name wouldn't be Hornbuckle anymore," Taylor points out.

"Isn't that the dumbest thing, how the wife ends up getting filed under the husband? The husband is not the most reliable thing for your friends to try and keep track of."

"Nobody holds a gun to your head, Mama," Taylor says. "Even if I married Jax, which I'm not going to, but what would I want with his stupid *name?* Just learning how to spell it is a big commitment."

"I'm going to call this whole list. One of them's got to know her, at least." Alice takes a deep breath and dials.

"I don't think *he* even ever spells it the same way twice."

Alice holds up her hand. "Ringing," she says. They both wait. After a moment they wait less breathlessly. Alice finally disconnects, then dials the next number on her list. "You've been picking on that boy all day long, Taylor," she says in a quiet voice, as if the ringing phone might otherwise hear her. "Either he's your boyfriend or he isn't, but don't just sit on the fence and run him down."

Taylor slumps in the swivel chair by the window and falls silent, twisting the chair slightly back and forth, while Alice tries two more numbers:

"I think they done dropped the bomb on Heaven, Oklahoma," she announces after getting no answer on number four. She scrutinizes her list, then glances up at Taylor, who is looking out the window with tears in her eyes.

"Hon, what is it? What I said about Jax?"

"I don't know if he is or he isn't. How can I have a boyfriend if I'm sleeping in motels and living in a car? No wonder Turtle wants to have a funeral for herself in the bathtub."

"This is going to pass," Alice says, beginning to dial again. "I know it's hard. But you and Turtle have a home back there waiting for you."

"Not waiting too hard," Taylor says without looking at Alice. "When I called last night he told me he'd gone to bed with the woman that collects our rent."

Alice's mouth falls open. She closes it, staring at Taylor, then suddenly blinks and says, "Hello? I'm a cousin of Sugar Hornbuckle's calling long distance, looking for her. She is? Good Lord. Yes, please."

Taylor looks up, her eyes still watery but changed, self-contained and inquiring.

"Don't give up the ship yet," Alice says. "We've found Sugar. It sounds like they're having a big old party in Heaven."

Sugar Hornbuckle hangs up the phone and goes cold at the sight of blue-lipped children, a host of them, running like a crowd of small ghosts stealing from the pantry. Letty shoos them off the peach pies and out of her kitchen, and Sugar blinks away what seemed like a bad omen.

"Who was that on the phone?" Letty asks.

Sugar backs up several stitches through her quilted thoughts. "Funniest thing. A cousin of mine I haven't seen since nineteen and forty-nine. She wants to come visit. She's got some business with the Nation but she didn't say what."

Letty's curiosity wakes up and knocks down the door. "Well, I wonder what that could be? She got some kind of a claim?"

"I doubt it. She's not from around here. We kind of grew up together down in Mississippi, as good as sisters. You ever been down South?"

"No. I heard it's hot."

Sugar laughs, wondering what could be hotter in summer than an Oklahoma woods.

"Could you give me a hand with these wild onions, hon?" Letty asks, not about to let her escape the kitchen yet with this thrilling news item. She crosses the kitchen to her freezer chest, walking like a bear; Letty is built square, with legs sticking out from the bottom of her dress that seem to be set two feet apart. She opens the freezer chest and bends over it, exposing the tops of her thick brown stockings rolled to her knees. A cloud of steam curls around her face and touches her hair with silver.

"Why'd you all go all the way down to Mississippi to get raised up?" Letty never leaves Heaven; as far as she is concerned, Mississippi might as well be India.

"It was the Depression," Sugar says. "Alice's mama had a hog farm."

"Hog farm? There's money in that, I guess."

"Oh, law, we never had three dollars at the same time. But we didn't have all that bad a time of it."

Letty grunts a little as she stoops deeply into the freezer. "Well, sure, you get by. I heard about them civil rights they had down there."

Sugar takes the frozen blocks Letty hands her, one by one, stacking them like cool firewood against her chest. She remembers helping Letty collect these wild onions in the spring, to be put away for a summer or fall hog fry. "It wasn't like they make it sound now. We were all more or less in the same boat, black and white. Or maybe we were just ignorant, but it seemed like we got along. My favorite thing in the world was going down to Jackson to see the maypoles and the State Fair. There'd be just hundreds of dark little children dressed up as angels, marching down the street, singing hymns. To this day, I swear that's the prettiest sight I ever saw."

"Mmhm." Letty is losing interest.

"Nobody had two bits, it was just like here. You didn't notice what you didn't have, because nobody was right there wagging it in your face."

"When's she coming?"

"She says just as soon as she can get here on the Greyhound bus."

Letty sighs. "Well, I'll bring over a pie, to say hello, soon as I help get Cash settled in."

Letty Hornbuckle is the nosiest person in three counties. Sugar knows why she'll bring over a pie—for the same reason she's been helping Cash: to snoop. She's probably been looking through all his things to see if he secretly got rich in Wyoming. Sugar helps Letty fill a pail and swish warm water over the freezer bags of wild onions. Letty will stir these into scrambled eggs, and Cash will declare he's never leaving home again. No, Letty can't possibly suspect her brother of having struck it rich. No Cherokee she's ever known would keep money a secret from relatives. Cash probably came back with the same nothing he bore away three years ago, and nobody will hold it against him. Especially not after all the funerals he went through. When they finish with the wild onions, Sugar slips quickly outside to find her husband and tell him about Alice.

The children she saw inside have joined a mob of others under Letty's big mulberry. She laughs at herself, her vision of ghosts. The children's hands and faces and soles are all inked blue from berries gulped and trampled.

Letty's yard is a small mowed clearing held in on every side by protective hickory woods. Sugar's husband, Roscoe, in the company of all the other old men, is standing watch over Letty's big iron washpot, which is settled like a hen on a white nest of coals. The fire adds more cruel heat to this hot day, quivering in the air around the men's boot leather and rising up into the arms of trees. Inside the enormous pot, a thousand thumb-sized pieces of what was yesterday a live fat hog swirl upward in the cracking oil. Sugar thinks: One more citizen of Heaven, making his contribution. Roscoe and his friends are studying the heat of the fire and the level of oil in the pot with the attitude men take on occasions like this, feeling the weight of their supervisory powers. Sugar smiles. A woman knows she can walk away from a pot to tend something else and the pot will go on boiling; if she couldn't, this world would end at once.

She stands alone under Letty's bent peach trees, wanting to be outside the crowd for a minute before it draws her back in. What will her cousin Alice make of this place? She can't imagine. Sugar looks fondly at the dark braids trailing down men's backs, the women's shoes lifted high in the uneven grass. Children are everywhere in sight. The ones too small to climb trees run low through the crowd, their smooth, dark heads passing under every hand. Sugar feels rocked in the bosom of family. All these people are related somehow to Roscoe and herself and her children. Probably she could pick out any two people in Cherokee County and track the human path that links their families. In fact, that's the favorite pastime of every old Cherokee, at gatherings of every kind. Even though she wasn't born here, Sugar has been a Hornbuckle long enough to do it as well as anyone: trace down Hornbuckles and Blackfeathers, Stones and Soaps and Swakes. She can remember, when she first moved here with her new husband, she felt she'd walked into an endless family reunion.

Her daughters, Quatie and Johnetta, are standing shoulder to shoulder in Letty's outdoor summer kitchen, Johnetta stirring the bean pot and Quatie working just as hard on some long tale she needs to tell. Quatie's husband's mother, Boma Mellowbug, is crossing the yard in a bright blue satin dress and a man's wool cap. She walks sideways like a crawdad, with her eyes on the sky. In Heaven it's a good thing to be related to Boma, because she sees things no one else does.

Earlier she saw Boma standing among the men, talking earnestly with Cash. Now she crosses to the grape arbor to talk to three boys and a girl that belonged to Bonnie Fourkiller, a dear friend of Sugar's now deceased. The girl has an odd haircut but still yet looks like Bonnie. Sugar can't remember any of these children's names except, strangely, the first baby boy who died—that was Soldier—and the youngest, Gabriel, who was taken off to Texas somehow, and killed, Sugar thinks, though she can't recall how. Today she can easily imagine those lost boys turning up here too, grown tall; she sees how their shoulders would fit into place between their brothers' and sister's.

The crowd is also missing Cash and Letty's mother, who died a few years back. She should be here ordering the children out of the pies and the old men away from idleness. In her last years she always organized gospel singing at the hog fries. For her whole life prior to that she went to the Locust Grove stomp dances, and wouldn't be persuaded to miss them for anything in this world, until her knees got bad; then she converted to Baptist. She said the kneeling and praying was trouble but still grieved her less than stomping. That was her way. So then they had to sing "Amazing Grace" and "Washed in the Blood" at every big occasion, with the Cherokee words, which were less appalling at least than the English. The obstinate practicality of old women pierces and fortifies these families like the steel rods buried in walls of powdery concrete. It astonishes Sugar that she's becoming one of these old women herself. She still feels pretty and young.

She jumps slightly, for Boma Mellowbug is standing beside her, reading her mind.

"Are you happy?" Boma asks, looking sideways at Sugar from under her wool cap and veil of white hair.

"I am, Boma. I haven't been sometimes, but now I am."

"Well, then, don't be tormented by the *kolon*. He's not always a bad thing."

Sugar looks up. "That bird?"

"That one flies over when somebody is going to die. You hear him call? He sounds like he's chewing bones."

A naked toddler wearing only red shoes moves from one group of adults to the next; none of them looks down, but each one honors the child's round head with a downstretched hand, as if it were a ripe melon that had rolled itself up from the field. Sugar stares at Boma, whose eyes are clear, light brown, and undisturbed. "I don't want anyone here to die," she tells her at last.

Boma blinks. "It's a big tribe. Somebody's always dying."

Sugar looks at the people gathered in this single green place and understands the price of love.

"All right then," she says. "Just so it's not one of the children."

"No," Boma says. "We're going to keep these children on."

20

THE WAR OF THE BIRDS AND BEES

IN ALICE'S OPINION, HEAVEN HAS gone to pigs and whistles. She has no idea what promise the town held in days gone by, but on the morning someone named it Heaven there could not have been, for example, a mess of mean dogs holed up under the Post Office porch.

"Watch that one pup with the stump tail," Sugar says, dancing a little on the stairs and swinging her purse at the dogs. "His name's Choppers."

Alice can't pick Choppers out of the lineup of his yellow brothers and sisters; they are all leaping up as if they'd been caught by the mouth on fishing lines. The two larger dogs merely stare, considering whether the food value in this pair of old women is worth the bother. "Why wouldn't somebody rout them out?" Alice asks, framing the question as tactfully as possible as she skirts sideways up the steps with her hands on her pants legs, watching her blind side.

"Oh, honey, they live here," Sugar explains. She pushes open the screen door and introduces Alice to her daughter Quatie, postmistress of Heaven, before Alice has quite finished looking out for rear-guard attacks.

The Post Office sells cigarettes and notions and smells a good deal like tuna fish. Quatie has a Camel going and a sandwich in one hand, which she wipes before holding it out to Alice. "Pleased to meet you," she says, once she has licked her front teeth. Quatie has her father's broad, brown face but her mother's eyes, sloped faintly down at the outside corners, giving a touch of sadness to her smile.

"Our cousin from way back when," Sugar tells Quatie, raising her hands to show it's been more years than she can count.

Quatie rolls her eyes at Alice in a friendly way. "Mama talks about Mississippi like it was kingdom come."

"Well, sure I do," cries Sugar. "Me and Alice were the belles of the ball. This morning we decided we'd come on downtown and paint the town red."

Quatie winks. "Reckon that took about a quart."

"Pardon?" Alice asks, still nervous.

"Of paint."

"Oh. Well, I'm used to small towns. Small is nothing new to me." But Alice is being polite. She thinks, as they leave the P.O. and head up the road toward Sugar's house, that this place has problems beyond being small. It looks like everybody here has been out of work for the last forty years, and in fact Sugar says that's about right. In the past, she claims, the eastern end of the state was a reservation, and fairly prosperous. But the federal government cut up the land into small packets and gave one to each family; since the people here had no thoughts of land as something to be given or taken permanently, they were persuaded by clever investors to trade their allotment papers for a mule or a stove or, in one case Sugar knows of, a crate of peaches and a copy of *The Leatherstocking Tales*. Since then, most of eastern Oklahoma has been more or less looking for a job. Sugar came here freshly married to Roscoe in 1950; it seems to Alice that they've lived mainly off Sugar's local fame as the

"Welcome to Heaven" poster girl, though it wouldn't have paid any bills.

Roscoe dropped Sugar and Alice downtown on his way to repairing a pump for some relatives in Locust Grove; Alice happily agreed that they could walk back. She wanted to get her bearings. Now she has got more bearings than she cares for. They pass houses that Alice only hopes have seen better times; front yards where chickens run free and cars with no wheels enjoy the rich, rust pelt of eternal life. They stop to rest a minute at the spot where Main crosses what Sugar calls "the uphill road" (which, Alice thinks, must surely run downhill for someone), in the shade of big oak trees whose limbs dangle vines like Tarzan's jungle.

"How'd that husband work out?" asks Sugar, politely avoiding the more obvious question of why she is here. Alice wants to mention Turtle, but can't. She's not yet at home with Sugar. They haven't seen each other for a lifetime. The cousin she's just met is a thin, humpbacked woman in canvas shoes and a blue cotton dress that hangs empty in the bosom. Alice recalls mention of sons in and out of trouble, and in their last correspondence, ten years ago, an account of surgery for breast cancer, but Sugar still has a pretty smile and eyes you look at twice. She wears her snow-white hair the way she did as a girl, in an Andrews Sisters roll across the back, and she has an almost flirty way of talking that makes Alice think of the Andrews Sisters shaking their fingers, making round "o's" with their mouths: "No, no, no, don't you sit under the apple tree with anyone else but me-ee!"

"Harland is his name," Alice confesses. "The fellow I married. It didn't amount to much. I finally just couldn't stand the quiet."

"Oh, honey, don't I know. I think Roscoe used up his whole vocabulary when he asked me to marry him. All that's left now is 'Where's it at?' and 'When's dinner?' "

Alice breathes a little deeper. Sympathizing over the behavior of men is the baking soda of women's friendships, it seems, the thing that makes them bubble and rise.

They pick up their feet and walk on past a Shell station and a building covered with pockmarked yellow siding that advertises HEAVEN MACHINE TOOLS NEW & USED. Then they are beyond the pale of what Alice would call town. It's small all right, but even so she feels Quatie underestimated the amount of paint called for.

"Where did the name Heaven come from?" she asks Sugar.

"Well, that's for the blue hole. A great big water hole down in the crick where the kids love to go jump in and fish and all. Catch crawdads, that kind of stuff. The grown-ups like to go too, really. It's the best place around. They used to just call it 'The best place,' in Cherokee, and when they went to turn that into English somebody thought people was talking about Heaven. But they wasn't, they just meant the best place *around here.*"

"Isn't that the way," Alice says. She feels relieved to know that "Heaven" as a value judgment is only relative.

"How about your girl?" Sugar asks. "Where's she now?"

It stuns Alice to realize she has no earthly idea. And can't go into it with Sugar, which makes her sadder still. "She's living out in Tucson, Arizona. Taylor's my pride."

"Oh, sure, they are. When they don't give you no trouble, they're a blessing."

The road becomes a lane, passing under a tunnel of locust trees. A creek runs beside them in the thick woods; Alice can hear its satisfied rush. Birds sing loudly in the trees, and there seem to be dozens of terrapins in the road. The trucks that come along swerve to miss them, and they pull in their heads and sit like rocks, their small hearts surely pounding from another near miss. But somehow they must make it across, otherwise the roads would be lined with box turtle tragedies.

"Well, look, there's poke," Sugar says, suddenly animated. She pulls a wadded plastic bag from her purse and shakes it open as she steps sideways down the bank. There in the ditch she squats and picks handfuls of new green leaves. A truck passes, and Sugar waves. Alice doesn't know what to do with herself, and half turns her back, as if her cousin were going to the bathroom down there. She knows you can eat poke, has known it all her life. But she has also known for many years what people would say about her if they saw her collecting her salad greens from the roadside.

Sugar climbs carefully back up the bank, triumphant, her bulging sack the size of a lumpy basketball. "There used to be a world of poke right up behind our place, where they cleared the woods out under the power lines," she tells Alice as she falls into step beside her, catching her breath. "But a few year ago they started coming along and spraying something poison under those lines that kilt all the poke. Now, why do you think they'd do that?" she asks.

Alice doesn't say, "To kill the weeds, what do you think?" She says, "It's hot, isn't it?"

Sugar wipes her brow. "I was just thinking how hot it used to get, back in those summers when we were kids. The grown-ups would live on the porch, and not hardly move."

"It *was* hot," Alice says. "It was Mississippi."

"My mommy wouldn't want the baby on her lap because it was too hot. We'd take the babies on *our* laps because we were big britches, playing mommies. I guess we didn't feel the heat so much, any more than we knew the half of what it was to be mommy."

Ahead of them, a huge black snake parts the weeds and starts to slide into the road, thinks better of it, loops back over itself like a shoelace, and slips away into the bush.

Alice speaks abruptly from her thoughts: "Do you know anybody named Fourkiller?"

"Oh, honey, you can't hardly walk around here without stepping on a Fourkiller. There's Ledger Fourkiller, he's a chief, just the nicest man you'd ever meet. He does the ceremonies over at Locust Grove and lives on a shantyboat. He's lived down there on the lake since the second war, Roscoe says. He's got a landing built all out of old tires. It's a wonderful thing to see."

They walk in silence, until Sugar asks, "Do you remember the maypoles in Jackson?"

"Oh, sure. The kids in white shoes, walking circles. The boys would go one way and the girls the other."

Sugar touches her hair. "The State Fair," she says. "Them parades. I never will forget. And remember that carnival?"

"The cow with a human face!" Alice cries.

"Rubber man! The hypnotist!"

"The Siamese calves, two bodies eight legs!"

"You wanted your money back on that one," Sugar says, "because it turned out to be dead and stuffed."

"I got it, too," Alice points out.

"You had spunk, I'll say that."

"Well, think about it. Dead and stuffed, they could have just sewed two regular ones together."

"I've been thinking about that for forty years, Alice."

"That dead calf?"

"No. You. Telling the man you wanted your nickel back. I wisht I'd had more of that. I feel like I didn't show my girls what I was made out of."

Alice is surprised to hear this admiration from her lively cousin. "Seems like they turned out all right."

"Oh, sure. The boys are a peck of trouble, but the girls, they're fine. You didn't meet Johnetta yet. She'll come over after she gets the bus drove. She's something, she's the type to get her money back." Sugar laughs. "She would have climbed over the rope to *see* if it was two cows sewed together."

Alice has on her jogging shoes, and she is used to getting where she needs to go, but she has to shorten her stride for Sugar, who seems to get winded easily. "You could get a big bowl of soup for five cents," Alice argues. "You couldn't just throw away a nickel."

"No. Still can't."

The two women walk through the shade, their elbows occasionally touching. Whenever they pass a little house and yard mowed out of the woods, Sugar waves at the people on the porch. They are liable to be of any age: a grandmother plucking greens from a bucket, or a man in his twenties with black, greased hands, kneeling over an engine as if he's about to deliver a baby out of it. And kids, by the score. They all wave back, calling Sugar by name. She has already introduced Alice to dozens of people, who seem to know already about Alice. Their names stilt and lean in her head like pictures from an old-time children's book: Pathkiller, Grass, Deal, Stillwater, Doublehead. Often she can't tell first names from last, or where the grandmother's name let off and the children's began. The young man with the engine is Able Swimmer. All of them seem to be related to Sugar through marriage or some catastrophe, or frequently both. Sugar is telling her right now, for instance, "Flossie Deal and I were at the courthouse in Tahlequah the day her son fell off the hotel they was building and busted his insides. Her other boy married Quatie's husband's sister."

Sugar slows her pace even more as they head uphill, and sighs a little.

"I loved that State Fair. Seems like ever time we went and sat in them bleachers, there wouldn't be a cloud in the sky."

"They had two fairs. First the State Fair, and after that the Black State Fair."

"Really? I never knew it was divided up."

Alice recalls that she used to find her beloved cousin sometimes naïve and in need of protection. "We only went to the second one. We liked it best, there was more music to it."

"There was. And the church floats."

"People dressed to beat the band, with hats and all. I liked all the hats."

"Remember those children that dressed like angels?"

Alice thinks. "No. I remember women dressed like bluebirds, in blue high-heeled oxfords. And I remember when they'd turn on those street-lights that were like light bulbs under fluted pie plates, and we'd dance in the street."

"Don't you remember those children? They'd sing 'When the Saints Go Marching In.' I just loved that."

Sugar and Alice pass by a dwelling that looks slightly more prosperous than most, though less interesting: a yellow brick rectangle set in a huge, flat lawn with nothing planted in it. A riding mower preens in the carport. "That's Les and June Courcy's, they're white," Sugar says, with neither favor nor disapproval, as if she'd simply said, "There goes a white rooster across the road." The two women walk on.

The land is steep. Everywhere Alice looks she sees long, dark loaves of hill cut with forested hollows. Around the houses, almost everyone has a goat to keep down the underbrush, although once in a while a front yard will sport an old orange mower alongside the satellite dish.

As they crest the hill, they're faced suddenly with a long mowed field surrounded by white fences, exactly like the horse farms Alice has seen in Kentucky. A brass sign on the white gate says HIDEAWAY FARMS. The shining asphalt drive trails proudly up the knoll to a stone house trimmed in white. The brass knocker on the front door is huge, as if to suggest you ought to be a fairly good-sized person to bother those within. Alice asks, "What's that place, racehorses?"

"Ostriches," Sugar replies.

Alice laughs at her cousin's sense of humor. "They get a good price for the meat?" she asks.

"No, the feathers. For ladies' hats and things."

Alice stares, but Sugar is not smiling. In fact, she looks irritated. "Ostriches?" Alice asks. "An ostrich farm?"

"That's what I'm a-telling you."

"Who ever heard of the like?"

"I never did," Sugar admits, "before this fellow name of Green come in from New Mexico or New Hampshire, one of the newer states, and says you can get rich on raising ostriches. He's been trying to get the state government in on it. The thing is, though, you have to be rich to *start* with, to raise ostriches. They cost you around twenty thousand dollar for a pair, just to set up housekeeping."

"Lord," Alice states. "Every feather on their hide must be worth a thousand."

"That's about it. The fellow was trying to sell the eggs for a hundred dollar, telling people around here they could hatch them out and get into the business that way." Sugar starts to giggle. She holds her fist in front of her mouth. "Roscoe's friend Cash, that just moved back here from Wyoming, told the man he'd buy one if Mr. Green would promise to set on it himself."

Alice feels intensely curious. She has never seen an ostrich, and combs the ridge for the sight of sassy tail feathers and a long pink neck, but she sees only velvet grass. "I don't reckon they're out today," she says at last, disappointed.

"Oh, you see them, some days," Sugar insists. "The kids like to pester them to pieces, to try and get them to run. Or spit, I heard they'll spit if they're mad. I don't know that a bird could spit, but they're an odd bird. They don't bury their heads, that's just a tale. Mr. Green says he's going to shoot the kids with rock salt, and that's *not* a tale, he'll do it. He said out loud in the grocery he'd like to see Boma Mellowbug drop dead tomorrow."

"Who?"

"Boma Mellowbug." Sugar nods at a great ramshackle house nested into the woods just over the fence from Hideaway Farms. The house itself is small, composed of wooden shingles, but it has many things tacked onto it to increase the living quarters, such as a school bus, very rusted. Alice can see chairs and a stovepipe inside the bus, and so many plants growing in there that their leaves jam against the windows and windshield like greenhouse plants. Horse trailers and refrigerators are parked in the yard among the huckleberry bushes. A trio of hens step primly around the splayed, spotted legs of a dead-looking beagle.

"What's the man got against Boma?" Alice asks, though she can guess. The white fence between the two properties could be the Iron Curtain. It's not clear to Alice, though, which country she'd want as her own, if she had to choose.

"Well, mostly he hates her bees. She's got bees living in her roof. He says they're going to kill his birds, but they wouldn't. They're good bees if you love them, and Boma does. A bird wouldn't know enough to hate a bee, I don't think. Do you?"

Alice has already decided that Heaven is a hard stone's throw beyond her ken. "I wouldn't know," she says, which is the truth. Nothing in her life has prepared her to make a judgment on a war between bees and ostriches. As they walk slowly past Boma's mailbox, which has been fashioned from a length of drainpipe and a wire egg basket, Alice hears the faint, distant thrum of the hive. She makes up her mind that for as long as her mission takes, on this stretch of Heaven's road at least, it would be a good idea to love Boma's bees.

FALL SEAS

21

SKID ROAD

TAYLOR TURNS THE HANDI-VAN UP Yesler Way, climbing the long hill above the waterfront. The streets are lined with dapple-trunked sycamores. From between the buildings come sliced glimpses of cold-looking water. A blind passenger in the seat behind her is telling Taylor about how she is forgetting the colors. She has lost all of them now but blue. "I *think* I recall blue," the woman says, "but I haven't seen it for forty years, so I have no idea how far off track I might really be."

Taylor stops carefully at a light. This morning she made a hard stop at a railroad crossing, and someone's seeing-eye dog slid all the way up the aisle from the back. She could hear the toenails scraping over the grooves in the rubber floor mat. After the van had come to a respectable standstill, the dog simply got up and walked back to the rear of the van, making Taylor feel terrible, the way people do when you step on their toes and they sigh but don't say a word.

"I never thought about that, that you might forget colors," Taylor says, trying to concentrate on her driving and also be friendly to the blind passenger, although this conversation is depressing her deeply. She recognizes the woman as a regular: Tuesdays and Fridays, for dialysis.

"Oh, you do, you forget," the woman insists. "It's not like forgetting somebody's name. It's more like you have in mind your idea of a certain color but it might drift, you know. The same way you can drift off the note a little bit when you're singing."

Taylor's radio comes on in a fit of static and demands to know her location.

"I just plussed at Pioneer Square and I'm ten-nineteen to Martin Luther King," she says. "I have two minuses at Swedish Hospital."

"Okay, Taylor, ten–twenty-seven after that," says the radio.

"Ten-four," she replies.

To get the job with Handi-Van, Taylor only needed a good driving record, a Washington State license, and three weeks of training, plus a course in CPR. The hardest part was learning to use the radio code, which she still feels is unnecessary. It doesn't actually save syllables, in Taylor's opinion; for instance, "ten–twenty-seven" is no easier to say than "return to base." It's probably less embarrassing to say "ten-twelve" than "I need a bathroom break," but the code doesn't keep any secrets, she has discovered. Yesterday the radio announced a 10-161, and all six of her passengers looked up and asked anxiously, "What's that?" Taylor had to read the code display on her sun visor to find out it meant an intersection obstructed by an injured animal. She could imagine every Handi-Van driver in the city looking up at the sun visor on that one.

On her way up Yesler, Taylor passes her own apartment, which resides in a long brown box of a building with twenty identical doors in the front, spaced every twenty feet or so like boxcars. The apartment is gloomy, with battle-scarred linoleum and precariously thin walls and neighbors on both sides who shout a lot in what sounds like Chinese; sometimes Taylor gets the feeling the two sets of neighbors are shouting at *each other*, using her apartment as a conduit for curses or strange instructions. But it's a roof over their heads, for now, and she's feeling more optimistic about finances. It took only about two-thirds of the $1,200 Alice gave her to pay the first month, get the lights on and move in. The rest she hid away inside a plastic cube on her night table that has family photos smiling on all six sides—Jax and Turtle back home in the Retarded Desert; Jax wearing his swimsuit and a paper bag over his head; a very old snapshot of Alice shelling out lima beans; that kind of thing. Taylor figures that's the last household object on earth a burglar would steal. Barbie is still with them, and was partly responsible for their winding up here; she insists the Pacific Northwest is on the verge of becoming very popular. She also agreed to use some of her loot to help cover expenses. For the time being, Barbie looks after Turtle in the daytime, and starting this week, Taylor is making eight dollars an hour.

She has decided she likes this city, which seems like Tucson's opposite, a place where no one will ever think to look for them. Bodies of water lie along every side, and snowy, triangular mountains crouch on the horizon, helping her to orient her mind's compass needle as she winds through unfamiliar city streets. Several times each day she has to drive the van across the lake on one of the floating bridges that bob like a long, narrow barge. Apparently they couldn't anchor them, as is usual with bridge construction, because the lakes are too silty and deep to sink concrete roots into. Taylor got this information and a world of other facts from Kevin, a fellow Handi-Van driver who has asked Taylor seven or eight times if she would like to go out with him. Kevin doesn't exactly float her boat; he's a pinkish young man whose jeans always appear brand new and never quite fit him. Kevin's main outside interest seems to be the pale mustache he is trying to grow. He talks in radio code even when he's off duty. In spite of all this, Taylor is about to relent. It's been so long since she had any fun she's afraid she'll forget how. The next time she talks to Jax, she wouldn't mind telling him she was dating someone. She makes her decision while she is helping the woman who has forgotten color find her way to the fire-engine-red door of the hospital: this Saturday, Taylor and Turtle will go somewhere with Kevin. If he didn't have Turtle in mind, that's his tough luck. He can go along with the idea, or he can turn himself around and 10-27.

Barbie and Turtle are out on the tiny patio behind the kitchen when Taylor gets home from work. Barbie has on a pink bikini and is lying on a bedspread, working on her tan. She looks like some kind of exotic bird tragically trapped in a rotten cage. Taylor slides open the stubborn glass door and drags out one of the falling-apart kitchen chairs, reminding herself to borrow a screwdriver and some screws from the garage at work. The late-afternoon light seems too weak to penetrate human skin, but it's the first time they've seen the sun in two rainy weeks, and Barbie claims she can't miss her window of opportunity. She says her tan is an important element of her personal identity. She has put Turtle to work cutting out gold foil stars and gluing them onto a short denim skirt Barbie found at a store called Second Hand Rose.

"That's going to fall apart the first time you wash it," Taylor observes.

Turtle stops cutting out stars. She lays the scissors carefully on the cracked concrete patio and comes over to sit on Taylor's lap.

"Oh, I know *that.*" Barbie is lying facedown and her voice is muffled. "I just won't ever wash it. See, Taylor, this is costuming, it's not like regular clothes."

As far as Taylor can see, everything Barbie wears is a costume. "What happens if it gets dirty?"

Barbie turns over on her side, looking a little peeved. "I'm careful, okay?"

"Okay. It's your skirt."

"This is going to be the All American ensemble," Barbie says patiently. "It goes with a red-and-white-striped halter top and a lace petticoat. It's just come out, we saw it today when we were scouting out what's new in the Barbie section. I'm like, this is so perfect, but it's not going to be easy to get lace like that. That's going to be a challenge."

Taylor is tuning out; she's learned when to stop listening to Barbie. She knows she won't get a quiz later on the All American ensemble. Kevin, the computer whiz, would say that Barbie is all output and no interface. Taylor strokes Turtle's hair. She's wearing the same green overalls she wore on the Oprah Winfrey show, though they are a good deal the worse for a summer of wear, and, Taylor notices, they're short in the leg and tight around the middle. Her toes have grown an inch or two past the ends of her sneakers; Taylor was horrified to realize Turtle was doubling up her toes in there, without complaint. Now she's wearing Barbie's size-six yellow flip-flops. She'll have to have new clothes before she starts school in a week and a half. More costs. Taylor feels defeated. If only Barbie's wardrobe talents could be put to civilian use.

"What did you do today?" she asks Turtle. "Besides scouting out the toy store and cutting out stars?"

"Nothing."

Taylor doesn't consider Barbie the ideal baby-sitter, but she's obviously short on choices. She hopes school will begin before Turtle gets warped by the world of fashion design. "You want to go to the beach or something on Saturday?" she asks.

"Yes." Turtle leans back against Taylor's chest. She takes both Taylor's hands in hers and crosses them in front of her.

"I've decided to go out with Kevin," she tells Barbie.

"Who?" Barbie asks, with genuine interest.

"That rabbity guy from work. Just mainly so he'll quit asking."

"Oh, right, Taylor. Like going out with somebody is a real wonderful way to give him the message you're not interested."

"I see your point."

"Did you bring a newspaper?" Barbie asks.

"I forgot."

"Tay*lor!* This is, like, the fiftieth time I've asked you. I wanted to look at the want ads."

"For a waitress job? But think about it, it's not worth it. You won't make as much as I'd have to pay for baby-sitting."

Turtle glances up at Taylor, her dark eyes showing a rim of white below the pupils and her mouth tucked like a made bed.

"Oh, I can make money all right," Barbie says. "And I don't mean waitressing, either. All I need is some job in an office with a color Xerox machine."

Taylor is afraid to ask for more details on this scheme, so she doesn't. But after a minute Barbie rolls over on her back and half sits up, so that the muscles form ridges in her narrow abdomen. She shades her eyes and looks at Taylor peculiarly.

"You want to know why I left Bakersfield?"

"You said there weren't enough career opportunities for Barbie look-alikes."

"Well, I lied," Barbie says flatly, her voice stripped of its usual friendly effort. "I was wanted for counterfeiting."

"Counterfeiting *money?*"

"What else can you counterfeit? Duh."

"How?"

"A color Xerox machine. It's so easy. Just come into the office a little early, lay out some twenties on the glass, copy them front and back, and blammo, you're ready to go shopping."

Taylor stares. "Are you kidding me?"

"Listen, I don't know why everybody in the world isn't doing this. My boss only found out because I left some messed-up bills in the trash once."

Taylor feels a little shaky. In these moments when Barbie's surface cracks, the feelings inside seem powerful and terrifying. Taylor wonders what it must have taken to turn someone's regular daughter into such a desperate, picture-perfect loner.

"Isn't that a federal crime?" she asks.

Barbie examines the end of her ponytail. "Oh, probably. I don't know."

"Are we going to start seeing your picture in the Post Office?"

"No way." She flips the ponytail behind her back and lies down again. "My boss won't press charges. I'd tell his wife what he tried to pull on me one day in his office."

Taylor glances down at Turtle, who unfortunately is taking everything in. "I don't think it's your boss you have to worry about. I think it's the U.S. Treasury Department."

"Well, don't you think they've got *criminals* to catch? I mean, it's not like I murdered somebody. I just stimulated the economy."

Taylor is never sure when to argue with Barbie, who behaves like a tourist from another solar system who only read a toy catalog before arriving here. You can't argue with someone like that about family values. But Taylor wishes Turtle weren't hearing this. The casino robbery seemed adventurous, like piracy or Robin Hood, but photocopying money sounds like a simple crime of greed.

Barbie, with her eyes carefully closed, presumably to get an even tan on her eyelids, feels around for the plastic glass near her elbow and rattles the ice cubes into her mouth.

"So why did you leave Bakersfield?" Taylor asks.

"They started putting up these signs in all the shopping malls, like 'Warning, warning!' I guess they started noticing the bills in their cash registers. Maybe when they tried to turn them in to the bank. I don't know. So I'm like, forget this! I have to leave town just to spend my money!"

Taylor doesn't know what to say. She would try to argue with Barbie, but she is bone-tired from driving the Handi-Van all day, strapping down wheelchairs and engaging in powerfully depressing conversations and enduring the superiority of seeing-eye dogs. She feels oppressed now by the ugly concrete patio. It's hardly big enough for a dog to turn around in, with a high brown fence separating it from the identical patios of the neighbors. She wonders if the color scheme of brown is some sort of international code for poverty. It would be more cheerful back here if she had a few plants, at least. A red geranium in a pot, or a tomato plant, something to use the free sunshine and give something back. But it will be weeks before they have even three extra dollars to spend on something like that. In the meantime, she thinks, who knows? Maybe Barbie has the right idea. Use the free sunshine yourself. Use whatever comes your way.

On Saturday, Kevin and Taylor and Turtle buy ice cream cones in Pioneer Square to celebrate Taylor's first paycheck. Taylor is not in a party mood: the check was much smaller than she expected, after what fell out for taxes and Social Security. She's working full time, and has no idea how she's going to cover both rent and food, unless Barbie helps. She's not crazy about using Barbie's money, either, considering the source.

"Look, Turtle, lick the side toward you. Like this." Taylor licks the crown of her own pistachio cone to demonstrate. Turtle nods, but goes right on turning her ice cream cone upside-down to lick the opposite side. A growing dampness is spreading outward from her chin onto her T-shirt like a full, green beard. Kevin, inscrutable as a traffic cop in his mirrored aviator sunglasses, has been ignoring Turtle.

It's a hot day, but the sycamore trees, with their mottled brown-and-white trunks leaning like the necks of tired giraffes, seem to know it's almost fall. Their leaves are browning mournfully at the edges, starting to give up the ghost. Quite a few have already fallen. They curl together in piles like brown-paper lunch bags, and Turtle kicks up noisy crowds of them as the three cross through the little park under a wrought-iron gazebo. Listless men and women sit on the benches in every kind of clothing—some in grubby overcoats, some in thin cotton trousers—but still they seem alike, with weathered faces and matted hair, as if these clothing styles were all variations of the uniform of homelessness. Kevin leads Taylor away from the benches toward the street, past a parked car that must have come from somewhere less rainy because it is covered in a deep tan fur of dust. Someone has written WASH ME across the rear window. Kevin takes this opportunity to explain to Taylor that the eastern part of the state is a virtual desert.

"Mom, here," Turtle says, holding up the lumpy remains of her ice cream.

"What, don't you want the rest of it?"

"I don't like ice cream."

"Turtle, sure you do. It's good for you. It's got calcium and helps your bones grow. Who ever heard of a kid that didn't like ice cream?"

Turtle looks at her mother with sorrowful eyes.

"Okay, there's a garbage can." Taylor takes the sodden offering and throws it away.

They cross the street in the shadow of a huge totem pole that overlooks the park. Taylor thinks for the first time in several days of Annawake Fourkiller. She imagines being quizzed on which kind of Indians carved totem poles, which ones lived in teepees, which ones hunted buffalo, which ones taught the Pilgrims to put two fish in the bottom of the hole with each corn plant. She feels ashamed. She has no idea what she should be telling Turtle about her ancestors. These days she hardly has the energy to tell her to eat right and get to bed on time.

"Yesler Way used to be called Skid Road," Kevin explains. Taylor notes that the green ice cream on his mustache makes it more noticeable. "They changed the name recently. This was actually the original skid row. In the old logging days they skidded the logs down this hill to the waterfront, to load them onto the ships, and I guess it was kind of a natural congregating place for out-of-work loggers, looking for a handout." He laughs thinly. "As you can see, it still is."

Across the street from them, some formidable paintings of Jesus adorn the windows of a storefront soup kitchen. Turtle pulls Taylor forward stickily by the finger, up the hill toward the imagined beach.

"I can't believe this sun," Taylor declares. "Two days in a row, even. I was starting to go crazy with all the rain."

"They thought changing the name of the street might clean the place up," Kevin says. "It doesn't help that those projects are right on the other side of the hill."

Kevin doesn't know that Taylor lives in one of the so-called projects. Kevin lives with his parents. His eight dollars an hour minus taxes goes mostly for home-computer equipment, from what Taylor gathers.

To reach Kevin's car they cross through another small park with two more totem poles: a gigantic wooden dog and man, facing each other with outstretched arms. They might be tossing an imaginary ball, but they don't seem happy. Their open, painted mouths are enormous, as if they might swallow the world. Taylor's eyes slip toward a woman on a bench with two stunned-looking children beside her. The woman has swollen knuckles and a stained red blouse and she bluntly follows Taylor with her eyes. Taylor looks down, feeling exactly as if she were carrying something stolen in her hands.

In Kevin's sleek blue Camaro they continue the travelogue up Yesler. "That's the Smith Tower," he says, "the white building with the pointy top. That would be the oldest skyscraper west of the Mississippi."

"Would be?"

"Is, I mean."

Taylor says nothing. They pass a grocery-deli, the school that will soon require Turtle's attendance, and a lot of signs in Chinese, then turn onto Martin Luther King Way, where the frame houses have peaked roofs and little yards of leggy flowers. She knows these streets. A man on her route goes to Rogers Thriftway every other day for Coca-Cola Classic, microwave popcorn, and Depends. Kevin doesn't have to tell Taylor that just a few blocks away, closer to the lakeshore and farther from Skid Road, the property values skid upward rather drastically.

They take Rainier Avenue south into a neighborhood where Taylor can't read any of the signs. Thai and Chinese, according to Kevin. "You wouldn't want to live down here," he says from behind his mirrored lenses, "but they have great noodle soup at that Mekong place."

"We lucked out with this sun," Taylor says. "I don't know if I'll ever get used to how cloudy it is here. I was thinking I might get that disease the Eskimos get from not seeing the sun enough. Where they go insane and start eating up their shoes."

"Never heard of that one," Kevin says, running a hand through the side of his white-blond hair. "Now this is the place to live."

Taylor can't argue. The lakefront neighborhood is breath-taking: elaborate houses with cedar-shake roofs and gardens of bonsai and flowering trees in the yards, banked steeply down to the street. It seems like you might need a passport to come over here from the other side of the hill.

They get out of the car and cross a long grassy area to the lake. Turtle is excited. She didn't have a swimsuit, but Barbie, in a generous moment, sacrificed a piece of blue lamé she'd been saving for a Prom Date ensemble, and turned out a bikini with impressive speed. Taylor had argued against a bikini for a six-year-old, but Barbie ignored her. Turtle runs ahead of them now, her feet flapping duckishly in Barbie's thongs. She pulls off her T-shirt as she goes, revealing a bony brown torso and two puffy bands of shiny blue fabric. She looks like a Mardi Gras dropout. With Taylor in tow she climbs down the concrete steps into the lake and stands knee deep on the pebbly bottom looking up with knocking knees and joy on her face.

"You like that?"

Turtle breathes in through shivering teeth, and nods.

"It's not too cold? I'm going to pull you out when your lips get as blue as your swimsuit."

"Okay," Turtle agrees, hugging herself.

"Kevin and I will be right over there, and I'll be watching you, okay? Stay here where the other kids are. Don't go any deeper."

Turtle shakes her head vigorously.

Taylor retreats to the beach towel Kevin has spread in the sun, without ever taking her eye off Turtle. Kids of every color run around her, screaming and jumping off the steps, but Turtle is immobile except for her shivers, only watching.

"Doesn't she know how to play in the water?" Kevin asks.

"She always takes a minute to get her bearings."

"So, is she one of these adopted Koreans, or what?" Kevin pulls four different tubes of sunscreen and an apple from his backpack and bites into the apple.

"She's adopted, yeah." Taylor sees her own stunned face in his reflectors, stupefied by the rudeness of a person who would bring a single apple on an outing with other people. Her shock doesn't seem to penetrate the lenses to sink into Kevin.

"Well, don't knock it," he says. "At least those people are industrious."

Taylor wasn't about to knock it. She would like to change the subject, though.

"I went out with a Korean girl once," he says. "I repeat, once. She was the valedictorian of our high school class. Kind of pretty. But Christ, what a tragedy, that family. You should see where they lived. Mung Bean Row."

Taylor unpacks the sandwiches she brought to share. She seriously resents having spent fifty-five cents on a can of tuna for this guy, after she and Turtle ate peanut-butter sandwiches all week. "Don't you think it might be possible to be a decent person but still not get anywhere?" she asks.

"Oh, sure. Some people are just not born with all that much upstairs. But Christ, if you know how to turn on the water faucet you can clean yourself up, is what I always say."

Taylor's stomach feels tight, like the beginning of a twenty-four-hour flu. She passes it off as merely a growing hatred of Kevin and nerves about Turtle in the water. In her mind she calculates the number of seconds it would take her to bound across the grass and down the steps, if Turtle should slip under.

"You know what I mean," Kevin says, with his mouth full of apple. "With all the opportunities that are available, and somebody's still sitting around staring at his navel on a park bench, you've got to admit they must be that way partly out of personal choice."

He should have gone out with Barbie, Taylor thinks. *The two of them could jabber at each other all day without ever risking human conversation.* She watches Turtle climb slowly onto the lowest step and jump back into the water, landing stiff-legged, following the lead of two tiny girls whose swimsuits are nearly as strange as hers. Taylor wants to tell her to bend her knees when she lands.

"You like tuna salad?" she asks Kevin.

"Okay," Kevin says, wolfing down the sandwich without looking at it, then licking his fingers with an appearance of slight distaste. He wipes his hands on his cutoffs and carefully takes off his sunglasses in order to rub clear, glossy sunscreen that smells like dog shampoo onto his face. He uses a different tube, white stuff, for his arms and legs. Taylor watches with very mild amazement. He pulls off his shirt and hands Taylor still *another* tube, marked Number 28.

"A lot of it's just poor money-management skills," he says, lying belly down on the towel, crossing his arms under his chin. "Know what I mean? Could you be real careful with the sunscreen? Don't miss any spots. One time I missed a little triangle on the bottom part of my back and it was there for the entire summer and fall."

"Poor money-management skills?"

"Well, yeah. It's a matter of putting in the effort, and being careful what you spend, right? And just having the basic attitude of going out and getting what you want."

"If you can dream it," Taylor says, "you can be it." She toys with the tube of sunscreen in her hands, reaching a conclusion that makes her stomach feel better instantly.

"Basically, that's the American reality," Kevin says. He closes his eyes and looks as if he plans to sleep.

Taylor rubs dry hands over Kevin's sweaty back, taking her time, until he begins to snore softly. Then she opens the tube of sunscreen, applies it to one finger, and carefully writes across his back: WASH ME.

The apartment is dark when they get home. Taylor clicks on all the lights to try to make herself feel less dark inside. "I guess Barbie went out, huh?"

"She probably went to get some Cheese Doritos with her pocketbook money," Turtle says.

"That's a safe bet. You feel like a peanut-butter sandwich? We'll go to the grocery tomorrow, I promise. I've got a paycheck, babycakes! We can buy anything we want."

"Chocolate cookies!"

"Lamb chops!" Taylor says.

"What's that?"

"Lamb. You know, baby sheep."

"Does it hurt the lamb to chop it?"

Taylor closes the refrigerator door, reluctantly. There is hardly anything inside, but she doesn't want to lose the light. Turtle is standing in the doorway, her eyebrows raised in their permanent question mark.

"Yeah," Taylor says. "I'm afraid it does. I don't know that it *hurts* the animals a lot, but they do kill them, before we eat them. That's where meat comes from. Didn't I ever tell you that?"

Turtle shrugs. "I guess."

"So how about peanut butter and strawberry jam?"

"Do they kill the peanuts so we can eat them?"

"No." Taylor thinks about this. "Well, yeah. I guess. A peanut isn't an animal, though."

"No, it's a plant. It's a seed. If we eat it, it doesn't get to grow up."

"Turtle, this is too sad. We can't just give up on eating. Let me make you a sandwich."

"Mom, I'm not hungry."

"At least a glass of milk, then, okay? They didn't kill anything to get milk, they just drained it out of a happy old mama cow."

"Mom, my tummy hurts."

"Okay, sweetheart. Go get ready for bed, if you want. I'll read you a book."

"We read all the books already."

"Back to the library tomorrow then. Promise."

Turtle leaves the kitchen. Taylor's stomach has begun hurting again, too. The sky outside the kitchen window is the shade of dark blue a blind person might imagine.

Turtle is back in the doorway, big-eyed. "Mom, why's it so clean in here?"

Taylor tries to understand. She follows Turtle into the living room. "I'll be darned, Barbie finally got in the mood to pick up all her stuff."

They are both quiet for a minute, not wanting to look any farther. Then Turtle goes to the door of Barbie's room.

"She cleaned up her room, too," Turtle says. "She took the sheets and everything."

"Damn it!" Taylor says. She sits on the broken brown sofa and tries hard not to cry. Those sheets were Taylor's; she brought them all the way from Tucson.

"Did she leave a note, Turtle?"

For a long time there is only the sound of Turtle opening and closing dresser drawers. She comes back to the living room. "No note," she says. "Remember when we found that note on our car? That said I'm sorry I didn't see you at Migget's and here's fifty dollars?"

Taylor begins to laugh or cry, she's not sure which. "Yeah," she says. "Barbie should have left us a note like that, don't you think?"

Turtle sits next to Taylor on the sofa, but stares into the darkness. "Mom, did I make her mad?"

Taylor pulls Turtle onto her lap. "Turtle, you had nothing to do with this. Look at me now, okay?" She strokes Turtle's hair and gently turns her head toward her. "Look at my eyes. Can you look at me? Don't go away."

With a great effort Turtle pulls her focus out of the darkness and fixes it on Taylor's face.

"That's it. Stay right here with me, and listen. Barbie liked you. She's just a nut case. She's the kind of person that can only think about herself, and she just decided she had to move on. We always knew that, remember? We decided we'd give her a ride that time in Las Vegas, but we always knew she wasn't going to come with us the whole way. Remember?"

Turtle nods.

Taylor rocks back and forth with Turtle in her arms. "Don't worry, you know I'm not going to leave you alone. You'll stay with me. Tomorrow's

Sunday, I don't have to go to work. And maybe on Monday they'll let you ride the van with me. You can help me drive, okay?"

"I don't know how to drive."

"I know, but we'll think of something." Taylor has no earthly idea what they'll think of. She knows it's against every regulation of the Handi-Van company to bring family members on board.

"Before you know it you're going to be starting first grade," she says.

"Mom, remember Lucky Buster?"

"I sure do."

"I saved him, right?"

"You saved his life."

"Will we ever see him again?"

"I don't see why not. Sure."

Turtle relaxes her hold on Taylor just a little.

"You think we should get ready for bed? I think it's past my bedtime too," Taylor says. She exhales deeply when Turtle finally releases her and goes into their room.

Taylor gets up and turns out all the lights. She doesn't want to look in Barbie's room, but she has to, to make herself believe. Sure enough, even the double bed is stripped down to the ugly blue-striped mattress. At least now she and Turtle can have separate rooms, Taylor thinks—she'll move in here and let Turtle have the room with the twin beds for herself. She will meet friends in school, and invite them over. They will be a normal American family. Taylor is less optimistic about her own possibilities for sharing the double bed. She misses Jax.

By the time she goes in to kiss Turtle goodnight, Turtle is in her in-between sleeptalking stage.

"Buster has to go home, Mom, this one in the water."

"Goodnight, Turtle. Sleep tight."

"My tummy hurts. Do those trees real or the dog was talking. Is it raining?"

"Yeah," Taylor says softly. "It's starting to rain again."

She undresses and climbs into the other twin bed. She'll have to figure out how to get new sheets for the double bed before she can move into the other bedroom. There is a lot more than too much to think about. She never imagined it would be this much of a problem to lose Barbie from her life. She should have known better. You don't adopt a wild animal and count it as family. Before Taylor turns off the light, she reaches over to her nightstand to take a look at Jax in his paper-bag ensemble.

The photo cube is gone.

22

WELCOME TO HEAVEN

"WELL, TAYLOR, YOU'VE BROUGHT YOUR pigs to a pretty market. How'd you lose your telephone?"

"Not the phone, Mama, the electricity. They couldn't shut the phone off because I didn't even have one yet. This number where you just called me back is a pay phone."

"Oh," Alice says, shifting the receiver. She's about decided her bad ear hears better than the good one. "Well, what's this other number I've got written down here?"

"That's the Handi-Van number. What I'm trying to tell you is you can't call me there anymore because I had to quit."

Alice is confused. It doesn't help that Sugar keeps coming in and out of the living room to ask questions. And this living room is crowded with enough furniture for two or three households. When Alice first peered into Sugar's huge china cabinet, she expected to see fancy dishes or Jesus stuff, but it isn't, it's Indian things of every kind. Old carvings, arrowheads, tacky little ceramic Indian boys. At least no headlamps.

"You quit that handicap job?" Alice asks, when it sinks in, what Taylor has just told her. "After you got trained in artificial retrucidation and everything?"

"Yeah, I had to, because Barbie left. There was nobody to take care of Turtle during my shift. I asked if I could take the week off, just till school started, but I was still on probation so they said they had to let me go."

"Well, that don't seem right."

"I know. It's okay. I just got hired as a cashier at Penney's. At least now after school Turtle can come here and hang out in Ladies' Wear till I get off work." Taylor laughs. "Until somebody gets wise and figures out that Turtle isn't going to buy any designer jeans."

A tall, thin girl with very long hair tromps through the front door and shouts, "Grandma!"

Sugar comes running. "What in the world?"

"Mama says you're not supposed to dance if you're on your period. I think that's an old wives' tale."

"Well, honey, it's all old wives' tales, if you think about it. I don't have your shackles done yet, anyway. Come here, I'll show you how far I've got."

The girl slumps on the couch. Alice is having a hard time concentrating. "Well," she tells Taylor, "you've been wanting to get shed of that Barbie since the day we run into her."

"I know. But I kind of needed her."

Sugar comes back carrying what looks like two masses of terrapin shells. They rattle heavily when she sits down with them on the couch next to her granddaughter.

"What's your new job like?" Alice asks.

"Above minimum wage, at least. Barely. It will come to around six hundred a month, I think, after what they take out. That's going to pay our rent and buy about three jars of peanut butter, but it's not going to get the utilities turned back on. I've got to figure out something else pretty soon. But at least I got a discount on school clothes for Turtle. She's starting first grade, Mama. Can you believe it?"

"You bought school clothes for Turtle instead of paying the electric bill?"

"Mama, I had to. I didn't want kids making fun of her. She looked like something off the streets."

"So I guess it's better to *be* out in the street than to *look* like something off the streets."

Taylor is quiet, and Alice feels terrible, understanding that what she just said is no joke. It's the truth. They are both stunned. A good deal of quiet static washes over the line before either one of them is willing to talk again.

"We're not living in the streets," Taylor finally says. "*Yet.* Mama, I feel bad enough, you don't have to tell me I've messed up."

"I'm sorry, Taylor. I hate to see you like this. Why don't you just come on down here and get it over with?"

"Mama, we don't even have gas money. And I'm not asking you to send any, either, because I know you left me all you had."

"What happened to that? The twelve hundred?"

"It's hard to explain. It's gone. It took most of it to get us moved into an apartment, because you have to pay a deposit and everything."

Alice senses that what Taylor just told her isn't completely true. But she lets it go. Trust only grows out of trusting.

"Have you met with that Annawake Fourkiller yet?" Taylor asks, her voice changed.

"I'm seeing her tomorrow. I'm so nervous I'm chasing my tail." Alice glances at Sugar and the girl, who are hunched together on the couch with the bright Oklahoma morning blazing in the window over their heads. Alice lowers her voice. "I didn't tell anybody yet, you know, what this is all about. I thought they'd make me spill the beans right off, but seems like people are willing to bide their time down here. They're all talking about me, seems like. Maybe they've all got their own explanations so they don't need mine."

"How'd you track down Miss Fourkiller?"

"There wasn't nothing to it. She just lives over here at Tahlequah, a little bit down the road. Everybody here knows everybody. I just called her up."

"What did she say?"

"Nothing. Just thanks for coming. She wants to buy me lunch and talk things over. She said she's been real worried about you and Turtle."

"I'll bet."

The girl gets up from the couch and goes. "Bye, Grandma," she calls, over the shriek of the screen-door hinge.

"Well, she could be," Alice says. "I'm not taking her side, but she sounded like she could be real worried."

"Don't tell her where we are, okay?"

"Taylor, honey, all you've given me is a phone number of a pay phone. For all I know you're at the North Pole."

"If we were, maybe Santa Claus would pull some strings and get our lights turned back on."

Alice feels the familiar deep frustration of loving someone by telephone. She wants to hug Taylor more than anything, and can't. So much voice and so little touch seems unnatural, like it could turn your skin inside out if you're not careful.

"Well, anyway, good luck when you talk to her, Mama. I better hang up on you now before you buy the phone company."

"Don't worry about it. I'm just putting it on Sugar's bill. She said we could work it out later on."

"Okay, Mama. Bye."

Alice waits. "Bye," she says, and then, "I love you," but the clear space at the other end of the line that held Taylor has already closed.

She sits slumped in the chair, feeling paralyzed. She feels the faces of Sugar's many grandchildren smiling at her from their frames on the wall. The ones who finished high school—mostly girls—Sugar has hung in the top row; below them, like a row of straight teeth, are the handsome, smiling, tricky-looking boys.

Sugar looks up. "Alice, honey, you look like you just run over your dog. How's that girl of yours?"

"She's all right. Having trouble making her payments."

"Isn't that the way," Sugar says, sounding as if this were an old joke. "Come over here and I'll show you what I'm making for Reena."

Alice sits next to Sugar and has a look: terrapin shells with holes drilled in them, and gravel rattling inside. "It's her shackles for the stomp dance," Sugar says. "The young girls wear them on their legs. She thinks it's the cat's meow. Most of the kids would just as soon go to the powwows, where they can drink beer, but Reena's real interested in the stomp dance."

Alice takes one of the shackles in her hands. It's surprisingly heavy. The fist-sized shells are sewn with leather thongs to the cut-off top of a cowboy boot, to make a sort of bumpy legging. The whole thing laces up the front with strips of gingham.

"Don't she get tired with all that weight on her legs?" Alice asks, not really seeing the point.

"Well, she'll have to practice. They wrap towels around their legs before they put them on, so they won't blister. These are training shackles, four shells on each one. As she gets better at it we'll add more, till she gets up to thirteen."

Alice hears the cough of a reluctant lawn mower starting up, then dying. "Why thirteen?"

Sugar thinks. "I don't know. Maybe Roscoe would know. That's just the number." She stands and looks outside, shading her eyes. "There's one of the grandkids come to cut my grass. I can't tell which one. You want some hot coffee?"

"No thanks," Alice says. "I'm jumpy enough already."

Sugar looks at her. "You are. Let's go take a walk down to the blue hole. You need to look at some water."

Alice is amazed by her cousin. Sugar is bent over with arthritis and doesn't move fast, but she never seems to stop moving. Today she is wearing a flowered apron that looks like a seed catalog, and cotton slippers instead of tennis shoes. She told Alice at breakfast she always knows when there's a storm coming in, because she can't get her shoes on.

Alice follows her out the door and down a worn path through the yard, to where a tall boy in huge unlaced sneakers is fiddling with the mower. He stands up and bends his head down for Sugar's kiss. A tiny blue butterfly lands on her shoulder.

"That means I'm gonna get a new apron," Sugar says, turning her head and pursing her lips to look at the butterfly before it darts away. Sugar's laugh is a wonderful, rising giggle.

She and Alice traipse down the hill past the outdoor kitchen, a wood stove with a pile of kindling beside it for cooking and canning when it's too hot indoors. "We planted this mulberry tree when we moved here," she tells Alice. "First thing Roscoe said we had to do."

"He likes mulberries?"

"No, he likes peaches. The birds like the mulberries better, so they'll leave the peaches to us. These here are Indian peaches, they call them. Blood red in the center." Sugar stops and looks at the dark mulberries scattered on the ground. "I wonder why chickens don't eat them."

"Maybe they'd rather have peaches," Alice says.

Sugar laughs. "No, a chicken's not that smart. Here's the fire pit where we have the hog fry."

"You fry hogs?"

"Oh, yeah. Cut him up first. For a special occasion. We had one here for me and Roscoe's anniversary, I'm sorry you missed that. Quatie organized it, she's the social director. We ate up the whole hog. Everybody came, all the kids and the grandkids and the husbands and the cousins. The only ones that didn't come was the ones that's dead." Sugar laughs.

Alice tries to imagine what it would take to get her family collected in one yard. "They come from far away?" she asks.

"I guess the furtherest anybody come was from Tahlequah. My kids all live right here." She points through the woods. "See them trailer houses? That one's Johnetta's, that's Quatie's, the two boys is on the other side of the road, they moved back in together since they both got divorced." She pauses and bites her lip. "No, one's divorced and the other one, his wife died. So they've got the kids up there. They's all right around."

"Why don't they move away?"

"Well, because they'd just end up coming back anyway, because this is where the family is. Why move away just to turn around and come back? Too much trouble."

"I never heard of a family that stuck together that much."

"Listen, in the old days they didn't even go across the yard. They just added onto the house. When you married, the daughter and the husband just built another room onto her folks' house. Roscoe says the houses just got longer and longer till there wasn't no place to sweep your dirt out. I think trailer houses was a right good invention."

Their trail has joined up with an old road, two mud tracks running through deep woods. Every mud puddle is surrounded by a prayer group of small blue butterflies. Alice is fascinated by their twitching wings. She wonders if the butterflies are all related to one another too. "How much of a piece of land have you got here?" she asks Sugar.

"It was Roscoe's mama's homestead land, sixty acres. Every one of them got sixty acres, back in the allotments. Most of them sold it or give it away or got it stole out from under them some way. I don't know why she didn't, probably didn't get no offers. So we ended up here. When the kids each one got big, we told them to find a place to set a trailer house and go ahead. They have to pay taxes. We don't. I don't know why, I guess because it's homestead land. Oh, look, there's poke."

Alice spies the purple-veined shoots clustered in a sunny spot beside the road.

"We'll have to be sure and pick those on our way back," Sugar says. "Roscoe told me there was a lot of them here. He come down here the other day looking for the eggs. We got one hen that's real bad about stealing the nest."

"That looks like a tobacco plant growing there," Alice says, pointing.

"Probably is. You might find marijuana, too." Sugar giggles.

The forest opens before them onto a grassy park with a long bank sloping down to the creek. Where the water is deep it stands a cool, turquoise blue. A steep limestone cliff pocked with caves rises behind the creek, and above the cliff, a wooded hill. Alice and Sugar stand a long time looking.

"I'll bet there's crawdads right in there." Sugar points to the shallows.

Alice feels herself relax, looking at the water. Bright orange dragonflies zip low and dive and stab their tails at their own reflections, then light in the rushes, transforming all that energy into perfect stillness. The sunlight reflected upward from the water lights the undersides of Sugar's and Alice's faces and the broad hickory leaves above them, as if they're all on a stage. "I can see why you'd call it Heaven," she says.

"Oh, this isn't the good one yet. This one they call the mushrat hole. I guess they used to trap a lot of mushrat and mink down here. Heaven's on down the trail a little bit," Sugar says, and she strikes out again downstream.

* * *

When Alice arrives in Heaven at last, a little breathless, she instantly begins to worry about boys cracking their skulls. Sugar is right, this blue hole is clearer, much larger and deeper, and the limestone cliff is alive with children leaping like frogs into the water. Sugar stands without a trace of worry on her face, watching small boys, most of whom are presumably her descendants, dive off twenty- and thirty-foot rocks. Some of the kids are barely past toddler age; they have more trouble climbing up the bank than jumping off. Alice is astonished. "Don't you worry about them?" she asks.

"Nobody's ever got drowned here," Sugar says. "They do sometimes up in the river, but not here."

The kids have noticed the two women; they wave their arms in wide arcs, shouting, "Hi, Grandma!" Sugar waves back, not very energetically, Alice thinks, as if it is no big deal to her to be acknowledged publicly by grandsons. Several older children stand knee-deep in water farther down the bank, fishing, and they, too, wave at Sugar. One boy crosses the creek and makes his way toward them carrying a heavy string of fish. He lays the fish on the grass in front of Sugar, just exactly the way Alice's old cat used to bring birds to lay at her doorstep. Alice can't get over what she is seeing: adolescent boys being polite. Even more than polite, they are demonstrating love.

Sugar makes over the fish. "Where'd you get all these? You must have been down here since Friday."

"No," he says, embarrassed. He is a stocky, long-haired teenager with broad shoulders and a gold razor blade on a chain hanging on his bare chest.

"What kind of fish are they?" Alice asks.

"The purple ones are perch," he tells her politely. "These are goggle-eyes. They go under rocks. The ones with the pink fins are chub." He turns back to Sugar, animated. "We caught a snapping turtle in the mud. Leon poked a stick at it and it bit it and wouldn't turn loose. We just pulled it right out of the water. Those things are *stout.*"

"They'll give you a stout bite, too, if you don't leave them be."

"I'll clean these and bring them up later, Grandma."

"Okay, Stand. Bring me some watercress, too. I see some growing down there by them red rocks."

"Okay." Stand walks away with his catch.

Sugar hobbles over to a pair of decrepit aluminum folding chairs that are leaning against a tree and shakes them open, setting them in the shade. "That Stand likes to get drunk, but he's a good boy. He loves to hunt. He brings me something every week. 'Grandma, I brung you this,' he'll say. He don't stay home. Junior is always taking him somewhere and dumping him off and then about three o'clock he'll go after him, he'll have something. Squirrel, or anything green, you know."

"He's your older son's boy?"

"No, not exactly, he's Quatie's, but she already had six or seven when he was born, so Junior adopted him. You know how people do. Share the kids around."

Alice doesn't exactly know, but she can gather.

"I wish he wouldn't drink, though. I swear he's the spit image of Roscoe, when I first met him."

"You must have fell hard for Roscoe," Alice says. "You wrote me you'd met him at the railroad yard, and then the next thing I know you'd run off and married him."

"Well, I was mad because you run off and got married first. And anyway I was sick of factory work."

"I'll tell you, Foster Greer wasn't anything to be jealous of. You've been a whole lot luckier in love than I ever was."

The two women sit still, watching slim brown bodies slip through air into water as if they were made for nothing more than this single amphibious act. Sugar sighs.

"He had shoulders just like that. Roscoe did. From carrying the ties."

"Railroad ties? That's a job."

"Mm-hmm. He used to cut ties and posts. Later on when we got married and come on back up here he cut cookstove wood. Just cut it right out of these woods around here. He'd sell it for fifty cents a rick. Now you get twenty-five dollars a rick."

"Isn't that something, what we used to pay for things?"

"Oh, Lordy! Remember when we worked in that mattress factory for fifteen cents a day?"

Alice laughs. "That was fun, though. More fun than you'd guess."

"No, what was fun was when we'd go to beer joints, or sneak in to watch them wrestling matches they organized in the barns."

"Oh, I liked those!" Alice says. "Those matches they have now on TV are just plain stupid. Like a costume party of grown-up men. I liked those tough-looking boys in the baggy shorts."

"You had a crush on that one, what was his name?"

"Rough and Tumble Ludwig. I did not." Both women cover their mouths and laugh.

"You know what I really loved?" Alice asks suddenly. "When we'd go out to the colored church with that girl Arnetta from the mattress factory."

"Your mama tanned our hides on that one," Sugar says.

"I didn't even care. I kept on going, even after you all left the farm. They sang gospel on Wednesday nights, and there was one woman in particular that always spoke in tongues."

"I've seen that, the speaking in tongues and the carrying on," Sugar says. "I wasn't much impressed."

"This one was different," Alice says, though she knows she can't explain it to Sugar. She leans back, closing her eyes and remembering, feeling the light from the creek playing on her face. That woman could be counted on. Her eyes would go soft and faraway, not agitated, and she would lay her hand on the head of a child, whoever happened to be near, because nobody was afraid, and she would speak out in a slow, meaty voice: "Bel-bagged oh Lessemenee! Yemett algeddy boolando!" And you would understand what she meant. *Yes, sister,* they would all cry. No one doubted she was receiving the spirit. In the years since, Alice, too, has seen the ones who shake and scream and roll their eyes back as if snakebit, but she has always doubted the sincerity of this. Anybody can get worked up, if they have the intention. It's *peacefulness* that is hard to come by on purpose.

Annawake stirs her coffee. Through the café window she can see Boma Mellowbug's bottle tree, with hundreds of glass bottles stuck onto the ends of its limbs. It's a little thin at the top where no one can reach, but once in a while someone from the volunteer fire department will bring a ladder and move some bottles to the upper branches to even things out.

She reaches for the cream pitcher and knocks over the sugar bowl at the same instant she sees the woman who must be the grandmother. She's wearing running shoes and polyester pants and a bright, African sort of shirt, and she is trying not to look lost. Annawake taps on the window and waves. The woman raises her head like a startled animal and changes her course, heading across the street toward the café. Annawake tries to spoon the sugar she has spilled back into the bowl. By the time Alice gets there, Annawake has created a crater in the small white mountain in the center of the table.

"I spilled the sugar," she says.

"Sugar's cheap," Alice says. "You could do worse things."

Annawake is caught off guard, forgiven before they even start. "Sit down, please," she says. She takes off her reading glasses and stands up to shake Alice's hand just as Alice is moving to sit down. They both bend awkwardly to accommodate the difference, and Alice laughs.

"I'm sorry. I'm nervous as a barn cat," she says, sliding into the booth across from Annawake.

"Me too," Annawake confesses. "How long have you been in Heaven? You finding your way around all three blocks of it?"

"I can't complain. Sugar's looking after me. My cousin. I mentioned her on the phone, didn't I?"

Annawake feels wary. She'd said Sugar Hornbuckle on the phone, but she hadn't said *cousin*. "So you and your daughter have ties here in the Nation?"

"Oh, no. Sugar and me grew up together down South. But I never knew Roscoe till he hollered howdy at me two days ago in the bus station."

"Oh," Annawake says, and they look each other in the eye.

Alice exhales slowly. "Well. I had all this stuff to say, that I was practicing on my way over here. I was supposed to start out being real high and mighty, but that's never been my long suit."

Annawake smiles. She has seen so many people show up for court armored in suits and lies. But this bright-eyed little old lady turns out for Greer vs. Fourkiller in an African-print dashiki from Wal-Mart, and an attitude to match. "I think I know what you were going to say," Annawake tells her. "Can I give it a shot?"

"Go ahead."

"Miss Fourkiller, you've got no business butting into our lives this way. You might think you know what's best for our little girl, because she's Indian and you are too, but that's just one little tiny part of what she is. You weren't there while she was growing up, and it's too late to be claiming her now, because she's already a person in our family."

Alice frowns. "I'll swan."

"Coffee, hon?" the waitress asks as she fills Alice's cup. She's a very short, very broad woman with blunt-cut black hair and a face as round and flat as a plate. "I don't think I know you. I'm Earlene."

"Earlene, this is Alice Greer," Annawake says. "She's come to town on some business."

"Uh-oh," Earlene says, noticing the sugar volcano.

"I made a little mess," Annawake admits.

"You know what that means. Means somebody's a-gettin' a new sweetheart." Earlene looks at the two women, beaming. "Which one, you reckon? I know Annawake's on the market. How about you, you married, hon?" she asks Alice.

"Not so's you'd notice," Alice replies. Earlene laughs so hard her bosom heaves and the coffee slides dangerously in the glass pot.

"I'll bring back a rag directly and get that up," she says. "I'm sorry if it takes me awhile to get back to you. I'm the only one here today. You all want the soup of the day? It's beef barley, it's real good."

"That would be fine," Alice says, and Annawake nods. Their water glasses vibrate with Earlene's footsteps as she makes her way back to the kitchen.

"There's one thing you left out," Alice says. "In my speech."

"What's that?" Annawake blows into her coffee.

Alice looks out the window when she speaks. "She was abused."

"I know. I'm sorry."

"Sorry?" Alice takes her straight on now. "That's not enough. You don't know what that child goes through. She's still not over it. Whenever she feels like she's done something wrong, or if she thinks Taylor's leaving, she just ... I don't know what you'd call it. It's like her body's still there but her mind gets disconnected some way. It's awful to watch."

"It must be," Annawake says.

"What I think," Alice says, folding her paper napkin, "is that you people had your chance, and now it's Taylor's turn. And she's doing a good job."

For the first time Annawake feels a stirring of animosity. "When you say 'you people,' who do you mean exactly? Indians in general, or just the Cherokee Nation?"

"I don't know. I just can't see how a thing like that could happen to a little baby girl."

"I don't know why it happens *here,* because we love our children more than money. And there are almost always enough good-hearted people in a family to fill in for the hardship cases."

"Everybody loves kids, that's nothing new under the sun," Alice states. "Except the ones that don't."

"I don't think you understand what I mean." Annawake's jaw tenses with this familiar frustration: explaining her culture to someone who believes America is all one country. She thinks about what she wants to say, and sees in her mind *family,* a color, a notion as fluid as *river.* She tells Alice, "I used to work at the Indian hospital at Claremore, checking people in. Sometimes it would be years before we'd get straight who a kid's mother was, because one aunt or another would bring him in. Maybe the mother was too young, so another family member raised him. It's not a big deal who's the exact mother."

Alice blinks, taking this in. "So with all this love going around, how does it happen that somebody walks up to my daughter's parked car one night and gives a baby away?"

Annawake watches two girls passing by outside on the street, Flossie Deal's granddaughters, she thinks. They are walking fast, with earnest, bobbing heads, the way only adolescent girls can move. Annawake also had speeches in her head, and she too has forgotten them, or lost her introductions. "God knows why," she says. "What's happened to us is that our chain of caretaking got interrupted. My mom's generation." Annawake feels her stomach harden. "Federal law put them in boarding school. Cut off their hair, taught them English, taught them to love Jesus, and made them spend their entire childhoods in a dormitory. They got to see their people maybe twice a year. Family has always been our highest value, but that generation of kids never learned how to be in a family. The past got broken off."

"Well, that's a shame," Alice says.

"Yeah. The ones my age are the casualties. We have to look farther back than our parents, sometimes, to find out how to behave." Annawake feels unsteady. "The woman who gave Turtle to your daughter, I think I could probably tell you her sad alcoholic one-bad-man-after-another story. She gave Turtle up because she had no idea how to save a baby from repeating that life. But I also know that baby fell out of a family that loved her, and she's missed."

Alice's expression changes. "You know that for sure? There's relatives here that want her back?"

Annawake touches the pad of her index finger into the sugar on the table, making a perfect circle, deciding how much to tell. "Yes," she says finally. "I could have told you, before I knew anything about the specifics of this case, that somebody here was missing that child. And it turns out I'm right. I found out just recently as a matter of fact, more or less by accident. At a hog fry. People talk about things here, and it comes around."

"Well," Alice says, glancing around, nervous again.

"It doesn't really change anything. The law is still the law, Turtle's adoption is invalid, whether relatives come forward or not. Our job is to figure out what's the next step."

"Does Turtle have any say-so in all this?"

"Sure she does. And I'm sure she would say she wants to stay with Taylor. I understand that." Annawake begins pushing the sugar into another shape, making a point on the bottom of the circle. "We're not going to decide anything today. The best we can hope for is just to get acquainted."

Alice takes the offensive. "What happened to your mama, after the boarding school?"

Annawake stares at the heart shape she has drawn in sugar on the table, wondering what in the world it is doing there. "Bonnie Fourkiller," she says. "Tried hard to be an all-American girl, but she had none of the assets and all the liabilities. Pregnant at sixteen with my brother Soldier, who they tell me was born blue and died pretty quick. She married a Kenwood kid with less talent for making money than she had for conceiving boys. Three more brothers, then me and my twin, Gabe. What I remember is Dad always somewhere tracking down work, and Mama begging us for mercy and drinking seven days a week. Lysol on Sunday mornings, so she wouldn't smell like liquor in church."

"Lord," Alice says.

"She was institutionalized at the age of thirty-five. But I was lucky, I had lots of people looking after me. My dad and brothers, and mainly my Uncle Ledger. He's a medicine man. Not a doctor. Kind of a minister. Have you heard of the stomp dances?"

"I've seen those turtle shells. Looks like that would be a chore, to dance with all that on your legs."

Annawake laughs. "It's work, but it's not a chore. I did that. But Uncle Ledger decided I would be the one of us who'd learn the white world. My brothers could do their reckless things, but I had to learn to listen to my head, every time. He made me speak English, and he pushed me to do well in school. He thought we needed an ambassador."

"The ambassador? That's what you are? Whatever you told my daughter Taylor scared her to death. She's a mess, all uprooted, and now she can't even make her payments."

"It didn't cross my mind that she would pack up and move."

"Well, she did. Last time I talked to her she didn't sound like herself. She's depressed. It's awful what happens when people run out of money. They start thinking they're no good."

"See that guy over there?" Annawake points across the street to the hardware store where Abe Charley is standing out front in his horsehide suit, talking to Cash Stillwater.

Alice leans, to look. "What's that, a cowskin he's got on?"

"Horsehide. There's a rendering plant over toward Leech where you can get horse leftovers pretty cheap. Abe made that suit himself. He's pretty proud of it."

"Taylor's boyfriend wears some odd getups, from what he's told me. But to tell you the truth, not as bad as that horsehide. Taylor just bought new school clothes for Turtle instead of paying her bills. She was scared to death of Turtle looking poor at school. You know how it is."

"Luckily I don't. I mean, growing up here, you don't have to bother much with pretending you're not poor."

Alice is tracking Abe Charley's flamboyant hide as he crosses the street.

Annawake refines the point on her sugar heart. "People say Indians are ungrateful welfare recipients, but what they really mean is we don't act embarrassed enough about being helped out. The young people like me, the radicals, we'll say it's because we had everything stolen from us and we deserve the scraps we're getting back. And that's true, but it's not the point. The old people around here, they're not thinking about Wounded Knee, they're just accepting what comes their way. For us, it's the most natural thing in the world to ask for help if we need it."

Alice has finally gotten her fingers into the sheet of sugar that is spreading across the table. She draws a pig, then puts a fence around it. "I was noticing that about my cousin Sugar," she says. "We were walking along and she saw some poke growing down in the ditch, and she just went right down there and got it. Didn't care who drove by and saw. I was thinking, 'Now, I'll eat poke if I have to, but I'd hate for anybody to see I was that hard up.' "

Annawake smiles, remembering summers of gathering greens with her uncle.

Alice puts another fence around the pig.

"Your cousin Sugar was my mother's best friend," Annawake says. "Ask her sometime if she remembers Bonnie Fourkiller."

"You had that brother that got sent away, didn't you?"

Annawake is startled to feel tears in her eyes. "How did you know that?"

"It was in that letter you wrote Jax. He read it over the phone."

Annawake wipes her nose with her napkin. "My other brothers are still around here, and a slew of nieces and nephews. My dad is still living, he's over in Adair now. What about you? Do you have other kids besides Taylor?"

"Nobody but Taylor. No son, no daddy, and no husband to speak of."

"None to speak of?"

"Well, I had me one, Harland, but he never talked. It was like trying to have a conversation with a ironing board. He just wanted to watch TV all the time. That's what ruint him, really, I think. TV does all the talking for you, and after a while you forget how to hold up your end."

Annawake smiles. "Interesting theory."

"So I left him. I doubt he's noticed yet. Now it's just back to me and Taylor and Turtle. Seems like we're doomed to be a family with no men in it."

"Could be worse. You could have a family with no women in it, like I grew up in."

"Now that's true, that would be worse."

They fall quiet. The window gives their eyes a place to go when they need to take a rest from each other.

"If you don't mind my asking," Alice pipes up, "what's going on with that tree over there?"

"That's Boma Mellowbug's bottle tree," Annawake says. "Our little thing of beauty. Boma is, I guess you'd say, the town lunatic."

"I think maybe I saw her. In a dress and a ski hat?"

"That was Boma. You really have to be sure you don't run over her with your car. Sometimes she'll stand in the middle of the street and have a conversation with the oaks. But everybody's crazy about Boma."

"She did all that by herself?"

"No. She got it going. Back when I was little, she started sticking old empties down over the ends of the branches of that redbud. And pretty soon somebody else would come along and add another one, and then we all got into it, keeping our eyes peeled for something special. Once I found an old blue milk bottle in a ditch, and another time, one of those fancy glass cups they used to have up on the electric lines. I couldn't wait for Uncle Ledger to drive me over here in his truck so I could put my things on the tree."

"Well," Alice says, "it's different."

"Not for here. For here it's just kind of normal." She laughs. "One time in law school we were discussing the concept of so-called irresponsible dependents. That a ward of society can't be a true citizen. I wanted to stand up and tell the class about Boma and the bottle tree. That there's another way of looking at it."

"What's that?"

"Just that you could love your crazy people, even admire them, instead of resenting that they're not self-sufficient."

"Why didn't you?"

Annawake shrugs. "There are things I can't explain to white people. Words aren't enough."

"Well, that's it, isn't it?" Alice says. "If we could get it across, we wouldn't be sitting here right now."

Earlene comes back carrying two bowls of soup and grinning from ear to ear. "Oops," she says, "I forgot to get up that sugar." She lumbers briskly away singing, "Here comes the bride!"

Annawake stares at Alice, the woman from the family without men, and hatches the most reckless plan of her life.

23

SECRET BUSINESS

Letty is standing in her garden with a butcher knife when Annawake drives up. She looks formidable, but Annawake kills the engine anyway and makes her way through the bean patch. She waves Letty's pie plate in the air. "I'm returning this to you," she says.

Letty puts a hand on top of her dead husband's hat and squints at Annawake, frowning, until her face lights with recognition. "Annawake, I swear I wouldn't have knowed you, except you was here at the hog fry. With that hair all cut off."

"Well, Letty, I'm growing it back. I'll look presentable in a year or two."

"I reckon you will." Now Letty stares at her pie plate. "How'd you get hold of that?"

"I took some of your sweet potato pie home from that hog fry you had for Cash. We took it home to Millie, remember? It's her favorite."

"Well, she should have come. She missed a good one."

"She wanted to, but the baby was cranky from getting his shots."

"Oh, that's a shame."

"He got over it. Millie says thanks for the pie. She wasn't going to return the plate till she had a chance to catch her breath and cook something to send back in it. But that's not going to happen for about twelve more years, so I snuck out with it this morning. I figured you'd rather just have the plate."

Letty laughs. "That's how it is with kids, all right. They're all over you like a bad itch. I miss mine, though, now that they's done growed."

Annawake looks around for evidence that a person might need a butcher knife to stand out here in the garden. There is no danger she can see. "You look like you're hunting for another hog to kill."

"I would, if one run through here, and that's no lie. Or a ostrich. Did you hear about that ostrich feather Boma Mellowbug's got hold of?"

"No."

"She says it fell on her side of the fence. That Green fellow figures she climbed over and got it, and he wants it back. He says he'll take her to court over it. Cash saw her downtown yesterday, a-wearin' it in her hat."

Annawake is sorry to have missed that. "How's Cash settling in, anyway?" she asks.

"Oh, I guess he's all right. I think he broods. I got him fixing up my roof for me to improve his disposition."

"That must be why I saw him yesterday talking to Abe Charley at the hardware store. You know, he's got a secret admirer."

Annawake can see Letty's ears rise half an inch in her head. "Who are you thinking of?"

"There's a woman staying over at Sugar and Roscoe's place. She's some kind of relative of Sugar's."

"Oh, honey, I know all about that. I was standing right over there in my own kitchen the day the woman called on my telephone and told Sugar she had to come here in a big old hurry. She's got some secret business with the Nation. A big claim. I can't tell you no more about it. I really oughtn't to go into it even that much."

Annawake smiles. "Well, she's dying to meet Cash Stillwater, that's what I heard."

"We ought to tell him, don't you think?"

"Oh, I don't think so," Annawake says. "He'd just be embarrassed, I imagine."

"Probably. Far be it from me to go butt in. What's she like, the cousin?"

"Alice Greer is her name. She's nice-looking, divorced. She despises watching TV, that's the main thing I know about her. She said she likes a man that will talk to her."

"Well, goodness me, Cash will talk your ear plumb off. I ought to know that."

"I gather she's going to be in town for a while," Annawake says. "They'll run into each other one way or another, don't you think?"

"Oh, sure," Letty says. Her knife blade catches the sun and winks in Annawake's eyes. "One way or another."

Annawake decides not to ask again about the knife. She will drop off the plate and go, leaving Letty to her own devices.

24

WILDLIFE MANAGEMENT

THE MAN WHO COLLECTS TAYLOR'S rent has pulled up in front of their apartment, just as she was about to leave to walk Turtle to school. His truck is loaded with strange things: large, long-handled nets, for example, and shipping crates. He gets out of the truck and steps snappily up the walk before Taylor can pretend she didn't see him.

"Hi," she says. "I was going to put it in the mail tomorrow."

"Well, they wanted me to get it from you today, if you don't mind. Since it's a week past due."

"Okay. Let me go in and get my checkbook."

The manager, a young man whose name she doesn't know, wears broad, flat-paned glasses that reflect the light, giving him a glassy-fronted appearance, like a storefront. Taylor actually feels a little sorry for him: what a hateful job. He once told her, apologetically, that his real job is in City Park Maintenance; he had to take on managing the apartments for extra cash after his wife had a baby. He has pale, uncommanding fuzz on his cheeks and seems too young to have all these worries.

She has just paid to get the electricity back on, so she dates the check for the middle of next week, after payday, and tries to think of something to say to distract him from looking at it too closely. "What's that on your truck?" she asks.

"Goose-catching stuff," he replies.

She tucks her checkbook into the back pocket of her jeans and returns her hand to Turtle's suspended grasp. "You catch geese?"

"We're having the big goose roundup today."

Taylor looks from his glassy face to the truck and back again, unsure of what one says in this exact situation.

"Canadian geese," he adds, to shed more light.

"Is that, like, a sport?"

"No, it's a citywide crisis," he says, hitching his brown Parks and Recreation jacket on his shoulders with the air of a man who considers himself something of a goose expert. "We've got these Canadian geese that come down here to the lakeshore," he explains knowledgeably, "while they're supposed to be on their way to somewhere else. Stopping for a little break, supposed to be. But everybody goes down there with their darling little child and a bag of day-old bread to feed the geese, and next thing you know, these birds have no intention of moving on. No intention whatsoever."

Turtle is tugging with a light pressure on Taylor's hand and looking at the toes of her new sneakers, which clearly want to head toward the schoolyard. But Taylor needs to be polite. This fellow may look nineteen, but his power over her life right now is infinite. "Well, I guess you wouldn't want every AWOL goose in Canada hanging out down by the docks."

"No, ma'am, you certainly do not. There's goose poop piled up to kingdom come down there. But our main interest is in protecting the welfare of these birds. It's poor wildlife management to allow a bird to live on handouts. A lot of these birds, and I'm not exaggerating this, ma'am, a lot of these birds have become too obese to fly."

Taylor clamps her teeth together so hard, to avoid smiling, she's afraid she's going to get a cramp. "Where are you taking them once you round them up?"

"Shipping them out to eastern Washington," he replies with satisfaction. "It's no party out there. Not a lot of rainfall. These geese will have to slim down and learn to fend for themselves, I'm telling you. Hard work will straighten out their bad habits pretty quick."

"What if they're just too lazy to learn better ways?" Taylor asks in a solemn voice. "You think they might just waddle on back west?"

"Oh, no, ma'am, there's no chance of them coming back here. No chance at all. Not where they're going. This trip is going to separate out the men from the boys, you might say."

"The sheep from the goats," Taylor says, nodding, a studied frown on her face.

"That's right," the manager says. He folds Taylor's check without a glance and places it carefully in his shirt pocket. "I have to be going now," he says.

"You certainly do," she says. "I sure hope you catch all the perpetrators."

Charged with Taylor's confidence, the manager practically sprints back to his truck and drives away in a hurry.

"I wish somebody'd give *us* some day-old bread," Taylor says to Turtle. "Don't you?"

She nods. "With strawberry jam."

The pair of them turn their toes out and pretend they are obese geese, waddling to school.

Late Saturday morning Taylor is headed south through steady rain toward the airport, wishing with all her might that she were flying somewhere too, instead of driving a man in a wheelchair to meet his plane. She's still on the Handi-Van roster as a substitute, and this morning she is filling in for Kevin. He isn't speaking to her but he let her drive his Saturday shift, since there was nobody else available, so he could go to a computer fair. Taylor feels uneasy about the baby-sitting she had to settle for; Turtle is with an elderly Chinese neighbor who wears a red wig and black stockings with brown plastic sandals. She sews uniforms for cheerleaders and baseball teams in her home, and seemed a safe enough bet. Unfortunately she doesn't speak English, so Taylor has no idea what she's being charged for the baby-sitting, and prays she'll come out ahead.

She has only one passenger at the moment, the man going to the airport. Taylor likes his looks: he's about her age, and has nice eyes that remind her a little of Jax. "You heading for someplace where the sun shines?" she asks him.

"Not likely," he says. "I work in the air traffic-control tower."

"You do?" She feels embarrassed; she had assumed he was just a passenger, not a working person. "What's that like? I heard that leads to heart attacks."

"Only if you let the planes run into each other. We try to discourage that."

"But how can you keep your eyes on everything at once? I think I'd be terrible at that job. I kind of freak out if the telephone and the doorbell both ring at the same time."

"We have radarscopes. You should come up to the control room sometime and see. Ask for Steven Kant."

She slows down to force a tailgater to pass. The windshield wipers are beating across the glass like a hypnotist's watch, instructing her to feel very, very sleepy. Taylor tries not to think about Turtle sitting in Mrs. Chin's dark apartment with no one to talk to, bearing mute witness to the flickering TV while Mrs. Chin's sewing machine plods through gaudy layers of satin. It would make Turtle's day if she could go see an air traffic control center. "Okay, I'll do that," Taylor says.

"Well, great."

The wide freeway is full of cars but empty of interest, merely blank and wet, the place where everyone on earth has surely been before. The air traffic controller doesn't seem to have anything more to say, which is too bad. In Taylor's opinion Steven Kant is probably the most upbeat passenger in the history of the Handi-Van corporation, and he's handsome, besides. "I'm Taylor, by the way," she tells him. "I don't usually drive this route. I guess you know that."

"No, I didn't. I don't usually go this route, either. My MG is in the shop."

"Oh, that's too bad."

"I don't mind the limo service once in a while." He catches her eye in the rearview mirror and smiles. "The service is friendly."

"Only the best. You just sit back there, sir, and pour yourself a glass of champagne."

"In my line of work they kind of frown on people showing up tipsy. But I'll take a rain check."

She looks in the mirror again, wondering if this is an invitation of some kind. She decides it is, but he's made it so gently that if she overlooks it neither one of them will feel bad. She supposes living in a wheelchair might train you in that kind of skill.

"You really drive an MG?"

"Yep. Convertible. Canary yellow, with wire wheels and hand controls and a very sporty wheelchair rack on the back."

"You got headers on that thing?"

"You bet. Headers and a glass pack."

"Whew. I'll bet she purrs."

"You know a lot about sports cars."

Taylor smiles. "Not a thing, really. I just used to sell them, a piece at a time."

Steven Kant laughs. "Sounds like a life of crime."

"No, nothing so profitable. A car-parts store." Taylor finds she can hardly remember working at Mattie's. She can picture herself in the store, joking with the men, among all those organized metal pieces of dream. But that saucy salesgirl seems to Taylor now like a confident older sister, rather than herself. Someone with her life well in hand.

"How about when your MG's fixed *you* can drive *me* someplace," she says. "Not to work, though. My other job is at the world's most hideous shopping mall."

"Okay. How about the locks?"

"The locks?"

"Yeah. Haven't you seen them before?"

"I've got about seven on my front door."

He laughs. "The locks between the sound and the lake, where the boats pass through. Really, you've never been there?"

"I'm new in town, sailor."

"Well, okay then, I'm going to show you the locks. And afterward I'll take you out for the freshest salmon of your life. What do you think, next Saturday?"

Taylor's stomach flips upstream when it hears about the salmon. Freshness is not the issue, either; right now she wouldn't be above taking home a salmon if she found one dead in the road. She's so tired of peanut butter she has stopped acting for Turtle's benefit like she cares about the murdered peanuts.

"Saturday would be good," she says, after pretending to think about it. "Only, I'm going to have to tell you right up front, I have a little girl that would love to come too. No husband or anything, but a kid. Would that be okay?"

"Two dates for the price of one," he says. "That's even better."

Taylor thinks: it won't be for the price of one. She eats too.

Jax has knocked over a nearly full bottle of beer into his synthesizer in the middle of "Dancing at the Zombie Zoo." He manages to play through to the last chords, touching the keys gingerly, not going for the demonstrative ending this time. He just hopes he won't get electrocuted. While they're fading on the final, he signals his lead guitarist for a break. Once the stage spots go off and they begin playing taped music through the house amps, Jax takes off his T-shirt and starts mopping the keyboard. He'll have to take the whole thing apart. He can't decide whether to start doing that now, before the beer has a chance to settle into the microprocessors, or wait until later. A young woman with terrible posture and limp, cherry-red hair hanging from exactly one half of her scalp is still dancing right in front of the stage. Or rather, she is doing shallow knee bends, bobbing in a slow rotation with her eyes closed. She has been drilling herself into the same spot for nearly an hour, annoying Jax for no particular reason. He picks up the beer bottle that committed its crime against music, and rolls it toward her, hoping it will fall off the stage and shatter her reverie. It merely clonks loudly and rolls past her. He takes his keyboard off its legs and kicks some amp cables out of the way to clear a space for it on the floor.

Rucker, the lead guitarist, crosses the stage and stands over him. "Man, you drowned it."

"Yeah. In beer, though, so it's happy. Do you know CPR?"

"No, man, I don't even *pay* my taxes."

"Rucker, you have no appreciable IQ."

"Jax, what do women see in you? The brunette working the bar sent you this note. She said it's urgent."

"Tell her I've got a disease, okay?" Jax takes a screwdriver out of his keyboard case and begins taking off the back plate.

"That's not funny."

"I'm only paid to entertain people with music here."

"What's wrong with you, some dog buried your bone? Did you see her? She's luminous."

"That's nice."

Rucker unfolds the note, which is inked on a cocktail napkin. "I'm reading this little love letter myself."

"I didn't know you could read." Jax kneels down with his head near the floor and peers inside his machine. It always amazes him: it can produce sounds exactly like a piano, a Hammond organ, a muted French horn, even breaking glass or a marble rolling down the inside of a pipe, and yet there is practically nothing inside. He remembers feeling this same astonishment the first time he took apart a TV.

"Who's Lou Ann?"

Jax looks up. "Let me see that."

"Lou Ann called," Rucker reads. "Super urgent emergency, call Taylor back at this number."

Jax swipes the napkin out of Rucker's hand and bounds off the stage, bumping into the bobbing half-bald dancer but still not waking her up. He makes a beeline for the pay phone between the bar and the kitchen. There's no hope of quiet, but he can't wait until he gets home. Taylor picks up on the first ring.

"Jax?"

"I'm going to die if I don't kiss your navel within one hour. Tell me you're calling from the Triple T Truck stop in south Tucson."

"I'm not. It kind of looks like the Triple T, though. I'm at a pay phone in the parking lot between a Kwik Mart and, I think, an open-air festival of drug users."

"Where's Turtle?"

"Asleep in the car. Hey, listen, you, I don't even know if I've forgiven you for screwing Gundi. Why would I let you kiss my navel?"

"Well, good, Taylor, you sound like yourself. You must be okay."

"I don't know if I am or not. I feel like I'm in hell. Do you have to pay rent and utilities in hell?"

"No. I think you make all the payments before you get there."

"Jax, my life's a mess."

"I wrote you another song. Listen."

"I don't know if I can listen to another broken-heart song."

"This one isn't as bad. Listen:

I made you happy,
I made you breakfast,
The only thing you ever made me was crazy.
I gave you flowers,
You gave me migraines,
Starting today you're going to give me the brushoff ..."

"Broken-heart song," Taylor diagnoses. "*Pissed-off* broken-heart song, which is worse. Jax, we've been over this. I didn't leave *you,* I left a situation."

"Would you mind writing that on the blackboard five hundred times?"

Her voice is quiet. "I miss you, Jax. Real bad. I get this aching in my throat sometimes and I'm not sure if you're real or not. It's been so long since I've seen you." Jax hears her blowing her nose, the most heartwarming sound he has heard in his life to date. He wishes he could program that nose blow into his synthesizer.

"I don't even have your picture anymore," she says. "Goddamn Barbie stole it."

"That's a crime against nature," says Jax. "She stole my photograph?"

"Well, there was money involved. It's kind of hard to explain."

"You had to *pay* someone to steal my photograph?"

A waitress with her blouse tied in a knot at the base of her rib cage passes Jax with a tray of dirty plates and gives him a look, running her eyes down his shirtless torso.

"I sacrificed my shirt to a medical emergency," he whispers.

She rolls her eyes as she wheels around and butts the kitchen door open with her hind end.

"I should have seen it coming," Taylor says. "That Barbie was petty larceny waiting to happen. I can't believe how bad I've screwed up here, Jax. Seems like I've made every wrong turn a person could make."

"You sound like a seven-car freeway pileup."

"I am. I didn't even tell you yet, I lost the van-driving job. I couldn't work out the baby-sitting. They kept me on the substitute board, but I don't get called much. Now I'm a cashier in a department store. Ladies Intimate Apparel, to be exact. Six dollars an hour."

"That's not so bad. Forty-eight dollars a day for selling undies. That's almost a thousand a month."

"Very good, math whiz, except it isn't. They take out some for taxes and Social Security and this mandatory insurance plan that I can't even use yet for six months. I'll get around seven hundred a month."

"Hey, that ought to melt away those unwanted pounds."

"I figured out a budget: our rent is three hundred and ninety, so if you figure in water and electricity and gas—we haven't turned on the heat yet, so I don't know what that will be—but say five hundred total, for rent and utilities. Then another fifty a month to keep the car going so I can get to work. If we can get by on a hundred a month for food, that should leave fifty dollars for emergencies. But Jax, we just keep getting behind. I had a car-insurance payment come due, and then today my register turned up forty-four dollars short, and they say they're going to take that out of my paycheck. I'm thinking, what paycheck?"

"That's robbery."

"No, it probably was my fault. I get distracted trying to keep an eye on Turtle in the store. They have this special aftercare program at her school for low-income, I guess that's me, but even that costs three dollars a day. Sixty a month. I don't have it."

"You're eating on twenty-five bucks a week?"

"Yeah. One dollar a meal for the two of us, plus Turtle's milk money that she has to take to school. We're not eating too high off the hog, as Mama would say."

"No, I'd say you were eating very low off the hog. I would say you are eating the hooves."

"Jax, poverty sucks."

"Can I quote you on that? Maybe a bumper sticker or something?"

"I know you're not rich either, but it was different there, with you and me to split the rent, and Lou Ann always around for baby-sitting."

"You should click your heels together and get your butt back home, Dorothy."

"Oh, I forgot to tell you the funny part. Now they're telling me I need to dress better for work. My supervisor says jeans and T-shirt is not acceptable attire for a cashier in Ladies' Wear. I wanted to tell her to shove her underwired bras and transfer me to Auto Repair. But if I lose this job we'll be living downtown on a bench, or in our car, and that's no joke. I swear I've considered shoplifting from the juniors department."

"Taylor, read my lips: Come home. I'll send you the money. I don't think this Annawake figure is going to come after you."

"You don't think so?"

"She seems more like the lurk-in-the-bushes and make-scary-noises type."

Taylor blows her nose again. "If I could get there on my own, Jax, I would. I feel tired all the time, like I could lie down and sleep a hundred years. But you can't be sending money. You don't have next month's rent."

"Don't be insulting. I could get it from Mattie."

"No!" Taylor cries.

"Well, Christ, keep your fingernails on. Mattie wouldn't mind."

"I mind," she says. "I'm going to make this work here. I have to. I'm not stupid, and I'm not lazy. I'm working so hard, Jax, but we never quite get caught up."

"It's not your fault, Taylor."

"Well, whose is it? I should be able to keep a roof over my own head. If I work at it."

"That's just a story. You're judging yourself by the great American cultural myth, but Horatio Alger is compost, honey. That standard no longer applies to reality."

"Right. Tell that to my landlord."

"What you need is a nice musician to take care of you."

"Now, there's a myth. Who did a musician ever take care of?"

"Not even his most beloved M1 synthesizer, at the moment. I just poured a beer down her front and left her gargling her final breaths on stage. We're on break right now."

"Well, guess what, I did meet this air traffic controller."

"Damn, I knew it. You're in love."

"No. But Turtle and I got to see the control room yesterday. It's this dark room full of little radar screens, with somebody in charge of each one. They sit there all day hunched over watching yellow blinking dots and drinking coffee and talking the pilots out of crashing into each other. What a life, huh? It looks kind of like a submarine."

"Is that what submarines look like? I always wondered."

"Well, I don't know. It seemed like it. It's called the Terminal Radar Approach Control. Turtle kept calling it the Terminal Roach Control. I'm not sure she had a real good understanding of the concepts."

"Don't be surprised if she did. Not much passes her by."

"That's true. It was kind of reassuring to see. At least somebody is in control of something in this world."

"Sounds like true love to me," Jax says miserably.

"Jax, I'm not in love with Steven Kant."

"Well, just make sure Steven Doesn't."

"That's great. You're telling me to be a nun, while you're finally getting the landlady interested in the plumbing."

Jax laughs, in spite of himself. "She's lost interest again, I promise you. Our toilet still defies the laws of hydrodynamics."

"Well, I'm sure glad to hear that. I wouldn't want to think she was showing you any special favors."

"You know what? I'm glad you're jealous. It makes me feel less remorseful about what I'm going to do to this Steven Can't when I locate his control tower."

"I'm not in love, Jax. He's nice, but he doesn't laugh at my jokes the way you do." She stops, but Jax knows from the quality of her silence to keep listening. She goes on. "I hate to say this, after what I just told you about making my own way, but he took Turtle and me to this nice restaurant in the airport, and I sat there thinking: everything on this menu costs more than our whole week's food budget. It was such a relief just to eat. Sometimes it's hard to separate that from love."

Jax can see through the bar to the stage, where his band is beginning to accumulate once again. Rucker and the drummer are standing over his synthesizer like forlorn relatives at a wake. The bobbing woman is still bobbing in a slow circle. Suddenly, as Jax watches, she keels like a mannequin and hits the floor with a somewhat frightening sound. Jax understands that he despises her because she is pitiful.

"I'm sending you two plane tickets home. Just tell me your address."

Taylor says nothing.

"I'm having trouble reading your lips."

"No. Don't send plane tickets. I can't just ditch the car here."

"This is not about your car."

"Jax, no."

"You damn proud little hillbilly."

She says nothing, and Jax holds his breath, afraid she'll hang up. Then her voice comes. "If that's what you want to call me, I don't care. I've hardly ever had a dime's worth of nickels but I always knew I could count on myself. If I bail out here, I won't even have that."

"You're breaking my heart," he tells Taylor.

"I'm breaking *mine,* Jax. I don't believe this is my life. I look in the mirror and I see a screwup."

Jax looks at the napkin in his hand that says, "Super urgent emergency, call Taylor." For once, Lou Ann hasn't exaggerated. He would give the world to know how to answer the call.

* * *

Something about the Seattle locks is reminiscent of the Hoover Dam. Taylor notices it right away, as they approach through a little park. The gate and entrance building have the same sturdy, antique look. Turtle has noticed too. "Remember those angels?" she asks.

"I sure do," Taylor says. "I was just thinking about those guys."

"What angels?" Steven asks.

"The guardian angels of the Hoover Dam," Taylor tells him. "They're sitting on this memorial for the people who died building it. Turtle and I were just there, not too long ago."

"You like public works, do you?" he ask Turtle.

"Uh-huh. I saw Lucky Buster fall down a big hole. We saved him, but then we had to run away from the Indians."

Steven laughs. "She's going to be a writer someday," he tells Taylor.

"Could be." Taylor squeezes Turtle's hand, a secret message. In her other hand she's holding Steven's umbrella, trying to give all three of them some protection from the drizzle. She feels a little self-conscious. It's the first time she has been on a date with two people whose heads reach about to her waist. She doesn't know whether to put her hand on Steven's chair, or just walk alongside. She was relieved when he popped open the umbrella and handed it to her.

They pass through the entry and Turtle runs a few feet ahead, for once excited, her black pigtails swinging like runaway jump ropes. She looks tall and impossibly thin in her new stretch kneepants and T-shirt and heavy white sneakers. It seems to Taylor as if something is pulling on Turtle's feet at night—she gets taller, but doesn't fill in. And her skin doesn't seem right. The worry surfaces at the front of Taylor's mind only at times like this, when she can watch Turtle with her full attention.

Inside the lock area, the three of them wait next to the rope, looking down into a long channel of water with a gate on either end. Despite the rain, there are jolly couples out boating: two sailboats already inside the lock, steadied by ropes, and a slender, aggressive-looking speedboat just now maneuvering itself in from the sound. A man in blue overalls directs the operation. Once everyone is secured, an alarm bell rings, the gate closes, and water rushes into the lock from underneath. The boats rise slowly on the crest of the engineered tide, from sea level to lake level. Taylor watches the voyagers bob like bathtub toys. "I guess around here you can't wait for a sunny day to go boating."

"You'd be waiting awhile," Steven says. "You should have seen it on the Fourth of July. Raining cats and dogs, and the traffic through here was still unbelievable. He had thirty or forty boats packed in at a time, like cars in a parking lot, all tied to each other."

"That sounds cozy."

"It was. There weren't three square feet of wasted space. You could have walked across, stepping from one deck to another. That guy is unbelievable," he says, pointing to the man in coveralls. "He can figure out how to pack forty boats in a quarter-block area, and then get them out again, without wasting an inch or a minute. He's got spatial skills that could get him into MIT."

"Is that so surprising? That a guy in overalls is brilliant?"

"Well, it's just ironic, considering what he gets paid."

"What do you think he gets paid?"

"I don't know, but I'm sure it's next to nothing."

Taylor already knew this, somehow. "I guess he should have gone to MIT," she says, feeling wounded, even though Steven has said nothing that could rightfully offend her.

The boats are nearly up to lake level now. The gate to the lake slowly opens and water rushes in, curling itself into eddies that make the boats rock from bow to stern. Steven leads Taylor and Turtle across the bridge to the other side.

"Now we get to see how the salmon do it," he says.

"Do what?" Turtle asks, looking at Taylor.

"Don't ask me. Ask him."

"Get from the ocean up into the lake," Steven says. "They live in the ocean all year, but then they have to swim back up into the rivers where they came from, to lay eggs."

"I've heard of that," Taylor says. "I heard they have to go back to the exact same place they were born."

"I don't know that they *have* to," Steven says. "Seems like they just always *want* to. Like all of us, I guess."

"Not me. I got out of Kentucky just as soon as I could get the tires of my car pointed rubber side down."

"And you'll never go back?"

"Oh, I might, I guess. You shouldn't forget who made you."

"How about you, Turtle, where were you born?" he asks.

"In a car," she says.

Steven looks at Taylor.

"It was a Plymouth," she tells him. "That's about all I know about it. She's adopted."

"I don't want to go back to live in a car," Turtle states.

Taylor thinks: Let's hope you don't have to.

They take the elevator down to the viewing area of the fish ladder. Steven explains that the fish have to swim up fourteen steps, against the strong current, to reach the lake. Through a thick window as high as a movie screen they see hundreds of grimacing, pale-bellied, pink-finned fish all headed the same way, working their bodies hard but barely moving forward. They look like birds trying to fly against a hurricane.

"Most of those are silver salmon," Steven says. "Those few you see that are bigger are king salmon."

They look beaten up, their fins bedraggled. "Poor things, why do they even come in here?" Taylor asks. "Seems like they'd be looking around for an easier way to go. A free ride in the locks, maybe."

"No, believe it or not, the strong gush of water flowing out at the bottom is what attracts them in here. The Corps of Engineers figured that out a few years back. They narrowed the channel to increase the flow, and a lot more fish came in. You know the really sad part?"

"What?"

"There are a couple of fat sea lions that like to hang around at the top, just licking their chops, waiting to meet these guys at the end of their hard day's work."

"That is so sad."

"Well, it's life, I guess. The law of the jungle."

The fish curve and buck and thrust themselves against the current, dying to get upstream and pass themselves on. Taylor stands flanked by Turtle and Steven. For a long time the three of them are very still before the glass, framed by greenish light and a wall of solid effort.

"I know how they feel," Steven says, his voice amused. "It's like getting into someplace that isn't wheelchair accessible."

I know how they feel, Taylor thinks, and it's not like getting into anywhere at all. It's working yourself for all you're worth to get ahead, and still going backward. She holds Turtle against her side so she won't look up and see her mother's tears.

25

PICKING

ALICE HAS A DATE. ANY minute now Cash Stillwater is going to pick her up and take her for a drive over to the huckleberry fields near Leech. She can't understand why, but there it is. Some out-and-out stranger has called her up and said, "Let's go pick berries."

Sugar insists he isn't a stranger—that Alice met Cash the day they were in town. She swears they spotted him opening the door for Pearl Grass coming out of the Sanitary Market, and went over to say hello. It must be so, she argues, because Roscoe's sister-in-law Letty claims Cash is sweet on Alice, and how could that be, if they hadn't met? Alice has to agree, it seems unlikely.

She is standing by the front window when his truck pulls up. His long legs come out first, in jeans and cowboy boots with curled-up toes, and then the rest of him. His face is flat and broad under the eyes, the dark skin creased rather than wrinkled. He wears gold-rimmed glasses that give him a kind, twinkling appearance. She has never laid eyes on this man in her life. But that's not to say she won't go for a ride with him, at least this one time. If someone is sweet on you without ever having met you, she reasons, you owe him that much.

She meets him at the door, gripping her purse for courage.

"You all set to go?" he asks. He seems to be looking her over just as thoroughly as she is eyeing him.

"Ready as I'll ever be," she states, looking down at her slacks and work-shirt. "Are these tennis shoes all right? If we're going to be in mud, I better borrow some boots from Roscoe. Sugar's wouldn't do me a bit of good, she wears a five. She always had the smallest feet of anybody."

"I don't expect we'll run into mud today, no. I think you'll do all right."

Alice follows him around to the passenger side of his truck, where he opens the door and gives her a hand up onto the running board. The truck is a wondrous, buttery copper color, though it seems about as old as anything with a motor could possibly be. The windshield is divided into two flat panes with a dark, puttied seam running down the center. Alice remembers Sugar's counseling, that Cash is a big talker, and she hurries to get some kind of conversation going. "You had this truck long?"

Cash starts it up. "All my life, near about. I keep putting new engines in her, and she keeps a-going. Wish I could do the same for myself." He pats his chest gently with his right hand, then reaches down to shift gears, which makes a sound like slamming the spoon drawer.

"They do that, now. Put new hearts and livers and stuff in people," Alice points out.

"I know. But that don't seem right, trading parts with dead folks just to keep yourself around, pestering the younguns. When you're wore out, I'd say that's a sure sign it's time to go."

"I agree," Alice says. She takes notice of some flower growing in the ditch that looks like a dandelion gone crazy, as big as a child's head.

"Ask me in ten year, though, and I might sing a different tune," Cash says, laughing.

"I know. It's hard to admit to being old, isn't it? I keep thinking, How'd this happen? Sixty-one! When I was young I looked at people this age and thought they must feel different inside. As different from me as a dog might feel, or a horse. I thought they would just naturally feel like they were wrinkled up and bent and way far along."

"It don't feel that way, though, does it?"

"No," Alice says, running a hand through her short hair. "It feels regular."

The trees crowd up against the road, each one a different shade of green. The oaks are the darkest. Their leaves angle downward and seem to absorb more light. Cash's truck rolls across a little bridge, and below them Alice can see a creek banked by a world of ferns, their spears all pointed straight up.

"You're kin to Sugar some way, is it?"

"We're cousins," Alice replies. "We grew up together, but we lost touch after I married."

"Well, it had to be Sugar's side you was related on, and not Roscoe's. If it was Roscoe's I'd of knowed you, because my sister Letty's the widowed wife of Roscoe's brother. Did you and your husband have a big family?"

"No, just my daughter. He didn't even quite stick around long enough to drive her home from the hospital." Alice laughs. "I had to get a nurse to drive us home. She was a great big woman with a Chevrolet as big as a barn. She said, 'I can drive home all the babies you want, Miz Greer.' I never will forget that. She made me wish I'd had twelve more, while I was at it."

"I wished that too. That we'd had more. We had the two girls, but then the doctor told my wife no more. Her blood was the wrong way, somehow. She had negative blood, is what he said. She always run to being peaked."

Alice feels embarrassed and amazed that within ten minutes of meeting one another they've gotten onto Cash Stillwater's dead wife's female problems. He doesn't seem bothered, though, only sad. She can feel sadness rising off him in waves, the way you feel heat from a child with a fever.

"Sugar tells me you've just moved back from someplace."

"Wyoming," he says.

They pass an old cemetery whose stone walls are covered with rose brambles, and then a white clapboard church set back in the woods. On a tree, a washed-out sign has been attached by a nail through its center, and rotated a quarter-turn clockwise. It crookedly advises: FLESTER DREADFULWATER FOR TRIBAL COUNCIL.

"Flester Dreadfulwater!" Alice says, hoping it's not impolite to laugh at someone's name who is no doubt some relative of someone related to Cash.

Apparently it isn't. "He lost the election," Cash says, smiling.

"Why'd you move to Wyoming?"

Cash stretches a little behind the wheel, though he never takes his eyes off the road. "I got restless after my wife died. I had this idea you can get ahead by being in a place where everbody's rich. That being close to good times is like *having* good times."

"My second husband was like that. He thought if he'd watched some loving on TV, he'd done had it." Alice instantly covers her eyes, feeling she has surely gone too far, but Cash only laughs.

"How long were you up there?" she asks, recovering. Riding through the woods with a talkative man is making her giddy.

"About two year," he says. "I despised it. Everbody rich, treating you like you was a backdoor dog. And not even happy with what they had. I did beadwork for a Indian jewelry store, and the owner one day up and took pills and killed himself clean dead. They say he was worth a million."

"Why'd he want to die, then?"

"I think he was depressed about the Indians being all gone." Cash points his thick hand at the windshield. "He should have come down here and had a look."

They pass a ragged little shack with a ragged little birdhouse on a post beside it, and Alice thinks: Then he would have taken the pills and shot himself too. But she knows that isn't entirely fair.

"They used to be a store up here," Cash says suddenly, as if he'd long forgotten this information himself. "A general store. I wonder what happened to that. We lived right down yander in them woods. We'd come up here for lard. You had to take a bucket. And me and mommy used to take fryers, we'd catch them and tie them up and walk to the store. And eggs."

"Oh, I remember carrying eggs," Alice cries. "That was just a criminal thing to do to a child. Make them carry eggs."

"Sounds like you know."

"Oh, yes. I was raised up on a hog farm in Mississippi. It wasn't just hogs, though. We raised a big garden, and we had chickens, and cows to milk. We'd sell sweet milk and cream. People would come in their wagons to get it."

"I miss that," Cash says. "Driving the mule. We had a mule team and a wagon."

"Well, sure," says Alice, feeling they've finally climbed onto safer ground. "Even up into the forties we still used horses or mules and the wagon. You'd see cars down in Jackson, but it wasn't the ordinary thing to have. We thought they were more for fun. For getting someplace, or hauling, you'd need the wagon and a team of mules."

"Wasn't that the time to be a kid?" Cash asks. "Our kids had to work out what to do with liquor and fast cars and fast movies and ever kind of thing. For us, the worst we could do was break a egg."

"Isn't that so," Alice agrees. "You know what seems funny to me, thinking about old times? We'd get excited over the least little thing. A man playing a fiddle and dancing a little wooden jigging doll with his foot. Even teenagers would stop and admire something like that. Now teenagers won't hardly stop and be entertained by a car accident. They've seen too much already."

"That's how I felt up at Jackson Hole. That's why I wanted to come back. Everbody acted like they'd done seen the show, and was just waiting to finish up the popcorn."

"Well, I met all Sugar's grandkids, and they seem interested in catching fish for their grandma. They're a nicer bunch than I'd ever in this world expect a teenager to be."

"Cherokee kids know the family, that's sure," Cash says. "They know the mother's birthday, the wedding anniversary, all that. We always have a big hog fry."

"You must enjoy your daughters."

"Well, we had a bad time of it in my family. My older daughter, Alma, is dead."

"Oh, I'm so sorry," Alice says, realizing she might have guessed this, from his stooped shoulders. She stops trying to talk for a while, since there is nothing to say about a lost child that can change one star in a father's lonely sky.

They pass clusters of little tin-roofed houses and trailer houses set near each other in clearings in the woods. Propane-gas tanks sit in the yards, and sometimes a wringer washer or a cookstove on the porch, or a weight-lifting bench in the driveway. There is really no predicting what you'll see here. One house seems to be hosting a family reunion: old folks sit around in lawn chairs, and six or seven kids are lined up straddling the silver propane tank as if it were a patient old pony.

"There's sassafras," Cash says, pointing at broad, mitten-shaped leaves sprouting among dark cedars in a hedgerow. "They use that in the medicine tea at the stomp dances."

"What's it do for you?"

"Oh, perks you up, mainly." Cash seems to be looking far down the road when he speaks. "My daddy, he knew all the wild roots to make ever kind of medicine. He tried to tell me what it's for, but I've done forgot about all of it. Back when I was a kid, I never did know people having operations for kidney and gallbladder and stuff, like they do now. Did you?"

"No," Alice says. "People didn't have so many operations. Mainly they got over it, or they died, one."

"When I had a bellyache he'd just get a flour sack, put ashes in that and put that on my side, and the pain would go away. People would always be coming to him, my dad. He died on New Year's day, nineteen and forty, and I didn't even know it for sixteen days. I was in boarding school."

"They didn't tell you?"

Cash doesn't answer for a while. Alice spies a black-and-white Appaloosa horse standing in the woods near the road, alone and apparently untethered; it raises its head as they pass by.

"I can't explain boarding school. The teachers were white, they didn't talk Cherokee, and seems like you got used to never knowing what was going on. You forgot about your family. We slept in a big dormitory, and after a few year, it was kindly like you got the feeling that's how kids got made. Just turned out in them lined-up beds like biscuits in a pan."

"That sounds awful. It sounds like a prison for children."

"It was, more or less. Half a day school, the other half-day work: sewing room, dining room, kitchen, laundry. Boys did the laundry. We didn't mix with girls. Except Sunday, when we had Sunday school, but sometime I couldn't go, I had to stay in the kitchen."

Alice tries to picture a herd of subdued little boys doing laundry and stirring pots. She can't. "Did you learn to cook, at least?"

"Not much. You know what got me through, though, after my daddy died? They had a big window on the west side of the dining room, and Miss Hay, she was the boss of the kitchen, she had a orange tree about two foot tall in a pot. She growed that from a seed. I watched it. There was two oranges on that tree when I left. They wasn't yellow yet, just green."

"Did you run away? I think I would have."

"I tried, a few times. But finally my mama said they needed me home, so they let me come on home. I just went up to seventh grade, that was all. I didn't learn too much English, even though they tried."

"Well, you sure speak it now," Alice says, surprised. Cash Stillwater talks more than any grown man she's met. She can't imagine how it would be if he spoke English any better.

"Oh, well, sure, you pick it up. We didn't talk Cherokee anymore at home after my girls started to get big."

"Why not?"

"I don't know. I talked to them when they were babies, and they knew it real good. But after a while it just all went blank. When they get up around four feet high and start mixing with the other kids, you know, in two weeks they can forget it. I feel like I done my girls wrong, some way. Like there was something they was waiting for me to tell them that I never could think of."

Alice feels his sadness again, and wishes she could lay a hand on top of his weathered brown paw on the gearshift. They've come out of the woods now into rolling, tall meadows of uncut timothy. At the head of a dirt road stands a hand-lettered sign: FIREWOOD. XMAS TREES. BLUEBERRYS HUCKLEBERRYS U PICK. As they turn in on the dirt track, a handful of quail run into the road and break into buzzing flight.

Alice feels excited, as if she has set sail for an unknown shore. She couldn't say why. The smallish bobbly heads of golden flowers are blowing in the wind, and the edges of the field are embroidered with tall white blossoms she remembers from childhood: Queen Anne's lace. They are as pretty as their name, but if you ever tried to take too close a look, they would sting your eye to tears.

It is nearly dusk when they get back to Sugar's with two full pails of huckleberries in the back of the truck. Alice ate some while they were picking, even though that's stealing, since you only pay for what you carry out. Cash teased her, warning that her blue tongue would give her away. She feels like a girl.

In Sugar's driveway, a banty rooster threatens to run under the wheels of the truck. Alice gasps a little.

"He'll run out of the way," Cash says. "If he don't, we'll make dumplings."

He turns off the key but the engine keeps chugging for a little while. Just like Cash, who can't seem to stop talking. "A week before Christmas, them roosters start crowing all night," he tells her. He reaches in his pocket and slips something into Alice's hand. It is dry and flat and sharp as a tooth. She examines it.

"An arrowhead? Where'd you get that?"

"Found it. While you was eating up all the berries."

"You take it home, then," she says, although she loves the feel of its ripply bite against her thumb, and doesn't want to give it up.

"No, you have it. I got about a hundred at home."

"You found that many?"

"No. Some I found, but most of them I made."

Alice turns the slim blade over in her hand. "How'd you learn to make arrowheads?"

"Well, it's a long story. I found my first one when I was five. A little white one about like that. It was broken, though, not much count. I got off my horse and picked it up, and then I picked up another piece of that same white flint, and later on I started knocking pieces off of it. I just kindly taught myself how. For a while I worked down there at Tahlequah making arrowheads for a tourist shop."

"I can't get over that. That's something."

"Oh, it isn't. We used to make ever kind of thing, when I was a kid.

We'd make blowguns out of river cane. Heat it over a fire, straighten it out. You blow a little arrow through there, it's good for killing a bird or a squirrel." Cash laughs. "Not that good, though. Now I use a rifle."

Alice wonders what it would be like to have a man go out and kill food for you. She opens the door and steps down from the truck before she can let herself think about it too long. Cash gets out too, and lifts one of the heavy pails out of the truck bed.

"There's a stomp dance coming up, Saturday week," he tells her.

"I know. Sugar's been talking about it."

"You planning on going?"

"I could."

"You want to plan on driving over there with me? I'd be happy to take you."

"All right," she says. "I'll see you."

Alice feels his eyes on her as she retreats to Sugar's front door. When she hears the truck kick up again, she turns and waves. His glasses twinkle as he pulls away with his arm trailing out the window.

Alice doesn't recall the sensation of romantic love; it has been so long she might not know it if it reared up and bit her. All she knows is that this man, Cash Stillwater, chose her. He saw her somewhere and picked her out. That single thought fills Alice with a combination of warmth and hope and indigestion that might very well be love.

26

OLD FLAME

ON THE NIGHT OF THE stomp dance, Cash comes to fetch Alice at a quarter to twelve. It had seemed to Alice a late hour to begin a date, but Sugar has assured her that the dances start late and run all night. "Cinderella wouldn't of had a chance with this crowd," Sugar tells her. "She'd of gone back all raggedy before anybody important even showed up."

Alice snaps on her pearl earrings and hopes for better luck. In Cash's truck, she teases about the hour as they drive through the woods. "I'm not so sure I know you well enough to stay out all night," she says.

"We'll have about two hundred chaperones," he says, a grin widening his broad face. "If I know my sister Letty, they'll all be keeping a pretty good eye on us."

Alice feels strangely excited by the idea that people are talking about herself and Cash.

"Can I ask you a question?" she asks.

"Shoot."

"I hope you don't mind my asking, but I'm sorry, I can't remember the first time we met."

He glances at her, and the dashboard lights glint on the curved lower rims of his glasses. "First time I seen *you* was on Sugar Hornbuckle's front stoop, the day we went berry picking."

"Well, how in the world?" Alice doesn't quite know how to go on.

"Did I think to call you up?" Cash asks.

"Yes."

"Letty told me." He looks at Alice again, bringing the truck to a complete, unnecessary stop at a quiet intersection on a thoroughly deserted road. Alice has her window rolled all the way down and can hear birds in the forest, fussing themselves into whatever activity it is birds perform at night. "She let me know you was interested," Cash says finally.

Alice is stupefied. "Well, I *would* have been, if I'd known you from the man in the moon, but I didn't. Sugar told me, she said Letty said ..." She can't finish.

Cash begins to laugh. He tips his straw cowboy hat far back on his head, smacks the top of the steering wheel with both his palms, and laughs some more. Alice merely stares.

"You have to know my sister Letty." He runs his index finger under his lower eyelids, behind his glasses. "Oh, law," he says. "If she had free run of this world, she'd like to get that Pope fellow fixed up with some nice widow woman."

Alice blushes deeply in the dark.

Cash reaches across and brushes Alice's cheek with the back of his hand before driving on. "And every once in a while," he says, "the old gal chases a pair of folks up the right stump."

A sign at the gate of the Ceremonial Grounds says: VISITORS WELCOME, NO DRINKING, NO ROWDINESS. Alice and Cash have fallen quiet. Several trucks are ahead of them and a station wagon behind, all rolling through the gate into a forest of small oaks. They pass a dozen or more open shelters with cedar-shake roofs and cookstoves inside, where women are gathered in thick, busy clumps. Above the roofs, the chimney pipes puff like smoking boys hiding out in the woods, giving away their location.

The dirt road ends at the edge of a clearing, and in its center Alice can see the round, raised altar made of swept ash, knee-high and eight feet across. The fire is already burning there, glowing inside a teepee of stout logs. At the edges of the fire a large log lies pointing in each of the four directions, giving it a serious, well-oriented look, like a compass. Cash has warned Alice that this fire is special. It's as old as the Cherokee people; someone carries off the embers in a bucket at the end of each ceremony and keeps them alive until the next monthly dance. Someone carried this fire over the Trail of Tears, he says, when they were driven out here from the east. Alice has only the faintest understanding of what that means, except that it's a long time to keep an old flame burning.

The altar is surrounded by a ring of bare earth some twenty yards across, and at its perimeter a circle of middle-aged oak trees stand graceful and straight-trunked, their upper limbs just touching. People are beginning to gather and settle on hewn log benches under the oaks, facing the fire. Cash gets out a pair of folding chairs and they settle down in front of the radiator grill. Alice can hear little overheated sighs and pops from the engine, and the buzz of a bee that has gotten tangled up there with the metal in an unlucky way.

"You reckon that's one of Boma's bees?" she asks Cash.

"Could be. We drove right by her place."

It was true. Alice saw her standing in her yard, wearing a fedora with a giant white ostrich feather cascading backward into a curl behind her left shoulder. It gave Boma a dashing look, like one of the three musketeers out checking the pressure on the propane tank. Alice feels a little guilty about the bee stuck here writhing on the radiator. "Sugar says Boma loves those bees," she says.

"Oh, she does. Bees are only going to stay living in your eaves if you have kind feelings toward them." He takes off his hat and gently swats the bee, putting it out of its noisy misery.

An old man ambles over to chat with Cash. He has a wonderfully round face and like every other man here wears a straw cowboy hat that has darkened and conformed itself to its master around the crown. Cash introduces him as Flat Bush, leaving Alice to wonder whether this is a first or last name, or both. The two men speak in Cherokee for a while. Alice is surprised that she can follow the general gist because of words like "Ace Hardware" and "distributor cap" that regularly spring up shiny and hard-edged from the strange soft music of the conversation.

People have begun to arrive now in a serious way, parking their trucks in a ring facing the fire, reminding Alice of a crew of friendly horses all tied nose in. She sneaks looks at the old women nested nearby in sag-seated lawn chairs. They all have on sprigged cotton dresses, dark stockings, dark shoes, and black or red sweaters. Their long white hair is pent up in the back with beaded clasps, and their arms are folded over their bosoms. Alice hopes she hasn't done anything wrong by wearing pants, or having short hair. But that's silly; no one has been anything but kind to her so far, or for that matter, looked at her twice. She listens in on the old women's conversation and it's the same over there, except that the hard, shiny words are "permapress" and "gallbladder" and "Crisco."

Roving bands of teenagers move through the woods from here to there: long-haired girls in jeans and Keds, and long-haired boys in jeans and complicated athletic shoes. Some of the boys are tough-looking, with black bandanas pushed high on their shiny foreheads and knotted in the back. They hail each other through the woods in English, but when they address the older people, their greetings are Cherokee. Even toddlers, when they run up to slap dark skirts with grubby hands, open their small mouths and let out strange little bitten-off Cherokee songs. Alice is fascinated. She thinks of the holy-roller churches in Mississippi, where people spoke in tongues, though of course in that case it was more or less every man for himself, whereas here they understand one another. She had no idea there was so much actual foreign language thriving right here under the red, white, and blue. The idea thrills her. She has always wished she had the nerve to travel to foreign lands. Whenever she suggested this to Harland, he reminded her that anything at all you could see in person you could see better on TV, because they let the cameras get right up close. She knew he was right, but always felt misunderstood, even so.

Suddenly there is a sense of quiet, although everyone is still talking.

The men are moving toward their trucks. Cash leans over to Alice as he gets up. "Ledger's just got here," he explains.

"Who?"

"Ledger Fourkiller. Our medicine chief. He's over by that standpipe."

Alice spots him: a small man in jeans and a hat and plaid flannel shirt, hardly one to stand out in the crowd. She doesn't know what she expected, surely not war paint, but still. "Where you going?" she asks Cash.

"Nowhere. Just to get my eagle feather."

The other men are doing the same: each producing a large brown feather from a glove compartment to tuck into a hatband. Alice would like to see Boma Mellowbug, but she doesn't. Instead, a woman with a walk like a she-bear is waddling over to Alice with two cups of coffee. She says something like "Siyo" to Cash. Cash introduces his sister Letty to Alice.

"Pleased to meet you," Alice says, though she actually feels just about every other known emotion besides "pleased." But she takes the coffee gratefully. The night has grown clear and chilly against her bare arms.

"You all looked cold. I thought you needed some hot coffee." She gives Cash some sort of look, but Alice has no idea what it means. Another woman, even shorter and broader than Letty, comes up behind them and reaches up high to clap Cash on the shoulder.

"This here's Alice," Letty tells the woman. "She's staying over at Hornbuckles'."

"My daddy's sister married a Hornbuckle," the woman tells Alice. "Did you know that?" she asks Letty.

"Well, now, sure I did. Leona Hornbuckle."

"No, not Leona. She was a Pigeon, before she married. I'm talking about Cordelia."

"Well, sure, Cordelia was your aunt. I knew that."

"She was a Grass. Cordelia Grass."

"Honey, I know it. I've got Grasses related to me through my oldest daughter."

"No, them's Adair Grasses. This is the Tahlequah Grasses."

Alice listens as the argument winds its way through Grasses, Goingsnakes, Fourkillers, and Tailbobs. At that point Cash touches his sister's arm and points to the fire circle. Both women give a little start and begin to move toward the fire. Cash leans down and touches Alice's hand. "I'm going to go smoke this pipe. I'll see you later on."

The benches have filled up entirely and the chief now stands by the fire. He's a man of slight build, maybe sixty, distinguished by the fact that a long, pale leather pouch hangs down from his belt. To Alice it looks like a bull's scrotum.

Sugar appears in the lawn chair next to Alice, out of breath. She leans over and grabs Alice's arm like a grammar-school girlfriend.

"I didn't want to interfere with anything."

Alice has had about enough of the entire Cherokee Nation organizing her love life. "What's that he's got on his belt?" she asks, nodding toward the chief. "Balls?"

"Naw, just tobacco and stuff. Plants. It's his medicine. They'll all smoke it directly. It isn't nothing bad."

"Well, I didn't think *that,*" Alice says. She wouldn't expect drugs; it has already struck her that there is no alcohol here. She can smell woodsmoke and coffee and the delicious animal scent of grease on a cooking fire, but none of that other familiar picnic odor. It's odd, in a way. A hundred pickup trucks on a Saturday night, and not one beer.

The chief raises his head suddenly and sends a high, clean blessing to the tree branches. His voice is so clear it seems to be coming from somewhere above his ears. When he paces to the east of the fire he seems to grow taller, just from taking long strides. He takes some tobacco from his pouch and offers it to the fire, speaking to the fire itself, the way you might coax a beloved old dog to take a rib bone out of your hand. The fire accepts his offering, and the chief paces some more, talking all the while. He fills a slender white pipe that's as long as Alice's arm. The old people move toward the fire, then nearly everyone else shuffles into single file behind them, making a line that circles the whole clearing.

Sugar leans to get up. "I got to go smoke the pipe now," she whispers. "Afterward, you come sit with me on the Bird Clan benches. You can't sit with Cash, he's not Bird, he's Wolf Clan." She winks at Alice. "Just as well. You can't marry inside your clan."

Sugar hurries to join the line, leaving Alice feeling bewildered and slightly annoyed. She surely had no idea she belonged to a clan. Also she's apparently the only person for miles around, besides Cash, who isn't making wedding plans.

The chief hands the pipe to the first old man, who closes his lips on the stem, closes his eyes, and breathes in. Then he rotates the pipe one complete turn, parallel with the ground. It's an odd-looking gesture that takes both hands. He hands the pipe to the woman behind him in line, the one who was debating Grasses with Letty. The old man walks five or six careful steps toward the east and takes a place at the edge of the clearing. When the woman has gone through the same motions, she joins him. One by one each person takes the pipe; even children do.

Alice spots Annawake in line behind a barrel-chested boy and a slew of kids, and there is Cash, looking like a tall, congenial weed among a cluster of chrysanthemum-shaped women. He seems round-shouldered and easy with himself each time he takes another little step forward. It's a slow process. Alice keeps her eye on two little twin girls dressed in identical frilled square-dancing skirts, moving patiently forward in the line. When their turn comes, the mother touches the pipe to her own mouth first, then holds it to her children's lips, helping each one to rotate it afterward. When the last person in line has smoked the pipe and everyone moves to sit down, Sugar motions Alice over to what she says are the Bird Clan benches. "Third ones from the east, counterclockwise," she points out with her finger. "So you can find them again."

"Well, it's a good enough seat, but I don't see what makes me belong here."

Sugar stares. "Alice Faye, you're just as much Bird as I am. Grandmother Stamper was full-blooded. You get your clan from your mother's line."

Alice never met her mother's mother, a woman of questionable reputation who died dramatically and young somehow in a boat. As the story is told, she didn't even own the clothes she drowned in; Alice hadn't especially thought this woman might leave her belonging to a clan. She doesn't argue, though, because the chief has begun to pray, or talk, again. With his arms crossed he paces back and forth on the bare dirt circle, sometimes looking up at the sky but mostly addressing the fire. His words seem very calm, more like conversation, Alice thinks, than preaching. Sugar says he is preaching, though. "He's saying how to be good, more or less. Everyday wrongs, and big wrongs. Don't be jealous, all that business," she confides. "Same stuff he always says."

Alice feels transported, though. His words blend together into an unbroken song, as smooth as water over stones. It *is* a little like those holy-roller churches she loved, where, when someone fell into a swoon, you *felt* their meaning; in the roof of your mouth and your fingertips you felt it, without needing to separate out the particular words.

A blue-tick hound walks across the clearing in front of the chief and lies down with a group of dogs near the fire. They all hold their heads up, watching him. Now and again a latecomer truck pulls up through the woods, joining the circle, and respectfully dims its lights. The focused attention in the clearing feels to Alice like something she could touch, a crystal vase, small at the ground and spreading as it goes up into the branches of the oaks.

All at once the chief raises his voice high, and something like a groan of assent rises up through the crowd and the glass is shattered. There is only quiet. Then babies start up with fretful cackles, and old men stand up to shake the hands of old women they didn't see earlier, and the dogs all rise and walk off toward the kitchens.

"Now we get to dance," Sugar says, excitedly. A dozen teenaged girls come out, checking each other seriously and adjusting side to side as they line up in a close circle around the fire. They're all wearing knee-length gingham skirts and the rattling leggings made of terrapin shells filled with stones. Alice is taken aback by how much bigger these are than the training shackles Sugar showed her; they bulge out like beehives from the girls' legs, below their dresses. They all begin to move with quick little double sliding steps, giving rise to a resounding hiss. Several old men fall into line behind them, nodding and singing a quick, perfect imitation of a whippoorwill. Alice feels chills dance on her backbone. The old men begin a song then, and the young women step, step, step, counterclockwise around the fire. As other people come into the circle, they take up hands behind the singers and shackle-bearers, making a long snake that coils languidly around the fire. All at once, when the chief holds up his hand, everyone's feet stop still in the dust and the dancers whoop. It's the sound of elation.

"Oh, that looks fun," Alice cries to Sugar. "Can't you do it?"

"Oh, I will, directly. You should too. You don't have to wait to be asked, just go on up any time you feel like it."

Another dance begins right away. The song sounds a little different, but the dance is still the same gentle stomping in a circle. Only the girls with the turtle-shell legs do the fancy step, concentrating hard, with no wasted motion in their upper bodies; everyone else just shuffles, old and young, pumping their arms a little, like slowed-down joggers. There are several rings of people around the fire now, and the crowd is growing. Alice is fascinated by the girls who remain in the inner circle by the fire, in the honored place, working so hard. This forest feels a hundred miles away from the magazine models with their twiggy long legs. These girls in their bulbous shackles have achieved a strange grace, Alice thinks—a kind of bowlegged femininity.

The dancing goes on and on. An old man produces a drum, and the music then is made up of a small skin drum and deep, mostly male voices and the hiss of the turtle shells above it all like a thrilling high wind. When Alice asked Cash, earlier, about the dance and the music, he said it would be music that sounds like the woods, and Alice decides this is right. No artificial flavorings. It's the first time she has witnessed an Indian spectacle, she realizes, that had nothing to do with tourism. This is simply people having a good time in each other's company, because they want to.

"What are the songs about?" she asks Sugar. To Alice they sound like "oh-oh-wey-yah," and sometimes the chief sings out in a sort of yodel. His voice breaks and rises very beautifully, and the crowd answers the same words back.

"I couldn't really tell you," Sugar answers, at last. "It's harder to understand than regular talking. Maybe it don't mean anything."

"Well, it would have to mean *something*, wouldn't it?"

Sugar seems untroubled by the idea that it might not. "Let's go," she says suddenly, grabbing Alice by the hand. "Just go in after the shackles," she instructs. "Don't get in front of the girls." Alice wouldn't dare.

She follows Sugar in, trembling with nerves, and then there she is, stomp dancing like anybody. At first she is aware of nothing beyond her own body, her self, and she watches other people, imitating the way they hold their arms. But she's also aware that she's doing a strange and unbelievable thing. It makes her feel entirely alive, in the roof of her mouth and her fingertips. She understands all at once, with a small shock, exactly what it is she always needed to tell Harland: being there in person is not the same as watching. You might *see* things better on television, but you'll never know if you were alive or dead while you watched.

Once in a while, Alice remembers Cash and feels a thrill in her stomach. She looks around for him, but can only see the people in front of her and those beside her in the snake's other coils. The song turns out to be a short one, and Alice is disappointed to see that when it ends everyone leaves the clearing and settles back down on the benches of their respective clans. Even after such a short time, her calves feel pinched. It's like an all-night workout on the Stairmaster she has seen advertised on Harland's shopping channel. A Stairmaster with a spiritual element.

While the dancers take a break, a young man stretches a hose from a spigot in one of the kitchen shelters, looping it through the trees, and attaches onto its end the kind of spray nozzle people use for gardening. He carefully hoses down the dirt floor of the dance area, beginning with the eastern part where the chief stood and paced, and working his way slowly around the clearing. He never sprays any water into the fire.

The fire seems to Alice like a quiet consciousness presiding. It's not like an old dog, after all, because it commands more prolonged attention. It's more like an old grandmother who never gets out of her chair.

Sugar is busy gnawing on a chicken wing and introducing Alice to everyone in sight. Alice is too tired to remember names, but she notices Sugar is very proud about pointing out Alice's connection to the Bird Clan.

"I know we had the same grandmother," Alice tells her finally, when all the Tailbobs and Earbobs have drifted away. "But you're forgetting I'm not Indian."

"You're as Indian as I am. Daddy was white, and Mama too except for what come down through the Stamper side."

"Bloodwise, I guess," Alice says, "but you married Roscoe and you've lived here near about your whole life. Don't you have to sign up somewhere to be Cherokee?"

"To vote you do." Sugar holds the chicken wing at arm's length, turning it this way and that as if it were some piece of sculpture she were working on. "You have to enroll. Which is easy. You've just got to show you come from people that's on the Census Rolls, from back in the 1800s. Which you do."

"Well, even if that's true, it don't seem right. I don't feel like an Indian."

Sugar places the chicken bones in a bag inside her purse, and touches a napkin to her mouth. "Well, that's up to you. But it's not like some country club or something. It's just family. It's kindly like joining the church. If you get around to deciding you're Cherokee, Alice, then that's what you are."

Alice can't believe it's 2:00 A.M. and people are still driving in. The crowd has grown to several hundred. The turtle-shell girls are assembling around the fire again, and when the dance starts, Sugar and Alice are among the first up. Alice feels endurance creeping up on her gradually. This time the singing lasts longer, and she forgets about her arms and legs. It's surprisingly easy to do. The music and movement are comforting and repetitious and hypnotic, and her body slips into its place in the endless motion. For the first time she can remember, Alice feels completely included.

The instant a dance stops, she becomes aware of her body again, her muscles and her sleepiness. She understands how, if she kept dancing, she could keep dancing. A keen, relaxed energy comes from forgetting your body. She sees how this will go on all night.

Midway through the next song, she realizes Cash has moved into the line behind her. She smiles as she moves her body through the siss-siss of the turtles. He is back there for a while, and then by the time another song begins, someone else is. She sees Annawake out to the side of her, once. She thinks she sees Boma Mellowbug too, without her feather. For a while she tries to keep tabs on where Cash is, but then she forgets to think about it, because she can't quite locate *herself* in this group either. She only knows she is inside of it.

At the end of each song the voices stop and then there is only the watershell hiss, vibrating inside a crystal jar of quiet. It's a sound that loses its individual parts, the way clapping becomes a roar in the hands of a crowd. It is as many pebbles as there are on a beach. Alice's life and aloneness and the things that have brought her here all drop away, as she feels herself overtaken by uncountable things. She feels a deep, tired love for the red embers curled in the center of this world. The beloved old fire that has lived through everything since the beginning, that someone carried over the Trail of Tears, and someone carried here tonight, and someone will carry home and bring back again to the church of ever was and ever shall be, if we only take care of it.

At home, with morning light seeping under the yellow-white shades in Sugar's spare room, Alice lies in bed hugging her own beating heart, afraid of falling asleep. She takes stock of where she is, without believing any of it. Her black suitcase yawns against the closet door, exposing a tangle of innards, and Sugar's ironing board stands near the bed under a pile of wrinkled laundry, burdened like a forward-leaning pack mule.

If she sleeps, the magic could be gone when she wakes up again in this room. She might be merely here, in a cousin's ironing room, with no memory of what has happened tonight. It seems like a fairy tale, and the stories say spells get broken and magic doesn't endure. That people don't really love one another and dance in the woods for no other reason than to promise goodness, and lose track of themselves, and keep an old fire burning.

27

FAMILY STORIES

A YOUNG WOMAN WEARING A lot of beads and a complicated hairdo leads Alice and Sugar through the basement hallway of the Cherokee Heritage Center. She unlocks the door to a small room with a huge oak table in the center.

"You need help finding anybody?" she asks. Alice has noticed that the girl is trying not to chew the gum in her mouth while they are looking. Is that what old women look like to the young? Their fifth grade teacher?

"No thanks, hon, I've done all this before," Sugar replies.

Their guide leaves them, chewing her gum earnestly to make up for lost time as she heads back upstairs to the gift shop. The big table is covered with old brown ring binders, sprawled out hodgepodge across one another like farmhands taking a break. One wall of the room is covered with an old-looking map of the Cherokee Nation districts, and some sort of film-viewing machine crouches against the other wall. Lined up across the back of the room are antique wooden cabinets of the type that might sit in a country doctor's office. Alice feels exactly that kind of nervousness—as if she's about to get a shot, for her own good.

Sugar sits down in one of the plastic chairs. "This here is the index for the Dawes Rolls," she says, picking up a ring binder thick enough for a toddler to sit on at the dinner table. "1902 to 1905," she reads. She straightens her glasses, licks her thumb, and begins to page through it.

"Are you sure we ought to be doing this?"

Sugar looks up at Alice over her glasses. "I swear, Alice, I don't know what's become of you. You used to make me sneak out to the beer joints on a double dog dare, and now you're scared of your shadow doing just a ordinary everyday thing."

"I don't want to break any rules."

"For heaven's sake, sit down here and look. This isn't nothing in the world but a long list of names. People that was living here and got allotments between certain years."

Alice sits down and scoots her chair toward Sugar, who is holding her chin high so she can see the small print through the bottom window of her bifocals. She looks like a proud little bird with a forties hairdo.

"I'm just going to show you your grandma's name. She's not going to reach out of the grave and tickle your feet."

"She might, if she knew I was trying to cheat the Cherokees."

"Alice Faye, you're not cheating."

Alice gets up and moves restlessly around the room, leaving Sugar to her search through the roll book. "What's this?" she asks, holding up a yellowed, antique-looking newspaper covered with strange curlicues.

Sugar looks up over her glasses. "The *Cherokee Advocate*. That's old, they don't run it anymore. That's what the writing looks like for the Cherokee. It's pretty, isn't it? I never did learn to read it. Roscoe does."

Alice studies the headlines, trying to connect their cursive roundness with the soft guttural voices she heard at the stomp dance. "They had their own paper?"

"Land, yes," Sugar says, without looking up again from her book. "It was the first newspaper in Oklahoma. The Cherokees got things all organized out here while everybody else was cowboys eating with their jackknifes, Roscoe tells me. Them big old brick buildings we passed by in Tahlequah this morning? That was the Cherokee capitol. Oh, look, here she is, right here." She motions Alice over, holding down Grandmother

Stamper under her fingertip. "Write down this enrollment number: 25844."

Alice digs in her purse for a pencil, licks the end of it, and dutifully records this number in her address book under the "Z's," since it seems unlikely she'll ever get close to anyone whose last name starts with a Z. For that matter, the whole address book is pretty much blank, except for three pages of crossed-out numbers for Taylor.

"Now all you've got to do is prove you're descended from her. Having the birth certificate is the best, but she didn't have one. What we did, when Roscoe helped me do this, was we writ to the records office down in Mississippi and we got the record of where she was drownded at. And then we just took that on down to the tribal recorder's office and explained how she was my grandma, and that was that. I think I showed them some family pictures and stuff. They're pretty understanding."

Alice stares at the book of names. She can't put a finger on who, exactly, she feels she's cheating. All the people on the list, to begin with, and the fact they are dead doesn't help. She wishes Sugar hadn't mentioned the business of coming out of graves and tickling feet. "It doesn't feel right to me," she says. "I always knew we were some little part Indian, but I never really thought it was blood enough to sign up."

"It don't have to be more than a drop. We're all so watered down here, anyway. Did you see them blond kids at the stomp dance, the Threadgills? They're signed up. Roy Booth over here at the gas station, he's enrolled, and he's not more than about one two-hundredth. And his kids are. But his wife, she's a quarter, but she's real Methodist, so she don't want to sign up. It's no big thing. Being Cherokee is more or less a mind-set."

"Well, maybe I have the wrong mind-set. What if I'm just doing it to get something I want?"

"Honey, the most you're ever going to get out of the Nation is a new roof, money-wise, and you might have to wait so long you'll go ahead and fix it yourself. There's the hospitals and stuff, but nobody's going to grudge you that. They'll collect from your insurance if you have it, no matter who you are."

Alice feels her secret swelling against her diaphragm from underneath, the way pregnancy felt toward the end. She is even starting to get the same acid indigestion. "Sugar, you're a good friend to me," she says. "I appreciate that you never have asked why I came here."

"Oh, I figured a bad marriage, whatever. Then when you asked after Fourkillers I thought you must be looking for Ledger, for some kind of cure." Sugar holds Alice steady in her gaze, and puts a hand on her forearm. "Everybody's got their troubles, and their reasons for getting a clean start. People's always curious for the details, but seem like that's just because we're hoping somebody else's life is a worst mess than ours."

Alice feels a pure ache to break down right there on the roll books and tell all. But she's so afraid. Sugar might withdraw that hand on her forearm and all the childhood hugs that stand behind it. A month ago, Alice wouldn't have thought any person alive would argue that Turtle belonged to anyone but Taylor. Now she sees there are plenty who would.

"My reasons for coming are different from anybody's you ever heard of," she tells Sugar. "I want to tell you, but I can't right yet. But what I'm thinking is that it could help my cause to sign up here and be Cherokee."

Sugar cocks her head, looking at Alice. "Well, then, you ought to do it. I don't reckon you have to say you're sorry for coming along and picking a apple off a tree."

Alice knows she has to pick the apple. But in her heart, or deeper, in her pinched stomach, she knows it will hurt the tree.

The afternoon is humid and buggy. Alice waves her hand around as she walks, to chase off the gnats that seem to spring right out of the air itself. She wishes she'd worn her shorts. Though when she pictures an old lady in baggy shorts walking down a dirt road to the river, waving her hands wildly, she comes up with something close to Boma Mellowbug. It's just as well she wore her double knits. She wants to make a good impression.

Alice asked Annawake if they could meet someplace besides the café in town; she's not crazy about having every Tailbob in sight overhear what she wants to discuss. Annawake suggested her Uncle Ledger's houseboat. Now Alice is fairly confident she's lost. Just when she arrives at the brink of serious worry, she sees the flat glare of the lake through the trees, and then the corrugated tin roof of what looks like a floating trailer home with a wooden veranda running all the way around. Thick ropes bind it to the shore, and thinner lines run from boat to treetops like the beginnings of spider webs, from which all kinds of things are hung: men's jeans with their legs spread as though they mean to stand their ground up there; and buckets, too, and long-handled spoons. She spies Annawake sitting on the edge of the porch with her legs sunk into the water.

"Yoo hoo," Alice calls, not wanting to startle Annawake, who looks at that moment like a child lost in the land of pretend. Annawake looks up and waves broadly, and Alice is struck by how pretty she is, in shorts and a velvety red T-shirt. Last time, in the café, Annawake showed sharp edges, a cross between a scared rabbit and the hound that hunts him, and her hair seemed deliberately shaggy. Between then and now she has had it trimmed into a glossy earlobe-length bob, and her maple-colored skin is beautiful.

Alice walks across the wobbly-planked bridge from bank to boat, hanging on to the coarse rope handrail to keep herself from falling in the water. The side of the boat is lined all around with old tires, like bumpers.

"You call this a lake?" Alice asks. "I could just about throw a rock to the other bank."

"Well, I guess at this point you could call it a glorified river," Annawake admits. "Did you have trouble finding us?"

"No." She looks around to locate the "us," but sees only Annawake and a lot of dragonflies. Annawake had said Ledger had to go bless a new truck in Locust Grove.

"Do you mind sitting out here? The mosquitoes will be here pretty soon, but the water feels great."

"Don't mind if I do." Alice sits beside Annawake and catches her breath, then takes off her tennis shoes and rolls her pants legs to her knees. When she plunges her feet into the cold, it feels like a new lease on life.

"That haircut looks real good," she tells Annawake, feeling motherly in spite of herself.

Annawake runs a hand through it. "Thanks," she says. "I kind of went crazy and cut it all off when I went to law school. I think I was in mourning, or something. Seems like it's growing back now."

"That was a good idea to meet out here. It's nice."

"Well, it's private. We used to come out here when we were kids, for the summer, and we felt like we'd gone to California. We thought it was a hundred miles to Uncle Ledger's. If anyone would have told me you could walk out here from town in half an hour I wouldn't have believed it. Because nobody ever does."

"Didn't even take that long. Twenty minutes."

"You're a fast walker."

"I always was. If you're going someplace, I figure you'd just as well go on and get there."

She and Annawake look each other in the eye for a second, then retreat.

"So, you've got something to tell me."

"To ask, really," Alice says.

"All right."

Alice takes a breath. "Would it make any difference about who gets to keep Turtle if I was, if her mother and I were enrolled?"

Annawake looks at Alice with her mouth slightly open. After a while she closes it, then asks, "You have Cherokee blood?"

"We do. I found my grandma yesterday in that roll book."

"The Dawes Rolls," Annawake says. She blinks, looking at the water. "This is a surprise. I thought I knew what you were coming here to tell me today, and this is not it."

"Well, would it make any difference? Would that make us Indian?"

"Let me think a minute." She runs her hand through the hair at her temple, pulling it back from her face. Finally she looks at Alice with a more lawyerly look. "First of all, yes, if you enrolled then you would be Cherokee. We're not into racial purity, as you've probably noticed. It's a funny thing about us eastern tribes, we've been mixed blood from way back, even a lot of our holy people and our historical leaders. Like John Ross. He was half-blood. It's no stigma at all."

"That just seems funny to me, that you can join up late. Wouldn't it seem like showing up at the party after they've done raised the barn?"

"I guess it could be seen as opportunistic, in your case." Annawake gives Alice the strangest grin, with the corners of her mouth turned down. "But generally there's no reason why enrollment should be restricted to full-bloods, or half-, or wherever you'd want to make a cutoff. Anybody who lives our way of life should have the chance to belong to the tribe. I *sure* don't think outsiders should tell us who can be enrolled."

"Don't it kind of dilute things, to let everybody in?"

Annawake laughs. "Believe me, people are not lined up on the Muskogee highway waiting to join the tribe."

"So I'd be as Cherokee as any soul here, if I signed up."

"Legally you would be. And I'll be honest with you, it couldn't hurt your case."

"Well, then, I'm going to enroll."

"But that's kind of missing the point, where your granddaughter is concerned. You'd be Cherokee legally, but not culturally."

"Is that the big deal?"

Annawake presses her fingertips together and stares at them. "When we place Cherokee kids with non-Indian foster parents, we have a list we give them, things they can do to help teach the child about her culture. Take her to the Cherokee Heritage Center, get Cherokee language tapes, take her to Cherokee National Holiday events, things like that. But that's just making the best of a bad situation. It's like saying, 'If you're going to adopt this baby elephant, you must promise to take it to the zoo once in a while.' Really, a baby elephant should be raised by elephants."

"She isn't an elephant. She's a little girl."

"But if she's raised in a totally white culture, there's going to come a time when she'll feel like one. And she'll get about as many dates as one. She'll come home from high school and throw herself on the bed and say, 'Why do I have this long, long nose?' "

Alice wants to argue that there are worse things, but she can't immediately think of any. She still doesn't want to buy it, though. "If I'm Cherokee, and Taylor is, a little bit, and we never knew it but lived to tell the tale, then why can't she?"

Annawake lays her dark wrist over Alice's. "Skin color. Isn't life simple? You have the option of whiteness, but Turtle doesn't. I only had to look at her for about ten seconds on TV to know she was Cherokee."

Alice crosses her arms over her chest.

"Alice, there's something else. I was going to call you in a couple of days. It turns out we have compelling reason to file a motion to vacate this adoption." She watches Alice carefully as she says this. "Someone has come to me asking that I help locate a missing relative who could be Turtle." She continues to look Alice in the eye.

"Oh," Alice says, feeling her heart pound.

"You didn't know about this?"

Alice's mouth feels dry. "No. Nobody would think to tell me about it. Sugar wouldn't, nor anybody, because there isn't a soul except you that knows what I'm here for."

"I see." Annawake looks back at her hands. "Well, we don't know for sure. All we have to go on really is the child's age, and the circumstances of her being removed from the family. The child they're looking for might be someone else entirely. But to tell you the truth, I think it's likely to be Turtle. I have grounds enough to subpoena Taylor and require her to bring the child here for identification."

Alice stares at the flat river where upside-down trees are dancing and cattails reach down toward the blue sky below them. There is a whole, earnest upside-down world around her feet.

"I thought you already told her she had to come here with Turtle."

"No. I suggested it, but I haven't filed the motion yet. What I'd like most is for Taylor to go ahead and do the right thing on her own. For the good of the child, I'd like to handle this with a minimum of antagonism."

"Well, Taylor's already done antagonized. She's living on the lam. That's the truth. I have to wait for her to call me. I don't even know what state she's in."

Annawake shakes her head slowly. "I keep thinking there has to be a way to explain this so it doesn't sound to you like we just want to tear a baby from a mother's arms."

"Well, what else is it?"

Annawake looks thoughtful. "Do you remember that surrogate baby case a few years back? Where the woman that gave birth to the baby wanted to keep it? But the judge awarded custody to the biological father and his wife."

"That made me mad! I never did understand it."

"I'll tell you what decided it. I read that case. The biological father stood up and told the jury his family history. He'd lost everybody, every single relative, in concentration camps during World War II. That baby was the last of his family's genes, and he was desperate to keep her so he could tell her about the people she came from." Annawake looks sideways at Alice. "That's us. Our tribe. We've been through a holocaust as devastating as what happened to the Jews, and we need to keep what's left of our family together."

Alice watches the water, where dozens of minnows have congregated around her calves. They wriggle their tiny bodies violently through the water, chasing each other away, fighting over the privilege of nibbling at the hairs on her legs. It feels oddly pleasant to be kissed by little jealous fish.

"You think I'm overstating the case?" Annawake asks.

"I don't know."

"Have you ever read about the Trail of Tears?"

"I heard of it. I don't know the story, though."

"It happened in 1838. We were forced out of our homelands in the southern Appalachians. North Carolina, Tennessee, around there. All our stories are set in those mountains, because we'd lived there since the beginning, until European immigrants decided our prior claim to the land was interfering with their farming. So the army knocked on our doors one morning, stole the crockery and the food supplies and then burned down the houses and took everybody into detention camps. Families were split up, nobody knew what was going on. The idea was to march everybody west to a worthless piece of land nobody else would ever want."

"They walked?" Alice asks. "I'd have thought at least they would take them on the train."

Annawake laughs through her nose. "No, they walked. Old people, babies, everybody. It was just a wall of people walking and dying. The camps had filthy blankets and slit trenches for bathrooms, covered with flies. The diet was nothing that forest people had ever eaten before, maggoty meal and salted pork, so everybody had diarrhea, and malaria from the mosquitoes along the river, because it was summer. The tribal elders begged the government to wait a few months until fall, so more people might survive the trip, but they wouldn't wait. There was smallpox, and just exhaustion. The old people and the nursing babies died first. Mothers would go on carrying dead children for days, out of delirium and loneliness, and because of the wolves following behind."

Alice uncrosses and crosses her arms over her chest, understanding more than she wants to. She knows she is hearing the story Annawake has carried around her whole life long. A speedboat whines past, far away on the other side of the river. Long after the boat and its noise are gone, they are rocked by the gash it cut in the water.

"They figure about two thousand died in the detention camps," Annawake says quietly. "And a lot more than that on the trail. Nobody knows."

A bright yellow wasp hovers over the water near their feet and then touches down, delicately as a helicopter. It floats with its clear wings akimbo, like stiff little sails.

Annawake gives an odd, bitter laugh. "When I was a kid, I read every account ever written about the Trail of Tears. It was my permanent project. In high school Civics I read the class what President Van Buren said to Congress about the removal, and asked our teacher why he didn't have us memorize that, instead of the Gettysburg Address. He said I was jaded and sarcastic."

"Were you?"

"You bet."

"Well. What did President Van Buren say?"

"He said: 'It affords me sincere pleasure to be able to apprise you of the removal of the Cherokee Nation of Indians to their new homes west of the Mississippi. The measures have had the happiest effect, and they have emigrated without any apparent resistance.' "

Alice feels she could just slide down into the water without stopping herself. It's monstrous, what one person will do to another.

Annawake and Alice sit without speaking, merely looking at the stretched-out body of Tenkiller Lake, drawing their own conclusions.

"Somebody must have made it," Alice says at last. "You're here. I saw the newspapers and all, that they had."

"Well, on the good side, we had the run of the place for a while with no interference. By the late 1800s we had our act together again. If you're really inclined to be Cherokee you should go down to the museum and have a look. We had the first free public school system in the world. For girls and boys both. In secondary school they taught physiology, music, history, algebra, Virgil."

"Shoot, that's more than they ever taught me."

"In 1886 we got the first telephone line west of the Mississippi into Tahlequah. They didn't want to have to look at ugly lines, so they ran it through the woods and strung it from trees."

Alice laughs. "Sounds like some high-class people."

"It's no joke. We had the highest literacy rate in the whole country."

"It's pretty, that writing." Alice can nearly taste the mysterious curled letters that kept their silence on the crumbling newspaper she saw. "Is it hard to read it?"

"They say it isn't, but I never learned. Don't tell anybody. It pisses me off that Uncle Ledger never taught me."

"You're bringing down the literacy rate."

"Yeah, I told him that. Although it's kind of down around our ankles now."

"What happened? If you don't mind my asking. I mean no offense, but Sugar showed me all the fancy old capitol buildings and stuff, and I was thinking it looked like a hurricane hit this place since then."

Annawake snorts. "Hurricane *Yonega.*"

"You can't blame every bad thing on white people," Alice says softly.

"Nineteen-ought-two, the railroad came in," Annawake replies, just as quietly. "Gee Dick and his band played for a stomp dance on the courthouse lawn, to celebrate the arrival of the first train. The first white folks stepped off the train and started poking around and probably couldn't believe they'd given us such a beautiful piece of real estate. No ugly telephone lines. Within four years, our tribal government was dissolved by federal order. The U.S. government started the Indian boarding schools, dividing up families, selling off land. You tell me, who do we blame?"

"I don't know. The times. Ignorance. The notion people always seem to get, that they know what's best for somebody else. At least that part's over, they're not moving you out anymore."

"No, now they just try to take our kids."

Alice feels stabbed. "Turtle was practically left for dead," she says. "My daughter saved her from starving in a parking lot, or worse. I'd think you might be grateful."

"I'm grateful that she's alive. But I'm not happy about the circumstances."

"Maybe you and me are just going to have to be enemies," Alice says.

"I don't think so. But I want you to understand how deep these feelings run. For this whole century, right up until 1978 when we got the Indian Child Welfare Act, social workers would come in here with no understanding of how our families worked. They would see a child who'd been left with someone outside the nuclear family, and they would call that neglect. To us, that is an insane rationale. We don't distinguish between father, uncle, mother, grandmother. We don't think of ourselves as having extended families. We look at you guys and think you have *contracted* families."

"That's true," Alice says, thinking of her empty address book. She can't deny it. It struck her back in Kentucky, when she wanted to leave Harland but couldn't think where else home might be.

"We couldn't understand why they were taking us apart. My brother Gabe, going to a man and woman in Texas when we had a whole family here. I've seen babies carried off with no more thought than you'd give a bag of brown sugar you picked up at the market. Just a nice little prize for some family. The Mormon families *love* our kids, because they think we're the lost tribe of Israel. Little pagan babies to raise up and escort you into heaven!"

Annawake's eyes are streaming tears. She looks up at the darkening sky. "These were our kids," she tells Alice, and the sky. "Thousands of them. We've lost more than a quarter of our living children."

There is a whole fleet of yellow wasps floating on the water now. A breeze too slight for Alice to feel causes them all to slide across the surface along the same diagonal. One by one, they lift off into the air.

Annawake wipes her face with the back of her wrist, and looks at Alice. "I concede your point that Turtle was abandoned. She wasn't stolen, she was lost and found. It's not the first time an Indian parent has given a child away, I have to admit that to you. There's a real important case, Choctaw *vs.* Holyfield, where that happened. But the way our law looks at it is, the mother or father doesn't have that right. It's like if I tried to give you, I don't know, a piece of the Tahlequah courthouse."

Alice hands Annawake a handkerchief. Young people never carry them, she's noticed. They haven't yet learned that heartbreak can catch up to you on any given day.

Annawake folds and unfolds the cotton square on her lap. "We see so many negative images of ourselves, Alice. Especially off-reservation. Sometimes these girls make a break for the city, thinking they'll learn to be blonde, I guess, but they develop such contempt for themselves they abandon their babies at hospitals or welfare departments. Or a parking lot. Rather than trust to family."

"It's a sad story," Alice says. "But if you make Turtle leave the only mama she knows now, you're going to wreck a couple of lives."

"I know that." Annawake looks down, tucking behind her ear a lock of hair that immediately falls out again. "I could also tell you that some wrecked lives would be made whole again. There's no easy answer. I'm trying everything I can think of to avoid legal intervention. I'd kind of cooked up an alternate plan, but it doesn't seem like it's working out." She gives Alice the same careful study again, looking for something.

"What does the law say?"

"That's easy. The ICWA says a child should be placed with relatives if they're available, or with other members of the child's tribe, or, third choice, with a member of another Native American tribe. The law is clear."

"How's your conscience?" Alice asks.

Annawake lifts her feet out of the water and splashes a little, causing the minnows to flee. "The thing is, I'm really not jaded and cynical. My boss thinks I'm a starry-eyed idealist. That's the whole reason I pursued this case, instead of minding my own business. At the time I met your daughter, I had never experienced a crisis of faith."

Alice looks up at the sky, so much brighter and more silent than the one reflected below. "I wish I could say I always knew what was right," she tells this mysterious child.

Annawake brushes Alice's hand so lightly she could have imagined it.

28

SURRENDER DOROTHY

THUNDER POUNDS IN THE DISTANCE and rain coats the Dodge's windshield, drifting across it in sheets like the hard spatter against a shower curtain. Taylor bangs on the steering wheel. "This isn't a city, it's a carwash!"

Turtle looks away, out the window on her side. They are parked in front of the Kwik Mart, held hostage by the rain, hoping it might lighten up enough to let Taylor make a call from the pay phone.

Taylor grips the steering wheel hard, until the weakness in her forearms runs in slow warm-water currents up into her shoulders and neck. She blows out air. "I'm sorry, sweetheart. I'm not mad at you, I'm mad at the rain."

Turtle mumbles something, rolling Mary idly in her lap.

"What?"

Still looking away, she pronounces: "You're always mad at something."

"Oh, Turtle." Taylor has to bite her tongue to keep from snapping, "I am not!" If she weren't so miserable, she would laugh at her terrible mothering skills. She stares out the window on her side, toward the washed-out vacant lot next door, empty tonight. Apparently the criminal element has the sense to stay home in this weather. They probably have nice homes, Taylor thinks, and VCRs. As drug dealers, they would have a decent income. Probably they're home watching *America's Most Wanted,* with their heat cranked up to seventy-five degrees.

"How was school today?"

"Okay, I guess."

"That's all?"

"Yeah."

Taylor turns in the seat to face Turtle, tucking her feet under her. She taps Turtle on the shoulder politely. "Listen, you, I want to talk about it."

Turtle slowly brings around her face, with its question-mark eyebrows.

"What was the best thing that happened?"

Turtle thinks about it. "There wasn't any best thing."

"Okay, what was the worst thing?"

"Lisa Crocker made fun of my pants."

"Your bicycle pants? What's wrong with those? All the kids wear those, I've seen them."

"She says I wear them every day."

"Well, that's not true. On the other days you wear your jeans."

Turtle pushes her palms against her thighs. "The other kids have more than two pairs."

"I know, Turtle. I used to get made fun of in school too. Mama cleaned people's houses, and they'd give her their kids' outgrown stuff for me to wear. They thought they were doing us a favor, but I ended up going to school looking like a clown."

Turtle slides her eyes sideways and suppresses a grin. "With a big red nose?"

"I should have worn a big red nose. I copped an attitude instead."

"What's that?"

Taylor notices that the rain is changing from a major to a minor key, maybe letting up a little.

"Copping an attitude? Oh, it just means I acted real tough. Like I *wanted* to look like that, and everybody else was ridiculous for wearing their little matching sweaters and skirts."

Turtle thinks this over. "I don't think I can cop an attitude," she says.

"You shouldn't have to! Kids your age should not even like the *idea* of clothing. You should still be trying to throw everything off and roll in the mud."

Turtle looks attentively skeptical.

"I'm telling you, this Lisa Crocker character is a social deviant."

"She's just like the other girls, Mom."

"Good grief, they're all going to grow up to be like Barbie! Can you imagine what that means for the future of our planet?"

"I want them to be my friends."

Taylor sighs and strokes Turtle's hair. "I think it's harder to be an underprivileged kid than it used to be."

"One time I wore the school's pants," Turtle says. "Those gray sweater pants with letters on them. When I had that accident."

"Well, that's true. That wasn't much fun, though, was it?"

"No."

"I'm glad your stomach's feeling better these days."

Turtle is quiet.

"Aren't you feeling better?"

"No," Turtle says faintly.

"No?" Taylor feels a wave of panic.

"It hurts mostly."

"Oh, Turtle. This doesn't make any sense. You've never been sick before."

"I'm sorry, Mom. I just get the stomach cramps. I can't help it."

"Oh, Turtle."

"Mom, it stopped raining. Look."

It's true, the noisy assault is over, but the windshield is still blurred with a serious drizzle. "You poor kid, you've forgotten what good weather is.

You think a sunny day is when you only need a raincoat instead of an umbrella."

"No, I don't. I remember sun."

"Remember Tucson?"

"Yeah."

"What do you remember best?"

Turtle closes her eyes for a long time. "There isn't any best," she says, finally. "I liked it all."

"But we didn't have much money then, either. I think you only had one or two pairs of pants even in Tucson."

"We had Jax, though. And Lou Ann and Dwayne Ray, and Mattie, down at your store."

"That's true. We had them."

"Will they let us come back?"

"We don't have enough money for gas. And we can't tell anybody where we are."

"But if we did have gas, I mean. Does Jax and everybody still want us to live there?"

"I think he does."

"He's not mad because we went away from home?"

Taylor rolls down the window and closes her eyes and lets the hissing night lick her face like a cat. "That's what home means, Turtle," she says. "Even if they get mad, they always have to take you back."

Alice answers the phone at last.

"Mama, I've been trying to call you all different times today. Where were you?"

"Law, Taylor, I couldn't even tell you. Someplace called Lip Flint Crick, or Flint Chip Lick, something. On a picnic."

"A *picnic?* I thought you were supposed to be arguing with the Fourkiller woman."

"I did. But then we went on a picnic."

"You argued, and then you went on a picnic?"

"No, not with her. I've got me a boyfriend."

"Mama, I swear, I can't turn my back on you for one minute!" Taylor hears a bitterness in her voice like green potato skins, but she can't stop up the place it's growing from.

Alice is quiet.

"I'm happy for you, Mama. Really. What's his name?"

A flat answer: "Cash."

"Oh, that sounds good. Is he rich?"

Alice laughs, finally. "Believe me, Taylor, this is not the place to come if you're looking to find you a millionaire typhoon."

"Tycoon, Mama. A typhoon is a hurricane, I think. Or maybe it's that kind of snake that strangles you."

"Well, they got more snakes here than you can shake your tail at, but no millionaire typhoons. The man-about-town is a fellow wears a horse-hide suit. He's a sight. It looks like he got up too early and put on the bath rug." She pauses. "How are you all doing? I been hoping you'd call."

"Not hoping bad enough to sit around by the phone, I notice."

Alice's voice changes. "Taylor, you got a bee in your bonnet. I don't know what you're mad at me for."

"I'm not mad at you. Turtle said that just a minute ago. She said I'm mad all the time. But I'm not. I've just fallen on some bad luck and landed jelly side down." Taylor digs in all of her jeans pockets for a handkerchief, but doesn't find one. She rips a yellow page from the damp directory underneath the pay phone. "I think I'm getting a cold."

"You still got that job?"

"Yeah, but they won't let Turtle hang around in Ladies' Wear anymore. She has to go out in the parking lot and sit in the Dodge for a couple hours, till I get off."

"In the car? Goodness, aren't you afraid she'll get lonesome and drive herself to Mexico or something? Remember when we read that in the paper when we was driving across Nevada? That six-year-old that drove the family car to Mexico?"

"That wasn't a newspaper, Mama, that was one of those supermarket things with Liz Taylor on the front. They make all those stories up."

"Well, stranger things have happened."

"I know. But I don't think Turtle's thinking in terms of Mexico."

"Well, good. But you might ought to leave her some stuff in there to play with, just in case."

"I do. I gave her some packing boxes and stuff from the store. She doesn't complain, you know how she is. But I feel like a murderer. Everything I've been doing, for this whole crazy summer, was just so I could keep Turtle. I thought that was the only thing that mattered, keeping the two of us together. But now I feel like that might not be true. I love her all right, but just her and me isn't enough. We're not a whole family."

"I don't know. Seems like half the families you see nowdays is just a mama and kids."

"Well, that's our tough luck. It doesn't give you anything to fall back on."

"What's that noise?"

"Oh, nothing. The Yellow Pages. I just blew my nose on half the landscape contractors in the city."

"Oh, well. I reckon you showed them."

"Mama, I'm thinking about going home."

"Don't hang up yet!"

"No, I mean back to Tucson. I'm at the end of the line here. Jax offered to send me money for gas. If my tires will just hold out. I'm worried about my tires."

"Oh, law, Taylor."

"What?"

"I've got some bad news."

Taylor feels numb. "What is it?"

"I talked to Annawake Fourkiller. She says there's somebody, relatives of a missing girl they think is Turtle, and they want to see her. Annawake said she was going to send you a, what was it? Something Italian sounding. A semolina? Papers, anyway. Saying you have to show up here in court."

"A subpoena?"

"That was it."

"Oh, God. Then I *can't* go home." Taylor feels blood rushing too fast out of her heart toward her limbs, a tidal wave. She stares at the symmetrical rows of holes in the metal back of the telephone hutch. Her life feels exactly that meaningless.

Alice's voice comes through the line, coaxing and maternal. "Taylor, don't get mad at me for something I'm fixing to say."

"Why does everybody think I'm mad? I'm not going to get mad. Tell me."

"I think you and Turtle ought to go on and come down here."

Taylor doesn't respond to this. She turns her back on the wall of holes and looks out through the rain at her car. She knows Turtle is in there but the blank, dark windows are glossed over like loveless eyes, revealing nothing.

"Go ahead and borry the gas money and come on. There isn't nothing to finding us here. Take the interstate to Tahlequah, Oklahoma, and ask around for Heaven. Everybody knows the way."

Taylor still doesn't speak.

"It would just be to talk things over."

"Mama, there's nothing to talk over with Annawake Fourkiller. I have no bargaining chips: there's just Turtle, and me. That's all." Taylor hangs up the phone.

Taylor has been waiting so long with Turtle in the free clinic waiting room she feels sure they've had time to pick up every disease known to science. One little boy keeps licking his hand and coming over to hold it up in front of Turtle, presumably to give her an unobstructed view of his germs. Each time, Turtle withdraws her face slightly on her neck like a farsighted woman trying to focus on small print. The little boy chuckles and pitches crazily back to his mother, his disposable diaper crackling as he goes.

Every now and then, the waiting-room door opens and they all look hopefully to the nurse as she reads off someone else's name. In the bright passage behind her, Taylor hears busy people scurrying and saying things like "The ear is in number nine. I put the ankle in two." The longer they wait, the more vividly Taylor can picture piles of body parts back there.

At last the nurse calls Turtle's name, in the slightly embarrassed way strangers always do, as if they expect the child answering to this name to have some defect or possibly a shell. As she follows Turtle down the hall, Taylor wonders if she did wrong, legalizing this odd name. She has no patience with people who saddle their children with names like "Rainbo" and "Sunflower" to suit some oddball agenda of their own. But "Turtle" was a name of Turtle's own doing, and it fits now, there is no getting around it.

They wind up in a room empty of body parts. The glass jars on the counter by the sink contain only cotton balls and wooden tongue depressors. Turtle climbs onto the examining table covered with white butcher paper while Taylor lists her symptoms and the nurse writes them on a clipboard. When she leaves them and closes the door, the room feels acutely small.

Turtle lies flat on her back, making crinkly paper noises. "Am I going to get a shot?"

"No. No shots today. Very unlikely."

"A operation?"

"Positively not. I can guarantee you that. This is a free clinic, and they don't give those out for free."

"Are babies free?"

Taylor follows Turtle's eyes to a poster on the wall, drawn in weak, cartoonish shades of pink, showing what amounts to one half a pregnant woman with an upside-down baby curled snugly into the oval capsule of her uterus. It reminds Taylor of the time she cut a peach in half and the rock-hard pit fell open too, revealing a little naked almond inside, secretly occupying the clean, small open space within the peach flesh.

"Are they what? Are babies free?"

"Yeah."

"Well, let me think how to answer that. You don't have to buy them. Just about anybody can get one to grow inside her. In fact, seems like the less money you have, the easier it is to get one. But after they come out, you have to buy all kinds of stuff for them."

"Food and diapers and stuff."

"Right."

"Do you think that's why the real mom that grew me inside her didn't want me?"

"No, she died. Remember? Her sister, the woman that put you into my car, told me your mother had died, and that's why they had to give you up. You told me one time you remembered seeing your first mama get buried."

"I do remember that," Turtle says. She continues to study the peach-pit baby poster. Taylor picks up a magazine and is startled to read news about a war, until she realizes the magazine is several years old.

"Hi, I'm Doctor Washington," says a tall woman in a white coat who breezes into the room as if she's run a long way and doesn't see any point in slowing down now. She has long flat feet in black loafers, and a short, neat Afro that curves around her head like a bicycle helmet. She looks around the room quickly, as if she might in fact be anticipating a blow to the head. Her eyes settle on Turtle for a moment, but the rest of her body remains tense. She holds the clipboard in one hand and a pencil in the other, poised between two fingers, jiggling in the air.

"Stomachache?" she says to Turtle. "Cramps, diarrhea? For two or three months?"

Turtle nods solemnly, owning up to all this.

"Let's take a look." Actually she looks at the ceiling, appearing to give it her full concentration as she pulls up Turtle's T-shirt and probes her belly with long, cold-looking hands.

"Here?"

Turtle nods, making a crackling sound as her head grinds against the white paper.

"How about here? This hurt?"

Turtle shakes her head.

Dr. Washington pulls down Turtle's shirt and turns to Taylor. "How is the child's diet." She states it, rather than asks.

Taylor feels her mind blank out, the way it used to in school during history tests. She tries to calm down. "I make sure she gets protein," she says. "We eat a lot of peanut butter. And tuna fish. And she always gets milk. Every single day, no matter what."

"Well, actually, that might be the problem."

"What, milk?"

The doctor turns to Turtle. "How do you feel about milk, kiddo?"

"I hate it," Turtle says to the ceiling.

"What kind do you give her?"

"I don't know," Taylor says defensively, feeling as if the two of them are ganging up. "The store brand. Two percent."

"Try leaving out the milk from now on. I think you'll see a difference right away. Bring her back in, in a week or two, and if that hasn't taken care of it we'll check on other possibilities. But I think cutting the milk's going to do it." She writes something on the clipboard.

Taylor senses that Dr. Washington is about to move on to an ear or an ankle. "Excuse me, but I don't get this," she says. "I thought milk was the perfect food. Vitamins and calcium and everything."

Dr. Washington slumps against the counter, losing a few of her imposing inches and visibly shifting into a slower gear. "Cow's milk is fine for white folks," she says, looking directly at Taylor when she says this, "but somewhere between sixty and ninety percent of the rest of us are lactose intolerant. That means we don't have the enzymes in our system to digest some of the sugar in cow's milk. So it ferments in the intestines and causes all kinds of problems."

"Uck. I never knew that."

"Yogurt may be okay, and aged cheeses. You can give them a try. And some kinds of orange juice are calcium-fortified, that can help you out some with her calcium. If you're determined to give her milk, you can get the kind that's lactose-reduced. There's a large Asian-American population in this city, so you can find that in most of the markets."

"My daughter isn't Asian-American. She's Cherokee."

The doctor lifts her shoulders in an offhand shrug. "Asian, Native American, African, we're all in the same boat. A lot of times it doesn't present until adulthood, but it can start showing up right around her age."

Taylor can't understand how such a major truth could have passed her by. "I always thought milk was the great health food. The people look so perky in those commercials."

The doctor taps her pencil eraser against her cheek and looks at Taylor with something that could be loosely defined as a smile. Her eyes are so dark the irises appear almost bluish around the edges, and her half-closed lids give her a lizardish look. "Who do you think makes those commercials?"

"The guardians of truth," Taylor says, sulkily. "Sorry, I didn't think about it."

For the first time, Dr. Washington's superior-reptile look melts into genuine sympathy. "Listen, nobody does. I break this news to parents of every color, a dozen times a week. You were doing what you thought was best, that's the main thing."

Her white coat is standing up straight again, then gone.

Turtle slides off the gift-wrapped examining table and bounds out the examining-room door like a puppy let out of its pen. Taylor finds she can't get up from her chair. She is paralyzed by the memory of Annawake Fourkiller's final warning, in Tucson, before she drove away: "I bet she hates milk."

Taylor catches up to Turtle outside the clinic. Turtle is shading her eyes and looking straight up at the sky, which for once is miraculously unclouded. A jet has left a white, rubbed-out gash of a trail, ugly as graffiti.

"An airplane makes that," Turtle informs her, and Taylor wonders how she knows this. It's one of several million things they have never yet spoken of, precisely. Did she learn it in school? Then again, do you have to be told every single thing about the world before you know it? The idea of rearing Turtle exhausts Taylor and makes her want to lie down, or live in a simpler world. She would like for the two of them to live in one of those old-time cartoons that have roundheaded animals bobbing all together to the music, and no background whatsoever.

"You're right," Taylor says. "A jet plane."

"Why is it doing that?"

Taylor wonders which level of answer Turtle wants. Why does a jet churn up white dust in the sky? (She doesn't know.) Or, what is this particular jet's motivation? (This, maybe nobody knows.)

"Remember in Dorothy, when the witch wrote in the sky?"

"Yeah, I do," Taylor says. "In the *Wizard of Oz*. She wrote, 'Surrender Dorothy.' "

"Did that mean they were supposed to give Dorothy to the witch?"

"That's what she was asking for. Yeah."

"Are you going to give me to the Indians?"

"No. I'll never do that. But I think we have to go back and talk to them. Are you scared?"

"Yeah."

"Me too."

29

THE SECRET OF CREATION

CASH MOVES THROUGH HIS KITCHEN the way a lanky squirrel might, if a squirrel could cook: stepping quickly from sink to stove, pausing, sensing the air. By comparison, Alice feels like the lazy squirrel wife, sitting at the table separating hickory nuts from their crushed shells. "Slow down, Cash," she tells him, smiling. "You're making my eyes hurt."

"I always do that to women," he says. "I'm just ugly, is all."

"Pish posh, you are not." Alice picks a nearly whole nut from the curled chambers of its shell and drops it into the bowl. For reasons she couldn't explain, the naked, curled little nuts remind her of babies waiting to get born.

Cash told her this log cabin was the original dwelling on his family's homestead. It has stood empty for years, and seemed the right size for him when he came back from Wyoming. It's all one room, with a kitchen at one end and a pair of parlor chairs flanking the lace curtain on the other end. For the summer he's moved his bed out to the porch, for air. His rifle, his toothbrush, and a lucky horseshoe hang over the stone fireplace. The cabin seems sturdy enough to stand through a tornado, or small enough to be overlooked by one in favor of the larger house that was built later on, where Letty now lives. The cabin has been occupied by most of Letty's children at one time or another; they were the ones who installed plumbing and strung out the electrical wire, which now supplies Cash's few light bulbs and—Alice was distressed to note—the little TV set that squats on the kitchen counter amongst the bowls and flour canisters. He did shut it off right away when she came in. She'll hand him that much.

"You don't have to get all them shells out. Just the big pieces," he tells her. "Are you watching this, now? You got to know how to make *kunutche,* if you're going to sign up to be Cherokee here in a while."

"Is that right? Will they give me a test?"

"Oh, I think so, probably. But if you decide not to enroll, then don't bother learning. No *yonega* would fool around with a thing that's this much trouble."

"Maybe I oughtn't to, then, and just go on letting you do all the work." Alice is startled to hear what she's just said, words that contain a presumption about the future. If Cash is in any way riled, he doesn't show it. He dumps the nuts with a clatter into a dented metal bucket and pounds them deftly with a wooden club, making a steady gritch-gritch like a cow chewing. The pounding club resembles a sawed-off baseball bat. Alice saw one in Sugar's kitchen and had no earthly notion what kind of cooking implement it might be. It looked so forceful.

"You pound it till it's powder, that's the way you start out," Cash instructs. "Then you roll it into balls about yay big." He holds up his right fist, wrist forward, to show her, looking to see that she has understood. "There's enough oil in it so it holds together good." He turns back to pounding, and goes on talking with a slightly breathless rhythm over the nutty gritching sound, which has now gone to more of a hiss. "When you get ready to fix it, you just break off a piece of the ball and add it to boiling water, and then you strain it through a good clean sock to get out the little bits of shell, and you mix it with rice, or hominy. It's kindly a soupy consistency."

"Sounds good," Alice says, reverently. In her life she has experienced neither men who talk a lot nor men who cook, and here is one doing both at once. She would have paid money to witness this, and not been disappointed.

"I love it with hominy," he adds. "It kindly puts you in the mood of fall, when you smell *kunutche.*"

"Did your wife teach you how to make it?"

"Well, now," he pauses and stares at the wall calendar. "I guess my mama did. My wife did the cooking, mostly, but I always pounded up the *kunutche.* She said all that grinding hurt her bones."

Alice stands up and wanders the length of the cabin, wishing for family pictures or some other hint of what Cash belongs to. Her eyes rest on his toothbrush, which seems small and stranded up there, and his gun. "You shoot anything with that rifle?"

"Oh, a squirrel now and then, if he'll set still long enough to get hit. My eyes isn't what they was. Usually I'll miss three or four time, and then one'll keel over and die of a heart attack."

Alice wants to give him a hug. If men only knew, modesty makes women fall in love faster than all the cock-a-doodling in the world. She touches her earrings, whose tiny beads shiver away from her fingers. They were delivered to her one morning in an envelope marked only, "From a secret admirer." Sugar, who had stood breathing on Alice's head while she ripped open the envelope, instantly identified the turquoise-and-silver beadwork as Cash's. She said he had been selling earrings just like that to the trading post at the Heritage Center.

Alice sent Cash back a note that said, "Many thanks and a special hug from your mystery date." She gave it to Sugar to mail at the P.O., and was mortified later to find that Sugar had run into Letty in town and asked her to hand-deliver it.

"Sugar says you do beadwork for the trading post. That a fact?"

"I do a little. It relaxes me at night."

"Somebody sent me these earrings. Can you imagine? Some fellow must think he can knock me over with a feather."

Cash grins. "I got your note."

"I'll bet Letty opened it up and read it first."

"Looked like it. She's not as professional as she used to be." Cash's face broadens under the eyes with a smile that seems to be settling in and getting comfortable.

"I guess I ought to try my hand at that," she says, coming over to stand next to him. "Either that, or sing for my supper. Of the two I think you'd ruther me mash nuts."

He positions her hands on the club, then stands back to watch. "I don't know about that. You got a real nice talking voice. I was thinking the other day, if I had a telephone I'd call up Alice just to listen at her voice. I bet you could sing like a bird."

"A turkey buzzard," Alice says.

"Now, you stop right there, I don't believe you. I'd pay a dollar to hear you sing 'Amazing Grace.' Or 'Don't Set Under the Apple Tree.' Here, it helps sometimes if you put more shoulder into it."

He stands behind her with his arms over hers, gripping her hands gently and pushing downward. The precise hissing sound returns to the kitchen, nut powder urged against metal. Alice feels a similar sound in her chest.

"You'd ask for your dollar back when I was done," she says.

Cash eases the pressure on her hands. "I wouldn't. Even if you did sound like a turkey buzzard, I wouldn't care."

Alice leans her head back against him at the same moment he lifts his arms across her chest, holding her there and dropping his face into the crown of her hair.

"Cash," she says.

"Hm?" He turns her around, keeping her within the circle of his arms. She looks up at his face, which at close range without her reading specs is blurry, except for the window-shaped lights in his eyes.

"You might be able to knock me over with a feather," she tells him. "It'd be worth a try."

Cash's cabin is in deep woods, a quarter-mile behind Letty's back garden. From his iron bed out on the screen porch, Alice wonders how it would be to wake up every morning to the sight of nothing but leaves.

"Did you hear what happened to that Mr. Green?"

"The ostrich rancher?" she asks. "I heard his ostriches like to sashay around and drop their feathers on the wrong side of the fence."

Cash runs a finger down Alice's nose. Without his glasses his eyes look soft and hopeful, like they're in need of something. Alice honestly can't remember the last time she was naked under the quilts with a man who was awake, but even so, neither she nor Cash seems to be in any big rush. It's such a pleasure just to realize they've gotten this far. And to listen to talk.

"He tried to break into Boma's house to get that feather back," Cash tells her.

"Lord! Was she home?"

"No. They was all at a wedding. Can you imagine? Reading about a wedding in the paper, he must have done, because he sure wasn't invited. And going over to burglarize the groom's own grandma?"

"Well, did he get it?"

"He got it all right." Cash rolls over onto his back and laughs, then clucks his tongue. "I oughtn't to laugh. He's in the hospital."

"With what?"

"Nine thousand bee stings."

Alice gasps. "And still no feather, I'll bet."

"Naw. It'd be like Boma to send it to him in a big vase of flowers, though. With a get-well card from the bees."

"Hope you're back in the pink soon, *honey,*" Alice says, getting the giggles.

"We're bad."

"We are," Alice says. "What would our kids think of us?"

The lines around Cash's eyes go soft, and he seems to drift for a moment. She traces the honed ridge of his breastbone with her finger, feeling deeply sad for whatever it is that takes him away, sometimes, at the mention of his family. She would do anything to ease that burden. She finds his hand, which was resting on her waist, and holds it against her lips. "I'm sorry," she says. "For whatever it is."

Cash moves forward to kiss her. He tastes like woodsmoke and the color of leaves. When he touches her breast, she feels the skin of her nipples gather itself in. She is pierced with a sharp, sweet memory of nursing

Taylor, and when he puts his mouth there she feels once again that longing to be drained, to give herself away entirely. Slowly Cash moves himself against her, and then very gently into her, and she feels the same longing coming through his body to hers. They rock against each other, holding on, and the birds in the forest raise their voices to drown out the secret of creation.

30

SIX PIGS AND ONE MOTHER

ALICE WAKES TO THE SOUND of voices inside, in the kitchen. Half of Cash appears in the doorway to the porch, his shirttail out, a smile on his face. He holds a spatula in his left hand, poised like a flyswatter. "How do you like your eggs?" he asks.

Alice, feeling confused, looks around as if she might have laid some eggs she's not aware of. "Who's that in your kitchen?"

"Kitty Carlisle."

"Kitty Carlisle lives in Oklahoma?"

"Naw. She's on 'Good Morning America.' "

Alice runs a hand through her hair, trying to get her bearings. She was in some dream with water and furry animals. "What do you need the TV on for?"

Cash shrugs. "No reason. Just for the company, I reckon."

"Well, I'll get up and keep you company." She begins to

gather up her limbs, testing to make sure of their four separate locations.

"No, you just set there another minute. I'm going to bring you breakfast in bed. I'll bring your coffee on out, as soon as you tell me 'sunny side up' or 'over easy.' "

She thinks. "Over hard, with the yolk broke, if you really want to know. Lord, breakfast in bed? I reckon if I was Kitty Carlisle I'd have me a frilly housecoat to put on."

"I'll bring you my bathrobe," he says, disappearing. Alice licks the roof of her mouth, looking at the leaves all pressed like happy spying faces against the screen. She feels she has died and gone to the Planet of Men Who Cook. Cash returns with an old flannel bathrobe, blue plaid, and settles it on her shoulders. She hugs it around her like a lady in church with a fur stole, and with her free hand accepts a cup of coffee. The first black sip arouses her throat and lungs.

Cash is busy moving things around. He sets a coffee table carefully beside the bed and covers it with plates of eggs, ham, toast, butter, and huckleberry jam. He pulls up a stool on the other side. Alice puts her arms through the sleeves of the bathrobe and sits up on the edge of the bed, facing him, so she won't feel like an invalid.

"I'm not used to being catered to," she says, smiling at her plate. "I'll try to tolerate it, though."

For a while they are quiet, making small clinking sounds with their forks. Cash blows on his coffee. A bird somewhere in the leaves asks, "Chit? Chit? Chit?"

"I been wondering how long a visit you're here for," he says finally.

"Oh, at Sugar's? I don't know. I guess till I wear out my welcome. I didn't really come just to visit Sugar, to tell you the truth. I had some business."

"With family?"

"No, with the Cherokee Nation. I don't know if it's with the Nation, exactly." She cuts into her eggs, which are perfect. Most people don't believe you really want broken yolks, and they won't go through with it; they'll keep it whole and runny for your own good. "I had some dealings to do with Annawake Fourkiller. It's something we have to settle about my daughter and granddaughter." Her heart pounds. She didn't decide to tell

Cash, she only knows that she's going to. "I have a little granddaughter that she saw on TV. You know Annawake?"

"Oh, sure. Her Uncle Ledger is the medicine man. You seen him at the stomp dance, didn't you?"

"Sure."

"That little Annawake used to follow him around like a calf." Cash chews his toast. "At the dance, when Ledger would get up to speak, she'd stand right up in front of him and holler out sermons."

Alice finds she can picture this. With Cash, it's easy to get derailed from a confession. "I guess she's going to be the next one, then."

"No, it's somebody younger. I don't know who yet, but they's already picked him out. It starts when you're too young to remember. The medicine man puts the medicine on you, and then when you're older you don't remember it, but it kindly influences how you grow. Later on, you get the training."

"Well, that seems dangerous, don't it? What if the kid that was all picked out to be the next preacher turns out to be a motorcycle hood?"

Cash seems very serious. "That wouldn't happen. The medicine man can tell from the child how they'll be. You don't want one that's real loud, a fighter or anything. You want one that's more quiet."

They return to their breakfast. Alice hears Kitty Carlisle, or someone at any rate, muttering to herself in the kitchen.

"How long were you and your wife married?" she asks.

"Oh, since we was too young to know a hawk from a handsaw. I met her at the stomp dance after I left boarding school. She come from over around Kenwood way." His whole body tilts slightly backward with the pleasure of memory. "Law, I'll tell you, I only started going up there to meet girls, and for the food. They cooked good food at the dances back then: bean balls, squirrel dumpling. Eggs. People went over and stayed all day. They'd come in the wagon and on horses. They'd put up a tent, put up long benches and put a quilt on it and sleep on that. I used to always go early, to play ball."

"Play ball?" Alice asks.

"They play a kind of ball game, before the dance. Did you see that big tall pole with a fish on the top, carved out of wood? Down there in the clearing at the stomp grounds, where the dirt's all beat up underneath."

Alice nods, because her mouth is full. The good thing about Cash is, you can eat big bites while you're listening to him.

"It's girls and women against boys and men. That's how they play. You throw the ball or sling it up there with a stick, and try to hit the fish. It's too hard for little kids and old people. It's kindly serious. I don't know how to explain it, quite. Keeping your body in good shape is part of being a good person, you could say. But back then I paid too much attention to trying to be the best one. Ever time you throw the ball and hit the fish, your side gets a point."

"Don't the boys always win out?"

"No, ma'am, they don't. You should see some of them girls. Now Annawake, she's a killer. And my wife was. That's how we met, playing ball. I won a point, and then she did, we went on like that for a whole game, so we figured out we'd have to get married."

Alice laughs. "Seems like a better reason than most kids have."

"I quit going for a while, after she died. I didn't tell you, but the other night, when we went over together, that's the first I been for a while."

"Why's that, Cash?"

"I couldn't tell you. I was gone away, and then after I come back it seemed too hard. It reminded me of the funerals."

"They have funerals at the stomp grounds?"

"Well, sure. They carry the casket around the fire three times, the same direction as you go when you're dancing, and then they carry it walking backwards, three times. I guess you're going back out of life the same door as you come in. And then you go to the cemetery for the burying. There's buckets of tea outside the cemetery, so when you go out you can wash your face and hands in the tea to wash off the grieving, and leave it there."

Cash looks sunk in misery. Alice says gently, "It don't seem like you left it all behind."

"Well, maybe they was too much of it come all at once. Four year ago, we had three funerals in the same season: my mama, well of course she was old. Then my wife, of the cancer. And then my oldest girl, Alma. She drove her car off a bridge and landed it upside down in the Arkansas River. She had a little bitty girl, when she done that. She left the baby behind that night with her sister, the one that run off with a no-count boy to Tulsa and don't talk to me no more. I kept on calling her up for a while. She was mean as she could be, but I had to call, because I was worried about Alma's baby. Lacey, her name was. But durn if one day she didn't up and give that baby away. She goes to a bar one night and hands her over to some girl passing through in a car."

Alice feels the breath knocked out of her, exactly as if she had fallen off a roof. She can't pull in air.

"The younger people have got bad problems, I'll be the first one to tell you. Monday mornings the jails are full of 'em. A lot of these kids think liquor is made for one purpose, to get drunk as quick as you can."

"How do you know she gave the baby away?"

"She told me. How do you like that? She tells me, 'Pop, I'm moving to Ponca City, could I use your truck next weekend? I done give Alma's baby away.' I felt so discouraged I just packed up my truck that same weekend and drove out of here. I couldn't stand to look at my own kin."

Alice puts a hand on her chest and gets her breath back. She has to say it before she thinks twice. "Cash, my daughter has that girl."

Cash puts down his coffee cup and looks at Alice. He doesn't for an instant disbelieve her.

"That's what I come here for," she tells him. "Annawake saw Taylor and the little girl on TV telling the story of how she got adopted. Annawake figured some way she belonged to the Cherokees, and she tracked them down. Taylor run off. They're living on the lam now so she won't have to give her up. She loves her, Cash. My daughter's been as good a mother to that child as ever you're going to find."

"Lord God in Heaven," Cash replies.

"I can't figure out what to think," Alice says.

"No, me neither."

"My brain's gone off somewhere. Are you fixing to be mad? Because I have to tell you where I stand. My daughter hasn't done a thing in the world wrong. She's protecting her child, like any living mother would do, man or beast."

"No," Cash says. "She ain't done wrong. I'm just trying to picture that Lacey's somewhere all in one piece. Walking, I guess. Lord, what am I saying? Walking, talking, picking up sticks. She'd be six and a half."

"She's not a Lacey. Not for love nor money. Her name's Turtle."

"Well, what kind of a name is that?"

"What kind of a name is Able Swimmer?" Alice fires back. "Or Stand Hornbuckle, or, or Flester Dreadfulwater!"

Cash ignores her. "It just don't seem real," he says. "After I come back here from Wyoming a little while ago, I talked to them girls down at Child Welfare about trying to find her. They said they might have a bite on the line, but I didn't hold for much hope. Lord God in Heaven. Us coming together like this, not even knowing."

He stares at Alice while the trees grow outside.

"Letty set this all up," he says. "She must have knowed."

"No, she didn't, Cash. Not a soul knew my side of it but Annawake. I didn't even tell Sugar."

"Well, how in the world?"

"I don't know," Alice says. "I'm suspicious of miracles. There's near about always something behind them."

"Sugar didn't know?"

"No. I swear on the Bible."

"I figured this business with you and me was something Sugar and Letty cooked up. Otherwise, Letty wouldn't have knowed you was fair game."

"Then it was Annawake," Alice says suddenly. "It was. She had to have done this. She said she'd been working on Plan B, I'll swan, I could tan her hide! She's trying to find a way around doing her rightful duty by Turtle."

Cash looks wary. "What is her rightful duty?"

Alice stares back, comprehending his position. "Nothing's settled, is it?"

Cash lays his knife across the edge of his plate. "No. Nothing's settled."

Alice has spent all Sunday afternoon with her teeth clenched and unkind intentions in her heart, hunting down Annawake. She feels like one of those Boston Stranglers you can read about. The first thing she did when she came home to Sugar was spill the whole story, start to finish, leaving out only the details of last night with Cash, which were nobody's business. Sugar agreed she ought to give Annawake a good talking to, for meddling. They enlisted Roscoe to drive over to Annawake's place in Tahlequah. Sugar sat in the cab between Alice and Roscoe, squeezing Alice's hand as if she were having a baby instead of about to lose one.

In Tahlequah, Sugar and Roscoe waited in the cab while Alice knocked on the door and talked to a heavyset girl holding a baby, who said Annawake was down at the Nation offices. They drove down the highway to Nation Headquarters, only to find the place deserted. There was one secretary in the whole place, who pointed them to Annawake's office across the street. It was locked. Alice tried to peer in, but saw only houseplants. She festered in the truck for nearly an hour, waiting, before deciding to drive back to talk again to the heavyset girl, who seemed, in all fairness, just as sweet as she could be. She said Annawake had come and gone again, fishing this time, down at her uncle's houseboat. Alice climbed back in the cab and surprised Sugar and Roscoe by claiming to know the way to Ledger Fourkiller's. When they dropped her off at the path running down to the river, they offered to wait, but Alice waved them on.

"I know my way. If she's not here, I'll just walk on back."

"Well, honey, that's miles and miles," Sugar had protested before they drove off. "And dark. You're liable to run into a skunk."

But Alice feels determined as she sets off down the path, skunk or no skunk. If she ran into one right now, he'd have to take his chances. She doesn't really expect to strangle Annawake once she finds her, but she hasn't ruled out the possibility.

Annawake has given up the pretense of fishing. Nothing down there is hungry, and to be honest, neither is she; it seems reasonable to call a truce. She swirls her legs in the water, watching the reflected stars tremble in each other's company. The water is warmer than the air, and moves against her skin as if it cared for her. She tries not to think how long it has been since she was hugged by someone who wasn't a relative.

She hears steps on the footbridge, or rather, feels their vibrations approaching, the way a spider knows the commerce of her web. "Ledger?" she calls out.

A human silhouette appears in the darkness at the edge of the porch, and it isn't Ledger Fourkiller. Smaller, meaner, not at home. Her heart thumps.

"Well! If it's not Miss Lonelyhearts."

Annawake knows the voice. Thinks hard.

"It was you, wasn't it? You set up me and Cash."

"Alice Greer?"

She approaches as slowly as a dog outside its territory, until she is standing five feet away, hands on her hips, both angry and hesitant.

"You're mad? I saw you two giggling like kids at the Sanitary Market. I thought you'd be sending me a thank-you card."

"That was a sly, sneak-handed business you did. You figured I'd take a shine to Cash and wouldn't want to take his baby away from him."

Annawake feels this woman's anger sharpened like a hunting knife. "Did you ever think it might work out the other way? That he might like *you* that much?"

"I don't think that's what you were aiming for."

"Can we sit down and talk it over?"

Alice hovers for a moment the way a female dragonfly will, before committing her future, laying her eggs on the water. Finally she plunges. Sits and takes off her shoes.

Annawake paddles her legs slowly back and forth. "To tell you the truth, Alice, I couldn't tell you what I was thinking. I don't think I *was* thinking, for once. I just followed my gut. I thought my Indian-white relations project needed a human touch."

"And me and Cash went like lambs to the slaughter."

"I didn't think it would take you so long to find out what you two have in common. I figured you'd tell him right away."

"Well, maybe us old folks don't just jump into things the way you kids do."

"Sounds to me like just the opposite. You were so busy jumping into things you forgot to state your business."

Unbelievably, Annawake hears Alice swallow a giggle.

"I guess I overstepped," she tells Alice. "I'm sorry."

In the very long silence, an owl calls from upriver. Annawake can picture its wide-open eyes, hunting. Stealing scraps of sight from the darkness.

"You probably didn't mean no harm."

"Believe me, I had a lot of help from Letty."

"That Letty," Alice agrees, with grudging humor. "She'd stick her nose in a grave if she thought there was still hope of warm gossip."

The adrenaline that rushed Annawake's limbs when she first saw anger in the dark is receding now, leaving her body with a longing to stretch. She arches her back. "Every town probably needs a Letty," she says. "Somebody to lubricate things, and then count backwards from nine every time a couple of newlyweds have a baby."

"Margie Spragg. That's who it was in Pittman. She was the phone operator for the longest time. It about killed her when they put in the dial tone."

"It's a public service, what those women do. Sometimes people have communication problems with their own hearts."

"Well," Alice says. "Nothing's settled, still."

"I know."

"Taylor's on her way. She called me from a truck stop in Denver."

"Is she?" Annawake feels curiously apprehensive. For months she hasn't been able to recall Taylor's appearance, having met her so briefly, but now, suddenly, she does. The fine-featured, trusting face, the long dark hair, the way she held perfectly still while listening. She remembers Taylor standing at the window curled forward with animal fear, and she imagines her in a telephone booth in Denver, curled forward with the receiver under a sheet of dark hair.

"I figured you'd be jumping for joy," Alice says.

"Oh, I'm not much of a jumper. I oftentimes have communication problems with my heart."

"Letty ever try to help you out on that?"

Annawake holds her hand in the air. "Don't even ask. Letty Hornbuckle has tried to fix me up with everything in this county that stands on two legs to pee. Unfortunately, that's not my problem."

"Oh."

Alice is now swirling her own legs through the water, creating crosscurrents that jostle the stars together in the water until Annawake can fairly hear them ringing.

"Look. There's the Little Dipper out there in the middle of the river, upside-down. See her?"

"I can't see good at night."

"You can see it in the sky, though. Straight up from that one dead oak that looks white, over there on the bank."

"I think I do see it," Alice says, in a voice thinned out from looking up.

"Don't look it straight head-on. Look a little off to one side, and it will be brighter. Uncle Ledger showed me that."

"Sure enough," Alice says in a minute. And then, "I'll swan. I can see all seven of the Seven Sisters, when I do that."

"You people! That must be why whites took over the world. You can see all seven of the Seven Sisters."

"What, you can't?"

"We call them the Six Pigs in Heaven."

"The what? The *pigs?*"

"It's a story. About six bad boys that got turned into pigs."

"Well, that must have made them think twice. What did they do to get turned into pigs?"

"Oh, you know. They didn't listen to their mothers, didn't do chores. Just played ball all the time. So their mothers cooked up something really nasty for them to eat, to try to teach them a lesson. Have you seen those little leather balls we use for playing stickball?"

"Cash showed me a real old one. It was all beat up, with hair coming out of it."

"Exactly. Animal hair. The mothers cooked up a stew made out of that, and fed it to the boys when they came home for lunch. The boys were disgusted. They said, 'This is pig food!' And the mothers said, 'Well, if that's true then you must be pigs.' The boys got up from the table and went down to the stomp grounds and ran in circles around the ball court, just yelling. The mothers ran after them, ready to forgive their rowdy boys and forget the whole thing, but right in front of their eyes the boys started turning into pigs."

"Law," Alice says earnestly. "They must of felt awful."

"They did. They tried to grab their sons by the tails, and they begged the spirits to bring them back, but it was too late. The pigs ran so fast they were just a blur, and they started rising up into the sky. The spirits put them up there to stay. To remind parents always to love their kids no matter what, I guess, and cut them a little slack."

Alice looks up for a long time. "I swear there's seven," she says.

The owl hoots again, nearer this time.

"Maybe so," Annawake says. "The Six Pigs in Heaven, and the one mother who wouldn't let go."

31

HEN APPLES

IN THE ROAD AHEAD, A dead armadillo lies with its four feet and tail all pointed at the heavens. The stiff, expectant curl of its body reminds Taylor of a teddy bear, abandoned there on its back. She reaches into the glove compartment and puts on her sunglasses so Turtle won't see her eyes.

Alice is backseat driving from the front seat, because she knows the roads. Turtle got used to the front seat on their long drive from the Northwest, and has now staked out a place between her mother and grandmother. She flatly refused the backseat when Taylor suggested it. Earlier today, Taylor confided to Alice that Turtle seems to be in a baffling new phase of wanting to have her own way; Alice replied, "About durn time."

"That was your turn right there. You missed it," Alice says.

"Well, great, Mama. Why didn't you let me get another mile down the road before you told me?"

Alice is quiet while Taylor turns the wheel, arm over arm, exaggerating the effort it takes to pull the Dodge around. Taylor can't stand it when she and Alice are at odds. The three female generations sit staring ahead at the Muskogee Highway, torn asunder, without a single idea of where the family is headed.

Alice speaks up again, this time well before the turn. "That stoplight up there. You'll turn into the parking lot right after that. Her office is in there next to a beauty shop, says Turnbo Legal something or other on the door."

Taylor pulls into a fast-food restaurant before the light. "I'm going to drop you two off right here, okay? I need to talk to her first. You can have a snack and play around a little bit, and come on over to the office in fifteen minutes or so. That sound okay, Turtle?"

"Yeah."

"No milk shake, okay, Mama? She's lactose intolerant."

"She's what?"

"She can't drink milk."

"It's because I'm Indian," Turtle says with satisfaction.

"Well, aren't you the one?" Alice asks, helping her out of the car, doting on Turtle as she has since their arrival in Oklahoma. The two of them are getting on like thieves, Taylor observes.

"Fifteen minutes, okay, Mama?"

"Right. We'll see you." She pauses before slamming the door, bending down to peer under the top of the doorframe at Taylor. "Hon, we're all upset. But you know I'm pulling for you. You never did yet let a thing slip away if you wanted it. I know you can do this."

Taylor pushes her sunglasses to the top of her head and wipes her eyes, suddenly flooded with tears. "Do you have a hanky?"

Alice shakes a wad of pale blue tissues out of her purse. "Here. One for the road."

"Mama, you're the best."

"You just think that cause I raised you." Alice reaches in to give Taylor's shoulder a squeeze, then closes the door. Turtle is already off, her pigtails whipping as she runs for the glassy box of a restaurant. Taylor takes a breath and drives the two final blocks to her destiny.

In the row of commercial fronts, between a realty office and a place called Killie's Hair Shack, she locates the law office. It seems deserted, but when she knocks on the glass door, Annawake appears suddenly behind the glare. The door slants open. Annawake's face is an open book of nerves, and her hair is different, a short, swinging black skirt of it around her face.

"I'm glad you made it," she says, throwing a glance at the parking lot, seeing the Dodge and no one else coming.

"She'll be here in a while," Taylor says. "I left Turtle with Mama across the street at a restaurant so I could tell you some stuff first."

"That's fine, come on in. Taylor, this is Cash Stillwater."

Taylor has to look twice before she sees the man in the corner sitting under the rubber tree. His worn, pointed-toe boots are planted on the carpet and his shoulders lean so that he seems drooped somehow, like a plant himself, needing more light.

"Taylor Greer," she says with urgently insincere friendliness, extending her hand. He leans forward and meets her halfway, then sags back into his chair. His dark face seems turned in on itself from shyness or pain, behind the gold-rimmed glasses.

Taylor sits in one of the chrome chairs, and Annawake clears her throat. "Cash has asked us to help find his granddaughter, Lacey Stillwater. I guess Alice might have told you that."

"Mama said there was maybe a relative. I don't know how you'd prove something like that."

"Well, there's blood testing, but I don't think we need to go into that at this point. Cash would just like for me to give you the information he has. His grandchild would be six now, seven next April. She was left in the custody of Cash's younger daughter, an alcoholic, after his older daughter died in a car accident. The child was given to a stranger in a bar north of Oklahoma City, three years ago last November. We have reason to believe that stranger might have been you."

"I can't say anything about that," Taylor says.

"We have no hard feelings toward you. But whether or not your adopted daughter is Cash's grandchild, there are some problems here. If the child is Cherokee, her adoption was conducted illegally. You didn't know the law, and I don't hold you responsible in any way. I'm angry at the professionals who gave you poor advice, because they've caused a lot of heartache."

Taylor is so far past heartache she could laugh out loud. At this moment she is afraid her heart will simply stop. "Can you just go ahead and say it? Do I have to give her up, or not?"

Annawake is sitting with her back to the window, and when she pushes her hair behind her ears they are pink-rimmed like a rabbit's. "It's not a simple yes or no. First, if she's Cherokee, the fate of the child is the tribe's jurisdiction. The tribe could decide either way, to allow you to keep her or ask you to return her to our custody. The important precedent here is a case called Mississippi Band of Choctaw *versus* Holyfield. I'll read you what the Supreme Court said."

She picks up her glasses and a thick stapled document from the desk behind her and flips through it, turning it sideways from time to time to read things written in the margins. Suddenly she reads: "The U.S. Supreme Court will not decide whether the trauma of removing these children from their adoptive family, with which they have lived for three years, should outweigh the interests of the tribe, and perhaps of the children themselves, in having them raised as part of the tribal community; instead, the Supreme Court must defer to the experience, wisdom, and compassion of the tribal court to fashion an appropriate remedy."

"So," Taylor says, trying not to look at the silent man under the rubber tree. "What does the voice of wisdom and compassion say?"

"I don't know. I'm not that voice. Child Welfare Services has the final say. They can give or withhold permission for a child to be adopted out. Assuming we're sure of jurisdiction here. Once we have all the facts, I'll make a recommendation to Andy Rainbelt in Child Welfare, and he'll make the decision."

"Do I get to talk to him?"

"Sure. He's planning on meeting you this afternoon. And I've agreed not to make any recommendations until I've heard what you have to say."

Taylor is aware of being the white person here. Since her arrival in Oklahoma, she has felt her color as a kind of noticeable heat rising off her skin, something like a light bulb mistakenly left on and burning in a roomful of people who might disapprove. She wonders if Turtle has always felt her skin this way, in a world of lighter people.

"Sir?" Taylor speaks to the man, Mr. Stillwater.

He leans forward a little.

"What was your granddaughter like?"

He crosses an ankle on his knee, looks at his hand. "I couldn't tell you.

She was small. Me and my wife, we looked after her a whole lot when she was a little bit of a thing. I'd say she was a right good baby. Smart as a honeybee. Right quiet."

"Did she ever talk?"

"Well, she started to. She'd say 'Mom-mom,' that's what she called her granny. Little baby words like that." His eyes light then, behind his glasses. "One time she said 'hen apple.' That's what I called eggs, to tease her, when we'd play in the kitchen. And one morning I had her with me down in the yard. One of the hens was stealing the nest, and I was looking for it, and she crawled off through the bean patch and into the weeds and here in a minute she hollers, 'Hen apple!' Just as clear as you please." He wipes the corner of his eye. "My wife never would believe me, but it's true."

Taylor and Annawake avoid looking at each other.

"Then after her mama died, seem like she quit talking. Of course, I didn't see a whole lot of her. She was with my other daughter and a young fella over to Tulsa."

Taylor bites her lip, then asks, "Did she go to her mother's funeral?"

He stares at her for a long time. "Everybody goes to the funerals. It's our way. The funeral is at the stomp grounds, and then the burying."

"Do you have any pictures?"

"What, of the funeral?"

"No. Of the child."

He folds himself forward like a jackknife and slides a curved brown wallet from his pocket. He flips through it for a moment like a small favorite book, pauses, then pulls out a tiny photograph, unevenly trimmed. Taylor takes it, afraid to look. But it has nothing of Turtle in it. It's merely a tiny, dark infant, her features screwed with fresh confusion. Her head is turned to the side and her wrinkled fist holds more defiance than Turtle ever mustered in her life. Until last week.

"Here's her mother, my daughter Alma. First day of school." He reaches across with another small photo, and she takes it.

Taylor makes a low noise in her throat, a little cry. It's a girl in saddle shoes and a plaid dress with a Peter Pan collar, standing tall on a front porch step, shoulders square. Her eyebrows hang an earnest question mark on her high forehead. The girl is Turtle.

Taylor holds the photograph by its corner and looks away. She feels she might not live through the next few minutes. The photo leaves her fingers, but she doesn't watch him put it away.

Taylor says, "The girl I've been raising came to me when she was about three. She had been hurt badly, before that. The night she came to me she had bruises all over her. That's the reason I kept her. Do you honestly think I should have given her back? Later on when I took her to a doctor, he said her arms had been broken. It was almost a year before she would talk, or look at people right, or play the way other kids do. She was sexually abused."

Mr. Stillwater speaks in the quietest possible voice to his boots. "I was afraid to death, when they took her to Tulsa. That boy beat up my daughter. She was in the hospital twice with a broke jaw." He clears his throat. "I should have gone and got her. But my wife was dead, and I didn't have the gumption. I should have. I done wrong."

There is a very long silence, and then a yellow leaf falls off the rubber tree. All three of them stare at it.

"I've let her down too," Taylor says. "In different ways. I made her drink milk even though I should have seen it was making her sick." She continues looking at the curled leaf on the floor, released from its branch. "Since all this came up, we've been living on the edge of what I could manage. I had to leave her alone in the car sometimes because I couldn't afford a sitter. We didn't have enough money, and we didn't have anybody to help us." Taylor tightens and releases her grip on the wadded blue tissue in her hand. "That's why I finally came here. Turtle needs the best in the world, after what she's been through, and I've been feeling like a bad mother." Her voice breaks, and she crosses her arms over her stomach, already feeling the blow. How life will be without Turtle. It will be impossible. Loveless, hopeless, blind. She will forget the colors.

She feels Annawake's eyes turned on her, wide, but no words.

When Taylor's own voice comes back to her, she hardly recognizes it or knows what it will say. "Turtle deserves better than what she's gotten, all the way around. I love her more than I can tell you, but just that I love her isn't enough, if I can't give her more. We don't have any backup. I don't want to go through with this thing anymore, hiding out and keeping her away from people. It's hurting her."

Taylor and Annawake gaze at each other like animals surprised by their own reflections.

Suddenly two shadows are at the door, tall and short. Annawake jumps up to lead them in. Turtle is hanging so close to Alice's knees they bump together like a three-legged race. Her eyes are round, and never look away from the man in the corner.

"Turtle, I want you to meet some people," Taylor says through the hoarseness in her throat.

Turtle takes a half step from behind Alice, and stares. Suddenly she holds up her arms to Cash like a baby who wants to be lifted into the clouds. She asks, "Pop-pop?"

Cash pulls off his glasses and drops his face into his hands.

32

THE SNAKE UK'TEN

"WHERE'D YOU GET A PRISSY name like Lacey from, anyway?"

"I don't know," Cash tells Alice, keeping his hands on the wheel and his eye trained ahead. "It was Alma thought of it. I think she liked that TV show with the lady cops. Lacey and somebody."

"Oh, if that don't beat all." Alice jerks herself around in the seat, facing away from him. She was more or less stuck for a ride home, since Taylor and Turtle had to go straight over to Cherokee Headquarters to see the man in Child Welfare. Annawake said her car was broken down and she was waiting for her brother to pick her up. That left Cash. She should have walked.

"She's so big," Cash says. "I can tell just how she is. The kind to keep her mind to herself, like her mother did."

They pass by fields of harvested hay that is rolled up for the winter in what looks like giant bedrolls. A barn in the middle of a pasture is leaning so far to the east it appears to be a freak of gravity.

"Are you going to go ahead and get enrolled, and get your voting card?" he asks.

"Might as well," Alice declares to the passing farms. "So I can get my roof fixed."

"Don't start talking to me about Indians on welfare."

"I wasn't."

"Well, don't. My people owned mansions in Georgia. They had to see it all burned down, and come over here to nothing but flint rocks and copperheads." Cash's voice rises to the pitch of a tenor in church.

"I can't believe I ever got mixed up with a family that names babies after TV shows!" Alice cries, just as loudly. "Kitty Carlisle in the kitchen. You can keep your Kitty Carlisle. I already had me one husband that was in love with his television set. Not again, no thanks!"

"Who was asking?"

"Well, I just didn't want you to waste your time."

As angry and heartbroken as she is, Alice feels something hard break loose down inside of her. She feels deeply gratified to yell at someone who is paying enough attention, at least, to yell back.

The Tribal Offices sit just off the highway in a simple modern arrangement of red brick and concrete slabs, with shrubs hugging the sidewalks. Taylor expected something more tribal, though she doesn't know what that might be.

Turtle holds tightly to her hand as they make their way around the long sidewalk, looking for the right entrance.

"You remember your grandpa, do you?" Taylor asks, talking to fend off approaching terror.

Turtle shrugs. "I dunno."

"It's okay if you do. You can say."

"Yeah."

"What else do you remember?"

"Nothing."

"Your first mother?"

Turtle shrugs again. "He's the good one. Pop-pop. He's not the bad one."

"You remember a man that hurt you?"

"I think I do."

"Turtle, that's good. I want you to remember. Remember him so you can throw him away."

Their shoes make soft, sticky sounds on the warm sidewalk. Turtle steps long to avoid the cracks. This building must be half a mile long, with entrances for every possible category of human problem. Health Care. Economic Development. Taylor can't believe the way life turns out. She has been waiting years for the revelation that just came to Turtle, and now it has happened, while they were walking along half distracted between a row of juniper hedges and the Muskogee Highway.

At last they find Child Welfare. Inside, the building is carpeted and seems more friendly. Receptionists sit at circular desks in the wide corridors, and pictures on the wall show the Tribal Council members, some in cowboy hats. When Taylor asks for directions to Andy Rainbelt's office, the receptionist gets up and leads the way. She wears low heels and has the disposition of a friendly housewife.

"This is his office here. If he was expecting you then I imagine he'll be on in here in a minute. He might be hung up with another appointment."

"Okay, thanks. We'll just wait."

But before they've sat down, they hear the receptionist greet Andy in the hall. He ducks in the doorway, smiling, huge, pony-tailed, dressed like a cleaned-up rodeo man in jeans and boots. Which is fine with Taylor. She prefers bull riding to social-worker interviews any day of the week.

"I'm Andy. Glad to meet you, Miz Greer. Turtle." His handshake is punctuated by a large turquoise ring on his index finger. When they sit, Turtle finds her way into Taylor's lap. Taylor hugs Turtle to her, trying not to look as off-center as she feels.

He leans forward on his elbows and just looks at Turtle for quite a while, smiling, until she has finished examining the floor, the doorknob, and the ceiling, and looks at Andy Rainbelt. He has kind, deep-set eyes under arched eyebrows. "So tell me about your family, Turtle."

"I don't have one."

Taylor earnestly wishes she were not alive.

"Well, who do you live with, then?"

"I live with my mom. And I have a grandma. I used to have Jax, too, back when we lived in a good house."

"Sounds like a family to me."

"And Barbie. She used to live with us. Barbie and all her clothes."

"Now, is she a real person or a doll?"

Turtle glances up at Taylor, who nearly laughs in spite of the dire circumstances. "She's both," Taylor answers for her. "She was a friend. Kind of clothes-oriented."

"What kind of things do you do for fun at your house?" he asks.

"Barbie played with me sometimes when Mom was at work," Turtle explains. "We made stuff. And clothes. She always ate Cheese Doritos and then went and throwed up in the bathroom."

"What? She did that?" Taylor feels ambushed. "I never knew that. Every time she ate?"

"I think every time."

"So that was her secret!" Taylor looks at Andy Rainbelt, feeling as if she might as well throw up too. "I guess we must sound like a pretty weird family."

"All families are weird," he says. "My job is to see which ones are good places for kids."

"Barbie is out of our lives, completely. I know it sounds bad that Turtle was exposed to that. I don't know what to tell you. She baby-sat for a while, while I was trying to get started in a new job. But she's gone."

"She took all our money," Turtle adds helpfully. "The guy that catches gooses had to take our electricity because we didn't pay."

Taylor knows her face must look like the cow in the corral who finally comprehends the slaughterhouse concept. "I was working full-time," she explains. "But somehow there just still wasn't enough money. It's probably hard for her to remember, but we had a pretty good life before all this happened."

Andy looks patient. "Listen. I hear everything in this office. I'm not grading you on what you say. I'm watching, more than listening, to tell you the truth. What I see is this little girl in your lap, looking pretty content there."

Taylor holds her so close she feels her own heart pounding against Turtle's slender, knobbed spine. "It's real hard on her to have to be separated from me. I just want to tell you that, for your records."

"I understand," he says.

"No, I mean it's terrible. Not like other kids. Sometimes Turtle lies in the bathtub with a blanket over her head for hours and hours, if she thinks I'm mad at her." She squeezes Turtle harder into her arms. "She went through some bad stuff when she was a baby, before I got her, and we're still kind of making up for lost time."

"Is that right, Turtle?"

Turtle is silent. Taylor waits for some awful new revelation, until it dawns on her that her daughter may be suffocating. She relaxes her hold, and Turtle breathes.

"Yeah," she says. "The bad one wasn't Pop-pop."

"She just met Mr. Stillwater. I mean, met him again. Her grandfather. I guess she's started remembering stuff from when she was little."

Andy has a way of looking Turtle in the eye that doesn't frighten her. Taylor is amazed. A giant who can make himself small. "Some tough times back then, huh?" he asks her.

"I don't know."

"It's okay to remember. Scares you though, sometimes, doesn't it?"

Turtle shrugs.

"Nobody's going to hurt you now."

Taylor closes her eyes and sees stars. She wishes on those stars that Andy Rainbelt could keep his promise.

Late that same afternoon, Taylor and Alice walk the dirt shoulder of the road out of Heaven. Turtle came back to Sugar's and fell into a hard sleep, but Taylor wanted to get out of the house for a while.

"I'm sorry you broke up with your new boyfriend," she tells Alice.

"Lord, what a soap opry," Alice declares. "All the fish out there, and I have to go for the one that's related to Turtle."

"Mama, that's not just bad luck. You were set up."

"Well, still, he didn't have to be so handy, did he? And related some way to Sugar?"

"To hear Sugar tell it, she's related some way to everybody from here to the Arkansas border. If they were determined to get you two together, it was bound to happen."

"Well, that's so. But I still have to say I got the worst darn luck in men."

"I'm not about to argue with that." Taylor has begun picking long-stemmed black-eyed Susans from the roadside as they walk along.

"The thing is, it's my own fault. I just can't put up with a person that won't go out of his way for me. And that's what a man is. Somebody that won't go out of his way for you. I bet it says that in the dictionary."

Taylor hands Alice a bouquet of orangey-yellow Susans and begins picking another one.

"It's the family misfortune," Alice says. "I handed it right on down to you."

"I called Jax," Taylor says, feeling faintly guilty.

"Well, honey, that's good. I mean it, I think he's tops. What's he up to?"

"His band is sort of breaking up. Their lead guitar quit, but they're getting an electric fiddle. Kind of going in a new direction, he says. He's trying to think of a new name with a country element. Renaissance Cowboys, something like that."

"Well, it beats the Irritated Babies all to pieces."

"Irascible Babies."

"What's that mean, irascible?"

"Irritated, I think."

"So I had the right idea, anyway."

"Yeah, I'm sure you did."

"And you forgave him for going to bed with that what's her name? That landlady gal?"

"Mama, I'd given him permission to do whatever he pleased. I told him when I left in June that we weren't, you know, anything long-term. So how could I hold it against him?"

A passing pickup truck, whose paint job looks very much like whitewash, slows down, then speeds on by when the driver doesn't recognize the two women carrying flowers.

"Mama, I've decided something about Jax. I've been missing him all summer long. Whether or not we get to keep Turtle, I've decided I want to start thinking of me and Jax as kind of more permanent."

"Well, that don't sound too definite."

"No, it is. I mean, I want us to be long-term. He's real happy. He wants to get married. I don't know if *married* is really the point, but you know what I mean."

"Well, Taylor, that's wonderful!" Alice cries, sounding ready enough to be wrong about men this once. She sings "Dum, dum da dum," to the tune of "Here Comes the Bride," and ties knots in the stems of her flowers, pulling each one through the next to make a crown. When it's finished she holds it out in her two hands like the cat's cradle, then places it on Taylor's dark hair. "There you go, all set."

"Mama, you're embarrassing me," Taylor says, but she leaves the flowers where they are.

"What changed your mind about Jax?"

Taylor uses her long bouquet like a horse's tail, to swish away gnats. "When the social worker asked Turtle about her family today, you know what she said? She said she didn't have one."

"That's not right! She was confused."

"Yeah. She's confused, because I'm confused. I *think* of Jax and Lou Ann and Dwayne Ray, and of course you, and Mattie, my boss at the tire store, all those people as my family. But when you never put a name on things, you're just accepting that it's okay for people to leave when they feel like it."

"They leave anyway," Alice says. "My husbands went like houses on fire."

"But you don't have to *accept* it," Taylor insists. "That's what your family is, the people you won't let go of for anything."

"Maybe."

"Like, look at Mr. Stillwater. Cash. He's still just aching for Turtle after all this time. I hate to admit it, and I'm not going to say I think he should have her. Turtle is mine now. But he doesn't accept that she's gone. You can see it."

Alice *has* seen it in Cash. She saw it long before she knew what it was. A man who would go out of his way.

Taylor has woven her flowers into a circle, and she crowns her mother with it. Alice reaches deep into herself and evinces a dramatic sigh. "Always the bridesmaid, never the bride."

A string of cars crackles by on the gravel, all following an old truck that is fairly crawling. The drivers stare, each one in turn, as they pass.

"Where's that sign?" Taylor asks.

"What sign?"

"The one that was in that magazine ad, remember? With Sugar, when she was young? You've showed me that fifty times."

"That sign that says WELCOME TO HEAVEN." Alice looks thoughtful. "You know, I haven't seen it."

"Maybe this isn't really Heaven!" Taylor says. "Maybe we're in the wrong place, and none of this is really happening."

"No, it's Heaven all right. It says so on the phone book."

"Shoot, then they ought to have that sign up. I wish we could go pose in front of it. Maybe somebody'd come along and take our picture."

"I wonder if they tore that down. I'll have to ask Sugar. I bet anything they did."

"Does that mean we're not welcome anymore?" Taylor asks.

Two more cars pass by, and this time Alice and Taylor smile and wave like Miss America contestants.

Alice says, "I reckon we'll stay till they run us out of town."

Some kind of fish jumps in the river. Annawake stares at the ring of disturbed water it left behind. "Uncle Ledger, just tell me what to do," she says.

Ledger is in his overstuffed chair on the porch of the houseboat, smoking his pipe. Annawake paces the planks silently in her moccasins.

"You never would let me tell you what to do before," he says through pursed lips, sucking his pipe stem. "Why would you start now?"

"I always knew what I was doing before."

"If you knew what you was doing before, you wouldn't be stumped now."

She sits down on the deck, then lies down, looking up at the sky.

"Did I ever tell you you looked like a plucked chicken, when you cut all your hair off?"

"I was mourning Gabriel. I thought somebody ought to."

"If you want to do something for Gabe, talk to Gabe."

"Gabe's in Leavenworth."

"What, they don't allow phone calls?"

Annawake looks up, startled. He means it. "I don't know. Yeah, I guess they do."

"Well, then, call him. Or go visit. Tell him you miss him. Organize a damn bust-out and bring him on back here."

Annawake feels something like round stones shifting inside her, settling into a new, more solid position. "I guess I could."

"Sure you could. If you got something to work out, then work it out. Don't take it out on the rest of the world by looking like a chicken."

"Thanks. Everybody always said I had your looks."

"Annawake, you're not as respectful as you used to be."

She sits up, but sees the light in his eye, so she can lie back down.

"Tell me a story," she says. "About a little lost girl whose mother is prepared to give her away, rather than go through any more hassle with Annawake Fourkiller."

"I'll tell you." He leans back in his chair, which once in its life was green brocade, before twenty summers of sun and rain. "Speak of lost children in low voices," he says. Annawake pulls herself up. He has slid over into Cherokee, and she has to sit up straight to follow him. "They say long ago there was a child claimed by two clan mothers. They carried the child to the Above Ones. They came with long cries and moans, both of them saying the child belonged to their own people. The mother from the plains brought corn, and the mother from the hills brought tobacco, both of them hoping to sweeten the thoughts of the Above Ones when they made their decision."

Ledger stops talking and merely stares at the sky for a time. His legs are splayed in front of him, forgotten, and his pipe dangles in his hand, still sending up a thread of smoke as a friendly reminder.

He goes on suddenly: "When the Above Ones spoke, they said, we will send down the snake Uk'ten."

Annawake leans forward with her arms around her knees, narrowing her eyes to listen. She wishes she had her glasses. She understands Cherokee better with her glasses on.

"We will send the snake Uk'ten to cut the child in half, and each clan can carry home one half of the child."

"Wait a minute," Annawake says.

"The mother from the grassland happily agreed. But the mother from the hill clan wept and said no, that she would give her half of the child to the plains clan, to keep the baby whole. And so the Above Ones knew which mother loved the child best."

Annawake pulls off a moccasin and throws it at Ledger, hitting him square in the chest. She pulls off the other and just misses his head, on purpose.

"What, you don't like my story?" He sits up startled, crossing his hands over his chest.

"Some old Cherokee story you've got there. That's King Solomon, from the Bible."

"Oh. Well, I knew I got it from someplace," he says, patting his pockets for matches to relight his pipe.

"It's a *yonega* story," she says.

"Is that true? Did a *yonega* write the Bible? I always wondered about that. It doesn't say on there, 'The Bible, by so-and-so.' "

"I don't know. Maybe it wasn't a *yonega*. I think it was a bunch of people that lived in the desert and fished for a living."

"If they lived in the desert and caught fish both, you better listen to them."

"Give me my shoes back."

He leans back to collect the one that flew over his shoulder, and tosses the pair. Annawake pulls them on over her bare feet and buttons them at the ankles.

"I've got to go down to the Council Chambers and give my recommendation in half an hour. And you haven't told me a thing."

"Not a thing, no."

"Except that maybe I don't want to jump for joy to see a baby cut in half. Which she's going to be, either way."

"Can I tell you something, little hothead?"

"What?"

"There's something else growing back with your hair."

"What's that?"

"Sense. Used to be, you wanted your side to win all the time."

"They taught me that in *yonega* law school."

"Must be. You never had a bit of it in you before. I never saw you knocking down your own brothers to hit the score in a stickball game."

"Okay, then, if you knew me so well, you never should have let me go to law school. If you knew it would just bring out my worst nature."

"If you have a frisky horse you put him in a race. You don't put him behind a plow."

Annawake gets up, dusts off her knees and her seat. "What do you know from horses, anyway? You're a Cherokee, not some war-whooping featherheaded Sioux."

"I know enough about horses. I know you want one that has a good heart."

"I hear Dellon's truck up on the road. He's driving me over to Headquarters. I'd better go."

"Annawake, you've got you a good heart. Run with it. Your whole life, you've been afraid of yourself." He is looking right at her. Not through her, like most people do, to the paper doll that is Annawake Fourkiller, but *into* her.

She stands with her mouth open, waiting for a word. Nothing comes. Then, "How did you know?"

Ledger seems entirely occupied with his pipe. He waves her off. "Birdy told me."

Dellon is idling with the radio on. He turns it down when she gets in. "So did Ledger blow smoke on you and bless you for the hunt?"

"He blew smoke all right. He aggravates me. Nobody ought to be that smart."

"Yeah, well, Annawake. That's what some people say about you." He rolls his eyes. "I wouldn't know who."

"If I'm so smart, how come I'm miserable?"

On the radio, Randy Travis's croony voice dips low over someone who's been gone for too long.

"You just need you a man, that's all," Dellon says.

Annawake exhales sharply. "I've had enough men in my life to last me about seven lifetimes. Think about it, Dell, growing up with all you guys, and Daddy, and Uncle Ledger. All those penises! You all had me surrounded like a picket fence."

Dellon shifts in his seat uncomfortably. "It wasn't *that* bad, was it?"

"No, Dellon, it's nothing personal against your body organs. But men are just not necessarily always the solution."

He stares at her until his truck runs into the ditch. He glances up and swerves back. "I'm going to have to put that in my pipe and smoke it awhile," he says.

She gives him the smile that has been knocking boys dead for twenty-seven years, with absence of malice. "You just do that."

33

THE GAMBLING AGENDA

THE MEETING THAT TOOK PLACE previously in the Council Chamber room must have been concerned with the Bingo question. On the blackboard at the front of the room someone has written in narrow, forward-slanting letters:

TODAY'S AGENDA—GAMING ON TRIBAL LAND, YAY OR NAY? PRESENTATIONS

1. Cyrus Stonecipher. "The pritfalls of gambling, a story too often told"
2. Betty Louise Squirrel. "BINGO, everybody wins!"

Annawake Fourkiller and Andy Rainbelt sit at the long speakers' table down in front with their backs to the chalkboard, apparently unaware of the gambling agenda. Andy Rainbelt seems festive in a blue calico shirt with satin ribbon trim at the yoke, similar to the one Annawake wore the day she and Taylor met. Taylor can remember exactly how she looked. Today she's a different person, in black-rimmed glasses and a haircut that seems worrisome to her. She keeps pushing it out of her way.

Turtle, Taylor, and Alice are sitting together in the red movie-theater chairs that fill the small auditorium. Turtle swings her legs so the toes of her sneakers drum out a steady *tha-bump* against the empty seat in front of her. The rows are set in a V-shape facing the speakers' table, with an aisle down the center. Those in attendance have assumed a wedding interpretation, in which the center aisle divides the two families; the seats on the other side are filling up briskly. Cash is over there and so is Letty, in a red dress with an imposing row of gold buttons down the front; countless other friends and relations have trailed in with children and greetings and messages for their neighbors. Boma Mellowbug is wearing a man's pinstriped suit and a baseball cap, looking very sporting. She holds the hand of an old, extremely thin man whose hair hangs between his shoulder blades in a white plait as thin and prickly as binder's twine. The heavyset woman who waited on Alice and Annawake in the coffee shop hustles in, leaning into Letty's row in a businesslike way to inform Letty that the half-size dress patterns are in at Woolworth's in Tahlequah.

"What *is* half-size, Aunt Earlene?" asks a young woman who's nursing a baby. "I always wondered that."

Earlene turns her back and speaks over her shoulder, reaching her hands around to her waist and the back of her neck to demonstrate. "It's when you've got less inches from here to here than you have in the inseam and the bust measurements."

"It's for when you're shorter than you are wide," says Roscoe.

"You hush," Letty tells him. "I don't know why Sugar feeds you."

Earlene plumps herself down next to the nursing mother. The baby is making a good deal of noise at his task, sounding like the squeaky wheel determined to get all the grease.

Sugar comes in late, long after Roscoe has taken the one vacant seat next to his sister-in-law Letty, and she seems uncertain where to go. She takes Alice's side at last, but a seat on the aisle, as close as possible to the Stillwaters.

The talking falls to a hush when a small woman in heels and a white silk blouse clicks in and takes her place at the front table next to Andy

Rainbelt. She has a good deal of hair, which she shakes when she sits down, as if it might have gathered dust somewhere along the road to this point. Annawake puts on her glasses, squares the pile of papers in front of her, and stands up. She looks out at the small assembled crowd and smiles oddly. "Have you all decided this is Stillwater versus Greer?"

The auditorium owns up to this by its silence.

She leans forward on the palms of her hands, peering out over her glasses, looking just like a lawyer in blue jeans. "Well, it isn't. This is not a court battle, it's just a hearing. I'm Annawake Fourkiller, you all know me here. I was hired by the tribe to oversee its interests in this case. This is Andy Rainbelt, who has jurisdiction as the appointed representative of Child Welfare Services. And this is his boss, Leona Swimmer, here to make sure we all do our jobs."

Leona Swimmer nods very slightly, apparently wishing to acknowledge nothing more than that she is, in fact, here.

Annawake goes on. "Mr. Rainbelt and I have conferred, and we're prepared to make a recommendation about the child known as Turtle Greer, also known as Lacey Stillwater."

Turtle stops swinging her legs. Taylor squeezes her hand so hard that for once Turtle knows herself what it's like to be bitten by those turtles that don't let go.

Annawake looks down at Andy. "Did you want to say anything?"

"No, you go ahead," he says. Leona Swimmer is craning her neck to read the blackboard behind her. BINGO, everybody wins! Taylor can just imagine this Betty Louise Squirrel. Some charmed, perky type whose tires never go flat and whose kids never get chicken pox. Taylor pictures her as an actual squirrel, in an apron.

Annawake speaks in the level sort of voice that takes practice to achieve. "There are two principal legal considerations here. First of all, the adoption of the child by Taylor Greer was improperly conducted. There was no malice on her part, but even so it was illegal. I've filed a motion in state court to invalidate the adoption."

The nursing baby lets out a small strangled cry. His mother moves him to her shoulder, patting and bouncing him there to get the air bubbles to rise according to the laws that govern babies.

"Secondly," Annawake says, "we've determined that the child is Cash Stillwater's granddaughter, Lacey Stillwater. She recognizes him, and bears a strong family resemblance."

"Isn't that so," moans Letty in a low, breathless tone as if receiving the spirit. Cash is perfectly still. He can't feel his hands, and wonders if he's having a quiet, unnoticeable kind of coronary.

"Given those facts," Annawake says, "we have to consider Cash Stillwater to be the child's legal guardian. If this were contested, a court would undoubtedly find in favor of Mr. Stillwater. The Indian Child Welfare Act clearly states that our children should stay within our tribe, and whenever possible, with their own relatives. In this instance the natural mother is dead and the father is unknown, so the obvious choice would be to assign guardianship to the grandfather."

Cash still hasn't moved. Taylor has stopped breathing.

"There's a complication in this case." Annawake picks up a ballpoint pen and clicks the point in and out, in and out. "The child has formed a strong attachment to Taylor Greer, the only mother she's known for the past three years. Mr. Rainbelt evaluated the adoptive setting, and after consulting with a psychiatrist, he feels it would be devastating to break this extreme attachment. He recommends counseling for the child, who suffered a period of abuse and neglect before she was abandoned and subsequently adopted. Counseling will be undertaken at the expense of the Nation. That's one of our duties to this child. Mr. Rainbelt suggests it would be valuable to the healing process, too, for her to spend time with her grandfather and other relatives."

Annawake holds the pen at arm's length and suddenly stares at it as if she had no idea of its purpose or origin.

"So," she says finally. "You can see."

No one in the audience makes any indication that she or he can see.

"You can see we have conflicting considerations here. Keeping the child in her own culture, and not disrupting her attachment to a non-Cherokee mother. We want to reinstate this child—who should be called Turtle, since she's grown to be a fine little person under her adopted mother's care, and that's the name she connects with her conscious memory of herself—we have to reinstate her as the granddaughter and legal ward of

Cash Stillwater. We recommend her legal name be recorded as Turtle Stillwater. So, we've figured out *who* she is. We've come that far."

Someone in the audience exhales. The baby emits a tiny belch.

Annawake takes off her glasses and looks at the ceiling as if in prayer. There is nothing up there but soundproof tile. No evidence of the Above Ones or the six bad boys who got turned into pigs, for whatever reason. The faces in front of her are wide open, waiting. She remembers wanting to be her Uncle Ledger, as a child, during the sermons. This is how it would be.

"I think we're looking at one of those rare chances life gives us to try and be the very best that we are," Annawake says. "The outside press, when they look at this case, will be asking only one thing: what is in the best interest of the child? But we're Cherokee and we look at things differently. We consider that the child is part of something larger, a tribe. Like a hand that belongs to the body. Before we cut it off, we have to ask how the body will take care of itself without that hand.

"The Indian Child Welfare Act was designed principally to protect the tribe from losing its members. Our children are our future. But we want them to grow up under the influence of kindness and generosity. Sometimes we have to put the needs of an individual in second place, behind the needs of the community. But we should never put them out of our mind entirely. What we have to do is satisfy the requirements of the tribe, without separating Turtle completely from the mother and grandmother she's come to love and trust."

Relatives and friends of Turtle Stillwater maintain a perfect silence.

Annawake puts down her glasses and pushes her hair behind her ears. "I'm going to go out on a limb here. Andy and I just cooked up an idea about fifteen minutes ago, right before this meeting. There's a precedent in these adoption cases for assigning joint custody. Sometimes it works, sometimes it's a mess. But we're going to go ahead and give Cash Stillwater legal guardianship of Turtle Stillwater, with the recommendation that Taylor Greer has shared custody. We're willing to work with both families on an agreeable custody arrangement. Last year, in the case of a Navajo child adopted by a family in Utah, the tribe allowed the child to spend the school year with her adoptive family and summers with her grandparents on the reservation." Annawake looks from Cash to Taylor; their faces look peculiarly identical. She bends down to confer quietly with Andy.

Andy Rainbelt doesn't stand, but nods, and Annawake speaks again. "Andy plans to continue on as Turtle's personal Indian social worker, and do follow-up evals to see how this custody deal is affecting her. He wants to stress that Turtle won't be separated from her adoptive family until she's ready to do that. But we're going to require the guardians to come up with a plan fairly soon that places Turtle here on the Nation at least three months out of the year."

Alice Greer blows her nose. Letty pulls out a lace handkerchief and blows hers also, with substantially more showmanship.

"Obviously," Annawake says, "with joint custody, everything depends on how well the two custodial parties are willing to cooperate. And whether or not the cooperation extends indefinitely into the future. I would hate to see this case ever go to court." She looks down at the papers in front of her. "I think that's about all I have."

After a moment of shell-shocked quiet, Boma Mellowbug lifts her voice into a long, rising whoop, the signal for ending the sermon and starting the dance.

"Thanks, Boma." Annawake smiles and sits down.

No one moves. Taylor takes her first breath of the too-thin air of the rest of her life—a life of sharing Turtle with strangers.

"This is your chance, people," Andy says. "You're allowed to speak up if you have suggestions or questions or just want to promote the general welfare. That's why we open these things up to the whole family."

Cash slowly finds his feet, facing front. "I have a suggestion. I suggest that if me and Alice Greer was to get married, then the little girl could still be seeing her grandma when she comes for the summers."

Alice's face drops open on all its hinges. So does Letty Hornbuckle's.

"Now wait a minute, Cash," Letty says, standing up, gripping the seat in front of her like a church pew. "You hain't knowed her but three weeks."

Cash turns on his sister like a bull would, seeing that red dress. "Letty, now you look here. You're the one started this whole business with her and me in the first place. You ought to be ashamed of yourself."

"No, now goodness me, I helped," Sugar says, pulling herself up as high as her humped back will allow for. "Letty, you're not being fair to Alice. She's my cousin. If they love each other, we ought to go on and let these kids get married." She turns and speaks to Alice. "I helped set it up, too. I made up some of that stuff I said about Cash itching to get to know you."

Annawake is smirking. "I hate to bring this up, Letty, but *I* gave you the idea of getting them together. Remember that day I brought back your pie plate? I just hit on it when I was talking to Alice downtown in the coffee shop one day, and spilled the sugar."

"Honey, don't you worry about that sugar," Earlene says. "That wasn't nothing. Floyd Tailbob throwed a whole fresh cup of coffee on Killie Deal one time in there, on a Easter Sunday. Don't even ask me how he done it."

Alice is standing with her mouth open, waiting. When Earlene has finished with Floyd Tailbob and Killie Deal, she asks, "Did anybody ask me if I *wanted* to marry Cash?"

All bosoms and shirt fronts turn to face Alice.

"Do I get a say-so here? Because I already made up my mind a long time ago, I don't want another husband that's glued to his everloving TV set. I have my own principles to think about." Alice sits down.

Annawake looks at Taylor. Andy Rainbelt is smiling broadly, exposing a wonderful gap between his front teeth. Taylor can hear him saying, *All families are weird.* She couldn't agree more. She's ready to grab Turtle and run for it, except she knows where that road ends.

"I just have one thing to say," Sugar announces. "If they do get married—I'm just saying *if*—then I think we ought to have the pig fry at my house. Because Letty's in the middle of getting her a new roof on, and that and a pig fry all at once would be too much to contend with if you ask me."

"Well, Sugar, it's Cash putting the roof on!" Letty cries. "Don't you think he's going to finish up a shingle job in time for his own wedding?"

The man with the white ponytail tells Earlene, "That was Flester that spilt his coffee on Killie Deal. I read about that in the paper."

"No, you did not. You're thinking of when he showed up with coffee all down his shirt sleeve when he was running for Tribal Council."

Leona Swimmer speaks up for the first time. "Now, why would either one of those things be in the paper? Could somebody tell me?"

Everyone turns to examine Leona. She looks very elegant and commanding, like a schoolteacher.

"Tribal politics, Leona," Roscoe tells her with polite impatience. "You know that as well as I do."

"Now, hear ye!" shouts Cash. "If this meeting is over with, which I'd say it pretty much is, I'm inviting Alice and everybody else here in this room to come over to my place right this minute and witness something I'm about to do."

He turns and walks out of the room. There is a moment of stupefied silence, then a neighborly stampede.

Taylor understands she has lost something she won't get back. Cash Stillwater is Turtle's legal guardian. No matter what.

Taylor can still remember the day when she first understood she'd received the absolute power of motherhood—that force that makes everyone else step back and agree that she knows what's best for Turtle. It scared her to death. But giving it up now makes her feel infinitely small and alone. She can't even count her losses yet; her heart is an empty canyon, so she puts her effort into driving.

Somehow she has ended up as caboose in the long line of cars following Cash's penny-colored pickup truck. She and Turtle seem to have been forgotten for the moment. It dawns on her that she could pull out of line now and head west, and not a soul would notice. But they're way past that point now. From now until the end of time she is connected to this family that's parading down Main Street, Heaven. One day soon she will lie in bed with Jax and tell him every detail of this day. The Renaissance Cowboys have got nothing on the Stillwaters, for entertainment value.

"Wait till we tell Jax we want him as your official daddy," she says to Turtle. "What do you think he'll do?"

"Maybe put his pants on his head and sing 'Happy Birthday' to himself."

"Yeah, maybe."

"Does that mean you're still my mom?"

"I am. But I have to share you with your grandpa now. He's going to have a big say in how you're raised."

"I know. So I can be a Cherokee when I grow up. Andy Rainbow told me."

"You like Andy?"

Turtle nods. "Those people in there? Were they Pop-pop's family?"

"Yep. *Your* family, to be exact."

"They're crazy."

"I know," Taylor says. "But they'll probably grow on you."

The one traffic light in town turns red on her, just after all the others have passed under. Taylor turns on her headlights so people will think it's a funeral, and floors it right on through the red. Nobody much was coming, anyway. If she gets separated from the others now, she'll never know how her life is going to come out.

Cash walks out the back door of his cabin carrying his television set, and with a vigorous wordlessness, sets it on a stump. It sits there not quite level, its short black cord hanging down in a defeated manner. While Cash stomps back inside, the witnesses arrange themselves in a semicircle facing the blank green eye. Nothing in this world, Alice notes, will get people organized and quiet faster than a TV set, even when there is nothing to plug it into but a tree stump.

Turtle takes a hop or two toward the TV, but the girl with the baby on her shoulder gently pulls her back. Taylor reaches forward and takes Turtle's hand.

Cash appears again, carrying his rifle. "You all move back," he says, and they waste no time.

"He's done lost his mind," Alice says calmly to Taylor.

"You better marry him, then," Taylor whispers back.

Cash stands a few feet in front of them with his feet wide apart. His shoulders curl forward, hunched and tense, as he lifts the rifle and takes aim. He remains frozen in this position for a very long time. Alice can see the gun barrel over his shoulder, wavering a little, and then she sees his shoulder thrown back at the same instant the gun's report roars over the clearing. Her ears feel the pain of a bell struck hard. The woods go unnaturally still. All the birds take note of the round black bullet wound in the TV screen, a little right of center but still fatal.

Alice's heart performs its duties strangely inside her chest, and she understands that her life sentence of household silence has been commuted. The family of women is about to open its doors to men. Men, children, cowboys, and Indians. It's all over now but the shouting.

BARBARA KINGSOLVER's nine published books include novels, collections of short stories, poetry, essays, and an oral history. Her work has also appeared in numerous literary anthologies and periodicals.

Kingsolver grew up in Kentucky and earned a graduate degree in biology before becoming a full-time writer. She and her husband, Steven Hopp, cowrite articles on science and natural history. With their two daughters, they divide their time between Tucson, Arizona, and a farm in southern Appalachia.